Once a reporter ~~~~ ~~~~~~~~~~~~~~~ ~~~~~~~~~~
News, Gerald Seymour is the author of eight
bestselling novels, including *Killing Ground*, *A
Line in the Sand* and, most recently, *Holding the
Zero*. His latest novel, *The Untouchable*, is now
available from Bantam Press. He lives in the
West Country. One of his novels, *The Waiting
Time*, has recently been adapted for Carlton
Television.

Also by Gerald Seymour

KINGFISHER
RED FOX
THE CONTRACT
ARCHANGEL
IN HONOUR BOUND
FIELD OF BLOOD
A SONG IN THE MORNING
AT CLOSE QUARTERS
HOME RUN
CONDITION BLACK
THE JOURNEYMAN TAILOR
THE FIGHTING MAN
THE HEART OF DANGER
KILLING GROUND
THE WAITING TIME
A LINE IN THE SAND
HOLDING THE ZERO

and published by Corgi Books

Harry's Game

AND

The Glory Boys

Gerald Seymour

HARRY'S GAME and THE GLORY BOYS
A CORGI BOOK : 0 552 14957 8

This WHSmith edition first published 2001
Copyright © Gerald Seymour 2001

1 3 5 7 9 10 8 6 4 2

including

HARRY'S GAME
Originally published in Great Britain by Collins
Copyright © Gerald Seymour 1975
Corgi edition published 1999
Set in 10/12pt Palatino by
Phoenix Typesetting, Ilkley, West Yorkshire.

THE GLORY BOYS
Originally published in Great Britain by Collins
Copyright © Gerald Seymour 1976
Corgi edition published 2000
Set in 10/12pt Palatino by
Kestrel Data, Exeter, Devon.

Corgi Books are published by Transworld Publishers,
61-63 Uxbridge Road, London W5 5SA,
a division of The Random House Group Ltd,
in Australia by Random House Australia (Pty) Ltd,
20 Alfred Street, Milsons Point, Sydney, NSW 2061, Australia,
in New Zealand by Random House New Zealand Ltd,
18 Poland Road, Glenfield, Auckland 10, New Zealand
and in South Africa by Random House (Pty) Ltd,
Endulini, 5a Jubilee Road, Parktown 2193, South Africa

WHSmith plc, Greenbridge Road, Swindon SN3 3LD.

www.whsmith.co.uk

Printed and bound in Great Britain by
Cox & Wyman Ltd, Reading, Berkshire.

Harry's Game

Gerald Seymour

To William Kean Seymour

Chapter One

The man was panting slightly, not from the exertion of pushing his way through the shapeless, ungiving mass of the crowd but from the frustration of the delay.

He drove himself at the knot of people that had formed a defensive wall round the Underground ticket machine, reaching out through their bodies with his money for the slot, only to be swept back as the crowd formed its own queue out of the rabble. It took him fifteen seconds more than two minutes to insert his ten-pence piece and draw out a ticket, but that was still quick set against the endless, shuffling line approaching the ticket kiosk.

He moved on to the next piece of gadgetry, the automatic barrier. He inserted his ticket into the machine, which reacted and bent upwards to admit him. There was space around him now. His stride lengthened. Bottled up amongst the mass on the far side of the barrier, with the clock moving, he'd felt the constriction, his inability to get away.

Now, in the open at last, he cannoned off an elderly man, deep in his paper, making him stumble. As he tried to sidestep his way out of the collision he knocked

7

into a girl loaded for the launderette, hitting her hard with his left elbow. She looked startled, half focusing on him, half concentrating on holding her balance, her arms out of action clinging to the plastic bag pressed into her breasts. He saw the look of surprise fill her face, watched her as she waited for the explanation, the mumbled apology and helping hand – the usual etiquette of Oxford Circus Station, top hall, at 8.45 in the morning.

He froze the words in his mouth, the discipline of his briefing winning through. They'd told him not to speak en route to the target. Act dumb, rude, anything, but don't open your big mouth, they'd said. It had been drilled into him – not to let anyone hear the hard, nasal accent of West Belfast.

As the man sped from the fracas, leaving the elderly man to grope amongst a mass of shoes for his paper, the girl to regain her feet with the help of a clutch of hands, he could sense the eyes of the witnesses boring into him; it was enough of an incident to be remembered. The briefing had said 'Don't speak . . .' but while the crowd acknowledged people's need to hurry it demanded at the least some slight apology for breaking the etiquette of the rush hour. The failure to conform was noted by the half-dozen or so close enough to examine the man, who now ran away towards the tunnel and the escalator leading to the Victoria Line. They'd had at least three seconds to see his face, to take in his clothes and, above all, to note the fear and tension in his face as their stares built up round him.

When he reached the escalator he swerved left to the walking side of the moving stairs and ducked down behind the moving line, past the stationary paper-readers and the bikini-advertisement watchers. Here the eyes were away from him, on the financial pages, the sports pics, or the hoardings floating tantalizingly by.

He was aware of his stupidity in the hall area, conscious that he'd antagonized people who would recognize him, and he felt the slight trembling again in his hands and feet that he'd noticed several times since he'd come across the water. With his right hand, awkwardly and across his body, he gripped the rubber escalator rail to steady himself. His fingers tightened on the hard rubber, holding on till he reached the bottom and skipped clear of the sieve where the stair drove its way under the floor. The movement and the push of a young man behind him made him stumble a little, and with his right hand he reached out for the shoulder of a woman in front of him. She smiled warmly and openly at him as he found his feet again, and a little hesitantly he smiled back, and was away. Better that time, he thought, no tension, no incident, no recognition. Cool it, sunshine. Take it easy. He walked through, carried forward by the crowd onto the platform. They'd timed the frequency of the trains; at worst he'd wait less than a minute.

His left arm, pressed against his chest, disappeared into the gap between the buttons of his raincoat. His left hand held tightly onto the barrel of the Kalashnikov automatic rifle he'd strapped to his body before leaving the North London boarding house two hours and twenty minutes earlier. In that time the hand had never left the cold metal and the skin under his thumb was numb with the indentation of the master sight. The barrel and weapon mechanism were little more than

9

twenty inches long, with the shoulder stock of tubular steel folded back alongside it. The magazine was in his hip pocket. The train blurted its way out of the darkened tunnel, braked, and the doors slid back. As he wormed his way into a seat and the doors closed, he edged his weight off the magazine, and the thirty live rounds inside it.

It was 8.51 by the cheap watch on his wrist, just visible if he moved the gun towards the coat buttonholes. Five minutes maximum to Victoria, three minutes from the Underground platform to the street, and, taking it gently, seven minutes from there to his target. 9.06 on location. The train pulled abruptly into Green Park Station, waited little more than forty-five seconds as a trickle of passengers got off, a few moments more to let others on, and the doors, to the shout of the big West Indian guard, were closing.

9.06 on location meant that he had two minutes in hand, perhaps three at the most, primarily to assemble the gun and pick his firing position. It was a close schedule now, and he began again to feel the trembling that had dogged him since Rosslare and the ferry, and that he had first felt acutely at Fishguard as he walked with the Kalashnikov past the cold eyes of the Special Branch section watching the ferry passengers coming over from Ireland. He'd gone right by them then, waving furiously to a non-existent relative in the middle distance beyond the checkpoint and suddenly realizing that he was through and on his way. At his briefing they'd told him the worst part before the shooting would be at Fishguard. He'd seen when he was at the back of the queue how they watched the men coming through, watched hard and expressionless, taking them apart. But no-one from his ferry, that he'd seen at any rate, had been stopped. At the briefing they explained that in his favour was his lack of form, never fingerprinted, never photographed, that he was an unknown face, that if he kept his nerve he'd get away with it and make it out as well. No sympathizers' homes in London were being used, no contact with anyone, keep it tight as an Orangeman's drum, one said. They'd all laughed. The train jolted to a halt, the carriage emptied. Victoria. He pulled himself up with his right hand on the pole support by the door, and stepped out onto the platform. Instinctively he began to hurry, then checked himself, slowed and headed for the neon 'Way Out' sign.

By the start of the nine o'clock news something approaching order was returning to the Minister's home. Three children already on their way to school, two more still wrestling with overcoats, scarfs, hockey sticks and satchels. The au pair in the hall with them. The Minister's Afghan tangled round their legs.

The Minister was alone at the long refectory table in the breakfast room, newspapers spread out where the children's cereal bowls had been. First he gutted the editorial columns, then on through the parliamentary reports, and finally to the front-page news. He read quickly, with little outward sign of annoyance or pleasure. It was said that only his closest parliamentary colleagues, and that meant about four in the Cabinet, could spot his moods at a time like this. But the selection of papers offered him little more than trivial interest in the fortunes of his colleagues. Since his eighteen months as second man in Belfast, and the

11

attendant publicity, his promotion to Social Services overlord and a place in the Cabinet had taken him back out of the public eye and reduced his exposure. His major speeches in the House were fully reported, but his monolithic department ticked along, barely feeling his touch at the helm. This morning he wasn't mentioned, and his department figured only in the continuing story of a grandmother in the North-East who had been taken to hospital penniless and suffering from malnutrition and then told local officials that she'd never drawn her pension, and believed people should look after themselves anyway. Lunatic, stupid woman, he muttered.

The news was mostly foreign: South Africa and the mine strike, Middle East cease-fire violations, Kremlin reshuffle. 'In Belfast' – suddenly he was concentrating – 'a city centre pub was destroyed by a car bomb. Two masked men had warned the customers to leave, but the bomb went off before the area could be fully evacuated. Three men were taken to hospital suffering from shock, but a spokesman said no-one was seriously hurt.' Belfast was pretty far down these days, he reflected. Just time left to see what football manager was leaving where, and then the weather, and it would be five-past. He shuffled his papers together and reached for his briefcase under the table; the car would be at the door in three minutes. 'Moving off, sweetheart,' he called, and made for the hall.

The Afghan was now sitting quietly on the doormat, the children ready, as the Minister put on his heavy, dark-blue overcoat, paused and contemplated the scarf on the hook, decided against it, gave his wife's offered cheek a kiss and opened the door into Belgrave Square.

12

The Afghan and au pair led the way down the steps to the pavement, then the children and after a moment the Minister and his wife. To his right he saw the black Austin Princess turning out of Halkin Street, seventy-five yards away, to pick him up. The children, dog and au pair walked left towards Chapel Street, and across the road a short, dark-haired man who had been leaning against the square's fence stiffened and moved forward.

The Minister's huge voice bellowed after his children: 'Have a nice day, darlings, and don't do any damage with those sticks.' He was still smiling at the over-the-shoulder grimace from the elder girl down the street, when he saw the rifle come from under the coat of the man across the street and move to his shoulder. He was out on the pavement now and some yards away from the house as he turned and looked for the sanctuary of the door in front of which his wife was standing, intent on her children.

He had started to shout a warning to her when the man fired his first shot. For the Minister the street exploded in noise, as he felt the sledge-hammer blow of the 7.62 mm shell crashing into his chest, searing into the soft flesh on its way through a splintered rib cage, puncturing the tissue of his lungs, gouging muscle and bone from his backbone, and bursting out through his clothes, before, a shapeless mass of lead, it buried itself in the white façade of the house. The force of that first shot spun and felled the Minister, causing the second shot to miss and fly into the hallway, fracturing a mirror beside the lounge door. As the man aimed for his third shot – 'Keep steady, aim,' they'd told him, 'don't blaze, and for Christ's sake be quick' – he heard the screaming. The Minister's wife was crawling down the steps to where her husband writhed in his attempt to get away from the pain. The man fired two more shots. This time there were no misses, and he watched with detached fascination as the back of the sleek, groomed head disintegrated. It was the last chance he had to see the target before the woman who had been screaming flung herself over it, swamping it from his view. He looked to his left and saw the big car stranded, its engine racing, in the middle of the road. To the right on the pavement he saw the children, immobile like statues, with the dog straining at its leash to escape the noise.

Automatically the man flicked the safety catch to 'on', deflated the catch at the top of the stock, bent the shoulder rest back alongside the barrel and dropped the weapon into the sheath they'd built to be strapped under his coat. Then he ran, jumping out of the way of a woman as he went. He turned into Chapel Street, sprinting now. Right next into Grosvenor Place. Must get across the road, get a line of traffic between you and them, he told himself. Alongside him was the high, spiked wall of Buckingham Palace. People saw him coming and moved out of his path. He clutched his unbuttoned coat tight to his body. The rifle was awkward now, with the curved magazine digging into his ribs. As he was running he was vulnerable, he knew that. His mind didn't tell him that no-one had cause to stop him, but focused almost exclusively on the road, the traffic, and at what moment he would see a hole in the river of buses and cabs and lorries. Get across Buckingham Palace Road and then into the safety and anonymity of the tube station at Victoria. Hard out of breath he stumbled into the station. He took a ten-pence piece from his pocket. Relaxed now, he could take his place in the queue. He pushed the coin into the automatic machine. Remember, they'd said, the law will expect a car; you're better on the tube. They'd given him a route, Victoria to Oxford Circus on the Victoria Line, then the Bakerloo Line to Baker Street, then the Metropolitan Line to Watford. He was on a train and moving and his watch showed 9.12.

The sirens of the patrol cars blotted out the screaming of the Minister's wife as she lay over the body. They'd been diverted there just ninety seconds before with the brief message, 'Man shot in Belgrave Square.' The two constables were still mentally tuned to the traffic blockages at the Knightsbridge underpass as they spilled out into the street. George Davies, twenty-two years old and only three years in the Metropolitan police, was first out. He saw the woman, the body of the man under her, and the brain tissue on the steps. The sight stopped him in mid-stride as he felt nausea rising into his mouth. Frank Smith, twice his age, screamed, 'Don't stop, *move*,' ran past him to the huddle on the steps, and pulled the Minister's wife from her husband's body. 'Give him air,' he yelled, before he took in the wrecked skull, the human debris on the flagstones and the woman's housecoat. Smith sucked in the air, mumbled inaudibly, and turned on his knees to the pale-faced Davies ten paces behind him. 'Ambulance, reinforcements, tell 'em it's big, and move it fast.' When Smith looked again at the Minister's wife he recognized her. 'It's Mrs Danby?' he whispered. It was a statement, but he put the question

15

into it. She nodded. 'Your husband?' She nodded again. She was silent now and the children had edged close to her.

Smith took the scene in. 'Get them inside, Ma'am.' It was an instruction, and they obeyed, slowly and numbly going through the door and off the street.

Smith got up off his knees and lumbered back to the squad car.

'Davies, don't let anyone near him. Get a description.'

On the radio he put out a staccato message: 'Tango George, in Belgrave Square. Henry Danby has been shot. He's dead, from all I can see. Ambulance and reinforcement already requested.'

The street was beginning to fill. The Ministry driver of the Austin Princess had recovered from the initial shock and was able to move the car into a parking-meter bay. Two more police cars pulled up, lights flashing, uniformed and CID men jumping clear before they'd stopped. The ambulance was sounding the warning of its approach on the half-mile journey from St George's Hospital at Hyde Park Corner. The Special Patrol Group Land-Rover, on standby at Scotland Yard, blocked the south side of the square. One of its constables stood beside it, his black, short-barrelled Smith & Wesson .38 calibre in his hand.

'You can put that away,' said his colleague, 'we're light years too bloody late.'

At Oxford Circus the man debated quickly whether to break his journey, head for the Gents and take the magazine off his Kalashnikov. He decided against it, and ran for the escalator to bring him up from the Victoria Line to the level of the Central Line. He thought there would be time to worry about the gun later. Now distance concerned him. His mind was still racing, unable to take in the violence of the scene behind him. His only reaction was that there had been something terribly simple about it all, that for all the work and preparation that had gone into it the killing should have been harder. He remembered the woman over the body, the children and the dog on the pavement, the old woman he had avoided on the pavement outside the house. But none of them registered: his only compulsion now was to get clear of the city.

The first reports of the shooting reached the Commissioner's desk a mile away at Scotland Yard at 9.25. He was slipping out of his coat after the chauffeured drive from Epsom when his aide came in with the first flashes. The Commissioner looked up sharply, noting there had been no knock on his door, before the young officer was in front of him, thrusting a piece of paper at him. As he read the message he saw it was torn at the bottom, ripped off a teleprinter. He said, 'Get me CI, Special Branch and SPG, here in five minutes.' He went over to his desk, pressed the intercom button, announced sharply, 'Prime Minister, please,' and flicked the switch back.

When the yellow light flashed in the centre of the console the Commissioner straightened a little in his seat, subconsciously adjusted his tie, and picked up his phone. A voice remote, Etonian and clipped, said on the line, 'Hello, Commissioner, we're just raking him up, won't be a second.' Then another click. 'Yes, right, you've found me. Good morning, Commissioner, what can I do for you?'

The Commissioner took it slowly. First reports, much regret, your colleague Henry Danby, dead on arrival in hospital. Seems on first impression the work of an assassin, very major police activity, but few other details available. He spoke quietly into the phone and was heard out in silence. When he finished the voice at the end of the line, in the first-floor office overlooking Downing Street and the Foreign Office arch, said 'Nothing else?' 'No, sir. It's early, though.' 'You'll shout if you want help – army, air force, intelligence, anything you need?'

There was no reply from the Commissioner. The Prime Minister went on: 'I'll get out of your hair – call me in half an hour. I'll get one of our people to put it out to the Press Association.'

The Commissioner smiled to himself bleakly. A press release straight away – the political mind taking stock. He grimaced, putting his phone down as the door opened and the three men he'd summoned came in. They headed critical departments: CI – the élite crime investigation unit; the Special Branch – Scotland Yard's counter-terrorist and surveillance force; and the Special Patrol Group – the specialist unit trained to deal with major incidents. All were Commanders, but only the head of the SPG was in uniform.

The Commissioner kept his office spartan and without frills, and the Commanders collected the armless chairs from the sides of the room and brought them towards the desk.

He spoke first to the Special Patrol Group Commander and asked him abruptly what was known.

'Not much, sir. Happened at 9.07. Danby comes down his front steps regular time, regular everything – he's waiting for the Ministry car. A man steps into the street on the other side, and lets fly, fires several shots, multiple wounds, and runs for it in the direction of Victoria. Not much good for eye-witnesses at this stage, not much about. There's a woman on the pavement had a good look at him, but she's a bit shocked at the moment. We've got he's about five-eight, younger than middle-aged, say thirtyish, and what she calls so far a pinched sort of face, dark hair. Clothes aren't much good – dark trousers under a biscuit-coloured mac. That's it.'

'And the gun?'

'Can't be definite.' It was the Special Branch man. 'Seems from what the woman said it's an AK47, usually called a Kalashnikov. Russians use it, VC in Vietnam, the Aden people, the Black September crowd. It's Czech-designed, quite old now, but it's never showed up here before. The IRA have tried to get them into Ulster, but always failed. The *Claudia* – that fishing boat up to the gills in arms – was running them when intercepted. It's a classic weapon, semi-automatic or virtually automatic – 400 rounds a minute, if you could get that many up the spout. Muzzle velocity around 2000 feet a second. Effective killing range comfortable at half a mile. The latest version has a folding stock – you could get it into a big briefcase. It's accurate and doesn't jam. It's a hell of a weapon for this sort of thing. Its calibre is fractionally bigger than ours so it fires Iron Curtain ammo, or ours at a pinch. We've found four shell cases, but no detail on them yet. It's got a noise all of its own, a crack that people who've heard it say is distinctive. From what the woman said to the people down there it fits with the Kalashnikov.'

'And the conclusion?'

'It's not an amateur's weapon. We haven't traced them coming in here yet. If it is a Kalashnikov we're not up against second division. If they can get one of these things then they're big and know what they're about.'

That struck the chord. All four stayed quiet for a moment; it was a depressing thought. A professional political assassin on their hands. It went through the Commissioner's mind before he spoke that a man who troubled to get the ideal gun for the killing, the most popular terrorist weapon in the world, would spend time on the other details of the operation.

He lit his first cigarette of the day, two hours ahead of the schedule he'd disciplined himself to after his last medical check, and broke the silence.

'He'll have thought out his escape route. It'll be good. Where are we, how do we block him?'

The murder squad chief took it up. 'Usual, sir, at this stage. Ports, ferries, airports, private strips as soon as we can get men to them. Phone calls ahead to the control towers. I've got as many men as possible concentrated on tube stations, and particularly exit points on the outskirts. He went towards Victoria, could be the tube, could be the train. We're trying to seal it, but that takes a bit . . .'

He tailed away. He'd said enough. The Commissioner drummed his desktop with the filter of his cigarette. The others waited, anxious now to get the meeting over and get back to their desks, their teams and the reports that were beginning to build.

The Commissioner reacted, sensing the mood.

'Right, I take it we all accept Danby was the target because of his work in Northern Ireland, though God knows a less controversial Minister I never met. Like a bloody willow tree. It's not a nut, because nutters don't get modern Commie assault rifles to run round Belgrave Square. So look for a top man, in the IRA. Right? I'm putting Charlie in overall control. He'll co-ordinate. By this afternoon I want the whole thing flooded, get the manpower out. Bank on Belfast, we'll get something out of there. Good luck.'

The last was a touch subdued. You couldn't give a pep talk to the three men he had in the room, yet for the first time since he'd eased himself into the Commissioner's chair he'd felt something was required of him. Stupid, he thought, as the door closed on the Special Patrol Group Commander.

His yellow light was flashing again on the telephone console. When he picked up his phone his secretary told him the Prime Minister had called an emergency Cabinet meeting for 2.30, and would require him to deliver a situation report to Ministers at the start of their meeting.

'Get me Assistant Commissioner Crime, Charlie Henderson,' he said, after he'd scribbled down the message from Downing Street on his memory pad.

At a quarter to eleven the BBC broke into its television transmissions to schools, and after two seconds of blank screen went to a 'Newsflash' caption. It then dissolved to a continuity announcer, who paused, hesitated for a moment, and then, head down on his script, read:

Here is a newsflash. Just after nine this morning a gunman shot and killed the Secretary of State for the Social Services, Mr Henry Danby. Mr Danby was about to leave his Belgrave Square home when he was fired on by a man apparently on the other side of the street. He was dead on arrival in hospital. Our outside broadcast unit is now outside Mr Danby's home and we go over there now to our reporter, James Lyons.

It's difficult from Belgrave Square to piece together exactly what happened this morning, as Mr Henry Danby, the Social Services Minister, left his home and was ambushed on his front doorstep. The police are at the moment keeping us a hundred yards back from the doorway as they comb the street for clues, particularly the cartridge cases of the murder weapon. But with me here is a lady who was walking her dog just round the corner of the Square when the first shot was fired.
Q. What did you see?
A. Well, I was walking the dog, and I heard the bang, the first bang, and I thought that doesn't sound like a car. And I came round the corner and I saw this man holding this little rifle or gun up to his—
Q. Could you see the Minister – Mr Danby?
A. I saw him, he was sort of crouched, this man in his doorway, he was trying to crawl, then came the second shot. I just stood there, and he fired again and again, and the woman—

Q. Mrs Danby?

A. The woman in the doorway was screaming. I've never heard such a noise, it was dreadful, dreadful . . . I can't say any more . . . he just ran. The poor man was lying there, bleeding. And the woman just went on screaming . . . it was awful.

Q. Did you see the man, the gunman?

A. Well, yes and no, he came past me, but he came fast, he was running.

Q. What did he look like?

A. Nothing special, he wasn't very tall, he was dark.

Q. How old, would you guess?

A. Not old, late twenties, but it was very fast.

Q. And what was he wearing? Could you see?

A. He had a brown mac on, a sort of fawn colour. I saw it had a tartan lining. I could see that he put the gun inside, in a sort of pouch. He just ran straight past me. I couldn't move. There's nothing more.

They'd told the man that simplicity would see him through. That if they kept it easy, with no frills, they'd get him back. He got off the train at Watford, and began to walk towards the barrier, eyes going 180° in front of him. The detectives he spotted were close to the ticket barricr, not looking down the platform, but intent on the passengers. He walked away from the barrier towards the Gents, went into the graffiti-scrawled cubicle, and took off the coat. He hung it carefully behind a door. He unfastened the shoulder strap, unclipped the magazine from the gun, took off his jacket and put the improvised holster back on. With the jacket over the top, the rifle fitted unseen close to his armpit. It gave him a stockiness that wasn't his, and showed his jacket as a poor fit; but that was all. Trembling again in his fingers, he walked towards the barrier. The CID men, both local, had been told the Minister had been shot at home in Belgrave Square, they'd been told the man might have got away by Underground, they'd been told he was in a fawn-brown macintosh and was carrying an automatic rifle. They hadn't been told that, if the killer was on the tube, his ticket might not have been issued at Victoria – could have been bought at another station during the journey. Nor had they been told the Kalashnikov could be folded. They ruled him out in the five yards before he handed over his ticket.

He walked away from them, panting quietly to himself, his forehead cold with sweat, waiting for the shout behind him, or the heavy hand falling on his shoulder, and felt nothing. He walked out of the station to the car park, where the Avis Cortina waited. He stowed the gun under his driving seat and set off for Heathrow. There's no way they'll get you if you stay cool. That was the advice.

In the late morning traffic the journey took him an hour. He'd anticipated it would, and he found he'd left himself ninety minutes for his flight when he'd left the car in the No. 1 terminal car park. He locked the car, leaving the rifle under his seat with its magazine along with it.

The police were staked out at all corners of the terminal. The man saw the different groups, reflected in their shoulder markings: Airport Police – AP, T. Division of the Metropolitan – T, and the Special Patrol

Group men – CO. He knew the last were armed, which gave him a chilled feeling in his belly. If they shouted and he ran, would they shoot him? . . . He clenched his fist and walked up to the BEA ticket desk.

'The name is Jones . . . you've a ticket waiting for me. The one o'clock to Amsterdam, BE 467.'

The girl behind the counter smiled, nodded, and began to beat out the instructions of the flight into her personal reservations computer. The flight was confirmed, and as she made the ticket out the terminal loudspeakers warned passengers of delays on all flights to Dublin, Cork, Shannon and Belfast. No reason was given. But that's where all the effort would be, they'd told him. They haven't the manpower for the lot.

The man brought out the new British passport supplied for him by his unit quartermaster and walked through immigration control.

Chapter Two

Normally the Commissioner travelled alone, with only the elderly driver for company. That afternoon sitting in the front with the driver was an armed detective. The car turned into Downing Street through the crash barriers that had been put into position half an hour after the shooting was reported. The dark, shaded street was empty of Ministerial cars, and sightseers were banned for the day. By the door two constables had established their will on the group of photographers gathered to record all comings and goings, and shepherded them into a line stretching from the railings, over the pavement and out into the parking area. The Commissioner was met in the hall, warm with its red carpets and chandeliers, and escorted to the lift. As he passed the small room to the right of the door, he noted the four plain-clothes men sitting there. His order that the Prime Minister's guard should be doubled had been carried out. Two floors later he was led into the Prime Minister's study.

'I just wanted to see if there was anything you wanted to say before we get involved in the main scene downstairs.'

'All I can do now, sir, is say what we know, what we're doing. Not much of the first, a lot of the second.'

'There'll be a fair amount of questioning about the security round the Minister . . .'

The Commissioner said nothing. It was an atmosphere he was not happy in; he reflected that in his three years as Commissioner and the country's top policeman he'd never got into this marble tower before, never got beyond the first-floor reception salons. On the way to Whitehall he had primed himself not to allow the police to become the scapegoat, and after thirty-six years in the Force his inclination was to be back at Scotland Yard hovering on the fifth floor by the control room, irregular as it was, but at least doing something.

There was little contact, and both acknowledged it. The Prime Minister rose and motioned with his hand to the door. 'Come on,' he murmured, 'let's go and meet them. Frank Scott of the RUC and General Fairbairn are coming in from Belfast in an hour or so. We'll hear them after you.'

The man was striding his way along the vast pier of Schipol Airport, Amsterdam, towards the central transit area. If his connections were working he had fifty-eight minutes till the Aer Lingus 727 took off for Dublin airport. He saw the special airport police with their short-barrelled, lightweight carbines patrolling the entrance to the pier where the El Al jumbo was loading, and had noticed the armoured personnel carriers on the aprons. All the precautions of the anti-hijack programme . . . but nothing to concern him. He went to the Aer Lingus desk, collected the ticket waiting for him, and drifted away to the duty-free lounge. They'd told him not to miss the duty-free lounge; the best in Europe, they'd said. Belgrave Square and the noise and the screaming were far away; for the first time in the day he felt a degree of calm.

In the first-floor Cabinet Room the Commissioner stood to deliver his briefing. He spoke slowly, picking his words with care, and aware that the Ministers were shocked, suspicious and even hostile to what he had to say. There was little comfort for them. On top of what they had seen on the television lunchtime news they were told that a new and better description was being circulated . . . for the first time the policeman had the full attention of his audience.

'There was a slight jostling incident at Oxford Circus this morning. A man barged his way through, nearly knocking people over, and noticeably didn't stop to apologize. Not the sort of thing that you'd expect people to remember, but two women independently saw the television interview from Belgrave Square this morning, and phoned the Yard – put the two together. It's the same sort of man they're talking about as we'd already heard of, but a better description. We'll have a photokit by four o'clock—'

He was interrupted by the slight knock on the door, and the arrival of the Royal Ulster Constabulary Chief Constable, Frank Scott, and General Sir Jocelyn Fairbairn, GOC Northern Ireland. When they'd sat down, crowded in at the far end of the table, the Prime Minister began.

'We all take it this is an IRA assassination. We don't know for what motive, whether it is the first of several

28

attempts or a one-off. I want the maximum effort to get the killer – and fast. I don't want an investigation that runs a month, two months, six months. Every day that these thugs get away with it is a massive plus to them. How it was that Danby's detective was withdrawn from him so soon after he'd left the Ulster job is a mystery to me. The Home Secretary will report to us tomorrow on that, and also on what else is being done to prevent a recurrence of such attacks.'

He stopped. The room was silent, disliking the schoolroom lecture. The Commissioner wondered for a moment whether to explain that Danby himself had decided to do without the armed guard, ridiculing the detective-sergeant's efforts to watch him. He thought better of it and decided to let the Prime Minister hear it from his Home Secretary.

The Prime Minister gestured to the RUC man.

'Well, sir . . . gentlemen,' he started in the soft Scots burr of so many of the Ulstermen. He tugged at the jacket of his bottle-green uniform and moved his blackthorn cane fractionally across the table. 'If he's in Belfast we'll get him. It may not be fast, but it's a village there. We'll hear, and we'll get him. It would be very difficult for them to organize an operation of this scale and not involve so many people that we'll grab one and he'll bend. It's a lot easier to make them talk these days. The hard men are locked up, the new generation talks. If he's in Belfast we'll get him.'

It was past five and dark outside when the Ministers, and the General and the Prime Minister again, had had their say. The Prime Minister had called a full meeting of all present for the day after tomorrow, and reiterated his demand for action and speed, when a

29

private secretary slipped into the room, whispered in the Commissioner's ear, and ushered him out. Those next to him had heard the word 'urgent' used.

When the Commissioner came back into the room two minutes later the Prime Minister saw his face and stopped in mid-sentence. The eyes of the eighteen politicians and the Ulster policeman and the General were on the Commissioner as he said:

'We have had some rather bad news. Police officers at Heathrow have discovered a hired car in the terminal car park near No. 1 building. Under the driver's seat was a Kalashnikov rifle. The car-park ticket would have given a passenger time to take flights to Vienna, Stockholm, Madrid, Rome and Amsterdam. The crew of the BEA flight to Amsterdam are already back at Heathrow, and we are sending a photokit down to the airport, it's on its way, but one of the stewardesses thinks a man who fits our primary description, the rough one we had at first, was in the fifteenth row in a window seat. We are also in touch with Schipol police, and are wiring the picture, but from the BEA flight there was ample time to make a Dublin connection. The Aer Lingus, Amsterdam/Dublin flight landed in Dublin twenty-five minutes ago, and they are holding all passengers in the baggage reclaim hall.'

There was a common gasp of relief round the Cabinet Room, as the Commissioner went on.

'But the Dublin airport police report that those passengers without baggage went through immigration control before we notified them.'

'Would he have had baggage?' It was the Prime Minister, speaking very quietly.

'I doubt it, sir, but we're trying to establish that

with the ticket desk and check-in counter.'

'What a cock-up.' The Prime Minister was virtually inaudible. 'We'll need some results, and soon.'

From Heathrow, the Kalashnikov, swaddled in a cellophane wrapping, was rushed by squad car to Woolwich on the far side of the city, to the police test firing range. It was still white from the chalk-like fingerprint powder brushed on at the airport police station, but the airport's resident fingerprint man declared it clean. 'Doesn't look like a gloves job,' he said, 'he must have wiped it – a cloth, or something. But it's thorough; he's missed nothing.'

In the suburbs of Dublin, in the big open-plan newsroom of RTE, the Republic of Ireland's television service, the central phone in the bank used by the news editor rang at exactly six o'clock.

'Listen carefully, I'm only going to say this once. This is a spokesman for the military wing of the Provisional IRA. An active service unit of the Provisional IRA today carried out a court-martial execution order on Henry DeLacey Danby, an enemy of the people of Ireland, and servant of the British occupation forces in Ireland. During the eighteen months Danby spent in Ireland one of his duties was responsibility for the concentration camp at Long Kesh. He was repeatedly warned that if the regime of the camp did not change, action would be taken against him. That's it.'

The phone clicked off, and the news editor began to read back his shorthand.

* * *

Ten hours later the Saracens and Pigs, on dimmed headlights, were moving off from the Belfast police stations, heading out of the sandbagged tin- and chicken-wire fortresses of Andersonstown, Hasting Street, Flax Street, Glenravel Street and Mount-pottinger. Sentries in steel helmets and shrapnel-proof jerkins, their automatic rifles strapped to their wrists, pulled aside the heavy wood and barbed-wire barri-cades at the entrances of the battalion and company headquarters and the convoys inched their way into the darkness. Inside the armoured cars the troops huddled together, their faces blackened with boot polish, their bodies laden with gas masks, emergency wound dress-ings, rubber-bullet guns, truncheons and the medieval Macron see-through shields. In addition they carried with them their high-velocity NATO rifles. Few of the men had slept more than a few hours, and that cat-napping in their uniforms, their only luxury that of being able to take off their boots. Their officers and senior NCOs, who had attended the operational brief-ings for the raids, had slept even less. There was no talk, no conversation, only the knowledge that the day would be long, tiring, cold and probably wet. There was nothing for the men to look at.

Each car was battened down against possible sniper attacks; only the driver, the rifleman beside him and the rifleman at the back, with his barrel poked through the fine visibility slit, had any sight of the darkened, rainswept streets. No house lights were on, no shop windows were illuminated, and only occasionally was there a high street lamp, one that had survived the attempts of both sides over the last four years to destroy its brightness.

Within a few minutes the convoys had swung off the main roads and were splitting up in the housing estates, all but one on the west side of the city. Two thousand troops, drawn from six battalions, were sealing off the streets that have the Falls Road as their spinal cord – the Catholic artery out of the west side of the city, and the route to Dublin. As the armoured cars pulled across the streets, paratroopers, marines and men from the old county infantry units flung open the reinforced doors and ran for the security of their fire positions. In the extreme west, on the Andersonstown and Suffolk border, where the houses are newer and the sight therefore more incongruous, the troops were from a heavy artillery unit – men more used to ma-nœuvring with the long-range Abbot gun than looking for cover in front gardens and behind dustbins. Away across the city from the Falls more troops were spreading into the Ardoyne, and across on the east side of the Lagan the Short Strand area was sealed.

When their men were in position the officers waited for first light. Cars that tried to enter or leave the cordoned streets were sent back. In a gradual drizzle the troops lay and crouched in the cover that they had found, thumb on the safety catch. The selected marksmen cradled their rifles, made heavier by the attachment of the Starscope, the night vision aid.

The noise started as the soldiers began the house-to-house searches. Women, mighty in dressing gowns with hair piled high by their bright plastic-coated curlers, surged from the houses to blow whistles, howl abuse and crash dustbin lids. Amid the cacophony came the beating of rifle butts on doors, and the thud of the axes and sledgehammers when there was no

33

ready answer. Within minutes there were as many civilians on the streets as soldiers, bouncing their epithets and insults off the unmoving faces of the military. Protected by small knots of soldiers were the unhappy-looking civilian police, usually with their panting, gelignite-sniffer Labradors close by. Occasionally there would come a shout of excitement from one of the small terraced houses, the accent North Country or Welsh or Cockney, and a small shining rifle or pistol would be carried into the street, wrapped to prevent the loss of clues that would convict the still half-asleep man bundled down the pavement and into the back of an armoured truck. But this was not often. Four years of searches and swoops and cordons and arrests had left little to find.

By dawn – and it comes late as far north as Belfast, and then takes a long time coming – there was little to show for the night's work. Some Japanese-made Armalite rifles, some pistols, a sackful of ammunition and crocodile lines of men for questioning by the Special Branch, along with the paraphernalia of terrorism – batteries, lengths of flex, alarm clocks, and sacks of potent weed killer. All were itemized and shipped back to the police stations.

With the light came the stones, and the semi-orderliness of the searches gave way to the crack of rubber bullets being fired; the streets swirled with CS gas, and always at the end of the narrow line of houses were the kids heaving their fractured paving stones at the military.

Unaware of the searches, bus drivers down the Falls Road, stopping at the lights, found youths climbing onto their cabs, a variety of pistols threatening them, and handed over their double-deckers. By nine o'clock the Falls was blocked in four places, and local radio bulletins were warning motorists once again to stick to alternative routes.

As the soldiers withdrew from the streets there were infrequent bursts of automatic fire, not pressed home, and causing no casualties. Only on one occasion did troops have enough of a target to fire back, and then they claimed no hit.

For both sides the raid had its achievements. The army and police had to stir up the pool, and muddy the water, get the top men on the other side on the move, perhaps panic one of them into a false step or a vital admission. The street leaders could also claim some benefit from the morning. After the lull of several weeks the army had arrived to kick in the doors, take away the men, break up the rooms, prise out the floor-boards. At street level that was valuable currency.

The man had seen the police convoy racing into the airport as he'd left, carrying as his sole possessions the Schipol duty-free bag with two hundred cigarettes and a bottle of Scotch. As he'd come through a young man had stepped forward and asked him if he were Mr Jones. He'd nodded, nothing more was required of him, and followed the young man out of the new terminal and into the car park.

It was as they had driven past the airport hotel they'd seen the Garda cars and a van go by. Neither driver nor passenger spoke. The man had been told he would be met, and reminded that he must not speak at all on the journey, not even on the home run. Speech is as ident-ifiable as a face, they explained. The car took the

Dundalk road, and then on the stretch between Drogheda and Dundalk turned left and inland towards the hills.

'We'll be away over near Forkhill,' muttered the driver. The man said nothing as the car bumped its way down the side road. After fifteen minutes at a crossroads, where the only building was a corrugated-iron-roofed store, the driver stopped, got out and went inside saying he'd be a minute and had to telephone. The man sat in the car, the light-headedness he'd felt at Schipol that afternoon suddenly gone; it was not that he was alone that worried him but that his movements and immediate future were not in his own hands. He had started to conjure up images of betrayal and capture, of himself left abandoned near the border and unarmed, when the driver walked back to the car and got in.

'Forkhill's tight, we're going farther down towards the Cullyhanna road. Don't worry, you're home and dry.'

The man felt ashamed that the stranger could sense his suspicion and nervousness. As a gesture he tried to sleep, leaning his head against his safety belt. He stayed in this position till their car jerked and flung his head hard against the window of the door. He shot forward.

'Don't worry' – again the self-assured, almost patronizing approach of the driver. 'That was the crater we filled in two years ago. You're in the North now. Home in two hours.'

The driver cut back to the east, through Bessbrook and on to the north of Newry and the main road to Belfast. The man allowed himself a smile. There was dual carriageway now, and a good fast road, till the driver pulled up outside Hillsborough and motioned to the duty-free bag on the back seat under the man's coat.

'Sorry, boy, I don't want that as we come into town. Ditch it.'

The man wound down his window and flung the plastic bag across the lay-by and into a hedge. The car was moving again. The next sign showed Belfast to be five miles away.

On his return from London the previous evening, the Chief Constable had put a picked team of detectives on standby to wait for information over the confidential phone, the heavily publicized Belfast phone numbers over which information is passed anonymously to the police. They waited through the day in their ready room, but the call they hoped for never came. There was the usual collection of breathy messages naming people in connection with bombs, shootings, locating the dumping of firearms . . . but not a word even of rumour about the Danby killing. In three pubs in the centre of Belfast, British army intelligence officers met their contacts and talked, huddled forward in the little cubicles they favoured. All were to report later that night to their controller that nothing was known. While they talked, threatening, cajoling, bribing their sources, military police Land-Rovers cruised close by. The red-caps had not been told who they were guarding, just detailed to watch and prevent the sudden entry of a number of men into those pubs.

The blowing of the laundry van intelligence surveillance unit, when soldiers kept watch on an IRA base area from the false ceiling of a laundry van while their colleagues plied for trade below, had woken the

37

operation directors to the needs for safeguards when their men were in the field. That was thirty months back. The tortured and mutilated body of a Royal Tank Regiment captain found just three months before had demonstrated the probability of a security leak close to the heart of the unit, and the public outcry at home at the exposing of soldiers to these out-of-uniform dangers had led to a Ministry directive that military personnel were no longer to infiltrate the Catholic community, but instead stay out and cultivate their informers. Funds and the availability of one-way air tickets to Canada were stepped up.

Quite separate from the military intelligence team, the RUC's Special Branch was also out that night – men who for three years had slept with their snub-nosed PPK Walthers on the bedside table, and kept a stock of spare number plates at the back of the garage, who stood to the side at the well-photographed police funerals. They too were to report that there was no talk about the Danby killing.

In the small hours Howard Rennie settled onto a hard wooden chair on the first floor of headquarters down the Stormont Road, and began with painful awkwardness to type out his first report. Some of his colleagues had already been in with the news that they had discovered nothing, that their informants were pleading total ignorance of this one; others would come after him to tell the same story. Even the recording tapes – the 'Confidential Line' – had failed them.

As a chief inspector, Rennie had been hammering the typewriter keys for statements, criminal assessments and incident report sheets for eighteen years, but he still maintained the right-index-finger, left-index-finger patter.

From his time in Special Branch Rennie knew the way the city would buzz after a Provisional spectacular, how rumour and gossip passed from ghetto to ghetto, carrying the message of success and with it a degree of indiscretion. That was where the Branch came in, men trained to be sensitive enough to pick up the murmurs of information. But the days of Special Branch glory in Belfast were long past.

Rennie could remember the courses he'd been on in the early days before it all went haywire, and the troops arrived, when he'd been told across in England by dour-faced men with biscuit tans from long service in the Far East and Africa that the inside work by the police was the only hope of breaking a terrorist movement in its infancy. 'When you get the army in, lording it over your heads, telling you what to do, knowing it all, then it's too late. It's out of your hands by that time. The military on the streets means the enemy are winning, and that you are no longer a force for the opposition to reckon with. The army are bad news for policemen, and the only way for a counter-terrorist operation to be successful is for the Special Branch to be in there, infiltrating, extracting knowledge at ground level.'

And they'd been right. Rennie could see that now. He and his colleagues didn't poke their noses into the corners and crannies of the Provisional heartland. They let the army do that with their fire-power and their armour plating, while the detectives sat back and contented themselves with the interrogation of the flow of arrested men. It was the next best thing, but not good enough.

He'd never been much for the cloak and dagger stuff himself. Too big, too heavy, too conspicuous, not a man to flake his way into a crowd, not ordinary enough. But there were others who had been good at it, till the funerals became too frequent, and the Chief Constable had called a halt.

One man, for instance, had been the king of the Branch men till he died up the Crumlin in a hail of automatic fire. Just watching the nightly riot when the sniper spotted him, and gone was a card-index memory, a walking filing system.

Rennie's report turned out to be a drab document. A succession of negatives after a score of calls and a search through the big tin drawers that carried the buff folders and the photographs and case histories. The Chief Constable came into the room as Rennie was pushing the typewriter back across the table.

'Nothing?'

'Nothing at all, sir. It's a blind alley so far. No-one saying anything. Not a word.'

'I told them in London that it'll come at this end, the man they're looking for. His equipment was too good for anyone based in London. He'll be here. How many do we know who're capable of it, capable of the discipline, of that sort of training?'

'There are quite a few,' said Rennie, 'but none of them out. I could name half a dozen in Long Kesh who we would be looking for if they were free. But, taking them out of the game, I can't see anyone. A bit ago, yes, but not now.'

'I'm calling for a very big effort, maximum effort,' the

Chief Constable had walked away from the table and was talking half to himself, half out into the darkness beyond the shatterproof taped windows. 'London have said in the past that they don't get the co-operation they're looking for when there's a big one in England, and they come here for our help. I don't want them saying that this time. God, it's a damned nuisance. All the manpower, all the effort, everything that has to be dropped for a thing like this. But we have to have him.'

He looked for a long time into the black distance beyond the floodlit perimeter fence. Then swung on his heel. 'Goodnight,' he said, and closed the door carefully behind him.

It'll go on a bit now, thought Rennie, every night here for the next few weeks, typing away, and with little to show for it, unless we're just lucky. Just lucky, and that doesn't happen often.

But just before midnight came the first positive identification of the killer back in the city. The duty major in intelligence section at Lisburn military headquarters, leafing through the situation reports of the evening, read that a patrol of the Lifeguards had for fifteen minutes closed the Hillsborough to Banbridge road while they investigated a package at the side of the road. It was cleared after the bomb disposal expert arrived and found the bag contained a carton of cigarettes and a bottle of Scotch, duty free and bought at Schipol airport. He hurriedly phoned his chief at home, and the RUC control centre. But, nagging at him, was the question of how such an operation as the Danby killing could have been mounted, with no word coming out.

* * *

The man was asleep now, in the spare back bedroom of a small terraced house off the Ballymurphy Bull Ring. He'd come at 11.25 up from Whiterock where he had stayed since arriving in Belfast. Round him a safety system was building, with the arrangement that he'd sleep till 5.30, then move again up into New Barnsley. The Brigade staff in Belfast were anxious not to keep him long in one place, to hustle him round. Only the Brigade commander knew the value of the man the precautions were made for . . . No-one else was told, and in the house he was greeted with silence. He came in fast over the back fence, avoiding the kids' bikes, ducked under the washing lines and made his way through the damp, filthy scullery into the back room. The family was gathered in semi-darkness with the television on loud – Channel 9. His escort whispered into the ear of the man of the house, and was gone, leaving him. The man was not from this part of the city, and was not known anyway.

His arrival and needs, after four years of warfare, were unremarkable. In the 'Murph' his name could be kept secret, not his reason for running – not after the Scotland Yard photokit had been flashed up on the screen during the late-night news. On orders from London the photo had been withheld until after the intelligence and Special Branch officers had attempted to identify the killer. With their failure the picture had been released.

The family gathered round the set to hear the announcer.

Scotland Yard have just issued a photokit picture of the man they wish to interview in connection

42

with the murder of Mr Henry Danby, the Minister of Social Security, at his home in central London yesterday morning. The picture has been compiled from the descriptions of several eye-witnesses. Scotland Yard say the man is aged about thirty, has short hair, with a parting on the left side, a narrow face, with what a witness calls 'pinched cheeks'. The man is of light build, and about five feet nine inches tall. When last seen he was wearing grey trousers and a dark brown jacket. He may also have a fawn-coloured macintosh with him. Anyone who can identify this man is asked to get in touch immediately with the police on the Confidential Line of Belfast 227756 or 226837.

High on the fireplace over the small fire grate was a carved and painted model of a Thompson machine-gun, a present to the family from their eldest son, Eamon, held for two years in Long Kesh. It was dated Christmas 1973. Below the gun the family registered no reaction to the picture shown on their screens.

In the small hours Theresa, Eamon's sister, tiptoed her way round the scarred door of the back room. She eased her path over the floorboards, still loosened and noisy since the army came to look for her brother. In the darkness she saw the face of the man, out from under his blankets with his arms wrapped around his pillow, as a child holds a favourite doll. She was shivering in the thin nightdress, transparent and reaching barely below her hips. She had selected it two hours before to put on before waiting to be sure her people were asleep. Very gently at first, she shook the shoulder of the man, till he

43

started half out of bed, gripped her wrist, and then in one movement pulled her down, but as a prisoner.

'Who's that?' he said it hard, tautly, with fear in his voice.

'It's Theresa.' There was silence, just the man's breathing, and still he held her wrist, vice-like. With her free hand she moved back the bedclothes and moved her body alongside his. He was naked and cold; across the room she saw his clothes strewn over the chair by the window.

'You can let go,' she said and tried to move closer to him, but only to find him backing away till the edge of the single bed stopped his movement.

'Why did you come?'

'To see you.'

'Why did you come?' Again harsher, louder.

'They showed your picture . . . on the telly . . . just now . . . on the late news.'

The hand released her wrist. The man flopped back on the pillow, tension draining out of him. Theresa pressed against his body, but found no response, no acknowledgement of her presence.

'You had to know, for when they move you on. I had to tell you . . . we aren't your enemies. You're safe with us . . . there's no danger.'

'There are six men in the city who know I'm here – and you . . .'

A little more nervously she whispered back, 'Don't worry yourself, there's no narks here, not in this street . . . not since the McCoy girl . . . they shot her.' It was an afterthought – Roisin McCoy, soldier's girl-friend, part-time informer, found shot dead under Divis mountain. Big outcry, no arrests.

'I'm not saying anything.'

'I didn't come to talk, and it's freezing, half out of the bloody clothes.'

He pulled her down, close now against him, the nylon of her nightdress riding up over her hips and breasts. She pushed against him, screwing her nipples against the black hair of his chest.

'Not much, are they?' she murmured. 'Couple of bloody bee stings.'

The man smiled, and the hand that had grasped her wrist to the point of half stopping the blood flow now stroked and rubbed urgently at the soft white inside of her thighs. She reached down and felt his stomach back away as she took hold of him, limp and lifeless, pliable in her hand. Slowly, then frantically, to match her own sensations she stroked and kneaded him, but without success.

Abruptly the man stopped his movements, pulled his hand away from the moist warmth.

'Get out. Bugger off. Get out.'

Theresa, nineteen years old, four of them spent on the mill weaving line, had heard and seen enough in her life to say, 'Was it that bad . . . London . . . was it . . . ?'

The interruption was a stinging blow across the right side of her face. His cheap onyx wedding ring gouged the skin below the eye. She was gone, out through the door across the passage to her bed; there she lay, legs clenched together, fascinated and horrified at the knowledge she had.

In her half-sleep she heard the whisper of voices and the footsteps on the stairs as the man was taken to his next place of hiding.

*   *   *

45

In the Cabinet Room the Prime Minister was showing little patience for the lack of a quick arrest. He had heard the Commissioner say that the case was static in London now, and that the main police effort was to establish how and where the man had entered the country. The boarding house in Euston where he had slept the night before the shooting had been searched, but nothing found. As expected the gun had yielded no fingerprints, and the same process of elimination was being used on the car. Here it was pointed out that the police had to identify the fingerprints of everyone who had handled the car over the previous six weeks or so before they could begin to come up with a worthwhile print and say this was the killer's. It would take a long time, said the Commissioner, and involved drivers, Avis staff, garage personnel. Nothing had been found on the basics – steering wheel, door handle, gear lever. He reported on the new security measures surrounding Ministers, pointed out that they were nearly if not totally a waste of time if politicians did not co-operate, and urged no repetitions of the situation by which the murdered Minister had been able to decide for himself that he no longer wanted protection. He finished by putting the proposition that the killer had no contact in Britain, and had operated completely on his own. Reservations for tickets in Dublin, Heathrow and Amsterdam had all been made over the phone and were untraceable. He fell back on the theme that the solving of the crime would happen in Belfast, and that yesterday a Chief Superintendent from the Murder Squad had gone to Belfast to liaise with the RUC.

Frank Scott, the Chief Constable, reported nothing

had come in on the confidential phones, and as yet there had been no whisper on the Special Branch net. 'Now we know he's in the city we'll get him, but it may not be fast – that's the situation.' It had been left to him to report the finding of the Amsterdam duty-free bag.

'That's what you said two days ago,' snapped the Prime Minister.

'And it's still the situation.' The Chief Constable was not prepared to give ground. The Northern Ireland Secretary chipped in, 'I think we all accept, Frank, that it's near impossible to stampede this sort of operation.'

'But I have to have results.' The Prime Minister drummed his knuckles on the table. 'We cannot let this one hang about.'

'I'm not hanging about, sir, and you well know that no-one in my force is.' The Ulster policeman's retort caused a certain fidgeting down the sides of the table from Ministers who had begun to feel their presence was irrelevant to the matter in hand – other than that by their arrivals and departures the cameras could witness the activity and firm hand of government. The Commissioner wished he'd come in faster. One up to the RUC.

The Prime Minister, too, sensed the chilliness of the situation, and invited the opinion of General Fairbairn. As the GOC Northern Ireland, commanding more than fifteen thousand men there, he expected to be listened to. He weighed his words.

'The problem, sir, is getting inside the areas the IRA dominate. Getting good information that we can trust and then can act on fast enough while the tips are still hot. Now, we can thrash around as we did yesterday morning, and as we have done to a more limited degree

47

this morning, and though we pick up a bit – a few bodies, a few guns, some bomb-making equipment – we're unlikely to get at the real thing. I would hazard the motive behind the killing was to get us to launch massive reprisal raids, cordon streets off, taking house after house to pieces, lock hundreds up. They want us to hammer them and build a new generation of mini-martyrs. It's been quiet there these last few weeks. They needed a major publicity-attracting operation, and then a big kick-back from us to involve people at street level who are beginning to want to disengage. The raids we have been mounting these last thirty-six hours are fair enough as an initial reaction, but if we keep them up we'll be in danger of reactivating the people who had begun to lose interest in the IRA.'

'What about your intelligence men, your men on the inside?'

'We don't go in for that sort of thing so much now, we tend to meet on the outside – after the young captain was murdered three months ago, horrible business . . . the Ministry wasn't happy, we suspended that sort of work.'

'Suspended it?' The Prime Minister deliberately accentuated the touch of horror in his voice.

'We haven't had an operation of anything like this size to handle for around a year; things have been running down. There hasn't been the need for intelligence operatives. Now we would have to set up a new unit completely – the men we have there at the moment are too compromised. I don't think in your time-scale, Prime Minister, we have the time to do it.'

He said the last drily, and with only the faintest hint of sarcasm, sufficiently guarded to be just about

48

permissible for a General in the Cabinet Room at No. 10 Downing Street.

'I want a man in there . . . nothing else to think about.' The Prime Minister was speaking deliberately, the Agriculture man thought – nice and slowly, just right for the transcript being scribbled in the corner.

'I want an experienced agent in there as fast as you can make it. A good man. If we've picked the killer up by then, nothing lost, if not . . . I know what you're going to say, General: if the man is discovered I will take the rap. That's understood. Well?'

The General had heard enough to realize that the interchange of ideas had been over several minutes earlier. This was an instruction by the Head of Government.

'For a start, sir, you can get the gentleman taking the notes over there by the door to take his last page out of the book, take it over to the fire and burn it. You can also remind everyone in the room of the small print of the Official Secrets Act. Thank you.'

The General got up, flushed high in his cheeks, and, followed hurriedly by the Chief Constable, who was sharing his RAF plane back to Belfast, left the room.

The Prime Minister waited for the door to close, and the angry footsteps to hasten down the corridor.

'They're free enough with the advice when they want us to play round with political initiatives, but the moment we come up with a suggestion . . . That's the way it's always been. I've had four generals in my time at Downing Street telling me it's all about over, that the Provisionals are beaten, that they're finished. They reel off the statistics. How many sticks of gelignite they've found, how many rifles, how many houses have been searched, how the back of the opposition is broken. I've heard it too often – too often to be satisfied with it.'

His eyes ranged up the shining mahogany table, along the line of embarrassed faces till they locked on to the Minister of Defence.

'Your people have the wherewithal for this sort of thing. Get it set up, please, and controlled from this end. If our friend the General doesn't like it, then he won't have to worry himself.'

That afternoon in an upper room above a newsagent's shop near the main square in Clones, just over the border in County Monaghan, half of the twelve-man Army Council of the Provisional IRA met to consider the operation mounted two days earlier in London. Initially there was some anger that the killing had not been discussed by all members in committee, as was normal. But the Chief of Staff, a distant, intense man with deep-set eyes and a reputation for success in pulling the movement together, glossed over the troubles. He emphasized that, now the shooting had taken place, the priority in the movement was to keep the man safe. Unknowingly he echoed the British Prime Minister five hundred miles away in Whitehall when he said, 'Every day we keep the man free is a victory. Right? They wanted to pull two battalions out next month; how can they when they can't find one man? We have to keep him moving and keep him close. He's a good man, he won't give himself away. But at all costs we have to keep their hands off him. He's better dead than in Long Kesh.'

*　　*　　*

It was getting dark when the RAF Comet took off from Tempelhof airport, Berlin, with its three passengers. Halfway back and sitting in an aisle seat Harry still felt bewildered. Two hours earlier he had been called to the Brigade commander's office at HQ under the shadow of the old Nazi Olympic stadium, and instructed he was going to London on urgent military business. He was told he wouldn't need to go home to get his bag, that was being done, and no, it would not be suitable for him to phone home at this moment, but it would be explained to his wife that he had been called away in a hurry.

Three and a half hours later the plane landed at Northolt and then taxied two hundred yards beyond the main reception area to an unmarked square of tarmac where a solitary set of steps and a civilian Morris 1800 were waiting.

For a captain in transport it was a very remarkable set of circumstances.

Chapter Three

Harry was awake at first light.

He was in a large room, painted soft pastel yellow with fine hard moulding round the ceiling. A study of a Victorian matron with a basket of apples and pears faced him from across the room. An empty bookcase against the same wall, a basin, small Ministry-issue thin towel hanging underneath it. There was a chair and table, both with his uniform draped over them. At the foot of the bed he could see the suitcase they said they'd packed for him, with no baggage labels attached to it.

They'd avoided all checks at Northolt, and Harry hadn't been asked to produce his passport or any travel documents. As soon as he was inside the car the two military policemen who had travelled with him had peeled away from his side and moved back into the shadows. He'd heard the boot bang shut to notify that his suitcase was aboard. Then the car had moved off.

'My name's Davidson.' The man in the front passenger seat was talking. 'Hope you had a good flight. We've got a bit of a drive now. Perhaps you'd like to sleep a bit.'

Harry had nodded, accepted the situation with what

grace his position allowed, and dozed off.

The car had gone fast out of London, the driver taking them on to the A3, then turning off down to Leatherhead, south to Dorking and then into the narrow winding side roads under Leith Hill. Davidson was beside the driver and Harry had the back seat to himself, and it was only when the night sky was blotted out by the arch of trees over the sunken road that he woke. The car had driven on some miles, with evident care, before it swept through the wrought-iron gates of one of those great houses buried deep amongst their own woods that lie hidden in the slopes. The drive was rough and in need of repair. Abruptly the rhododendrons gave way to lawns and the car pulled up at a huge porticoed front door.

'Bit formidable, isn't it? The Ministry maintains it's all they could get. Delusions of grandeur. A convent school went broke. Kids all died of exposure, more likely. Come on in.'

Davidson, who had opened the door for him, was speaking. Harry was aware of several other men hovering in the background. The bag was collected, and Davidson went in, followed by Harry.

'We've a long day tomorrow. Lots of talking to do. Let's call it quits, have a good night, and breakfast at seven. OK?'

Sandwiches and a vacuum flask of coffee were waiting in Harry's room.

The plate and dirtied cup were on the rug by his bed. He put his feet down gingerly and moved to his case. His shaving bag was on top of his neatly folded clothes. He wondered what on earth Mary was making of all this. If they'd sent that dreadful adjutant down to tell her he was called away on urgent business it would be enough to get him a divorce – better be someone with a little experience in the world of untruths.

No-one he'd seen last night had been in uniform. After shaving he put on a checked shirt, Transport Corps tie and his grey suit. He folded away his uniform in the wardrobe and dispersed his other clothes to the various drawers and cupboards. He sat by the window waiting for someone to come to tell him breakfast was served. From his room on the second floor he could see he was at the back of the house. Overgrown tennis courts. A vegetable garden. A great line of trees before the ridge of Surrey hills.

Harry was not naïve and had realized he was to be briefed for an intelligence mission. That didn't bother him, he'd decided. It was a little flattering, and was welcome after brigade transport. Perhaps the remarks about nervous collapse had been rather overstressed on his post-Aden reports. Anyway, little had come his way that had stretched him to the degree he thought he was capable of. If they'd brought him from Germany then the hard assumption would be that they were going to use him for something in Berlin. This pleased him, as he prided himself that he had taken the trouble to learn passable German, have a near taxi-driver knowledge of the city and keep himself discreetly abreast of the trade techniques. His thoughts were full of the Reichstag, watchtowers, walls and clumps of flowers by the little crosses when the sharp knock came and the door opened.

*   *   *

It began in earnest in what must once have been the drawing room, now furnished in the fashion of the Defence Ministry. Heavy tables, sofas with big pink flowers all over them and deep armchairs with cloth squares at the back to prevent greased hair marking the covers.

Davidson was there, and three others.

Harry was given the armchair to the right of the fireplace, dominated by an oil painting of the Retreat from Kabul in the snows of the Afghanistan passes. One man sat behind him by the window; another, not ostentatiously, close to the door. The third sat at a central table, his files spread out on the drapes that covered the polished oak surface. One was of stiff blue cardboard, its top crossed with red tape. 'SECRET' had been written across the front in large letters, and underneath were the words: 'BROWN, HARRY JAMES, CAPT.' Four sheets of closely-typed paper were inside – Harry's life history and the assessments of his performance by each of his commanding officers. The first page carried the information they had sought when they had begun the search for the officer they wanted.

Name: Brown Harry James
Current rank: Captain
Age: 34 years
Born: Portadown, NI, November 1940
Distinguishing marks and description: 5'11" height, medium build, brown hair, blue eyes, no distinguishing marks, no operation scars
Service UK: Catterick, Plymouth, Tidworth, Ministry of Defence

Service Overseas: Cyprus (2nd Lt), Borneo (2nd Lt), Aden (1st Lt), Berlin (Capt)
Decorations: Cyprus – Mentioned in Despatches, Aden – Military Cross

In the last quarter of the page was the passage that ensured that Harry came into the operation.

Aden citation: For three months this officer lived as a native in the Arab quarter of Sheik Othman, moving inside the community there and supplying most valuable intelligence concerning terrorist operations. As a result of his work many important arrests were made. It should be stressed that this work was extremely dangerous to the officer, and there was a constant risk that if discovered he would face certain torture and death.

Too right, Harry would have thought if anyone had let him see the file. Day after day, living with those filthy bastards, eating with them, talking with them, crapping with them. Watching for new cars, watching for movement after curfew, observing the huddles in the coffee shops. And always the fear, and the horror if they came too close to him, seemed too interested, talked too much. The terrible fear of discovery, and the pain that would follow. And the know-alls in intelligence back at headquarters who only met an NLF man when he was neatly parcelled up in their basement cells, and who pass discreet little messages – about hanging on a few more days, just a little bit longer. They'd seemed surprised when he just walked up to an army patrol one hot, stinking morning, and introduced himself, and walked out of thirteen weeks of naked terror. And no mention in the files on him of the nervous breakdown, and the days of sick leave. Just a metal cross and an inch square of purple and white cloth to dangle it from, all there was to show for it.

Davidson was moving about the room in sharp darts around the obstacles of furniture.

'I don't have to tell you from your past experience that everything that is said in this room this morning goes under the Official Secrets Act. But I'll remind you of that anyway. What we say in here, the people you've seen here, and the building and its location are all secret.

'Your name was put forward when we came into the market for a new man for an infiltration job. We've seen the files on the Aden experience, and the need has now come up for a man unconnected with any of the normal channels to go in and work in a most sensitive area. The work has been demanded by the Prime Minister. Yesterday afternoon he authorized the mission, and I must say frankly it was against, as I understand it, the advice of his closest military advisers. Perhaps that's putting it a bit strong, but there's some scepticism . . . the PM had a brother in SOE thirty years ago, he has heard over Sunday lunch how the infiltration of agents into enemy country won the war, and they say he's had a bee about it ever since.

'He wants to put a man into the heart of Provo-land, into the Falls in Belfast – a man who is quite clean and has no form in that world at all. The man should not be handled by any of the existing intelligence and under-cover groups. He'd be quite new, and to all intents he'd be on his own as far as looking after himself is concerned. I think anyone who has thought even a little about what the PM is asking for knows that the job he has asked us to do is bloody dangerous. I haven't gilded it, Harry. It's a job we've been asked to do, and we all think from what we've read of you that you are the ideal man for it. Putting it formally, this is the bit where you either stand up and say "Not effing likely", and walk out through the door and we'll have you on a flight to Berlin in three hours. Or it's the time when you come in and then stay in.'

The man at the table with the files shuffled his papers. Harry was a long way from a rational evaluation of the job, whatever it was they were offering. He was just thinking how large a file they'd got on him when he became aware of the silence in the room.

Harry said, 'I'll try it.'

'You appreciate, Harry, once you say "yes", that's it. That has to be the definitive decision.'

'Yes, I said yes. I'll try it.' Harry was almost impatient with Davidson's caution.

The atmosphere in the room seemed to change. The man behind Harry coughed. Davidson was on the move again, the file now open in his hand.

'We're going to put you into the Falls with the express and only job of listening for any word of the man who shot the Minister, Danby, three days ago. Why aren't they doing it from Belfast? Basic reason is they've no longer got an infiltration set-up that we're happy with. They used to do it, lost out, and have pretty much withdrawn their men to let them stooge on the outside and collect the stuff they want from informers. The activity has been down over the last few months, and with the risk that exists – I'm being straight with you, Harry – of an undercover man being picked off, and the hullabaloo when it hits the fan, those sort of operations have been scaled down. There is a thought that the intelligence division over there is not as tight as it ought to be. We've been asked to set up a new operation. Intelligence in Belfast won't handle you, we will. The Special Branch over there won't have heard of you. Whatever else your problems may be they won't be that someone is going to drop you in it over there, because no-one will know of your existence. If you have a message you pass it to us. A phone call to us, on the numbers we give you, will be as fast – if you want to alert the military – as anything you could do if you were plugged into the regular Lisburn net, working under their control.

'I stress again, this is the PM's idea. He raised it at the security meeting yesterday and insisted we push it forward. The RUC don't want you, and the military regard it as something of a joke. We reckon we'll need you here for two weeks before we fly you in, and in that time they may have the man, or at least have a name on him. If that happens then we call the whole thing off, and you can relax and go back to Germany. It's not a bad thing that they don't want to know – we won't have to tell them anything till it's ripe, and that way we keep it tight.'

He'd wondered whether to mention the Prime Minister's involvement, and thought about it at length the previous evening. If this man were to be captured and talk under torture the balloon would be sky high, the reverberations catastrophic. But there was another side to it. Any man asked to do as dangerous a job as the one envisaged had the right to know where the orders originated; to be certain he wasn't the puppet on the end of wire manipulated for the benefit of a second-rate operation. It was Davidson's own inclination to be open, and he reckoned that apart from everything else a man in these circumstances needed all the morale-building he could get.

'So far the police and military have put out pictures, appeals, rewards, launched raids, checked all the usual angles, and they haven't come up with anything. I don't know whether you would. The PM's decided we try and that's what's going to happen.

'I'm sorry, but on this there cannot be a phone call to your wife. We've told her you've been called away on urgent posting. This morning she's been told you're on your way to Muscat, because of your special Aden knowledge. We have some postcards you can write to her later and we'll get them posted by the RAF for you.

'I said at the beginning this would be dangerous. I don't want to minimize that. The IRA shoot intelligence men they get their hands on. They don't rough them up and leave them for a patrol to find, they kill them. The last man of ours that they took was tortured. Catholics who work for us have been beaten up, burned, lacerated, hooded and then killed. They're hard bastards . . . but we want this man badly.'

Davidson paused in his stride, jolting Harry's attention. Harry fidgeted and shifted in the chair. He hated the pep talks. This one was damn near a carbon copy of the one he'd had in Aden, though then the PM's name had been left out, and they were quoting top secret instructions from GOC Land Forces Mid East.

Davidson suggested coffee. The work would start after the break.

The Prime Minister had been hearing a report on the latest speech to a Bulawayo farming conference of the rebel Prime Minister – his 'illegal counterpart', as he liked to call him. He scanned the pages quickly and deftly, assimilating the nuances the Rhodesian's speech writers had written in for the reader on the other side of the world. It was a static situation, he decided, not one for a further initiative at this stage. When his secretary had left him he turned back to his desk from the window and dialled an unlisted number at the Ministry of Defence.

The conversation was short and obviously to the point. It lasted about twenty-five seconds. The Prime Minister put his opening question, listened, and rang off after saying, 'No . . . no . . . I don't want to know any more . . . only that it's happening. Thank you, you'll keep me informed, thank you.'

Off the Broadway, halfway up the Falls, the man and his minder locked the doors of the stolen and resprayed Cortina and moved through the protective cordon of white-painted petrol drums to the door of the pub. The minder had been there from the morning, not knowing and not asking who was the man he had been set to protect. With the job went the PPK Walther that pulled down his coat pocket. The gun was a prize symbol of the old success days of the local IRA company – taken from the body of a Special Branch constable ambushed as he cruised late at night in the Springfield Road. It was now prized, partly for its fire power, partly for its value as a trophy.

The man led the way into the pub. It was the first time he had walked the streets of the city since his return, and after two days on the move from house to house and not a straight night's sleep at any of them he showed the signs of a life on the run. The Army Council had anticipated this and had decided that for his own safety the man should as soon as possible be reintroduced to his old haunts, as the longer he was away the more likely it was that his name could become associated with the shooting in London.

The pub boasted a single bar, dark, shabby and with a pall of smoke hanging between shoulder height and the low ceiling. A sparse covering of worn lino was on the floor, pocked with cigarette burns. As always most eyes were facing the door, and conversation died as the man walked in and went towards the snug, away to the left of the serving area. The minder gripped him by the arm, and mouthed quickly in his ear.

'They said in the middle of the bar. Show yourself. That's what they told me.'

The man nodded his head, turned to the bar and ordered his drinks. He was known only slightly here, but the man with him was local, and that was the passport to acceptance. The man felt the tension easing out of him, as the conversation again spread through the bar.

Later he was asked by one old man how come he'd not been in. He replied loudly, and with the warm beer moving through him, that his Mam in Cork had been unwell. He'd been to see her, she was better now and he was back. His Mam was better known in these streets than he was, and it was remembered by a few that she'd married a railwayman in Cork three years after her first husband died, and moved away to the South from Belfast. Lucky I was too, she'd say. The railwayman himself had died now, but she had stayed south. The man's explanation was more than adequate. There were mutterings of sympathy, and the subject closed.

His main worry had been the photokit picture. He had seen it reproduced on the front page of the Belfast *Newsletter* on his second day back and read of the efforts to track him down. He'd seen pictures of the troops sealing streets off, looking for him, and looked at quarter-page advertisements taken by the Northern Ireland Office urging people to tell all they know about the killing to the police via the Confidential phone. There were reports that a huge reward was to be offered for his capture, but if any of the men in the bar linked him with the picture there was no sign of it. The man had decided himself that the picture was not that similar to his features, too pinched in the face, the word the woman had used, with the hair parting too accentuated.

He was on his third pint when the patrol came into the pub.

Eight soldiers, crowding the small area, ordered everyone to stay still and keep their hands out of their pockets. With the shouting from the troops and the general noise of their entry, no-one noticed the minder leaning against the bar slide his gun down towards the washing-up bowl. Nor did they see the publican, ostensibly drying his hands before displaying them to the troops, put his cloth over the dark gun-metal. With his final action he flicked cloth and gun onto the floor and kicked them hard towards the kitchen door. The design of the building prevented any of the soldiers seeing the young girl's hand that reached round the door in answer to her father's short whistle, gather up the gun, and run with it to the coal shed. The men in the bar were lined against the side wall by the empty fireplace and searched. The man's search was no more, no less thorough than that of the other men. They searched the minder very thoroughly, perhaps because he was sweating, a veil of moisture across his forehead, as he waited for their decision on him, not knowing what had happened to the gun that bore his palm prints and could earn him five years plus in the Crumlin Road.

Then, as suddenly as the soldiers had come they were out, barging their way past the tables, running into the street, and back to their regular routine of patrolling. There was noise again in the bar. The publican pushed the washing-up cloth, now filthy with coal smuts, across the wooden bar to the minder. The man felt good. He'd come through the first big test.

At the big house in Surrey the team round Harry had worked him hard the first day. They'd started by discussing what cover he would want, and rejected the alternatives in favour of a merchant seaman home after five years, but with his parents dead some years back.

'It's too small a place for us to give you a completely safe identity you could rely on. It would mean we'd have to bring other people in who would swear by you. It gets too big that way. We start taking a risk, unnecessarily.'

Davidson was adamant that the only identity Harry

would have would be the one he carried round on his back. If anyone started looking into his story really deeply then there was no way in which he could survive, strong background story or not.

Harry himself supplied most of what they needed. He'd been born a Catholic in one of the little terraces off Obin Street in Portadown. The houses had been pulled down some years ago, and replaced by anonymous blocks of flats and small houses, now daubed with the slogans of revolution. With the destruction of the old buildings inevitably the people had become dispersed.

Portadown, the Orangeman's town with the ghetto round the long sloping passage of Obin Street, still had its vivid teenage memories for Harry. He'd spent his childhood there from the age of five, after his parents had been killed in a car crash. They'd been driving back to Portadown when a local businessman late home on his way back from Armagh had cut across them and sent his father into a ditch and telegraph pole. Harry had stayed with an aunt for twelve years in the Catholic street before joining the army. But his childhood in the town gave him adequate knowledge – enough, Davidson decided, for his cover.

For four hours after lunch they quizzed him on his knowledge of the intricacies of Irish affairs, sharpened him on the names of the new political figures. The major terrorist acts since the summer of 1969 were neatly catalogued on three closely-typed sheets. They briefed him particularly on the grievances of the minority.

'You'll want to know what they're beefing about. You know this, they're walking encyclopaedias on every shot we fired at them. There's going to be a lot more, but this is the refresher.'

Davidson was warming to it now, enjoying these initial stages of the preparation, the thoroughness of which would be the deciding factor whether their agent survived. Davidson had been through this before. Never with Ulster as the target, but in Aden before Harry's duty there, and Cyprus, and once when a Czech refugee was sent into his former homeland. That last time they heard nothing, till the man's execution was reported by the Czech news agency half an hour after a stony protest note was delivered to the British Ambassador in Prague. Post-war Albania had involved him too. Now it was a new operation, breeding the same compulsion as the first cigarette of the day to an inveterate smoker.

Harry had come up to the table. The papers were spread out in front of him, fingers reaching and pointing at the different essentials for him to take in.

Later he was to take many of them to his room, ask for some sandwiches and coffee and, sprawled in front of the gas fire, read them into the small hours till they were second nature. On his own for the first time in the day he too was able to assess the importance of the preparation he was undergoing, and alone in the room he allowed himself to think of the hazards of the operation in which he was now involved.

It was past two in the morning when he undressed and climbed into bed, the papers still strewn on the rug in front of the fire.

Chapter Four

Over the next fortnight the street scene in Belfast returned to its pre-Danby level of violence. It was widely recognized that in the wake of the killing the level of army activity had risen sharply, initially in the use of major cordon and search operations, merging into an increase in the number of spot raids on the homes of known republicans on the run. The army activity meant more men were charged with offences, but alongside their appearances in court was an upsurge in street rioting, something that had previously been almost eradicated. The army's posture was sharply criticized by the minority politicians, who accused the troops of venting on innocent Catholic householders their frustrations at not being able to find Danby's murderer.

The Secretary of State for Northern Ireland agreed to appear on the local Independent TV station and the regional BBC news programme to answer the allegations of Protestant papers that not enough was being done – that a British Cabinet Minister had been shot down in cold blood in front of his wife and children yet his killers were allowed to go free for fear of offending Catholic opinion.

Before appearing on television the Secretary of State called a meeting of his security chiefs, and heard both Frank Scott and General Fairbairn urge caution and patience. The General in particular was concerned lest a show of strength spread over several weeks undo the gradual return to something like normality. The three men were soon to leave for their various destinations – the politician for the studio, the General for Lisburn and the Chief Constable for his modern police head-quarters – but first they walked on the lawn outside the Stormont residence of the Secretary of State. Away from the listening ears of secretaries, aides and body-guards the General reported that his intelligence section had heard nothing of the killer in Belfast and there was some concern about whether the man they sought was even in the city. The Chief Constable added to the politician's cross in reporting that his men too had been unable to uncover any hard information on the man. But the head of his Special Branch favoured the belief that the killer was in the city, and probably back in circulation. The Chief Superintendent in charge of picked detectives had a fair insight into the workings of his enemies' minds, and had correctly read the desire of the Provisional IRA Army Council to get their man back into the mainstream.

For three minutes they talked in the centre of the lawn. The conversation ended when the Secretary of State quietly, and more than a little hesitantly, asked the General:

'Jocelyn, no news I suppose on what the PM was talking about?'

'None, nor will there be.'

The General made his way back to his car, turned and shouted a brusque farewell.

As the military convoy pulled away, the politician turned to the policeman. 'We have to have this bastard soon. The political scene won't hold up long otherwise. And there's a lot of restiveness among the Loyalists. We need him quick, Frank, if the sectarianism isn't to start up again. There's not much time . . .'

He walked quickly now to his big maroon Rover with its reinforced sides and extra thick windows, with machine-guns, field dressings and gas masks alongside his official cases in the boot. He nodded to his driver, and then winced as the detective sitting in front of him loaded the clip of bullets into the butt of the 9mm Browning.

The car swung out into the open road for the drive into the city, with his escort close behind to prevent any other car slipping between them. 'What a bloody carry-on,' the politician observed as they swept through the traffic towards the television studios.

The interview of the Secretary of State was embargoed until 18.01 hours; its full text was issued by the Northern Ireland press office to Belfast newspapers. In essence the BBC and ITV transmissions were the same, and the public relations men put out only the BBC interview.

Q. Secretary of State, can you report any progress in the hunt for Mr Danby's killer?
A. Well, I want to emphasize that the security forces are working flat out on this one. I myself

have had a meeting just before this broadcast with the army commander and chief constable, and I am perfectly satisfied with the investigation and follow-up operations they are mounting. I'm confident we'll round up this gang of thugs quickly.

Q. But have you any leads yet to who the killers are?

A. I think we know who the killers are, they're the Provisional IRA, but I'm sure you wouldn't expect me to talk on television about the details of a police investigation.

Q. It's been pretty quiet for some time in Belfast, and we were led to believe that most of the IRA commanders were imprisoned . . . Isn't it justifiable to expect rather quicker action, even results at this stage?

A. If you mean to imply we have claimed the IRA weren't capable of mounting this sort of operation I don't think we have ever made that sort of assumption. We think this is the work of a small group, a very small group. We'll get them soon . . . there's nothing to panic about – (It was a bad word, panic, he saw it as soon as he said it. The interviewer nudged him forward.)

Q. I haven't heard the word 'panic' used before. Are you implying the public have overreacted towards the killing of a Cabinet Minister in broad daylight in front of his children?

A. Of course, this was a dreadful crime. This was a colleague of mine. Of course, people should feel strongly; what I'm saying is that this is a last fling of the IRA—

Q. A pretty successful last fling.

A. Mr Danby was unarmed—

Q. In Loyalist areas of the city the government are accused of not going in hard to find the killer because the results could antagonize Catholic opinion.

A. That's untrue, quite untrue. When we have identified the man we intend to get him. There'll be no holding off.

Q. Secretary of State, thank you very much.

A. Thank you.

Most of the young Protestants who gathered in the side streets off the Albert Bridge Road, pelting the armoured vehicles as they went by, hadn't seen the interview. But word had quickly spread through the Loyalist heartlands in the east and west of the city that the British had in some way glossed over the killing, not shown the determination to rout out those Provie rats who could murder a man in front of his bairns. The battalion on duty in Mountpottinger police station was put on fifteen minute readiness, and those making their way to the prosperous suburbs far out to the east of Belfast took long diversions, lest their cars became part of the sprouting barricades that the army crash-charged with their Saracens. Three soldiers were hurt by flying debris and the Minister's broadcast was put down as the kindling point to the brushfire that was to smoulder for more than a week in the Protestant community.

Meanwhile Harry was being prepared for the awesome moment when he would leave the woods of Surrey and fly to Belfast, on his own, leaving the back-up team that now worked with him as assiduously as any heavy-weight champion's.

Early on Davidson had brought him a cassette recorder, complete with four ninety-minute tapes of Belfast accents. They'd been gathered by students from Queen's University who believed they were taking part in a national phonetics study, and had taken their microphones into pubs, launderettes, working men's clubs and supermarkets. Wherever there were groups gathered and talking in the harsh, cutting accent of Belfast, so different to the slower more gentle Southern speech, tapes had attempted to pick up the voices and record them. The tapes had been passed to the army press officer via a lecturer at the University, whose brother was on duty on the Brigade commander's staff, and then, addressed to a fictitious major, flown to the Ministry of Defence. The sergeant on Davidson's staff travelled to London to collect them from the dead-letter box in the postal section of the Ministry.

Night after night Harry listened to the tapes, mouthing over the phrases and trying to lock his speech into the accents he heard. After sixteen years in the army little of it seemed real. He learned again of the abbreviations, the slang, the swearing. He heard the way that years of conflict and alertness had stunted normal conversation; talk was kept to a minimum as people hurried away from shops once their business was done, and barely waited around for a quiet gossip. In the pubs he noticed that men lectured each other, seldom listening to replies, or interested in opinions different to their own. His accent would be critical to him, the sort of thing that could awake the first inkling of suspicion that might lead to the further

72

check he knew his cover could not sustain.

His walls, almost bare when he arrived at the big house, were soon covered by aerial photographs of Belfast. For perhaps an hour a day he was left to memorize the photographs, learn the street patterns of the geometric divisions of the artisan cottages that had been allowed to sprawl out from the centre of the city. The developers of the nineteenth century had flung together the narrow streets and their back-to-back terraces along the main roads out of the city. Most relevant to Harry were those on either side of the city's two great ribbons of the Falls and Shankill. Pictures of astonishing clarity taken from RAF cameras showed the continuous peace line, or the 'interface', as the army called it, the sheets of silvery corrugated iron that separated Protestant from Catholic in the no man's land between the roads.

The photographs gave an idea of total calm, and left no impression of the hatred, terror and bestiality that existed on the ground. The open spaces of bombed devastation in any other British city would have been marked down as clearance areas for urban improvement.

From the distance of Germany – where theorists worked out war games in terms of divisions, tank skirmishes, limited nuclear warheads, and the possibility of chemical agents being thrown into a critical battle – it had become difficult for Harry to realize why the twenty or so thousand British soldiers deployed in the province were not able to wind up the Provisional campaign in a matter of months. When he took in the rabbit warren revealed by the reconnaissance photographs he began to comprehend the complexity of the problem. Displayed on his walls was the perfect guerrilla fighting base. A maze of escape routes, ambush positions, back entries, cul-de-sacs and, at strategic crossroads, great towering blocks of flats commanding the approaches to terrorist strongholds.

It was the adventure playground par excellence for the urban terrorist, Davidson would say, as he fired questions at Harry till he could wheel out at will all the street names they wanted from him, so many commemorating the former greatness of British arms – Balkan, Raglan, Alma, Balaclava – their locations, and the quickest way to get there. By the second week the knowledge was there and the consolidation towards perfection was under way. Davidson and his colleagues felt now that the filing system had worked well, that this man, given the impossible brief he was working under, would do as well as any.

Also in the bedroom, and facing him as he lay in bed, was the 'tribal map' of the city. That was the army phrase, and another beloved by Davidson. It took up sixteen square feet of space, with Catholic streets marked in a gentle grass-green, the fierce loyalist strongholds in the hard orange that symbolized their heritage, and the rest in a mustard compromise. Forget that lot, Davidson had said. That had meant something in the early days when the maps were drawn up.

'Nowadays you're in one camp or the other. There are no uncommitted. Mixed areas are three years out of date. In some it's the Prods who've run, in others the other crowd.'

It had been so simple in Sheik Othman, when Harry had lived amongst the Adeni Arabs. The business of survival had occupied him so fully that the sophisti-

74

cations they were teaching him now were unnecessary. And there he had been so far from the help of British troops that he had become totally self-reliant. In Belfast he knew he must guard against the feeling that salvation was always a street corner away. He must reject that and burrow his way into the community if he was to achieve anything.

Outside the privacy of his room Harry seldom escaped the enthusiasm of Davidson, who personally supervised every aspect of his preparation. He followed Harry in the second week beyond the vegetable garden to the old and battered greenhouse, yards long and with its glass roofing missing, and what was left coated in the deep moss-green compost that fell from the trees. There were no nurtured tomatoes growing here, no cosseted strawberry cuttings, only a pile of sandbags at the opposite end to the door with a circular coloured target, virgin new, propped against them. Here they retaught Harry the art of pistol shooting.

'You'll have to have a gun over there – and not to wave about, Harry,' Davidson laughed. 'Just to have. You'd be the only physically fit male specimen in the province without one if you didn't have a firearm of some sort. It's a must, I'm afraid.'

'I didn't have one in Aden. Ridiculous, I suppose, but no-one suggested it.'

He took the gun from the instructor, grey-haired, hard-faced, lined from weather, wearing a blue, all-enveloping boiler suit and unmarked beret. He went through the precautionary drills, breaking the gun, flicking the revolving chamber that was empty, greased and black. The instructor counted out the first six shells.

Five times he reloaded the gun till the target was peppered and holed and askew.

'It's not the accuracy that counts so much with the first ones, sir,' said the older man, pulling off his ear-muffs, 'it's the speed you get the first one or two away. If you're shooting straight enough for your opponent to hear them going by his ear that tends to be enough to get his head back a bit. But it's getting the first one away that matters. Gets the initiative for you. There aren't many men as will stand still and aim as you're pulling the trigger for the first one. Get 'em going back and then worry about the aim for the third and fourth shot. And try not to fire more than the first four straight off. It's nice to keep a couple just so that you have a chance to do something about it if things don't turn out that well. Remember with this one it's a great little gun, but it's slow to load. That's its problem. Everything else is OK.'

They went over the firing positions. Sometimes the classic right-arm-extended, sideways-on stance. 'That's if you've got all night, sir, and you don't think he's armed. Take your time and make sure. Doesn't happen that often.' Then they worked on the standard revolver-shooting posture. Legs apart, body hunched, arms extended, meeting in front of the eye line, butt held in both hands, the whole torso lunging at the target. 'You're small yourself then, sir, and you've got your whole body thrown in with the gun to get it away straight. You won't miss often from that, and if you do you'll give 'im such a hell of a fright that he won't do much about it.'

'What's he like, Chief?' Davidson said to the instructor.

'We've had better through here, sir, and we've had

worse. He's quite straight but a bit slow as of now. I wouldn't worry about that. If he has to use it he'll be faster. Everyone is when it's real.'

Harry followed Davidson out of the greenhouse and they walked together up the brick and weed path amongst the vegetables. It was mild for November; the trees, huge above them, were already without their load of leaves and above the trees the soft meandering grey clouds.

'I think it's going quite well, Harry – no, I mean very well at the moment. But I don't want to minimize anything that you're going to have to go through. It's all very well here, swotting for an exam if you like . . . but the questions themselves are very tough when you get to the actual paper. Forgive the metaphor, Harry, but it's not an easy road over there, however much we do for you here. There are some things we can iron out at this end. Accent. It's critical for immediate and long-term survival. You can spare your blushes but I think that's coming along very well. Your background knowledge is fine, detail of events, names, folklore – that is all good. But there are other more complex factors, about which we cannot really do very much, and which are just as vital.'

They stopped now some twenty-five yards from the house on the edge of the old tennis court. Davidson was looking for the words. Harry wasn't going to help him; that wasn't his style.

'Look, Harry. Just as important as the accent, and getting the background right, and knowing what the hullabaloo is about, is how you are going to stand up to this yourself. It's my job to send you in there as perfectly equipped as possible. Right? Well, the thing I cannot actually gauge is how you'll soak up the punishment of just existing there. You could have an isolation problem . . . loneliness, basically. No-one to confide in, not part of a local team, completely on your own. This could be a problem. I don't know the answer to it, I don't think you're liable to suffer too greatly from it – that's my reading of your file. Sorry, but we go through it most nights with a fine blade. Unless you're aware of it, and bolt it down, there'll come a time when you'll want to tell someone about yourself, however obliquely, however much at a tangent. You'll say now, never, never in a month of whatevers, but believe me it'll happen, and you have to watch it.'

Harry searched his face, noting for the first time since he'd come to the big house the concern of the other man. Davidson went on, 'After Aden we're pretty confident in your ability to look after yourself. There's a lot in the file on that. I've no reason to disbelieve it, you've shown me none. The simple day-to-day business won't be pleasant but will be bearable. The other thing you have to consider is if you're discovered – what happens then? There is a fair chance that if they spot you we may be getting some sort of feedback as they build up information and we'll have time to shift you out in a hurry. You may notice something, a tail, a man watching you, questions being asked. Don't hang about then, just come back. What I'm getting at is difficult enough to say, but you have to face it, and you'll be better for facing it. You have to work out how you'll react if they take you alive.'

Harry grimaced weakly. The older man was fumbling about trying to say the most obvious thing of the whole operation, stumbling in his care not to scratch the varnish of morale that was coated some-times thickly, sometimes sparsely on all these jobs.

'I think I can help you,' Harry smiled at him. 'You want to know whether I've considered the question of being taken, tortured and shot. Yes. You want to know whether I'm going to tell them all about here, you and everything else. Answer, I don't know. I think not, I hope not. But I don't know. You don't know these things, and there's no absolute statement I can make that would be of any use. But I've thought of it, and I know what you'd hope from me. Whether you'll get it I just don't know.'

They began to walk again. Davidson swung his right arm round behind Harry's back and slapped his far shoulder. Like a father, thought Harry, and he's scared stiff. It's always been nice and comfortable for him, sitting at a desk packing the nameless numbered men off to heaven-knows where, but this time the jungle's been creeping a bit close.

'Thank you, Harry. That was very fairly put. Very fair. There's things that have to be discussed if one's to keep these things professional. I'm grateful to you. I think your attitude is about right.' Thank God for that, Harry thought, now he's done his duty. We've had our facts of life talk, ready to go out into the big nasty world, and don't put your hands up little girls' skirts. God, he's relieved he's got that little lot over.

As they came to the paint-chipped back door, Davidson started again. 'You know, Harry, you haven't told us much about home, about your wife. The family. It's an aspect we haven't really had time to go into.'

'There's nothing to worry about there. Not that I know of. I suppose you never do till it's too late to be

79

worrying about that sort of thing. She's very level. Not complicated. That sounds pretty patronizing, but I don't mean that. She's used to me going away in a hurry, at least was used to it when we were younger. It's not been so frequent over the last few years, but I think she's OK.'

'Did she know what you were doing in Aden?'

Harry said it slowly, thoughtfully, 'No. Not really. I didn't have time or the opportunity to write. There had been those little sods rolling grenades into the married quarters and smuggling bombs in with the food and things like that. The families went home before I became involved in the special stuff. I didn't tell her much about it when it was all over. There wasn't much to tell, not in my terms.'

'I'm sorry you had to come over here without being able to see her.'

'Inevitable. It's the way it is. She's not very service-minded. Doesn't live off married mess nights. Doesn't really get involved with the army scene. I think I prefer it that way. She'd like me out, but I tell her earning anyone else's shilling than the Queen's isn't that easy these days. I think she understands that.'

'The postcards will start arriving soon. The first lot that you did. And you'd better do some more before you move on.' Davidson sounded anxious, wanting to do it right, thought Harry. As if there was anything he could say about – what was the word he used? – this 'aspect' of the job. Of course she'd want to know where he was, of course if she knew she would be stunned with worry. What else could she be, and what could be done about it? Nothing.

They hesitated outside the door of the big room

where the work was done.

Davidson said, 'I wanted to be sure that you wouldn't be too concerned about your family while you're over there. It could be important. I once had a man—'

Harry cut in, 'It's not a problem. Not compared with the other ones. She'll cope.'

They went into the room where the others were waiting. Davidson thought to himself, he's a cold enough fish to succeed. It went through Harry's mind that his controller was either very thorough or on the reverse slope and going a touch soft. It was the only time the two men had anything approaching a personal conversation.

Later that afternoon it was suggested that Harry should personally meet the eye-witnesses who had been in Belgrave Square, or who had reported the jostling incident with the hurrying man in the Underground ticket area at Oxford Circus. Harry could have gone in the guise of a detective, but Davidson, after mulling it over for thirty-six hours, decided it was an unnecessary risk and sent a video camera from the Ministry round to their homes with one of the young officers in order that they could relive the moments they had been face to face with the gunman. For about fifteen minutes the elderly man who had seen a flash of the face while reading his paper, the girl with the bag of laundry, the woman exercizing her dog, the driver of the ministry car and the woman who had stood immobile as the man weaved a way past her had spelled out their recollections. They were taken again and again through the short experience, milked till their impatience with their questioner grew pointed, and then left wondering why so much equipment and time was spent in merely reiterating the statement they had made to the police the previous week.

Endlessly the tapes were rerun, so that the strength of each witness's description could be tested. Hesitations about hair styles, eye colours, cheekbone make-up, nose size, all the details that make each face unique as a fingerprint were analysed. Davidson made up a chart where all the strong points were listed in green ink, the next category in red, the doubtful points in blue. These were placed against the photo-kit picture already issued by the Royal Ulster Constabulary and Scotland Yard.

There were differences, they found. Differences that would have been sufficient to prevent the young soldiers in the pub off the Broadway eight days earlier from connecting the picture they had memorized with the man they had studied, arms up and legs apart, against the wall.

'You have to know him,' said Davidson – so often it became like a holed record – 'You have to know about him, have a sense that when he's on the pavement and you're at the other side you'll have him straight away. It's chemistry, my boy.'

Harry thought of it a different way. He thought in a job as daft as this you need everything on your side. He reckoned his chances of seeing the man about minus nil, though he maintained a more public optimism with Davidson.

The Ministry had designed their own photokit of the man, using the Scotland Yard one as a basis, but from the eye-witness tapes they slightly altered various features, particularly the profile of the face. Their own picture was displayed around treble life-size in the rooms where the team worked, the big living room, and the dining area at the back – and more space on Harry's wall was taken up with it, alongside the maps and aerial photographs.

By the fifteenth day they were ready to push Harry out into the field, and cut the cord that held him to the security of the big house amongst the trees. Other than his sleeping time, and those hours he'd worked in his room on the voice tapes and the maps, he'd been allowed to spend little time on his own. That was Davidson's idea – 'For Christ's sake, don't let him brood on it,' he told the others.

Davidson had wondered whether there ought to be some celebration on Harry's last night, and then decided against it in favour of a few glasses of beer after their final session, and another early night.

'Don't believe all that *Daily Telegraph* stuff about them being beaten, smashed, in their final death throes. It's nonsense. They need time to regroup, and they needed a big morale booster. They've got that, not in the killing itself, but in our failure to nab their man and lock him up. The Prods are restless now, not critical yet, but stirring the pot – just as the Provos want it.

'To be frank, Harry, we all thought they'd have had the killer by now, and for thc first week at least we may have handled your preparation on that basis. The word I had last night is they haven't identified any positive clue yet. No-one's losing anything by you going in. But in a strange idiotic way you have a better chance than the military clumping round and the police. It's not a great chance, but worth taking.'

They wished him luck. A little formal. Harry said nothing, nodded and walked into the hall and up the stairs to his room. They let him go alone.

The fire position was in the roof of a derelict house just to the north of the Falls Road, beyond its junction with Springfield. Four of the houses had been demolished when a nineteen-year-old volunteer in the First Battalion had stumbled, knocking the arm of the battalion's explosives officer as he was putting the final touches to a seventy-five-pound gelignite bomb. The officer's fingers had moved some three-eighths of an inch, enough to connect momentarily with the terminals that in another few minutes would have been attached to the face of a cheap alarm clock.

The explosion had left a gouged hole in the line of the street. The first house to the right after the gap was left naked and exposed to the open air. The next house down was in better shape. There was a door still in place, and the roof was largely intact. The house was empty because local housing officials had condemned it as unsafe, and gas and electricity had been switched off. The five houses beyond were occupied.

The man had wedged himself in the angle between the beams and the horizontal struts of the roof. Part of the time his legs were astride the struts, which cut deep into his thighs in spite of the cushions he had brought with him. Otherwise he knelt, spreading his weight over two of the struts. In that position his balance was more stable, but it hurt more.

Looking down he could see through a gap in the roof where a tile had slid down into the street, shaken loose by the blast from the explosion. The tile had been only slightly above the level of the guttering and from his position his eyes were little more than four feet from it. From the hole his line of visibility took him left to the corner of the street, and across to the right the length of the frontage of three houses. On the same side of the street as the man's hiding place was the home of a Mrs Mulvenna, whose husband was currently held in Long Kesh. She always kept her front-room light on, with the curtains drawn back, so that the light illuminated the pavement just beyond the extremity of the man's field of fire, and threw shadows into the area covered by his line of vision. It was his hope that a night patrol, their faces blackened, rubber soles on their boots, would edge away from the brightness in favour of the side of the road where they could find some false refuge in the greyness, but where they would be covered by the man's sights. He knew enough of the habits of the soldiers to be able to bank on one of the troops in the middle of the patrol lingering uncertainly on the corner. The soldier would need to pause for only two or three seconds to make the man's vigil worthwhile.

The army were never consistent with their patrol patterns, and in the three days that he had been in the roof the man had seen only one group of soldiers. That had been in mid-morning and then, without Mrs Mulvenna's light to drive them across the street, they had come by, right underneath the hideout, and virtually out of sight. He had seen one of them momentarily then, heard their fresh, young English country voices as they passed by unaware of his presence above.

Across the man's knee was an Armalite rifle. Small, light-weight, with shocking high velocity hitting power. The bodywork of the rifle was of black plastic, made in Japan, built under licence as a copy of the American infantry's M16 weapon. The Kalashnikov in London had been a luxury, an eccentricity . . . for the more routine job in which he was now engaged the Armalite was totally suitable.

And so he waited in the dark and freezing draughts of the roof for the twenty seconds or so it would take an eight-man patrol to move past the shadows of the three houses opposite. His eyes strained at the darkness, his ears keen to the noise of feet and the different types of shoes the civilians wore. He had cat-napped through the day to reserve his concentration for the time, fast and silent, that the soldiers would come.

Chapter Five

The lady who had been walking her dog in Belgrave Square now left it at home each morning when she went to the doctor's surgery. The elderly GP allowed her to talk for at least ten minutes each morning before gently shooing her back to her flat and the hysteria and depression that had engulfed her since the shooting. The doctor appreciated the need of the widow, who had been his casual and infrequent patient for twenty-three years, to talk to some friend who could comprehend her meticulous description of the screaming woman, the man with that awful banging gun at his shoulder, the petrified children, the sirens, and the shouting, helpless policemen.

He gave her mild sedatives, but had been unwilling to prescribe habit-forming doses in the hope that time would eventually erode the images of the killing. He had been surprised and annoyed when she had told him that the detectives had been to see her again, a clear week after they had received her signature on what was described as the final and definitive statement she would need to make. She had told the doctor of the queer equipment they had brought, and how over and over she had been made to describe the man with the gun.

It had been sufficient of an ordeal for her, this last visit, to set back her recovery, and accordingly the doctor had phoned the Scotland Yard officer who was named in the papers as heading the enquiry. But such was the pressure on his time, and the size of his register, that he had taken the matter no further when told that no policeman had been to visit his patient in the last nine days. He had blustered a bit when he was told that, protested about the obvious inconsistency between the police story and his patient's, and then rung off. It still puzzled him.

The Secretary of State for Defence was in his office early, clearing his desk for the start of a short holiday, and arming himself with persuasive and informed argument that he would need for his nine holes with the Prime Minister. The civil servant who was briefing him on the missile gap and the sagging morale of denuded units in Germany continued his lecture in his usual professorial manner. He had a turn of phrase that had infuriated a series of Ministers as the civil servant had progressed upwards to his position of a Man Who Ran Things. His role in the vast department was all-commanding, his power and influence huge. One of the smaller cogs in his well-oiled machine was Davidson, and one of the less frequently mentioned properties on his books was the house near Dorking.

Tentatively the Minister spoke to him.

'That suggestion of the PM about the Danby killing – you remember, putting a chap in there. He'll want to know . . . what's happening?'

'Yes. He phoned last week. I wouldn't worry about it, Minister. We're still going over feasibility et cetera at the moment. It's not a fast business, you know; not a thing we can successfully knock off overnight.'

'Nothing definite yet, then? You've already spoken to him? That's a bit odd, isn't it? On to you direct, and by-passing me? He may be in charge of security and all that, but it's a bit off. What did you tell him?'

'That things were in hand. That he'd get a briefing the moment there was something to report, when there were developments.'

'I think you see me as some sort of security risk or something.' The Minister grimaced. The civil servant smiled generously. The subject was terminated. It was back to rocketry and more conventional theatres of war.

Twenty-five thousand feet up, between Liverpool and the Isle of Man, Harry was working things out. The reality of it all had been brutally clear as he had stood in the queue waiting to be searched by the Securicor team at the departure gate. Whoever heard of an agent getting his own bags taken apart by his own bloody side? It was painfully clear why his promised Smith & Wesson would have to be picked up at the Belfast main post office, where Davidson was to send it to await collection. He tried to concentrate on his cover story. Merchant seaman going home after years away, land in turmoil, oppression over the minority. Time for all true Irishmen to get back to back, together to withstand the English bastards. Three hundred years post Cromwell, and nothing changed. Blood of martyrs on the streets again. Would anyone be daft enough to come back to that stinking hole, just because things were getting worse? Be out of their minds. Irish might be daft enough, have to be daft. One thing – bloody English wouldn't come home, they'd all go off to Australia or South Africa. Wouldn't catch them risking their precious lilywhite backsides.

The story was as firm in his mind as it ever would be.

He lay, half awake, half asleep, in no man's land. What of the commitment he had taken on? Motivation was vague and unthought-out. It wouldn't be as strong as the other side's. No chance. Motivation was against the code with which he had been instilled. Officers didn't need motivation. It wasn't all clear.

Rights and wrongs, pluses and minuses, blacks and whites were all vague. In Northern Ireland things don't divide and coalesce neatly. That's too easy. What was it the politicians had said? 'Anyone who thinks he knows the answer to Northern Ireland is ill-informed.' Good, that. Lots of ill-informed types in the mess in Germany then. Came back with the solution worked out. One big swoop, one big push, the tough hand, the gentle hand, the 'saturate them', the 'pull the plug and leave them'. All the answers, none the same, but all spoken with such authority. Amazing how you can learn three hundred years' bigotry in four months looking after five blocks in a scruffy council estate.

Harry, heavy with sarcasm, had once congratulated a brother in uniform on the good fortune the other had in being able to see things so clearly. To be able with such confidence to apportion his blame and praise, culpability and credit – that made him a lucky man. In Mansoura, just out of Sheik Othman, where the gunmen were running round while the boyos in Ulster were still on their iced lollies and sing-songs, it had been so much easier. The Red Cross man from Switzerland, in his little white suit, even with a big bright cross on his hat so they wouldn't throw a grenade at him from a rooftop, had come to visit the unit once. He'd said to the colonel something like, 'One man's terrorist is another man's freedom fighter.' The colonel hadn't liked that. Pretty heady stuff, they all thought in the mess. Such rubbish. Terrorists they were then, wog terrorists at that.

But in Aden Harry had thought it was obvious to even the most stupid that British society was in no way being protected by their efforts . . . business perhaps, but nothing else.

Whatever else men died for in the sharp staccato engagements of small-arms fire, the green fields of home were a touch removed from the Mansoura roundabout picket, Checkpoint Golf or the Chartered Bank in Crater. As an Ulsterman, and so never allowed a posting home to fight, Harry had often wondered whether soldiering there was any different to Aden. Did all the stuff about duty, purpose and reason mean that much more just because the fighting was down by the local supermarket and not six hours away on a VC10? He reckoned he was as disinterested now in the welfare of the great body of society as he had been then. He had been given a job to do, and he was doing it because someone had to, and by a series of accidents he was better equipped than most.

But by the time the Trident was arching over the landfall to the south of Strangford Lough, Harry had decided he was not a little flattered he'd been asked. He had been chosen for a mission, after all, called for by the

Prime Minister. In the close heat of the plane he thought of his wife, warmth and closeness flooding through him. It was a pity she couldn't share in his pride. The passenger across the aisle noticed the slow smile spreading across the cheeks of the man slumped by the window.

For a few more seconds Harry indulged himself, conscious of the softness of the moment. He knew from the other times of great danger that he had faced that he could cocoon himself in sentimentality for his family, for Mary and the boys. It was part of the mechanism of protection which Harry understood and cherished.

As the airliner began its approach across the small fields towards Aldergrove Harry fastened his belt strap, and let his thoughts turn to the man whose image was imprinted in his mind. He could see the man, could put flesh and colour and dimensions on to the dark lines of the photokit. The target. Was he an enemy? Not really. What, then, if not an enemy? Just a target. Still to be killed, no question of that. *Eliminate* – it rolled off Harry's silent tongue. It was the word he liked.

He was jolted awake as the wheels suspended below the wings banged down onto the scarred tarmac. The plane surged forward in the air at a little more than ninety miles an hour, bounced again, and began to slow with the application of the engine's reverse thrust.

Terminal 1, Heathrow, the first-floor cafeteria. Davidson was breakfasting with the team who had come up to see Harry off. It was a subdued meal without the frills of conversation. Not much had been said after Harry had disappeared towards the security checks. Davidson had muttered, almost audibly, 'Gutsy little sod.'

'I'll take the bill,' he had added, as they rose from the table, and then, as an afterthought, 'I think we've told him all we could in three weeks, but it's bloody little time. To do that job properly you'd need six months. And then you couldn't be sure. Always the same when the politicians dip their toes in – short cuts. That's the order of the day. To come through with three weeks behind him he'll need to be lucky, bloody lucky.'

The anomaly of going to war in your own country was not lost on Harry. He came down the steep steps from the plane and hurried past the RAF Regiment corporal, who held his rifle diagonally across his thighs, right-hand forefinger extended along the trigger guard. There were coils of barbed wire at the flanks of the terminal building, sprawled across the flower beds that had once been sufficient in themselves to mark the perimeters of the taxi-ing area. The viewing gallery where people used to wave to their friends and relatives was now fenced with high chicken wire to prevent a missile being thrown onto the apron; it was out of bounds to civilians, anyway. After getting his bag in the concourse Harry walked out towards the coach pick-up point. Around him was an avenue of white oil drums with heavy planks slung between them – a defence against car bombers moving their lethal loads against the walls of the buildings. He moved by a line of passengers waiting to take the Trident back to London. They stood outside, occasionally shuffling forward with their baggage. Up at the front the searches went on in two green prefab huts. Only rarely did the faces of the travellers match the brightness of their going-away clothes: children silent, women with their eyes darting round, the men concerned with getting the cases to the search and then eventually to the plane. Greyness, anxiety, exhaustion.

Harry climbed on the bus, and was quick enough to ensure himself a window seat near the back.

By the time the coach had left the fields behind and was into the top of the Crumlin Road the man directly behind Harry was in full voice. Taking upon himself the role of guide and raconteur, outmatching those who lead crocodiles of tourists round the Tower of London and Hampton Court, he capitalized on the quiet of the bus to demonstrate his intimate knowledge of the campaign as fought so far.

'Down there on the right – you see the small lane – just round the corner where you can't see – that's where the three Scottish soldiers were murdered . . . the pub . . . the one that's blown up – the one we're passing – they took 'em from there and killed them down the road when they were having a slash. There's nothing to see there now . . . people used to put flowers, but not now, nothing to see except there's no grass in the ditch where they got it . . . Army dug it all up looking for bullets, and it never grew since. Now on the left, where the road climbs up, towards the quarry, that's where the senator was killed . . . the Catholic senator with the girl, they were killed up there, stabbed. Last year it was, just before the elections. Look now in front, there she is, the greatest city on earth. Down below, left, not hard left, that's Ardoyne . . . over to the right that's Ballymurphy . . . we're coming into Ligoniel now.'

It'll be bus trips for the Japanese next, thought Harry.

Once they've stopped looking round Vietnam you'll be able to flog them Belfast. By special demand after the world's greatest jungle conflict, we offer you reduced rate to the longest-ever urban guerrilla war. Roll up! Roll up! Get your tickets now!

'Now wait for the bumps.' The man behind was away again, as the bus had slowed to a crawl. 'Here we go now. See we're outside a barracks . . . there on the left . . . they all have bumps outside now . . . stops the Provos belting past and giving the sentry a burst with a Thompson. They used to have luminous paint on them, the bumps, that's gone now . . . if you don't know where they are you give the car a hell of a bang . . . hit one of those at fifty and you know about it . . . that's Ardoyne, now, over on the left, where the policeman is. That's a sight for the English, policemen with bullet-proof coats and machine-guns . . . won't use the army flak jackets, have their own. We cut across now, they don't rate going down the Crumlin in Ulster buses. We'll use the Shankill. Looks all right, doesn't it, quiet enough? See that hole on the right? That's the Four Steps bar . . . killed a fair few when that went up. Not a breath of a warning. Look there on the same side, see it? That hole . . . that was a furniture shop . . . two kiddies died there – not old enough to walk.'

'Shut up, Joe, nobody wants to know. Just wrap it.'

Perhaps Joe felt he had given his virtuoso performance. He fell silent. Harry watched out of the window, fascinated by the sights. At the traffic lights the driver nudged up to the white line alongside a Saracen armoured car. Soldiers were crouched inside the half-open steel back doors, rifles in hand. On the other side of the crossroads he watched a patrol inching its way through the shopping crowds. On all sides were the yards of pale-brown hardboard that had taken over from glass in the display windows of the stores. The policemen here had discarded their sub-machine-guns, but let their right hands rest securely inside their heavy dark coats. It surprised Harry how much there was to see that could have been a part of any other British industrial city – buses, cars, people, clothes, paper stands – all merging in with the great military umbrella that had settled itself on Belfast.

At the bus station Harry switched to another single-decker that went high up on the Antrim Road to the north, speeding past the troubled New Lodge Junction before cutting into residential suburbs. The houses were big, old, tall, red-brick and fading. Davidson had given him the name of a boarding house where he'd said Harry could get a room, three stops up past the New Lodge.

Harry got off the bus at the stop, and looked round to find his bearings. He spotted the house they had chosen for him and moved away from it farther down the long hill till he was about a hundred and fifty yards from the seedy board with its 'vacancies' sign. Then he waited. He watched the front door for twenty-five minutes before he saw what he'd half expected. A young man came out down the steps that led to the short front path. Clothes not quite right, walk too long, hair a fair bit too short.

Harry boiled. 'Stupid bastards. Davidson, you prime bastard. Send me to one of your own bloody places. Nice safe little billet for soldiers in a nice Proddy area. Somewhere you won't find anything out, but you won't get shot. No, not Davidson, some bugger in intelligence in Belfast, having his own back because it isn't his caper. Sod 'em. I'm not going through all this to sit on my arse in Proddyland and come out in a month with nothing to show. No way.'

He took the next bus into central Belfast from the other side of the road, walked across to the taxi rank in Castle Street, and asked for a lift up to mid-Falls. Not Davidson's game, that. He wouldn't know addresses in Belfast, it would have to be one of the minions, flicking through his card index, this looks right to keep him out of mischief. Couldn't infiltrate Mansoura from bloody Steamer Point, nor the Falls from Prod country.

To the cab driver he said, 'I'm working about halfway up, and looking for someone who takes in lodgers. Not too pricey. Yer know anyone? About halfway, near the Broadway. Is there anyone?'

He waited in the cab for several minutes for the other seats to be taken up in the shuttle service that had now largely replaced the inconsistencies of the bus timetable. The journey he'd made in from the airport, out onto the Antrim Road, his wait there, the trip back, the walk to the taxi rank, that delay sitting in the back waiting to go, all had taken their toll in time.

Deep greyness was settling over the city, rubbing out its sharp lines, when the taxi, at last full, pulled away.

The first soldier in the patrol was up to the corner and round it before the man had reacted to the movement. The second gave him a chance to identify it as an army patrol. On the third and fourth he had begun to get an aim, and for the next man he was ready. Rifle at the shoulder. The upper part of the shadow cut out by the V of the leaf mechanism of his rear sight, and sliced by the upward thrust of the front sight at the far tip of the barrel. The fifth soldier had come fast round the corner, too close to his colleague in front, and paused for the other to move farther away before starting off again himself. He was stationary for one and a half seconds before the man fired. The shadow fell out from the darkness of the wall towards the corridor of light from Mrs Mulvenna's front room.

The man had time to see the stillness of the form, half on the pavement and half on the street, before he wormed and scrambled his way to the centre of the roof space – and ran. His escape route took him along a catwalk of planks set across the gaps between the roof beams, in all traversing the roof space of four homes. In the last house the light shone up among the eaves where the ceiling door had been left open for him. He swung down onto the landing, and then moved to the stairs leading to the back of the house and the kitchen. The Armalite was grabbed from him by a teenager who had been listening for the clatter of the escape across the ceiling. Within three minutes it would be in a plastic bag, sealed, and dropped under the grating in the back yard, with a thin line of dark cord tied to the bars to retrieve it later.

The man went out into the back yard, scrambled over the five-foot-high fence, ducked across the back entry, and felt for the rear doors on the far side till he came to the one off the hook. It remained for him to cut through that house, and he was out in the next street. Here he didn't run, but ambled the three hundred yards farther away from the killing where he rang a front-door bell. A youth came out immediately, motioned him to a waiting car, and drove him away.

There had been no pursuit. No soldier had seen the fractional flash of the barrel as the man fired. Five of them, shouting and waving, fear in their eyes, had sunk to firing positions in the doorways of the street. Two more gathered beside their dead colleague. Before the ambulance came it was plain that their efforts were pointless, but they fumbled the medical dressing clear from his webbing belt and placed it over the bloody chest wound.

Harry heard the single shot from far up the road when the taxi was caught in stationary traffic at the lights just beyond the huge bulk of the hospital building. As the taxi stayed unmoving, log-jammed in the sea of vehicles, a convoy of armoured cars swept by up the wrong side of the road, horns blaring and headlights on. Soldiers jumped from the moving column to take up their shooting positions on the main road, while others poured into the side streets. Harry saw the blue flashing light of an ambulance swing sharply out of a side street, one hundred and fifty yards up on the right, and turn down towards them. The ambulance was a Saracen with huge red crosses on a white background painted on the sides. Turning his head, Harry saw through the flapping open doors at the back two dark shapes bent over the top end of the stretcher. The handles of the stretcher, between them a pair of boots, stuck out beyond the tailboard of the armoured car.

It was some minutes before the traffic moved again. None of the other passengers in the cab – the old lady with her month's shopping, or the two office girls from Andersonstown – spoke a word. When the cab reached the street corner where the ambulance had emerged the soldier in the middle of the road waved them out and to the wall. He ran his hands fast and effectively over the shoulders, torsos and legs of Harry and the driver, contenting himself with examining the woman's shopping holders and the girls' bags. He looked very young to Harry.

'What happened?' Harry asked.

'Shut your face, you pig-arsed Mick.'

The taxi dropped him off seventy-five yards farther on. He was to try Mrs Duncan's. First left, twelfth door on the right: 'Delrosa'.

It didn't take Harry long to settle into the small room that Mrs Duncan showed him at the back of her two-storey house – about as long as it takes to unpack the contents of a small suitcase and put them into a medium-size chest of drawers and a wardrobe. She suggested he wash his hands and then come down to the big room where the other guests would gather, first for tea, then to watch television. She asked no questions about him, obviously prepared to give the stranger time to fill in his background at his own pace.

Looking across from his window, Harry could see the Falls Road where the army Land-Rovers and Saracens still criss-crossed back and forth.

There were six at tea, all eating urgently and with concentration. The way to avoid talking, thought Harry. Stuff your face, with just a mutter for the milk or the sugar, or the fresh-cut bread, and you don't have to say anything. No-one mentioned the shooting, but it came into the room with the BBC local television news. Mrs Duncan came from the kitchen to the doorway, leaning there, arms folded, in her apron. A single shot had killed the first soldier to die in Northern Ireland for three weeks. The pictures showed troops illuminated in doorways and manning roadblocks. Over the sound-track but half drowned by the report came the words 'Put that bloody light off.' Then there was only the meaningless picture of the tarmacadam with the dark stain on it, something for the colour-TV people but just a shapeless island on Mrs Duncan's set. Then out of the blackness the overlit whitened face of the young reporter as the hand light picked him up at close range.

He had little to say. A routine foot patrol in the Broadway district of the Falls had been ambushed. A single shot had been fired, fatally wounding a soldier just as darkness was falling. He said that an extensive follow-up operation was still in progress, that the area had been cordoned off, and that all cars leaving it were being searched. The camera cut to a harassed-looking officer.

Q. What happened here, Colonel?
A. This is really a most shocking attack, a most cowardly murder. One of my soldiers was shot down in cold blood, quite without warning. A horrible, despicable crime.
Q. Did your men get a sight of the gunman?
A. No, it wasn't till we were engaged in an exten-sive follow-up operation – which you will have seen for yourself – that we found the place where the gunman was hiding. He was up in the roof of a derelict house, and he aimed at my patrol through the gap left by a missing tile.
Q. Would this have been the work of an expert?

A. An expert – in terrorism, yes, in killing, yes. We found sixty-eight cigarette butts in the roof. He'd been there some time. He'd put four chairs on the staircase of the house – it's very narrow anyway. If we'd been chasing him and had run into the building those chairs would have lost us several seconds. That's the work of an expert killer. He'd chosen a house which had a communicating passage down the length of the terrace roof. That's the way he got out.

Q. Did anyone see anything on the street?

A. I'm sure half the street knew what was going on. Lots of people, masses of them, must have known a young man was going to be shot down in the gutter outside their homes. But I think your question is, did they identify the gunman to us? The answer there is decisively, No, they didn't. But many of them must know who the killer is – I appeal to them to use the police Confidential phone and stamp out this type of cruel, cowardly attack.

Q. Thank you, Colonel.

The programme changed to an interview in the studio. A Protestant politician and a Catholic politician were arguing over the same ground, with some minute variations, that they'd been debating on the same channel for the last four years. Between them was a linkman who had been hosting them, feeding them their questions and winding them up over the same period. Before the talk was a minute old Mrs Duncan came forward like a battleship under power, and reached for the off switch.

'There's enough politics on the street without bringing them into my house. Just words. Won't do that young man any good. Mother of Jesus rest with him.'

A youngish man, across the table from Harry, said, 'If they stayed in their barracks they wouldn't get shot. If they weren't here there wouldn't be any shooting. You saw what they did when they came round here a few days ago. Taking the houses apart, lifting men, and blocking the streets. Claimed then it was because of that man that got shot in London. But the searches they did were nothing to do with it. Aggro, what they were looking for, nothing more. Harassment.'

Nobody in the room responded. The young man looked round for someone to join in argument with. Harry sided with him. 'If they were as busy chasing the Prods as us, they'd find things easier for themselves.'

The other looked at him, surprised to find support, if not a little disappointed that it was an ally who had put his cap in the ring. Harry went on, 'I've been away a long time, but I can see in the few hours that I've been back where all the troops are. I've been abroad, but you still read the papers, you still see the news on the telly bought from the BBC. You get to feel the way things are going. Nothing's done about those Prods, only us.'

It was not easy for Harry, that first time. With practice he would gain the facility to sing the praises of the IRA. But the first time round it was hard going. Never like this in Mansoura. Never went down the souk and shouted the odds, about what a fine bloke Quahtan As-Shaabi was, victory to the NLF, out with

103

the imperialists. Just kept quiet there, and scuffed around in the dirt, and watched. But a different scene here. Got to be in the crowd. He excused himself, saying he was tired and had been travelling all day, and went to his room.

Chapter Six

It was just after seven when Harry woke. He knew soon enough that this was the day he started working and move on to active service. The euphoria of the farewells, the back-slaps and good-luck calls, were over. He had arrived. Now would begin the hard work of moving on to the inside. He checked his watch. Well, twenty minutes more and then it could all begin, then he would get up.

He'd known since his training started that the initial period of infiltration was going to be the difficult part. This was where the expertise and skill entered in his file after Mansoura would count. They had chosen him after going over those files, and those of a dozen other men, because they had thought that he above all of them stood the best chance of being able to adapt in those early critical hours in the new environment.

They'd told him he must take it slowly, not lambast his way in. Not make so much of his presence that he attracted attention and with that, inevitably, investigation. But they also stressed that time was against him. They pointed to the enormous benefits the opposition were gaining from the failure of the vast military force to catch the assassin.

The dilemma was spelled out to him. How much speed could he generate? How fast could he move into that fringe world which had contact with the gunmen? How far into that world must he go to get near the nucleus of the organization where the man he hunted was operating? These were his decisions. The advice had been given, but now he had to control his own planning.

They had emphasized again and again at Dorking that his own death would be bad news all round. Enormous embarrassment to HMG. No risks should be taken unless absolutely essential. It had amused him, drily. You send a man to infiltrate the most successful urban terrorist movement in the world over the last twenty-five years, and tell him if he gets shot it would be awkward. Not much time to mess about with the frills. They'd said if it was going to work out for him it would be in the first three weeks. By then they expected something to bite on . . . not necessarily the man's full name but a regular haunt, the address of a friend. A hint. Anything on to which they could turn the huge and formal military and police machine. The great force was poised and waiting for him to tell it where to hit, and that pleased him.

He was starting with little enough to go on. The same available to everyone else in the city – or virtually the same. He had in his mind the photokit picture, with the knowledge that it was superior to the one issued in police stations and army posts. But that was all that tipped the scales in his favour. Nothing else, and not much to set against the disadvantages of arriving as a stranger in a community beset by informers and on its guard against them. His first problem would be the infiltration of the Catholic population, let alone the IRA, and becoming known to people already haunted by the fear of army plain-clothes units cruising in unmarked cars, laundry vans and ice-cream trucks with hidden spy holes, of the Protestant UVF and UFF killer squads. He had to win a degree of confidence among some small segment of these people before he could hope to operate with success.

Davidson had struck a chord when he said, 'They seem to have the ability to smell an outsider. They close ranks well. It's like the instinct of a fox that's learned to react when there's a hostile being close by. God knows how they do it, but they have a feeling for danger. Much of it is how you look, the way you walk, the way you go along the pavement. Whether you can look as though you belong. You need confidence. You have to believe that you're not the centre of attention the whole time. The first trick is to get yourself a base. Establish yourself there, and then work outwards. Like an upside-down pyramid.'

The base was clearly to be the good Mrs Duncan. She was in the kitchen and washing up the first sitting of breakfast when Harry came down the stairs.

'Well, it's good to be back, Mrs Duncan. I've been away a while too long, I feel. You miss Ireland when you're away, whatever sort of place it is now. You get tired of the travelling and the journeys. You want to be back here. If these bastard British would leave us to lead our own lives then this would be a great wee country. But it can't be easy for you, Mrs Duncan, running a business in these times?'

107

The previous evening he had formally given his name as Harry McEvoy. That was what she called him when she replied.

'Well, Mr McEvoy, they're not the easiest of times, to be sure. One minute it's all quiet and the place is full. Then you'll have a thing like last night, and who is going to come and sleep a hundred yards or so from where a soldier was shot dead? The travellers from the south find all this a bit near. They like it a bit further away from where it all happens. Having it full like it is now is a luxury. What did you say your business was? I was flustered up a bit when you came, getting the teas and all, yesterday.'

'I've been away, ten years or so, just under in fact, at sea. In the Merchant Navy. Down in the South Atlantic and Indian Ocean, mainly.'

'There's a lot you'll see has changed. The fighting's been hard these last years.'

'Our people have taken a bad time, and all.'

'The Catholic people have taken a bad time, and now the Protestants hate us as never before. It'll take a long time to sort it out.'

'The English don't understand us, never have, never will.'

'Of course they don't, Mr McEvoy.' She flipped his egg over expertly, set it on the plate beside the halved tomatoes, the skinned sausage, the mushrooms and the crisp fried bread. 'Look at all the ballyhoo and palava when that man of theirs was shot – Danby. You'd think it was the first man who had died since the troubles. Here they are, close to a thousand dead and all, and one English politician gets killed . . . you should have seen the searches they did, troops all over. Never found damn all.'

'He wasn't mourned much over here.' Harry said it as a statement.

'How could he be? He was the man that ran the Maze, Long Kesh. He brought all his English warders over here to run the place for him. There was no faith in him here, and not a tear shed.'

'They've not caught a man yet for it?'

'Nor will they. The boys will keep it close. Not many will know who did it. There's been too much informing. They keep things like that tight these days. But that's enough talk of all that. If you want to talk politics you can do it outside the door and on the streets all the hours that God gave. There's no shortage of fools here to do the talking. I try and keep it out of the house. If you're back from the sea, what are you going to do now? Have you a job to be away to?'

Before answering, Harry complimented her on the breakfast. He handed her the empty plate. Then he said, 'Well, I can drive. I hoped I could pick up a job like that round here. Earn enough so that with a bit of luck I can pay you something regular, and we can agree on a rate. I want to work up this end of town if I can, not in the centre of town. Seems safer in our own part. I thought I might try something temporary for a bit while I look round for something permanent.'

'There's enough men round here would like a job, permanent or not.'

'I think I'll walk around a bit this morning. I'll do the bed first . . . an old habit at sea. Tomorrow I'll try round for a job. Wonderful breakfast, thanks.'

Mrs Duncan had noticed he'd been away. And a long time at that, she was certain. Something grated on her ear, tuned to three decades of welcoming visitors and apportioning them to their birthplace to within a few miles. She was curious, now, because she couldn't place what had happened to his accent. Like the sea he talked of, she was aware it came in waves – ebbed in its pitch. Pure Belfast for a few words, or a phrase, then falling off into something that was close to Ulster but softer, without the harshness. It was this that nagged as she dusted round the house and cleaned the downstairs hall, while above her Harry moved about in his room. She thought about it a lot during the morning, and decided that what she couldn't quite understand was the way he seemed to change his accent so slightly mid-sentence. If he was away on a boat so long then of course he would have lost the Belfast in his voice – that must have happened. But then in contradiction there were the times when he was pure Belfast. She soundlessly muttered the different words that emphasized her puzzlement to herself, uncomprehending.

They don't waste time in Belfast lingering over the previous day. By the time Harry was out on the pavements of the Falls Road and walking towards town there was nothing to show that a large-scale military operation had followed the killing of a young soldier the previous evening. The traffic was on the move, women with their children in tow were moving down towards the shops at the bottom end of the Springfield Road, and on the corners groups of youths with time on their hands and no work to go to were gathering to watch the day's events. Harry was wearing a pair of old jeans he had brought from Germany, and that he'd used for jobs round his quarters in the base, and a holed pullover that he'd last worn when painting the white surrounds to the staircase at home. They were some of the clothes the officer had collected when he'd called and told his wife that her husband was on his way to the Middle East.

The clothes were right, and he walked down the road – watched, but not greatly attracting attention. The time had been noted when he came out of the side road where Mrs Duncan had her guest house, and into the Falls. Nothing went on paper, but the youth that saw him from behind the neat muslin curtain at the junction would remember him when he came back, and mentally clock him in. There was every reason why he should be noticed, as the only new face to come out of the road that morning. Last night when he had arrived it had been too late to get a decent look at him. All Mrs Duncan's other guests were regulars, discreetly vetted and cleared by the time they'd slept in her house enough for a pattern to emerge.

Harry had decided to walk this first morning, partly because he thought it would do him good but more importantly to familiarize himself with his immediate surroundings. Reconnaissance. Time well spent. It might save your life, they'd said. Know your way round. He came down past the old Broadway cinema where no films had been shown for two years since the fire bomb exploded outside the ticket kiosk, and the open space of the one-time petrol station forecourt where pumps, reception area and garages had all long since been flattened. Across the road was the convent

111

school. Children were laughing and shouting in the playground. Harry remembered seeing that same playground, then empty and desolated, on West German television when the newsreader had described the attack by two IRA motorcyclists on William Staunton. The Catholic magistrate had just dropped his two girls at school and was watching them from his car as they moved along the pavement to the gate when he was shot. He had lingered for three months before he died, and then one of the papers had published a poem written by the dead man's twelve-year-old daughter. Harry had read it in the mess, and thought it of rare simplicity and beauty, and not forgotten it.

'Don't cry,' Mummy said
'They're not real.'
But Daddy was
And he's not here.

'Don't be bitter,' Mummy said
'They've hurt themselves much more.'
But they can walk and run –
Daddy can't.

'Forgive them and forget,' Mummy said
But can Daddy know I do?
'Smile for Daddy, kiss him well,' Mummy said,
But can I ever?

He was still mouthing the words as the Royal Victoria Hospital loomed up, part modern, part the dark close red-brick of old Belfast. Staunton and scores of others had been rushed here down the curved hill

112

that swung into the rubber doors of Casualty.

Harry turned left into Grosvenor Road, hurrying his step. Most of the windows on either side of the street showed the signs of the conflict, boarded up, bricked up, sealed to squatters, too dangerous for habitation, but remaining available and ideal for the snipers. The pubs on the right, a hundred yards or so down from the main gate of the RVH, had figured in Davidson's briefings. After a Proddy bomb had gone off the local Provos had found a young bank clerk on the scene. He came from out of town and said he'd brought a cameraman to witness the devastation. The explanation hadn't satisfied. After four hours of torture, and questioning, and mutilation, they shot him, and dumped him in Cullingtree Street, a little farther down towards the city centre.

Davidson had emphasized that story, used it as an example of the wrong person just turning up and being unable to explain himself. In the hysteria and suspicion of the Falls that night it was sufficient to get him killed.

The half-mile of the street Harry was walking down was fixed in his mind. In the log of the history of the troubles since August 1969 that they'd given him to read, that half-mile had taken up fifteen separate entries.

Harry produced a driving licence made out in the name of McEvoy and the post office counter clerk gave him the brown paper parcel. Harry recognized Davidson's neat copperplate on the outside – 'Hold for collection.' Inside was a .38 calibre Smith & Wesson revolver. Accurate and a man-stopper. One of nine hundred thousand run off in the first two years of the Second World War. Untraceable. If Harry had shaken

113

the package violently he would have heard the rattling of the forty-two rounds of ammunition. He didn't open the parcel. His instructions were very plain on that. He was to keep the gun wrapped till he got back to his base, and only when he had found a good hiding place was he to remove it from the wrapping. That made sense, nothing special, just ordinary common sense, but the way they'd gone on about it you'd have thought the paper would be stripped off and the gun waved all over Royal Avenue. At times Davidson treated everyone around him like children. 'Once it's hidden,' Davidson had warned, 'leave it there unless you think there's a real crisis. For God's sake don't go carrying it round. And be certain if you use it. Remember, if you want to fire the damn thing, the yellow card and all that's writ thereon applies as much to you, my boy, as to every pimpled squaddie in the Pioneers.'

With the parcel under his arm, for all the world like a father bringing home a child's birthday present, Harry walked back from the centre of the city to the Broadway. He wanted a drink. Could justify it too, on professional grounds, need to be there, get the tempo of things, and to let a pint wash down the dryness of his throat after what he'd been through the last thirty-six hours. The 'local' was down the street from Mrs Duncan's corner. Over the last few paces to the paint-scraped door his resolve went haywire, weakened so that he would have dearly loved to walk past the door and regain the security of the little back room he had rented. He checked himself. Breathing hard, and feeling the tightness in his stomach and the lack of breath that comes from acute fear, he pushed the door open and went into the pub. God, what a miserable place! From the brightness outside his eyes took a few moments to acclimatize to the darkness within. The talk stopped and he saw the faces follow him from the door to the counter. He asked for a bottle of Guinness, anxiously projecting his voice, conscious that fear is most easily noticed from speech. Nobody spoke to him as he sipped his drink. Bloody good to drink, but you'd need to be an alcoholic to come in here to take it. The glass was two-thirds empty by the time desultory conversation started up again. The voices were muted, as if everything was confidential. The people, Harry recognized, had come to talk, as of an art, from the sides of their mouths. Not much eavesdropping in here. Need to Watergate the place.

Across the room two young men watched Harry drink. Both were volunteers in E Company of the First Battalion of the Provisional IRA, Belfast Brigade. They had heard of the cover story Harry was using earlier in the morning just after he'd gone out for his walk. The source, though unwittingly, was Mrs Duncan. She had talked over the washing line, as she did most mornings, with her neighbour. The neighbour's son, who now stood in the bar watching Harry, had asked his mother to find out from Mrs Duncan who the new lodger was, where he came from, and whether he was staying long. Mrs Duncan enjoyed these morning chats, and seldom hurried with her sheets and pegs unless rain was threatening. It was cold and bright. She told how the new guest had turned up out of the blue, how he hoped to find a job and stay indefinitely, had already paid three weeks in advance. He was a seaman, the English Merchant Navy, and had been abroad for many years. But he was from the North, and had come home now. From Portadown he was.

'He's been away all right,' she shouted over the fence to her friend, who was masked by the big, green-striped sheet suspended in the centre of the line, 'you can see that, hear it rather, every time he opens his mouth. You can tell he's been away, a long time and all, lucky beggar. What we should have done, missus. Now he says he's come back because Ireland, so he says, is the place in times of trouble.' She laughed again. She and her friend were always pretending they'd like to leave the North for good, but both were so wedded to Belfast that a week together at a boarding house north of Dublin in the third week of August was all they ever managed . . . then they were full of regrets all the way back to Victoria Street station.

The son had had this conversation relayed to him painfully slowly and in verbatim detail by his mother. Now he watched and listened, expressionless, as Harry finished his drink and asked for another bottle. In two days' time he would go to a routine meeting with his company's intelligence officer, by then sure in his mind if there was anything to report about the new lodger next door.

Harry walked quickly back to Delrosa after the second glass of Guinness. He'd never been fond of the stuff. Treacly muck, he told himself. He rang the doorbell, and a tall, willowy girl opened the door.

'Hullo, McEvoy's the name. I'm staying here. The room at the back.'

She smiled and made way for him, stepping back into the hall. Black hair down to the shoulders, high

116

cheekbones, and dark eyes set deep above them. She stood very straight, back arched, and breasts angled into the tight sweater before it moulded with her waist, and was lost in the wide leather belt threaded through the straps of her jeans.

'I'm Josephine. I help Mrs Duncan. Give her a hand round the house. She said there was someone new in. I do the general cleaning, most days in the week, and help with the teas.'

He looked at her blatantly and unashamed. 'Could you make me one now? A cup of tea?' Not very adequate, he thought, not for an opening chat-up to a rather beautiful girl.

She walked through into the kitchen, and he followed a pace or so behind, catching the smell of the cheap scent.

'What else do you do?' Perfunctory, imbecile, but keeps it going.

'Work at the mill, down the Falls, the big one. I do early shift, then come round and do a bit with Mrs Duncan. She's an old friend of my Mam's. I've been coming a long time now.'

'There's not much about for people here now, 'cept work, and not enough of that,' Harry waded in, 'what with the troubles and that. Do you go out much, do you find much to do?'

'Oh, there's bits and pieces. The world didn't end, and we adapted, I suppose. We don't go into town much – that's just about over. There's not much point, really. Go to a film and there'll be a bomb threat and you're cleared out. The Tartans run the centre anyway, so you have to run for dear life to get back into the Falls. The army don't protect us, they look the other

117

way when the Tartans come, Proddy scum. There's nothing to go to town for anyway 'cept the clothes, and they're not cheap.'

'I've been away a long time,' said Harry, 'people have been through an awful time. I thought it time to get back home. You can't be an Irishman and spend your time away right now.'

She looked hard at him. The prettiness and youth of her face hardened into something more frightening to Harry. Imperceptibly he saw the age and weariness on the smooth skin of the girl, spreading like the refocusing of a lens, and then gone as the face lightened. She reached into the hip pocket of her jeans, straining them taut as her fingers found a crumpled handkerchief. She shook it loose and dabbed it against her nose. Harry saw the green embroidered shamrocks in the corners, and fractionally caught the motif in the middle of the square. Crossed black and brown Thompson machine-guns. She was aware he was staring at her.

'There's nothing special about these. Doesn't mean I'm a rebel and that. They sell them to raise funds for the men and their families, the men that are held in the Kesh. "The Men Behind the Wire." Look. It's very good, isn't it – a bit delicate? You wouldn't think a cowardly, murdering thug would have the patience to work at a thing so difficult, be so careful. They think we're all pigs, just pigs. "Fenian pigs", they call us.'

She spat the words out, the lines round her face hard and clear cut now, then the tension of the exchange was gone. She relaxed.

'We make our own entertainment. There's the clubs, social nights. There's not much mid-week, but

118

Saturday night is OK. Only the bloody army comes belting in most times. They always say they're looking for the great commander of the IRA. They take ten boys out, and they're all back free in twenty-four hours. They stir us up, try to provoke us. We manage. I suppose all you've heard since coming back is people talking about their problems, how grim it is. But we manage.'

'That handkerchief,' said Harry, 'does that mean you follow the boyos, have you a man in the prisons?'

'Not bloody likely. It doesn't mean a damn. Just try and not buy one. You'll find out. If you don't buy one there's arguing and haggling. It's easier to pay up. You've got to have a snot-rag, right? Might as well be one of these and no argument, right? I'm not one of those heated-up little bitches that runs round after the cowboys. When I settle it'll be with a feller with more future than a detention order, I can tell you. And I'm not one of those that runs around with a magazine in my knickers and an Armalite up my trousers, either. There are enough who want to do that.'

'What sort of evenings do you have now? What sort of fun do you make for yourselves?'

'We have the caelis,' she said, 'not the sort they have in the country or in the Free State, not the proper thing. But there's dancing, and a bit of a band, and a singer and a bar. The army come lumping in, the bastards, but they don't stay long. You've been away, at sea, right? Well, we've got rid of the old songs now . . . 1916 and 1922 are in the back seat, out of the hit parade. We've "The Men Behind the Wire" – that's internment. "Bloody Sunday." "Provie Birdie", when the three boys were lifted out of Mountjoy by helicopter. Did you hear about it? Three big men and a helicopter come right down into the exercise yard and lifts them out . . . and the screws was shouting "Shut the gates!" Must have been a laugh, and all. Understand me, I'm not for joining them, the Provos. But I'm not against them. I don't want the bastard British here.'

'On the helicopter, I was going through the Middle East. I saw it in the English paper in Beirut.'

She was impressed, seemed so anyway. Not that he'd been to an exotic sounding place like Beirut, but that the fame of Seamus Twomey, Joe O'Hagen and Kevin Mallon had spread that far.

'Do the army always come and bust in, at the evenings?'

'Just about always. They think they'll find the big boys. They don't know who they're looking for. Put on specs, tint your hair, do the parting the wrong way, don't shave, do shave . . . that's enough, that sorts them out.'

Harry had weighed her up as gently committed – not out of conviction but out of habit. A little in love with the glamour of the men with Armalites, and the rawness of the times they lived in, but unwilling to go too close in case the tinsel dulled.

'I think I'd like to come,' said Harry. 'I think it would do me good. I'm a bit out of date in my politics right now, and my voice is a bit off tune. James Connolly was being propped up in his chair in Kilmainham in my time, and they were wearing all their Green. It's time I updated and put myself back in touch. A lot of brave boys have died since I was last here. It's time to stand

120

up and be counted in this place. That's why I came back.'

'I'll take you. I'll pick you up here, Saturday, round half seven. Cheers.'

She was away into the kitchen, and Harry to his room.

Chapter Seven

The man was moving the last few yards to his home. It was just after two in the morning. Two men had checked the streets near his house and given an all-clear on the presence of army foot patrols.

It was his first visit back into his native Ardoyne since he had left to go to London nearly a month ago. His absence had been noted by the local British army battalion that operated out of the towering, near-derelict, Flax Street mill complex on the edge of the Ardoyne. It was entered in the comprehensive files the intelligence section maintained on the several thousand people that lived in the area, and a week before two Land-Rovers had pulled up outside the man's house, made their way to the half-opened front door and confronted his wife. She could have told them little even if she had felt inclined to. She didn't, anyway.

She told them to 'Go fuck yourselves, you British pigs'. She then added, nervous perhaps of the impact of her initial outburst, that her husband was away in the South working for a living. The army had searched the house without enthusiasm, but this was routine, and nothing was found, nor really expected to be. The intelligence officer noted the report of the sergeant who had led the raid, noted too that it would be nice to talk to the occupant of No. 41 Ypres Avenue at some later date. That was as far as it had been taken.

If Harry had been chosen for his role because he was clean, the same criterion had operated with the other man's superiors when they had put the cross against his name midway up the list of twenty or so who were capable of going to London and killing Danby.

Ypres Avenue was a little different from the mass of streets that made up the Ardoyne. The battle it was named after gave a clue to its age, and so its state of repair was superior to those streets up in the Falls where Downs had been hiding the last three weeks and where the streets took their names from the Crimean and Indian Mutiny battles, along with the British generals who had led a liberal stock of Ulstermen into their late-nineteenth-century fighting. But fifty-nine years is still a long time for an artisan cottage to survive without major repairs, and none had been carried out on any considerable scale in the Avenue since the day they had been put up to provide dwellings for those working in the mill, where the army now slept. The houses were joined in groups of four, with, in between, a narrow passage running through to the high-walled back entrance that came along behind the tiny yards at the rear.

The blast bombs, nail bombs and petrol bombs of four years of fighting had taken their toll, and several of the houses had been walled up. The bottom eight feet of a wall at the end of the Avenue had been white-washed, the work of housewives late at night at internment time, so that at night, in the near darkness of the Ardoyne, a soldier's silhouette would stand out all the more clearly and give the boyos a better chance with a rifle. Most corners in the area had been given the same treatment, and the army had come out in force a week later and painted the whitened walls black. The women had then been out again, then again the army, before both sides called a mutual but unspoken truce. The walls were left filthy and disfigured from the daubings.

The army sat heavily on the Ardoyne, and the Provos, as they themselves admitted, had had a hard time of it. This was good for the man. A main activist would not be expected to live in an area dominated by the military and where IRA operations had virtually ceased. He had been careful to link all his work with the Falls, away in a quite separate Catholic area from the Ardoyne.

Each house was small, unshaped, and built to last. Comfort played only a small part in its design. A front hall, with a front room off it, led towards a living area with kitchen and scullery two later additions and under asbestos roofing. The toilet was the most recent arrival and was in the yard against the far wall in a breeze-block cubicle. Upstairs each house boasted two rooms and a tiny landing. Bathing was in the kitchen. This was Belfast housing, perfect for the ideological launching of the gunman, perfect too as the model ground for him to pursue his work.

In the years the man had lived there he could find his way by the counting of his footsteps and by touch, when he came to the door of his own yard. The door had been recently greased, and made no sound when it swung on its hinges. He slipped towards the kitchen and unlocked the back door and went upstairs. That back door was never bolted, just locked, so that he could come in through it at any time.

It was the longest he had ever been away. The relief was total. He was back.

He moved cat-like up from the base of the stairs, three steps, then waited and listened. The house was completely dark and he had found the banister rail by touch. There were the familiar smells of the house, strong in his nose – the smell of cold tea and cold chips, older fat, of the damp that came into the walls, of the lino and scraps of carpet where that damp had eaten and corroded. On the stairs while he waited he could hear the sound of his family clustered together in the two rooms, the rhythm of their sleep broken by the hacking cough of one of the girls.

There was no question of using the lights. Any illumination through the sparse curtains would alert the army to the fact that someone in the house was on the move unusually late, coming home or going out. A little enough thing, but sufficient to go down into the files and card system that the intelligence men pored over, and which gave them their results. In the blackness the man inched his way up the stairs, conscious that no-one would have told his wife he was coming home this particular night, and anxious not to frighten her.

He moved slowly on the landing, pushed open the door of the back room where he and his wife slept, and came inside. His eyes were now accustomed to the dark. He made out her hair on the pillow, and beside it the two small shapes, huddled close together for warmth and comfort. He watched them a long time. One of the children wriggled and then subsided with the cough. It had just been coming on when he had left home. He felt no emotion, only inhibition over how to break in and intrude on their sleep. Gradually his wife became aware of his presence. At first she was frightened, moving quickly and jerking the head of one of the sleeping children. She was defensive in her movement, the mother hen protecting her nest. The aggression went when she saw it was him. With a half-strangled sob she reached out for her man and pulled him down onto the bed.

Beneath him he felt the children slide away to continue their sleep uninterrupted.

'Hullo, my love, I'm back. I'm OK. Safe now. I've come back to you.'

He mouthed the words pressed hard into the pit of her neck, his voice sandwiched between her shoulder and ear. She held him very tightly, pulling at him as if some force were working to get him away from her again.

'It's all right, love. I'm home. It's over.'

He rose to his knees and kicked off his shoes, wrenched at his socks and pulled away the trousers, jacket and shirt. She passed one of the sleeping children over her body and pulled back the clothes of the bed for him to come into the empty space.

Desperately she clung to him there, squeezing the hardness and bitterness and strength out of him, demolishing the barriers of coldness and callousness with which he had surrounded himself, working at the emotions that had been so suppressed in the last month.

'Where've you been?'

'Don't . . . don't . . . I've missed you, I've wanted you.'

126

'No, where've you been?' she persisted. 'We thought you were gone – were dead. There was no word, not anything. Where? There's always been a word before when you've gone.'

He clung to her, holding onto the one person that he loved and whom he needed as his lifeline, particularly over the last weeks of tension and fear. He felt the tautness draining out of him as he pressed down onto her body. It was some moments before he realized that she was lying quite still, rigid and yielding nothing. His grip on her slackened and he rose a little from the bedclothes to see her face, but when he was high enough to look down at her eyes, she turned them away from him towards her sleeping children.

'What's the matter? What's this for?'

'It's where you've been. Why you've been away. That's the matter. I know now, don't I?'

'Know what . . . ?' He hesitated. Stupid bitch, what was she blathering for? He was here. Flesh and blood. But what did she know? He was uncertain. How much had she realized through the frenzy in which he had held her? What had that crude and desperate weight of worry communicated to her?

'Are you going to tell me about it?' she said.

'About what?' His anger was rising.

'Where you've been . . .'

'I've told you. Once more. Then the end of it. I was in the South. Finish, that's it.'

'You won't tell me, then?'

'I've said it's finished. There's no more. Leave it. I'm home – that should be enough. Don't you want me here?'

'It said in the papers that his children were there.

And his wife. They saw it all. That the man went on shooting long after he'd gone down. That the children were screaming, so was his wife. It said she covered him from the bullets. Put herself right over him.'

She was sitting right up now with her hands splayed behind her, back straight, and her breasts, deep from the children she had suckled, bulging forward under the intricate pattern of her nightdress. Downs's longing for her had gone, sapped from him by her accusation. The moment he had waited for, which had become his goal over the last few days on the run, was destroyed.

She went on, looking not at him but straight in front of her into the darkness. 'They said that if it took them five years they'd get the man who did it. They said he must have been an animal to shoot like that across the street. They said they'd hunt for him till they found him, then lock him up for the rest of his natural. You stupid, daft bastard.'

Her point of focus was in the middle distance way beyond the walls and confines of their back bedroom. In his churning mind the replies and counter-attacks flooded through him. But there was no voice. When he spoke it was without fight.

'Someone had to do it. It happened it was me. Danby had it coming. Little bastard he was. There's not a tear shed for him; they haven't a clue to bring them to me. There's no line on me. The picture's no good. The kids wouldn't recognize me on that. They didn't, did they?'

'Don't be so stupid. Do you think I'd hold up two four-year-olds and show them a picture and say "Do you recognize your Dad? He's a killer, shot a man in front of his kids." That what you want me to do?'

128

'Shut your face. Finish it. I told you there'll be no more. You shouldn't have known. You didn't need to know.'

'It'll be bloody marvellous. The return of the great and famous hero, with half the sodding army after him. What a future! "We weren't supposed to know." What sort of statement is that? If they shoot you when they get you there'll be a bloody song about you. Just right for Saturday nights when they're all pissed, so keep the verses short and the words not too long. What a hero. You'll want me to teach the kids the words, and all. Is that the future for us?'

She sank back onto the pillow, and holding the nearest of the two children, began to weep, in slight convulsive shudders, noiselessly.

He rose from the bed and put on his underclothes, shirt and trousers, before moving in his bare feet across the room to the door. He went down the stairs and into the front room. Checking an instinctive movement towards the light switch, he groped his way to his armchair by the grate and lowered himself gingerly down onto it. There were newspapers there, and he pushed them down onto the floor. He sat there very still, exhausted by the emotion of the last few minutes. She'd clobbered him, kicked him in the crutch, and when the pain had sped all over him come back and kicked him again. Since Danby all he had wanted was to get back here, to her, to the kids, the totalness of the family. To be safe with them. The bitch had destroyed it.

In the dark he could relive the moments of the shooting. He found the actual happenings hard to be exact about.

They had faded, and he was uncertain whether the picture he put together was from his memory or his imagination. The immediate sensations were still clear. The kicking of the Kalashnikov, the force driving into his shoulder – that was as vivid as the day and the time itself, the impact feeling. So, too, was the frozen tableau of the woman on her husband. The children. That enormous, useless dog. That was all still there. He saw the incident as a series of still frames, separate episodes. Some of the pictures were in panorama, as when Danby came down the steps and was looking right for the car and waving left at the children. Others were in close up – the face of the woman he had run past. Fear, disbelief, shock and horror. He could see every wrinkle and line on the silly cow's face down to the brown mole above her right cheek. He remembered the blood, but with detachment. Inevitable. Unimportant.

He wanted congratulations for a job well done. He'd thought that out and decided he was justified in some plaudits. It had been professionally done. The movement would be proud of the effort. He knew that himself, but yearned to be told so out loud. She should have bestowed the accolade. Of course she would guess, no way she wouldn't. Dates were right, the picture. She should have been the one with a nod, and an innuendo. She had guessed. She had to. But she called him a 'stupid, daft bastard'. He was hurt and numbed by that.

They had never talked about the Provos. Right from the start that had been laid down. She didn't want to know. Wasn't interested. No word on the nights he was going out. Went and buried herself in the kitchen, played with the children, got out of his way. She accepted, though, that he needed her strength and support when he came home. That was the concession she gave him. But that was not exceptional in the Ardoyne.

The women would hear the shots out in the streets where the battlefield was just beyond the front-room curtains. There would be the high crack of the Armalite, fired once, twice or perhaps three times. Within seconds would come the hard thump of the answering army rifles, a quite different and heavier noise. If the man was not home by dawn the women would listen to the first news broadcast of the day, and hear what had happened. Sometimes there would be an agony of time between hearing that the army returned fire and claimed hits and the savoured moment when the man came in untouched.

Then there would be no words, only warmth and comfort and the attempt to calm the trembling hands.

His wife had once shown him an article in a London women's magazine which told of the effect on the morale of the army wives stationed in Germany that those same early broadcasts had. He had read how fast word spread around the married quarters that the unit had been in action, and how the women then waited at their windows to see if the officer came round and which house he went to. They would know if one of the men had been killed because the chaplain or the doctor would be with the officer, and they would go to a neighbour's house first, have a quick word on the doorstep, then move next door and knock, and when the door opened go inside. The news would be round the houses and maisonettes and flats within minutes.

The man had been responsible for two of those visits.

On the first occasion he had watched the funeral on television, seen the forty-five-second clip that showed the coffin with the flag on it, and a young widow clutching the arm of a relative as she walked surrounded by officers and local dignitaries. Then the staccato crack of rifle fire from the honour party. That was all. The other soldier he'd killed last week had been buried without a news team there to record the event. Interest had been lost. Whether he saw it or not was of no importance to him. He extracted no satisfaction either way.

It left him unmoved. He could imagine no soldier weeping if it were he who were shot dead. He had long accepted that it could happen and, apart from the tension of the actual moments of combat and the bow-string excitement afterwards, he had learned a fatalism about the risks he took.

He had started like most others as a teenager throwing rocks and abuse in the early days at those wonderful, heaven-sent targets . . . the British army, with their yellow cards forbidding them to shoot in almost every situation, their heavy Macron shields, which ruled out effective pursuit, and their lack of knowledge of the geography of the side streets. All the boys in Ypres Avenue threw stones at the soldiers, and it would have been almost impossible to have been uninvolved. The mood had changed when a youth from the other end of the street and the opposite side of the road was shot dead in the act of lighting a petrol bomb. He had been one form above the man in secondary school. Later that night four men had arrived at the far end of Ypres Avenue to the rioting, and the word had spread fast that the kids should get off the streets. Then the shooting had started. In all, fifteen shots had been fired, echoing up the deserted street. He was eighteen then, and with other teenagers had lain in an open doorway and cheered at the urgent shouts of the soldiers who had taken cover behind the Pigs. Abruptly a hurrying, shadowy figure had crawled to the doorway, pushed towards him the long shape of a Springfield rifle, and whispered an address and street number.

He had made his way through the back of the houses, part way down the entry, and through another row of houses where a family had stared at the television, ignoring him as he padded across their living space before closing the door onto the street behind him. When he reached the address he had handed the rifle to the woman who answered his knock. She said nothing and he had made his way back to Ypres Avenue.

That had been the start.

Many of his contemporaries in the street had thrust themselves forward into the IRA. They would meet together on Saturday nights at the clubs, standing apart from the other young men to discuss in secretive voices their experiences over the previous days. Some were now dead, some in remand homes or prison, a very few had made it to junior officer rank in the IRA and after their capture had been served with indefinite detention orders to Long Kesh. The man had kept apart from them, and been noticed by those older, shadowy figures who ran the movement. He had been marked down as someone out of the ordinary, who didn't need to run with the herd. He had been used sparingly and never with the cannon fodder that carried the bombs

133

into the town shoe shops and supermarkets, or held up the post offices for a few hundred pounds. He'd been married on his twentieth birthday when he was acting as bodyguard to a member of the Brigade staff, at a time when relations between the divided Provisionals and officials were at an all-time low. After the wedding he had not been called out for some months, as his superiors let him mature, confident that he would, like good wine, repay well the time they gave him. They used him first shortly before the twins were born. Then he took part in an escape attempt at Long Kesh, waiting through much of the night in a stolen car on the M1 motorway for a man to come through the wire and across the fields. They had stayed seven minutes after a cacophony of barking dogs on the perimeter fence six hundred yards away had spelled out the failure of the attempt. With two others he had been used for the assassination of a policeman as he left his house in the suburb of Glengormley. It was his first command, and he was allowed to select his own ambush point, collect the firearm from the Brigade quartermaster, and lead the getaway on his own route. After that came attacks on police stations, where he was among those who gave covering fire with the Armalites to the blast of the RPG rocket launcher.

On those early occasions he had often missed with the crucial first shot, firing too hurriedly, and then had to run like a mad thing with the noise and shouting of the soldiers behind him. They were heady moments, hearing the voices of the English troops with their strange accents bellowing in pursuit as he weaved and ducked his way clear.

Amongst a small group, though, his reputation had

improved and his future value was reckoned as such that for nearly a year he had been left to lead what amounted to a normal life in the Ardoyne. Around him the army removed all but a tight hard core of activists. He was left at home, his name not figuring on the army files, his photograph absent from the wanted lists.

In their four years of marriage his wife had borne him twins, both boys, and conceived some weeks before their wedding, and two daughters. The time that he was away preparing for London, in the English capital, and then hiding in Northern Ireland before coming back to Ypres Avenue was the longest he had ever been away from his family. As he sat in the room where the light began to filter its gentle way through the thin cotton curtains he reflected on the hugeness of his disappointment at the way his wife had reacted.

He was still slumped in his chair when she came downstairs, a little after six. She came into the room on tiptoe and up behind the chair, and leaned over and kissed him on his forehead.

'We'll have to forget it all,' she said. 'The kids'll be awake soon. They've been upset, you being away so long, and the wee one has the cough. They'll be excited. There's a dance at the club on Saturday. Let's go. Mam'll come down, and sit. We'll have some drinks, forget it ever happened.'

She kissed him again.

'We need some tea, kettle's up.'

He followed her into the kitchen.

For Davidson, in his offices above a paint store in Covent Garden, it was to be a bad morning. He had asked for an appointment with the Permanent

Under-Secretary at the Ministry of Defence. The Boss. The Gaffer. Appointments with subordinates only when there was a fiasco or a potential fiasco. Davidson had to explain that their operator had gone missing and had never checked into the address that had been suggested to him.

Davidson had been hoping for a phone call, or failing that at least a letter or postcard to the office, saying, if nothing else, that Harry was installed and working. The complete silence was beginning to unnerve him. The previous day he authorized the checking of the Antrim Road guest house – discreetly, by telephone – for a Mr McEvoy, but the word had come back that no-one of that name had been near the building. There was no way Davidson could find out in a hurry whether the package containing the pistol sent for collection had in fact been picked up. He told himself there was no positive foundation to his fears, but the possibility, however faint, that Harry was already blown or dead or both nagged at Davidson. Nagged enough for him to seek a rare audience in the Ministry.

By early afternoon the brandies were on the table in the restaurant of the big hotel on the outskirts of the city. Both the Brigadier and the Chief Superintendent were in their own clothes and mildly celebrating the promotion and transfer of the army officer from second in command of the Brigade with responsibilities for Belfast to a new appointment in Germany. Both knew from their own intelligence-gathering agencies in vague terms of the sending of Harry and the Prime Minister's directive – it had come in a terse, brief message from the GOC's headquarters. There was little

136

more to it than the statement that a special team had been set up to spearhead the hunt for Danby's killer, and that all other operations in this direction should continue as before. During the serving of the food neither had spoken of it, as the waiters hovered round them. But with the coffee cups full, and the brandy glasses topped up, the subject was inevitably fielded.

'There's been nothing from that fellow the PM launched,' muttered the Brigadier. 'Long shot at the best of times. No word, I'm told, and Frost in intelligence is still leaping about. Called it a bloody insult. See his point.'

'Sunk without trace, probably. They sniff them out, smell them a mile off. Poor devil. I feel for him. How was he supposed to solve it when SB and intelligence don't have a line in? If our trained people can't get in there, how's this chap?'

'Bloody ridiculous.'

'He'll end up dead, and it'll be another life thrown away. I hope he doesn't, but if he sticks at it they'll get him.'

'I expect your SB were the same, but intelligence weren't exactly thrilled. What really peeved them was that at first they weren't supposed to know anything, then it leaked. I think the Old Man himself put it out, then came the message, and there wasn't much to show from that. Frost stayed behind after the Old Man's conference last Friday and demanded to know what was going on. Said it was an indication of no confidence in his section. Threatened his commission and everything on it. GOC calmed him down, but it took a bit of time.'

The music was loud in the dining room, and both

men needed to speak firmly to hear each other above the canned violin strings. The policeman spoke:

'I think Frost's got a case. So have we for that matter' . . . in mid-chord and without warning the tape ran out . . . 'to put a special operator in on the ground without telling . . .' Dramatically conscious of the way his voice had carried in the sudden moment of silence he cut himself short.

Awkwardly the two men waited for the half-minute or so that it took the reception staff away in the front hall to loop up the reverse side of the three-hour tape, then the talking began again.

The eighteen-year-old waiter serving the next table their courgettes had clearly heard the second half of the sentence. He repeated the words to himself as he went round the table – 'Special operator on the ground without telling.' He said it five times to himself as he circled the table, fearful that he would forget the crucial words. Then he hurried with the emptied dish to the kitchen, scribbling the words in large spidery writing on the back of his order pad.

He went off duty at 3.30, and seventy-five minutes later the message of what he had overheard and its context were on their way to the intelligence officer of the Provisionals' Third Battalion.

Chapter Eight

Harry spent a long time getting himself ready to go out that Saturday night. He bathed, and put on clean clothes, even changing his socks from the ones he'd been wearing through the rest of the day, took a clean shirt from the wardrobe and brushed down the one suit he'd brought with him. In the time that he'd been in Belfast he had tried to stop thinking in the terms of an army officer, even when he was on his own and relaxed. He attempted to make his first impulses those of the ex-merchant seaman or lorry driver that he hoped to become. As he straightened his tie, though, he allowed himself the luxury of thinking that this was a touch different from a mess night with the rest of the regiment at base camp in Germany.

He'd spent a difficult and nearly unproductive first week. He'd visited a score of firms looking for driver's work with no success till Friday when he had come across a scrap merchant on the far side of Andersonstown. There they'd said they might be able to use him, but he should come back on Monday morning when he would get a definite answer. He had been in the pub on the corner several times, but though

139

he was now accepted enough for him to stand and take his drink without the whole bar lapsing into a silent stare none of the locals initiated any conversation with him, and the opening remarks he made to them from time to time were generally rebutted with non-committal answers.

It had been both hard and frustrating, and he felt that the one bright spot that stood out was this Saturday night. Taking Josephine out. Like a kid out of school and going down the disco, you silly bugger. At your age, off to a peasant hop. As he dressed himself he began to liven up. One good night out was what he needed before the tedium of next week. Nearly six days gone, and not a thing to hook on to. Davidson said three weeks and something ought to show. Must have been the pep talk chat. He came down a little after seven and sat in the chair by the fire in the front room that was available to guests. He was on his own. All the others scurried away on Friday morning with their bags packed and homes to get to after a half-day's work at the end of the week. Not hanging about up here, not in the front line.

When the doorbell rang he slipped quickly out into the hall, and opened the door. Josephine stood there, breathing heavily.

'I'm sorry I'm late. Couldn't get a bus. They've cut them down a bit, I think. I'm not very late, am I?'

'I think all the buses are on the scrap yards up the road, stacks of them there, doubles and singles. I'd only just come down. I reckon you're dead on time. Let's go straight away.'

He shouted back towards the kitchen that he was on

his way out, that he had his key, and not to worry if he was a bit late.

'How do we get there?' he asked. 'It's all a bit strange to me moving about the city still, especially at night.'

'No problem. We'll walk down to the hospital, get a cab there into town, and in Castle Street we'll get another cab up the Crumlin. It's just a short walk from there. It won't take long, we'll be there in forty-five minutes. It's a bit roundabout, that's all.'

In Ypres Avenue the man and his wife were making their final preparations to go out. There had been an uneasy understanding between them since their talk in the early hours after his homecoming, and no further word on the subject had been spoken. Both seemed to accept that the wounds of that night could only be healed by time and silence. She had lain in bed the first three mornings waiting for the high whine of the Saracens, expecting the troops to come breaking in to tear her man from their bed. But they didn't come, and now she began to believe what he had told her. Perhaps there was no clue, perhaps the photokit really did look as little like him as she, his wife, believed. Her mother was busying herself at the back of the house round the stove, where she kept a perpetual pot of freshened tea. All the children were now in bed, the twins complaining that it was too early. To both of them the evening was something to look forward to, a change from the oppressiveness of the atmosphere as the man sat about his house, too small for privacy or for him to absent himself from the rest of the family. It had been laid down by his superiors that he was not to try to make contact with his colleagues in the movement, or in any way expose himself to danger of arrest. It meant long hours of waiting, fiddling time uselessly away. Already he felt restless, but hurrying things was futile. That's how they all got taken, going off at half-cock when things weren't ready for them. Not like London. All the planning was there. No impatience, just when it suited and not a day earlier. Boredom was his great enemy, and the need was for discipline, discipline as befits the member of an army.

With his wife on his· arm, and in her best trouser suit, he walked up his street towards the hut with the corrugated-iron roof that was the social club. He could relax here, among his own. Drain his pints. Talk to people. It was back to the ordinary. To living again.

By the time Harry and Josephine arrived at the club, it was nearly full, with most of the tables taken. The girl said she'd find somewhere to sit, and he pushed his way towards the long trestle tables at the far end from the door where three men were hard at it in their shirt sleeves taking the tops off bottles and pouring drinks. Harry forced his way through the shoulders of the men standing close to the makeshift bar, made it to the front and called for a pint of Guinness and a gin and orange.

As he was struggling back to the table where Josephine was sitting he saw a man come up to her and gesture towards him. After they'd spoken a few words he'd nodded his head, smiled at the girl and moved back towards the door.

'Someone you know?' he said when he sat down, shifting her coat onto the back of the seat.

'It's just they like to know who's who round here.

Can't blame them. He wanted to know who you were, that's all.'

'What did you tell him?'

'Just who you were, that's all.'

Everything was subdued at this stage of the evening, but the effects of the drink and the belting of the four-piece band and their electrically-amplified instruments began to have a gradual livening effect. By nine some of the younger couples were ignoring the protests of the older people and had begun to pile up the tables and chairs at the far end of the room to the bar, exposing a crude, unpolished set of nail-ridden boards. That was the dance floor. The band quickened the tempo, intensified the beat. When he felt that the small talk they were making was next to impossible, Harry asked the girl if she'd like to dance.

She led the way through the jungle of tables and chairs. Near the floor Harry paused as Josephine slowed and squeezed by a girl in a bright-yellow trouser suit. It was striking enough in its colour for Harry to notice it. Then, as his eyes moved to the table where she was sitting, he saw the young man at her side.

There was intuitive, deep-based recognition for a moment, and Harry couldn't place it. He looked at the man, who stared straight back at him, challenging. Josephine was out on the floor now waiting for him to come by the girl in yellow. He looked away from the face that was still staring back at him, holding and returning his glance, mouthed an apology and was away to the floor. Once more he looked at the man, who still watched him, cold and expressionless – then Harry rejected the suspicion of the likeness. Hair wrong. Face

143

too full. Eyes too close. Mouth was right. That was all. The mouth, and nothing else.

The floor pounded with the motion of a cattle stampede – as it seemed to Harry, who was used to more ordered dances at the base. At first he was nearly swamped, but survived after throwing off what decorum he had ever learned as he and Josephine were buffeted and shoved from one set of shoulders to another. Sweat and scent were already taking over from the beer and smoke. When the band switched to an Irish ballad he gasped his relief, and round them the frenetic movements slowed in pace. He could concentrate now on the girl close against him.

She danced with her head back, looking up at him and talking. Looking the whole time, not burying herself away from him. She was wearing a black skirt, full and flared, so that she had the freedom to swing her hips to the music. Above that a tight polka dot blouse. The top four buttons were unfastened. There were no Josephines in Aden, no Josephines taking an interest in married transport captains in Germany.

They talked dance-floor small talk, Harry launched into a series of concocted anecdotes about the ports he'd visited when he was at sea, and she laughed a lot. Twice a nagging uncertainty took his attention away from her to where the man was sitting quietly at the table with the girl in the yellow trouser suit, glasses in front of them, eyes roving, but not talking. The second time he decided the likeness was superficial. It didn't hold up. Face, eyes, hair – all wrong. Before he turned back to Josephine he saw the mouth again. That was right. It amused him. Coincidence. And his attention was diverted to the girl, her prettiness and inevitable promise.

The man too had noticed Harry's attention. It had been pronounced enough to make him fidget a little in his chair, and for him to feel the hot perspiration surge over his legs inside the thick cloth of his best suit. He had seen the doorminder talk to the girl who brought him in, and presumably clear the stranger. But his nerves had calmed when he had seen Harry on the dance floor, no longer interested, but totally involved in the girl he was with. The man could not dance, had never been taught. He and his wife would sit at the table all evening as a succession of friends and neighbours came to join them to talk for a few minutes and then move on. Along the wall to the right of the door and near the bar were a group of youths, some of them volunteers in the Provisionals, some couriers and some lookouts. These were the expendables of the movement. The teenage girls were gathered round them, attracted by the glamour of the profession of terrorism, hanging on the boys' sneers and cracks and boasts. None of the boys would rise high in the upper echelons but each was necessary as part of the supply chain that kept the planners and marksmen in the field. None knew the man except by name. None knew of his involvement.

First through the door was the big sergeant, a Stirling sub-machine-gun in his right hand. He'd hit the door with all the impetus of his two hundred pounds gathered in a six-foot run. Behind him came a lieutenant, clutching his Browning automatic pistol, and then eight soldiers. They came in fast and fanned out in a protective screen round the officer. Some of the soldiers carried rifles, others the large-barrelled, rubber-bullet guns.

The officer shouted in the general direction of the band.

'Cut that din. Wrap it up. I want all the men against the far wall. Facing the wall. Hands right up. Ladies, where you are please.'

From the middle of the dance floor a glass curved its way through the crowd and towards the troops. It hit high on the bridge of a nose creeping under the protective rim of a helmet. Blood was forming from the wound by the time the glass hit the floor. A rubber bullet, solid, unbending, six inches long, was fired into the crowd, and amid the screams there was a stampede away from the troops as tables and chairs were thrown aside to make way.

'Come on. No games, please. Let's get it over with. Now, the men line up at that wall – and *now*.'

More soldiers had come through the door. There were perhaps twenty of them in the hall by the time the line of men had formed up, legs wide apart and fingers and palms on the wall high above their heads. Harry and the man were close to each other, separated by three others. At her table the girl in the yellow trouser suit sat very still. She was one of the few who wasn't barracking the army with a medley of obscenities and insults. Her fingers were tight round the stem of her glass, her eyes flicking continuously from the troops to her husband.

Josephine's table had been knocked aside in the scramble to get clear from the firing of the rubber bullet, and she stood on the dance floor interested to see what the army made of her merchant-seaman escort.

Six of the soldiers, working in pairs, split up the line of men against the wall and started to quiz each man on his name, age and address. One soldier asked the questions, the other wrote down the answers. The lieutenant moved between the three groups, checking the procedure, while his sergeant marshalled his other men in the room to prevent any sudden break for the exits.

Private David Jones, number 278649, eighteen months of his nine-year signing served, and Lance-Corporal James Llewellyn, 512387, were working over the group of men nearest the dance floor. The man and Harry were there. The way the line had formed itself they would come to the man first. It was very slow. Conscientious, plodding. The wife was in agony. Charade, that's all. A game of cat and mouse. They had come for him, and these were the preliminaries, the way they dressed it up. But they'd come for him. They had to know.

The lance-corporal tapped the man's shoulder.

'Come on, let's have you.' Not unkindly. It was quiet in the Ardoyne now, and the soldiers acknowledged it.

The man swung round, bringing his hands down to his side, fists clenched tight, avoiding the pleading face of his wife a few feet away. Llewellyn was asking the questions, Jones writing the answers down.

'Name?'

'Billy Downs.'

'Age?'

'Twenty-three.'

'Address?'

147

'Forty-one, Ypres Avenue.'

Llewellyn paused as Jones struggled in his notebook with the blunted pencil he had brought with him. The lieutenant walked towards them. He looked hard at the man, then down into Jones's notebook, deciphering the smudged writing.

'Billy Downs?'

'That's it.'

'We were calling for you the other morning. Expected to find you home, but you weren't there.'

He stared into the young man's face. That was the question he posed. There was no reply.

'Where were you, Mr Downs? Your good wife whom I see sitting over there didn't seem too sure.'

'I went down to see my mother in the South. It's on your files. You can check that.'

'But you've been away a fair few days, Downs boy. Fond of her, are you?'

'She's not been well, and you know that. She's a heart condition. That's in your files and all. It wasn't made any better when there weren't any of you lot around when the Prods came and burned her out . . . and that's in your files too.'

'Steady, boy. What's her address?'

'Forty, Dublin Road, Cork.' He said it loud enough for his wife to hear the address given. His voice was raised now, and she listened to the message that was in it. 'She'll tell you I've been there for a month. That I was with her till four days ago.'

The lieutenant still gazed into Downs's face, searching for weakness, evasion, inconsistency. If there was fear there he betrayed none of it to the soldier a bare year older than himself.

'Put him in the truck,' the lieutenant said. Jones and Llewellyn hustled Downs across the room and towards the door. His wife rose up out of her chair and rushed across to him.

'Don't worry, girl, once the Garda have checked with Mam I'll be home. I'll see you later.' And he was out into the night to where the Saracen was parked.

The two soldiers came back to the line, and the lieutenant moved away to the other end where the youths, resigned to a ride back to barracks and an interrogation session at the end of it, snapped back sullen replies to the questions.

Llewellyn touched Harry's shoulder.

'Name?'

'Harry McEvoy.'

'Age?'

'Thirty-three.'

'Address?'

Jones had had his eyes down on his notebook till that moment. He glanced up to hear the answer. Harry saw an expression of astonishment take hold of him, then change to suspicion, then back to bewilderment.

'Bloody hell, what are you doing—?'

Harry's right foot moved the seven inches into Jones's left ankle. As the private ducked forward, caught off balance by the sudden pain, Harry lurched into him.

'Shut your face,' he hissed into the soldier's ear.

Jones's face came up and met Harry's stare. Imperceptibly he saw the head move. A quick shake, left to right and twice.

'I'm sorry,' said Harry. 'Forget it. I hope you'll forget it.'

149

The last words were very quiet and straight into Jones's ear. The men in the line, waiting to be questioned, still faced the wall; the women, sitting at their tables, were out of earshot. The exchange between Harry and Jones seemed to have passed unnoticed.

Llewellyn had been diverted by a commotion down at the far end of the hall, where four youths were half carried and half dragged towards the doorway. He was concentrating again now.

'Come on – what's the address?'

'Delrosa Guest House, in the Broadway. Just up from Beachmount.'

Harry's eyes were fixed, snake-like, on Jones.

'Bit off course, aren't you?' said Llewellyn.

'My girl's local.'

'Which one?'

'In the polka dot, the dark-haired girl.' Harry gazed past Llewellyn, his eyes never leaving Jones. Twice the younger soldier's eyes came up from his notebook, met Harry's, and dived back to the writing.

'Lucky bastard,' said Llewellyn, and moved on.

Apart from Downs, the army had taken nine youths when the officer shouted for his men to leave the club. They went out in single file, the last going out backwards with his rifle covering the crowd. As the door swung to after him a hail of empty bottles and glasses cannoned into the woodwork.

A tall man at the far end from Harry shouted a protest.

'Now come on, folks, we can do better than that. Lob things at the bastards, yes, but not so we cover *our* floor with *our* bottles and *our* glasses and *our* beer. Now, we're not going to let those swine spoil the evening for us. Let's move it all back and tidy up, and see if we can't get something out of the evening.'

It was a good effort on the part of the community leader, but doomed to failure.

Harry noticed that the girl in yellow was gone before the floor was half cleared. He shifted in his seat.

'We can't go yet. It's the principle of the thing,' said Josephine. 'You cannot let the bastards wreck everything. What did you say to that soldier?'

'I just tripped against him, that's all.'

'You're lucky. You might have got a rifle butt across your face. There's men taken to the barracks for less.'

The band had started up again, attempting to capitalize on the angry mood of those left behind.

Armoured cars and tanks and guns,

Came to take away our sons . . .

'Will it wake up again, or is this the lot for the evening?' asked Harry.

. . . Through the little streets so narrow . . .

'I doubt it,' she said, 'but it's best to give it a few minutes. Let's see, anyway.'

. . . Cromwell's men are here again . . .

'It's not that bad, is it?' said Harry. 'I heard it in the Baltic when we were working out of a Swedish port. They used to play it about every third disc. Got to quite like it. We had a mate on board who said his son was in the army here. He used to get right steamed up just listening to it.'

. . . The men behind the wire . . .

People were edging towards the door. Harry sensed there would be little more of a night out for any of them.

'Come on, let's quit. We don't want to stay here for the funeral.'

151

'I'm going to powder my nose, then,' Josephine said.

'Looks all right to me. Don't hang about.'

She smiled, got up from the table and went out through a side door where a gaggle of girls younger than Josephine had gathered. The band was still trying, but was competing with a wave of talk particularly from a large group that had gathered round a local primary schoolteacher who was taking down the names of all those lifted by the military. He was promising to go round to the barracks to see what had happened to them.

It was a cold clear night as Harry, with Josephine on his arm, walked out of the hall and off towards the all-night taxi rank for the drive down to Castle Street. Then there would be another taxi, and a walk up the last part of the Falls to Mrs Duncan's.

Harry and Josephine were naked, entwined and asleep, when 275 miles to the south the Garda squad car drew up outside the stone terraced house in the Dublin Road in Cork. There was the sharp mustiness of the docks in the pre-dawn air, as the two policemen fumbled their way from the car to the front doorstep.

'It's a sod of a time, God help us, to be getting this poor dear out of her bed.'

The sergeant rang the door bell, twice and firmly, and waited. A light came on upstairs, not fast, then in the hall, and after that the noise of the bolts in the door grating open.

'From the sound of it you'd think she'd got the Bank of England in there,' muttered the sergeant into his gloves.

'Good morning, my love. I'm sorry to be coming at

such a time as this to wake you. But a message has come down over the telephone from Dublin and I'm to ask you some questions. Won't take a moment now. Shall we come on in, out of that wind?'

'We'll do what business you have here. You should be ashamed of yerselves coming at this time . . .'

'That's not our affair, my love. Now, are you ready? We want to ask you when was your boy last here.'

'Billy, you mean?'

'That's the lad, love. That's the one they want to know about.'

'He was down till the middle of the week. Been here a month, and just gone back. Why do you need to come at this time of night to ask that?'

'You're sure of that now, my dear? No mistakes?'

'Of course I'm sure. Billy was here for a month. And those are bloody silly questions to be asking at this time of night.'

She closed the door on them. The two Garda men knocked at the next-door house and again waited for the door to open. They took away the same message. Billy Downs had been there for a month.

The alibi had been passed on to the old lady and her four immediate neighbours some forty-five minutes before the police car had arrived. The wife's phone call to a friend of her man in Belfast had started the chain. Another call had been made to Dublin, another one from there to Cork, and a young man who had left his car two streets away from the Dublin Road had completed the process. The Provisionals' lines of communication were somewhat faster than the complicated and official process of liaison between North and South.

Downs had been interrogated twice, maintaining quietly and without fuss that he had been at his mother's in the South. He was kept apart from the other prisoners with the officers who had questioned him unsure whether they ought to have pulled him in or not. They heard at 5.30 the results of the checks in Cork, gave him back his coat and his tie and his shoes and told him to get away home.

Chapter Nine

They'd come into the house on tiptoe and holding their shoes. Both knew the prim well-scrubbed hallway and stairs well enough to estimate where the boards creaked, and where it was safe to put down their full weight. Harry held the girl's hand very tight. At first they had tried to go up the stairs together, and then, finding that impossible, he had gently led the way. There had been no talk about what they should do, where they should go when they left the taxi, no discussion whether she should come back to Delrosa with him. He had looked into her face at the doorway as he rummaged with his free hand for the latch key, seen those mocking, querying eyes turned up to his face, looking as if to challenge or dare him to take her inside. He'd squeezed her hand, and they'd gone in together. The message of silence was implicit.

Once in his back room a floorboard had erupted in protest at her foot and he had pulled her away from the place near the basin where she was standing wriggling out of her coat. That was where it would creak. That was the place where he had prised up the planks two days earlier to find a secure hiding place for his Smith & Wesson revolver.

She slung the coat across his easy chair by the window, and stood waiting for him to move towards her. He felt a tightness streaming through him. Clumsy. Gauche. Inhibited. He reached out towards the tall girl who gazed back at him, her expression one of interest, curiosity to see what he had to offer.

'You make me feel . . . a bit like someone who's forgotten most of it,' he whispered into her ear, one hand holding the back of her neck, the other flattened into the small of her back.

'You haven't made me feel anything yet.'

'Cheeky girl.'

'Try a bit of cheek yourself. Might take you a long way.'

He pulled his left hand round, drawing back from her to give himself room to unbutton the few remaining buttons on her blouse.

'Not much of an obstacle course here,' he murmured as he flicked the buttons, small and transparent, through the opened holes of the fabric.

'Who said they were supposed to be?'

His hand had moved inside her blouse, and he began to ease the soft cotton over her shoulders and down her arms.

'I was never very much one for this. Getting everything off in the right order, like a bloody production line in reverse.'

'And it takes so much more time. Let's see to it ourselves. I'll meet you under the sheets in forty-five seconds from now.'

In a welter of tights, pants, black skirt, shoes and bra

156

she stripped herself and was away in the bed waiting for him. Harry was fighting with his right cuff link. She had started to follow the second hand of her watch with exaggerated interest before he climbed into the narrow bed alongside her.

'You took thirty seconds over the limit. Bad marks for that, sailor boy.'

'Wasn't for lack of trying.'

He had curved his arms round her, as she came close to against him. His fingers ran their course across her skin, tight, cool and firm. Beautiful girl. Her eyes closed. She moaned. Calling for him, hurrying him. That first time there were few preliminaries, few subtleties. He found her fast, deep, easy. He poured himself into her. Both engaged in a frantic, uncaring race. He sagged away. Disastrous. Bloody Belfast. Like everything else – crude and rushed. No future for tenderness or patience.

'Got a bus to catch?'

'It'll be better next time,' he said, 'it happened too quick for me. And I never got round to asking you whether . . . you know, whether you take anything . . . or what?'

'There's Catholics and good Catholics here. I'm one of the first. You don't have to worry about that.'

The second time was better. Softer, calmer. Slower. He took a long time finding the routes and depths and contours of her body. Finding where she moved and squirmed, and when she thrust herself at him. Heat against his chest and his thighs. She called the time she was ready for him to come into her, called quietly in his ear. Her mouth open, almost soundless. He smiled down at her as he felt himself slipping away into the

157

void. It was over and they lay together. Her hair strewn with the sweat out on the pillow, he on her softness waiting for the limpness to come. Still locked together.

'You've no worries, then?' she asked.

'What do you mean? I don't think so.'

'You can't screw if you're really worried. Did you know that?'

'Old wives. Where did you hear that? Who told you that?'

'Just what one of the girls said in the bog tonight.'

'Tell me what she said.' He lay straddled across her, her mouth an inch or so from his ear.

'She said she'd tried to do it with one of the big men, but he couldn't manage it. She said he was all so tied up he couldn't make it. She was ever so upset.'

Harry grimaced in disbelief.

'No, that's what she said. She was there tonight. She told me in the loo. She's a bit frantic at the best of times. Then the army nicked the fellow who'd have had her on the way home. Peeved her a bit. On her own on Saturday night. Not right for her. That's what she said. Big hero. Big deal. I'm all for cowards in this city.'

'I don't believe you,' said Harry, very still now. 'Which girl was it?'

'I'm not telling you the best lay in Ballymurphy!'

'I don't believe you. You're making it up.'

She pushed him back sideways. In the small bed there was hardly enough room, and he clung to her to save himself from disappearing on the floor. She rolled over onto him, half her weight supported by his hips and waist and the other half supported by an elbow.

'It was Theresa. In pink. She had the tight skirt? Remember her? Believe me. You'll be up to Ballymurphy sniffing round now. Randy bugger.'

'I'd believe anything said by anyone as lovely as you,' said Harry.

'Bullshit,' she said.

'Who was the big man that didn't slake wee Theresa's thirst?' His hands were on the move again now, seeking the closeness between her thighs. She rolled and rose beneath him.

'Just like that. Go on. Just like that. The big man, the one they're all looking for. The London man. The one that did the politician in London. Don't stop there. Just like that. Faster! There's bugger all time. The old girl's alarm'll be off in half an hour. She's out like a flash then. Makes enough noise to wake half the folks in Milltown Cemetery.'

Minutes later she was out of bed, dressed and making her way quietly down the stairs to the front door. She refused to let Harry come and see her off, gave him a sisterly kiss on the forehead and was gone. He stood at his bedroom window and saw her some moments later walking along the main road under the street lights. When she had gone beyond the gap he lost sight of her.

After she had left Harry lay in his bed, stretching out his legs, searching out the new-found room, working over in his mind the information she had given him. No problem for the intelligence guys. A girl called Theresa, about eighteen or nineteen, in Ballymurphy. Sleeps around a bit. No problem. Should wrap up the whole thing. Not bad; one good screw in the line of duty, and the big *coup*. He could scarcely believe his luck – getting so far so quickly – all falling into his lap – and on a night out, at that. And the old woman, Davidson, who didn't rate his chances, who fussed and clucked over him, what would he be thinking when Harry called through? A moment to savour, that would be. I'd like to see his face, thought Harry.

There was still the worry over being recognized by that stupid, gawping soldier. But they should have the man within forty-eight hours, and then what the soldier saw wouldn't matter. All be academic by then. But where did the soldier come from? He turned over in his mind the military situations he'd been in over the last two years, trying to work out where he had seen the young man who had no doubts about him. Davidson would sort it out. Ring him in the morning. Let him know it's just about wrapped up.

For the first time since he had come to Belfast he felt the excitement that had been the hallmark of the Sheik Othman operation.

He used to leave little pencilled messages in English in an old fruit tin on the Sheik Othman-to-Mansoura road. Nothing as luxurious as a telephone. Sometimes he'd stay around in the afternoon heat the next day when the town was sleepy and out of gear and watch the military come bulldozing into the town in their Saladins and Saracens. He would watch the leather-faced, expressionless men hustled away into the armoured cars, resisting the show of force that came to get them only with the contempt in their eyes. That was the reward for the strange job he did – to see the clumsy boot of the army stepping into the exact footprints he had silently prepared for them.

It was a good two and a quarter hours before Davidson would be in the office. He had told Harry that for the first three weeks at least he would be there every day, Sundays included, at eight in the morning and stay till ten at night. Must be playing havoc with his marriage, thought Harry. Can't really see Davidson with a wife, though.

He'd go into town, he decided, and make the call from one of those anonymous call boxes in the city centre. Now two hours' sleep. That bloody woman. He was exhausted.

But she was a bit special.

Not like that at home. Couldn't be really. Nothing in married life vegetating round a barracks square in a line of neat, desiccated quarters that matched the drawn bowstring of the city at war. Too many bombs, too many snipers, too many mutilations for people to hang about on the preliminaries. You'd want a few memories as you bumped about in the box up the Falls to Milltown Cemetery. That was the philosophy of life for Belfast. And not a bad one, thought Harry.

Across in Germany they'd be asleep now. The wife and the kids, tucked up in their rooms, the familiar bits and pieces round them. The things, semi-junk, that they'd collected from the duty-free lounge and the market places where they went shopping when he was off duty. Knick-knacks that brightened the service furniture they lived off. Josephine didn't fit in there, was outside that world. They'd be up soon. Always had an early breakfast on Sundays. Someone would take the boys out for football. That was regular. And his wife . . . how would she spend a cold Sunday in North Germany? Harry was half asleep. Not quite dreaming but close. She'd go visiting, walk out along the line of officers' detached houses for a coffee in mid-morning, and stay for a drink before lunch, and have to make her

161

excuses, and there'd be laughter when she'd flap about the lunch in the oven. Perhaps someone would ask her to stay and share theirs. That would be par for the course. And they'd say how sorry they were that Harry was away, and how suddenly he'd gone, and fish for an explanation. The questions would confuse her, and embarrass her, because they'd expect her at least to have an idea of why he'd vanished so quickly. And she wouldn't have an answer.

Could she comprehend it even if she did know? Could she assimilate this tatty, rotten job? Could she understand the man that was hunted, and the need to kill him? Could she accept what might happen to Harry? 'I don't know,' Harry said to himself. 'God knows how many years we've been married, and I don't know. She'd be calm enough, not throw any tantrums, but what it would all mean to her, I've not the faintest idea.'

That would all sort itself. And when the answers had to be given then Josey would be a fantasy, and over.

Billy Downs was in his bed now, and asleep. He'd come back to find his wife sobbing into her pillow, disbelieving he could be freed, still suffering from the strain of the phone call she had made hours earlier. Many times he told her it was just routine, that there was nothing for them to fear. Relax, they know nothing. It's clean. The trail is old and cold and clean. She held onto him as if uncertain that he was really there after she had mentally prepared herself for not seeing him again as a free man. The terror of losing him was a long time thawing. He put a brave face on it, but didn't know himself the significance of his arrest. But to run now

162

would be suicide. He would stay put. Act normally. And stay very cool.

As soon as he came off duty, in the small hours of Sunday morning, Jones asked to see his commanding officer. His platoon lieutenant asked him why, and about what, but the shuffling private merely replied that it was a security matter and that he must see the colonel as soon as he woke. He was marched up the wide steps of the mill, enclosed with the dripping walls festooned with fire- and parcel-bomb warnings and urging the soldiers to be ever vigilant, and shown into the colonel's office. The colonel was shaving electrically and continued with the modern ritual as the soldier put together his report. Jones said that while searching a social club the previous night he had seen a man he definitely recognized as having been the transport officer at a base in Germany where his unit had refitted after a NATO exercise. He said that the man had given his name as McEvoy, and he explained about the kicked ankle, and the instruction to forget what he had seen. There was a long pause while the officer scraped the razor round his face, doubtful what action to take, and how he should react. The minute or so that he thought about the problem seemed to the young private an eternity. Then he gave his orders. Jones was to make no further mention of this incident to any other soldier, and was confined to barracks till further notice.

'Please, sir. What do I tell the sergeant-major?'

'Tell him the MO says you've a cold. That's all, and keep your mouth shut. That's important.'

When the soldier had about-turned and stamped his way out of the office the colonel asked for his second in command to come and see him. Sunday was normally the quiet morning, and the chance of a modest stay in bed. The second in command came in still wearing his dressing gown. To the colonel the position was now clear.

'There's all these chaps running round in civvies. I think we've trampled on one. If we say we've done it, there's going to be a hell of a scene all the way round, lot of fluff flying and problems. I'm going to ship Jones out to Germany this afternoon and have the page of his log destroyed. We can take care of this our own way and with rather less palava than if it goes up to old Frost at HQ.'

The second in command agreed. He would ask for the log book, and deal with the offending page personally. Before his breakfast.

Early Sunday morning in Belfast is formidable. To Harry it was like the set of one of those films where there has been a nerve gas attack and no-one is left alive. Nothing but grey, heavy buildings, some crazily angled from the bomb blasts, others held up at the ends by huge timber props. Outside the city hall, vast and enormous and apparently deserted, the pigeons had gathered on the lawns. They too were immobile except when they ducked their heads while searching for imaginary worms in the ground. No buses. No taxis. No cars. No people. Harry found himself scurrying to get away from so much silence and emptiness. It was almost with a sense of relief that he saw a joint RUC and Military Police patrol cruising towards him. This typified the difference for him between Aden and here. When he was on his own in Mansoura he had shut himself away from the safety of the military and accepted that the run for home would be way too long if his cover was blown or he gave himself away. Now he had the army and police all round him. He was part of their arm, an extension of their operations.

Yet he felt the very closeness of the security forces was unnerving. The agent operating in hostile territory has to be self-sufficient and self-supporting. All just as applicable to the British agent working in Great Britain. Can't be like the little boy with the bloody nose running home to Mum. In Mansoura it had been quite conventional and therefore more acceptable.

Not only was the city deserted of people. It was battened down for the day. Iron railings, their tops split into sharp tridents, blocked off the shopping streets that fanned off Royal Avenue. The turnstile gates into the security precincts were padlocked. Shops inside and outside the barricades had their windows barricaded and shuttered.

Down near the post office he found a bank of empty phone boxes, with only the work of vandals to prevent him taking his pick from a choice of six. It was cold inside the booth, with the wind cutting through the gaps left where the kids had kicked out the glass in the days before the army operated in strength in the city centre.

He took from his pocket a pile of ten-pence pieces and arrayed them in formation like fish scales on the top of the money box, and dialled the London number he had memorized in Dorking. If he had gone through an operator some of his call might have been overheard. This was the safe way. The phone rang a long time before it was answered.

Davidson heard the ringing when he was at the bottom of the stairs.

Against its shrill persistence he fumbled with his key ring to release the three separate locks on the heavy door, and stumbled across the darkened room where the blinds were still down. He picked up the receiver.

'Four-seven-zero-four-six-eight-one. Can I help you?'

'It's Harry. How are the family?'

'Very well, they liked the postcards, I'm told.'

That was the routine they had agreed. Two sentences' chatter to show the other that he was a free agent and able to talk.

'How's it going, Harry boy?'

'Middling. I'll get the report over first. Then we'll talk. Going in ten from now.'

That was time enough for Davidson to get the drawer in the leg of his desk open, switch on the cassette recorder and plug in the lead to the telephone receiver.

'Going now, OK? The man is in Belfast still. I'm sure of that. He is apparently under great stress and while on the run shortly after the shooting was with a girl called Theresa. No second name. She's from the Ballymurphy area. He tried to screw her, and she's telling her friends that he couldn't make it, because he was so wound up about the shooting. She's late teens or early twenties. She was at a dance last night in a green-painted hut in the Ardoyne. She was wearing pink, tight skirt. The army heifered their way in, and picked up about a dozen blokes, some of them in Theresa's group. They should be holding them still, unless they work bloody fast. One of them can identify her. So she's worth a bit of chat and then I think we'll be homeward bound. Seems straight sailing from here. That's the plus side. Now the anti. In the club I was lined up for an ID check. Lance-Corporal from Wales asking questions, a young boy writing down the answers. The boy recognized me. God knows from when, but he did. I'd like it sorted out. I'm going to lie low for today, but I may have a job of sorts coming up. That's about it, basically.'

'Harry, we were worried when we didn't hear anything.'

'I didn't want to call in till I had something to say.'

'I won't mess you about. But I know you're not staying where we planned for you.'

'Too bloody right. Right little army rest house. Right out of the interesting areas, and I take a peep at the place and out comes some squaddie in plains. Shambles that was. You should crucify whoever sold you that pup.'

'Thanks, Harry. I'll kill them for it. I'll go high on it.'

'I've made it on my own. Quite snug, on the other side of town. Let's leave it that way. I'll call you if anything else shows up.'

'We'll do it your way. It's not usual, but OK. Nothing more?'

'Only tell the people who pick the girl up to go a bit quietly. Don't ask me what the source of this is, but I don't want it too obvious. If you can get her in without a razzamatazz you should have your man before anyone knows she's gone, and can link her to him.'

'I'll pass that on. Anything else?'

'Nothing more. Cheers. Good hunting.'

Davidson heard the phone click down. The call had lasted one minute and fifty-five seconds.

Harry let the receiver stay a moment in his hand after he'd pressed down the twin buttons with his fingers to end the call. He would have liked to talk with Davidson, unimportant small talk. But that would be unprofessional. Dangerous. Soft. Diverting. Pray God they would get the bastard now. He began to walk back to a lonely day at Delrosa, as the city on half-cylinder sparked to life.

Davidson had been surprised that Harry had rung off so fast. He reached down into his drawer and spun back the spools of his tape a few revolutions to check that the recording had operated correctly. He then wound the tape back to the beginning and played it from start to finish, taking a careful shorthand note of the conversation. He then rewound the tape again and played it once more, this time against his shorthand. Only when he was satisfied that he had correctly taken down every word spoken by Harry did he disconnect the leads between the tape and the telephone. He searched in his diary, at the back in the addresses and useful numbers section, for the home phone number of the Permanent Under-Secretary.

'I thought you'd want to know, after our talk the other day. He's surfaced. There's some quite useful stuff. Should give a good lead. He sounded a bit rough. Not having much of a joyride, I fancy. I'll call you in the office tomorrow. I'm quite hopeful we may be on to something. Yes . . . I'm going to pass it on now.'

His next call was to an unlisted extension in the Ministry of Defence.

Minutes later Harry's message was on a coded tele-type machine in the red-brick, two-storey building that housed the intelligence unit at army headquarters, Lisburn. It was of sufficient immediate importance for Colonel George Frost to be called from his breakfast. Cursing about amateurs and lack of consultation he set up an urgent and high-level conference. He summoned his own men, the 39 Brigade duty operations officer, Police Special Branch, and the army officer commanding the unit that controlled the Ardoyne. The meeting was called for nine, and the unit officer was given no information as to why he was wanted at HQ, only told that on no account were any of last night's suspects to be released. Davidson had somewhat short-ened Harry's message. Believing that an arrest was imminent now, he too had decided that the report of the recognition should be suppressed and should go no further. A million-to-one chance. It could happen again. Could be forgotten. Only cause a flap if it went official.

Whilst he was waiting for the meeting Frost reflected on the punched capitals in front of him, deciphered from the code by one of the duty typists. It was detailed enough to impress him, improbable enough to sound likely, and the sort of material you didn't pick up sitting on your backside in the front lounge. When he had read his riot act at the General about being kept out of the picture he'd heard of the three weeks' crash training course, and been told the arrival date. The source was now about to start his second week. Five lines of print that might be the breakthrough – and might not.

It was the sort of operation Frost detested. Ill-conceived and, worst of all, with the need for fast results dictated by political masters. If he's working at this pace, involved enough to get his nose stuck into this sort of stuff, then Frost reckoned he had about another week to go. That would be par for the course on a job like this. That was always the way. Crash in hard while the trail is still warm. You might get something when you stir the bottom up. But not discreet. No, and not safe either.

Poor bastard.

Frost had seen the body of the Armoured Corps captain, found shot and hooded, dumped outside Belfast. He had been working with a full team behind him. All the back-up he needed. Time on his side. Now this nameless and faceless man was trying to do what the whole army and police couldn't. Stupid. Idiotic. Irresponsible. All of those things, that's how Frost rated it. And there'd be a mess. And he'd have to clear it up.

Harry was nearly at his digs by the time the meeting Frost had called was under way. He had decided this was to be his day off. Tomorrow he would chase the job and try to get a bit of permanence into his life.

But today the pubs were closed. Nothing to do but eat Mrs Duncan's mighty roast and sit in his room and read. And listen to the news bulletins.

The platoon commander briefed to go and arrest the girl deep in the network of the Ballymurphy housing estate had stood his ground when asked to take the minimum number of troops needed for the pick-up.

'We've had four patrols shot at from that street or the alleys off it in the last eighteen days. If we have to search for her we'll be in there twenty minutes or so, and I can't just leave a couple of men outside to play Aunt Sallys. If I take a Saracen and a Pig they'll carry sixteen, and that way I can have enough men round the house, and enough to search the place as well.'

'They've asked for it to be discreet,' said his company commander.

'Well, what do they want us to do, have the padre drive a Cortina up to the front door and ask her to come for a picnic with him? Who is the girl anyway, sir?'

'Don't know why they want her. We hardly know her. The CO went up to Brigade this morning about something, and then came on the net with the instruction to pick her out.'

'However we do it, the whole street will know inside five minutes. It's Sunday, so we can't take her on the way back from work, wherever that is. If we're going into those streets we ought to have a proper back-up. Can they wait till dark?'

'No, the instruction is for immediate. That's quite clear. I take your point. Have as many men as you want, but be fast in there, and don't for God's sake start a riot.'

Theresa and her family were at lunch when the army arrived. The armoured troop carriers outside the tiny overgrown front garden, soldiers in fire positions behind the hedge and wall that divided the grass from next door's. Four soldiers went into the house. They called her name, and when she stood up took her by the arms, the policeman at the back intoning the Special

171

Powers Act. While the rest of the family sat motionless she was taken out to the back of the armoured car. It was moving before her mother, the first to react, had reached the front door.

None of the soldiers who surrounded the girl in the darkened steel-cased Saracen spoke to her, and none would have been able to tell her why she had been singled out for this specific army raid. From the Saracen she was taken into a fortified police station, through the back entrance, and down the stairs to the cells. A policewoman was locked in with her to prevent any attempt at communication with other prisoners in the row. An hour or so earlier the nine boys taken from the club the previous night had been freed after sleeping in identical cells on the other side of the city. One of their number, pressed to identify someone who would swear he had been in the club all evening, had unwittingly given Theresa's second name and address.

The decision had already been taken that she would be kept in custody at least until the intelligence operation that had produced the information was completed.

Chapter Ten

Seamus Duffryn, the latest of the intelligence officers of E Company, Third Battalion Provisional IRA, had made Sunday his main working day. It was the fourth weekend he'd been in the job, with a long list of predecessors in Long Kesh and the Crumlin Road prison. Duffryn was in work, a rarity in the movement, holding down employment as mate to a lorry driver. It took him out of town several days a week, sometimes right down to the border and occasionally into the Republic. Being out of circulation he reckoned would extend his chances of remaining undetected longer than the average of nine weeks that most company-level officers lasted. He encouraged those with information for him to sift through to leave it at his house during the week where his mother would put it in a plastic laundry bag under the grate of the made-up but unlit front-room fire. He kept the meagre files he had pieced together out in the coal shed. There was a fair chance if the military came and he was out that they would stop short of scattering the old lady's fuel to the four winds in an off-the-cuff search.

On Sunday afternoons his mother sat at the back of the house with her radio while Duffryn took over the front-room table, and under the fading coloured print of the Madonna and Child laid out the messages that had been sent to him. They were a fair hotch-potch, and at this level the first real sorting of the relevant and irrelevant took place. They concerned the amounts of money held at the end of the week at small post offices, usually a guess and an overestimate, the occasions when a recognized man of some importance drove down the company's section of the Falls, the times that patrols came out of the barracks. Then there was the group that fell into no natural pattern, but had seemed important enough for some volunteer to write down and send in for consideration.

He kept this last group for his final work, preferring to spend the greater part of the afternoon on the detail of the job that he liked best, checking over the information from his couriers and the eyes that reported back on what was happening at street-corner level. His sifted reports would then go to his company commanding officer, a year younger and three and a half years out of school. The best and most interesting would go up the chain to Battalion.

The afternoon had nearly exhausted itself by the time he came to the final group, and the one report in particular that was to take him time. He read it slowly in the bad light of the room, and then went back and reread it looking for the innuendo in the ambiguous message. It was a page and a half long, written in pencil and unsigned by name. There was a number underneath which denoted which volunteer had sent it in. He went through the report of probably only one hundred words for the third time till he was satisfied he had caught its full flavour and meaning. Then he began to weigh its importance.

Strangers were the traditional enemies in the village-sized Catholic communities of Belfast. The Short Strand, the Markets, the Ardoyne, Divis, Ballymurphy . . . all were self-sufficient, integral units. Small, difficult to penetrate, because unless you belonged you had no business or reason to come. They boasted no wandering, shifting groups, no cuckoos to come and feed off them. Those who were admitted after being burned out or intimidated away from their homes came because there were relatives who would put roofs over their heads. There were no strangers. You were either known or not admitted.

What concerned Duffryn now was the report on the stranger in the Beachmount and Broadway area. He was said to be looking for a job and getting long-term rates at Delrosa with Mrs Duncan. There was a question about his speech. The scribbled writing of the report had the second name of McEvoy. First name of Harry. Merchant seaman, orphaned and brought up in Portadown. No harm in that and checkable presumably. The interest in the report came later. The flaw in the set-up, the bit that didn't ring true. Accent, something wrong with the accent. Something that had been noticed as not right. It was put crudely, the reason Duffryn read it so many times to get the flavour of the writer's opinion:

'Seems to talk OK, then loses us for a moment, or a word, or sometimes in the middle of a word, and then comes back . . . his talk's like us mostly but it comes and goes . . . it's not just as if he'd been away as he says. Then

175

all his talk would have gone, but it only happens with odd words.'

It was enough to cause him anxiety, and it took him half an hour to make out a painstaking report for his superiors setting down all the information he had available on the man called McEvoy. The responsibility would rest higher up the chain of command as to whether or not further action was taken. He would keep up surveillance when he had the manpower.

There were difficulties of communication in the city and it would be some days before his message could be passed on.

Private Jones was on board the 15.30 Trident One back to Heathrow. He was out of uniform but conspicuous in his short haircut and neatly pressed flannels. He had been told he would be met by service transport at Heathrow and taken to Northolt where he would be put on the first flight to Berlin and his new posting. It had been impressed on him that he was to speak to no-one of his encounter the previous night. The incident was erased.

Interrogation was an art of which Howard Rennie had made himself a master, an authority, skilled at drawing out the half-truth and capitalizing on it till the flood-gates of information burst. He knew the various techniques; the bully, the friend, the quiet business-like man across the table – all the approaches that softened the different types of people who sat at the bare table opposite him. The first session with the girl had been a gentle one, polite and paternal. It had taken him nowhere. Before they went into the interview room for the second time Rennie had explained his new tactics to the officer from army intelligence. Rennie would attack, and the Englishman capitalize on it. Two men, each offering a separate tempo, and combining together to confuse the suspect.

The detective could recognize his own irritability. A bad sign. One that demonstrated the hours he'd put in that week, the sleep he had forfeited. And the girl was playing him up. They'd given her the easy way. If she wanted to play it like the boyos did, then good luck to her. But she was tired now, dazed by the surroundings and the lights, and hungry, having earlier defiantly refused the sandwiches they brought her.

'We'll start at the beginning again, right? . . . You were at the dance last night?'

'Yes.'

'What were you wearing? We'll have that again.'

'My pink dress.'

That much was established again by the detective. They'd got that far before. He'd done the talking. The army captain had said nothing as he sat behind the girl. A policewoman was also in the interview room, seated to the side of the desk and taking no part in the questioning. The questions came from the big man, directly opposite Theresa, just across the table.

'Your home in Ballymurphy . . . it's a hideout?'

'No.'

'It's used as a hideout. We know that. It's more we want. But it's where the boyos lie up?'

'No.'

'We know it is, you stupid bitch. We know they stay there.'

'Why ask me, then?' she shouted back.

177

'It's used as a hideout?'

'You say you know it is.'

'How often?'

'Not often.'

'How many times in the last month? Ten times?'

'No, nothing like that.'

'Five times, would that be about right? In the last month, Theresa?'

'Not as often as that.'

'How about just once, Theresa? That's the one we're interested in, just the once.' It was the officer behind her who spoke. English. Soft voice, different to those RUC bastards. She sat motionless on the wooden chair, hands clenched together round the soaked and stained handkerchief from the cuff in her blouse.

'I think we know one man came.'

'How can I tell you . . . ?'

'We know he came, girl, the one man,' the big Branch man took over again. 'One man, there was one man, wasn't there? Say three weeks ago. For a night or so. One man, yes or no?'

She said nothing.

'Look, girl, one man and we know he was there.'

Her eyes stayed on her hands. The light was very bright, the tiredness was ebbing over her, swallowing her into itself.

'One man, you stupid cow, there was one man. We know it.'

No reply. Still the silence. The policewoman fidgeted in her seat.

'You agreed with us that people came, right? Not as many as five, that was agreed. Not as many as ten, we got that far. Now, understand this, we say that one man

178

came about three weeks ago. One man. A big man. He slept in the house, yes or no? Look at me, now.'

Her head came up slowly now to look at the policeman directly in front of her. Rennie kept talking. It was about to happen, he could sense it. The poor girl had damn all left to offer. One more shove and it would roll out.

'You don't think we sent out all those troops and pigs just for one girl if we don't have it cast iron why we want to talk to her. Give us a bit of common. Now the man. Take your time. Yes or no?'

'Yes.' It was barely audible, her lips framing the word with a fractional fluttering of the chin. The army man behind her could not hear the answer, it was so softly spoken. He read it instead on the face of the detective as he sighed with relief.

'Say it again,' Rennie said. Rub it in, make the girl hear herself coughing, squealing. That keeps the tap flowing. Once they start keep up the momentum.

'Yes.'

The detective's face lost some of its hostility. He leaned forward on the table. 'What was his name? What did you call the man?'

She laughed. Too loud, hysterically.

'What are you trying to do to me? You trying to get me done in? Don't you know I can't . . . I couldn't anyway, I don't know it.'

'We want his name.' Cut the softness. The crisis of the interrogation. She has to go on from here. But the little bitch was sticking.

'I don't know his name. He was hardly there. He just came and went. It was only about six hours, in the middle of the night.'

'He was in your house. Slept . . . where did he sleep? . . . in the back room? . . . yes, we know that. He's on the run, and you don't know his name? Don't you know anything about him? Come on, Theresa, better than that.'

'I don't know. I don't *know*. I tell you I just don't . . . that's honest to God. He came in and went upstairs. He was gone before morning. We didn't see him again. We weren't told anything. There was no need for us to know his name, and when he came we didn't talk to him. That's the truth.'

Behind the girl, and out of her sight, the army officer put up his hand for Rennie to hold his questions a moment. His voice was mellow, more reasonable and understanding to the exhausted girl in the chair four feet in front of him.

'But your father, Theresa, he'd know that man's name. We don't want to bring him in. We know what happened that night, up in this man's room. We know all about that. We'd have to mention it. They'd all know at home. How would your Dad stand up to all this, at his age? There's your brother. You must think of him as well. It's a long time he's been in the Maze . . . it would go well for him.'

'I don't know. I don't. You have to believe me. He never said his name. It's because he wasn't known that he came, don't you see that? It was safe that way. Dad doesn't know who he was. None of us did.'

'You know why we want him?' the detective clipped back in, swinging her attention back into the light of the room away from the peace she found in the shadows round the soldier.

'I know.'

180

'You're sure. You know what he did?'

'I know.'

'Did he tell you what he'd done?'

'No.'

'How did you know?'

'It was obvious. I've never seen a man like it. He had a hand like an old man's. It was all tied up. Like a claw. I can't say how he was . . . it was horrible.'

'What was his name? We want his name.'

'You'll get me killed for what I've said. So help me, Mother of Jesus, he never said his name.'

The inspector pulled a photokit picture of the man from a brown envelope, and flipped it across the table to the girl. She looked at it briefly and nodded. Then she pushed it back to him.

'Take her down,' he said to the policewoman. The two went out of the interview room and away towards the station's cells. He went on, 'Bugger it. I thought we had her. I thought it was all going to flow. I have a horrible feeling the little bitch is telling the truth. We'll have another go at her in two our three hours or so, but I don't think she knows any more than she's said. It makes sense. A strange house, strange people. They're alerted someone is coming. They stick their noses into the box, and he's a bed for the night. Come on. Let's get a nap for a bit, and then one last bash at her.'

After they had gone Theresa sat a long time in her cell. She was alone now, as the policewoman had left her. In her own eyes the position was very clear. The army had pulled her into the station to question her about the man who had stayed at the house, the man she had gone to in the middle of the night. The man who

181

had killed in London, was on the run, hunted, and in bed couldn't screw. They had pulled her in because they thought something she knew was the key to their finding the man, arresting him, charging him, sentencing him, and locking him away to become a folk hero in the ghetto, however many years he rotted in a cell like this one. If she was not vital to their case then, as they said themselves, would they have sent the troops and the pigs to collect her? When he was arrested and charged and all Ballymurphy knew she had spent two days in the station being questioned . . . what would they say? Who would listen when she denied she had ever known his name? Who would walk away satisfied when she said she had given no information that in any way led to his capture? Who would believe her?

In the legend they'd weave her name would figure. She went back again over all that she could remember of what she had said to that bastard copper. The one who shouted in the front. Nothing, she'd said nothing that helped them. She'd looked at the photograph, but they knew that he was the man. All they needed was his name, and they didn't know that, and she hadn't told them. But how had they learned of the night? She had told girls, some, a few, not many. Would they betray her? Her friends in a chatter in the bog or over coffee break at the mill, would they tout to the military?

So who was going to believe her now?

She had heard what the IRA did to informers. All Ballymurphy knew. It was part of the folklore, not just there, but all over the city where the Provos operated. The vengeance of the young men against their own people who betrayed them was vicious and complete.

There'd been a girl, left at a lamp post. Tarred and feathered, they'd called it. Black paint and the feathers from a stinking old eiderdown. Hair cut off. She'd talked to a soldier. Not loved him – not cuddled or kissed him. Just talked to him, standing with him outside the barracks in the shadows. A boy who lived on the street, they'd shot him through the kneecaps. He hadn't even been an informer. 'Thief' was the word on the card they hung round the gatepost where they left him. Provo justice. She hadn't known him, just knew his face. She remembered him on the hospital crutches when he was discharged. Ostracized and frightened. They killed girls, she knew that, and men whom they reckoned were informers. They shot them and dumped their bodies, sometimes rigged with wires and batteries. Making a stiff into a bomb hoax. Then they lay a long time in the ditch waiting for the bomb disposal man to work his way through his overnight list and come and declare the body harmless. And all the reporters and photographers were there.

It was very easy to imagine. A kangaroo court in a lock-up garage. Young men with dark glasses at a table. Hurricane lamp for illumination. Arms tied behind her. Shouting her innocence, and who listens? Pulled from the garage, and the sweet smelliness of the hood going over her head, and bundled into a car for the drive to the dumping ground and the single shot.

She wanted to scream, but there was no sound. She quivered on the bed, silhouetted against the light biscuit-coloured regulation blanket with the barred-over light bulb shining down on her. If she had screamed at that moment she would probably have lived. The policewoman would have come and sat with her till the next interrogation. But in her terror she had no voice.

She knew that they would come again and talk to her, perhaps in another hour, perhaps longer. They had taken her watch and she had no sense of time now. When they came again they would ask her if she had ever seen the man on any other occasion. They would ask that over and over again, however many times she maintained she'd not set eyes on him since the night at her house. They would go on asking that question till they had their answer. They would know when she was lying, especially the quiet one behind her, the Englishman. She was tired, so tired, and slipping away. Could she keep up her denials? They would know and she would say. Before morning they would know about the dance, how the man had been there with his wife. They had taken him away. So why did they still need the name? Confusion and complicated argument swayed and tossed through the girl. They had taken him but they didn't know him. Perhaps they had not made the connection, and then what she might say in her exhaustion would weave the net round him. Betray him. Play the Judas. If she told the English officer it would be treachery to her own. The pigs would be out for him, pulling him into another police station, and she would wear the brand. Tout. Informer. Despised.

She looked round the brick and tile walls of the cell till she came to the heavy metal bar attached to the cell window that moved backwards and forwards a distance of two inches to allow ventilation to the cell. As it was winter and the window tight shut, the bar protruded from the fitting. She estimated that if she stood on her bed and stretched up she could reach the bar. Very deliberately she sat up on the bed. She moved her skirt up over her hips and began to peel down the thick warm tights she was wearing.

When the policewoman came to her cell to wake her for the next round of questions Theresa was very dead. Her mouth was open, and her eyes bulged as if they were trying to escape from the agony of the contortions. The nylon had buried itself deep into her throat, leaving a reddened collar rimming the brown tights. Her feet hung between the side of the bed and the wall, some seven inches above the floor.

Frost was wakened by the duty officer in intelligence headquarters without explanation. The message was simply that he should be in headquarters, and that 'all hell is about to break loose'. By the time he reached the building there was a report from the police station waiting for him. It covered only one sheet, was slashed to a minimum and was signed by his own man who had been present at the interrogation.

Theresa . . . was interrogated twice while in police custody in the presence of myself, Detective Inspector Howard Rennie, Detective Sergeant Herbert McDonald and Policewoman Gwen Myerscough. During questioning she identified the photokit picture of a man wanted in connection with the Danby killing as a man who had stayed in her father's house around three weeks ago. After the second session of questions she was returned to her cell. She was found later hanging in the cell, and was dead by the time medical attention reached her.

Signed,
Fairclough, Arthur. Capt., Intelligence Corps.

No marks for grammar, thought Frost, as he read it through.

'Where's Fairclough?' he snapped at the duty officer.

'On his way back here, sir.' It was a time for short direct answers when the big man was in this sort of mood.

'How long?'

'Should be here in about ten minutes, sir.' Then the sparks will come. Poor old Fairclough, thought the duty officer. Rather him than me.

The colonel went to the filing cabinet behind his desk and unlocked the top drawer, pulling it out on its metal runners and rummaging around for his dog-eared Ministry of Defence extension numbers book. It was a classified document and also listed the home telephone numbers of senior staff at the Ministry, military and civilian. He found the number of the Permanent Under-Secretary that Davidson worked to, and dialled the Surrey area code and then the six digits.

'My name's Frost. Army intelligence in Lisburn. It's a hell of an hour but something has come up which you should be aware of. This is not a secure line, but I'll tell you what I can. We were passed some information from a section of yours about a girl. That was yesterday morning. She was brought in yesterday afternoon and questioned twice. You know what about. She knew the man we want, identified the picture, and said he'd stayed in her house within the last month. Found her about three-quarters of an hour ago hanging in her cell. Very dead. That's all I have. But I wouldn't care to be in your man's shoes when the opposition find out about all this. Thought you ought to know. Sounds a bit of a cock-up to me. Cheers.'

The Permanent Under-Secretary had thanked him for the call and rung off.

Frost locked away his directory and pocketed the keys as Fairclough came in a fraction behind his knock.

'Let's have it, Arthur.'

'We got it out of her that the man stayed at her old man's place. She said they weren't given his name, and that she never knew his name. I think she was levelling with us. We left her for a couple of hours and when they came to get her out to bring her back up she'd strung herself up with her stockings. One thing should be straight, sir. She was treated quite correctly. She wasn't touched, and there was a policewoman present the whole time.'

'Right. Put it all down on paper, and soon. I want our version on this out fast. The information from London, on which we pulled her in. It seems to have stood up? It was real stuff?'

'No doubt about that. She'd been with him, all right. No doubt.'

Fairclough went out of the colonel's office to type his report. Frost went back on the phone to army public relations, another bedside telephone waking the early morning sleeper-in. He suggested that when the press enquiries started coming the men on the information desk should treat this very much as a police matter involving a girl picked up by the army for

187

routine interrogation. He then called the head of Special Branch, first at his home where he was told he was already at Knock Road headquarters, and then at his office there. His own people had briefed him. With the slight diplomacy that he could command he made the same suggestion about press desk treatment as he had made to his own people.

'You want our people to take the can?' said the policeman.

'Inevitable, isn't it? Your police station, your interrogation. Don't see how we can end up with it.'

'Your bloody info set the thing up.'

'And good stuff it was too. There should be an enquiry at that damned station as to how it happened.'

'The Chief Constable in his wisdom had made that point. I think we should meet for a talk about the next move, if there is one, or this trail will be dead in no time.'

'I'll call you back,' said Frost, and rang off.

Half-cock operation and the poor sod, whatever his name is, puts it right under our noses. And we drop it. Poor devil. And on top of that we let the girl kill herself, which puts a noose round his neck and a bag over his head. We've done him well today. Desertion's the least he's justified in doing.

Harry heard about the girl, with the rest of the province, on the early morning radio news bulletin. It was second story after the European Economic Community all-night talks. The item was brief and without explanation.

'In Belfast a girl has died after being taken to a police station in the Falls Road area. She was found early this morning hanging in her cell and was dead by the time she reached hospital. Police named her as nineteen-year-old Theresa McCorrigan from Ballymurphy. An investigation is being carried out to find what happened. The Northern Ireland Civil Rights Association have issued a statement calling for a full and independent enquiry into the death. They allege two armoured cars and troops were used yesterday afternoon to arrest the dead girl from her home.'

Harry switched off the radio. He felt numb. No more playing about. No more kindergarten. These were the powers of the forces at work. A simple, ordinary, decent girl. Wants to get screwed by a bloke who cannot make it. Tells the girls in the loo about it, bit of a giggle, have a laugh together. Thirty hours later she's so terrified that she puts something round her neck and steps off. Throttled. A bit randy, and talks too much . . . and now she's dead. Harry remembered her. Across the far side of the club: in with the toughies and the big kids near the bar. Rolling a bit. Too much gin, and not enough chips to soak it up.

He was the cause of the fear. He was responsible for the agony of the girl, before she slung whatever it was underneath her chin, and swung off into the void. Had she even been questioned by then, he wondered? Had she been able to say anything? Or was it all a lot of boasting?

They all listen to those bulletins, Harry reflected, every last one of them, catching up on the night's disasters, funding themselves with conversation for the day. Josephine would be no different. She would hear it, making her face up, having her breakfast, washing her smalls, but the transistor would be somewhere in her home. She'd hear it, and she'd put it together. Was she that fast, that clever? Had to be, it was there on a plate, and what then?

Harry would have to wait to find out. She wasn't doing tea this week, had a different shift at work. He'd have to wait till the weekend and their next date. Have to sit it out, Harry boy, and sweat it out, and see how bright she is, and if she is bright what's she going to do about it.

He went down the staircase, across the hall, and out to the street. He heard Mrs Duncan calling after him about his breakfast, and ignored her as he kept on going up the pavement and turned left towards Andersonstown. It took him a good hundred yards to swallow the emotion and regain control. As he walked he set out the position, making in his mind a chess-board of his job. Pawns, that's where she rated, and pawns were expendable. Bishops and knights hurt more but they could also be lost. He and the man he was hunting were the queens of his game. The superstars, and second only to the kings, who were sacred and inviolate. If, as the queens were moved round the board, the pawns toppled over, then that was the nature of the game he and the man played. There was no time to lament the loss of pawns.

The old theme song. It had been different in Aden. There had been no involvement there. Nothing personal. A clear enemy, all that was on the board was black or white but definite. Now all the squares were grey, and the figures too. Even the two queens. There would be a problem for an outsider in picking one set of pieces from another.

190

Chapter Eleven

Within four hours of the first broadcast of Theresa's death a soldier had been killed and heavy rioting had broken out in the Ballymurphy, Whiterock, Turf Lodge and New Barnsley estates.

The soldier had died when he was hit by a burst of shots fired at close range from a Thompson sub-machine-gun. He was last man in a patrol in Ballymurphy, and the gunman was apparently operating from the top floor of an empty council house. Some of the photographers who had gathered outside Theresa's house to get a picture of her parents and collect a holiday snapshot of the girl herself ran in the direction of the shooting. The fleetest managed a few hurried frames as the soldiers lifted the body of their colleague into the back of a Saracen.

In the Falls and Springfield Roads, groups of youths had hijacked buses, driven them into the middle of the street, and set fire to them. After that the army moved in. Armoured cars and Land-Rovers were pelted with milk bottles and rocks by the crowds who had gathered on the pavements. The army responded by driving at them, firing volleys of rubber bullets from mountings

191

beside the driver. At one building site a barricade of rocks and oil drums had been assembled by the time the Saracens arrived. They'd crashed into the flimsy wall, fracturing it and scattering the drums crazily across the street, when a lone youth, at the controls of a brilliant-yellow excavator-digger machine, charged back defiantly. The troops, who had been advancing behind the cover of the armoured cars, fell back as the mechanical dinosaur accelerated down a slight hill towards the toad-like armoured cars. A few feet from the impact the youth jumped clear, leaving his runaway digger to collide head on with the Saracens. The armoured cars, acting in strange concert for things so large, edged it against a wall, where it spent its force revving in demented futility.

The stoning went on a long time. Unit commanders made it clear in their situation reports to Brigade head-quarters at Lisburn that they detected a genuine anger among people. Those who over the last months had shown disinclination to abuse and pelt the military were back with a vengeance. There were rumours, they said, sweeping the Catholic areas, that the girl who had killed herself in the police station had been tortured to a degree that she could stand no more, and that she had then killed herself. Provisional sympathizers were on the move off the main roads where the army patrolled, and behind the crowds, giving instructions.

Theresa's parents were on lunchtime television, maintaining that their daughter had never belonged to any Republican organization. They described graphically how she had been taken from the lunch table the previous day. The army press desk received scores of calls, and stalled by saying this was a police matter, that the army was not involved, and pointing out that the girl had died in a police station. At police headquarters the harassed man on the receiving end told reporters that an investigation was still going on, and that the officers who were carrying out that investigation had not called back yet.

Both at army headquarters and amongst the Secretariat that administered the Secretary of State's office at Stormont Castle there was a realization that something rather better by way of explanation was going to have to come out before the day was over.

Faced with crises the Prime Minister had a well-tried formula to fall back upon. Identify the problem. Focus all attention on it. Solve it, and then leave it alone. When he finally concentrated on any one subject his aides found he had enormous capacity to wrestle with whatever political abscess was causing the pain. But they also found that once he thought the situation dealt with then his interest faded as fast as it had risen. Northern Ireland, comparatively quiet for months, was now on the shelved list. It teetered close to what a politician had once called the 'acceptable level of violence'. So the transcripts of the lunchtime news bulletins that were brought to him he resented as an intrusion. Violence back again. Streets closed. Casualties. The distasteful death of a young girl in the police cell. It was his habit to be direct.

From the back room office overlooking the Downing Street gardens, insipid in the November light, too many leaves left around, he called the army commander in Lisburn. Without any interruption he listened to a rundown of the morning's events, and made no comment either when the General launched into the background of the girl's arrest. He was told for the first time of the intelligence reports that had been fed in from London, of her questioning, what little she had admitted to knowing, and then of the finding of the body.

'Is this the first we've had from our chap?'

'First that I've heard of. Certainly we've received nothing else we could act on.'

'And it was good stuff, accurate. Something we hadn't had before, right?'

'The information was factual. It didn't take us as far as we'd hoped it might at first. I understand, though, that this is the first positive line we've had on the fellow we're looking for.'

'Seems we set a bit of a trap, and it's rather missed its target. We'll have to decide whether our chap's had as much out of the pot as he's going to get. Problem is at what stage to get him out, whether we've compromised him already.' He was enjoying this, just like the way it was in the war. SOE and all that. The general cut across the line.

'It's not so easy, Prime Minister. It's faintly ridiculous, but I'm told his controllers don't know where he is, don't even know where to get in touch with him. You appreciate that this chap is not being controlled from here. Your instructions were interpreted very strictly on this point. It's London's responsibility. He calls in, they don't call him. But my advice would be that he stays. For the moment, at least. When you begin this sort of thing you stick with it. There's no out, in midstream, because it's a bit too hot. He'll have to finish it, or dry up completely.'

194

The Prime Minister came back, 'We've no reason to believe yet that he's been compromised? But it would be difficult, very difficult, if he were to be identified in this context.'

'Those were the sorts of questions I assume had been answered before the instruction was given to launch this operation, Prime Minister.'

The sarcasm bit down the line.

The Prime Minister banged the phone down, then immediately flipped the console button on his desk and asked abruptly for the Secretary of State in Stormont Castle. After forty-one years in politics he could see the storm clouds gathering long before they were upon him. He knew the time had come to pull in some sail, and close down the hatches. The combination of an agent working to the Prime Minister's orders and a teenage girl hanging herself in a cell were better ingredients than most for a political scandal of major proportions. He must start to plan his defensive lines if the worst should happen and the chap they'd sent over there should be discovered. That bloody General, not much time to run over there and his next appointment already confirmed. Entrenched, which was why he was so free with the advice. But all the same, in spite of his eminence, it must have hurt him to admit that this was the best information they'd had so far . . . and for all that they'd loused it up.

'He won't have liked it. One bright thing today,' and then he turned his attention to the search for a fail-safe system. Call the Under-Secretary, the man in charge of this incredible non-communication set-up. In the event of catastrophe no statement till the civil servant had cleared it, and get that away to Lisburn. No acknowledgement for the agent, of course, if all goes wrong . . . deny all knowledge of the mission.

The Secretary of State was on the line. The Prime Minister wasted no time on pleasantries.

'I've been hearing about the troubles today, and the girl. Difficult situation. I thought we were weak at lunchtime, too defensive. We need to be more positive. I've a suggestion to make. It's only a suggestion, mind you, and you should bounce it off your security people and see how they react. But I think you should say something like this – get a note of it and I'll read over what I've drafted. Along these lines, now. That the girl was a known associate of the man we are hunting in connection with the killing of Danby. That she was brought in quite correctly for questioning, and had been spoken to briefly before being left in the cells for the night. You must emphasize that she was not touched. Leak it that you're prepared to offer an independent post-mortem from one of the hospitals, if you think that'll help. But my thought is to bring it back to Danby. By the by, his memorial service is at St Paul's this week. You'll be there, I hope. It'll all be in the public gaze again. We'll be all right if we play a bit bold, and attack. Worst thing we can do is to get on the defensive.'

The linking of the killing of the British Cabinet Minister with the death of the teenager in the Falls Road police station was splashed across the last edition of the *Belfast Telegraph*, and extensively reported on later television and radio news bulletins. The few men in the city who knew of Harry's existence were uncertain what effect the disclosure would have on the agent's work and safety. They acknowledged an immediate lifting of the pressure on their public relations set-up for more

196

information concerning the circumstances of the death.

Harry was not the only man in the city with pawns on the chequerboard.

The scrap merchant would take Harry on to his payroll. He'd obviously liked the look of him. He said he had a brother at sea, and asked Harry if he could start there and then. There was not a word about National Insurance cards or stamps, and twenty pounds a week was offered as pay. Harry was told he'd need to spend a month or so in the yard to see the way the place was run. There was to be expansion, more lorries. When they came, if it all worked out, there would be a driving job, and more money.

On his first morning Harry prowled round the mountains of burned and rusted cars. These were the stock-in-trade of the scrapman, heap upon heap of rough, angled metal.

Harry said to the neat dapper little man who was his new boss, 'Is this what the business is? Just cars? You've enough of them.'

'No problems with the supplies of that. You must have seen it, though you've been away. Terrible driving here. If you take the number of cars, they say, and work it out against a percentage of all the people that own them, and the number of accidents . . . then it's worse than anywhere else in the whole of England or Ireland. Maniacs they are here. The boyos down the road do the rest. We'll have a dozen wrecks in tomorrow morning. There'll be a double-decker, as well, like as not, but they're bastards to cut up.'

He smiled. Small, chirpy, long silk scarf round his neck, choker style, hat flat on his head. They're all the same, thought Harry, likeable rogues.

The scrap merchant went on, 'It's an ill wind. Scrapmen, builders, glaziers . . . we're all minting it. Shouldn't say so, but that's how it is. The military dump the cars that are burned out, up there on the open ground. We send a truck up and pull them down here. Not formal, you know. Just an understanding. They want them off the street and know if they put them there I'll shift them. We'll have a few more today, and all.'

He looked up at Harry, with the brightness evacuating his eyes. 'People are powerful angry about this girl. You'll find that. They get killed in hundreds here. Most of the time it doesn't mean a damn, however big the procession. But this girl has got them steamed again.'

Harry said, 'It's a terrible thing pulling a girl like that out of her house.'

'Poor wee thing. She must have been awful scared of something to want to do that to herself. Mother of Jesus rest her. Still, no politics in this yard, and no troubles. Those are the rules of the yard, Harry boy. No politics, and that way we get some work done.'

He walked round with Harry and introduced him to the other men in the yard, six of them, and Harry shook hands formally. They greeted him with reserve, but without hostility. When his escort went back to the office to look to the papers Harry was free to browse. At one stage as he meandered amongst the cars he was within eight feet of a Russian-made rocket launcher. It was the RPG 7 variety, complete with two missiles and wrapped in sacking and cellophane, locked into the boot of a car. There were always people coming into the yard, and the cover was good. Access was easy at night. The launcher, sealed against the wet, had been placed there after the Provisional unit to whom it had been issued had found it inaccurate and unreliable. It had been abandoned until they could come across a more up-to-date manual of operation, preferably not written in Russian or Arabic.

As the little man said, no politics, no troubles. That first day Harry abided faithfully by it, taking his cue from the other men in the yard. Slowly does it here. The high column of black smoke from a blazing Ulster bus was ignored.

The rest of the first week that Harry was there was quite uneventful. He was accepted to a limited degree as far as small talk went, and nothing more. His few attempts to broaden the conversation were gently ignored and not pressed on his part. The death of Theresa and the start of the job probably meant, thought Harry, the start of the next phase. No immediate pointers for him to follow, only the long-term penetration remaining. Three weeks. What idiot said it could be done in three weeks? Three months if he was lucky. And it relaxed him. Going up the road each day and having the work to occupy his mind would ease him. Better than sitting in that bloody guest house. Claustrophobia.

And each day he was watched by Seamus Duffryn's volunteers from Delrosa to the yard, and back again.

Downs was in the kitchen swilling his face in the sink, Monday-morning wash, when his wife came in white-faced, shutting the door behind her on the noise of the playing children.

'It's just been on the radio, about you. About a girl. The girl who killed herself.'

'What do you mean? What about me?'

'This girl from the Murph, it says she was linked with the man that did the London killing.'

'It didn't actually mention me?'

'Said you was linked. Connected.'

'What was her name?'

'Theresa something. I didn't catch it.'

'Well, I don't know her.'

'It said she was being questioned about him because she was a known associate. That was another word they used – "associate". God rest her, poor kid. She was just a child.'

'Well, I don't know her, and that's the truth.'

'That's what they're saying on the radio . . . loud and clear . . . where any bloody ape can hear it.'

'Well, it's all balls, bullshit.'

'When you're shouting, you're always lying. Who was she? What was she to do with it?'

'I don't know her. I tell you, I just don't know her.'

'Billy, I'm not daft. You were in town a long time before you came back here. I haven't asked you where you were, before you came home. Who is she?'

'What did you say her name was?'

'Don't play the fool with me. You heard the first time.'

'If it's Ballymurphy, I stayed there one night. I came in darkness while the family was round the box. There was a girl there. Just a kid who brought me some food in the room. I was away by five-thirty.'

'Just brought some food, did she?'

200

"Course, she did . . . don't bloody question me . . . like the fucking Branch.'

'Just on the strength of that, brought her in and questioned her, just because she brought you some grub? Didn't get her father in – he's giving interviews. Just took her in.'

'Leave it,' he snapped at her. He wanted out. Escape.

'Just tell me who the little bitch was and what she meant to you.'

'She's just a child a minute ago, now she's a little bitch. She was nothing. Nothing. Must have blabbed her mouth off. Squealed, the little cow.'

'How did she know who you were?'

She shouted the last question at him. She would have taken it back once the words were out and had crumpled against him. The noise and aggression slewed out of him. Beseeching. Pleading. Don't make me answer. The found-out child and the hollow victory.

'I'm sorry,' she said. 'Just forget it.'

She turned away, back towards the door into the living room where the children were fighting, and one was hungry, and another crying.

'I'll tell you what happened . . .' She shook her head, but he went on, 'This is once and for all, never ask again. If I'd wanted her I couldn't have done anything about it. I was so screwed up. I was sort of cold, frozen, shivering. I couldn't do anything for her. She asked if it was me in London. I hit her. Across the face. She went back to her room. I've only seen her once since then. She was at the dance at the club on Saturday night. I suppose she saw me.'

201

He walked across to his wife and put his arms round her. The children still cried and the pitch was growing. He pulled her head against his shoulder. There was no response, but she was pliant against him, totally passive.

Downs went on, 'That's when she must have talked. Going home after the dance. Must have said that she knew the man that had been in London. Then some rat, some bastard, squealed. A fucking spy, a tout. Right there at one of our dances, some bastard who'll shop you. That's what must have happened.'

'Forget it. We have to forget all these things. There's nothing left otherwise.'

He held her for a long time in the darkened kitchen, lit by the inadequate bulb hanging without a shade from the wire flex. At first she wept silently and without dramatic effect, keeping her grief private, not using it as a weapon to cudgel him with. She controlled herself, and clung to him. Nothing would be different, nothing in his way of life would change.

'You'll go back?'

'When they want me.'

'You could end it all now. You've done your share.'

'There's no way that could happen.'

He needed her now, to recharge him. When the dose was enough he would go back into his own vicious, lonely world. Of which she was no part.

She was one of the crowd. The crowd of women who had so little influence over their men that it was pointless, indecent, to beg them to stay off the streets. She was still luckier than most. Her man was still with her. The bus that came each Thursday lunchtime to the top end of Ypres Avenue was well enough known. It took the women to Long Kesh to talk to their men for half an hour, across a table.

That night Billy Downs opened his door to a treble knock. He was given an envelope by a youth and saw him scurry away into the darkness. His wife stayed in the kitchen, as she too had recognized the call sign of the fist against the door. She heard him switch the hall light on, pause a few moments and then the sound of tearing paper, over and over again.

He went into the front room and threw the half-inch squares of paper that had made up the single sheet of writing into the fire. The message was from Brigade. It was short and to the point. For the moment he was to stay at home. It was believed that the girl had hanged herself before identifying him.

Davidson had had a bad week. He admitted it to the young man who was drafted in to share the office with him. The fiasco of the girl had started it off. The Permanent Under-Secretary had been on as well, laying the smokescreen that would be used if the operation went aground. Davidson had tried to counter-attack with complaints about the original lodgings and then the foul-up over the girl, but had been rejected out of hand. There was silence from Harry himself for six days after his first call. Davidson and the aide sat in the office reading papers, making coffee, devouring takeaway fish and chips, takeaway Indian, takeaway Chinese. The number that had been given to Harry was kept permanently free from all other calls.

When he did call, on the Saturday afternoon, the effect was electric. Davidson started up from his easy chair, pitching it sideways, tipping a coffee beaker off his desk as he lunged for the telephone. Papers drifted to the floor.

'Hello, is that four-seven-zero-four-six-eight-one?'

'Harry?'

'How are the family?'

'Very well. They liked the postcards, I'm told.'

Davidson was on his knees, his head level with the drawer where the recording apparatus was kept. He pulled up the lead and plugged it into the telephone's body. The cassette was rolling.

'Anything for us?'

'Nothing, old chap. No, I'm just digging in a bit. I think it may go all quiet for a few days, so I'm settling into some sort of a routine.'

'We're worried about you in the wake of that bloody girl. We're wondering whether we should pull you out.'

'No way. Just getting acclimatized.'

'I think we all feel at this end that you did very well last weekend. But we want some way to get in touch with you. This may suit you, but it's ridiculous for us. Quite daft. We're sitting here like a row of virgins waiting for you to call us up.'

'It's the way I'm happiest. I've been bitten, remember. On the first house. It's going to be a touch trickier getting something further out of this, and this is the way I want it to be. Bit silly, you might say, but that's the way it is.'

Davidson backed down and switched the subject.

'Are they sniffing round you at all?'

'I don't think so. No particular sign of it yet, but I don't know. More of a problem is that I don't see where

204

the next break is going to come from – what direction. I was very lucky last time, and look where the thing got us. It can't be on a plate like that again.'

'You're not following anything particular at the moment, then?'

'No, just entrenching. Getting ready for the siege.'

'Perhaps it's time you should come out. Like this weekend. I don't want you hanging about wasting time. Look, Harry, we know it's bloody difficult in there, but you've given the military and security people a lead that they ought to be able to do something about . . . Come out now. Get yourself up to Aldergrove and get the hell out . . .'

The phone clicked dead in his hand, before the dialling tone purred back at him. Despairingly he flicked the receiver buttons. The call was over.

Bugger. Played it wrong. Unsettled him. Just when he needs lifting. Silly, bloody fool. Should have made it an order, not a suggestion, or not mentioned it at all. The military should be following this now. The girl must have left a trail a mile wide.

Davidson could see through his uncurtained window that it was now dark outside. He thought of Harry walking back up the Falls to his digs. Past the shadows and the wreckage and the crowds and the troops, the legacy of the spluttering week-long street fighting he had been the spark to. Keep your head down, Harry boy.

Chapter Twelve

It was acknowledged at the highest levels of the IRA's Belfast Brigade command that the campaign was at a crucial stage, the impetus of the struggle consistently harder to maintain. The leadership detected a weariness among the people on whom they relied so greatly for the success of their attacks. But the differences between the people at street level and their protectors, as the Provisionals saw themselves, were growing. Money was harder to collect for the families of those imprisoned, doors generally left unlocked for the gunman or blast bombers to escape through were now bolted, and the confidential phones to police headquarters where the informers left their anonymous messages were kept busy with tip-offs that could only come from the Catholic heartland.

As the pressure grew to a near intolerable degree on the shoulders of the Provisionals' leadership so it was understood that the days of gallantry and chivalry were gone, too. Once a British officer had stood in the turret of his armoured car, stiffly upright with his right arm in the salute position as the coffin of an IRA man was carried past him, draped in the tricolour. Once

British officers after an evening's celebration and in their slacks and sports jackets found they had wandered into the Bogside, were captured and returned safely to their embarrassed seniors.

That was all over now. As the IRA fought back against the growing strength and experience of the security forces arrayed against them, so the attacks became more vicious and more calculated to shock.

It was the Brigade commander who made the reluctant decision to call Billy Downs out from the Ardoyne and from inactivity. It was accepted that he was of greatest value when used sparingly, but within seventy-two hours of the earlier instruction he was given new orders.

The subject of the Brigade's death sentence was an RUC inspector. A priority was put on his death, and it was reckoned important enough to risk the exposure of one of the movement's top cards.

The policeman they wanted shot was Howard Rennie, CID, transferred to Special Branch. Their dossier reported him as coming from the hills of County Antrim, near the coast. He had been unknown in Belfast till recently when word had begun to seep into the information system from the holding centres and prisons about a detective with sufficient ability as an interrogator that he was directly responsible for the failure of several suspects to keep their mouths shut.

It had taken a long time once they'd started for the Brigade intelligence section to identify Rennie, locate his headquarters at the holding centre in Castlereagh barracks, and put a plan into operation against him. The final decision to eliminate him was taken after a company intelligence officer reported on the list of police cars' number plates and models that had left the police station after the death of the girl in her cell. One was similar in model and colour to that driven by the detective. His association with the events of that night was sufficient to put him several places up the list of priorities, and would win the movement nothing but support when he was killed.

Billy Downs was given a dossier to read but not to keep. The caller who came to his house late, after the wife and the children had gone upstairs, was to bring it away with him when Downs had done his reading. His wife came down the stairs to see who the visitor was, paled at the sight of the long-haired youth in jeans and heavy quilted anorak who returned her stare and then turned away without speaking to her. She went into the kitchen, aware that the front room was no place for her. When she moved upstairs again she could hear the voices, talking hurriedly, hushed and with urgency.

Downs was shown a picture of Rennie. Taken five years ago, and one of a group. It had been gained from the copious files of a photographer in the small town where Rennie had then been stationed. It was a fair bet they'd find such a picture when they went into the photographer's shop with guns in their hands, and the competence of the filing system saw them through. The picture was of a group of policemen all celebrating their promotion to sergeant. The picture would not help Downs that much, as it suffered seriously in the enlargement, but it gave him an idea of the build, the hair and the shape of the face of the policeman that he had been ordered to kill. The car the detective would be using was a Triumph 2000 and bottle-green, but the file on Rennie carried a list of a minimum of eight number plates that he might use. He read that Rennie lived in a small, detached house in Dunmurry, down a cul-de-sac. The house right at the bottom of the 'U' of the close. Difficult for surveillance and for ambush. The dossier said he used a door direct into the garage. Wife opened the garage doors from the inside and he drove straight out in the mornings. They would be open when Rennie came home. The policeman would be armed.

The problems of the ambush were made clear to him. 'It'll not be easy to get the whore. None of them is easy. They often go together – lift each other to work. They'll be using different routes and all. They've guns, too. One of them would get a shot in if you try it then. They know how to use them. Rennie's a trained shot. And clever – won't be easy to nail the bastard. No chance of sitting down his road: all those women flappin' their curtains from not enough to do, they'd see you and be on the phone straight off. And you don't have time to set it up, next week, next month, when you like. They want it, and fast. Brigade's order. It's a special one, and they want you for it.'

His unpolished ankle-length boots were beside the chair. Jeans crumpled and not washed nor ironed since he came home. Shirt was off-white and dirty, collar frayed. The fire was small now, needing help to stay alive. He had put the light out when the courier had gone, so that he could concentrate the better on the policeman, Rennie, that they had put him against. He had memorized much of the detail of the file and now he savoured the problem they had set him, seeking out

209

a plan of action. Like a mathematician attempting the answer to a complex formula, he stayed in the chair thinking on the method and the manner by which Rennie would be assassinated. He was surprised to have been called out, but the implication was clear. This was a vital and important operation, he was a vital and important operator.

His wife stayed upstairs, aware that this was no time for her to go down to the front room and try to break the spell her husband was weaving for himself as his mind took up attack tactics and the weapons he would use.

She drifted into an uneasy sleep that night, tossing through an immediate nightmare. She saw her man cut down by a burst of bullets, caricatures of grotesque soldiers standing over him. Life throbbing away in the gutter. Feet pushing and manœuvring him. When she reached across to see if he had come upstairs yet she found only the emptiness of the sheets beside her. Back in her half-sleep she witnessed over and over again the firing of those perpetual rifles, and the agony and throes of her man. And then exhaustion and fear took her beyond the stage of the dreams and left her in deep sleep till the morning.

That was how he found her when he came upstairs with a plan maturing well in his mind. He was impressing himself with the cleverness of what he would do. Excited and pleased with his solution to a technical problem.

He lay on his back, elbows outstretched on the pillow, his hands under his neck, going back over his plan, testing each point in it for flaws. He was tired but elated enough to find none as he checked over each aspect of the killing, each aspect bar the final one – the killing itself. He shut that out of his mind. The actuality of the killing, the pulling and squeezing of the trigger.

He seldom tried to work out the values of the killings he performed to the movement that he served. Tasks and projects set for him by his superiors. Others determined the morality. Others had the hatred. Others turned his work into victories. He did as he was told, expertise his trade mark. The soldier in his army.

There were some in the movement, men that he had met or, in other cases, heard of, who were said to relish the physical side of the killing. There were stories that they tortured the demented minds of their victims after the sentence of the kangaroo court. Demonstrate the firearm. Go right up to the moment of shooting and then fire with an empty gun. There were beatings-up, knifings and cigarette burnings. That was no part of Billy Downs. His killing was different. Clever. Organized. Against major targets. His feelings were known and respected by the top men. The ritual was for others. He belonged in the field. His mind reverted to the reconstruction and progress of the murder of Rennie, his plans racing far ahead. It was close to dawn before he slept.

In a room above a chip shop in Monaghan town, just over the border into the Republic, the Army Council met for the first time in a fortnight. Eight men round a table. Businesslike, with their pencils and notebooks round them. There was much talk of what they had seen on the earlier television news bulletins, of the film taken on the steps of St Paul's of the arrival of government ministers and Cabinet members to the memorial service for Henry Danby.

'Hardly what you'd call security. Sod-all protection.'

'They all had 'tecs with them, but by the look of it only one each. Not the big man, though. He had a couple. Little film stars, you get to know them.'

'Right open, if we wanted to put a man in again.'

'Wide open. What those bloody papermen call a wall of steel. Nothing.'

'It would only be a repetition. Took a lot of planning last time. Manpower. What do we achieve? There was good reason for that bastard Danby, but another man, what for?'

'It did a fair bit for us when we got Danby. Keeping our man on the loose, that's not done us bad.'

'There was no sympathy for Danby. There's no-one else we can get who is in that crowd where we would get the same reaction. The bastard was hated. Even the Prods loathed him.'

'In London there's no way they can guard the politicos, no way at all. They have to be out and be seen to be about. They can't lock themselves away. You can do that from the White House, but not from Downing Street.'

'Let's have some talk about what we'd get from hitting them again in London.' It was the Chief of Staff who spoke, terminating the knockabout round the table.

He made only rare incursions into the talk, preferring to let it ripple round him while he weighed the ideas before coming down in support of any one in particular. He was a hard man with few feelings that did not involve the end product. Like some cost-effectiveness expert or a time-and-motion superman, he demanded value for effort. His training in military tactics had been thorough, and he had risen to corporal in the parachute regiment of the British army. He was in his mid-thirties now and had seen active service in Aden and Borneo. He'd bought himself out at the start of the troubles and set up briefly as a painter and decorator, before going underground. When he had been voted into the number one position in the Provisionals by his colleagues it was because they knew they could guarantee he would pursue a tough, ruthless campaign. Those who believed in the continuation of the war of attrition on British public opinion had felt threatened by those they thought might compromise. The new commander was their safeguard. He was no strategist, but had learned enough of tactics on the streets of the Lower Falls where he came from. He had sanctioned the killing of Danby, and was well pleased with the dividends.

The quartermaster took it up. 'It's the trouble with all spectaculars. You launch them, and they succeed, and where do you go from there? Only upwards.'

The older man in the group, a veteran of '56, who lived now in Cork, said, 'It stirs the pot well and truly. How many bombs, how many "another soldier tonight" add up to a British Cabinet Minister?'

The quartermaster across the table was not impressed. 'But what's the reaction? If we did it again, they'd tear the bloody place apart. We'd not survive it. They'd be all over us. Down here as much as in the North.'

'That's what we have to weigh. What would happen to the whole structure? They'd go mad, knock bloody shit out of us.' The speaker was from Derry. Young, from the Creggan estate. Interned once and then released in an amnesty to mark the arrival of a new Secretary of State. He had been in the Republic's prisons as well, and now lived on the run as much in County Donegal as in the maze of streets in the Creggan housing estate. 'Our need at this moment is not to go killing Cabinet Ministers from Westminster, but winning back what we lost at Motorman when the army came into Bogside and Creggan. We have to play on the tiredness of those people across the water. There's no stomach there for this war. They're soft there, no guts. They'll get weary of hearing another soldier, another policeman, another bomb, another tout. It's the repetition that hurts them. Not another big killing. All that does is get them going. It affronts their bloody dignity. Unites them against us. We have to bore them.'

'The bigger man you get the better.' It was a Belfast man. He was of the new school, and had come a long way since Long Kesh opened. He had pitiless eyes, wide apart above his ferret nose, and a thin, bloodless mouth. He chain-smoked, lighting cigarettes one after another from the butt of the one he was discarding. 'The big man himself wouldn't hurt. They never believe we mean it over there. Somehow the fucking Micks won't actually get round to it, they say. Get the old bugger, himself, that would sort them.'

That quietened it. Then the Chief of Staff chipped in, cutting through the indecision of the meeting as he brought it to heel and away from the abstract.

'We'll think about it. It has attractions. Big attractions. Total war, that's what it would mean. Davie and

214

Sean, you'll work for a bit on it. Have something for us in a fortnight with something concrete. I don't want it done hasty . . . something in a bit of detail. Right?'

They moved on to other business.

The process of arrests went on with seeming inevitability, with frequent reunions in the Crumlin and Long Kesh. The Provisionals' intelligence officer, who should have seen the report of that conversation between the army Brigadier and the policeman overheard at their hotel lunch, was taken into custody before the message reached him. When there was an arrest those still in the field shifted round their weapons, explosives, equipment and files, lest their former colleague should crack under interrogation and reveal the hiding places.

That message, closely written on two sheets of notepaper, remained in a safe house in the communication chain while the Third Battalion worked round to an appointment for the vacant position. The clogging in the system lasted more than a week, and when the new man came to sort through the backlog he had a table covered with reports and documents to wade through. He was into his second day before he got to the paper written by the waiter.

He was sharp enough to sense immediately the importance of what was in front of him. He read it carefully.

The man with the thin moustache looked like an army man, and from the kitchens I could see the big Ford out in the car park with the uniformed escort sitting there in the front. The other one was talking when the music stopped. He was a policeman, I think. That's when I heard him say, 'Special operator on the ground without telling.' He must have realized I was standing there, and he just stopped and didn't say anything else until I was right away from him. He looked very bothered . . .

That was the guts of the message. The intelligence officer had read it once, gone slightly beyond and then rapidly coursed his eyes back over it. He could imagine the situation. Military and police, not taken in on the act, and feeding their bloody faces, weeping on each other's shoulders, stuffing the food in far away from the 'Careless Talk Costs Lives' bit. It was the sort of place you'd expect to hear a major indiscretion uttered, when they couldn't keep their big mouths shut. That was why the waiter had been introduced onto the staff of the hotel.

Undercover men working for the army or D16 were the particular dislike of the Provisionals. They believed there was a much greater secret intelligence and surveillance operation against them than in fact existed. Their traditional hatred was for the plain-clothes army squads who cruised at night round the backstreets of the ghettos in unmarked cars, looking for the top men in the movement. But this had a more important ring about it to the intelligence officer than squaddies out in jeans and sweaters and armed. If a Brigadier and a top copper were not in on the act, and thought they ought to have been, it meant first it was top secret, and second that they considered it important enough for them to have been briefed. Something of critical value to those English swine, so sensitive that top-ranking men had been left out in the cold.

Farther down the waiter's report was a paragraph explaining that the tone of the exchange across the lunch table had been critical.

The officer wrote a three-line covering note on a separate piece of paper, clipped it to the original report and sealed it in a plain brown envelope. A courier would take it that night to the next man up the chain, someone on the Brigade staff.

Twenty-two hours later he met Seamus Duffryn for the first time. Duffryn had originally intended that his message should go by hand, but the combination of the new appointment and the nagging worry about this man, Harry McEvoy, had led to the direct meeting, risky as it was.

They met in a pub in the heart of the broken-up and ravaged triangle of the Lower Falls. Taking their pints of beer with them, Duffryn led the other to a corner table. With their heads huddled together he spoke of the stranger that had come to the guest house farther up the Falls. Looking for work. Said he'd been away a long time. Had this strange accent that was noted by those when he first came, but which his latest reports said was not so pronounced. When Duffryn mentioned the accent, the Battalion officer looked at him intrigued, and the junior man explained the apparent lapses in speech. Duffryn said that his men who followed McEvoy and heard him talk in the pubs, said the oddness about the speech was something very much of the past. Ironed out, muttered Duffryn. He had come to the end of his patience on the matter and wanted a decision. Either the man should be cleared or there would have to be authorization for more surveillance with all its problems of manpower. Duffryn himself had personally tried to observe McEvoy by spending three successive evenings in the pub on the corner where it was reported that the stranger came to drink, but he'd stayed alone these evenings, and the man he wanted to see had not shown himself.

'I'm not sure what it means,' said the man from Battalion. 'You never know about these things. It could mean he's a man put in to infiltrate us. It could be nothing. It counts against the bugger that his accent is improving. Would do, wouldn't it? With each day he spends here, it would improve. There's something else we have that indicated a few days ago that they could have put an undercover man in. He'll be a big bloody fish if it's right. He'll be a bloody whale if what we think about him is right.'

He hesitated as to whether he should bring the young Duffryn further into the web of reports and information that was forming in his mind. He dismissed it. The golden rule of the movement was 'need to know'. Duffryn needed to know no more than he already knew.

'That's enough. From now on – and this is important – and I want it bloody well obeyed to the letter – no more following this McEvoy. Let him ride on his own a bit. I don't want the bugger flushed before we're ready for him. We'll just leave him alone for a bit, and if we have to we'll move when it's all nice and relaxed. I want it taken gently, very gently, you see? Just log him in and out of the guest house, and that's the lot.'

*   *   *

Harry had not been aware of the watchers before they were called off, and therefore had no idea that he had thrown off a tail when he had gone through the city centre shopping crowds to a telephone kiosk to call Davidson. On the Friday night when he had been in the city nearly three weeks he came down past the cemetery towards Broadway with his wage packet in his hip pocket, and the knowledge that there seemed to be no sign of suspicion towards him from the men he was working with. He had a hired car booked for Saturday for his date with Josephine.

There was a Sinn Fein meeting that Friday night up on the junction of the Falls, and after he'd had his tea Harry wandered up to listen to the speeches. There were some familiar faces on the lorry that was being used as a speaker's platform. The oratory was simple and effective and the message brutally clear. Amongst the committed there would be no easing in the struggle, the war would go on till the British were gone. The crimes of the British army, the Stormont administration and the Free State government were catalogued, but the crowd of three or four hundred seemed lukewarm to it all. They'd been listening to this stuff for five years or so now, Harry reflected. He'd be a bloody good orator to give them something new at this stage. The army stayed away and after hearing the first four speeches Harry left. He'd clapped with the rest, and cheered by consensus, but no-one spoke to him. He was just there, ignored. God, how do you get into this bloody mob? How does it all happen like Davidson said, in that magic three weeks? It'll take months, till the face is known and the background and every other bloody thing.

A long haul. He wouldn't call Davidson this weekend. Nothing to say. Those buggers had sent him here, they could sit and stew for a bit and wonder what was going on. The trail of the man he sought was well chilled now. It would be very slow, and his own survival would take some thinking about. But there'd be no coming out, no trotting up to Aldergrove. One-way to Heathrow please, my nerve's gone and so has that of my controller, thank you very much.

No way. You stay in for the whole way, Harry boy.

Chapter Thirteen

She was waiting at the lights at the junction of Grosvenor and the Falls when he pulled up in the hired Cortina. Tall in the brittle sunlight, her hair blown round her face, and shivering in the mock sheepskin coat over the sweaters and jeans he'd told her to wear.

'Come on, get that door open. I'm frozen out here.' A bit distant, perhaps too off-hand, but not the clamouring alarm bells Harry had steeled himself to face.

He was laughing as he reached across the passenger seat and unlocked the nearside door, and pushed the handle across to open it. She came inside, a bundle of coat and cold air, stealing the warmth he had built up since he had collected the car.

'All right then, sunshine?' He leaned over to kiss her, but she turned her head away, presenting her cheek for what he hadn't intended to be the brotherly peck they ended up with.

'Enough of that. Where are we going?' she said. She straightened her back in the seat, and began to fasten her seat belt.

'You said you wanted some country. Somewhere we

can stretch ourselves a bit, walk around. Where do you suggest?'

'Let's off to the Sperrins. About an hour down the Derry and Dungiven road. That's wild country, real Ulster stock. You've seen the slogans on the Proddy walls before the troubles started, "We will not exchange the blue skies of Ulster for the grey mists of the Republic," well, the blue skies are over the Sperrins.'

'Well, if it's OK for the Prods it'll do for us second-class Micks.'

'I was brought up down there. My Dad had a bit of land. Not much but enough for a living. It's a hard living down there. It's yourself and that's all, to do the work. We cut peat down there and had some cows and sheep. Stupid bloody creatures. We were always losing the little buggers. There was no mains, no gas, no electricity, no water when I was born. He's dead, now, the old man, and my Mam came to Belfast.'

'Were you involved at all, with the politics? Was the old man?'

'Not at all. Not a flicker. Most of the farmers round were Prods but that didn't make much difference. The market was "non-sectarian", as they'd say these days. Different schools, different dances. I couldn't walk out with Prod boys when I lived at home. But that's years back now. There was no politics down there, just hard work.'

He drove slowly out of town, on to the M2 motorway which runs within minutes into the open countryside, leaving the city with its smoke and its gibbet-like cranes and its grey slate roofs away behind the Black Mountain that dominates the south of the city. It was the first time Harry had seen the fields and hedgerows, farms and cottages since he came in on the airport bus. The starkness of the contrast staggered him. It was near-impossible to believe that this was a country ravaged by what some called civil war. For a moment the impressions were tarnished by the rock-filled petrol drums outside a pub, but that was a flash of the eye, near-subliminal, and then was gone in favour of the hills and the green of well-grassed winter fields.

Josephine slept in her seat, head back against the column dividing the front and rear doors, her seat belt like some pompous decoration strapped across her breasts. Harry let his eyes stray from the endless, empty road to her.

'Just follow the Derry road, and wake me up when we get to the top of the Glenshane,' she'd said.

The road slipped economically through the countryside till Harry reached Toome, where the Bann came through, high and flooded from the winter rain, forcing its strength against the medieval eel-trapping cages that were the lifeblood of the town. He slowed almost to a halt as he gingerly took the car over the ramps set across the road in front of the small, whitewashed police station. Yards of bright corrugated-iron sheeting and mounds of sandbags surrounded the building. It looked deserted. No bulbs showing at the top. After Toome he began to pick up speed. The road was straight again, and there was no other traffic. In front was the long climb up to Glenshane in the heart of the Sperrins. The rain gathered on the windscreen, horizontal when it came but light and occasional.

As he came to the hills that divided the Protestant farmlands of the Ulster hinterland from Catholic

Dungiven and Derry, Harry spotted a damp, out-of-season picnic site on his right, and pulled into the car park. There was a sign marking the Pass and its altitude, a thousand feet above sea level. He stopped and shook Josephine's shoulder.

'Not so much of the blue skies and the promised land here. Looks more like it's going to tip down,' he said.

'Doesn't matter. Come on, Mr McEvoy, we're going to do some walking and talking. Walking first. Up there.' She pointed far out to the right of the road where the hill's squat summit merged towards the dark clouds.

'It's a hell of a way,' he said, pulling on a heavy anorak.

'Won't do you any harm. Come on.'

She led the way across the road and then up the bank and through the gap in the cheap wire fence where a succession of walkers had made a way.

Farther on there was a path of sorts to the top of the hill, made by the peat cutters at first and then carried on by the rabbits and the sheep. The wind picked up from the open ground and surged against them. Josephine had pushed her arm through the crook of his elbow and walked in step half a pace behind him, using him part as shelter and part as battering ram as they forced their way forward into the near gale. High above, a buzzard with an awesome dignity allowed itself to be carried on the thrusts and flows of the currents. Its huge wings moved with only a minimum of effort, holding position a hundred and fifty feet or so above the tiny runs fashioned by the creatures the bird lived off. The wind stung across Harry's face, pulling his hair back over his ears and slashing at his nose and eyes.

'I haven't been anywhere in a wind like this in years,' he shouted across the few inches that separated them.

No reply. Just the wind hitting and buffeting against him.

'I said I haven't been in a wind like this in years. It's marvellous.'

She rose on her toes, so that her mouth was in under his ear.

'Wasn't it like this at sea, sometimes. Weren't there any gales and things all those years you were at sea?'

The cutting edge of it chopped into him. Retreat. Back out.

'That was different. It's always different, sea wind, not like this.'

Poor. Stupid. Not good and not convincing. He felt the tightening deep in his balls as he went on against the wind. Up a cul-de-sac and got cornered. Slackness. The elementary error. He flashed a look down and behind to where her head nestled into his coat. He contorted his head to look into her eyes, and saw what he expected. Quizzical, half-confused, half-amused: she had spotted it. The inconsistency that he'd known the moment he'd uttered it. Phrase by phrase he went over it in his mind, seeking to undo the mistake, and evaluate its damage. The second time he'd said it, that was when she would have been sure. The first time, not certain. The second time, certain. He'd semaphored it then.

There were no more words as they went on to the summit. The low jigsaw of clouds scudded above them as they clung together against the power of the gale. In

225

spite of the heaviness of the cloud there was a clarity to the light of the day. The horizon was huge. Mountains to the north and south of them, the road leading back into the civilization of the hill farms to east and west.

A few yards beyond the cairn of stones that marked the hilltop the rain running down over the years had sliced out a gully. They slid down into it, pushing against the sandy earth till they were at last sheltered. For a long time she stayed buried in his coat, pressed against his chest with only her black tossed hair for him to see. He felt the warmth from her seeping through the layers of clothes. For Harry it was a moment of beauty and isolation and complete tenderness with the girl. She broke it suddenly, crudely and fast.

'You slipped up a bit there, Harry boy. Didn't you? Not what I'd have expected from you.'

Her face was still away from his. He couldn't see into her eyes. It hit home. He said nothing.

'A bit mixed up then, weren't you, Harry? Your story was, anyway. Merchant seaman who was never in a storm like they have in the Sperrins? A bit of a cock-up, Harry.'

She'd relaxed in her voice now. Easy. In her stride. Matter-of-fact.

'Harry,' and she twisted under him to turn into his face and look at him. Big eyes, mocking and piercing at the same time, and staring at him. 'I'm saying you made something of a slip-up there. Not the first that you've had. But a good old balls-up, a right big one. Harry, it's a great bloody lie you're living. Right?'

He willed her now to let it go. Don't take it to the brink where explanation or action is necessary. Leave the loophole for the shrug and the open door.

226

In the town his inclination would have been to kill her, close his fingers on that white, long throat, remove the threat that jeopardized his operation. But on the mountain it was different. On the moorland of the upper hills, still crouched in the gouged-out hollow, and the wind singing its high note above and around them, it seemed to Harry ridiculous and time-wasting to deny what she had said. It wasn't in his orders to go strangling girls. That was logical as the solution, but not here. Out of context.

'It's a bad place this for strangers these days, Harry. It would be rather worse if the boyos find your story isn't quite so pat as it should be. If they find you're rather more of a handful than they took you for, then it could be a very bad place. We're not all stupid here, you know. I'm not stupid. It didn't take the world to put eight and eight together after Saturday night, or ten and ten, or whatever you thought too much for an "eejit" Mick girl who's an easy lay. It wasn't much I said to you. Just a little bit of chat. But there's half the British army round the wee girl's house for Sunday lunch. What did they find to talk to her about? God knows. Do you know, Harry? It was enough for the poor wee bitch to hang herself, God rest her. I mean, you weren't exactly covering your tracks, were you, Harry?'

The eyes that drove into him were still bright and relaxed, looking for his reaction. As he listened she grew in strength and boldness. She would close for the kill. She would make the point. Sure of her ground, she began to goad him.

'There had to be something odd about you. Obvious. No family. But you come right back into the centre of Belfast. But you've no friends. No-one knows you.

People might have gone to a quiet place on the outskirts if they just wanted to come back and work. You've not come to fight, not for the Provos. They don't go to war from a guest house. The voice worried me, till Theresa died. I thought about it and worked it out then. The accent. It's good now. Very polished. You're quite Belfast, but you didn't use to be. So I don't reckon your chances, Harry, not when the Provos get a hold of you. There is some who can talk their way out of it, but I don't reckon you've a chance. Not unless you run.'

Harry knew he should kill her. He looked fascinated at the soft skin, and the delicate line that searched down on either side of the little mound in her throat, saw the suspicion of a vein beneath the gentle surface. But there was no fear there, no terror in her face, no expectation of death.

They'd chosen Harry as a hard man, as a professional, able to do what was necessary, to go to the limits for his own survival. He could kill a man either in heat or from cold logic, and if the man's eyes betrayed his fear that would make it easier, remove the complications.

The endless strands of black hair were playing across her face, taken past her eyes, encircling her mouth . . . and the warmth of her body close to him . . .

There had not been women who had to die in Aden. He was now in an area beyond his experience. Harry had heard it said once that to kill in close combat you had to act instinctively, there were no second chances, the will to cause death evaporates quickly, and does not come again except to the psychopath.

His hands were numbed and useless in the big gloves, and the moment had passed. He looked out on to the moorlands where the spears of sunlight played down from the cloud gaps. He had hesitated, and that would be enough. The buzzard still hovered high above him, and she was still talking.

She was tall, but not strong, he thought. She wouldn't be able to fight him off. He could kill her now. While she yapped on. It would be a long time before they found her. Could be the spring. She'd struggle a bit but she had no chance. But she knew he wouldn't. He could see that. There was no fear in her. A moment had come earlier when he might have put his hands to her. It was gone now.

'If I went to the bookies more often,' she went on, 'I'd say you were a real slow horse. I'd say not to put any money on you reaching the finish. I mean it, Harry. I'm not just trying to frighten you, or anything daft. That's the way it is. If I was in your shoes I'd be carrying spare knickers in my pocket. Well, don't just sit there. Say something, Harry.'

'There's not much to say, is there? What would you like to hear me say? If you go off to Portadown and see people there, they'll tell you who I am. Yes, I've been away a long time. That's why the accent was strange. I'm acclimatized. The girl – I can't explain that. How could I? I've no idea about it.'

He could not have explained why he had gone back on the resolution he'd made so few minutes earlier not to get involved in a charade of deception. There was no conviction, no belief, and he communicated it to the girl.

'Balls,' she said. She smiled at him and turned away to put her head back into the roughness of his coat. 'That won't do, Harry. I don't believe you, neither do you. You're not a good enough liar. Whoever recruited you, and for whatever, did a poor job there.'

'Let it go, then. Forget it, drop it.' Pathetic. Was that all he had to say to the girl?

'Who are you, Harry? What did you come here for? When you touted on young Theresa it was after I mentioned the man that did the killing in London. Is that why you're here? You're not just run-of-the-mill intelligence. There's more than that, I hope. I'd want to think my feller was a wee bit special. What's the handle? The Man who Tracked the Most Wanted Man in Britain?' She snorted with amusement.

'But seriously, Harry, is that what you are? A little bit special? The Danby killing?'

She gave him time now. He was not ready. As an afterthought she said, 'You don't have to worry, you know. I won't split on you or anything like that. It's the national characteristic . . . the Ulster Catholics, we don't inform. But they don't take well to spies here, Harry. If they find you, God help you. And you'll need him.'

Harry started to move.

'There's not very much to say. What do you expect me to say? Confess, dramatic revelations? Shout you down? Walk away and leave you? Strangle you? What the hell do you want me to say?'

He got up out of the ditch and moved back towards the summit of the hill, where the wind took him and fought him, coming in crude rushes that caused him to hesitate and sometimes give ground. The rain had intensified while they had been in the ditch and now it lashed across his body. He looked only at his feet, head hunched forward, with his anorak hood up as he stumbled across the gorse and the heather, slipping and falling because he would not give the attention to the ground in front of him. He'd gone a hundred and fifty yards from her when she caught him and thrust her arm into his. They went together down the hill to the car, hurrying along the worn-out shape of the path.

They ran the last few yards to the car. She stood shaking by the passenger door as he looked for the keys. It was raining hard now and once they were inside he switched on the heater. The water ran down the windows in wide streams, and they were as cocooned and private as they had been on the hill.

'What are you going to do if you find him?' she said.

'Are we serious now, or sparring still?'

'Serious now. Really serious. What will you do?'

'I'll kill him. Take him out. He's not for capturing. We pretend he is, and they mount the thing on that assumption. But he's dead if we get close enough to him.'

'Just like that.'

'Not just like that. I've got to find him first. I thought we had him after the dance. It hasn't moved from there. Up a bit of a blind alley now. Perhaps that's just talk about killing him. It should happen that way, but likely it won't. He'll be picked up, and it'll have sod-all to do with me.'

'Is that what you came for? Because a man kills a politico in England, then they send for you, and you come over here?'

'That's what I came for.'

'There's a thousand and more have died here since it all started. And you come because of one of them. He was . . . wait for it, I'm working it out . . . yes, he was a tenth of one per cent of all the people that have died here. That's not a bad statistic, is it? A tenth of a per cent. He wasn't mourned here, you know. No-one gave a damn. Pompous bugger. Always on the box telling us how well he was doing flushing out the gunmen from off our backs. Why was he so special? They didn't send the big team over when they shot the Senator in Strabane, or the UDR man who had all the land down the road in Derry. So why have you come?'

'They put the glove down, didn't they? That's what shooting Danby was about. To make us react and see how effectively we would counter-attack. They killed him as a test of strength. We have to get the man and the team that did it. Either we do, or they've won. That's the game.'

'So it's not just Queen and Country? Forces of Right against Forces of Evil?'

'It's nothing to do with that. They've challenged us. Given us a bait we cannot ignore. That's why we're in there kicking. We have to get the killer before the next time.'

'Who are you then, Harry? Who do you work for? Who pays your cheque?'

'You won't get that. You've too much already. Christ only knows why, I've—'

'And where does little Theresa fit into this big act? You're here to avenge a death. There's been one more already. How many more people get hurt, getting in the way, to make it still worthwhile for you?'

'Quite a lot.'

'So, even in death, some count for more than others.'

'Right.'

She shifted the ground, and softened the attack.

'What sort of fellow is he, this man you're looking for?'

'I don't know much about him. I've an idea what he looks like, but not a good description. I don't know his name. He's a cool customer, and he'll be a crack shot. One of the top men, but they'll have kept him out of the main eye of things.'

'When Theresa talked about him, do you know what it was made her say it?'

"Course I don't know. How could I?'

'I mean, she wouldn't just bring a thing like that out of the blue, now would she? She said to me that the man that did the London killing was at that dance. He was there the whole time with his wife. She was looking such a misery that Theresa said she couldn't have been getting enough. That's how it all started. She said the cow couldn't be having it away, then she went into her own bit. That was to back her story up. She didn't know anything else.'

'That's the truth, Josephine?'

'She didn't have to die, alone like that, just with those bastard coppers around her. All she knew was what I said. I doubt she even knew the man's name.'

She had started to shout again, spitting out the unsaid accusation at Harry. The weakness had gone. The heat of her attack burst round the tiny marooned inside of the car.

'You might as well have killed her yourself, Harry. She wasn't involved in any way at all. You came here with your challenges, and the bloody games you play. And a wee girl dies who had nothing to do with it. There's enough innocent people killed here without

233

strangers coming and putting their fingers in and digging out more shit.'

She crumpled then. Sobbing rhythmically and noiselessly. Gazing into the steamed-up window beside her. The rain was still falling.

Harry was deciding what he should do on his return to Belfast. His ego was rumpled by the way the girl had broken through him. He ought to have killed her up there on the hill, but she had said she was no threat to him and he believed it. His ego was of less importance, though, than the news she had just given him. The man who he searched for had been at the caeli the previous weekend.

She shook herself, trying to shrug away her misery.

'Come on, I want a drink. There's a pub just down the road. You can't stop for the dead. Not in Ulster. Like they say, it all goes on. I should have dropped it ages ago. Come on, let's go have a couple of hot tods.'

She leaned over and kissed him lightly, again on the cheek.

Then she began to adjust her face, working with deftness from the little pouch that came out of her bag, painting over the reddened and flushed valleys under her eyes.

When she had finished she said, 'Don't worry, hero boy, I won't tell the big bad Provies about you. But if you've ever taken advice, I'm telling you, don't hang about. Or whatever medal you're after will have to go in the box with you.'

They drove down the hill to where the pub and petrol station were nestled in a redoubt cut out from the stone. He ordered the drinks she wanted – Irish, with hot water and sugar and lemon.

The faint sunlight that had seen them out of Belfast was long since gone as Harry drove back on the shiny, watered road into the city. They spoke hardly a word all the way, and Harry dropped her off where he had met her in the morning, on the corner of Grosvenor and the Falls. Just before he stopped he asked her where she lived, so that he could drop her at the door. She said it would be better at the main road.

'When will I see you again?' he said, as she climbed out of the car. The traffic was hustling them.

'Next week, at Mrs Duncan's. You'll see me there.'

'And we'll go out somewhere? Have a drink?'

'Perhaps.'

She knew so much more than she had wanted to, or was equipped to handle. What had started as something of a game had become considerable enough to subdue her into a morose silence most of the way home. She darted out of the car, and without a wave disappeared into the Clonard side streets.

Harry dropped the car off at the garage and walked back to Delrosa. His mind was filled with that conversation he'd had with Davidson in the garden. The loneliness factor. Sounded so astonishing when the old chap was trying to put it over as a problem. What had he said? 'Unless you're aware of it, there will come a time when you want to tell someone.' Fumbling his way into it because it embarrassed him that his chosen man could possibly fall into so well-signposted a pit, embarrassed even to suggest it. And that's the way it was, because Davidson knew what it was about, was the only one of them who knew what it was about. How many of the others could transpose themselves into the hostility of this community, live day-in, day-out with the fear and the strain and the isolation?

Don't go on with it, Harry boy, let it rest there. Don't let it infect you. The cancer of doubt spreads fast enough, Harry. Drop it.

Billy Downs decided he would go for Rennie the next day, Sunday.

The reports that were available from the minders who had been cautiously watching the policeman suggested that he made a habit of going to the interrogation centre on Sunday afternoons. He stayed a few hours and reached home around seven in the evening. It fitted with the plan that Downs had made. He discussed none of this with his wife, but as his pre-occupation with the killing grew so they moved about their house, two strangers under the same roof. Life was carried on with a series of gestures and mono-syllabic phrases.

Downs had been informed of the arrangement by which he would take possession of the Armalite rifle that he would use for the attack, and he had reported up the chain on the timing and the date that he would want the operation set in motion. It had been suggested to him that the Armalite was an unsuitable weapon for a close-quarter killing, but in the face of his wishes the point had not been pressed.

The huge power of the weapon excited him to such a degree that he could think of taking no other. The bullet that he intended should kill Rennie would leave the barrel at a muzzle velocity of 3250 feet per second. The statistics that he had read in a sales brochure astounded and exhilarated him. It weighed slightly less than seven pounds and would fit comfortably into the poacher-style pocket he had fashioned on the inside of his raincoat. And he would be far from his safe base area: if he were intercepted by the army or police then the sharp crack of the Armalite would be enough to send his enemy scurrying for cover for the few seconds he might need to get clear. He had asked for two thirty-round magazines for the weapon, just in case.

A brandy in hand, Frost was sitting on his own in a corner of the mess at Lisburn mulling over the magazines of weekly comment with which he prided himself he kept abreast. He made a point of working his way through the dog-eared *Spectator*, *Economist* and *Statesman*, and it had become sufficient of a ritual for other officers of equal rank to leave him to himself, when on any other evening they would have joined him.

The mess waiter came over and hesitated beside the chair, before plunging in.

'Excuse me, sir. Sorry to trouble you. There's a reporter from *The Times* on the phone. Says he needs to speak to you. Says it's urgent. He said to say he was sorry to trouble you, but he thought you'd want to hear what he had to say.'

Frost nodded, pulled himself up and followed the waiter to the phone cubicle.

'Hello, Frost here. Ah, yes, we've met. A leaving party, in the summer, right? What can I do for you?'

He listened without interruption as the reporter read over to him the story that was being prepared for Monday's editions. The Provisional IRA had tipped off one of their favoured reporters in Belfast that they believed the British had infiltrated a new secret agent into the city on a mission so sensitive that only the GOC, General Fairbairn, had been told of it. The Provos were claiming that the operation had caused great anger among British army staff officers in HQ. On Monday the story would appear in Dublin papers as well as British ones, and the IRA would be calling for special vigilance from the people to seek out the spy. The Provos, Frost was told, were saying this was a special operation and one quite different from anything mounted before.

'I'm not expecting you to comment on anything, Colonel. This is a private call, just to let you know what's going on. Good night.'

The colonel mouthed his thanks.

He flicked the receiver's buttons up and down till the operator came on the line.

'Evening. Frost here. GOC at home, please.' When he was connected he told the General he needed to see him immediately. There was no hint of an apology for disturbing the senior soldier in Northern Ireland at that time of night. That would not have been Frost's style. His early-warning antennae were already jangling with the possibility of a major intelligence scandal.

The General and Frost talked for an hour, and agreed to have another meeting at eight on Sunday morning with the benefit of further information. They would then, they thought, get on to the MOD and demand Harry's immediate recall before the awkward business became necessary of dragging him out of some hedgerow with an IRA bullet in the back of his head.

Across the city in Mrs Duncan's boarding house Harry was asleep. He had been somewhat unnerved by the brutality with which his cover had been stripped aside by the girl. On his return he had lifted the carpets and floorboards at the place where the revolver was hidden. The Smith & Wesson, with its six chambers loaded, was now wrapped in a towel under his pillow, in the corner over by the wall. As a day it had been a fiasco. A shambles. Back in the reality of the city with the hardness of the gun near to him he felt lunatic at what had passed between him and the girl in the wind and rain on the hillside. Out of his tiny mind.

Chapter Fourteen

Harry was up early again that Sunday morning, and out of the house well before eight to make his way down to the city centre and the phone that he could use to talk to Davidson. This time he took the revolver with him, in his coat pocket, with the roughness of its shape shielded by the length of the covering anorak. The decision to take the gun had been an instinctive one, but now that he had it, and out on the streets and loaded, the situation that he faced was all the more clear. For the first time since they had flown him in from Germany he felt uncertain. That was the girl. Up that mountain talking a load of slop when he should have been concentrating, then letting her go last night, back into the warren that she shared with his opposition. Madness, and it aggravated him. Perhaps also there was the knowledge that the trail that had seemed so warm a week ago had now chilled.

The Smith & Wesson jarred against him as he stepped out down the Falls to the phone and communication with Davidson. There were no eyes watching him after he left Delrosa: the orders of the Battalion intelligence officer were being strictly obeyed.

He dialled the number, four-seven-zero-four-six-eight-one. After several desultory clicks he heard it ringing at the other end. It was answered.

'It's Harry here. How are the family?'

Davidson was in early too, and hoping for the call. 'Very well, they liked the postcards.'

'I've got a bit of a problem.' Pause. 'I've been blown by this girl, the one that helped me with the business I gave you last week. What a cock-up that was.' Pause. 'But anyway, putting the finger on that bird has led this girl straight back to me. She knows what I am. Not who I am, but what we're here for. I want you to take her out. Get her out of the scene for the duration. You can do that, can't you? She tells me that the man we want was at the same dance that we were at, a fortnight ago. I half-felt I remembered him. But the face wasn't quite right on the photokit. If it's the man then the army pulled him in, but that looked routine. He was just one of the ones that were rounded up. He had a woman with him, presumably his wife, in a yellow trouser suit. Have you got all that?'

'I've got it on tape, Harry. Anything else?'

'Hell, what more do you want? No, that's all I have at the moment. But look, I don't want the living daylights bashed out of this girl. I just want her lifted out so she doesn't get involved any more. She's Josephine Laverty, lives with her mother in one of those little streets in Clonard, up off the Springfield on the right. You'll find her, but get to her quick, there's a good lad.'

'We'll work something out. Don't worry.'

'There's not really much else. It's a bit chill here at the moment but I think I'm settled in here OK. If you don't

241

wrap it up on what I've just given you then it'll be a very long time. Do we have time for that?'

'We've plenty, as long as you think it worth it, Harry. But we ought, as you say, to kill it this time. It was a hell of a balls-up over the other girl. There was a lot of praise at this end for what you got. Great satisfaction. You're all right yourself, are you? No-one following you about, no awkward questioning? Our assessment is that they would be right up to you by now if they were about to blow you, and that you'd probably have been aware of something. That's not just supposed to cheer you up, but if no-one is sniffing around you then it should mean you're OK.'

'No, there's nothing like that,' Harry said. 'I'm working too. Job in a scrap yard in Andersonstown, and paying well. Back to the scene, then.'

'Harry, look, you ought to know this. I got well and truly chewed up over your living arrangements, us not knowing. It's not only unusual, it's unprofessional as well. Very unprofessional.'

'The whole thing's unprofessional,' Harry replied. 'Nothing's going to change. You're not going to order me, are you? I don't think it would help, and it's my neck. Thanks very much for caring. Cheers, maestro.'

''Bye, Harry, I understand. No-one else does. Take care, and listen to the news. As soon as you hear we've got him, come whistling out. Give me a call first if you can, but head on up to the airport like you've got a bomb up your backside. Take care.'

Harry put the phone down, and hurried out into the cold and the long walk back up the Falls. He was concerned that they should get the girl out of the quag-

242

mire, and fast, before her involvement became too great for her to extricate herself . . . before she followed the other girl he'd brought into the game.

But things did move fast that Sunday.

Twenty minutes after Harry had rung off Davidson called the Permanent Under-Secretary. He caught the civil servant on the point of going to early morning service. The bad news first. Always play it that way, Davidson liked to say. Kick them a bit, then produce the magic sponge. They like it better. The agent was still declining to name a contact point. Not refusing, but declining. Don't want to make an order of it. Told him it's stupid, but can't do more than that. As he says, it's his neck. Our scandal if he catches it, mind, but his neck for all that. Now the bonus. Good information out of our chap. He'll like that.

'Keep that for a moment,' snapped the civil servant. 'I've had calls in the night. GOC has been on, and that man of his, Frost of intelligence. Bloody misnomer that. They want our fellow out, and kicking up a hell of a scene. They think he's blown.'

Davidson bit his tongue. He heard at the end of the line the call for the rest of the family to go on.

'There's been some sort of leak. Like a sieve, that place. The papers have got a story from the opposition that they know a big man has been put in. There's panic stations over there. Anyway the order is get the chap out or the General says he'll go to the PM. Consolation is that the men over there say they don't think the IRA have a name. But that'll come soon enough. And you haven't an idea where we could go and just take hold of him?'

243

'All I have is that he works in a scrap merchant's in Andersonstown. Nothing more.'

'That won't do us much good till Monday morning.'

'He's done well again, our chap. The man we want was actually at the dance where Harry was the other night. The military had him, and must have let him go, or are holding him on something else . . .'

'Look, for God's sake, Davidson, I'm at home. I'm going to church. There's no point feeding me that sort of material over the phone. Talk to Frost direct. He'll be in his office, prancing about. He's having a field day. But if this Harry man should call again, get him out. That now is an instruction.'

Davidson had always had to admit that he enjoyed the complicated paraphernalia of introducing the agent into the operations theatre. He could reflect on it now, with the phone quiet, and his superior racing down the country lanes late for his communion. Davidson had been on the old Albania team. There had been the months with the undercover Greeks and Turks in Cyprus. Three years' secondment to the Singapore government to train bright-faced little policemen in the techniques of urban infiltration and maintaining men in a hostile environment. There was a gap in his wide experience. He recognized it. The men he sent into the field or discussed sending were all, as Davidson saw them, foreigners. The involvement with the men who listened to his lectures or acted under his orders was loose, and in no way binding.

With Harry it had become quite different. The danger that he now knew his agent to be facing numbed Davidson to a degree that almost shamed him. He had long seen himself as a tough, near-ruthless figure, the man in charge who put his agents onto the ground without sentiment or personal feeling. His defensive walls were being breached, he realized, as he thought of his man across the water, with the enemy closing on him.

And Harry didn't just not know of it: he'd just been told that all was well and looked good. That made him vulnerable.

Davidson had a growing feeling of nausea when he remembered how Harry had been brought to Dorking. Damn-all chance he'd had of backing out of the operation. The Prime Minister personally authorized the setting up of the team, and we've chosen you as the most suitable man. What chance did he have of sidestepping that little lot? He'd been belted off on the plane on a wild-goose chase. If he's not out of there soon he'll be number one thousand and bloody something pushing up daisies.

He picked up his phone and called Frost direct, in his office where he'd been told he'd be. At the other end of the line the serving colonel in intelligence left the London-based civilian with no illusions as to what he thought of armchair administrators organizing undercover work without consultation or know-how. Davidson resigned himself to it, letting it blaze over him. Between the interruptions he read over the transcript of Harry's message. He ended on a high note.

'He did pretty well with the first lot of stuff we gave you. We were disappointed in our team it didn't come to much. You should have it sewn up this time, don't you think, old boy?'

Frost didn't rise. It was a juicy and wriggling bait, but the office was crowded, and it was not the day for

245

telephone brawling. That would come after this merry little show was wrapped up and in mothballs – what was left of it. He called the Springfield Road police to request the locating and picking up of the girl Josephine Laverty of Clonard, and then turned his attention to the matter of the man having been in and presumably out of military hands on Saturday night two weeks back. Cool bastard he must be, appraised the colonel. In between the calls he cancelled his Sunday-morning nine holes with G2 Ops.

Other operations had gone wrong before, Davidson recalled. There were those endless nights when they parachuted Albanians into the marshlands between the sea and Tirana and waited in vain with their CIA colleagues for the chatter of radio signals that would let them know all was well. When the Cypriot agents he had controlled had disappeared there had been days of nagging uncertainty until the bodies showed up – generally tortured, and always shot through the back of the head. But they were only aliens, so that the recriminations were short-lived, the reprisals muted. But if they lost Harry then the ramifications would be huge, and public. The round-up of scapegoats would be spectacular, Davidson had no doubt of that. The Permanent Under-Secretary would have faded from the picture by then, would have fetched his sliding carpet out. The old hack would be left holding the baby.

He called his assistant in from the outer office where, thank God, the man spent most of his time, and told him to watch the phones. He was to tape all calls, regardless, on the cassette recorder, whichever phone they came through on. He slipped out of the building. Sunday morning in Covent Garden. Some sunlight about on the upper reaches of the big buildings. Piles of fruit and vegetable boxes. No people. Davidson walked to the small grocer that he knew would be open to serve the flats, big and grey-smeared, to the north of the market square. He bought bread, and cartons of milk, coffee and biscuits, some butter, and lemon curd. He'd liked that ever since boarding school thirty-five years ago. The total was about all his cooking facilities would cope with.

There had been no calls when he returned. He phoned his wife, told her he would be in town for a day or so, and not to worry. She didn't sound as if she was. There was an army-issue camp bed kept in the wardrobe behind his desk, excruciatingly uncomfortable but better than nothing. It would be a long wait, and no-one to spend it with but the boring young man they'd sent along to give him a hand. Davidson had realized soon that they had not fully briefed his assistant on what was happening. He had no intention himself of enlightening him. They were on stand-by now, operational twenty-four hours.

The boys ran intricately between the towering regimented lines of the pine trunks, hurtling their way over the bending carpet of needles and cones in perpetual games of chase and hide and seek. Their voices were shrill, loud as if to fight off the cold attacking wind that heralded the real winter of the great plain east of Hanover. This was where Harry liked to bring them, to search for trout in the streams in high summer and spend weekends in a wooden chalet, to run round to keep warm in the early winter, and then, when the snow came, to bring their toboggans. Sometimes they would set up a fox that had hidden in the sparse, stunted undergrowth under the pine umbrella hoping to avoid detection, then when its nerve went and it bounded clear there would be the noisy, clumsy chase, the ground giving under their boots before the quarry made its escape. It would take them deep into the forest, and when the brown flash was well lost they would stop and ponder and think of the direction of the fire-break path where they had left their mother, Mary Brown.

She had brought sandwiches full of sausage and a Thermos of tomato soup today, and they would have that later sitting at a wooden table in the picnic area beside the car park.

From the wide path she could hear the distant noise of their voices, as she walked with a taller, older woman, her mother. A week after Harry had gone she had written to her home in the English midlands countryside. There the three-page letter had been recognized as a distress flare, a call for help. Arrangements had been made. Father could look after himself for a week, cook his own meals, get the garden into shape for the long winter lay-off.

When the children were in bed the conversation often, and hardly accidentally, strayed to Harry's abrupt departure, and now that they were again out of earshot it continued.

'It's just so difficult to understand,' said Mary's mother, 'that no-one should be able to tell you anything about it. You'd have thought someone could have had the gumption, even the courtesy, to say something to you.'

'There's been nothing,' said Mary, 'not a word

248

from anyone since they came and packed his case. Rummaged around in the wardrobe, right down the bottom where his old things are – half of them should have gone this week to the sergeants' wives' jumble sale – things he'd only wear if he was gardening or painting or cleaning out the cellar, or something like that. We've had two postcards from somewhere down the Gulf, and otherwise nothing.'

The postcards had shown a camel corps contingent of the Sultan, and a gold-domed mosque. The messages had been brief and facetious. 'Having a wonderful time, got a very red nose from the heat, don't think there'll be snow here this Christmas, love to the boys and to you, my darling, Harry,' and 'Giving church parade a miss this week. Missing you all. Sorry about the nonsense but it will all seem clear when I'm home. Love you all, Harry.' They'd taken a long time to arrive, and now they decorated the mantelpiece above the fire in their front room.

'But tell me again, dear, exactly what they said when you asked the people in the office.' Mother had the infuriating habit of demanding endless, word-by-word repetitions of conversations she'd already heard umpteen times.

'Just what I told you. That it was as a result of a signal from London, that everyone here was as much in the dark as I was. That Harry would be away six weeks' minimum, probably not more than eight. And that if I were short of anything or having problems not to hesitate to call the Families Officer. He's an awful old bore – a passed-over major. I'd really be on my last legs if I called him. I just don't think they know.'

'It must be to do with the Aden business, I suppose.

The thing he was awarded the Military Cross for. Your father and I were very proud for you—'

Mary cut in, 'I cannot believe it's anything to do with that. It was years ago, and Harry was really knocked out by that. He had weeks of sick leave. He doesn't talk much about it. But it must have been awful from what I was told. He just lived in amongst them then, wasn't even fluent on Arabic. Passable but not fluent.'

'Well, it has to be something secret.'

'Has to be.' She was wearing her hair up, and the wind was pulling it away from the big tortoiseshell clip at the back of her head. It was whisping away – she hadn't taken enough time to settle it properly in the hurry to get the food ready and the kids dressed for the expedition. She had little make-up on, lipstick untidy. Not how she'd want Harry to see her. 'But I don't think he'd volunteer for anything like this now, and I cannot for the life of me see why anyone would just pick him out over all the people they've got and rush him down to the Gulf. It just doesn't make sense. I thought he'd burned all the spook stuff out of him.'

'Still, it's not long now, only a fortnight or so,' comforted her mother.

'That's what they said. We've no option but to believe them.'

Mary Brown could not confide the depth of her unhappiness to her mother. Too many years of marriage and before that secretarial college in London had dulled the relationship. Their marriage was too confidential to gossip about. What hurt most was that she had thought she had understood the man she had been living with for so long, and now she had discovered that there was a different compartment in his make-up.

'Well, at least we know he can look after himself,' said her mother, sensing the barriers going up.

'Let's hope he doesn't have to. We'll get the kids back and have lunch.'

She called for them, and when they emerged filthy from the forest they all walked back to the car.

That same lunchtime Seamus Duffryn was summoned to a house in Beachmount and told by the Battalion intelligence officer to resume close surveillance on McEvoy. Duffryn was told a squad was going out in the afternoon to find a friend of McEvoy, a girl who had been out with him. Josephine Laverty from Clonard.

A few hundred yards away in the Springfield Road the British army unit that had been asked to find the girl was puzzled that it had no record of her or her mother living in the area. There was no reason why they should have done, as the house was in the name of Josephine's uncle, Michael O'Leary. A little after three o'clock the unit reported in that it had been unable to locate the girl. By then a critical amount of the available time had run out.

It took more than two hours from the time Frost called the army headquarters dominating the Ardoyne and told them of the tip to the moment Billy Downs was identified. First the troops who had taken part in the search operation at the caeli had to be located. The lieutenant who had led the raid was in Norfolk on weekend leave, and there was no answer to his telephone. The sergeant, the next senior man out, recalled that he had busied himself near the door on security, but he was able to name the six soldiers who had carried out the split-up question-and-answer work. Private Jones was now in Berlin, but Lance-Corporal James Llewellyn was picked up by a Saracen from a foot patrol on the far side of the Battalion area. There was no written record, of course. That, along with Jones, were the only two pieces of evidence of the confrontation, and both had now disappeared. Llewellyn stared at the photokit issued in London that had been brought up from the guardroom.

'That's the one it's like, if it's any of them. It's Downs. It's not a great likeness. It's not easy to pick him on that picture. But if he was there that's the one it was. There was his woman there, in yellow. She ran out across to him.'

With the name they attacked the filing system. Billy Downs. Ypres Avenue, number 41. There'd been a spot-check on his story about being down in Cork with his mother. The Garda had been fast for a change, and had cleared him of involvement. They said he'd been there through that period. There'd been a query about him because he was away from home. Otherwise, clean with nothing known. The net inside the headquarters spread wider, to include the policeman who had seen him that night in the small hours.

'He was very cool. Not even sweat on his palms. I know, as I looked.'

It was into the afternoon that they called Frost back.

'We think we've located the man you want. He's Billy Downs, without an "e" on the end. Ypres Avenue, wife and kids. Very quiet, from what we've seen of him. Unemployed. His story stuck after the Garda ran a check on the alibi he gave us to account for his long absence from the area. There was no other reason to hold him. Like to point out that the chaps that have actually seen this fellow say that he's not that like the pics you put out. Much fatter in the face, I'm told. Perhaps you'll let us know what you want done. We've a platoon on immediate. We can see pretty much down that street: I've an OP in the roof of a mill, right up the top.'

Frost growled back into the phone, 'I'd be interested in knowing if Mr Downs is currently at home.'

'Wait one.' As he held on for the answer Frost could hear the distant sounds of the unit operations room as they called up the OP on a field telephone. 'Not quite so hot, I'm afraid. They log comings and goings. We think Downs left his home, that's number forty-one, around twenty-five minutes ago. That's fifteen-o-five hours precisely that he went out. But he goes in and out pretty regularly. No reason to think he won't be back in a bit.'

'I'd like it watched,' said Frost, 'but don't move in yet, please. This number will be manned through the evening and the night. Call me as soon as you see him.'

Downs was on his way by car up the Lisburn Road at the time that the observation post overlooking Ypres Avenue was warned to look out for him. There were several subsequent entries in the exercise book the two soldiers kept for logging the comings and goings in the street. They had noted him as soon as he came from his front door and began the walk up the hill away from them to one of the decreed exits from the Ardoyne. When the message came through on the radio-telephone to the troops, Downs was just out of the heartland, standing in the no-man's ground at the top of the Crumlin waiting for his pick-up. This was neither Protestant nor Catholic territory. Side streets on either side of the road shut off with great daubed sheets of corrugated iron. Two worlds split by a four-lane road with barricades to keep people from each other's throats. Scrawled on one side was 'Up the Provos', and 'British Army Out', and beyond the opposite pavement the messages of 'Fuck the Pope' and 'UVF'.

He was edgy waiting there in daylight beside such a busy road, one used heavily by military traffic, and the relief showed in his face when the Cortina pulled up alongside him, and the driver bent sideways to open the passenger door. The car had been hijacked in the Falls thirty-five minutes earlier.

A moment later they moved off, weaving their way through the city. By the crossroads in the centre of the sprawling, middle-class suburb the car turned left and up one of the lanes that lead to the Down countryside through a small belt of woods. They turned off among the trees.

The driver unlocked the boot and handed over the Armalite. It was wrapped in a transparent plastic bag. Downs checked the firing mechanism. It was a different weapon to the one that he had used before in his attack on the patrol, and was issued by a quite unconnected quartermaster. But the rifle came from the same original source – Howa Industries, of Nagoya in Japan. It had been designed as a hunting weapon, and that astonished him. What sort of animal did you take a killing machine of this proven performance to hunt? He released the catch on the stock to check that the folding hinge was in working order. That reduced the length of the weapon by eleven inches, bringing it down to less than two-and-a-half feet, so that it would comfortably fit into the padded inside pocket of his coat. He was passed the two magazines, glanced them over and fitted one deep into the attachment slot under the belly of the gun. He activated a bullet up into the breach, and flicked with his thumb at the safety catch to ensure it was engaged. The volunteer at the wheel watched the preparations with fascination.

With the stock folded, Downs pushed the rifle down into the hidden pocket.

'I don't know how long I'll be,' he said. 'For God's sake don't suddenly clear off or anything smart. Stick here. At least till midnight.'

They were the only words Downs spoke before he disappeared into the growing darkness to walk the half-mile towards Rennie's house. The only words of the whole journey. The teenager left behind with the car amongst the trees subsided, shivering, into the driver's seat to wait for his return.

The regular Sunday afternoon visit to the office to clear the accumulation of paper work off his desk was no longer a source of controversy between the policeman and Janet Rennie. It had been at first, with accusations of 'putting the family into second place' being levelled. The increasing depression of the security situation in the province had caused her to relent.

It was now understood that she and the two girls, Margaret and Fiona, would have their tea, watch some television and then wait for him to get home before bedtime.

Over the last four years Janet Rennie had become used to the problems of being a policeman's wife. A familiar sight now was the shoulder holster slung over the bedside chair when he had an extra hour in bed on Saturday mornings, before the weekly trip to the out-of-town supermarket. So too were the registration plates in the garage, which he alternated on the car, and around the house the mortise locks on all the doors, inside and out. At night all these were locked with a formal ritual of order and precedence, lest one should be forgotten, and the detective's personal firearm lay in the half-opened drawer of the bedside table, on which rested the telephone which, as often as not, would ring deep into the night.

Promotion and transfer to Belfast had been hard at first. The frequency of the police funerals they attended along with the general level of danger in the city had intimidated her. But out of the fear had come a fierce-rooted hatred of the IRA enemy.

Janet Rennie had long since accepted that her husband might not last through the troubles, might be assassinated by one of those wild-eyed, cold-faced young men whose photographs she saw attached to the outside of the files he brought home in the evenings and at weekends. She didn't shrink from the possi-bility that she might ride in the black Austin Princess behind the flag and the band to a grey, country church-yard. When he was late home she attacked her way through the knitting, her therapy along with the tele-vision set. He was often out late, seldom in before eight or nine – and that was a good evening. But she felt pride for the work he did, and shared something of his commitment.

The girls, seven and five, were in the bright, warm living room of the bungalow, kneeling together on the treated sheepskin rug in front of the open fire, watching the television, when the doorbell rang.

'Mama! Mama! Front-doorbell!' Margaret shouted to her mother at the back, too absorbed to drag herself away from the set.

Janet Rennie was making sandwiches for tea, her mind taken by fish-paste fillings and the neatness of the arrangement of the little bread triangles. They had become a treat, these Sunday teas, the girls and their mother playing at gentility with enthusiasm. With annoyance she wondered who it could be. Which of the girls from the close was calling right at teatime?

The bell rang again.

'Come on, Mama. It's the front door.' Margaret resigned herself. 'Do you want me to go?'

'No, I'll do it. You stay inside, and you're not going out to play on your bikes at this time of night.'

She wiped her hands on the cloth hanging beside the sink. Right from the start she ignored the basic rule of procedure that her husband had laid down. As her hand came up towards the Yale lock that was always on, she noticed that the chain had been left off since the children came back from playing with their friends of three doors down. It should have been fastened. She should have fastened it before she opened the door. But she ignored the rules and pulled the door back.

'Excuse me, is it Mrs Rennie?'

She looked at the shortish man standing there on her front doorstep, hands in his coat pockets, an open smile round his face, dark hair nicely parted.

'Yes, that's right.'

Very quietly he said, 'Put your hands behind your head, keep them there and don't shout. Don't make any move. I know the kids are here.'

She watched helplessly as through his coat, unbuttoned and open, he drew out the ugly squat black shape of the Armalite. Holding it in one hand, with the stock still folded, he prodded her with the barrel back into the hallway. She felt strange, detached from what was happening, as if it were a scenario. She had no control over the situation, she knew that. He came across the carpet past the stairs towards her, flicking the door closed with his heel. It clattered as it swung to, the lock engaging behind him.

'Who is it, Mama?' From behind the closed door of the lounge Fiona called out.

'We'll go in there now. Just remember this. If you try anything I'll kill you. You, and the children. Don't forget it when you want to play the bloody heroine. We're going to sit in there, and wait for that bastard husband of yours. Right? Is the message all plain and clear and understood?'

The narrow barrel of the Armalite dug into her flesh just above the hip as he pushed past her to the door and opened it. Their mother was half into the room before Fiona turned, words part out of her mouth but frozen when she saw the man with the rifle. Even to a child three months off her fifth birthday the message was brilliantly obvious. The girl rose up on her knees, her face clouding from astonishment to terror. As if in slow motion her elder sister registered the new mood. Wide-eyed, and with the brightness fading from her, she saw first her sister's face then her mother standing hunched, as if bowed down by some great weight, and behind

258

her Downs with the small shiny rifle in his right hand.

Too frightened to scream the elder girl remained stock-still till her mother reached her, gathered the children to her, and took them to the sofa.

The three of them held tightly to each other as on the other side of the room Downs eased himself down into Rennie's chair. From there he was directly facing the family, who were huddled away in the front corner of the sofa to be as far as possible from him. He also had a clear view of the door into the room, and of the window beyond it at the far edge of the lounge. It was there that he expected the first sign of Rennie's return, the headlights of the policeman's car.

'I'll warn you for the last time, missus. Any moves, anything clever, and you'll be dead, the lot of you. Don't think, Mrs Rennie, when it comes to it, that you're the only one at risk. That would be getting it very wrong, a bad miscalculation. If I shoot you I do the kids as well. We'll leave the TV on, and you'll sit there. And just remember I'm watching you. Watching you all the time. So be very careful. Right, missus?'

Billy Downs paused and let the effect of his words sink in on the small room.

'We're just going to wait,' he said.

Chapter Fifteen

The four men sent to question Josephine Laverty had none of the problems finding her that the British army unit in the Springfield Road had encountered. Smiling broadly, the oldest in the group, and the leader, suggested that old Mrs Laverty might care to go into the kitchen and take herself a good long cup of tea.

They took Josephine up to her bedroom far from the mother's ears. One of the younger men drew the curtains, cutting out the frail shafts of sunlight, and took up his position by the window. Another stood at the door. The third of the volunteers stood behind the chair they suggested Josephine should sit in. The older man they called Frank, and they treated him with respect and with caution.

The girl was poorly equipped to handle an interrogation. Frank's opening question had been harmless enough, and he was as astonished as the other three boys in the room at the way she collapsed.

Perhaps it was because she was one of the uninvolved, those few in the city who tried to weave a life outside the troubles. Her lack of commitment had built up a fear of violence, second nature to so many, and therefore not so terrifying. Without loyalties there was only self-preservation, and there was little anyone could do now to help her in the face of the unspoken brutality of the men who had crowded round her. Cold, cruel faces, pallid, expressionless, used and trained in begetting pain. There was only one reason they would come to her . . . because of Harry, sweet and beautiful and chatty Harry. She looked at their hands, big, dirty, broken fingernails, roughened with usage. Their boots, hard and bruised from wear, drab from the rain outside. Men who would hurt her, punch her, kick her. And for what? For a few minutes' delay in the inevitable. She would tell them what they had come to find out. They were far outside her experience, the men who stood around her, moving among her possessions as if there by right. They did have the right, she thought. Yesterday on the Sperrins she had become involved in their territory, and that was why they had come.

'This fellow McEvoy, that you've been going with. Who is he?'

There had been no reply, only a dissolve as her head went down to her lap and she buried her cheeks and her eyes and ears into the palms of her hands.

'Who is he?' Frank was insistent. 'Who is he, where does he come from?'

'You know who he is. Why come to me for it? You know well enough.'

Frank paced up and down, short steps, continually twisting round towards the girl when he lost sight of her, moving back and forward between the window and the door, skirting the single bed littered with the girl's clothes.

261

'I want you to tell me.' He emphasized it. Like an owl with a scarce-whelped mouse, a stoat with a rabbit, he dominated the cringing girl on the wooden chair before him.

'I want it from you. D'yer hear? I've not much time.'

Josephine shook her head, partly from the convulsion of her collapse, and reeled away from him as he swung his clenched fist back-handed across her face. Her knuckles took much of the force of the blow, but through the splayed fingers across her eyes she saw the blood welling close and then breaking the skin at the back of her hands.

Frank could see that what had been put to him as somewhat of a routine questioning had become rather more complex. The fear and hesitation of the girl had alerted him. Her inability to answer a simple explicit question. Frank knew McEvoy only as a lodger at the girl's employer's guest house . . . been out with him once or twice. A fair-looking piece, he'd probably knocked her off, but that wouldn't be enough to put her there doubled up and sniffling.

'I'm getting impatient, girl. To him you owe none of the loyalty you should give to us.'

He weighed up whether he would need to hit her again.

She nodded her head, very slightly at first, then merging into the positive mood of acquiescence and surrender. Frank held back. He would not have to hit her again.

She straightened up, steadying herself as she prepared the words.

'He's with the British, isn't he? You knew that. He's British. I don't know what he does, but he's been sent to live amongst us. He's looking for the man that killed the politico. Over in London. That's his job. To find that man. He said when he found him he'd exterminate him.'

She stopped, leaving the shadowy little room quiet. Below she could hear her mother about the kitchen, picking things up and putting them down.

Josephine saw the enormity of what she had said. She'd told him, hadn't she, that his truth was safe with her. One backhander and she spilled it all. She remembered it, outside the pub on the hill at Glenshane. She'd promised it then, when she'd told him to quit.

Frank stared intently at her.

'His job was as an agent in here? He's a British agent? Sent in to infiltrate us? . . . Holy Jesus!'

'You knew? You knew, didn't you? You wouldn't have come if you hadn't known.'

The room was near-dark now. Josephine could barely make out the men in the room – only the one silhouetted at the window by the early street light. Her mother called up for tea for her visitors. No-one answered. The old lady lingered at the bottom of the stairs waiting for the reply, then went back to the kitchen, accepting and perhaps understanding the situation and unable to intervene.

The girl wavered one last time in her loyalties and her allegiance. Upbringing, tradition, community all came down heavily on the scales against the balance of the laugh and adulthood and bed of Harry. But there was the wee girl with the tossing feet and the tightening stocking, and the obscenity and the misery of death in the police cell, and that wiped Harry from the slate. She spoke again.

'He was the one that shopped Theresa, the girl that hung herself. She said she'd been with the man that did the London killing, but he couldn't perform. Harry tipped the army about it. He said the killing was a challenge to the British, and they had to get the man who did it, and kill him. Something like that, just to show who ran things. He told me this yesterday.'

The volunteers said nothing, their imagination stretched by what the girl said. Frank spoke. 'Was he close to the man he was looking for? Did he know his name? Where he lived? What he looked like? Just how much did the bastard know?'

'He said he thought he knew what he looked like.' She saw Theresa again in her mind, heard her giggling in the small space round the basin outside the lock-up closet. That was the justification, that was enough . . . to see the girl's face. Hear her choking. 'He said he was a good shot, and a cool bugger, that's what he called him. And, yes, they were looking, he said, for a man who would be out of the main eye of things. That was the exact phrase he used.'

'And you, how did you spot this highly-trained British assassin, little girl?'

'I spotted him because of a silly thing. You have to believe me, but we were on the Sperrins yesterday. He said he'd been in the Merchant Navy, and sailed all over, but the gale on the mountain seemed to shake him a bit. I said to him it wasn't very good if he'd been to sea as much as he said. Then he didn't hide it any more. He seemed to want to talk about it.'

Clever little bitch, thought Frank.

'Is he in regular touch, communication, with his controller?'

264

'I don't know.'

'Is he armed?'

'I don't know that either. I never saw a gun. I've told you all I know. That's God's truth.'

'There's one little problem for you, Miss Josephine.' Frank's voice had a cutting edge to it now, something metallic, cold and smooth. 'You haven't explained to me yet how this British agent came to hear about Theresa and what she was saying about the London man. You may need a bit of time for that, you bastard whore. Treacherous little bitch.'

He came very close to her now. She could smell the tobacco and beer on his breath and the staleness of sweat on his clothes. He hadn't shaved that day, and his face was a prickled, lumpy mass.

'Just work it out,' he said. 'Then tell the lads, because they'll be waiting for an answer. To us you're nothing, dirt, scum, shit. You've shopped one of your own . . . a wee girl who hanged herself rather than talk to the fucking British. You betrayed her. You betrayed your lover boy as well. We'll put it about, you know, and we'll let the military know as well. You'll find somewhere to run, but there'll be sod-all people to help you get there, you little cow. But then, when these lads have finished with you, you'll be thinking twice before you go drop your knickers to another Britisher.'

Frank turned away and walked to the door. He said to the man who was standing there, 'It's just a lesson this time, Jamie. Nothing permanent and nothing that shows. Something just for her to remember, to think about for a long time. Then lose yourselves. If we need you later we know where you'll be, so split from here. And, little girl, if you've half an inch of sense in your double-dealing painted head you'll not mention what's happened here tonight, nor what's going to.'

He went out of the door and down the steep staircase. In the hall the old woman saw him, as she turned in her chair by the fire and looked at him. He smiled at her.

'Don't worry, lady,' he said, 'I can find my way out. You just stay where you are.'

The three younger men followed him through the door fifteen minutes later. They left Josephine doubled up on the bed wheezing for air and holding the soft solar plexus of her stomach. She lay a long time in the room, fighting the pain and willing it away. Her clothes lay scattered in the corner of the room where the men had ripped them from her.

'Right on your bloody flesh, you little bitch, where it hurts, and where it'll last.'

She'd thought they were going to rape her, but instead they simply beat her. She curled herself up, foetal position, her arms protecting her breasts and lower stomach, thighs clamped together. That was how she stayed after they'd gone. Her breath came back to her soon, and after that there was the long, deep aching of the muscles, and, mingled with it, the agony of the betrayal. Betrayal of Theresa. Betrayal of Harry.

Perhaps the men had been sensitive about beating up a girl, perhaps it was the sight of her nakedness, but the job was not thoroughly done. The effect soon faded. There was time to think then. Frank would have gone straight to the house to find Harry. He'd be taken, tortured, and shot; that would come later, or tomorrow morning. Her reasoning made any thought of warning Harry irrelevant. They would have him already, but did she want to warn him? One good screw, and what

266

had he done? Lifted her bedroom tattle from pillow confidence to military intelligence information. Let him rot with it.

When her mother came up the stairs late in the evening she was still doubled up, still holding her stomach, and cold now on her skin. The old lady looped the girl's nightdress over her head, and twisted her feet under the clothes. She spent some minutes picking the clothes up from the floor, showing no more interest in those that were torn than in those that formed the general muddle on the floor.

Twice during the Sunday evening Davidson phoned through to Frost. The first-floor office had, with the coming of darkness, taken on the appearance of a bunker. The telephone that was specified for outgoing outside calls was on the floor beside the canvas camp bed, now erected.

Davidson was curtly told there was no information, and reminded that he'd already been told that he would be notified as soon as anything was known. The earlier elation had left him, and he allowed Frost the last word on an operation so inefficient that you cannot even get in touch with your man when you need to get him out.

But for all his bark Frost was now sufficiently involved in the operation to call Springfield Road, wait while the commanding officer was brought to speak to him, and stress the urgency with which the girl Laverty should be found.

In their eyrie high above the Ardoyne two soldiers looked down on Ypres Avenue. There were no street lights, old casualties of the conflict, but they watched the front door of No. 41 from the image intensifier, a sophisticated visual aid that washed everything with a greenish haze and which enabled them to see the doorway with great clarity. On the hour they whispered the same message into their field telephone. No-one had used the front door of the house.

Frank did not go near Delrosa that night. On his bicycle he had ridden up to Andersonstown in search of his Battalion commander. It was arranged that at midnight he would be taken to meet the Belfast Brigade commander. Frank knew his name, but had never met him.

From his home the Permanent Under-Secretary had authorized the sending of a photograph of Harry to Belfast. The next morning, Monday, it was to be issued to troops who would raid the various Andersonstown scrap merchants'. Less than half a dozen people in the province would know the reason for the swoops but each search party would have several three-inch-by-four pictures of Harry. It had originally shown him in uniform, but that had been painted out.

The big television in the corner of the room droned on, its Sunday message of hope and charity, goodwill and universal kindness expounded by ranks of singers and earnest balding parsons. The family sat quite still on the sofa watching the man with the Armalite.

The pictures claimed no part of the attention of Janet Rennie as she stared, minute after minute, at the man with the rifle across his knee, but for long moments

the children's concentration was occasionally taken
by the images on the screen before being jerked to the
nightmare facing them across the carpet. It was a new
degree of fear that the children felt, one they were not
able to cope with or assimilate. They held fast to their
mother, waiting to see what would happen, what
she would do. To the two girls the man opposite
represented something quite apart from anything they
had experienced before, but they recognized him as
their father's enemy. Their eyes seldom left his face,
held with fascination by the greyness of his skin, its lack
of colour, its deadness. This was where they saw the
difference between the intruder and their world. There
was none of the ruddiness and weight, the life and
colour that they knew from their friends' fathers
and the men that came home with their father.

In the first twenty minutes that Downs had been in
the room, Fiona, who traded on her ability to charm,
had attempted to win the stranger with a smile. He
looked right through her, gap-toothed grin and all.
She'd tried just once, then subsided against her mother.

He's never come out into the light, the elder girl,
Margaret, told herself. He's been locked up, and like a
creature he's escaped from wherever they've kept him.
This man was across the wall, but she knew little of the
causes of the separation and the walling-off. She
studied the deepness of his eyes, intent and careful,
uninvolved as they took in the room, traversing it like
the light on a prison camp watchtower, without order
or reason but hovering, moving, perpetually expecting
the unpredictable. She saw his clothes too. A coat with
a darned tear in the sleeve, the buttons off the cuffs,
trousers without creases and shiny in the knees, frayed

269

at the turn-ups and with mud inside the lower leg. To children, suits were for best, for work, not for getting dirty and shabby. His shoes were strange to them, too. Cleaned after a fashion by the rain on the winter pavements, but like his face without lustre, misused.

Margaret understood that the gun on Downs's lap was to kill her father. Her sister, twenty months younger, was unable to finish off the equation and so was left in a limbo of expectancy, aware only of an incomprehensible awfulness. Margaret had enough contact with the boys at school who played their war games in the school yard to recognize the weapon as a rifle.

He'll be a hard bastard, Janet Rennie had decided. One of the big men sent in for a killing like this. Won't be able to distract him with argument or discussion enough to unsettle him. He's hard enough to carry out his threat. She saw the wedding ring on his finger. Would have his own kids, breed like rats the Catholics, have his own at home. But he'd still shoot hers. She felt the fingers of her daughters gripping through her blouse. But she kept her head straight, and her gaze fastened on Downs. There was no response to her stare, only the indifference of the professional, the craftsman who has been set a task and time limit and who has arrived early and therefore must wait to begin. Faster than her children she had taken in the man, searched him for weakness, but the gun across his knees now held her attention. If he were nervous or under great strain then she would notice the fidgeting of the hands or the reflection of the perspiration on the stock or barrel of the gun. But there was no movement, no reflection.

He held the gun lightly, his left hand halfway along the shaft and his fingers loose round the black plastic that cradled the hard rifled steel of the barrel. His hand was just above the magazine and her eyes wandered to the engineered emplacement where the capsule of ammunition nestled into the base of the gun. Just after he had sat down, Downs had eased the safety catch off with his right index finger, which now lay spanning the half-moon of the trigger guard. Like a man come to give an estimate on the plumbing, or life insurance, she thought. None of the tensions she would have expected on display. Thirty minutes or so before she thought her husband might be arriving home she decided to talk.

'We have no quarrel with you. You've none with us. We've done nothing to you. If you go now you'll be clean away. You know that. You'll be right out of here and gone before my husband gets back.' That was her start. Poor, she told herself, it wouldn't divert a flea.

He looked back with amused detachment.

'If you go through with this they'll get you. They always get them now. It's a fact. You'll be in the Kesh for the rest of your life. Is that what you want?'

'Save it, Mrs Rennie. Save it and listen to the hymns.'

She persisted. 'It'll get you nowhere. It's the Provisionals, isn't it? You're beaten. One more cruel killing, senseless. It won't do any good.'

'Shut up.' He said it quietly. 'Just shut up and sit still.'

She came again. 'Why do you come here? Why to this house? Who are you?'

'It's a pity your man never told you what he did when he went to work of a morning. That's late in the day now, though. Quiet yourself and stay where you are.'

271

He motioned at her with the rifle, still gently, still in control. The movement was definitive. Stay on the sofa with the children. He sensed that the crisis was coming for her, and that she knew it. With growing desperation she took up the same theme.

'But you're beaten now. It'll soon be all over. All your big men are gone. There'll have to be a cease-fire soon, then talking. More killing won't help anything.' Keep it calm, don't grovel to him, talk as an equal with something on your side. There's nothing to counter-balance that Armalite but you have to make believe he doesn't hold everything.

'We're not beaten. It's not over. We've more men than we can handle. There'll be no talks, and no cease-fire. Got the message? Nothing. Not while there are pigs like your man running round free and live.'

The children beside her started up at the way the crouched stranger spoke of their father. Janet Rennie was an intelligent woman and hardened by her country upbringing. That she would fight for her husband's life was obvious: the problem had been in finding the medium. For the first time in nearly two hours she believed she stood a chance. She still watched the hands and the rifle. The hands were in a new position on the Armalite. From resting against the gun they were now gripping it. Attack, and how can he hit back before Rennie comes home?

'There's no future for you boys. Your best men are all locked up. The people are sick and tired of you. You know that. Even in your own rat holes they've had enough of you—'

'You don't know a bloody thing about what goes on. Not a bloody thing. You know nothing. Nothing.

Shut up. Shut your bloody face . . .'

She taunted him, trying to act it with her voice to overcome the fear. 'They don't want you any more. You're outnumbered, living off the backs of people. Without your guns you're nothing—'

He shouted back across to her. 'What do you know of the way we live? What do you know of what support we have? All you see is what's on the bloody television. You don't know what life is like in the Falls, with murdering bastards like your husband to beat the shit out of boys and girls. We're doing people a service when we kill fucking swine like that husband of yours.'

'My husband never killed anyone.' She said it as a statement of fact. Safe.

'He told you that, did he?' Very precise, low and hissing the words out. 'Pity you never asked him what sort of little chat he had with the wee girl that hanged herself in the cells at Springfield.'

She had built herself towards the climax. Now he watched with relish the demolition. She remembered reading about the girl, though it had not been mentioned at home. Work rarely was. The rebuttal caught her hard, draining her. The hands. Hold on to the hands, and concentrate on them. The only lifeline is the hands. The left knuckle was white on the barrel, blood drained out from round the bones. He was holding the rifle with both hands as he brought it up across his face to wipe his forehead with the sleeve on his right arm. He was sweating.

'You're nothing, are you? That's all you're fit for. Sitting in people's homes with guns, guarding women and wee bairns. You're a rat, a creeping, disease-ridden

273

little rat. Is that what the great movement is about? Killing people in their homes?'

Her voice was battering it out now, watching the anger rise first in his neck and spread through the lower jaw, tension, veins hardening and protruding. Safe. What can the gun do now that would not rouse the neighbours who lived through the thin brick-and-cement walls of the estate just a few feet from her own bungalow?

'You've made it all out wrong, Mrs Rennie. Whatever your bloody man says you don't kill the Provos just by locking a few up. We are of the people. Don't you know that? The people are with us. You've lost, you are the losers. Your way of life, God-given superiority, is over and finished, not us . . . We're winning. We're winning because the people support us. Go into Andytown, or the Murph or the Ardoyne or Turf Lodge. Go in there and ask them about Provo rule. Then ask them what they think of RUC scum.'

He was shouting, half-rising out of the flower-covered seat of the chair. The rifle was now only in the right hand, but with the finger still close to the trigger. His left arm was waving above his head.

The hatred between the two was total. His fury was fanned by the calmness she showed in face of the rifle, and the way she had made him shout and the speed with which he had lost his control. Her loathing for the Republicans, bred into her from the cradle, gave her strength. With something near detachment she weighed the pluses and minuses of rushing him there and then. He was gripping the gun, but it was pointed away from the family. There was no possibility that she could succeed. She felt the children's grip on her arms.

274

If she surged suddenly across the room she would carry them like two anchors halfway with her.

He was not so calm now, and she saw the hint in his eye that he felt the claustrophobia of the room, that the time he had sat in the chair had sapped that sense of initiative and control that were so important to him. She remembered a young Catholic boy who had come round her father's store, idling or loitering or just with nothing to do, and how her father had pulled him up by the front of his collar, and shaken him like an animal to find what he was doing there, on the corner outside the shop. And there had been then the trapped-rodent fear of the youth, of the second-grade boy, who accepted that this would happen, and ran when released, feeling himself lucky not to be thrashed. In the eyes of the man across from her was the hint that he knew he no longer dominated the situation.

When Rennie turned into the cul-de-sac he noted immediately that the garage interior light was not switched on. He stopped his car forty yards from the bottom of the road, and turned off his engine and lights. The bungalow seemed quite normal. The curtains were drawn, but there was a slice of light through the gap where they had been pulled not quite together, from the hall light filtering through the patterned and coloured glass. Everything as it should be.

But no light in the garage. For months now it had been a set routine that an hour or so before he was expected Janet would go into the kitchen and switch on the light in the garage. They kept the garage empty, without the clutter that the neighbours stored there. That way there was no hiding place for an assassin.

The detective sat in the car, watching, allowing himself some minutes just to look at the house and search in front of him in detail for any flaw other than the unlit garage. There was no light upstairs. Perhaps there should have been, perhaps not. Usually Fiona would be having her bath by now, but only darkness there. That was another cautionary factor.

Over the years Howard Rennie had been to enough full-dress police funerals to wonder how it could happen to himself. There was only one way. The epitaphs of the dead men were clear enough. Carelessness. Somewhere, for some time, usually minuscule, they had slackened. Not all, but most, grew overconfident and fell into the convenience of routine, began to believe in their own safety. A few were killed in closely-planned attacks, but most as Rennie knew well presented themselves as casual targets.

This was why he had a light fitted for the garage that should now be on, and why he noticed it was not lit.

His wife was a meticulous and careful person. Not one to make a silly mistake about the garage. It was the dilemma of the life they led that he wondered constantly how far as a family they should take their personal security. On the one hand there could be something drastically wrong that had prevented his wife from switching on a light as agreed. On the other she could be next door for sugar or milk, and stayed to gossip while the children played or watched television.

But it was quite out of character for her to forget.

He eased out of the car, pushing the door to but not engaging the lock, and reached for the PPK Walther in his shoulder holster. He had loaded and checked it before starting his drive home from Castlereagh, but he again looked for the safety-catch mechanism to see it was in the 'on' position. On the balls of his feet he went towards the front gate. The gate was wrought-iron and had never hung well – it rattled and needed a lifting, forcing movement to open it. Rennie instead went to the far side of the gatepost before the hedge thickened, through a gap, past the roses and onto the grass. The run up to the front door was gravel and he kept to the grass, fearful of any noise his feet might make. Though the window showed the light from inside, the gap between the curtains was not enough for him to see through.

There were no voices at the moment he reached the window, just the hymn-singing on the television. Rennie came off the grass and stepped onto the tiled step of the doorway. The Walther was in his right hand, as with the left he found his Yale key and inserted it gently into the opening. Steady now, boy. This is the crucial time. If you're noisy now it's blown – if there's anything to blow. For a moment he felt sheepish at the stupidity of tiptoeing across his own front lawn. Had the neighbours seen? The door opened, just enough to get him inside. To the lounge door. It was off the latch, and the aperture of an inch or so acted as a funnel to the final crescendo of the programme, and the choir's lusty singing. As the sound tailed away he heard his wife speak. 'Great hero, aren't you? With your bloody rifle. Need it to make a man of you . . .'

The voice, shrill and aggressive, was enough to deaden the tiny amount of sound Rennie made as he leaned into the door, and the man in his chair was aware of nothing till the door started swinging on its hinges towards him.

Downs saw the door moving long before the woman and her children.

His body stiffened as he fought to take hold of himself, and for concentration after seeing his control debilitated long before by the argument across the room. He was still raising his rifle into the fire position when Rennie came in, low and fast, to hit the carpet and roll in one continuous action towards the heavy armchair between the fireplace and the window.

The movement was too fast for Billy Downs, who fired three times into the space by the door before checking to realize that the policeman was no longer there. He struggled up from the sitting position in the deep soft armchair, flooded with the sudden panic that he had fired and missed, and didn't know where his target was.

The metallic click of Rennie's safety catch, and the single shot that howled by his ear and into the French windows behind, located the target.

Rennie was not a marksman. He had been on pistol-shooting courses, most of which simulated a street situation. Only once they'd practised storming a room. When you go in, they'd said, dive and roll as soon as you hit the floor, and keep rolling till you find cover. You're difficult to hit while you're moving. The first shot came as he balanced momentarily on his left side, his right arm free to fire in the general direction of the dark shape across the carpet. But his momentum carried him on till he cannoned into the solid bulk of the big chair. He was on his right side, the Walther driving into the softness of his thigh when he realized his impetus had wedged him between the wall and the chair. He twisted his head, seeing for the first time with agonizing clarity the man, his wife and the children, as he struggled helplessly to swivel his body round. His survival depended on that movement.

The rifle was against Downs's shoulder now, eye down the barrel, not bothering with the complicated sight device, just using the barrel to give him a line. He poised himself to fire. Wait for it, you bastard copper, wait for it, now. The triumph of the mission was there now, the bloody slug of the copper on the deck, soft, fat and vulnerable. And dead.

Rennie was screaming. 'No, no. Keep away.'

For the two children the room had disintegrated in speed and noise. When Fiona saw her father some four seconds after he had come through the door she fled from the sofa across the middle of the room towards him.

It was the moment that the man had chosen to fire.

Fractionally his vision, misted and unclear, of the man that he had come to kill was blocked by the chequered dress and the long golden hair.

He hesitated. Staring at the body feverishly trying to get the child behind it and away. It was the time to shoot, a perfect target. Still he hesitated.

He saw the child with pin-point clarity, as sharp as the mummified kids back in the street in London. Not part of the bloody war. He couldn't see the face of the girl as she writhed closer to her father, only the brightness of her dress, the freshness of the white socks, the pink health of the moving skin on the small legs. Couldn't destroy it. Rennie was struggling to pull the child under him to protect her. Downs could see that, and when he'd done so the big policeman would be free to fire himself. Downs knew that. It had no effect. Not shoot a child, no way he could do it. He felt himself drifting away from the reality of the room, concentrating now on his wife. Kids at home, not as clean, scrubbed as these, but the same. If his wife knew he'd slaughtered a small one . . . He saw the slight body fade under the shape of the detective, and the other man's firing arm come up to aim.

Behind the man were the French windows and the light framework of wood. He spun and dived at the centre of one of the glass panels. The wall of wood and glass squares gave way. Rennie, the child spread-eagled under him, emptied the pistol in the direction of the window.

It was the fifth or sixth shot that caught Downs in the muscle of the left arm, just above the elbow. The impact heaved him forward through the obstacle of wood and glass splinters and across the neat patio towards the well-cut back lawn.

The pain was searing hot as Downs ran across the lawn. At the bottom, among the vegetables still in the ground, he crooked the rifle under his injured arm and with his right levered himself over the fence and into a cut-through lane.

Struggling for breath he ran down the lane and then across a field to get to the road where the car was parked. Pushing him forward was the fear of capture, and the knowledge that the failed shooting would bring massive retaliation down on him. Like the fox discovered at work in the chicken coop who flees empty-handed, the sense of survival dominated. The experience in the house, coupled with the exhaustion of the running and the pain in his arm combined to create a confusion of images all returning to the looming blond head of the child thrust into his line of fire as the detective lay on the ground. It merged with the memory of the muted stunned children in London as he fired at their father. Again and again, though, as with a film loop, came the face of the child across the room, throwing herself at her prone father. And after that, as he neared the car, was the knowledge that if he had fired he would have killed the policeman. He might have hit the child, that was the area of doubt: he would have killed the policeman, that was certainty. He had hesitated, and through his hesitation his target was alive. It was weakness, and he had thought himself above that.

The young driver was asleep when he felt his shoulder shaken violently and above him the frantic and blood-etched face of the man.

'Come on. Get the fucking thing moving. Don't hang about. Get it out of this bloody place.'

'Aren't you going to do something about that—?' the youth pointed to the still-assembled Armalite, but cut off when he saw the blood on the arm that was holding the rifle.

'Just get moving. Mind your own bloody business and drive.'

The boy surged the car forward and out onto the road in the direction of Andersonstown.

'Did it go OK?' he asked.

Chapter Sixteen

The Belfast Brigade still met in a semi-detached corporation house in the centre of the conglomeration of avenues, crescents, walks and terraces that make up the huge housing estate of Andersonstown. It was very different country to the Falls and the Ardoyne. Landscaped roads, and flanking them a jigsaw of neat red-brick homes. Ostensibly the war had not come here with the same force as in the older battlegrounds closer to the city centre, but such an impression would be false. This was the Provo redoubt, where the Brigade officers and top bomb-makers had their hideouts, where the master snipers lay up between operations, where five thousand people voted for a Provisional supporter in a Westminster election. Cups of tea were rare for the troops here, and it was the tough and experienced battalions who were asked to hold the ring with the most dedicated and intransigent of the enemy.

The particular house where the Brigade met had been chosen with care. It had been noticed that the combination of a twist in the road and a slight lip shielded both the front and rear doors of the house from the army camp some three hundred yards away.

The house could be approached from the rear with virtual impunity.

The Brigade commanders were key figures in the campaign in the main urban area of Northern Ireland. Some, like Joe Cahill and Seamus Twomey, had become household names round the world, famous as the men who had converted the guerrilla wars of South East Asia and the Middle East and Latin America into West European terms. Promotion had exposed younger men to the job, none of them any the less hardliners for their youth ... Adams, Bell, Convery. All had learned assiduously the arts of concealment and disguise. Their capture called for rounds of drinks and celebration toasts in the mess of the army unit concerned, and articles in the national press maintaining that the Provos were about to fold up. But within a week of the one-time commander being carried off to Long Kesh so another young man moved forward into the scene to take over. During their reign in office, however short, they would set the tone of the administration. One would favour car bombs, another would limit attacks only to military and police targets, or direct operations towards spectaculars such as big fires, major shoot-outs and prison escapes.

Each left his imprint on the situation, and all went into the mythology of the movement. The one common factor was their ability to move, almost at will, round the rambling Andersonstown estate. Their names were well known to the troops, but their faces were blurs taken for the most part from out-of-date photographs. One had ordered his wife to destroy all family pictures that included him, and given all his briefings from behind curtains and drapes, so that under the rigours of cross-examination his lieutenants would not be able to give an accurate description of him. The most famous of all had sufficient mastery of impersonation to be able to win an apology for inconvenience from a young officer who had led a search party through the house where the Brigade commander was giving an interview to a reporter from a London Sunday.

To a portion of the community their names provoked unchecked admiration, while to those less well disposed they sowed an atmosphere of fear. There were enough youths with 'kneecap jobs' and daubed slogans of 'Touts will be shot dead' for the message not to have to be repeated that often.

That there were a few prepared to risk the automatic hooding and assassination was a constant source of surprise to the army intelligence officers. Money was mostly the reason that men would whisper a message into a telephone booth, but not even then big sums. There was seldom the wish to rid the community of the Provisionals . . . Men who felt that way stayed silent, kept their peace, and went about their lives. It was because the Brigade commander and his principal lieutenants could never be totally certain of the loyalty of the men and women who lived in Andersonstown that they delayed their meeting till midnight, though their arrival at the house had been staggered over the previous seventy minutes.

None was armed. All were of sufficient importance to face sentences of up to a dozen years if caught in possession of a firearm. If arrested without a specific criminal offence provable against them they could only be detained in the Kesh – with the constant likelihood of amnesties.

They took over a back bedroom while below the lady of the house made them a pot of tea. She took it up the stairs on a tray with beakers and milk and sugar. They had stopped talking when she came in and said nothing till she had placed the tray on the flat top of a clothes chest, and turned to the door.

'Thanks, mam,' the Brigade commander spoke, the others nodding and murmuring in agreement. She was away down the stairs to busy herself with her sewing and late-night television. When that was over she would sleep in her chair, waiting for the last man to leave the house to tell her the talking was over. The woman asked no questions and received no explanations other than the obvious one that the positioning of the house made it necessary that the men should use it.

There were six men in the room when the meeting started. The Brigade commander sat on the bed with two others, and one more stood. Frank and Seamus Duffryn were on the wooden chairs that, apart from the bed and the chest, represented the only furniture in the room. The present commander had been in office more than six months, and his general features were better known than was common. He scorned the flamboyance of masks. From the pocket of his dark anorak he brought a small transistor radio of the sort with a corded loop to be slipped over the wrist so that he could walk along the pavement with it pressed to his ear. This was how he kept abreast of the activities of the ASUs, the Active Service Units.

The crucial listening times of the day for him were 7.50 a.m., the 12.55 lunchtime summary, and then five to midnight. Each day the BBC's Northern Ireland news listed with minute detail the successes and failures of his men. Shootings, hijackings, blast bombs, arms finds, stone-throwing incidents, all were listed and chronicled for him. The lead story that night was of the shooting at a policeman's house in Dunmurry.

The men in the room listened absorbed to the firm English accent of the announcer.

The gunman had apparently held Mrs Rennie and her two children at gunpoint in their house for some hours while he waited for her husband to return from duty. A police spokesman said that when Mr Rennie entered the living room of his home the gunman fired at him. Mr Rennie dived for shelter behind an armchair just as his younger daughter ran towards him. It seems the child ran into the field of fire of the terrorist, who then stopped shooting and ran from the house. Mr Rennie told detectives that when the girl moved he thought she was going to be killed as the gunman was on the point of firing at him. The family are said to be suffering from shock and are staying the night with friends.

In the Shantallow district of Londonderry a blast bomb slightly wounded . . .

The commander switched off the set.

'That's not like bloody Downs from the Ardoyne. Not like him to lose his nerve. Why should he do that?'

'Stupid bastard. We needed Rennie killed. Put a lot of planning in and a deal of work to have him rubbed. Then it's screwed. Could be they're just feeding us this crap.' It was the Brigade quartermaster who came in.

'Doesn't sound like that. Sounds like Downs just threw it. Hardly going to fool us, are they? The bugger Rennie, he's alive or he's dead. We sent for him to be killed, he's not. So that means it's failure, can't be any other answer. What matters is that our man couldn't finish it.'

He pondered on the decision he was about to take as the other men waited for him. He alone knew of the link between Danby in London and the man Downs from the Ardoyne. Later perhaps he would include the others in the knowledge, he decided, but not now. At this stage, he felt the fewer the better. Some of the commanders ran the office by committee, but not the man who now spoke again.

'On from there. What about the man they've put in? What do we have?'

'I think it's watertight.' Frank had taken the cue and come in. Frank had been with the Provisionals since the split with the Officials, the 'Stickies' as they called them, but this was the first time he had been in such élite company. It slightly unnerved him. 'The girl he was laying spilt it all. It's incredible, what he told her. She was saying that he says to her that he was sent over to get the man that shot Danby in London. She told him about the girl, the one that was picked up and taken to Springfield, the one that hanged herself. It was because he shopped her that she was taken in. She says she challenged him about it yesterday afternoon. He admitted it.'

The Brigade intelligence officer was sitting on the bed beside the commander. Hard face, tight pencil lips, and darting, pig-like eyes.

'What's his name, the Englishman?'

287

'The name he's using is Harry McEvoy. I doubt if it's real or—'

"Course it isn't. Doesn't matter that. They must be a bit touched up then over there, if they send a man over on his own, to find us just like that.'

Duffryn spoke.

'But it all fits with what we had from the hotel. The army man and the RUC. The bit we had about them putting a man in and then not telling the brass. We thought we'd caught the buggers griping about it. It has to be some nonsense drawn up by one of them bastards sat behind a desk in London, in the Ministry.'

Duffryn was little more than a name to the commander. He looked at him with interest.

'You had a line on the man first, right? Through his accent? Where is he now? What's covering him?'

'He's at the guest house, where he has his lodgings. It's called "Delrosa", run by Mrs Duncan, off the Broadway. She's all right. He's there in a back room that he rents. The front and back are watched at the moment and the lads have been told in the last hour or so that if he goes out he's to be tailed. But they must stay right back.'

'And the girl you've talked to, won't she warn him?'

'We told her not to. I think she understood. She won't do anything,' Frank said.

The commander lit his fourth cigarette in less than half an hour, pulled at it, forcing the smoke down into his throat.

'I think we want him before we hood him. We would like to talk to him for a bit first. Pick him up and bring him in for a talk. Does he work?'

'In a scrap yard. He leaves to walk there about

eight, just a few minutes after perhaps.'

'Take him when he's walking. On the main road, get him into a car and take him up the Whiterock, into the Crescent, the house there we've used. I don't want him killed unless it's that or he's away. Remember that, I want him chatted with.'

For Frank and Seamus it seemed the end of their part in the evening. They rose out of the chairs, but were waved down by the commander.

'Where's Downs now?'

The Brigade quartermaster said, 'The message came through just before I left to come here. The wound he got, it's a light one, in the arm. Flesh. It's being fixed up now by the quack in the Murph. He's OK, but he hasn't gone home yet. The quack will want to keep an eye on him for the next few hours.'

The Brigade commander talked to no-one in particular.

'What do they say when a driver's been in a crash? A lorry driver, bus, heavy truck? That sort of thing. What do they say? Send him straight back out again. Don't hang about fidgeting and mumbling about it. Get stuck in again. Downs can go on this one. His nerve wasn't too good last night. He'll need this to get him back into scratch again. He'll want to retrieve himself a bit. Get him here in an hour. Downs can finish him after the talking to.'

It amused him: the fox turning back on the hound.

For Frank and Seamus the briefing was finished. They went out through the back of the house to where a car was parked some three hundred yards away, keys in the dash. Frank would drive on to the doctor and drop Seamus near his home.

Seamus Duffryn was frightened for the first time since he had become involved with the movement. He'd been present three months earlier at an interrogation. A kid from up in Lenadoon. The charge was that he had betrayed colleagues in the movement to the military. The muffled screaming of the youth was still in his ears, bouncing and ricocheting about. They'd burned his naked stomach with cigarette ends while he was strapped in a chair, with a blanket over his head folded several times to deaden the noise. He'd screamed each time the glowing ash met his skin, from a deep animal desperation and not with hope of release. Seamus Duffryn had become involved that night, and would become involved again tomorrow. The paper stuff he did, that was unimportant. This is when it mattered and you were either in the movement or you were out of it. There had been an awful, shaming thrill through his entire body when he saw the light grey material of the boy's trousers turn to heavy charcoal. As the urine ran down the kid's leg there'd been the steam rising through the trousers, and the hood had gone on, and the gun had been cocked. At the moment they shot him the kid was still screaming but uncontrolled.

If McEvoy was British army, how would he take it? Duffryn wondered. That was a nothing from Lenadoon. McEvoy would be different. How would he stand up to their interrogation and the ritual end?

He would find out by tomorrow night. He hurried on his way through the night to his home and his mother.

After he'd made his phone call to London Harry had spent the rest of the day in his room. Before dark he gazed mindlessly into the abstract of roofs and walls that was the view from his window. He had not gone down to Sunday high tea, and to Mrs Duncan's enquiries only replied that he thought he had something of a chill coming on. He was going to have an early night, he shouted through the door. She had wanted to bring him a hot drink in his room, but through the closed door he managed to persuade her that there was no need.

He wanted to be alone, shutting out the perpetual tension of moving in company and living the falsehood that had been planned for him. That girl. It had upset him. Created imbalance in the delicate poise he had taken up. Blown by a silly girl who couldn't stop talking. Up on a mountain, wind and rain, like some cigarette advertisement, and he'd chucked the whole operation. Ridiculous and, worse, so bloody unprofessional. He brooded away the hours. He'd put faith down on the line of a girl whose address he didn't even know. What in Christ's name would they be thinking in London when he put the request in for the special treatment for Harry's bit of tail? Go raving mad, wouldn't they? And reckon he'd twisted. No way they wouldn't. And they'd want to get him out.

He'd heard all the radio broadcasts, searching for the formula announcement that would end it all. Arrest . . . Man wanted for questioning . . . London murder . . . Big operation . . . Tip off . . . Appear in court. That would be the jargon. There had been nothing.

He had steeled himself to what he would do if he heard of the capture of the man. He'd be out of the front door, straight out, with no farewells or packing of luggage, on to the Falls, and turn right along the main road, and then right again before the hospital and on down to the Broadway barracks, and in through the front door . . . But without the news he couldn't end it all. He had to stay, finish the job. No arrest and it was all a failure, abject and complete. Not worth going back for, just to report how it all got boobed. Didn't really matter what Davidson said. No arrest, no return.

But where was the bloody army? Why wasn't it all wrapped up? Big enough, weren't they? Got enough men, and guns, and trucks. He's out there just waiting for you to go and get him. The National bulletins traced their way round the news; there was nothing from Northern Ireland.

The frustration mounted in Harry, welling up against his reason and his training. How much information had he pushed at them in London over the last two, three weeks? How much did they *want*? All sewn up, it should be, cut and dried, taped and parcelled – and now more delay. Through Josephine, streak of bloody luck there, about as much information had come out as he was ever likely to get his hands on. The long-term adrenalin was fading . . . he wanted out . . . he wanted it over . . . but when it was finished.

As the dusk came he unwrapped the Smith & Wesson. After locking the door he took the weapon to pieces and laid it out on a handkerchief on the bed. With a second, dirtied handkerchief from his pocket he cleaned the firing mechanism, then reassembled the gun. He would take it with him next morning to the yard. Put it in the bag where the sandwich box went. It was a sort of therapy, the gun, the instant pick-me-up. It had gone wrong. Nothing on the radio when there should have been. The girl, that was where it had gone wrong, with that bloody girl.

Lovely face, lovely body, lovely girl, but that was where it all loused up. Nothing else, that's the only point where it's gone wrong, but that's enough. Gossip, don't they, and she won't keep her mouth shut any more than the rest of them. Like she talked about Theresa, so she'll talk about me. A lonely man in a backroom bedsitter. The gun was insurance, the disaster was less distinct.

When he went to bed he lay a long time in the dark of the room thinking about Germany, the family, home and the people with whom he worked. The other officers, easy and relaxed, none of them knowing where Harry was, and few caring. He envied them, yet felt his dislike of that easy way of life. His distrust of the others not committed to the front, as he was now, was all-consuming. It was only rarely that he turned his mind to his wife and the children. It took him time, and with difficulty he re-created them and home on the NATO base. The chasm between their environment and Harry's was too difficult for him to bridge. Too tired, too exhausted.

His final thought was salvation and made sleep possible. Of course the man was in custody, but they'd be questioning him. It would take thirty-six hours at least. They wouldn't rush it, they'd want to get it right. Tomorrow evening they would be announcing it, and then home, and out of the hole; another forty-eight hours perhaps, and then out.

In the early hours of that Monday morning, while Harry alternately dozed and dreamed in his bed, and while the Brigade nucleus sat up in Andersonstown waiting for Downs to come, Davidson in the Covent

Garden office was scanning the first London editions of the papers.

Both *The Times* and the *Guardian* carried reports from Northern Ireland that the Provisional IRA were claiming that British intelligence had launched a special agent into the Catholic areas, and that people in those areas had been warned to be especially vigilant. Both the writers under whose bylines the stories appeared emphasized that, whether true or false, the claim would have the effect of further reducing the minimal trust between the people of the minority areas, the front-line housing estates of the city and the security forces. There was much other news competing for space – on the diplomatic front, the state of the economy, and the general 'human interest claptrap' that Davidson raged about. The Belfast copy was not prominently displayed, but to the man propped up on his camp bed it presented a shattering blow. He lay deep in newsprint and pondered his telephone, wondering whether there were calls he should make, anything he could usefully do.

Those bungling idiots had still failed to pick up the chap Downs and the girl Josephine. Near a day to get them, and nothing to show for it. He was astonished, too long after the war, too long after the organization had run down, too many civilians who'd never been up the sharp end. Without the arrest the scheme of which he was an integral part would collapse, and at a rate of knots. In all conscience he could not ring that man Frost again, supercilious bastard, and once more expose himself to that sarcasm. On the wall by the door the clock showed after two. For a moment he comforted himself that Harry might see the report for himself and do a bunk on his own.

No, that wouldn't fit, scrap men don't take *The Times* or the *Guardian*, that wouldn't match the cover.

Davidson tried to shut the problem out of his mind, and closed his eyes. He fumbled unseeing above him till his fingers caught at the string that hung down from the light switch. By the time he drifted into sleep he had worked out his immediate future. The early retirement and professional disgrace, and all because that hoof-footed army couldn't pick one man up. The unfairness of it all.

Frost had gone to bed a little after midnight, and lain half awake expecting the phone to ring, and unwilling to commit himself to the task of sleeping. It had to come, the message that either the man or the girl had been found. The bell's shrill insistence eventually woke him. The army in the Ardoyne reported no known entries or departures at the house in Ypres Avenue. He authorized the unit to move in and search at 05.30 hours.

After that he slept, safe in the knowledge that Monday would be a real day, a real bugger.

The doctor had cleaned the wound. He'd found the damage slight, lessened further as the cotton wool and spirit cleaned away the caked blood that had smeared itself on the upper part of the left arm. A small portion of flesh had been ripped clear close by the smallpox vaccination scar. There was an entry and exit wound, almost together and one, and after he had cleaned it thoroughly the doctor put a light lint dressing over the pale numbed skin.

'You can move yourself around a bit. If you need to, that is. But if possible you should stay still, take it quiet. Go put yourself in the easy chair out the back, and get a rest or something.'

'Is it serious? Will I be left with anything?' asked Downs.

'If you look after it you'll be OK, nothing to worry about, nothing at all. But you must go easy to start with. The only problem is if it gets infected at this early stage. But we'll see that doesn't happen – yes?'

The doctor had been associated with the fringes of the movement since the start of the violence. He asked no questions, and needed few answers. Once every fortnight or so he would hear the square of gravel flick once, twice, against his bedroom window, and in his dressing gown he would open the door to a casualty too sensitive to face ordinary hospital treatment. He had made his attitude clear at least three years earlier, that there was no point them bringing men to him who were already close to death. Take them to the RVH, he'd said. If their wounds were that bad they'd be out of it for months anyway, so better for them to get top medical treatment in the best hospital than the hand-to-mouth service he could provide. He handled a succession of minor gunshot wounds, was able to remove bullets, clean wounds and prevent sepsis setting in.

He was sympathetic to the Provisionals but he gave them no material support other than the late-night *ex officio* surgery. Perhaps if he had been born into the ghetto he would have been one of them, but he came from off the hill, and went to medical school after sixth-form secondary education. Though they had his sympathy he reflected he was a very different person from the hard, wild-eyed men who came to him for treatment.

Downs was very white in the chair, his shirt ripped away on the left side and his coat, holed and bloody, draped over the back. He heard the faint knock at the door down the corridor at the front of the house. There was a whispered dispute in the hall. He heard that distinctly and twisted himself round in the chair to see two men push their way past the doctor and into the room.

There was a tall man, in jeans and a roll-neck sweater. 'The Chief wants you. He's waiting in Andytown now. Said he wants to see you straight away.'

The doctor remonstrated, 'Look at the state he's in. You can see that for yourself. He should be here all night, then go and rest. He's in shock.'

'No chance. He's wanted at a meeting. There'll be no permanent damage if we take him?'

'You're setting back recovery time, and adding to the risk of infection.'

'We'll see you get a look at him tomorrow. Right now we have to go. Come on.'

This last was to Downs. Twice he looked backwards and forwards from the messenger to the doctor, willing the doctor to be more insistent. The doctor didn't meet him, avoiding the pleading in the man's eyes. The tall man and his colleague took hold of Downs under his armpits and gently but decisively lifted him towards the door.

The doctor said, 'You may need these to pull him up

a bit, if there's something that he has to do. Not more than a couple at a time, after that he has to sleep. If he takes them they'll help him for a few hours, then it's doubly important that he rests.'

From the high wall cabinet in the back room he took down a brown pill bottle, half filled with tablets, half with a wad of cotton wool.

They always said they'd come back, but few did. If they needed further treatment they headed south, where they could lie up more easily away from the daily tensions of the perpetual hunt by the military for men on the wanted list. The doctor watched them carry the man to the car and ease him into the back, propped up against the arm-rest in the centre of the seat. He wagered himself the pills would be in use before lunchtime.

The drive between the doctor's house and the meeting place in Andersonstown took twenty minutes. They helped the wounded man out of the car and in through the back entrance the way the night's other visitors had come. Irritably he shrugged them off once he was inside the scullery, and independently followed their instructions to go up the stairs and in through the second door on the left of the landing.

Only the Brigade commander had remained to see him.

'How are you, Billy? Have they fixed you up all right?'

'Not so bad. It's only in the flesh. Not much more than a graze, the thing went straight on through. It's bandaged up now and the doc says it's clean.'

'I heard a bit about it on the radio. Said you didn't get a shot into the bastard, you didn't hit him. Said his brat got in the way and you didn't fire. Is that right?'

'It's not as simple as that.' Oh Christ, not an inquest now. Not why, wherefore, how and when at this time of night. 'I fired once and missed, then when I had a clear shot at him the kid came right across. She was right in front of his body and his head. I couldn't see him so I didn't fire.'

The Brigade commander was still smoking, in front of him the clear glass ashtray mounted with a score of filtered ends steeped in the grey powder he flicked continuously into the bowl. The debris was left in a circle round the ashtray where it balanced on the blanket over the bed.

'If you'd just fired, child and all . . . then you would have got him, yes? If you'd just gone right on through with it Rennie would be dead, right?'

'Is that what they said on the radio?' Downs was peeved by the reception, not used to being challenged and questioned. 'Is that what Rennie is saying, on the radio? If I had fired through the kid then I would have killed him?'

Who did this bugger think he was, thought Downs. When was this miserable sod out with an ASU? When did he expose himself? All right for those who give orders and send kids out to carry bombs into tuppenny-ha'penny supermarkets. Get out on the streets at night, know the silence of waiting, the terrible noise of action, feel a nine-millimetre slug hit you. Then come quizzing me. Anger rose in him, but not sufficient for him to shout, to release him from the discipline inculcated into him. Can't shout at the Brigade commander. That's mutiny.

'I don't know what Rennie is saying,' said the

commander. 'The radio said the child was in the way and that you didn't fire. That's all. There's no criticism of you. I know of no cause for criticism.'

Cunning sod. 'There shouldn't be. Rennie was no soft one. He moved bloody well.'

'One or two people, who don't know the facts as we do, might feel if they only had half the story that Billy Downs had ballsed it up, gone soft on the job. If they hadn't the big picture, and knew it all, they might say Billy Downs was sent on a job, and when one of the copper's brats got in the way that then he held his fire.' Downs didn't really know the commander, he was from a different part of the city. They had had no real dealings before, but rank separated them, and dictated that he must let him have his say. 'These people, they might recall that when we shot Sean Russell, of the UDR, in New Barnsley, that he had his kids draped all over him. Now two of them were wounded, but Russell was still shot dead. The order had been to shoot him. Now we all know that it wouldn't be fair to put your escapade tonight in the same category. And we know that your nerve is as good as ever. That you are one of the top soldiers we have. We know that, don't we, Billy?'

'You know it's balls,' said Downs. 'I'm not soft. My nerve hasn't gone. We're not fighting five-year-olds. Is that what you're saying, that we kill wee girls? Are you saying that I should have fired straight through the girl? Is that what you think I ought to have done?'

'Don't get ratty, Billy. It's just we have to be careful that people who don't know the circumstances might think that. They might point out that getting you that close to Rennie took a deal of time, and that then the

300

front runner botched the whole bloody thing . . . because a kiddie got in the way. That's nonsense, Billy.' The voice droned on, repetition of failure dragging itself through Downs. He had to sleep, to rest, to escape from this room with this boring and nagging whore of a man.

'We know it's not true, Billy. We know there was a good reason for you not to shoot. We know you couldn't see the target. We know Rennie wasn't straightforward. I don't know how many other people feel the same way. But that's enough of that. Nobody will have a leg to stand on by tomorrow night. Right, Billy? We have a little job tomorrow, and by the time that's done they'll be silenced.'

Downs looked away, broken by the twisting of the screw. Self-doubt rampant. The commander crushed the ego out of him.

'I'm the only one of Brigade group that knows about London. We've kept it tight for your protection. It's worked pretty well . . . up to now. There's a difficulty come up. The Brits have put a man in to find you. An agent. McEvoy. Harry McEvoy. Lodging down in Broadway. There's a split in their top ranks about him. We think London wanted him but Lisburn didn't.'

He let it sink in, watched the colour return to the man's face, watched the fear come back to his eyes and saw the hands begin to clasp and unclasp.

'His job, the agent's job, is to find you. Perhaps to kill you, perhaps to take you in, or just tell them where to go. We fancy he wants to kill you. He's been near to you already. He tipped the troops that picked up the girl that hanged herself. We think she did that rather than tell about you. Rennie was the one that questioned her.

301

He chatted to that girl till she was ready to hang herself. You couldn't kill him when his brat jumped in the way. You had no cause to be soft with Rennie. You'll have a chance to let people know what you're made of, Billy. Tomorrow we're going to lift this fellow that's come for you, and we'll talk to him, then we'll hood him. That's where you come in. You'll shoot him, like you shot Danby, like you should have shot Rennie.'

Downs felt faint now, exhausted by the sarcasm of the top man. He nodded, sweat rising from his crotch across his body.

'When it's over we'll send you down to Donegal. Sleep it all off, and get fit again. Tonight you'll stay in Andersonstown. They'll pick you up at six-fifteen. They'll have the guns when they meet you. This will sort it out, I think. Be just the right answer to those who say that Billy Downs has gone soft.'

He wanted out, and this was the chance. They were showing him the way. The way to do it properly, not so as you were looking over your shoulder for half a lifetime, and running. The official way, that was how it was done. One more day, one more job. Then out. Leave it to the cowboys. The heroes who didn't hold their fire, who shot wee kids. Squeeze the trigger right through the scream of a five-year-old. Was that Pearse's revolution, or Connolly's or Plunkett's? Was it, hell. Leave it to the cowboys after one more day.

Chapter Seventeen

The long night was coming to its close when B Company swarmed into Ypres Avenue. The column of armoured cars had split up some hundreds of yards from the street, and guided by co-ordinated radio messages had arrived at each end of the row of bleak terraced houses simultaneously. The first troops out sprinted down the back entrances behind the houses, taking up positions every fifteen yards or so of the debris-strewn pathways. From the tops of the Land-Rovers searchlights played across the fronts of the houses as the noise and banging in the street brought the upstairs lights flickering on.

The major who commanded the company had received only a short briefing. He had been told the man they were looking for was named Billy Downs, the address of his house, and that he was expected to search several houses. He was thirty-three years old, on his fourth tour to Northern Ireland, and as a company commander in South Armagh on his last visit had witnessed four of his men killed in a culvert bomb explosion. His hatred of the Provisionals was deep-rooted and lasting. Unlike some of his brother officers who respected the expertise of the opposition he felt only consuming contempt.

What Downs was wanted for he hadn't been told, nor what his status was in the IRA. He'd only guessed the reason for the raid when they had unpinned the picture from the guardroom wall and given it to him. It was the photokit that had gone up five weeks earlier after the London shooting and remained top of the soldiers' priority list. The intelligence officer down from Lisburn noticed the flash of recognition spread across his face as he looked down at the picture.

Once the street was sealed there was time to work carefully and slowly along the road. No. 41 was the third house they came to. The soldiers banged on the door with their rifle butts. The few who had seen the picture of the man they wanted were hanging on the moment of anticipation, wondering who would come and open the door.

From upstairs came the noise of crying, steadily increasing to screaming pitch as the family woke to the battering at the wooden panels. Downs's wife came to the door, thin and frail in her nightdress and cotton dressing gown. A tiny figure became silhouetted against the light from the top of the stairs when she drew back the bolts, turned the key and stood against the soldiers. The troops in the search party pushed past her, huge in their boots and helmets and flak jackets. They raced up the stairs, equipment catching and bouncing off the banisters. A lieutenant and two sergeants. All had seen the picture, all knew what they were there for. The officer, his Browning pistol cocked and fastened to his body by a lanyard, swung his left shoulder into the front bedroom door, and bullocked his way to the window. The man behind switched on the light, covering the bed with his automatic rifle.

Two faces peered back at the intruders. Saucer-eyed, mouths open, and motionless. The troops patted the bodies of the children and pressed down the bedclothes round them, isolating the little humps they made with the blankets. They looked under the bed and in the wardrobe. There were no other hiding places in the room.

They had come in hard and fast, and now they stopped, halted by the anticlimax of the moment.

The lieutenant went to the top of the stairs and shouted down.

'Not here, sir.'

'Wait there, I'll come up.'

The major came in and looked slowly round the room.

'Right, not here now. But he has been, or she's a dirty little bitch round the house. There, his pants, vest, socks. I wouldn't imagine they lie round the house too long.'

By the window was the crumpled pile of dirty clothes underneath the chair that Downs used to hang his coat and trousers on at night.

'Get her up here,' said the major. 'And get the floorboard chaps. He's been here pretty recently. May still be in the house. If he's about I want him found, wherever he is, roof, basement if there is one, wherever.'

She came into the room, her two younger children hanging like monkeys over her shoulders, thumbs in mouths. Like their mother they were white-faced, and shivering in the cold away from their bedclothes.

'We were wondering where we might find your husband, Mrs Downs.'

'He's not here. You've poked your bloody noses in, and you can see that. Now get out of here.'

'His clothes are here, Mrs Downs, you and I can both see that. I wouldn't expect a nice girl like you to leave his dirty pants lying on the floor that many days.'

'Don't be bloody clever with me,' she snarled back at him. 'He's not here, and you can see that, now get your soldiers out of here.'

'The problem, Mrs Downs, is that we think your husband could still be here. That would be the explanation for his clothes being on the floor. I'm afraid we're going to have to search round a bit. We'll cause as little disruption as possible. I assure you of that.'

'Big heroes, aren't you, when you have your tanks and guns. Big and bloody brave.'

The soldier with the crowbar mouthed an apology as he came past her. He flipped up a corner of the thread-worn carpet and with a rending scrape pulled up the board at the end of the room. In four separate places he took the planks up before disappearing to his hips down the holes he had made. The major and his soldiers waited above for him to emerge with his torch for the last time and announce with an air of professional disappointment that the floor space was clear. Using ladders, they went up into the loft, shaking the beams above the major and the man's wife, and swinging the light fitting.

'Nothing up there either, sir.'

The ground floor was of stone and tile, so that stayed put, while the expert banged on the walls with his hammer in search of cavities. The coal bunker out in the yard was cleared out, the wooden framework under the sink taken down.

'It's clean, sir.'

That was the cue for her to return to the attack.

'Are you through now, you bastards? All these men and one little house, and one wee girl alone with her kids, and it takes all of you and your bloody guns and Saracens—'

'You know why we want him?' The major lashed out. 'You know what he did? We'll go on till we get him. If we have to rip this house to pieces each week till we get him, we'll do that. Doesn't he tell you where he's going at night? Doesn't he tell you what he did last month? Try asking him one day.'

He strode out through the house, followed by his search team. It was three minutes after six o'clock. Failure and frustration was how the majority of these raids ended. He knew that, and he'd never lost his temper before, never gone overboard as he'd done with the woman in No. 41. He comforted himself on two points. It needed saying; and the intelligence officer who had tagged along hadn't heard it.

Once the army had gone a clutch of neighbours moved into the house to gather round the woman and commiserate on the damage left behind. None knew of the importance of Billy Downs among the Provisionals and so news of the army outrage at the house would travel fast through the community. Yet those that came to dress the children and help in the clearing up and the making of tea and breakfast noted how subdued was their friend. Cowed by what had happened. That was not the usual way. The familiar reaction was to greet the going of the soldiers with a hail of insults and

307

obscenities at their backs. But not this woman.

Once the friends and neighbours had left her, to get their own families ready for work or school or just dressed and fed, the words of the officer returned to ring in her ears. Quietly she padded about the house, her children in a crocodile procession behind her, checking to see which of her few possessions were damaged or tarnished or moved.

This was the confirmation. God, this was what she had feared. Right back to the first night back home after London, she had been waiting. So much wind this confidence he had, that no-one knew him. Like a rat he was, waiting in a barn with the door shut for the farmer to come in the morning with his gun and his dogs. The big, fresh-faced officer, with the smears on his cheeks, with his suspicion of a moustache and posh accent, who hated her, he had laid down the future. He had mirrored her nightmares and hallucinations while she lay sleepless beside her man. They would come, and come again for him, and keep on till they found him.

Last night he had not slept beside her. On the radio in the back room she heard the early news. A policeman shot at . . . an intruder hit . . . in the middle evening. That was the top story. Whoever had been involved should have been home now. Her man was usually home by now, or he would have said something.

Around the passage and stairs and landing of the house she thought of her man. Wounded, maimed, alone in the dawn of the city. What hurt most was that she was so unable to influence events.

News carried across the city. With the efficiency of

tribal tom-toms word passed over the sprawling urban conglomeration that the terraced house in Ypres Avenue had been raided. Less than an hour after the major had walked through the front door and to his armoured Land-Rover Billy Downs would hear of it. Brigade staff had decided that he should know. They felt it could only enhance his motivation for the job at hand.

Harry's alarm clock dragged him from the comfort of his dreaming, and woke him to the blackness of his room. His dreams had been of home, wife and children, makeshift garden behind his quarters, holidays in timber forest chalets, fishing out in the cool before the sun came up, trout barbecued for breakfast. With consciousness came the knowledge of another Monday morning. It was three weeks to the day that he had left the house at Dorking with the view of the hills and vegetable garden. Twenty-one days exactly. 'Must have been out of my mind,' he muttered to the emptiness of the room.

Over the weekend he had thought of what Josephine had said to him. She'd accused him of interfering in something that was basically none of his concern, of causing death when he should have stayed uninvolved. Stupid bitch should have passed the same message to the man who came to London with the Kalashnikov.

He examined his position and its natural courses. He wanted to finish it. End it properly. End it with a shooting, with the man in the picture with his black and white-lined face, dead. That was not emotional, there was no wild spirit of revenge, just that such an ending was the only finite one, otherwise the job was incomplete.

In Aden, good old Aden, it had been so much more simple. British lives at stake, the justification of everything, with the enemy clearly defined – Arabs, gollies. But here, who was the enemy? Why was he the enemy? Did you have to know why to take his life? It churned over and over, unanswered, like pebbles in a coffee machine, grating, ill-fitting and indigestible.

In spite of the fact that Harry came originally from a country town an hour or so's drive from Belfast the army's mould had been the real fashioning influence overreaching his childhood. Like his brother officers in the mess he was still perplexed at the staying power of the opposition. But here he parted company. To the others they were the enemy, to Harry they were still the opposition. You could kill them if it was necessary, or if that was demanded for operational reasons, but they remained the opposition. They didn't have to be the enemy to make them worth killing.

But how did they keep it up? What made them prepared to risk their lives on the streets when they took on the power of a British army infantry section? What led them to sacrifice most of the creature-comforts of life to go on the run? What made them feel the God-given right to take life, and torture a man in front of his family?

They're not heroes. Bloody lunatics, he said to himself as he pulled the sweater over his head. They rejected all the ordinary things that ordinary people search for, and chose to go on against these massive odds. It didn't involve Harry. The man he was searching for was quite straightforward. He was a killer. He was a challenge. Simple and clean. Harry could focus on that.

'A cup of tea, Mr McEvoy?' Mrs Duncan at the door cut short his thoughts. 'What would you be wanting for breakfast? There's the lot if you can manage it. Sausages, bacon, tomatoes, eggs, and I've some soda bread?—'

'Just toast and coffee, thanks. I'll be away down in a moment.'

'That won't get you far. It's a raw day, right enough.'

'Nothing more, thank you, Mrs Duncan. Really, that's all I want. I'll be right down.'

'Please yourself then. Bathroom's clear. Coffee's made, and remember to wrap up well. It's a cold one.'

After he'd shaved there was not much to the dressing. Sweater already on and damp from the soap and flannel, faded jeans, his socks and boots and his anorak. He took the face towel from the rail in the bathroom, brought it back into his room and when he had finished dressing laid it out on the bed. About two feet by one and a half, it was bigger than the one the Smith & Wesson was already wrapped in, and he changed them over, putting the revolver in the new towel.

'Silly bugger,' he thought, 'clean towel just to wrap a gun in.' He needed a towel to disguise the outline of the weapon when it sat in the deep pocket of his anorak on the way to work. But he didn't need a clean towel. That's the army for you: everything clean on a Monday morning. Funny if he got stopped at a roadblock. He thought of that and a whole band of disappointed squaddies having to hand him over. Wouldn't have cried overmuch either. Last night, late, he'd decided to put the gun in his coat, easier access than the food bag slung over his shoulder, and the bag with the sandwiches and flask would be lying about in the rest hut through the day, and God knows who could be rummaging around in there. When the revolver was wrapped it was light and blunt, though still bulky and hard to ignore, bigger than a spectacle case, bigger than twenty cigarettes and the large box of matches that most men carried.

He breezed into the kitchen.

'Morning, Mrs Duncan, all right then?'

'Not so bad, little enough to complain about. You're sure about the toast and coffee?' Disappointment clouded her face when he nodded. Harry had been in the bathroom during the seven o'clock news bulletin, and through the closed door he had heard her radio playing faintly downstairs, loud enough to be aware of it, but too indistinct to hear the actual words.

'Anything on the news, then?'

'Nothing to note, just the usual. It goes on. A policeman chased a man out of his house and shot him. That's his version, anyway, up Dunmurry way, more trouble in the Unionists. Never change their spots, that crowd. They've given nothing to us without it being wrung out—'

Harry laughed. 'They haven't caught the big man yet then, top of the Provos?'

'Well, Mr McEvoy, if they have, they didn't say so, which means they haven't. They'd be trumpeting it if they had, but that's all the news is, the troubles. Makes you wonder what they used to put in before it all started. I can hardly remember. There must have been something else for them to talk about, but they've forgotten it now, right enough.'

'Well, then, no big man in the net—'

'They don't get the real big men, only the shrimps.'

'No, it's just that I read in one of the papers I saw up at the yard that they were mounting an effort to rake in the big fish.'

'They say they're doing that each week, and nothing comes of it.'

Harry had banked a lot on the man being in custody. It was twenty-one hours after the call to London, to Davidson. Couldn't be that difficult to pick the bastard up. Shouldn't be taxing the might of the British army. They must have him, but they weren't saying yet, had to be that way. They wouldn't say yet, too early, of course it was. The explanation was facile but enough to tide him over his breakfast.

It was Monday morning and he was the only guest. Tonight, round teatime, the travellers and the others would be back in the front room. The place then was not quite his own as on Saturdays and Sundays. Lord and master of the household was how he felt over the weekend. Delusions of grandeur.

'Will Josephine be in this afternoon?' He sounded casual, matter-of-fact.

'Should be, Mr McEvoy. Should be here in time to help me with the teas and a bit of tidying up that I haven't got round to. She's back on early shift this week. You wanted to see her?'

Shrewd old goat, thought Harry. Beautiful throw-away, real afterthought.

'I'd said I'd lend her a book,' he lied gracefully.

'She'll be here when you get back. I'll need her today,

313

and all. We're full tonight. It's the way it should be, but work all the same.'

'And money, Mrs Duncan.' It was as much familiarity as was permitted.

'Your sandwiches are there on the sideboard.' She wasn't drawn. 'Bovril as you like them, horrid stuff, and some coffee in the flask. I put a boiled egg in, too, and an apple.'

'Very naughty, Mrs Duncan, you'll make me into an elephant.'

She liked the banter and was still laughing with him as he walked into the hall and to the front door.

'You've got enough clothes on, then? We don't want you with a cold and that.'

'Don't you fuss, Mrs Duncan.'

The Prime Minister liked to start the day with his papers, a cup of tea and the first radio news bulletin. He amused himself by making that first news the commercial one, maintaining to all those who expressed surprise that he was not locked on to the BBC, that he was a capitalist, and as head of a capitalist government he should hear the capitalist-funded station. The radio acted as window dressing to his reading, the spoken version of canned music. He could not do without it, hated silence, but it took an almighty news story to distract his attention from the newspapers. Like all politicians he had a consummate appetite for newsprint, able to take in, extract, cross-reference or ignore the thousands of words that made up his daily diet. Included in the pile that rested on his lap in the middle of the bed were the *Western Mail* and the *Scotsman*. He would have liked the *Belfast News*

Letter, but the printing times and transportation problems across the Irish Sea made it impossible, so he compromised by having the previous afternoon's *Telegraph* sent over. He waded through the politics, diplomatic, economic, pausing fractionally longer on the gossip columns than he would have wanted others to know, and through sport where he delayed no longer than it took him to turn the pages. The pace was enormous, nothing read twice unless it had major impact.

The frown began deep between the overbearing bushiness of the eyebrows. The degree of concentration extended. The mixture written on his stubbly face was of puzzlement and anger.

The Times had put it on page two, and not given it much. Eight paragraphs.

He found the same story in the *Guardian*, a little longer, and above it the resident staff reporter's name. The length of the copy had relatively little importance or significance to the Prime Minister. The content flabbergasted him. He read three, four times that a British agent had been identified by the Provisional IRA, and the population in the ghetto areas alerted so that they might be on their guard against him.

For Christ's sake. Five weeks since Danby was killed. Outcry and outrage over, gone with the memorial service. Whole wretched business faded and, just as well, no leak that Danby himself had asked for his detective to be taken off. And now the prospect of it all back again, supercharged, and with what drifting out? Heaven only knows. With a surge he swept the bedclothes from him and leaned across the bed. He never had been able to make a telephone call lying

315

on his side. He slung the dressing gown over his shoulders and sat on the edge of the single bed he had occupied since his wife died, feet dangling, and picked up the telephone.

'Morning, Jennifer, first of the day.' Always something friendly to the girls on the switchboard, worked wonders with them. 'Secretary of State for Northern Ireland. Quick as you can, there's a good girl.'

He sat for two-and-a-half minutes, reading other papers but unable to turn his full attention to them till the telephone buzzed angrily in its console.

'The Secretary of State, sir. Seems he's in the air at the moment. Left Northolt about eight minutes ago. He'll be down at Aldergrove in forty-one minutes. He's early this morning because he's going straight down to an industrial estate in Londonderry, opening something. There's a helicopter waiting to lift him down there. That's his immediate programme.'

'Get him to phone me as soon as he reaches Aldergrove. Let them know I'd like it on a secure line.'

He considered calling the Ministry of Defence or Fairbairn in Lisburn, and then dismissed it. Protocol up the spout if he did. If they were to be dropped in a monumental balls-up then the Secretary of State should do some of the lifting, and take a bit of the weight. Time to play things straight down the middle, the Prime Minister reflected.

Across London Davidson was shaving. Wet. With a brush and new blade. He had read his papers again in the daylight. He knew, since he had not been woken from his sleep by the telephone, that in Belfast Billy Downs and the girl were still at large. He could not be certain at this stage to what level of danger Harry was exposed. When he ditched his logical appraisal the only conclusion was that the situation must be slightly worse than critical. He said that out loud; the aide was in the other half of the office and would not hear him. The words rolled off his tongue, giving him that almost sexual pleasure that excitement and tension carry in their wake. He stood there in his trousers, socks and vest, with the bowl of tepid water in front of him . . . all so much like the war. The Albania operation, Cyprus. But how to reconcile that when advanced base headquarters, ABHQ, they used to call it, was in Covent Garden, West One, Central London?

He patted his face, reddened by the sharpness of the blade and the cool water. Putting on his shirt, he dialled Lisburn military direct. When the WRAC operator came on the line he asked for Frost. The intelligence colonel was already in his office.

'Morning, Colonel. I wanted to ring you to find the up-to-date situation. I fancy there'll be various meetings in the morning. People will want to know. I take it there's been no positive news or you would have called me.'

'Right, Mr Davidson.' Had to be the 'Mister', didn't it? Doesn't miss them. Not a chance of twisting it. 'There is no news. We haven't found the girl. We did Downs's home, and the report an hour ago said he wasn't there, but had been a few hours earlier. There's an off-chance he's in trouble. A man of his description attacked a policeman's home late yesterday and botched it up. The policeman thinks he hit him with a single revolver shot as he was escaping. There are one or two blood spots on the escape trail, but we won't get much from them for a bit till the follow-up report is in. It doesn't seem enough to indicate a serious wound. As for your man, well, we're taking out the Andersonstown scrap merchants in about forty minutes. I've nothing else.'

'Are you putting it that there's a good chance Downs was out on this shooting last night, or not?'

'There are similarities, but it's not a positive identification. Hair's not the same as the picture, so the policeman's wife says. She was a long time with him. Face is similar. The policeman himself is not able to be very helpful as he was moving most of the time and getting his gun out and being shot at. He didn't get much of a look. We have the picture you sent us, it's with the unit now that's going to try to round your fellow up.'

'Thank you very much, Colonel.'

'That's all right, Mr Davidson. I'm sure we'll never have the opportunity again of providing a similar service to your organization.'

Davidson put the phone down.

'Stupid, pompous bugger. Bloody man, does he think we're having a picnic at this end?'

He said it with enough ferocity to wake his assistant in the armchair by the door on the other side of the partition. The younger man shrugged himself out of his sleep.

'Any news?'

'Not a bloody dicky bird that matters.'

The men on duty in the intelligence section moved quietly round the room, unwilling to attract Frost's attention. He was slumped ungracefully in his chair, his eyes half closed, half focused on the ceiling. He was a man of method and neatness, following his own individual rule book, but following it closely, and expecting others to ape him. Harry McEvoy violated the rule book. The theory, the preparation and the execution of the McEvoy operation all contravened the requirements of this sort of business. His subordinates had detected the inner anger and knew enough to keep their distance.

Frost could see the weakness in the whole affair. This lunatic fighting between departments and services. Point-scoring at a grand level and at the expense of the man out there on the streets. He was as guilty as any. But the issue had to be settled so there would be no repetition. That was where it was all so amateurish. The Prime Minister and the GOC ... They should have their heads knocked together. But rivalries don't come from a victory march, they don't surface when the show's going well, they're the product of long-drawn-out failure.

The chatter of the teletype machines and the noise of men shuffling round the room, doors opening, muted talk were insufficient to disturb his train of thought.

It's because we're all lashing around, stranded by the tide, looking for the way out when there isn't one, that a damn-fool thing like this gets launched. And after five endless years of it, and the promise of how many more to come, the inevitability that the professionals are going to be cold-shouldered, that the outsiders will want to have their say. Inevitable. And the price we pay for it is having that poor devil McEvoy or whatever his

319

real name is out there on the streets, working for God knows who.

Frost straightened up in his chair. 'Get me some coffee, please. Black, and make sure there's plenty there this morning.' He was tired, exhausted by it all. They all were.

The postcard was lying on the mat, colour side down, when Mary Brown responded to the flap of the letter box in the front door.

'There's a card from Daddy, darlings,' she called into the back of the house where the boys were having their breakfast.

'Not a letter, Mum?' her elder boy shouted back.

'No, just a card. You know how awful your father is about letters.'

There was a market scene on the card. Men in kaffiyehs and futahs staring blankly from the gold market that stood in the middle distance.

'Hope to see you all soon. Still very hot, and not much to do. Love you all, Harry.' That was all there was on the card, written in Biro and in Harry's large hand.

Josephine Laverty was late, and hurried in a frantic mixture of a run and a walk down the Falls to the mill where she worked. She couldn't go fast as the pain still bit into her ribs. She too had heard the early radio news, half expecting in an uninvolved sort of way to hear that Harry McEvoy had been found face down, hooded and dead. It had surprised her that there was no mention of him. This morning she had wondered for a wild moment whether to go to see if he was still at Delrosa, but there was no will power and the emotion he had created was now drained from her.

Perhaps she would go to Mrs Duncan's tonight to help with the teas. Perhaps not, but that could be a later decision. There was now an irrelevance about Harry McEvoy. Forget him. The pillow eavesdropper who had a girl killed. Forget the sod.

With their photographs of Harry the troops from Fort Monagh raided the five scrap yards in Andersonstown. No-one in the operation had been told why they were to pick up the smiling man in the picture who wore his hair shorter than their more general customers. The orders were that if the man was found he was to be taken straight to Battalion headquarters and handed over. Amongst those NCOs who were the foremen of the military factory floor and who knew most of what mattered there was surprise that so many men were occupied in looking for a man whose picture was not on the operations room wall, whose name was completely fresh. They had their regular batch of photographs, top ten for the week, top thirty for the month, four for each day of the week. Made up on little cards and issued to the troops to study before they went out on patrol. But this face had never been among them.

At the scrap yards the employees who had arrived before the troops stood sullenly against the walls of the huts, hands above their heads, as they were searched and then matched with the photograph. From the five locations the initial report was that a blank had been drawn. But the troops would lie up in the yards till nine at least in the hope that the man they wanted would still come – was just late. At the yard where Harry in fact worked there was disbelief when they were shown the picture. Never involved, never talking politics, just an ordinary man, too old to be with the cowboys. The little man who ran the yard looked round the armoured cars, and the soldiers, reckoned Harry must be important and determined to say nothing. He confirmed the picture, that he employed a man called Harry McEvoy, that he had started work recently, that was all. Let them find the rest out for themselves.

'Where does he live?' the lieutenant who led the raid asked him.

'Don't know. He never said. Just down the road somewhere, that's all he said.'

'He must have given some impression where he lived?'

'Nothing.'

'What about his stamps, his insurance?'

The little man looked embarrassed. The answer was clear enough.

The lieutenant was new to Northern Ireland. The man opposite him seemed of substance, a cut above the yobbos, respectable even.

'Look, we need this man rather badly.' He said it quietly, out of earshot of the other men.

'Well, you'll have to wait for him, won't you.'

But time was ticking on its way, and as the soldiers crouched behind the wrecked cars and buses and waited there was no sign of the face in the photograph. Even the little man became worried by Harry's non-arrival. His first reaction had been that it was a case of mistaken identity, but that Harry should be absent at the same time that the military launched this reception led him to suppose that his newest hand was a rather more complex figure than he had believed.

The soldiers radioed in, hung about a few more minutes and drove back, empty-handed, to Fort Monagh.

Chapter Eighteen

The Secretary of State spoke to Downing Street from the
single-storeyed red-brick building that was the RAF
Reception at Aldergrove. They'd offered him a car to
take him to the officers' quarters and the use of the
group captain's phone, but he'd declined. The message
waiting for him was of the sort the Prime Minister
rarely burdened him with, must be important and
should be returned at speed.

It took several minutes for the connection to come
through. The delay came from the need to patch in the
speech distortion apparatus that would safeguard
the security of the call and prevent any casual telephone user listening in on the conversation. When the
instrument rang out in the partitioned office indicating
that the call was ready the service aides discreetly
backed out through the door. The Secretary of State's
men stayed with him.

'Morning, Prime Minister. I'm returning your call.'

'I won't keep you long. I wondered how thoroughly
you'd read your papers this morning. *Guardian*
and *Times*. Provisionals claiming they've identified
an agent of ours, warning the population. All a bit

324

melodramatic but enough to cause anxiety.'

'I haven't seen it, I'm afraid.'

The Prime Minister replied, 'We're a little anxious at this end that it could be the fellow we sent over for Danby. Could be difficult if they nabbed him, and he talked.'

'Trifle awkward, no doubt about that. Well, we'll get the people who run him to move him out right away. Get him back to UK and snappy. That's the simple answer.'

'The problem lies right there,' said the Prime Minister. 'It's a bit incredible, but the chaps controlling him in London cannot contact him. Seems he just calls in when he has something to say.'

The Secretary of State winced. 'Bit unusual that, isn't it? Bit unique. Not standard procedure. What you are saying is that he may not know he's blown if in fact he is. That we may not be hearing too much from him in the future.'

'You're not a million miles away from it.'

'And what do we do . . . ? Sorry, I'll rephrase that one. What do you want done about it?'

'I'm just letting you know the situation. There's not very much we can do about it beyond the obvious. Stand by to catch the cradle.'

'If it comes, it'll be from a fair altitude.' The Secretary of State played a slow smile round his lips at the head of government's discomfiture.

'Could be a bit tricky.' The Prime Minister was sounding old, tired, and a long way away.

'I'm glad it wasn't down to me, this one,' he paused, to let it sink home. 'Still, we'll see what comes out of it. It may be just a kite they're flying. They often do that.

I'll keep a weather eye out for the storm clouds. Goodbye, Prime Minister.'

There were no confidences with his staff as the group left the building and walked to the big Puma helicopter for the ride to Londonderry. He asked his army liaison officer to keep him informed if there should be any assassination victims during the day.

His remark of 'hare-brained scheme at the best of times' was heard only by the Scotland Yard detective, his bodyguard, sitting next to him as he adjusted his safety harness while the rotor blades gathered their impetus.

The ambush was in position.

It was a proven, brutally simple piece of organization. A stolen Ford Escort was parked sixty yards up from Delrosa just before the junction with the Falls Road. The car was empty and unlikely to cause suspicion. The number plates had been changed. Harry would walk along on the opposite side of the pavement and turn into the main road. He would be watched by three men who had placed themselves behind the lace curtains of the house in front of which the car was parked. With Harry safely round the corner the men could come out of the house, start up the car, and cruise up from behind him to surprise their target. It was a fast and effective method and over the years had come to be considered fail-safe. The three men in the room, back from the lace curtains, were Downs, Frank and Duffryn. All were at this stage without their guns, but in the Escort's glove compartment was a Luger, and underneath the driver's seat a folded-down Armalite, placed in position, ready loaded and cocked.

To both Frank and Duffryn this was a novel situation. Neither had ever been entrusted with a mission of such importance before, and the tension they felt was reflected in the frequency with which both of them came forward and tugged at the flimsiness of the curtain to view the other side of the road. They talked quietly in staccato style to each other, avoiding the eyes and attention of Downs, who stayed at the back behind them. Neither Frank nor Duffryn knew the third man's name, only vaguely his reputation as a marksman. That was something both had reflected on overnight to comfort themselves, as the few hours slipped away before the rendezvous.

Since he had been told of the operation Downs had had little to say. He burned up his anger and frustration inside himself till he was as taut as a stretched catapult. The pain of his injury told on him, too, and though that was slightly compensated for by the tablets he had taken he felt weak and, above all, disorganized.

Both Frank and Duffryn looked to the third man for leadership, but he buried himself away from them, not communicating the confidence and expertise they were looking for. He wore a loose overall sweater, with his left arm in a sling underneath it, with the sleeve hanging free at his side. He knew he was not fit enough to get into a fire-fight like that, but for a pick-up and at close range he'd see it through. To back him up he had the strength and fitness of the other two men. He would sit in the front with Duffryn to drive, and Frank in the back with the Englishman for the short ride from Broadway to Whiterock.

Frank said, 'He's late now. He can't be much longer.

He's a big fellow. We'll not miss him. He's the only visitor at the house.'

'How long do we leave him after he's away round the corner?' Duffryn asked. He'd been told the answer three times but kept on asking with the insecurity of a small boy who needs to quiz his teacher in class so that she won't forget his presence.

'Hardly at all,' said Frank. 'Just a few yards. We want to pick him on the bend near the cemetery, so we need him to move about a hundred yards, not much more.'

'Hope the bloody car starts,' Duffryn giggled weakly, and looked at Downs. 'You done this sort of thing before?'

Duffryn saw the pale, pinched, hating face. Sensed the quality of his anger and hostility.

'Yes,' said Downs.

'It works like they plan it, does it? I mean, it all seems so straightforward when you put it on paper and work out a timetable and that. But does it really happen as easily as that?'

'Sometimes. Other times it doesn't.'

'The thing that worries me –' like a bloody tap, drip, drip, drip, thought Downs as Duffryn chattered on – 'is if they have a Pig going by as we jump him. Christ knows what we do then.'

He said the last to himself, as the anxiety built up in him about the calibre of the morose and injured man that he and Frank were depending on for success. Just as Duffryn put it out of his mind, Frank stiffened and edged forward again towards the window.

'He's coming. Here comes the English bastard.'

Duffryn pushed his friend to the side to see for himself. The tall figure in the distance, blurred and in soft focus, closing the wicket gate at the front of Delrosa behind him, that was their enemy. He'd thought about him most of the night, about the killing of him, now he came, walking straight without a sideways glance. Looks as if he owns the place, thought Duffryn.

'Keep back from the window, you stupid buggers,' the man behind them hissed.

Harry was stepping out, aware of his slow start to the morning, and conscious that whatever speed he walked to the yard he would still be late. The combination of Mrs Duncan's chatter and her insistence on the fresh coffee that had percolated interminably had delayed him. He came up the familiar pavement fast, with his sandwiches and flask in the bag bouncing on his shoulder and the weight of the wrapped revolver thudding against his right hip.

He saw the car, one of several parked on the other side of the road. It was small, neat and well kept, but slightly different, something strange . . . the keys left in the ignition. Daft idiot, who leaves keys in his car down the Falls. People didn't leave the keys in the ignition round here unless they'd gone inside for something shorter than a quick crap.

Harry moved on past the car and up to the junction of the side street and the Falls, where the Catholic community came into town, and where the traffic snarl-ups were beginning.

The side of the road that Harry walked on, though, was virtually clear, with just an occasional car speeding past him. He was a punctual man. The army and his aunt's upbringing had disciplined him in this, and his lateness this Monday morning annoyed him. He checked with his left wrist to see how far behind the morning schedule he was, and realized with a suppressed oath that he had left his watch behind . . . Where? . . . Not in his room, not at breakfast . . . in the bathroom after shaving. He was thirty yards into the Falls, the guest house some seventy-five back round the corner. Damn and blast it. Only a hundred yards back to get it. He wavered. And then, a hundred yards back to where he was now. Two hundred yards. Nothing. It's a naked feeling without a watch. Not as bad as leaving glasses behind, or your fly unzipped, but an irritation. Harry swung on his heel and walked back towards Delrosa.

As he turned the corner Duffryn was beside the driver's door of the car, at the handle and in the process of opening it. Frank was already in the back seat, and the man coming out of the house last was halfway between the front door and the car.

For a moment all four men froze.

Harry, mind racing like a flywheel, trying to put a situation and background to the familiarity of the face in front of him.

Where? Where did that face come from? Find it.

It was fractional, the lapse of doubt before the image slotted. The dance, the woman in yellow, the army crashing in, and as the concentration lasted so the face confronting him across the street suffused into the detail of the photokit picture. Outline of cheekbone structure, that matched. More so than when the man had been at the club, the contours of the flesh on the face merged with the painstaking impression built up in London. Perhaps it was the strain Downs had been under these last hours, or the pain from the wound, but the features at last resembled those the old lady had seen in the park, that the girl in the Underground station had stared at as she fought to keep her balance.

The first movement. Harry reached into his anorak pocket, thrust deep with both hands to pull out the pistol. He dragged at the white towelling, and ripped it from the blackness of the gun, tearing a ladder of bright cotton on the foresight. Thirty feet away Duffryn flung himself face down behind the car, his mind clouded by the sight of the gun in the enemy's hand. Frank jack-knifed his body over the front passenger seat to open the glove compartment where the Luger lay, stretching himself over the obstacle of the headrest. Downs bent low, ducking forward towards the back of the car. Out of sight and to the rear right door beyond which his beloved Armalite was resting.

Aimed shots, Harry boy. Don't blaze. Aim and you'll hit the buggers. He shrugged the duffel bag from his shoulder onto the paving stones, and, legs squat and apart, brought the revolver up to the aim position. Knees slightly bent, body weight forward, both arms extended and coming together with the gun at eye level. The classic killing position. Hands and gun as one complete sighting apparatus. Squeeze, don't jerk the trigger. Take it gently. The thumb of the right hand fumbled forward, rested on the safety catch in the 'on' position, and eased it forward.

In the big 'V' of the arms, reaching to the barrel of the revolver, was the contorted shape of Frank, still stretching for the Luger. Harry steadied as the man lurched back into the rear seat with the gun in his hand, and fired his first shot. The left side of the rear window disintegrated, and Frank jolted as the bullet hit him in the throat. The effort of getting at the Luger had denied him a clear look at Harry. Bewilderment was spread over his face as he subsided onto the back seat with a rivulet of crimson flooding down onto the collar of his shirt. Not in itself a fatal shot, but it would become one if Frank did not get immediate hospital treatment. He was out of Harry's sight now. The Englishman stood stock-still, looking for the next target. Come out, you bastards. Show yourselves. Where's the bloody man we want? Which of you has the next gun? Who shoots next? Steady, Harry boy. You're like a big lamp-post up there, you berk, right in the open. Get some cover.

Harry knelt on the pavement.

'Come out with your hands above your heads. Any attempt to escape and I'll shoot.'

Good control, Harry, dominate the buggers.

Downs whispered to Duffryn as they huddled on the reverse side of the car.

'Make a run down the hill. He'll not hit you with a hand gun. But for God's sake run – and now!'

He pulled Duffryn past him and shoved him out into the open and away from the sanctuary of the car. Downs shouted after him, 'Run, you little bastard, and weave . . .'

Duffryn, in deep terror, bolted from the cover. Out of control and conscious only of the empty space around him he sprinted down the street in the direction of Delrosa. His intention was to shift direction from right to left and to change his speed at the same time. The effect was to slow him down and make him the easier target. Harry fired four times. By the time he pulled the trigger for the second time he had sensed that he was after a man who had never faced this type of situation

332

before. He heard Duffryn sob out as he ran, pleading, merging with his shout as the third shot caught him between the shoulder blades. Duffryn cannoned forward into the lamp-post, leant spread-eagled against it for a few seconds, and then slid down to become a shapeless mass at its base. The fourth bullet, unnecessary, jolted into his sluggish body. Duffryn would live; neither of the hitting bullets had found a critical resting place.

Now that he was down and stationary the confusion ebbed, and clarity came to the young intelligence officer. The enemy would kill him. No doubt – certainty. It seemed not to matter. There was hurt but not so much as Duffryn had expected. He was puzzled he could barely picture the face of the Englishman who had shot him. The clothes he could see, and the gun resting between the hands and the kick as it rocked back when Frank was shot. But there had been no face. The gun obscured it. He had not even seen his enemy. He never would now.

The moment that Duffryn had run Downs eased open the front door of the Escort, forced himself upwards into the driving seat and started the engine. The four shots that Harry had fired at the decoy – the hare with the job of distracting him – had given Downs sufficient time to get the car rolling in the direction of the Falls.

Harry swung the revolver round tracking his attention away from the fallen boy to the moving car. He saw Downs's head low over the wheel before it swung lower still, below the dashboard. That was the moment he fired, knowing instinctively as he did so that he was going too high. The bullet struck the angle of the roof of the car, exited and thudded into the wall of the house opposite. Count your shots, they always drilled that. He had done, and he was out, chamber empty, finished, exhausted. Three more cartridges in the picnic bag, down at the bottom below the plastic food box and the coffee flask. Frantically he broke the gun and pushed the used cases out so that they clattered and shone on the pavement. He slid in the three replacements, copper-plated ends and grey snub-nosed tips.

Downs was out in the traffic of the Falls, desperate to avoid the cars round him, but unable to escape from the conformity of the Catholic route into town. As a reflex Harry ran after him, revolver still in hand. He saw cars shy away from him as he came out into the traffic lanes, heard the grind of gears and scraping of brakes as men tried to put space between him and themselves. It was as though he had some plague or disease and could kill by contact. His man was edging away when Harry worked out the equation. Nine cars back was a Cortina Estate, crawling with the others and unwilling to come past the man waving his revolver. Harry ran to the passenger door. It was unlocked. As he looked into the driver's eyes he shouted at him.

'This is loaded. You're to follow that car. The white Escort in front and follow it close. For your own safety don't bugger about. I'm army, but that won't help you if you mess me.'

Donal McKeogh, aged twenty-seven, a plastics salesman living outside Dungannon, forty miles down the motorway, gave a mechanical, numbed response. The car trickled forward, its driver's mind still blank. Harry saw the Escort drawing away.

'Don't mess me, you clever bugger,' he screamed at the face a few inches away, and to reinforce the effect of his intentions fired a single shot through the roof of the car. McKeogh surged forward towards the Springfield Road lights. The message was understood now, and would not need repeating. He might have seen me coming out into the traffic, reckoned Harry, but he's unlikely to have seen which car is following him. Little chance of that. McKeogh swerving through on the inside, crossing the double lines in the centre and drawing angry shouts from other drivers, had closed the gap to five cars by the time they reached the lights.

Two bullets remained in the Smith & Wesson.

It had taken Billy Downs little time to work out where he was going. The failure to kill the Englishman dictated the decision. He was going home. Blown, finished, out.

He was tired. Needing a corner to sleep away the stabbing pains and biting disappointments of the last few hours, he needed quiet, and silence. Away from the guns, and the firing, and the blood. Above all he wanted to get away from the noise of the weapons that blasted out close to his ears, screwing up his guts with tension, then releasing them like an unplugged bladder, flat and winded.

Away from it all, and the only place he could go was home. To his wife. To his children. To his house. To Ypres Avenue. The logic and will power and control that had caused him to be chosen for London were drained from him. No emotion, no sensitivity left. Even the slight bubbling coughs of Frank in the back seat could not disturb him.

Failure. Failure from the man considered so valuable that only the most important work was earmarked for him. Failure from the élitist. More important, failure against the enemy who was working to kill, eliminate, exterminate, execute *him*. The words kept tempo with the throbbing of the arm wound. Christ, how it hurt. A bad, dangerous pain that dug at him, then went, but came again with renewed force, chewing at his strength and resolve.

The Armalite was still in the car, untouched under his seat, but useless now. It had no further part to play. The Armalite days were over, they didn't settle things. It was over. Concluded, done with, half a lifetime ago.

Driving was hard. He had to stretch his left arm to the gear handle every few seconds, and even the movement from the second to third aggravated the injury. He mapped out a route for himself. Down to Divis, then across the top fringe of town to Unity flats, and then on to Carlyle Circus. Could park there, on the roundabout. It was a walk to the Ardoyne then, and the car and Frank would be close to the Mater, their own people's hospital. Frank would be found quickly there, and would get the treatment he needed. There were no roadblocks and he moved with the traffic, Frank too low down to be seen and the bullet holes failing to draw people into involvement.

It was nine minutes to the Circus where the Crumlin and the Antrim Road came together, and where cars could be left unattended. He drove on to the space and stopped the car. To get out he had to lever himself up with his right hand, then he looked behind and into the back. Frank was very white, with much of his blood pooled beside his face on the plastic seating. In his eyes was just enough light to signal recognition.

'Don't worry, Frank boy. You're close to the Mater. You'll be there in five minutes. I'm going to call them. I'm going now, and don't worry. God bless. It's all OK, you'll be safe. A few minutes, that's all.'

Frank could say nothing.

Downs left the engine running and the driver's door open as he ran away from the car. It was enough to ensure that someone would look inside. The broken window would clinch it. The Armalite was still under the driver's seat, and the Luger lay beneath Frank's body. He ran up the Crumlin, Mater hospital on his right, huge and red and cleansed, giving way to the prison. High walls, coils of barbed wire, reinforced stone sentry towers and, dominating it all, the great gatehouse. Downs went on by them, and past the soldiers on guard duty, and the policemen guarding the courthouse opposite with their flak jackets and Stirlings. None spared him a glance as he ran.

The sprint gave way to a jog, then to little more than a stumble as he neared the safety of the Ardoyne at the top of the long hill. The weight of his legs seemed to pin him back as he forced his feet forward, separating himself from the chaos and disaster behind him. His breath came in great sobs and gulps as he struggled to keep up momentum. The only demand he made of himself now was to get to his home, to his wife, and bury himself in her warmth. The Circus and the hospital and the prison were far behind down the road when he reached the iron sheeting that divided Shankill from the Ardoyne, where he had stood the previous afternoon waiting for the lift that took him to Rennie's home. God rot that bastard copper and his bloody children. That was where it had all collapsed. The child in the way, smack in the way, never a clear sight at the copper, only the kid's head. Panting and wrenching for air, he slowed up to walk the last few yards.

They were right. He'd lost his nerve. Billy Downs, the one selected by the Chief of Staff, had slipped it because of a child's head.

And then, this morning . . . Frank with his voice shot out, and the young bugger they'd sent him, down on the pavement, shredded. And you, you clever sod, you told him to run to make room for yourself, and he did, and he bloody bought it.

In the race across the city McKeogh had several times fallen back in the traffic stream, losing completely the sight of the white Escort before spotting it again far to the front manœuvring among the lorries and vans and cars. Then Harry screamed and threatened McKeogh, and the salesman would speed up. He doubted his hijacker was a member of the British army but was undecided whether he was IRA or UVF. That he would be killed if he didn't follow the bellowed instructions, he was certain. As they came out of the town and reached the Circus the Escort was gone. Four major routes come together there, including the Crumlin leading up to the Ardoyne and the Antrim Road running up to the nearer, equally hard-line, New Lodge. New Lodge offered the quicker refuge, and Harry aimed his arm that way, as McKeogh swung round the Circus and then up the wide road. They drove a mile and fast up beyond the scorched entrance to the ghetto before Harry indicated they should turn back.

'Try the Crumlin, it has to be that way.'

'He could have got away from us and still be in this road. If he went up the Crumlin he'll be out of the city by now, up in Ligoniel, halfway to the airport,' said McKeogh.

'I know where he can be. Just drive and close your attention on that,' Harry snapped back. He would be lucky now to find him again. He knew that, but didn't need any bloody driver telling him. Neither saw the Escort still parked among the other cars on the Circus, and they turned up the long haul of the Crumlin. Harry was forward in his seat now, peering right and left as McKeogh swept up the road. At the top he shouted. The exultation of a master of hounds throwing off the frustration of a lost quarry.

'There he is, at the tin wall.'

McKeogh slowed the car in against the near pavement.

'Who is he?' he said.

Harry looked at him, didn't reply and bolted from the car. He ran across the road and disappeared from McKeogh's view through the gap in the silver corrugated fence. Downs had a start of less than a hundred yards.

Talk of the initial shooting straddled the city. The first officer into the road was taken by a lance-corporal to meet the tear-swamped Mrs Duncan. Between gulps and pauses to blow her nose she told the immediate story that formed the basis of the situation report.

'He'd just left for work, Mr McEvoy, and I heard the shooting, and I ran to the door. Up the end of the street was Mr McEvoy with a gun, and one man seemed to

339

run down the street towards this end, and he was shot. Mr McEvoy just aimed and shot him. Then another man got into the car and started to drive away, and Mr McEvoy fired at him too, and I don't know whether he was hit or not. It was so fast. Then Mr McEvoy ran into the road waving and shouting at people in cars. Then I came indoors.'

'Who is this Mr McEvoy?' the bemused subaltern asked automatically.

'He's my lodger, been here three weeks. Quiet as a mouse, and a gentleman, a real proper man. Never spoke to anyone, and then there he was crouched behind his gun and shooting it over and over.'

The ambulance took Duffryn to hospital, and bulletins later in the day spoke of his condition as 'critical'.

Frost, still in the 39 Brigade Operations Room at Lisburn, saw the reports coming in over the teletype. In rapid succession he spoke to the GOC, the Brigade commander in Londonderry – in order that the Secretary of State could be briefed when he arrived there – and finally to Davidson in London. In each case the message was substantially the same.

'At first sight it looks as though they mounted some sort of ambush for McEvoy this morning. There was a balls-up on the job, and our fellow ended up shooting at least one of theirs. He's in hospital injured. Another chap escaped in a car, and when last seen McEvoy was standing out in the Falls trying the old tack of waving down a spot of transport, civilian, for hot pursuit. It gets a bit more droll each stage. He'd holed up in a small guest house just off the Falls in the Broadway section. So he's on the loose again, and it's my wager that by lunchtime the place will be buzzing a bit.'

Four minutes later the teletype was chattering again. A shot-up car had been discovered in Carlyle Circus, and a man had been taken from the back with serious gunshot wounds.

'This McEvoy, he's one of ours,' said Frost to the major from his department who stood beside him.

'Working for us?' said the other man in astonishment. The clerks and corporals and duty officers strained to listen.

'Not as simple. Working for our side, but not working for us, not for this department. It's involved and complicated and a cock-up. The guts are that the Prime Minister wanted an outsider with good cover and uncompromised, to move in and operate while controlled from London. He had a specific task, to locate the man that killed Danby. I think he did it and all the trimmings as well. It's a boy called Billy Downs, from the Ardoyne. The place is watched now, and we did a raid this morning but that was negative. But the whole thing went sour. This man, McEvoy, had little faith in his controller and not much more in us. Can't blame him for that. The talk I've had with his controller shows him as stupid as they come. So we had a ludicrous situation, lunatic, with McEvoy phoning his controller and passing over information but not saying where he could be contacted. In between his weekly messages not a word from him. Revolutionary tactics, OK. Then it leaked to the opposition – how they got hold of it I don't know – complete secrecy was supposed to be the strength of the whole enterprise, and the Provos still heard about it. There was the bit in the papers this morning, that was the tip of it.'

341

The major nodded. He'd seen the cutting already, snipped out and noted.

Frost went on.

'Well, it seems the boyos went for McEvoy this morning to try to get him on the way to a job he'd picked up. He's cool enough, this lad. There's been quite a shoot-out. McEvoy shot at least one of them. Maybe more, there's another half stiff turned up beside the Mater in a car with guns in it. It may be something to do with it. Could well be.'

One of the desk sergeants came towards the colonel pushing a telephone trolley across the floor of the ops room, a light set in the handle flashing brilliantly.

'Call for you, sir.'

Frost took the phone, identified himself, and listened rather more than a minute. Then he thanked the caller, asked him quietly not to move anything, and said he would be on his way.

'There's been shooting in Ypres Avenue, that's Billy Downs's street. Looks a bit like *High Noon* apparently, bodies and plenty all over the place.' Frost rattled it out, hard and composed. 'I think I'll go down there, so hold the fort, please. And call RUC HQ, Special Branch. Ask for Rennie, Howard Rennie. He might want to come up there. It'll take me about fifteen minutes to get there. But if there's any word of McEvoy let me know right away.'

And he was gone before the major could stand on any of his dignity and complain about being kept in the dark. That Frost traditionally kept things close to his chest was small consolation. Suddenly the operations room was alive. It was seldom the staff on the first floor of headquarters were able to feel the tension of street-level operations. Frost had brought them into it, though at the expense of his famous discretion. The sergeant brought the trolley over once more.

'It's a call for Colonel Frost, sir. They say it's London and personal and urgent. A Mr Davidson. The colonel called him a few minutes ago. Will you take it?'

The major took the phone. 'It's his deputy here.' He waited while the question was framed at the other end, then went on, 'We have another wounded man, and a shooting in Downs's street in the Ardoyne. Bodies but no names to match them with is the order of the morning so far. You'll have to wait half an hour or so, and then we might have the answers. Sorry, old chap, but that's the way it is.'

Chapter Nineteen

Feverish in the torment of her uncertainty, Billy Downs's wife had sent two of her children to the community crèche, and dumped the others with her neighbours. In her threadbare green coat and with her bag and purse she had taken herself to the shops at the top of the Ardoyne. The screw had been well twisted on her exhausted nerves.

The news programme less than two hours earlier had carried reports of the shooting at the policeman's house, amplified by eye-witness accounts. The BBC had sent a man to the house, and his story made much of the gunman who hesitated, the intervention of the child, and the wounding of the gunman. There had been a trail of blood and the policeman was a trained marksman, the report said. The *Irish News*, which she had seen when she took the young ones three doors down, had shown a floodlit picture of the neat bungalow and white-faced detectives working with their fingerprint kits by the front door. The paper had also spoken of the wounding of the would-be assassin.

Men from the community association would come in later in the day to help repair the boards pulled up at dawn by the army, but for now the debris and confusion in the house and the noise of the children coupled with the danger to her husband to defeat her.

But the single factor that weighed most with her was the knowledge that the military knew of her husband, had identified him, and that their life together was effectively over. If he had survived last night then he would be on the run and go underground, otherwise the future held only the prospect of years in the Kesh or the Crumlin.

And for what?

She was not one of the militant women of the streets who blew the whistles and beat the dustbins, and marched down the Falls, and screamed at the soldiers and sent food parcels to the prisons. At the start the cause had not interested her, till parallel with the growing involvement of her husband she had become passively hostile to the movement. That a Cabinet minister should die in London, a soldier in Broadway or a policeman in Dunmurry was not the fuel that fired her. Her conviction was of far too low a grade to sustain her in her present misery.

Her purse had been full from the social security last Thursday. Now most of it was spent, with only enough for the basics of bread and milk bolstered by sausages and baked beans and tins. At the shops as she queued many eyes were on her. Word had passed in the streets that the army had raided her house, that they were looking for her man, that he had been out all night. Over the years it had become a familiar enough situation in the little community, but that it was this family that was at the centre of the morning's swoop caused the stares, the muttered comments and the pulling aside of the front window curtains.

She glared back at them, embarrassing the lookers enough to deflect their eyes. She paid for her food, pecking in her purse for the exact money, and swung out of the door and back to the street. She had forty yards to walk to the top of Ypres Avenue.

When she turned into the narrow long street the observation post spotted her. The soldiers were concealed in the roof of the mill, disused and now converted into warehouse space. They came and went by the back stairs, and where the boards were too rotten hauled themselves up by rope ladder. Once in position they put a heavy padlock on the door behind them, locking themselves in the roughly-fashioned cubicle, constructed out of sandbags, blankets and sacking. They had some protection and some warmth: that was all. To see down the Avenue they lay on their stomachs with their heads forward into the angle of the roof with a missing tile providing the vantage point. The two men in the post did twelve hours there at a stretch, and with three other teams would rotate in the position, familiarizing themselves enough with the street so that eventually they would know each man and woman and child who lived there. The comings and goings were logged, laboriously, in a notebook in pencil, then sifted each evening by their battalion's intelligence officer. A synopsis of life in the street was sent each week to headquarters for evaluation. It was a process repeated in scores of streets in the Catholic areas of Belfast, as the security forces built up their enormous and comprehensive dossiers on the minority community.

Lance-Corporal David Burns and Private George Smith had been in the mill since six that morning. They arrived in darkness and would leave long after the few street lights had come back on. They had been in Belfast eleven weeks on this tour, five more to go. Thirty-four days to be exact.

To the OP they'd brought sandwiches and a flask of sugared tea plus the powerful German binoculars they used, a folded card that expanded to show a montage of the faces of wanted men, the rifles with daytime telescopic sights and also the bulging image intensifier for night work. They carried everything they needed for the day up the rope ladder to the roof. Only the radio telephone and the bulk treacle tin for emergency nature calls were permanent fixtures.

Burns, face intent behind the glasses, called out the details on the slight woman walking towards him.

'The bird from forty-one. Must have been shopping. Didn't go for long. Can't be ten minutes since she went. Looks a bit rough. Didn't find her husband, did they?'

The soldier squirmed closer to the aperture, pressing the glasses against his eyebrows, face contorted with concentration.

'Hey, Smithie, behind her. I think he's coming. Right up the top there. Sort of running. That is her old man, isn't it? Looks like him. Have a squint yourself.'

'I'm not sure, not at this range. We'll be definite when he gets down the road a bit.' Smith had taken over the hole. 'Is he a shoot-on-sight, or what?'

'Don't know. They didn't say nothing about that. I'm sure enough now it's him. Get HQ on the radio. Looks like he's run a bloody marathon. Knackered, he is.'

* * *

347

It was the pounding of his feet that first broke through her preoccupations. The urgency of footsteps dragged the woman away from the images of her wounded husband and the breaking of her home. She turned towards the noise, and stopped still at the sight.

Downs was struggling to run now, head rolling from side to side and the rhythm of his arm movements lost. His legs flailed forward over the last few paces to her, unco-ordinated and wild. The stitch in his right side bit into the stomach wall. The pallor of his face was slug-like, excavated from under something of permanence. His face was hollow at the cheeks as he pulled the air inside his lungs, eyes fearful and vivid, and round them the skin glistened with a sheen of sweat. He was shape-less, the big sweater worn over the left shoulder and arm giving him a grotesque breadth. But as he came towards her it was the eyes that held her. Their desperation, loneliness and dependence.

She put down her shopping bag on the paving, careful that it should not topple over, and held out her arms for her man. He fell against her, stumbling, and she reeled with the sudden weight as she took the strain. Against her he convulsed as his lungs forced down the air they needed. There were words, but she could not understand them as they buried themselves in the shoulder of her coat. Far distant, on the top street corner a knot of women had gathered.

'They came for you, you know, this morning.'

'I know.'

'They searched all over, and they said they'd come again. Again and again till they got you.' He nodded, numbed and shocked by the pain of the running and the throbbing in his arm. 'They know, don't they? They know it all. They're not so daft as you said.'

'I was told.' The voice, the speaking, was a little easier now. The air was there, coming more naturally, and the legs steadied.

As she twisted herself against him, working away from the sharpness of his collarbone against her cheek, she felt him wince and tear away his left arm.

'Is that where they hit you? Last night it was you. At the policeman's home. Did he hit you?' The pain came and went, surging and then sagging. 'Has it been looked at? Have you seen a doctor?' Again he nodded.

'Where are you going now? What are you going to do?'

'I'm going home. It's over, finished. I just want to go home.'

'But they came this morning for you,' she screamed, her voice high, hysterical that he could not understand something so simple. 'They'll be back as soon as you walk through the door. They'll take you. They were crawling all through, under the floorboards and into the roof, looking for you. They took the place apart trying to find you.'

He wasn't listening. 'They put a man in, just to find me.' He said it with wonder, as if surprised that the enemy would classify him of such importance that they would take a step so great. 'We found him first. We went to get him this morning, and it just ballsed-up. There's two boys shot by him, the Englishman. And last night that was another cock-up. That bloody copper, he—'

'I heard it on the radio.'

'Well, there's no point in running now. I'm finished

349

with it. There'd be a reason to run if I was going on, but I'm not.'

'You mean all this? It's not just because you're hurt? We can get you away from here, the boys will shift you.'

'It's definite,' he said. He was very tired now, deeply tired and needing to sit down, to take the great weight from his legs. He picked up her shopping bag with his right hand, and draped the injured left arm over the small woman's shoulder. They began to walk by the terraced doors and the chipped and daubed red brick of the street. It was a grey Belfast morning, rain threatening, wind cold and from the east, coming in over the Lough. The two threaded a path over the fractured paving stones, past the endless heaps of dogs' mess towards the house that had become Downs's goal.

The moment the two had created for each other was broken by the footsteps behind. Instinctively both knew the noise of pursuit. In the Ardoyne the knack of recognizing it was inbred.

The women on the corner were silent as Harry ran by them down the gentle incline towards where the man and his wife were walking away from him. He held the revolver close to him, reassured by the hardness of the wooden handle, roughened with age and usage. He pulled up twenty feet short of them. The pair swung round to face him.

'Don't move. Don't try to run or get your firearm. If you do I'll shoot.'

Harry barked the instructions. The harshness of his tone and its assurance surprised him. He felt almost detached from the orders he was shouting.

'Put the bag down and begin to walk towards me,

and slowly. Your hands on your head. The woman –
she stays where she is.'

Be strong. Don't mess about with him. You'll be a
long time before you shift the bastard. Don't let him
dominate you. Keep the gun on him, look at his hands
the whole time. Watch the hands, and keep the gun in
line. Keep it so it's only got to come straight up to fire,
and the catch off. Check with the thumb that the catch
is off. It is, certain. Now separate them, don't let them
be together so she can shield him. She'll do that, they
all will, throw themselves at you to give him a yard.
And shoot. If he moves shoot him. Don't hesitate. Stay
still yourself. Don't march about. That disorganizes
the shot you may make. Two bullets only. One up the
spout, and the other in the next chamber, that's all.

Harry studied him hard. The other man, the opposition. Dirty, cowed and frightened – is that the
terrorist? Is that all he is? Is that the killer in all
his glory? Not much to look at, not much without his
Kalashnikov.

'Start walking now, and remember: keep it very cool,
or I shoot. What's your name?'

'Billy Downs. You're the Englishman they sent for
me? The one that had the girl killed?' They'd told him
the Britisher hadn't come to take him, not to put him in
the Kesh, but to kill him. The fight of survival was
returning, steadily and surely. 'You won't get out of
here, you know. Not with me on the end of your pistol,
you won't.'

He looked past Harry and seemed to nod his head
into the middle distance. It was cleverly done. Good
try, Billy boy. But you're with the professionals now,
lad. A squaddie might have turned and given you the

351

third of a second you needed to jump him. Not Harry. Pivot round. Get your back to the wall. Keep going till you feel the brickwork. But watch the bastard. All the time keep your eyes on his hands.

Faced with troops in uniform, Downs would probably have submitted without a struggle and climbed into the armoured car to start whatever segment of his lifetime in captivity they intended for him. But not this way. No surrender to a single hack sent from London to kill him watched by his wife and in his own road. For a year it would be talked about – the day when a lone Englishman came into the Ardoyne and shot down meek little Billy Downs. The day the boy's nerve went.

He was formidable, this Englishman, in his old jeans and dark anorak, with the clear-cut face, softer than those fashioned in the bitterness of Belfast. He had not been reared through the anguish of the troubles, and it showed in the freshness of his features. But he was hard, Downs had no doubt on that. They'd trained him and sent him from London for this moment, and Downs knew his life rested on his capacity to read the expressionless mouth of his enemy. When he made his break all would depend on how well the Englishman could shoot, and, when he fired, how straight. Downs made his assessment . . . he'll fire, but fire late, and he'll miss. He turned himself now from the waist only, and very slowly, towards his wife. He was close to her, much closer than Harry, and with his face in profile he mouthed from the far side of his lips, the one word:

'Scream.'

She read it in the shape of his mouth, the way the lips and gums twisted out the message. Harry didn't see the instruction, and was still concentrating on the man's hands when she yelled. It came from deep down, a fierce noise from so small a woman. Harry jerked from his preoccupation with Downs as he searched for the source of the noise, his eyes shifting direction.

Downs had made his decision. Now or not at all, either now or the bastard has you in his own time, to shoot like a rat in a cage. He pushed his wife violently towards Harry and started for the freedom of the open street down the hill. His first two strides took him to the edge of the pavement. A flood of adrenalin . . . anticipating the shot, head down, shoulders crouched. This was the moment. Either he fires now or I make it, three, four more paces then the range and accuracy of the revolver is stretched. His eyes half closed, he saw nothing in front of him as his left foot hit hard on the steep edge of the pavement. For his heel there was support, for his sole there was nothing, only the gap between the flagstones and the gutter eight inches below. His weight was all there, all concentrated on that foot, as he catapulted himself forward, the momentum taking over.

He realized the way he was falling, and tried to twist round onto his back, but there was no time, no room. He hit the rough gravel of the road on his left arm, right on the spot where the flesh had been twice torn open by Rennie's bullet. The frail lint bandage gave no protection. With his right arm he clawed at the road surface trying to push himself up and away from Harry, who was coming to him, revolver outstretched . . .

Harry saw the pain reach over and cover the man's face. He saw the hand scruffing under the body. If the man had a gun that was where it would be, down by

353

the waist, where the hand was fumbling now. It wasn't a difficult decision any more. He raised the revolver so that the line went down from his right eye, down his right arm to the 'V' of the back sight and along the black barrel to the sharp foresight, and then on to the man's upper chest. He held the aim just long enough for his hand to steady, then squeezed the trigger gently into the cup of his forefinger. The noise was not great. The revolver gave only a slight kick, jolting down the rigid arm to Harry's shoulder. Below him Downs's body began to twitch, giving way to spasmodic convulsions. The blood found its own pathway from the side of his mouth out onto the greyness of the road. Like water tracking across dry earth it kept its course, faster, thicker, wider as the road discoloured with its brightness.

There was no need for the second bullet, Harry could see that.

'Why did you shoot him? He had no gun. Why did you kill him?' She was moving towards Downs, looking at Harry as she spoke. 'You didn't have to shoot. You could have run after him, and caught him. You know he was shot last night, and hit. He wasn't much opposition to you, you Britisher sod.'

She knelt down beside her husband, her stocking dragging on the harsh surface of the road. He lay on his side, and she could not cradle him as she would have wanted. Both her hands touched the face of her man, unmarked in his death, fingering his nose and ears and eyes.

Harry felt no part of the scene; but something was demanded of him, and painstakingly he began to explain.

'He knew the rules. He knew the game he was playing. He came to London and murdered the Cabinet Minister. In cold blood. Shot him down in front of his house. Then he went to ground. It was a challenge to us. He must have known we had to get him – you must have known that. It was a test of will. There was no way we could lose – we couldn't afford to.'

Harry had wondered how this moment would be. How he would feel if the man were dead, destroyed. There was no hatred, no loathing for the slight body that lay on the grit of the tarmac. There was no elation, either, that his world and his system had beaten that of the young man who they had told him was the enemy, evil, vermin. Harry felt only emptiness. All the training, all the fear, all the agony, directed to killing this awkward, shapeless nonentity. And now nothingness. He looked again at the wife as she stayed bent over her lifeless man, and began to walk up the hill out of the Ardoyne.

She was watching him, hands still on the man's body, when the shot came. Simultaneously with the crack she saw Harry stagger, appear to regain his balance, and then career backwards, before thudding against the front wall of a house. His arms were pressed against the middle of his chest. Then he toppled in slow motion over onto the pavement.

In the OP it was Smith who was at the aperture, giving a continuous description to the lance-corporal who relayed the message back to headquarters over the radio telephone.

'There's a man running up behind Downs. With a shooter. A revolver, looks like, a little one. Tell 'em to shift 'emselves back at HQ. Downs has his hands up, and they're talking. Not much, but saying something.'

From the telephone set Burns called, 'What about the other bloke, they want to know, what's he look like?'

'Civvies, anorak and jeans. It's a short-barrel revolver he's got, not Downs . . . the other man. Scruffy-looking. He's making a run for it, Downs is. Bloody hell, he's down, tripped himself. Fuck me, he's going to shoot him, he's going to shoot him!'

High in the hidden observation post Burns heard the single shot.

'I can get the bugger, can't I, Dave? He just shot the other bastard. Waving a gun about and all that, it's enough.'

Smith was manœuvring his rifle into position. The old Lee Enfield with the big telescopic sight, the sniper's weapon, the marksman's choice.

'I've a good line on him from here. No problem.' Smith was talking to himself, whispering into the butt of the rifle. Burns was motionless and watched from the back of the OP, nestled among the blankets and sacking as Smith drew back the bolt action, and settled himself, shifting his hips from side to side to get comfortable for the shot. He was a long time aiming, wanting to be certain the first time. The firing echoed round under the roof of the mill.

'Did you get him?' urged Burns.

'A real bloody peach.'

The sharpness of the pain numbed Harry. As he lay, stomach down on the pavement, he could feel nothing, his head was facing the walls of the houses away from the street. Green moss rubbed close to his nose, and beyond that lay the jagged edge of a milk bottle, and, huge and high, a front doorstep. There was no understanding of what had happened. Just the noise, and the helpless collapse, the blow that had carried him from his feet.

He worked his right hand slowly from under him where it had gripped his chest. The fingers were scarlet and shiny. The effort was so great. No strength left, no power, and endless labour just to move an arm. The action of all the muscles, all working in his biceps, his heavy shoulders, and deep behind the ravaged rib cage, combined to bring on the first stabs of agony. Bruised from his fall, his face contorted with pain, the upper teeth clamping on the softness of his lip, he struggled to control the spasms.

And with the pain came the realization of what had happened. They've had you, Harry. As you stood there like a big idiot, consumed in your inviolability, they took you. So silly. Just standing there, in the heart of the Ardoyne, standing and waiting, and they obliged. His mind was clearing as the flesh and tissue round the great wound torn by the bullet throbbed out its protest. This is the way it ends, he knew that. Here against the dampened pavings, by the weeds and the fractured glass, among hatred and loathing. Some little swine out there with a rifle, taking a long time, waiting for the moment, not hurrying. That was the way death comes, Harry. Billy Downs already dead, the woman beside him; that was somewhere in the greater distance, away beyond.

Other faces were closer, sharp-etched now . . . Davidson, in the garden near Dorking – it'll be dangerous, he had said. Hadn't wanted to say it, thought it might frighten . . . Mary came closer to him, and the boys, big faces happy with laughter, all noise and running to him. Take hold, Harry, fight it.

The impact of the shot had flung Harry several feet back before it felled him. His hands with animal instinct had closed on his stricken body, the revolver careering from his fist and bouncing into the roadway where it rested.

Harry forced himself upwards, using his right hand to provide the lever till he could jackknife his lower body under him and spread the great weight from the arm onto his knees. The first time he failed, collapsing back into the pool of blood. Again he attempted it, this time with greater success, till, like a pantomime dog, he began to work his way up the hill. There were people at the doorways now, but none moved or spoke as the Englishman dragged his way past. A single child screamed as his opened coat slipped from his left hand fingers, and permitted a flow of blood down onto the ground and over the hardness of the pavement before his knees smeared its ordered passage.

A hundred pairs of eyes watched Harry move away, aware that this was the effort of a man already doomed but unable to accept it. These people knew the inevitability of death, knew how a man fought to stave off its coming, and knew from the signs when he would win, and when lose. The Englishman they knew would lose, the blood told them that, the whiteness of his face, the breathing, irregular and bubbling. And then they saw Billy Downs's wife rise up from the road where her man lay and walk with quick, neat steps towards Harry. They saw that in her path was the revolver.

She bent down and picked it up. It was heavy,

cumbersome in her small hand. Her index finger had to strain forward to find by feel the metal coldness of the trigger arm. She didn't look at the gun, or check it as a man used to handling firearms would have done. Those people at their doors who saw themselves in line with her and Harry backed away, seeking the safety of their front doors, but the uninvolved stayed to see what would happen.

Eighteen inches from his head a door slammed, its noise breaking Harry's thought, diverting his attention from his sole preoccupation of taking himself beyond the pain of Ypres Avenue, and then he heard the brush of her feet, scurrying closer to him. She walked on past him and then spun round, blocking his way till his face was close to her legs. Harry subsided backwards, his hand still holding his body up, but his weight down on his hips. He could see all of her from there, not just the legs and the feet, but her coat that was old and tired, her face once pretty and now hideous from the grief and shock of the last few minutes, and her short narrow arm, and the tight, pale-skinned clenched fist. And the revolver, too big for her, grotesque.

The barrel of the gun was steady, so were her eyes, nothing distracting her from the man near-prone in front of her.

She said, 'You didn't have to shoot my man. What was Billy to you? What did it matter to you, what happened to him? He was finished, broken, and you cut him down like a rat in the gutter. And you talk about rules and challenges. What rule was that, to kill Billy, hurt and unarmed?'

There was no fear in Harry now. It had all evaporated a long time back. The words came hard to him. 'You know why he died, what he did. He was against us. Each was determined to destroy the other. He understood that.'

'You never knew anything of him – what sort of man he was, how good he was to us. And yet you come to our street, and shoot him down, defenceless.'

Harry struggled to speak again to her. So difficult, so exhausting, this twisted, shattered face above him, not understanding the world of her man, not understanding the war that was being fought out on her own streets. It was all so simple, so easy, but Harry felt the waves of tiredness pouring over him, and no longer had the strength to reason with the woman.

She went on: 'You think we're all animals over here. But what's it to you if Danby gets killed, or a soldier, or a policeman, what's it to you, over from England? Do you think you're any better than our people?'

Harry stayed silent a long time as he struggled to concentrate his thoughts.

'He deserved to die. He was an evil little bastard. He's better off—'

The fingers wrenched at the trigger. The noise mingled with her sobs as Harry rolled slowly and with precision over onto his back. At the top of Ypres Avenue the first two Saracens were arriving.

The soldiers looked over the two bodies, made the decision that both were beyond medical help, and left them where they had fallen. Both Harry Brown and Billy Downs were in the awkward, sack-like form that the troops could recognize as death. Downs lay a few feet from the kerb, out in the road. The blood had run from him to create a lake, dammed from escaping farther by the debris of the gutter. His wife was beside him again, and still holding the revolver loosely and without interest. The sergeant of the platoon walked towards her and, with nervousness showing in his voice, asked her to hand over the gun. She opened her fingers and it clattered noisily on the road. When the soldier spoke again to her there was no reply. She stood, quite still, swamped by her emotions.

Harry was sprawled face up close to the wall of a house, his head beneath the front room window from which a face, old but without the softness of compassion, looked down on him. The women of the street edged their way closer to Billy Downs's wife, the men gathered in clumps, leaving the business of comforting and abusing to their women.

In their shawls and head scarves and short skirts they shouted at the officer who came with the platoon. 'He's one of yours. That bastard dead over there.'

'He's a fucking Englishman.'

'Shot a man without a gun.'

'SAS killer squads.'

'Killed an unarmed man. In front of his wife, and he never in trouble before.'

The crescendo gathered round the young man. In a few moments his Company commander and Battalion commander would be there, and he would be spared, but till then he would take the brunt of their fury. Faced with the accusation that Harry was one of theirs the soldiers looked curiously at the body of the big man. They knew a certain amount about the undercover operations of the army, particularly the Mobile Reconnaissance Force (MRF), but to the men in uniform it was a different and basically distasteful world. The

361

soldiers had their rules and regulations to abide by. The book was near to God.

In exasperation the lieutenant shouted above the babble:

'Well, if you say the chap who shot Downs is one of ours, who shot him then?' He'd phrased it clumsily, said it in anger and expected no answer.

The chorus came back, gloating, satisfied. 'The Provies got him. A Provie gunman. One shot. From the bottom of the street.'

The far end of the street down the hill was deserted, dominated only by the massive red-brick wall and grey-slate roof of the old mill. The lieutenant looked up at it, and winced.

'Bloody hell,' he said.

His sergeant, who had been examining Harry, came over to him. 'The chap on the pavement, sir. He's been hit twice. First I would say was high velocity, there is an entry and exit wound and a big blood marker, looks as if he tried to get away, you can follow the trail, about fifteen yards to where he is now. He was shot again then, right in the head, no exit, and it must have been a hand gun or something, that killed him.'

'Thank you, sergeant. The woman who was holding the pistol, you'd better put her in the Saracen. Go easy with her, she's in shock, and I don't want a riot here.'

'It's just as we found it, as you requested,' they told Frost when he arrived.

The Battalion commander briefed him. 'The chap by the wall shoots Downs and then is shot himself. I'm not a hundred per cent sure where the second shot comes from. Still waiting for all the reports. Indications are that it's my OP in the mill roof. We're rather quiet about that position, but I haven't spoken to the men up there yet. Seems they wounded the fellow, then Downs's wife, she's in the Saracen now, came in and finished him off.'

There was no reaction on Frost's face. His eyes travelled round the street taking in the faces and the scene. He walked over from one body to the other, his bodyguards hovering at each shoulder. He recognized Harry from the photograph that had been sent the previous evening from England. It should never have worked, but it had. And now right at the end was all loused up. Poor devil.

He paused where Downs lay, looking into the profile of the face and running a check against the picture they'd issued. We'd have been lucky to spot him from that, the colonel thought, not really good enough, something to be learned from that. He went past the open door of the Saracen. Mrs Downs sat huddled deep in the shadow of the interior. She sat totally still, staring at the armour-plated sides, festooned with pick-axes, CS gas-grenade canisters, ammunition boxes. Two soldiers guarded her.

'It's not for general release,' he said to the Battalion commander, 'but you'll hear about it soon enough anyway. The Prime Minister ordered a special man put in, with the sole job of finding Danby's killer, right? The Cabinet Minister shot in London, what is it? six or so weeks ago. Downs was the assassin. By something of a miracle, and a quite unaccountable amount of good luck, the agent tracked him down. That's not a generous assessment, but that's how I evaluate it. He

363

tracked him and shot him dead about fifteen minutes ago. I think your OP has just shot the Prime Minister's man.'

Frost knew how to play his moment. He stopped there, let it sink, then went on.

'We'll deflect it as much as we can, but I suggest you leave it to Lisburn to make the statements. It may be some consolation to you, but I didn't know much about the agent either. He wasn't working to me. I wouldn't worry about the role of the OP in all this.'

'I wasn't worrying—'

Frost cut across him.

'It's happened before, it'll happen again. Marines shot their own crowd in the New Lodge. RUC have shot our people, we've killed theirs. Bound to happen.'

The other man considered. They stood alone in the street away from the people of Ypres Avenue, with the bodyguards and troops giving them room to talk. He remembered now the soldier they had sent to Berlin; what he had seen in the green-topped social club less than three hundred yards from where they stood. There was nothing to say, nothing that would help the prone figure by the wall, nothing that would achieve anything beyond unnecessary involvement. Business-like, brisk as always, he said to Frost:

'Is there any reason for us not to clean this lot up now? Our photographer has done his stuff, and the RUC people won't want to come in here.'

'No reason at all. Get it out of the way before the press and cameras start showing up.'

'Will there be much aggro, the fact that this fellow Downs wasn't armed when he was killed?'

'I wouldn't have thought so,' said Frost, 'there isn't

usually when we get one of the real ones. They seem to accept that, part of the game. Right at the beginning there used to be mayhem. But they've become tired of saying it. They're all unarmed men – that's the charm. Doesn't work them up any more. Be interesting to see what sort of show he gets in the death notices in the press tomorrow morning. We'll see how highly they regarded him then. A big man can get three or four columns. Be interesting. Come from the Brigade command, their Battalions, Companies and a good number from the Kesh. Costs them a fortune – and keeps the papers going.'

They walked together back towards Frost's Land-Rover.

Frost was gone by the time Rennie was brought to Ypres Avenue in a Saracen from Battalion head-quarters. He climbed gingerly out of the protection of the personnel carrier and jumped down onto the road. First time in the Ardoyne for sixteen months. The Special Branch had no love for parading their faces on the streets of the Provisional heartland. He was conspicuous, he knew that. Anyone in civilian clothes who needed five soldiers and a three-ton armoured car to take him in and out would attract attention. He was conscious of the eyes at the doors, blank and subdued but watching him.

'Are the bodies still here?' he asked the Battalion commander.

'We've shifted them, I'm afraid. My people have taken the necessary pictures. There's not much to see now. That's where Downs died, the blood on the road. The other fellow, McEvoy, he was shot on the pavement by number twenty-nine. There's a small blood pool there.'

'Who's McEvoy?' said the detective.

'I fancy you'll hear more of him from your own office. But he's a rather sensitive creature right now. One of ours, they tell me. Trailed Downs back here and shot him. I'm still waiting for the details on the rest. Looks a bit black, though. I think one of my OPs shot him. McEvoy was waving a gun round, in civilian clothes. It's pretty definite.'

He had no need to ask about Downs. The wild, staring face that had confronted him fourteen hours earlier across the width of his bright living room remained vivid in his mind.

But Downs was dead now. Rennie thanked the officer and hurried back to the Saracen.

The press statement from Lisburn was short and took something more than two hours to prepare. It was the result of a series of compromises but owed most of its drafting to the civilian deputy head of the army public relations department who had recently transferred from the Treasury, and had experience of the art of communiqué writing.

Billy Downs, a known IRA gunman, was shot dead at 09.10 hours in Ypres Avenue where he lived. He was involved in an exchange of shots with a member of the security forces, an officer engaged in plain-clothes surveillance duties. The officer, who will not be named till his next of kin have been informed, was hit by a single shot in the chest and died before medical treatment reached him.

Downs was high on the army's wanted list in Northern Ireland, and was also wanted in London for questioning by detectives investigating the murder of Mr Henry Danby.

The main object was to keep it short, pack it with information and deflect the press away from the sensitive bit. There was, he said when he had finished typing it, more than enough for the scribes to bite on without them needing to go digging round any more.

A solitary journalist moved towards the delicate area that first day, but without knowing it, and was easily put off.

'Then this man Downs was carrying a gun?' he asked the duty press officer.

'Obviously, old man, it says in our statement that there was an exchange of shots. Have to be armed, wouldn't he?'

There were no other questions to be asked. Amongst the resident reporters in McGlade's pub that night interest was warm but not exceptional, and the treatment of the story was straight and factual.

Locally it was denied that Downs had been armed, and three hours of rock-throwing followed the news bulletin that contained the army statement. By then it had started to rain.

Chapter Twenty

The Prime Minister learned the news at lunchtime. The message had been framed by the Under-Secretary, Ministry of Defence, with an eye to the political master's taste, and the order in which he would read of the events in Ypres Avenue had been carefully thought out. First, Billy Downs as the killer of Henry Danby had been shot dead. Second, he had been identified by the agent specifically sent to Northern Ireland by the Prime Minister. Third, and unfortunately, the agent had been shot in the chest during the incident and had died.

As he read the message that the aide gave him his attentive smile had switched to a frown of public concern, studied by the bankers round the table with him in the first-floor salon of No. 10. They looked for a clue as to the contents and information that was important enough to intercede in discussions on the progress of the floating pound, albeit the end of the discussions. The Prime Minister noted their anticipation and was anxious to satisfy it.

'Just on a final note, gentlemen.' He refolded the typewritten sheet. 'You will all be reading it in the papers tomorrow morning, but you might be interested to hear that we have caught and killed the man that assassinated Henry Danby. He was shot in Belfast this morning after being hunted down as part of a special investigation that was launched from this building a few hours after our colleague was murdered.'

There was a murmur of applause round the table and a banging of the palms of hands on the paper-strewn mahogany surface.

'But you will be sorry to hear, as I am, that the man we sent to find this terrorist was himself killed in the shooting exchange. He'd been operating under cover there for some weeks, and obviously carried out a difficult task extremely successfully and with great bravery. The whole concept of this intelligence operation really goes back to the last war. My family were involved in Special Operations – you know, the crowd that put agents into the occupied countries. I had a hell of a job getting the military and police to agree to it. But it just shows, you sometimes need a fresh approach to these things. Perhaps we should get that general over there, who always seems to be wanting more troops, to have a try at banking and running a budget!'

There was general and polite laughter.

'He'll get a medal, won't he? The man you sent over there? They look after the families and all that sort of thing, I suppose?' the elegantly-dressed deputy chairman of the Bank of England said.

'Oh, I'm sure he will. Well, I think we can adjourn now. Perhaps you would care to join me for a drink. I have a luncheon, but I'm not off to that till I've had a drop of something.'

Later in the day he called the Under-Secretary to

express his appreciation of the way the operation had been handled.

'It'll get a good show in the papers, I trust,' said the Prime Minister. 'We ought to blow our own trumpets a bit when we chalk one up.'

'I don't think there will be too much of that, sir.' The civil servant replied decisively. 'MOD have put out a short statement only. I think their feeling is that undercover is bad news in Ulster, and that apart from anything else it was a damn close thing whether our man got theirs first or vice versa. They're playing it rather low key I'm afraid, sir.'

'As you like. Though I sometimes feel we don't give ourselves the pat on the back we deserve. I'll concede that. One more thing. The man we sent over there, I'd like a medal for him now it's over. What sort of chap was he, by the way?'

'I'll see to that. He already had an MC from Aden. We could make it a bar to that, but perhaps that's a bit on the short side. I personally would favour the OBE. The George Cross is a bit more than we usually go for in these circumstances, and it would obviously provoke a deal of talk. You asked what sort of chap. Pretty straightforward, not too bright. Dedicated, conscientious, and a lot of guts. He was the right man.'

The Prime Minister thanked him and rang off. He hurried from his study to the Humber waiting outside the front door of the official residence. He was late for the House.

The Army Council of the Provisional IRA, the top planning wing of the military side of the movement, had noted the killing of Downs. The Chief of Staff had

370

received a letter from the Brigade commander in Belfast relaying the collapse of their man's morale and his failure in the last two missions assigned to him.

The two members of the Council who had been asked to report on the practicality and desirability of further assassinations in the political arena, particularly the plan involving the British Prime Minister, delivered their assessment at the first meeting of all members after the Ardoyne shoot-out.

They advised against the continuation of attacks on the style of the Danby assassination. It had, they said, been disastrous for fund-raising in the United States: the picture of Mrs Danby and her children at the funeral had been flashed across the Atlantic and coast to coast by the wire syndication services. The Provisionals' supporters in the States reported that November's fund-raising and on into December would show a marked drop. They said that if there were a repeat or a stepping-up of the tactics the results could prove disastrous. And money was always a key factor for the movement: RPG7s and their rockets did not come cheap, not from Czechoslovakia or Libya nor from anywhere else.

The Chief of Staff summed up that in the foreseeable future they would not consider a repetition of the Danby attack, but he finished: 'I still defend the attack we carried out against Danby. That bastard deserved to go. He was a straight, legitimate target, and it was well done, well carried out. They acknowledge that on their side, too. There's been no trumpeting on their side even though they've shot our lad. They've been keeping their heads down for more than a week.'

There was criticism in the Council, that had not been

371

voiced while Downs was still on the run, of the way the Chief of Staff had monopolized the planning of the attack. That would stand against him in the future, being one of the factors in his eventual replacement and consequent demotion.

Little of the credit for the killing of Billy Downs landed on Davidson's desk. It jumped with no small agility to the name of Harry McEvoy via the desk of the Permanent Under-Secretary.

Frost put in a long and detailed complaint about the amount of work the independent and, for so many days, unidentified agent had meant for the security services. He logged the man-hours involved in the search for Harry at the scrap yards, and for the girl round the Clonard, and described them as wasteful and unprofessional. The control of the agent received scathing criticism, particularly the inability of London to reach their man when they wanted to draw him out. The paper concluded with the demand that such an operation should not be repeated during the following eighteen months that Frost would be on the staff of Northern Ireland headquarters.

The Under-Secretary who had a copy of the document forwarded to him read it over the phone to Davidson. The response was predictably angry.

'He forgets it was over there and on his side of the fence that some big mouth let the cat out of the bag.' Davidson already had the transcript of the interrogation of the stricken Duffryn. Still suffering from shock, the young man had given Special Branch all of his limited knowledge of the Provisional IRA and its affairs relating to Harry McEvoy.

'He forgets that our man got the fellow, not all their troops and police and Special Branch and SIB, and whatever they call themselves, SAS and the others.' Davidson roared it into the receiver.

The Under-Secretary soothed. 'They have a point, you know. This bit how you couldn't reach him, and he didn't stay where he was supposed to, that was a bit irregular.'

'The way they clod about over there, I'm not surprised he didn't go to the house they fixed for him. The fact is we were set a mission, and carried it out, with success. Is that cause for a bloody inquest?'

Davidson had not been told how Harry had died. That was to be kept very close in London. 'Need to Know' was being applied with rigour. The Under-Secretary decided that if the PM wasn't on the list then Davidson ranked no greater priority.

'Of course the mission was a success, but it's put a great strain on inter-service and inter-department co-operation. The feeling at MOD is that a similar operation would not be mounted again. That means, I greatly regret to say, that the team we set up to direct our man will have to be dismantled.' There was no change in his voice as he delivered the hammer blow. It gave him no pleasure, but Davidson was so excitable that one really did have to spell it out in simple words and get it over with. He went on: 'I did have hopes at one stage that if this went off without a hitch we might have had something a bit more regular going through Dorking. Make a habit out of the place. But that's not to be.'

Davidson could recognize the shut-out. The shouting was over. He asked, 'And what now? What happens to me?'

373

'It's recognized here, Davidson, that in fact you did very well on this one, particularly in the preparation of our man. You made him ready for a difficult and dangerous task, which was subsequently carried out with great expertise. You must not take all that Frost says too seriously. You've a great deal of experience to offer, and this showed in the way you got the fellow ready. I want you to think about it carefully, and not come to any hasty decision, but the feeling is that there's a good opening abroad for you.'

Here it comes, the old pay off, reckoned Davidson. What would they have for him, sewing blankets in the Aleutians?

'You've built up great experience of counter-terrorist operations.' The civil servant kept going – don't lose pace, don't let him interrupt – 'I won't beat about the bush. Hong Kong wants a man who can advise them on the posture they should be in. Now don't say anything hasty, the terms are first class. You'd get more than I'm getting. Good allowances, good accommodation, and pretty much of a free hand. Probably live off expenses and bank the rest, I'd say. Don't give me an answer now, but sleep on it and call me in the morning. Cheers, and we all think you did well.'

The conversation was over.

Davidson ranged round the office, fumbling at his papers, diving into the drawers of the old wooden desk. He aimed a kick at the folded camp bed away in the corner, not used since the last Sunday night of his vigil. It took around an hour to find the will and inclination to exert some order to the anger of his feelings. The documents and maps of the operation filled two briefcases. The rest was government property.

Some bloody man could clear that up. Sort it out themselves.

He made a call to his wife. Didn't speak much, just said he'd be home early, that he had some news, they would be going out for a meal. Then he locked up. He'd thought about Harry considerably since the shooting, and by the time he had reached his commuter train his rage had subsided and he brooded in a corner over the evening paper about the young man who had died in Belfast . . . sent away across the water with all that damn-fool optimism coursing through him.

For days Mrs Duncan talked of little more than the strange events that preceded the death of her favourite lodger.

That the man who shared her bathroom, her front room and occasionally her kitchen, who lived in her best back bedroom should have turned out to be an English agent was rather too much for her to serve out in a single session of conversation. Her neighbours came several times to hear the full saga, culminating in the eye-witness description of the final shoot-out beyond the front garden gate.

She was to remain unaware of her full role in the death of Harry and Billy Downs. She never discovered that it was her chatter over the back fence about the strange accent of the man who lived under her roof that was to start the process that led, near-directly, to the gunfire in the street (interrupting her late Monday morning breakfast). She told those who came to listen to her that the thing she found the strangest was the confidence and authority with which Harry was holding the gun as he shot down Duffryn against the lamp-post (a few feet from where she stood at the door). The cold methodical power with which that quiet man, a man she had grown to like but knew little about, executed the youngster, had shaken her more than any of the other horrors of five years of living on the Falls.

The army had come mid-morning and backed a Saracen right up to the gate. Two men in civilian clothes had waited till the doors were opened and screened them from casual view from the pavements, then hurried into the house. They had searched Harry's room slowly and carefully while soldiers hovered round the house and the street was sealed to all cars. When the men left it was with all Harry's possessions slung together into big transparent plastic bags.

Later that same day Josephine arrived to help with the teas. It was a wasted visit, as the guests had cried off. There were no takers for the lodging used by British intelligence. Some telephoned their apologies and listed excuses, others simply failed to turn up. Instead Josephine was told the events of the day. She listened without comment, and sat on a straight chair in the kitchen, sipping her tea, and smoking a cigarette. She was another who would never learn her full part in the affair. She went home that night believing her information alone had led the Provisionals to Harry. In the months ahead she was to stay distant from any connection with politics and with violence. Left alone by the IRA, she took to remaining at home in the evenings with her mother, shutting out the memories of the few hours she had spent with Harry, of how he had betrayed her, and of how she had betrayed him.

Billy Downs's funeral was a bigger day than any in his young life. A huge and winding crocodile of relatives and friends marched behind his tricolour-draped coffin up the Falls Road. It had been the army's intention to prevent the firing of the traditional volley over the body, but the procession diverted into the back streets of the Lower Falls and before it emerged again the shots had been fired. Photographers were icily warned of the consequences of taking pictures.

Eight men from Ypres Avenue took the weight of the coffin on their shoulders for the first part of the journey to Milltown Cemetery. Grim, set faces, they marched at the head of a crowd estimated by police at around three thousand. Behind them came the display of force, youths and girls in semi-uniform, the green motif dominating, polished Sam Brownes, shouted commands and the tramping of feet.

At the bleak, over-ornate, Milltown gates faces in the crowd were recorded by the Asahi cameras of the military from behind the sandbags on top of the walls of the Andersonstown bus station. Inside the cemetery the Chief of Staff of the movement, who arrived and departed unseen by those who were hunting him, delivered the graveside oration. They played the 'Last Post' while small children in their best clothes played and skipped among the stones that marked the last resting place of other heroes of the Cause.

As weeks and months passed by, so increased the adulation and estimation in which Billy Downs was held. They named a club after him, and wove his picture into a big, wide banner. It was some eight feet across, with slots for two poles, one at each end, so that it could be carried high in procession on the marches the Provisionals organized.

The songs followed, sung with the nasal lament in the bars of Andersonstown and the Ardoyne to drinkers who sat silent and rapt. They were heavy with sentiment, helping to cement the legend that in Ulster solidifies so quickly. The brave soldier of the songs had been gunned down by the British killer squads while his woman and bairns were round him. It was as his wife had said it would be.

The Secretary of State had refused the request by Billy Downs's wife that she be allowed to attend the funeral of her husband.

Early on the morning of her husband's burial she was transferred from the police station where she had initially been held to Armagh women's prison. She was declared an 'A' category prisoner, an automatic classification that took into account what she was accused of, not her potential as an escape risk. They flew her, with a prison escort, by Wessex helicopter from Belfast to the parade square of Gough barracks in the old cathedral town. When she stepped out onto the tarmac, half deafened by the rotor blades, and dominated by the armed men round her, she seemed to some who watched a pitiful and harmless creature. She still wore the green coat that she had put on the previous Monday morning to go and get her groceries from the shop on the corner in Ypres Avenue. By the time they had hustled her from the helicopter to the armoured car that waited on the edge of the square, she was shivering. It would be warmer when they reached the cells just down the road, and she would get a mug of tea then.

The Royal Air Force flew Harry out on a Hercules trans-porter, along with a cargo of freight and two private soldiers going home on compassionate leave.

The two boys, both in their teens and only just old enough to serve in the province, huddled in their canvas seats away from the tin box wrapped in sacking and strapped down with webbing to the floor of the aircraft. There was a brown label attached to the box, filled in with neat handwriting.

'Says he's a captain.'

'It's the one that did that shooting on Monday morning, and got it himself.'

'Says on here he's got an MC and all.'

'Took one of their big men with him, didn't he?'

'He tracked this joker for weeks. The officers were talking about it. I heard it when I was on dinner-waiting. Lived right in amongst them.'

'This is the first time I've been over, but I've nearly had a full tour, done three and a half months, but I've never seen an IRA man, or anything like one. All we do is patrol, patrol, patrol, but we never find much.'

'Undercover agent, they called him in the paper.'

'Didn't do him much good, whatever he was.'

That terminated it. They spoke no more of Harry as the plane brought them down to Northolt, where it had all started six weeks earlier.

They buried Harry Brown in the village churchyard close to where his wife's parents lived. By army standards it was a conventional funeral. There was an honour party, immaculate and creased. A staccato volley was fired over the grave. An army chaplain gave a short address by arrangement with the local vicar. In the event it was not much different from the funeral accorded to Billy Downs. Smaller, less stylized, less sentimental, but with all the same ingredients.

There were few civilians present. Mostly soldiers in uniform, stiffly upright as the bugler played the final haunting farewell. There was a wreath from the Prime Minister, and Davidson took time from his packing to attend. Frost was there too. Both stayed back from the graveside, and neither introduced themselves to the family.

Mary walked away supported by her mother and father. She had had two large brandies before coming, and could tell herself she had borne herself well. As she climbed into the large black car the public side was over. She could weep, leaning heavily on her mother's shoulder.

And she could say, 'Why in heaven's name did they choose Harry? He was lovely, precious to me, nothing special to them. They could have chosen a thousand men in front of him. Why did it have to be Harry?'

By the time they had gone, dispersing in their different directions and leaving the covering of flowers over the heaped-up earth, the evening was bearing down on the day. And across the water the truce that runs to heel with the daylight was coming to an end. A few more minutes and the darkness would have engulfed the Falls, the Murph, Andytown and the New Lodge. The young men were preparing to draw their rifles, receive their orders, move out onto the streets. Later a policeman would be killed, and a pub be destroyed by explosives. The life and death of Billy Downs changed none of that, nor the brief entry into his world of Harry Brown.

THE END

The Glory Boys

Gerald Seymour

To Rosalind Wade

Chapter One

There was quiet in the car now, attention riveted on the twin headlights far behind in the darkness. The man in the back seat had swivelled round, wiped the condensation from the back window, and peered hard into the void of the retreating road. The passenger in the front had also twisted round in an attempt to follow the passage of the lights, while the driver scanned the tilted mirror to his front. The road was not straight, and on the sharp curves where the high hedges came close to the tarmac they would lose the lights, and then find them again as the course of their route levelled out.

For the three men the tension had begun some fifteen kilometres back. The driver had been the first to speak, but that was long after his companions had noted his continual and hurried glances up at his mirror. He had spoken in the slow, high-pitched dialect of the pure Palestinian Arab.

'It's been with us a long time, the car behind. I've surged three times, pushed the speed up seven or eight ks an hour. It doesn't affect him – he's just maintaining the same distance. By the big farm, near the wood, you remember, I slowed then.

Right down, cut back by about twenty. He didn't close up.'

That was when they had started to take notice. Picked up the two powerful beams away in the distance, begun to sweat a little, allowed the nervous silence to take over.

The front passenger pulled the glove hatch open and rummaged for the plastic envelope containing the maps that had been supplied with the car. He felt in his pocket for his cigarette lighter, and then with the maps and the small flame he bent double, the papers down on the floor and the light shielded by his body. He ran quickly through the pages that showed in detailed and intricate pattern the road system of northern France. He hesitated on one of the maps, his finger tracing a line with difficulty in the flickering, shaking light.

'We're just past Béthune – that was the last town. Another two or three kilometres there's a turn-off to the left. Runs through some villages. Auchy . . . Estrées. It's difficult to see like this. It looks as though the road winds round the villages, a bypass. It's a broken line on the map, not for lorries. We can get through that way, and still be in good time for the boat. We have the time?'

'There's time enough.' The man in the back spoke, his words carrying away from the other two as he continued to search the road behind. 'He's still there. I lost him a moment, but he's there again.'

The road was straight now. Clear and fast, high trees on either side, the headlamps swinging past the tall trunks and melting away into the night across the fields. There was an occasional lighted cottage or farmhouse, but that was all. Three in the morning, and with the soulless cold of the early hours settled deep on the countryside. The men in the car shivered, the fear they felt accentuating the chill. From the back came the request for the heater to go on, declined by the driver.

'We've just cleared the mist on the windows. I don't want it again. I want to be able to see all the windows. I want to be able to see all the way round.'

As if to emphasize the point he wound down the window on his door, letting the bitter night air flood into the saloon. There was a howled protest as the wind and draught cut in from the space above the glass.

'Don't worry,' shouted the driver, lifting his voice above the noise. 'The turn-off is very soon now. He'll be gone then. Look for the signs and remember the names of those villages.' Optimism, the way they all wanted it.

The man beside him said, 'Auchy and Estrées, those are the two we want.'

They came too fast to the junction, and the driver had to brake hard to avoid overshooting the narrow road that curved away to the right. The car protested fiercely as it was swung round, tyres indenting the gravel chips. The man in the back was flung across the wide seat. To steady himself he clung to the heavy grip-bag that shared the seat with him. When he looked again the twin lights had disappeared.

It was a winding, delaying road now. An uneven surface, pocked by the use of tractors and heavy farm machinery. Hay from the fields showed up high in the overhanging trees where it had been whisked from the carts by the branches. The speed came

9

down. The driver still returned to his mirror, but saw only darkness.

'We'll not know for a bit yet. The curves are too quick . . . he'd have to be right up our bottoms for us to know he was there. Right up.'

He laughed, and the others joined him. Too loud to maintain the pretence that they were still calm: the apprehension came through with the successive giggles. It had been a long drive, three days of it already gone, across hundreds of kilometres of Italian and French roads. So little distance left. Less than two hours to the ferry port, far less. And now the first crisis, the initial moment of the unexpected.

The minutes went by as the driver carefully threaded his way along the centre of the road. The man in the back allowed his eyes to wander, the compulsion of his vigil at the rear window waning.

'Can we have the window closed now? I'm frozen here. All right for you bastards, but here I'll die of cold.'

'Just a few more minutes. Till we're sure we will keep the air coming in and the windows clear. You should not feel it that hard. You said you spent your winters in the Jordan mountains, you will have known the cold then, the snow on the hills—'

'Not the Jordon mountains, the mountains of Palestine.'

The laughter spread through the car. The driver turned behind him, his face huge with the smile.

'Accepted. There was no snow, no mountains for it to fall upon in Haifa. Palestine Haifa. No cold there.'

'What can you know of Haifa? Too long ago when you left for you to have memories there.'

The driver said, 'No, I have a slight memory of it. I

was four years when we left. There is a memory, though it is faint. One does not know how much is memory and how much is the image of what one has been told in the camps of the former life.'

'I have been to Haifa,' the front passenger interrupted. 'I went by lorry to work there on a site, a building project. They took us daily from Jenin. It must have been beautiful once. They were spreading concrete over the earth when we came. It was stop-gap work before I went to Beirut to study, just to fill in the time while I waited.'

They drove down a gentle incline into a tight-knit, snug village. Big church, civic building, market across to the right, and a ribbon of houses. Few lights. A grey, hostile, closed hedgehog community, battened down for the night to repel strangers, no movement except for the long-legged dog that scurried from their path. They laughed again as they saw the animal race away into the shadows. This was a private place, offering no refuge to visitors. The road ran straight through, without hesitation. There was a bridge and then they were past the village and climbing again.

The driver was still smiling as he looked again into his mirror. Two bright circles of light, perfectly and symmetrically framed in the chrome fitting. He stared hard, watching their progress down the same hill they had travelled over on their way into the village. He said nothing, but flicked his head between the view in front and the mirror. The man in the back saw his movements and swung round heavily in his seat.

'It's still there,' he said. 'The bastard is still with us. Coming into the village now, perhaps three, four hundred metres behind us. Go faster, while he's dawdling through the village, get some distance between us.'

The car surged forward, the power of its engine pulling it over the road surface. There was no consideration now for the ruts and holes. The chassis jolted and bounced as the wheels undulated on the uneven tarmac, lurching where the deeper pits had been half-filled with stones. The driver was totally concentrating now, his hands far up on the wheel, feet alternating between brake and accelerator, body deep into the well of the seat. The new speed communicated his anxiety to his passengers.

'Get me a route mapped out,' he snapped, eyes not diverted from the front. 'We don't want to find ourselves boxed in in some miserable farmyard. I want all the options, and good notice before the turnings.'

The front passenger had the maps on the floor again, and was struggling with the lighter.

'I can't do it, not with the wind, and not with the banging. I can't see a thing, the scale is too small.'

'You can have the window up, but I can't slow it, not now. What's at the back?' He yelled the last question over his shoulder.

'He's there still. The lights were gone for a moment just as he was coming out of the village, but they're back again. You can see them yourself, now we're on the ridge and in the open. Staying with us. As we've speeded so have they. Who do you think they could be? What bastards are they?'

Questioning, lack of decision.

That angered the driver. 'Don't waste yourself worrying over that sort of nonsense. Makes no difference who the bastards are. What matters now is that we know what road we are on and where it goes to. Shut up about everything else.'

Tortuously the man with the maps traced out a path. He had folded the sheets so that only that part of the region they traversed was visible. It made a small square. His eyes were very close to the paper, but it was some time before the flame of the lighter, stronger now the windows had been wound up, permitted him to find the route they were taking. Every movement of the car jolted his finger from the lines he was tracing out for them. He was aware of the frustration building up inside the car as his colleagues waited for his information, but it was a network of country lanes and minor roads that they were asking him to ferret through. He took his time. Perhaps no opportunity to rectify a mistake: one alone would be disastrous. Let them wait till he was ready, and certain. When at last he was satisfied he drew an envelope from an inner pocket of his anorak and began to write. He had trouble with the spelling of the villages, the printing was so miniature, and several times he was obliged to look again and work slowly through the longer words. He flicked the lighter closed.

'It will be the last time we can manage it for such a long time. The flame has little more power. We are well, I think. We are on the road to Fauquembergues. First we must pass through Estrées, but it looks to be the same road. At Fauquembergues there are three roads that divide just above the village. We take the most northerly, the one to the right. After that, on to Liane and so to Samer. Boulogne must be signed there.'

'How far to Estrées?' said the driver.

'Two, three kilometres, perhaps. We go straight through. Then Fauquem . . .' His voice tailed away as once again he sought to read his scribblings in the half light of the dashboard illumination.

'You're sure, now? No doubts about the route?'

'None at all,' the passenger snapped back.

He felt irritated. We hardly know each other, he thought, we've been together for days now but have no personal contact. Had never met before the planning of this mission. Had only talked in the most general and superficial way; that was as it was intended. Each one dependent on the other, needing to trust totally in the skill and resolution of his colleagues, but without the deep-rooted certainty that comes from long-standing knowledge and companionship.

The driver swerved on a bend, nearly taking them off the made-up surface and on to the raised and heavily-grassed verge. Preoccupation and anxiety bent him away from his principal role of driving the motor. Friction would follow, increased by the man who sat beside the driver, quiet and resentful at the lack of faith shown in him. In the back the third man gazed out through the window at the lights, held as if by elastic at the same unincreasing, undiminishing distance.

It was standard in these operations, the three men knew, that the attack team would come together only at the final stage, that they would have been drawn from different camps and different backgrounds. They were briefed to keep clear of questioning their comrades on personal histories. From involvement follow breakdown and collapse under interrogation. Know the code-name only, what more do you need to know? they had said. But without an understanding of each other the strains in adversity were that much greater, fuelling the apprehension inside the car.

The driver stamped his foot on the brake. On the speedometer the needle sagged back from beyond a hundred kilometres to below forty. Both his passengers hung on to their seats.

Straddling across the road was the solid, unyielding mass of a Friesian herd. Perhaps on their way to milking, perhaps being transferred from one field to another further away, perhaps being collected for market, perhaps . . .

'Murdering hell, what in the whore's mother's name do we do with this?'

'Blast the horn. Get the old fool in the front to shift them.'

'The car behind, it's closing quickly.'

'Use the grass at the side of the road.'

'The bloody peasant with them, at the front . . .'

'Get on the grass, that's the only way round.'

'The car behind us, it's less than one hundred and fifty metres. It's slowing but still closing on us.'

Inside the car there was a babble of shouting. To the front the herd seemed unmoved. Sad and heavy eyes looked at the car, then back to the black and white dog that snapped and yelped at the cows' hooves.

'Shut up! Shut up! Stop goddam-well talking,' yelled the driver.

He wrenched the car across onto the grass. Momentarily the wheels began to spin, then bit into the soft ground.

'Take it easily, slowly, or we'll be stuck.' More instructions for the driver. But he alone of the three was remaining cool, closing his mind to the shouting.

The car moved on, bumping over the loose earth that had been excavated from the ditch that ran beyond the grass and short of the field's hedge. The bumper nudged aside a cow, sending it butting its way amongst the safety of its fellow creatures. Huge, dark figures, snorting and scraping their bodies against the paintwork of the vehicle. Their smell crept into the sealed saloon, drawing twisted grimaces from the men inside.

'He's right on us. Not sixty metres away . . .' The shout from the back was cut off as the glare of the pursuing headlights illuminated the interior of the car. The passengers ducked down, only the driver remaining upright.

'All right. All right. We're nearly out now. He has to come through this crowd too.' Before he was clear of the herd he was changing up, running through the gears, weaving to avoid the leading animals before bursting back on to the open road. He caught only the briefest sight of the farmer, walking proud and straight at the head of his herd.

The car rushed forward. Ahead the road stretched into the emptiness beyond the reach of their lights. It was then the three men heard, all together, the first blast on the siren as the vehicle behind them attempted to untangle itself from the shuffling barricade. The piercing, sing-song wail of the amplified call drove through the windows and doors and roof of the car, filling it with noise, and they could see flashing among the confusion of the cows' backs and heads was the blue, rotating police lamp.

The man in the back pulled the grip towards him,

slid back the fastener and plunged his hand in amongst the shirts and socks and underpants and books, before he fastened on the hardness of the Luger pistol. Some of the grip's contents spilled out onto the leather seat-work, snagging on the raised foresight of the gun as he pulled it from the case. The magazine was in position.

'There's your answer,' he said quietly. 'Now we know who we have running with us.'

There was no reply from the front. He cocked the gun.

From his office in police headquarters in St Omer, twenty-five kilometres to the north, the man who had been issuing orders for the last hour could plot exactly the position of the fleeing car. His size, not grotesque but huge, belied the efficiency of his work. The big wall map where an aide continually moved coloured pins demonstrated this. The position of the car, kept up-to-date by the constant radio calls from the pursuing police vehicle, was shown by a yellow marker; his own men, barely separated, by a red one. Stretched out ahead of the path of the three Arabs was a near-continuous line of blue pins, straddling the minor and principal roads that led to the coast and to the port of Boulogne.

He had not expected the car to turn off from the main coast road across which his major force was concentrated, but as a precaution he had placed single police cars, each manned by two officers, on all parallel B routes. It had been his intention that the car that held his interest would be unaware that it was under surveillance before it was stopped by any one of the sixteen blocks now in place. The use of the

17

pursuit car's siren and lamp had changed that.

It had been a brutal day's work since the teletype message bearing the instructions from Paris had forewarned him of the need to set a major operation in readiness. By late afternoon, at a time when he would normally have been thinking of home and his supper, the fleet of black Citroëns had started to arrive in the discreet yard at the back of his headquarters. He had shaken several hands. Men from the Ministry, from the security services. There had been one who wore no tie, was dressed in creased jacket and slacks, and to whom everything was relayed. That one spoke his French adequately, but was not fluent, had a Central European accent and dangled a silver, six-pointed Star of David round his neck. He was treated with something close to deference.

The local man had been told little, informed of only a part of the background to the event, but had established, and forcibly, that if a car was negotiating his personal territory then it was preferable to have his own man on its tail.

'These lanes will swallow you up,' he'd said with the certainty of intimate knowledge. 'If you have no local experience, you will lose them, easy as a flea in a rug.'

The point had been accepted. One of the canniest of his drivers had taken over from the security services' surveillance that had shadowed the car across two-thirds of French territory. It had been going well, earning congratulations from the big men of the Paris counter-espionage division, until the angry and staccato bursts over the radio had warned of the intervention of the cows. But little, he had reflected, was lost. The men he hunted were still being shepherded into the fine mesh net that he had laid for them.

'When will they reach the blocking point, on their present route?' He spoke to his aide.

'Four to five minutes, sir. Not longer. Just the far side of Fauquembergues, at the crossroads. Where the petrol station and the café are.'

'Two men?'

'Two, sir. Roben and Miniux. We're in touch with them. They are alerted and have been told they have only to hold the *fedayeen* a few minutes. The larger force is already heading toward the point.'

'Tell them to go carefuly,' he said, adding as an aside – because he too was now consumed with concern – 'it was not intended only two should make the interception.'

It was the driver who spotted the red light in the centre of the road.

It was being waved slowly up and down, the international sign to halt. As he closed the distance the gendarme's fluorescent arm-band gleamed back at him above the brightness of the torch. He shouted to the others.

'There in the front. A police check. They're waving us down.'

It was the moment for one of the three to take control. The man in the back was the first to react, perhaps because it was he who clasped the only firearm in the car. Someone had to lead. There had been too much indecision in the previous few minutes, too many voices raised, his own among them. He leaned forward, head and shoulders pressing over the

19

top of the front seat. His voice was shrill, but clear and commanding.

'Burst right past him. Don't hesitate, don't slow at all. Go to his left and speed faster as we go by. He'll be armed, so keep your bodies low as you can . . . right down. Don't hesitate . . . and when you get very close, put down the front lights, then on again.'

The car hurtled towards the lone policeman, bearing down on him at some twenty-seven metres a second. The driver could see the whiteness of his face above the dark of the uniform and rain cape, could see the shape of the torch, beam now agitated, and the movement of the illuminated arm wrestling with the webbing strap across the right shoulder. The driver could see the fear fill the face, the eyes grow large. His feet were rooted to the ground, rabbit-like, transfixed.

'Kill the lights!'

The command was barked from the back of the car, and the driver instinctively carried out the instruction. Too much initiative had been heaped on his shoulders before; now he was just able to obey, to react. Fifty metres in front of him the policeman disappeared into the blackness. Almost immediately came the next order.

'On again, the lights.'

The driver shrieked with horror. Ten paces beyond the front of the car was the policeman, directly in their path, his sub-machine-gun close to his hip, pointed directly at the windscreen. He never fired.

The radiator of the car smashed into his upper thighs. His body jack-knifed into the air. The car recoiled from the impact, then shuddered again as the policeman clipped the roof before spiralling over the top of the car. The driver swerved across to the right, late and with effort, just avoiding the blue patrol car parked at an angle and filling the road. The man beside him felt the nausea rising deep in his intestines and into the constricted pipe of his throat. The third man had closed his eyes just before the fragile, toy-like figure was brushed aside, trying to shut out the vision of the gaping, incredulous mouth of the policeman.

As Roben hit the road surface, shattering his vertebrae, and destroying what faint source of life was left to him, Miniux opened fire.

From the car they saw the policeman who crouched back from the road and close to the ditch. At his shoulder was the steel-framed butt of the squat MAT 49. There were thirty-two nine-millimetre rounds in the magazine, and he fired them all at the car, moving his finger from the trigger only when the hammering kick of the weapon subsided. The bullets ploughed their way first into the engine of the car, then worked their pattern back toward the interior. The first to die was the front passenger, four shells hitting him in the chest. The driver too was struck, feeling the pain spreading from his left arm and then into the torn wounds in his side. But the man behind, protected by the bodywork and the seats of the car, survived the low velocity spray.

The car veered first to the left, then wove a way down the centre of the road as the driver fought to maintain a direction against the contradictions of the damaged steering system. His head went down once, but he jerked it upward, taking in again the contours of road, hedges and fields. A few more metres, perhaps, but not a journey. He was incapable of that, he knew. Strong enough only to get clear of the awfulness of the noise of the bullets, and the smell that they brought, and the terror that followed the collapse of the windscreen and the side windows.

He managed another three hundred metres down the road, then with great effort dragged his foot across to the brake. It took so much force to bring the car to a stop. Vermilion blood, his own blood, billowed and spilled across his knees, and ran to a pool on the rubber mat under his feet. That was death, he could recognize that. There was no way to staunch that life-flow. He looked at it, abstracted, the desire to rest supreme. The rear door opened and he saw a face at his window and then his own door gaping open. He felt himself sliding out, the rough earth coming to meet him. A hand arrested his fall and held him upright. A voice – familiar, but he could not put a name to it – was close to his ear.

'Dani, Dani, can you hear me? We have to run from here. Bouchi is dead, he has to be – he's so still. The siren is closing. But I can help you . . .'

The driver shook his head, very slowly, very deliberately.

'You go alone.' He paused, seeming to suck in air that his carved lungs could not accept. 'For Palestine, for a free Palestine. You'll remember that when you meet with him. Remember Palestine, and remember me, when you meet with the Mushroom Man.'

His eyes blinked. There was not enough strength to laugh any more, just enough to move the delicate, soft, brown eyelids, and he died.

The sirens came no closer. Must have stopped at the block, the survivor thought, as he reached inside the back of the car and pulled clear the grip. The Luger was now in his pocket. He ran to the back of the car, unscrewed the petrol tank guard, and thrust his hand into his trousers for a packet of cigarettes. He crumpled the carton, enough for it to fit comfortably into the petrol aperture. With his matches he lit the thickened paper, dropped it into the hole, and sprinted for the comfort of the darkness. He heard the explosion behind him, but didn't turn.

An official black car brought the Israeli secret service officer to the crossroads. Roben still lay in the road, a policeman's coat draped over his face, and the car skirted him at crawling pace. Further up was the parked patrol car with a knot of uniformed men round it. They were feeding Miniux with brandy from a flask. A long way beyond that, difficult to see clearly, was the smoking skeleton of the burned-out vehicle.

'How many have we found here . . . of them?' The Israeli pointed down the road.

'We found the two men. They are still inside – unrecognizable, of course. There will be problems of identification. The car reached that far, the policeman who fired on it says after it stopped it caught fire. That could be expected: it took many bullets.'

The Israeli looked back at the detective who had spoken, then stared out into the short horizon that would soon be broken in the first pencil-line of dawn. He said, 'It's very strange. Just two of them. The information that we gave in Paris was that there were three travelling. Perhaps we have lost one. Mislaid him somewhere on the way.'

Chapter Two

The young Arab's sole preoccupation was to put distance between himself and his pursuers. He had sprinted the first few hundred metres till the sodden fields and the churned mud of the farm animals had taken their toll of his strength. His feet sunk into the softened ground, causing him to heave and pull to withdraw them. Soon he had switched to a more gentle trot – not to safeguard his strength, but simply because he was not capable of faster movement. He punched his way through thick hedges, tore his coat on a strand of wire, fell once when trying to keep up his momentum and clear a dried-out ditch. But all the time he kept on his way.

He reasoned that if he were fortunate there would be no search in daylight, and that the gendarmes would be satisfied with the debris of the car. They would poke about among the charred bodies, and find little justification in launching a manhunt for him. That was if he was lucky. If they were coming after him now it meant that the following car had spotted the three of them when the lights swept the inside the second before they ducked down to avoid the brightness and the recognition.

Or the one who had fired from the side of the road, the one they had never seen, what if he had seen them in silhouette as they sped past him? If he had counted three, then they would now be massing with their dogs, and their cordons, and their large-scale maps. The bag that dragged him down with its weight – that would be his salvation. Here was the vital change of clothes, the travel documents, the mould back into society when he arrived at the ferry port.

Once, when he slipped past a darkened farm-house, old, rectangular and alien, there was barking, but otherwise his journey was a silent one. There would be no help for him in this wet and clammy countryside. He must keep going, however much the pain in his stomach, from the violent exertion without food, slowed him down. It would be difficult to move once the sun rose away behind him – where the car was, where Bouchi and Dani lay – but till then he must continue to run.

This was what the training had all been for. This was why they had urged and pummelled the recruits up the soft shale hills of Fatahland, why they had screamed and kicked them to the point beyond exhaustion, toed them into activity when they collapsed, and then, when they could move no more, left them to find their own slow path back to the tented camps. And the next morning it had been the same, and the next . . . and the next . . . They had gone on driving the young men till their stomach sinews had hardened, their lungs were cavernous, and their thigh muscles rippled and rolled in use. After that, and only then, they taught them weapon drills, the craft of being in open country. Then had

come the sophistications of disguise and concealment.

When he had first arrived at his camp, he had
been a raw, attractive and intelligent young man,
but they had spotted the bitterness, and turned his
hatred of Israel into an obsession. It had not taken
them long: seven weeks of the intensive course had
been enough. The product was then ready for use.
The determination sharpened, the viciousness
honed: the mark of the killer. That was the role they
had fashioned for Abdel-El-Famy. They were pleased
with what they saw, and confident of success when
they gave him his orders.

The man who now struggled and heaved his
way over the fields of northern France, hugging
the hedgerows for protection from the eyes of
the country people who would soon be rising from
their beds, was a very small pawn in the complex
power-game of the Middle East. Individually he was
insignificant, unexceptional. Under his given name
he featured on one of the tens of thousands of
personal files maintained by the Israelis and Western
European intelligence services.

Back in Nablus, the sprawling valley town on the
Israeli-occupied West Bank of the Jordan river, he
had flung stones at the Israeli soldiers who every
afternoon a little before one o'clock massed close to
the school gates. There was nothing particular about
that. All the High School children did it, all were at
some stage caught in the pincer nets of sprinting
Jewish soldiers, thwacked on the head and shoulders
by the billy sticks, and taken off in lorries to the
barbed-wire compound and left to cool their heels
for a few hours. He'd been through the process,

known that when the officer and the 'political adviser' came to interview them it was not the time for insolence. He'd bided his silence then, and been sent home – with an army boot in the seat of his jeans to help him on his way. Nobody filled in papers about boys like that; it would have tied up the bureaucracy for a lifetime.

But the regular afternoon rock-throwing, and the sprint back to the safety of the labyrinth of alleys and deep shops in the casbah, affected young people in a different way. Some grew beyond it, learned to control their dislike of the occupying force, and as age and responsibilities increased were able to co-exist with the new order. A few, a very few, were left scarred by the experience. Abdel-El-Famy was one of those, and tilted, half-consciously, away from passive acceptance. At eighteen he had left Nablus, had taken the bus that wound into the Jordan valley and crawled for fourteen hours across the Jordanian and Syrian plains before dropping down through the winding Lebanese hills to Beirut. There were always places in the Palestinian-orientated univer-sities for those from the Occupied West Bank. Those who had lived under Israeli rule, and rejected it to come out, were traditionally lionized. He enrolled for a course in English studies, was a good student, but throughout was brushing against a quite new science, one that away in Nablus the military governor had effectively stamped out: the science of revolutionary politics.

Through the long, hot afternoons after classes, the students sat at the café on the Corniche disputing the road to the recovery of Palestine. Choking them from the exhausts were the huge Fords and Cadillacs that paraded the tourists and visitors through the city. A few hundred yards down the road was the looming bulk of the United States of America's embassy complex, complete with heavily-armed personnel carriers manned by Lebanese troops. The open jeeps of the Squad 16 militia, with their angled, crimson berets and toy-like Armalite rifles, would cruise past the young people, eyeing them, letting them have no doubt that they were in a foreign country, without rights and without privileges. They were strangers; tolerated, but not welcomed. They could only afford the thin, upright bottles of Pepsi-Cola, which they had to drink with patience and restraint to make last. And while they sat and watched the affluence and arrogance of another country, they argued and bickered over the way to regain their own State. In the old days it had been clear that the answer lay in violence, and they had clubbed together their piastres to buy the papers – Arabic, French language and in English – that carried the long and detailed reports of the activities of Black September and the Popular Front for the Liberation of Palestine. Two bottles had lasted all day in the roadside café where they had settled with their papers and a transistor radio to hear the news of the assault on the Olympic Village in Germany. Fifth September, 1972: it had been a drawn-out and heroic day. They had worshipped the *fedayeen* who died on the airport apron at Furstenfeldbruck, reviled what they called the 'treachery' of the German police in ambushing them, rejoiced at the death of eleven Israeli sportsmen.

But out of the violence of Munich was born a respectability for the Palestine cause; and the leaders, so the young people in the cafés said, were beginning to anticipate the leathered seats around the conference tables, the scent of the huge black official cars that would carry them there, were wanting to finger the gold-cased pens that signed and initialled treaties. The arguments in the bright heat, with the sea shimmering up to the beach front, became more bitter, more divided. There were some who said any Palestinian State was better than nothing, however small, however much an exercise in diplomatic geometry, wherever the lines were drawn. There were others who saw only the complete return to their former lands as being sufficient, the argument of no compromise. This was the view of Abdel-El-Famy. He understood that the table-based arguments would only sap his resolve and desire for revenge. His presence at the cafés became less and less frequent, as he sought out the men untainted by weakness who were prepared to fight on regardless of any moves by the leadership of the Palestinian refugee community towards a half-peace.

He joined the Popular Front for the Liberation of Palestine General Command, a small but deadly organ in the so-called 'Rejection Front'. He became one of fifty-five young men, aged between seventeen and twenty-five, who had taken a solemn oath of initiation, who knew they would be sent on missions with little prospect of return or survival. It was as he had wanted it.

Just eight days ago he had been called forward from morning parade and instructed to present himself at the tent of the General Command's leader. There were three others inside when he opened the flap door, their faces all in shadow from the diffused light that passed through the grey canvas roofing. Apart from the man who directed the General Command's operations, the only figures he knew were those of 'Bouchi' and 'Dani' – new arrivals, placed with different training sections, and therefore virtual strangers. They were told they would be travelling to London, that their mission was regarded as of the utmost importance to the whole Arab movement. They were given a code-name, and an operational plan to work to, and a target to seek out. Abdel-El-Famy was no longer a penniless refugee, from a bare bungalow in the hill above the market place of Nablus. His existence had taken on a new purpose, and, like a stoat hungry for rabbit's blood, he was not to be easily deflected. His threat to the uneasy peace of the Middle East was enormous, and if he succeeded the reverberations of his action would be felt by millions throughout the Western world.

Famy lay high up among the bales in the roof of the barn. It was past eight, and he had been resting there for more than twenty minutes, yet still the breath came hard for him, and the sweat rolled in great rivers from the shiny, dank hair down across his face and onto his shoulders. He had stripped off his clothes, except his yellow underpants, and lay prone on the hard, irritating surface of the packed straw. He estimated he had travelled twenty-five kilometres. Four hours. One more such effort and he would be in Boulogne and ready for the ferry. He had decided it was better to arrive a day late in England by roughing it across country to the ferry port rather than risking all in the hope of finding a bus and a lift on the roads in the immediate aftermath of the interception. He would stay in the barn all day, emerging only as darkness fell again over the fields.

He heard children playing far away, high-pitched voices carrying to him, and when he moved to peer through a hole in the wooden planking he saw them, bright in their school clothes, and with their satchels on their backs, skipping and playing as they went away up the road. Harmless and unseeing, they offered no threat. And he began to rest, body splayed out on the bales. Once he was aroused from his sleep by a dog's sharp bark, and from the same vantage-point he watched the progress of a farmer across his land, with the dog far in front trailing a scent. Otherwise there was nothing to disturb the tranquillity he needed. In his sleep he was far away; in the hills above the town where he had been born, playing on the slopes and rolling stones down at the imperturbable goats, playing at football in the dusty school yard, working beside his father on Saturdays in their ramshackle garage.

Perhaps it was the evening coming on, as the sun dipped, and the warmth fled from the ageing timbers of his refuge, but his dream switched abruptly in mood from the happiness of his childhood to the day just after his fourteenth birthday when the big tanks had rumbled their way into the square at Nablus. He recalled the echoing machine-gun and rifle fire, the wail of the Red Crescent ambulances, and the fear on the faces that huddled in steel-shuttered doorways. It was the first time in his life he had seen terror on grown men's faces. He would not forget it. He was not asleep much longer, waking quickly but then finding himself confused

31

and needing a minute to work out his situation, where he was, and why.

It was dark in the barn when he set off. It was difficult to walk at first, as the stiffness and damp of the previous night seemed to have locked the suppleness of his knees. It would be a hard trek again, but at dawn if he pushed himself once more he should be near to the boat, ready to dispose of the muddied, drenched clothes and to substitute the precious, clean garments he carried in his grip. With laundered clothes he could assume his final identity, and take on the name of Saleh Mohammed, Algerian passport Number 478625, born 22 August 1953 at Oran.

There is a restaurant, specializing in fish delicacies, that overlooks the sea at Sidon. It is roughly half-way between Beirut and the nest of tents far to the south where the General Command maintained its headquarters. Before the Palestinians took their war into Israel, and before the retaliatory air strikes and commando raids that inevitably followed, this was a place in which tourists delighted. But the package holiday-makers, the tour operators discovered, were not seeking any great excitement when they paid out their dollars and francs and marks. They were prepared to give the possible excitement of the war zone a very wide miss. Flights of Israeli Phantoms this far north were rare, but the sightseers needed more convincing.

So the restaurant is near-deserted, and the square Crusader castle that stands just to the front of the white tablecloths no longer suffers the armies of stilletos and sandals. Out on the terrace is as comfortable and as discreet a place to discuss matters greatly confidential as any in the town.

The leader of the General Command seldom came to Beirut. His independent stand had won him many enemies inside the overall Palestinian movement, and his presence in the Lebanese capital would make him vulnerable to the attentions of the Israeli agents who at a few hours' notice could call in their country's assassination squads from the sea. He was high on their death list, perhaps given the ranking of Number Three after George Habash and Abou Iyyad. He had received a phone call on a secret unlisted number in the little village close to his tent camp in mid-morning urging him to make the rendezvous. The message was from a journalist who sympathized with the politics of the General Command and who was on the staff of one of Beirut's biggest dailies with its offices and printing works on the chic, well-heeled Rue Hamra in the heart of the most fashionable part of the Lebanese capital.

As he picked the flesh from a small, bone-packed mullet the journalist passed to the intense-eyed man opposite him a piece of news-agency copy ripped from the teleprinter in his office that carried exclusively the reports of the Agence France Presse. He was aware of basic details in the organization's operations, and had realized the significance of the eight-line story. It was the first news the General Command had had of the progress of their unit since it had flown from Beirut to Athens, and they had started their overland journey to London.

'They are reliable, this Agency?' asked the General Command leader, through a mouthful of fish.

'One has to believe them. They are taking just the

main points from all French sources, but most of this story is taken direct from the Sûreté statement. There would be little room for error. But the other agencies, Associated Press and UPI, are carrying much the same. In less detail it was carried on the Overseas Service of the BBC as well. The facts are not in dispute.'

'It speaks of road blocks. Roadblocks stopping them. Of the car being machine-gunned. Now at that time in the morning why are there roadblocks, why have countryside police been issued with weapons of the size of sub-machine-guns? There is only one interpretation, I think you will agree. There is only one explanation for such precautions to be taken in circumstances such as these.'

The journalist nodded, and sipped at the water in the narrow-stemmed glass in front of him. He said quietly: 'It has to be the Israeli service. Our people have been compromised. The French would do nothing on their own. If our people were going right through France they would be allowed to do so. The Israelis have prodded the French, poked them into action. Did they have arms?' It was a bold question for him to ask; normally he would not be privy to such minute mission details.

The leader smiled. 'Not much, perhaps a pistol, not more than one. No grenades, no explosives, no rifles. They are further on down the road: to be collected. But that is not for your paper. Perhaps you could let it be known from 'a high source in the men's movement' that they were not armed. But not identify the group. Yes?'

'There is no difficulty in that. "Two unarmed Palestinians gunned down by the French police" –

34

that will make good reading. Perhaps the Paris office of our paper can work up the involvement of the Israeli Secret Service, and the two can be married together.' The journalist began to take a quick note in his pocket-sized pad of the form of words he would use.

The two men attacked their meal, pulling with their fingers at the larger bones, spitting out the smaller ones, and dousing their hands in the bowls provided. The terrace was quite empty, other than the two diners at this one table. When he had finished the commando leaned forward. There was no-one within yards who could have overheard what he said, but old habits die hard.

'The reports speak of two men being found in the car. There could be no doubt of that one fact?'

'No doubt at all. That is common to all the stories.'

'And if they had captured a prisoner, a third man, would they have released that information?'

'Most likely,' the journalist replied. 'It is not the sort of thing they are going to hold secret. There is no reason for them to.'

Again the smile played around the mouth of the General Command's leader, dallied there a little, and then faded. He was not one given to conventional humour. One would not expect that from the man who was responsible for a morning's carnage at the bright modern Fiumincino Airport of Rome that left thirty-one dead, nor from the man who ordered his subordinates into the northern Israeli settlement of Kiryat Shmona, an operation that filled seventeen coffins. But irony amused him. And it would be ironic if the death of that man's colleagues were to enhance his own safety. It was no part of the journalist's role in the movement that he should be aware of such interests.

The leader said: 'I would be interested to hear if there are any further arrests, or sightings, or . . .' He let it tail away. He had said enough. The journalist waved his arm at a distant figure who hovered at the entrance to the kitchens, gestured a writing motion with his hands to signify that the meal was over and that he wished to accept the bill.

'Before you leave there is a message I want you to deliver. It is sensitive. I want it handed only to the man whose name I shall give you. It is in Beirut, and must reach him this afternoon.' The leader drew a sheaf of papers from inside his khaki combat jacket, revealing for a moment the polished, light-brown shoulder holster he wore through all his working hours, and with a ball-point pen began to write. Had he looked the waiter who brought the reckoning for the meal could not have seen what was being written, as the leader protected the message with his hands. The pen moved hurriedly and with bold strokes across the paper, the Arabic symbols firm and decisive.

While the bank notes were away being sorted out at the cash till he said: 'It must go straight away to the commercial secretary of the embassy that I have named on the folded paper. I will tell you what it says; you'll want to open it if I don't tell you, and I would rather not have it delivered as if it's been half-way through the *souk* in Baghdad.' He laughed, and the journalist shuffled in embarrassment, and muttered his protestations. 'No, I know you, you are all the same. It merely says that we go on as before, but at reduced strength. There; that tells you all or nothing. For you, my good friend, I think it tells you nothing. Nothing. And you should be happy that way.'

And he was away, striding between the tables inside the restaurant towards the car park where his Fiat waited. Once he raised his right arm above his shoulder, a final farewell to his luncheon informant. One of his bodyguards had stayed at the front door of the building, and he now fell in behind. Two more were sitting in the car. As the leader settled into his seat the driver engaged the gears, and they moved off.

'We have to be patient a while,' he said. 'Two of the men on the European operation have been intercepted. They are dead. There is no word of the third, nor of whether the French even know of his existence. If there were to be one who has survived, and could go on with the task, which one would you select?' He was speaking with the man who sat beside him, an older man whose judgement he trusted.

'Of those three?' the other paused for a moment's reflection. 'It would be the one we code-named "Saleh". Saleh Mohammed. The one that calls himself "Famy".'

'That is a good judgement. Pray to God it is that one who lives. They were all fine boys, but he was the best. The youngest, but still superior. It is a great problem that he faces, the one who has lived, if that is indeed the case.'

His companion stroked the sleek, steel darkness of the barrel of the Klashnikov rifle that lay across his lap, his eyes playing on the cars that flashed by them. The leader was talking softly, half to himself, and there were no interruptions.

'Much will depend on the people that he meets there. These Irishmen, they represent an unknown factor, and one man on his own must be more dependent on them than we had planned. More is required now than a simple availability of weapons, explosives, transport and a safe house. The foreigners must provide a different dimension. They must become involved.'

He was silent. The other man said: 'Will they provide that?'

'It is imponderable,' said the leader. 'Probably, but I cannot say with certainty. In Tripoli they were friendly enough. They wanted to co-operate then – were anxious to buy weapons. They were making a geture towards us then. That was the conception of the plan. They have killed many times in their own struggle, but always have been fearful of the scale of missions that we are prepared to stage. Perhaps their cause is only worth fighting for, not worth dying for. There were promises in Tripoli, endless promises. As I have said, we shall have to be patient.'

Again the smile.

After their swim the young man and the girl had taken their towels, draped them on the grass away from the pool and close to the high wooden fence that shut it off from the road and the car park, and sprawled down on them. It was hot that evening in London's south-west suburbs, and facilities were overstretched. But few wanted to be in the shade, far from the water, and so the couple found the privacy they searched for.

Five-and-a-quarter miles down the road were the main runways of Heathrow Airport, and every few seconds the couple's voices would be drowned, losing the competition with the Rolls-Royce and Pratt and Whitney engines that surged overhead. But in between the cacophony there was time to talk, not of anything special, nothing heady, just the kind of things that were being endlessly repeated by other couples who shared the grass with them but were out of earshot.

She was seventeen-and-a-half, was called Norah, and punched a cash register in a supermarket from eight-thirty in the morning till five-fifteen in the afternoon. She lived at home, and thought the boy she had met beside the pool the previous evening quite the most interesting she had encountered in her limited experience. She wore last year's bikini, which had been right for Benidorm and the ten days of concentrated Spanish Mediterranean heat, but now seemed tight and restricting, as if unable to cope with the developments of the previous twelve months. He seemed to like it, though; his eyes were seldom off it. Most of the time they lay on their backs, stretched out and relaxed, fingers touching, his short-cut nails searching out the lines on her wrist, the crannies between her fingers, the soft sensitive places on the underside of her knuckles. He'd kissed her last night, quietly and gently in the lane behind her house, after the cinema and the ditching of her friend. He'd held her loosely with none of the frantic endeavour she was used to from the series of boyfriends who took her for a coffee and a dance or a film and then believed it their right to maul and explore her afterwards as due return for a pound's expenditure.

This one was different. No thigh pressed hard

between her legs, no fumbling under her blouse, no hand trying to get inside her jeans. The boy had kissed her, long and easily, seemed to think that was what they both wanted, was right, had told her he'd see her tomorrow, same place. She'd come to the pool, and he'd been there, where he'd said he'd be, looked happy enough to see her again.

She had done most of the talking, last night and again this afternoon. He seemed to want that, didn't interrupt, looked interested. He said very little himself as she chattered about her holiday, her friends, her mother and father, her work, the prices in the shops, the television programmes she saw when she was at home, the films she went to on her nights out. He didn't reciprocate. Last night, in her bed at the back of the semi-detached house a mile-and-a-half away, she'd blamed herself for that. "Course he didn't say anything, didn't give him much of a chance to get a word in,' she'd said to herself.

Soon the dew would be forming on the grass, and the coolness of the middle evening was beginning to embrace her bared shoulders. She shivered a little, and reached out for the jersey she had brought with her. She'd come equipped this time to be out late in the open air, uncertain what the next few hours would bring, but excited and expectant.

'I'll catch my death, dressed with nothing, like this,' she giggled, and turned toward the boy anticipating he would be smiling back at her. But he was sitting up now, his head arched back, neck taut, long fair hair pressed against his shoulder blades, eyes staring and intent on the huge obliterating frame of the Boeing 747 three thousand feet above them.

'You're late, big bird,' he said soundlessly against

40

the roar of the aircraft. 'Don't be late next week, not for the plucking of the Mushroom Man.'

'What did you say?' she shouted, wriggling closer to him to hear his reply.

'Nothing, nothing. Just that they're flying late tonight.' Her ear was close to his mouth, and he spoke softly, with his delicate Irish brogue flavouring the words.

'What plane is that?' she said, watching over his shoulder the vast airborne mass, almost beautiful with its white fuselage and the deep sky-blue livery line running its length, tail erect and crowned with the simple star on the pure background.

'That, my little girl, is a Boeing seven-four-seven, manufactured at Seattle, in the State of Washington, USA. It's valued at a little more than fifteen million pounds, and that one is flying in Israel's colour. El Al, and late again.'

He got up from the grass, and began to pull on his trousers over the dried-out swim suit. Before he draped his shirt over his shoulders she saw again the reddened disfigurement of the healed wound, in diameter little more than a pencil width, low to the left side of his chest. She had asked about it the day before, and been told of a stumble while carrying a pitchfork, on the farm, many years back.

'Are we doing anything tonight?' She mentioned it hesitantly, though she'd already told her mother she'd be out late, at her friend's home.

'I'm sorry,' he said, seeing her face fall open with the disappointment. 'I'm sorry, I really am, but I can't tonight. I have to meet a man . . .'

'About a dog,' she said.

'No, it's real. I have to meet a man tonight. It's

been planned a long time, and he's coming over from abroad to see me. Really. There's some business I have to do, take a few days. I'll see you then, again. Definitely. Definitely. Come on, I'll walk you down to the bus stop.'

She was near to tears when he left her, waiting for a red double-decker to take her back to an early night at home.

For two hours Ciaran McCoy stayed beside the train departure board at Waterloo Station, waiting for the man he was to meet to come forward and introduce himself. He had fulfilled all his instructions. Red tie, light raincoat over his right arm, Avis Rentacar sign displayed in his hand. Endless faces scurried past him, running to catch their trains, running away from them, all anxious not to stay a minute longer in the belly of the great terminus than was necessary. It was futile and frustrating. He'd been buffeted, pushed and shoved by those who saw him as an obstruction in their path, but never noticed, not acknowledged. Close to midnight, he walked across the now near-empty concourse to the battery of telephone booths and dialled the seven-figure number he had been given.

His call was answered by a switchboard deep behind the Edwardian façade that housed a North African embassy in a smart SW7 address overlooking the favoured Rotten Row and the spaces of Hyde Park. McCoy asked for an extension, was surprised when the operator did not demur that there would be no-one there at this hour, and was further surprised when the phone was promptly answered. He couldn't remember the word he was supposed to

42

give. Been waiting too long, too wrought up to remember it. Bloody foreign word, and he didn't know what it meant.

'It's McCoy here. Ciaran McCoy. I was told to call this number. Our friend hasn't shown.'

The voice at the other end was calm, reassuring, in perfect English. Unmindful of the lack of the code-word. There had been a delay. The situation was uncertain. The project might be called off, might not. Developments were awaited. He should telephone again tomorrow evening, but not so late. The voice wished him good night, and the call was terminated.

Five seconds after McCoy put the receiver back into its rest the tape recorder stopped rolling. It was standard procedure that all calls to that number were automatically monitored; and had been so ever since the extension number was obtained from a second officer of that embassy in exchange for Foreign Office silence about his drinking habits. The diplomat had done well from the bargain; the conservative Moslem government he represented in London would have looked badly upon his be-haviour.

The tape would be one of scores of conver-sations recorded that night that would be replayed by shorthand typists working from the basement of a substantial building in Curzon Street, Mayfair, a bare mile from the embassy.

Chapter Three

David Sokarev always carried the Mauser pistol in the glove compartment of his car. It rested there on top of the maps and the packet of boiled sweets that his wife had bought him as an aid to ending his smoking habit. On top of the gun and hiding it was the rag that he used to clean the overnight moisture from his windscreen. The pistol was loaded, but with the safety catch in force, and was used only twice a year, when he went on the shooting range east of Beersheba. Left to himself he would have placed it in a drawer and forgotten about it, but he had been ordered to possess a gun, and therefore it was easier simply to leave it in the car. If the occasion had arisen when he was obliged to fire in anger he would probably have missed. His chunky iron-rimmed spectacles were a witness to his poor eyesight. The pistol was never disturbed, rejected like the boiled sweets, but, like them, of insufficient importance to have an issue made of it.

There had been a suggestion that his work made him too sensitive a man to be driving himself to work, and there had been talk that he should have a driver pick him up from his home, take him to the

44

laboratory, and then late in the day bring him back to Beersheba. He had railed at that as preposterous, asked them whether there were so many able-bodied men without proper jobs to do that they could spare one for such sterile activity. He had won his case, and drove himself.

He was a careful and methodical man, and unlike so many of his fellow-countrymen drove slowly and with circumspection. It took him between forty-seven and fifty minutes from the time he left his flat on the third floor of the block till he presented his identity card at the gate of Dimona. Colleagues using the same route would flash past him, hoot their horns and wave cheerfully at old 'Tortoise', as they had nicknamed him. It was a boring ride to have made most days a week, and most weeks a year for the last sixteen years, but his mind was seldom concerned with the other traffic. The problems of plutonium, sub-critical masses, fission, isotope separation, neutrons – they were what enveloped him, as the little car trudged its way back and forth the twenty-four miles across the Negev desert. He would read, too, as he drove, the book propped against the steering wheel. He was able, apparently, to take in the printed word while successfully avoiding the fast-moving hazards which shared his road; but few of his colleagues lightly accepted the offer of a lift.

When he had started work at Dimona the project had been at the apex of Israel's secret list. He had not been able to tell any family friends where he went each day, nor the nature of his work. The buildings, tucked away among the sandhills and placed well back from the road, were described to the outside world as housing a textile factory, and no-one who knew him could comprehend a link between David Sokarev and man-made fibres.

But the Bedouin who used to pass, listlessly urging their camels between the dunes, had taken the news of the cranes and bulldozers and cement-making apparatus across the border to the military governor of the Egyptian town of El Arish. The message had gone to Cairo of huge construction works deep in the Negev desert, of wire fences sprouting up, of armed troops patrolling. The concern in Cairo was passed to the American State Department in Washington. There, too, anxiety was expressed and the foolproof system of international espionage set in motion.

From a United States Air Force base in northern Iran a U2 plane had taken off with orders to fly over Dimona and photograph the new complex. The pilot had violated Israeli air space at an altitude of fractionally more than fifteen miles. At the IAF field which had specific responsibility for Dimona they could only watch the radar blip of the American reconnaissance aircraft and contain the frustration that it was beyond their own operational ceiling. It had been a brilliantly hot October day, back in 1960, when the photographs were taken. Sokarev had been working in his temporary, prefabricated wooden offices, awaiting the fulfilment of the Director's promise that he was high on the list for more suitable and permanent premises. He, like everyone else who pored over charts and diagrams and formulae, was unaware of the pictures being recorded in the upper stratosphere.

After the U2 landed in Turkey the rolls of film

were rushed under conditions of great secrecy direct from the cameras in the plane's nose to another aircraft standing ready and fuelled to fly to Washington. They showed the little wooden hut where Sokarev worked – or at least its roof – but there was small interest in that compared with the bulky shape discernible a hundred yards away across the sand and surrounded by the lorries that were needed to bring up the materials. The men expert in interpreting altitude photography identified a medium-sized nuclear reactor, the integral plant necessary in the manufacture of the plutonium that is at the heart of an atomic explosion.

When Dimona was washed out into the open the news made slight adjustments to Sokarev's life. The degree of security that had wrapped round the very existence of the project was relaxed. The Israeli Government issued statements about the requirement for nuclear energy for peaceful uses, ranging from electricity power to the extended life of vegetables on shop counters. Sokarev was pleased. Fewer of his friends regarded him with such curiosity. Life became more normal.

In the halcyon days after the June Victory of 1967, when the nation's defences seemed secure and the Arabs had taken a bloodied, broken nose, been pushed back far from the Israeli settlements, across the great buffer zones of Sinai, the Jordan valley, and the Golan Heights, then there was little to concern Sokarev about the pace of his work. He was at forty-one a young man for his job, on the up, regarded by his colleagues as brilliant and directing his energies toward what his project director blithely called the 'agro-nuclear complexes': the reclaiming of

47

desert land through the use of thousands of millions of gallons of sea water, distilled through nuclear power. The project did not last.

The war of attrition across the Suez waterway exacted a toll both from human life and from the fragile Israeli economy. New tensions rose along the Egyptian and Syrian borders. And on the day in October 1973 when Sokarev and his family were at prayer, Yom Kippur Day, the Arab armies breached the great defensive lines that lay along the Canal and which bestrode the Golan. The peace was hard-won this time; none of the trumpeting of 1967 followed the cease-fire. Reports filtered through the foreign press of new, far-reaching Soviet rockets, sited on the plains behind Damascus and protected by nests of anti-aircraft missiles, rockets that could reach any Israeli town, either with a conventional high-explosive warhead or armed with a localized nuclear device. To Sokarev and to many of his team it was clear the time had come to consider intensely, if perhaps belatedly, what was called in the common rooms round the world where men specialized in physics, the 'nuclear option'.

The days at Dimona started earlier, ended later. Sokarev and the team that was built around him wrestled with the problems of abbreviations in time and expenditure for the fashioning of the bomb. Extraction of uranium from the phosphate ores of the Negev was increased, as the plant gulped up more than twenty-five tons a year. Some of the ablest men in the department were sent to the United States, and then to West Germany to study at the European nuclear centre. As a result the costly Jericho missile system was developed with a range of more than three hundred miles, the country's own and independent delivery weapon.

The politicians began to talk. 'The possibility of nuclear weapons moving into the Middle East theatre should not be eliminated,' said Moshe Dayan. Israel's President proudly announced that his country had assembled the knowledge and equipment to construct the bomb.

And from the reactor in the desert came the tiny quantities of plutonium 239, at little more than eight kilograms a year, in bulk the size of a fruit from the Beersheba orangeries, yet with the capability to create a twenty kiloton explosion. The bombs, equivalent in destructive capacity to those dropped more than thirty years earlier on Hiroshima and Nagasaki, could not be tested, but at least the stockpile was starting.

It had been a brutal twenty months for Sokarev, of fierce hours, interminable arguments over government money, that never extended to the budgetry minimum he maintained his department must have if research were to continue. He took his papers home at night, but increasingly they were covered with the columns of figures that represented the finances of the programme and were expressed in the currency of the inflated Israeli lira. He longed for the days when his working brain had been overwhelmed only by the horizontal characters of the equations he sought to set up and then disprove, and, if he could not find the flaw, then rejoice in the knowledge of perfection.

That he was tired showed. His face was greyer and had the pallid yellowness that comes from perpetual artificial light, denial of sunlight, and the harassment of worry. His trousers fitted him poorly and had stretched, while his shirt bulged over his belly; the tennis that he had played twice a week, and which had been his principal form of enjoyment, was now denied him.

But the guard who stopped him that Thursday morning at the first of the security perimeter gates and who knew the personnel who came and went at the plant noted that the normally worn face of David Sokarev was a little brighter, a little livelier. As he looked into the scientist's window, waiting for the Polaroid identity card to be produced, he saw almost a spark of recognition in the other man's eyes. Generally there was no acknowledgement, but today there was an inclination of the head, near to a greeting.

'You're looking well today, Professor,' the guard said, as he handed the plastic-coated card back to the waiting hand.

'So I should be. Off out of here for a few days. My last day and then away for a bit.'

'Holidays?' the guard asked, before moving back to swing up the red and white painted 'Stop' barrier that blocked advance.

'Of a fashion. A few days in London, then on to New York and perhaps San Francisco after that. The last isn't finalized. A few lectures, to meet old friends. Something of a holiday, yes.'

Twice more the car was stopped by grey-brown uniformed guards. Each time they swung their submachine-guns across their backs, and walked forward to check the card. All three men who spoke to the professor as he arrived that morning were to notice the fractional bounce that had lifted him.

'I'm late in,' he said to his secretary in the outer office. 'Was held up talking to the man on the gate.' She said nothing. It was one minute past eight o'clock.

'What have we today?'

'Mostly meetings. The Director wants to see you as well, preferably in the afternoon. Two sub-committees in the morning, so that will fit well. And there was a call a few minutes ago from the Foreign Ministry. They want to drive down from Jerusalem to see you, but they'd like us to fix a time for the afternoon, and call them back. I would suggest about four, after you've seen the Director.' She was a pretty girl, tall and straight-backed, and wearing an eye-riveting miniskirt high up on her sun-browned thighs. Efficient as well, and the office was chaos every time she went for military service.

'What do they want in Jerusalem?' He was behind his desk now, scooping at the papers from his tray, and scattering them over the wooden surface.

'It was the security division from the Foreign Ministry. Protection Branch. They said they wanted to talk about your trip.'

It was closer to six in the evening, and many of the Dimona workers were already on their way home, before David Sokarev's desk was clear enough for him to feel able to abandon his work for the three weeks of his visit to Europe and North America. There were no more letters to sign, charts to check, scribblings to be made in the margin of reports. No more excuses to prevent him seeing the two men who waited in his outer office.

He saw they were both young when they came through the door. Fit and good-looking. They shook his hand. He neither apologized for keeping them so long nor did they seem to expect it. Joseph Mackowicz had come to talk, Gad Elkin to listen.

Mackowicz said, 'I am glad you could see us, Professor. We are both to be travelling with you throughout your journey. We will be very close to you at all times. It is best on these visits that we get to meet the people we accompany before we leave, rather than meeting at the airport, just seeing each other a few minutes before departure. I think you have little experience of being escorted on a visit abroad?'

'I have not been away for some years. It was a long time ago and then I travelled only with my secretary.' He saw Elkin smile from his chair. 'Not the one I have now, I can assure you. A rather more formidable lady. When I indented to take Anna to handle my correspondence, type my speeches, things like that, it was refused. Not enough money for her to go, I was told. I did not anticipate that if they could not scrape together the lire for Anna they would be able to send two gentlemen such as yourselves. I had resigned myself to travelling on my own.'

'Your typing will be taken care of; the embassies will find a girl for that.' Mackowicz did not react, was not one to rise to even the most gentle humour. 'We have the places that you will be visiting, and we will supervise your programme. What we want for the moment is a guarantee that you will afford us your co-operation, and take most seriously our advice.'

The professor looked hard at the young man, adjusted his glasses, then pushed them back to the bridge of his nose.

'I would never knowingly not co-operate.'

'That, Professor, is excellent news. Not everybody in a similar position to yours is happy to have us in such proximity. Some talk of embarrassment for their foreign colleagues. I can assure you if there is embarrassment it is something we must suffer.'

'I had not given myself such importance,' said the professor slowly, a tinge of sadness in his voice. 'Nor had I realized that I might be at risk. It is not the sort of situation that one considers.'

Mackowicz said, 'We had not considered our athletes at Munich to be either politically important or at risk. We knew, we'd been told, that an Arab attack, from the Black September faction, would come at about that time somewhere in Europe, at some international gathering. No-one put the sum together, and no guard was given to our people. They died defenceless, and it will not happen again. A single tennis player, or swimmer or runner, if they represent Israel, then they are protected. It was all laid down in the reorganization that followed Munich. Inevitably, so too for a politician, a diplomat, or a scientist of your status.'

Anna carried in a tray with coffee. No milk, too expensive, sugar, coarse and with the granules over-large. The men stopped talking while she was in the room and handing out the mugs. The professor thanked her, said he would send a postcard, and see her on his return. She should go home, he told her. He could lock up. She waved, a small feminine gesture, at the door, closing it behind her.

53

'Gentlemen,' said Sokarev. 'I am only a scientist, perhaps only a technician. Not versed in the ways outside Dimona. I read the paper, not often, but I read it, and I listen to the wireless in the evening. Though I had not imagined it before I can accept the possibility of threat. But I would not take it as a great one, a small risk only. So I ask myself these questions. First: why did you come here tonight, a long journey – and we have discussed nothing of importance so far? Second, I say: why do we need two men to look after me? Why cannot this be done by our own people from the embassies when I get off the plane, or by the police forces of the countries that I visit?'

There was silence in the room. Sokarev continued to gaze at Mackowicz, waiting for the answer. He watched him light his cigarette, unhurried, patient with the ignorance. In the distance there was the noise of a car starting up. The other scientists would be gone soon, and the cleaners would be on their rounds. Permeating the room came the semi-audible moan of a far-off electric generator. A fly played around the professor's nose till he swatted it away.

It was Elkin this time who spoke. 'It had been intended there would be just one of us. The situation changed, and we have to change with it. You are regarded by the Government as a high-risk category. You have much specialized knowledge from your work here. You head an important team. All those things make you an important target, but then all those things we knew weeks ago when your itinerary was filed. Since that time there have been movements – information – that have suggested to us that your protection should be increased. Our work, in a way, can be considered perhaps as sensitive as yours. You would not wish me to say more.'

'You have said nothing,' retorted Sokarev.

'We have listening posts,' Mackowicz cut in. 'We have people who listen for us, and we have people who interpret what they hear. It's a difficult, drawn-out process, and many times we are wrong. Often there are several factors in the air at the same time; rarely do they come to land together. But from what we learn we try to form a shape, to anticipate their actions. This is what we are doing at the moment. The pattern is not yet whole in this instance, but it has a form, an outline.'

'Specifically, there is a threat to me?' There was puzzlement from Sokarev, his confidence about to drain.

'We cannot take it that far yet,' said Elkin. 'We know a squad from one of the Palestinian terror groups has been moving north across Europe. They were intercepted on our advice by the French authorities. At least two of them died. We believed from our informants that there were three. If so, one is not yet accounted for. They were on the road to Boulogne when they were blocked. It is reasonable to assume from that route that their destination was a cross-Channel ferry, and Britain. We have no political leaders, no military men in Britain in the next month. Only yourself, Professor.'

Sokarev was quiet, subdued and unhappy in the presence of these chilling young men, and growing resentful of the message they brought. The silence, long and perceptible, even to the point of shuffled feet, was broken by Mackowicz. 'You will not have read about this, nor will you need to repeat it. Six nights ago the same group that has held our interest in Europe mounted a raid from their advance base in Lebanon across the fence towards Ramot Naftali, south of Kiryat Shmona. They were ambushed by an army patrol. There were five in all and we captured one. The rest we killed in the action. The IDF statement that evening announced that one of the terrorists had escaped, though he was in fact in our hands. Under interrogation he talked to us. They often do, you know. We gave him his life by barter. He would survive but he would take back with him a radio transmitter. He could give us further information about operations. That was the agreement we made. There were no messages, and he is dead. We have many eyes and ears in Fatahland, and yesterday we were told. He died not nicely, but in pain, and choking because his testicles were blocking his windpipe. You will see from what I say that information is not easy to come by, and when we do have access then we listen to what we are told.'

Sokarev felt he wanted to vomit. He rose up unsteadily from his chair and moved across the room. By the door he switched on the light, banishing the spreading shadows, flooding the office from the fluorescent bar hung from the ceiling. Apart from a single photograph and a chart that showed him which members of his team had booked their annual leave or were on extended sick leave the walls were bare. As he wanted his office – uncomplicated. The photograph showed his three children; two girls in army slacks and regulation V-necked navy blue sweaters, and between them his son, a head taller and in light, air-force summer khaki, with his pilot's wings on his chest. Home together for a 'shabbat' leave, and they'd be together again, same opportunity tomorrow. They expected to fight, could comprehend the modern war fought crawling at belly-level beyond the frontiers of their country. But to Sokarev the dark and sinister images that the two security men had introduced to his office were hostile and alien.

'You are presumably going to tell me what this terrorist said under questioning?' He had stayed by the door.

Mackowicz and Elkin stood up. Mackowicz said, 'He told us they had been planning an attack in Europe. He did not know the location, he did not know the target. He knew only the code-word for the operation. Under extreme interrogation he gave it to us. The PFLP General Command are the terrorist grouping, and they have given this operation the word "kima". It is an Arabic word, of the Palestinian dialect. Translated, it is "mushroom". Not the small button-shaped one of the kitchen, but the larger, free-growing plant that magnifies and flourishes. That is why we consider a man from Dimona to be at risk. And why where will be two of us at your side when you travel.'

After they had gone David Sokarev sat a long time in the room.

Then he collected together the papers he would require for his journey, packed them into the old, frayed briefcase, and locked the door behind him. There were only a few lights on in the office blocks and laboratories but all around were the brilliantly-lit wire fences. The watch-towers were manned after darkness, and as he walked to his car he could see the men high up on the stilted platforms, and below them the dog-handlers with the proven attack alsatians. This was the oasis that he knew, safe, rewarding, isolated.

When he reached for his keys he found that his hands were trembling, that he had difficulty in selecting the correct key to open the door. He got in and sat in the seat for a few moments, to calm himself and mollify the breathiness that affected him. Then he drove off for the gates, and the road, and home. At the three check-points the guards called out a greeting, but this time won no response.

He drove home faster than usual, arriving at the flat a full eight minutes earlier than his established habit would have permitted. His wife noticed the drawn look in his face and the tension about his eyes. For the first time in his adult life he was experiencing fear. It was a fear of the unknown. Of a strange city of millions of people, but where one man, or two, or three, or four, had a solitary and inflexible purpose, the destruction of David Sokarev, of himself. He had seen the photographs of these men in the *Jerusalem Post* and the afternoon paper, *Yediot Aharonot*; they were on their backs, broken and spent, cut down by gunfire, surrounded by some circle of elated soldiers. They always died, always seemed to end their missions dragged by the ankles to an army jeep, flung onto a bloody stretcher with the reverence of a turnip sack. Garbage. But there was no reason that Sokarev could see to believe their commitment would be any the less in a foreign capital.

She brought him his meal. Some liver, the money for it dug deep from the housekeeping purse, and watched the way he toyed with the meat, eating to please her. He told her nothing of Mackowicz and Elkin, and what they had said inside the office.

Chapter Four

A city is a vulnerable, flaccid target for an act of
terrorism. Huge and preoccupied and indifferent –
the ideal hunting ground, and never more so than if
the stalkers are a small, motivated group of men
whose numbers can be counted on the fingers of
one hand. In time of war a city can be mobilized,
organized and put into uniform with specific tasks
to perform. But when peace reigns it absorbs the
danger, turns the other cheek, has too much with
which to concern itself to be agitated by the tiny
cancer flowing at will in its body.

The Provisional IRA proved conclusively how
defenceless is a great international capital. One hundred and forty-eight bombs in twenty-two months
and the mighty carcase barely knew it was under
attack. Cars packed with gelignite disintegrating
among shopping crowds, duffle-bags exploding on
busy railway platforms, mutilated bodies ferried
away in fleets of ambulances. But the next time
the sirens went the crowds still gathered to watch,
sometimes amused, always interested, never involved.

Where eight million people are gathered together

over an area of some four hundred square miles everyone is a stranger. For the terrorist there is anonymity here, the opportunity to blend into whatever background he chooses. If he has funds he will take a smart flat – Mayfair or Belgravia – where a porter will salute as he goes out, but will ask no questions. Otherwise he can turn to the myriad of small hotels behind the big railway termini of North London, pay when he registers, and be left in total privacy. In the big city the man who is careful and patient, and skilled in the art of guerrilla warfare, should survive. He can blame only himself if he fails.

The forces ranged against him are meagre. The principal and most obvious bastion that he must avoid is the civilian police force, with its headquarters at Scotland Yard, close to Victoria Station. Confronted with the increasing problems of conventional crime, serious and minor, of public apathy and lack of manpower, the metropolitan police have been forced into a crash-course in combating international violence. They started without experience and it was a hard road to make up ground when the luxury of time was not permitted. The whole concept of fighting such an enemy had been far from officials' minds when they moved their offices and files and laboratories into a towering, glass-faced structure so vulnerable to car-bomb attack that policemen had to patrol the pavement outside to prevent any vehicle parking unattended within fifty feet of its walls. But, of the hundreds of detectives who scurry in and out of the main swing doors, flashing their warrant cards at the bemedalled commissionaires, relatively few are engaged in anti-terrorist operations. Those that are belong to Special Branch, the wing formed close on a hundred years ago to counter the Irish Fenian threat.

The Irish problem still dominates their work – tying men down on the long-drawn-out surveilance of buildings, meetings, pubs, airports and homes, along with the constant search for reliable informers.

The Branch men have also to concern themselves with the potential of subversion, and keep their paperwork up to date on the fringe anarchist groups, the most militant of the background trade union officials, the activities of the Iron Curtain-bloc diplomats. They are responsible for the protection of principal Britons, from the Prime Minister downwards, and also of foreign persons of rank arriving in the country. They are not generously endowed with funds, or with manpower. Less than five hundred men, and the country to cover.

They had been informed of the planned visit of David Sokarev to Britain, but with four days to go to his arrival at Heathrow Airport they were unaware of his crucial importance to Israel, and of the extent of the threat against him. At a later stage there would be a discussion over the telephone between the Middle East desk and the Security Attaché at the Israeli embassy, probably the night before the professor flew in. In the normal way of things the decision on the need for protection would be taken then, with consideration given to the availability of officers, and more pressing priorities.

But for the survival of David Sokarev on his journey through London there was another group of men far more important than the officers of the Special Branch. They worked from little-known premises in one of the most fashionable districts of the capital. Close to the Playboy Club, the London Hilton and the Londonderry Hotel, is a gaunt five-storey building. It is in need of fresh paint, pointing and general repairs. The windows, in the uniform metal-rimmed rows so beloved by architects of the twenties and thirties, are shielded by lace curtains; those on the lower floors are protected by half-inch thick concertina steel meshes. Side entrances to the block have been bricked up, as have upper windows at the corners of the building that still show the rifle-aiming slits, hurriedly fitted in 1940. There is no plaque on the walls beside the main doorway to give a clue to the occupation of those who work in the building. The parking meters set into the pavements outside the front entrance are masked by red plastic hoods to prevent the casual motorist from leaving his car there. Above the doorway, and needing the attention of the cleaners, are the words 'Leconfield House'. The building carries no other visual identi-fication. It is the nerve-centre of the country's most secret organization, the one responsible for deep undercover counter-espionage and counter-terrorist operations; the British Security Service works from here.

Eleven hours after the tape recording of Ciaran McCoy's conversation with the Arab diplomat had been completed the spools were on the desk of a man who used a small office on the second floor of Leconfield House. A transcript had been taken by the duty clerks, who were the first to listen to the play-back, and that too lay on the high-polished oakwood surface. The room occupied by Philip Willoughby-

Jones was bare to the point of starkness. A regulation square of carpet, determined by his Civil Service grade, covered the centre of the floor and was surrounded by ageing though systematically polished linoleum. The door to the room was set opposite the only window; on the third wall was a calendar sent out by a firm that specialized in the postal sales of garden bulbs; against the fourth was a steel filing cabinet. Grouped in a semicircle in front of the desk were four chairs, framed in metal tubing, seats covered with yellow plastic, not designed for comfort but for working men who would leave them when their business was completed. The chair behind the desk offered only a slight concession in two vaguely-cushioned armrests.

Jones – he detested the hyphenated name his father had taken to using after his admittance to the masonic order of a small, East Midlands industrial town – was short and sparely built. He had a sharp gull nose that jutted out above his brush moustache, a legacy of his Royal Air Force days. His thin cheeks, merging into the shape of his bone structure, had neither colour nor verve, and were evidence of a man who had spent most of his time indoors. His hair, wispy and greying, was tended hurriedly and carelessly each morning, and remained in shape only for as long as the water used on his comb maintained order. The brightness lay in his eyes; narrow, deep-set, but alert and alive. It was his lower jaw that separated him from other men, the way the skin, lacking in wrinkles and hair, had been transposed from his right buttock to cover the incinerated layer that he had lost so many years before. The replacement had no gloss or animation, and at the point where the new skin had been grafted to the old it irritated and annoyed. Jones was responsible for the general surveillance of the activities of Middle East embassies located in London.

Duggan, of Irish Affairs, would be down in fifteen minutes to talk with him, along with Fairclough, Arab Affairs (Palestinian). Before they came there was time to look again at the file on the embassy in Princes Gate. So much of his work was done from the files; the most thorough and successful course of action followed invariably from the writing down of minutiae – that was the Director General's belief, and the way he expected his subordinates to operate. Jones unlocked the second of the three drawers of the cabinet, and rolled it back. Hundreds of typed reports confronted him. Observations, assessments, personal biographies, transcripts of recorded telephone conversations. At this particular embassy several telephone lines were listened to, each extension warranting a separate brown folder. He flicked through them till he came to the one he wanted and lifted it out. Few sheets there. The number was only recently known, and it had been noted that little traffic came through it. Back at his desk he began to read, quickly and expertly, occasionally writing a few words in a neat trained hand on the memory-pad. There was time for a pipe before the others came, and he lit up, sucking far down into the charred wood of the bowl.

Wait till there's a big party, then move, they'd told him. Abdel-El-Famy had delayed going through the French customs and immigration, waiting till the student group swamped the blue-uniformed officials.

65

He had merged with them, one moment on their fringe, the next right among them. But the checks at Boulogne were casual, guided only by the report from St Omer that they should watch for someone mud-spattered and probably unshaven. Famy's delaying tactics were unnecessary. His real protection came in the orange shirt he now wore, which had been neatly ironed and that had not suffered from its time in the grip-case; and in his laundered jeans and hip-length navy corduroy jacket. He had shaved, too, so that he fitted none of the descriptions that had been issued to the harbour police. The pistol and the soiled clothes were buried beneath the previous autumn's windfall of leaves in a wood to the east of the town. They would be found, eventually – but long after he had completed the task that had been set for him.

On the crossing Famy had made a conscious attempt to talk to a section of the party. His knowledge of French was variable, but sufficient to allow him to strike up conversation. It was the start of a holiday and so spirits were high; there was no shortage of young people to laugh and joke with. The lecturer looking after the students for their eight days in London was vaguely aware that a tall, swarthy man, a little older than the others, and now among them, had not been at the station in Paris. It puzzled him, but he knew only a few of the group, and had had little time on the Paris-to-Boulogne leg of the journey to get close to them. He shrugged it off; perhaps a friend from home, or from school . . .

Famy saw the white ribbon of cliff as the boat swung to port, beginning its run to the long jetty.

Not the clear white he had expected, not the formidable barrier he had read of in the university at Beirut, but shallow and with fields coming down toward the sea. The castle caught his eye, powerful, squat and old-fashioned. He smiled to himself, savouring it; that was his enemy, tired now, outdated, unable to compete in the new and modern world that he was seeking, unable to comprehend the hitting power of the Palestinian movement, unable to defend itself against the new philosophy of revolution and attack.

The two girls from Orléans and the boy from St Etienne were a long time getting their bagggage together after the complicated process of docking and tying up. Famy was patient, the rest of the group less so. From the lecturer and other students came cries for the three to hurry themselves. It suited Famy well. Out of the delay would come anxiety about the train connections for London, and that would mean a concentrated, excited rush at the customs and immigration barriers.

And that was how it was. As Customs quizzed the first four of the party the lecturer began to shout and wave the folder with the rail tickets. Other students joined in, all hugely enjoying the performance. The officials were good-humoured enough, and the party went through. Famy handed over the white immigration card, duly filled in, at the desk, and was talking deeply with the two girls as they swept past the Port Watch Special Branch men. He didn't rate a glance from them. His passport was still in his inner pocket, unrequired, unexamined.

For Famy there was now a moment of indecision. His orders, the orders for the three of them when they left Beirut, had been specific about the next stage of the journey. The instruction was that under no circumstances were they to travel via the direct Dover-to-London rail connection. If for any reason you are suspected, they had said, the authorities have two-and-a-half-hours' grace to make up their minds and intercept at the terminal at Victoria. His people had been adamant about this, and thorough enough to provide the bus timetable that would enable the squad to move down the coast and then link up with a train not connected with the cross-channel services.

Famy reasoned that although he was travelling a full day behind schedule the timetables would remain constant. He had felt safe with the group and was reluctant to leave them, but his orders made no allowance for personal initiative at this stage. When the girls looked round for him he had disappeared.

There were endless waits at bus stops, interspersing the tedious stages of the journey. Dover to Folkestone, seven miles. Folkestone to Ashford, seventeen miles. Ashford to Maidstone, eighteen miles. And in all that time nobody, with the exception of the ticket men, spoke a word to him – not a greeting, not a smile, not a syllable of conversation.

In Maidstone, a dull, boring little town, it looked to him, as he walked through the streets busy with Friday afternoon shoppers, he reverted to the railway system, and a slow stopping train to London. As he climbed into the carriage he reflected with satisfaction that he was within an hour of his destination, and the streets on which it had been determined that David Sokarev would die.

It was a difficult meeting in Leconfield House – three men round the one desk, close to their copies of the transcript, attempting to read more into the badly-typed words than they could find. There were many silences, and an adjournment was forced on them by the necessity for Duggan and Fairclough to return to their offices to search for anything that might throw light on the single brief conversation they had been given. After an hour of sparring round the problem Jones had felt it was time for summary and analysis.

'Let's just stop a minute,' he said, wanting to be back with specifics. 'Let's establish what we have from our own material before we start going else-where and picking other people's stuff. First, the number our friend McCoy telephoned is rarely used, but was considered of some importance or that little sod who gave it us wouldn't have looked as though he thought he was doing us the favour. When we spoke to him last he seemed to think we were getting the bargain out of it. So, it's sensitive. That's borne out by our second point of reference, the call itself. It's different to other calls on the line, on the number. They've been in some code, but we haven't enough on that yet, and it's not broken.'

He reached among his own papers, taking from one of the files four foolscap sheets, each printed over only three lines.

'Stuff like this. Doesn't make much sense, but this

is what we have. "Accommodation one-seven-three, six-five, one-six-two." That was put over three days ago, bit of preamble, not much. English accent, probably disguised. Next night something similar, same sort of style. "Rendezvous as arranged, seven-seven, one, six." Both times it's the incoming calls that are given the information. On to the message last night. To my mind it represents a failure of rendezvous – clear to the deaf that, nothing remarkable in that piece of deduction. But where the pattern breaks down is that though the voice is the same as the first two calls this time he uses a name. Introduces himself. Doesn't use a code-word, bursts straight in.'

Fairclough spoke. 'Try the simplest way through. McCoy, the name we have and which is perhaps genuine, he's hanging about last night. Cools his heels waiting for someone. Gets fed up. Wants to know what's happening and calls the number, the contact number he's been given. Uses the call box. But he's got to be angry, hopping bloody mad. Too angry to remember the drill he's been given. What's the code-word used in the first two calls?' That he couldn't remember it annoyed Fairclough; a concise, organized man, he liked to have things at his fingers.

'Just one word, it seems,' said Jones. 'Just the word "Mushroom", then straight into the message, and whatever that means. No delay; very professional. No possibility of a trace on a call of the length they've been using.'

'Bloody impossible,' interjected Duggan, who didn't like the way events were shaping – the pattern that was building. Too ominous, too much that smacked of planning, and who was it that plans even on such unimportant details?

'Back to the scene, back to the facts.' Jones knew the way a meeting could disintegrate into side-tracking, into theory, and end up with a morning gone.

'We establish that for last night's call there is no use of the code. We also establish that our little diplomat feels it worth sitting in his miserable hutch half the evening waiting for the incomings, long after the crowd he works with are off swigging sherbet and tomato juice on the merry-go-round. When we look at him, what we have on him, there's damn all. New here, within the last few months. Ostensibly small job – visas and passports. Oil men and few businessmen, not that many, but he has a phone line of his own and an extension not listed in their directory. Takes calls at any time, either arranged or he sleeps in there.'

He paused. He was talking too much, doing his schoolmaster bit again. Shouldn't be like that with his colleagues, but he'd caught the Duggan chill, and didn't want it to spread. Even among friends doubt and apprehension are corrosive. Bloody daft though, wasn't it? Three grown men, playing schoolboy riddles, working on a braintease. Fun this one, because they've torn up the answers, won't tell you whether you're right or not. Can change the questions half-way through, can't they, just when you're warming? Their initiative, always the same, always the bastards have the initiative. And the three of them were there, pushing the hot air up, seeking another justification for another lost weekend. Ought to have one's head examined, working oneself into a lather, eighty-hour week, another fraught telephone call home. Bloody stupid. Plough on, Jonesey, they're all waiting.

'So we come finally to the complication. Mystery Irish voice, the magic accent that gives us all wet dreams at night.' Duggan looked pained; Fairclough smiled.

Jones went on, 'What is McCoy doing – waiting for his mate and, when the blind date doesn't show, phoning a confidential embassy number? Thoughts, gentlemen?'

He'd finished. Let the others pick the bones out of that lot. Nasty smell it left, not too tangible yet, but enough of a stench to alert him.

Duggan's turn. He'd contributed little so far. The area he covered in his work was very different to that of the other two men. They were long-range, working on hypotheses, dealing with the possible, but the unlikely. His concern was the probable, and exact and known threat, that went under the initials of 'PIRA' – Provisional Irish Republican Army. When he had slipped back to his office earlier he had checked against his own list of suspects, and the cross-references, looking for any mentions of Ciaran McCoy. None existed. He had telephoned the headquarters of Military Intelligence at Lisburn, County Down, in Northern Ireland. They would begin their searches, feed his request into the computer. 'Negative' or 'Positive' would be on the telex by lunch-time at the earliest, mid-afternoon by the latest.

'If the boy's PIRA it's difficult to explain. They've had contacts with this Government. Bought arms there. The Claudia and the Klashnikovs that we intercepted, they were from this source. They've had meetings there, discussions, but their politics are the width of the Sahara apart. If there is a liaison then it would be of direct necessity. It's to do one thing, then forget it. They couldn't hold together for anything sustained. But we have to know about this boy, we have to localize him.'

'It's the place we have to start,' Fairclough chipped in. 'Only bloody place we can begin, it's from McCoy we start pulling the pieces together. But if they're talking about a link-up then we're not far off the spectacular. After rendezvous they don't hang about knitting, they move on to target. That's the Arab way – what we have to be thinking about if we believe the liaison exists. They come in late and they hit and they shift. Munich's the best example. The crowd that went into the Olympic village arrived two and three days before the attack. But they'll have done the planning, and with thoroughness. Go back to Munich again: they were setting that up *seven months* earlier.'

'Don't know why we bother,' Duggan, determined to depress.

'Perhaps they're not available to come at all,' Jones murmured, a smile playing round his lips, contorted a little on the graft line, and accentuating the divisions in the age of the skin. 'You saw the morning papers. Shoot-out near Boulogne. Two men believed Arabs cut up at a roadblock. But nothing from the "Firm" yet.'

'Nice thought,' agreed Fairclough.

There was a gentle knock on the door. The girl who came in was tall, a little plump, fair hair back over her shoulders. Her skirt was an inch too long, her sweater an inch too tight. Too many bulges. She was Helen Anderson, and had been personal secretary to Jones for the last eight years.

'Sorry to interrupt, sir,' she said quietly.

No, you bloody aren't, thought Duggan. You run this bloody office, come and go when you please. Sorry, my arse.

She repeated, 'Sorry, sir, I didn't put it through, but there's been a message for Mr Fairclough, from Foreign Office. The Israelis have made a contact with our people in Cyprus. The report will be coming over the wire later on. When they've put it through the mincer, found the right code-book, it'll be sent over. They said it was important, that you should wait on for it.'

She nodded her head, accepted that the message had been understood, and was gone.

'That's the bloody evening gone, for the lot of us,' said Fairclough. 'You'll be waiting all ears and pencils for this phone chat-up, Duggan for trace, me flogging through this lot.'

They all laughed. They bitched and moaned every Friday night when work saturated their desks, and they always stayed.

Only a very few of the businessmen who dropped in for a quick one with their wives or secretaries or mistresses to the White Elephant or the Curzon House Club on the other side of the street would have had any inkling of the work of the men whose light burned late into the night in the gaunt building opposite.

The Israeli who had flown to the Akrotiri Royal Air Force base in south-west Cyprus was travelling under the direct instructions of the Director of Military Intelligence in Tel Aviv. He came anonymously, the only passenger in an ageing nine-seater Aero Commander. Much of the exchange of information between the various wings of Israel's security services and the British Secret Intelligence Service – SIS or 'the Firm', as the trade called it – was conducted in the immense, sprawling RAF camp. To meet him was one of the resident British team who had driven the seventy-five miles from Nicosia in response to a telephone message from the Israeli embassy there to the British High Commission. The British took note of the warnings that were flashed to London from the island; on at least a half of the occasions that troops had been drafted into Heathrow Airport it followed close on information received via the harsh sun-reflecting tarmac at Akrotiri.

That evening the two men wasted little time, and the Israeli was in the air again less than twenty-five minutes after their conversation had begun. It was sufficient for him to make five points. First, a Palestinian assassination squad had been intercepted on its way through northern France. Second, the Israeli security representative in Paris was both unhappy with the French authorities' follow-up of the incident and uncertain that all the members of the gang had been accounted for. Third, the Israelis had gained the knowledge that the operation was code-named 'Mushroom'. Fourth, his country's premier but largely unknown nuclear scientist would be leaving Tel Aviv for Britain on the following Monday to fulfil a long-standing speaking engagement. And fifth, his Government would react extremely unfavourably if any incident should mar the visit. Understatement was the man's style, but he repeated the last three times.

'He is important to us – very important in certain fields that we consider vital to our national defence. You understand what I have said?'

The Englishman looked across at the ground crew standing beside the plane – out of earshot, but curious about the two men.

He asked, 'If he's so important and the threat exists, why not call the visit off, and forget about it?'

'If we did that every time there was a threat we would become immured, sterilized. We don't bend the knee to these bastards, and we expect the support of your agencies in the United Kingdom.'

'Anything else that could help us?' said the Englishman. He thought, the little sod, he's enjoying it. Always do when they can wrap someone else up in their interminable problems.

'Nothing more. Just keep it tight round him, our Professor. As you would say, tight as a guinea-pig's arse.'

Always the same, thought the Englishman. They revel in it – the rest of the world jumping to their bloody orders. He too would have a destroyed evening, writing and then encoding his report, but unlike the men in London he would be scratching out of a cocktail party. The big girl from Chancery would have . . . made you bloody sick.

The information Duggan had requested was brought from the basement bank of teletype machines at four o'clock. He read the paper with care, the frown deepening on his forehead as he waded through the lines of blue-punched capitals.

Timing: 15.52 hours. Friday 28/6.
Subject: McCoy, Ciaran Patrick Aloysius.
Address: Ballynafeigh fm, nr Crossmaglen, S Armagh, NI.
Age/DOB: 22 years, 14.3.54.
Security File: For last three years McCoy has been member Crossmaglen Bn PIRA . . . After one year was reported I/C Active Service Unit operating Cullyhanna area. Believed expert rifle shot, natural leader. Arrested Sec Forces 8/12/74. ICO and detention order. Held HM Prison Maze where became PIRA cage commandant. Freed on Sec of State's instruction 3/7/75. Since then active in political work and would return again to violence should situation deteriorate. Last is Mil Intelligence and SB assessment. Believed responsible for shootings incidents in S Armagh area, specifically RUC patrol car 17/8/74 and sniping of paratroop killed 10/10/74. Pix and Prints following.
Background: Undermentioned is person-to-person confidential from Mil Intelligence HQ 3BDE, Lurgan, NI and not for release outside your department.
We astonished at release of McCoy and protests were via Commander Land Forces to appropriate political offices. Reply was that as McCoy only detainee from that area and response to local PIRA required in existing cease-fire situation he was being freed. Exclaimer. Regarded as of high calibre and exception to colleagues in that has good educational standards with full secondary

77

education from Armagh City. Deceptive in manner and could pass well in all company.

Re your specific requests:

1. Last seen in area approx 10/12 days ago.
2. No known visits to London, but sister once worked St Mary's Hosp, Paddington London W2.
3. Would have considerable disguise capabilities witness long period before pick-up.
4. Last interrogated by Maj Ian Stewart, Int Corps Rtd, address obtainable Ministry of Defence (Personnel).

Upsummer: Hard boy. Bestest luck.

Duggan photocopied the paper three times. One for Jones, one for Fairclough, one for his departmental head. The original he put into the new folder, marked with McCoy's name on the outside, and which up till then had contained only the transcripts of the phone calls to the embassy.

He read the information again, interpreting the officialese of the message. The implications were fearsome. A top man, in a top-grade Provisional set-up, leader of an active service unit, arrested, served with an Interim Custody Order, then a detention order, and then released by some bloody politician in order to keep a cease-fire going when everyone knew the bastards were on their knees and suing for peace. Responsible for at least two deaths. Poor devils, gunned down, and not even the satisfaction of having their man spend the rest of his natural behind bars. Not even the General able to get the decision reversed. Made you want to pack it in.

So what was little McCoy doing running round London, calling up embassies, missing his links? Duggan hurried to the lift and the floor below where Jones had his office.

Chapter Five

Sokarev's wife had noted the preoccupation that gripped her husband. There was his listlessness, the unwillingness to contribute anything in conversation, the desire just to slump in his chair, the books at his desk unopened. There were often times when his work had seemed to force him down, literally bowing his shoulders with the pressures of the speed and intricacy and finesse required for the study of nuclear action.

On previous occasions the signs of extreme exhaustion and depression had been well telegraphed, and they had been able to discuss them, thereby lessening the load. But not this time. Her gentle feelers for information were shrugged off, and she was left feeling frustrated and inadequate. She hoped that the arrival later in the day of 'the children', as she still called them, would be enough to rouse him.

Sokarev himself thought continuously of what the security men had told him, wondered why they had found it necessary to take him into their confidence, regretted that they had. He was not used to fear, and could not remember a similar sensation of such intensity. Like an infant afraid to be left alone in an unfamiliar room, he had come in the last twenty-four hours to dread his London visit.

When, just before nightfall succeeded dusk, his wife suggested they should take a walk together he shook his head, heavy with the negative. He heard her sigh her disappointment as she fidgeted with a duster behind his chair.

'We've time,' she said, 'before the children come. We could go down to the new swimming pool, just a few hundred metres, a few minutes. We'll be back well before them.'

He shook his head again, and she left it.

He sat alone for a few more minutes, then got up abruptly.

'I'd like a walk,' he said quietly. 'I'd like to go on my own. I won't be long.' Her face clouded, and he watched the pain he had inflicted. Her jaw seemed to tighten, her eyes to close a little. 'There is a problem. I have to think about it. It has no place for you. Not long-term. I'll resolve it very soon. I'm sorry.'

Out on the street there was a warm, dry heat. The children were on the pavement playing football, but they made way for the professor. Hot, spiced smells came to him from the kitchens as he walked mingling with the scents from the flowering trees that had been planted when the flats were built. There was noise: high above him, a couple shouted abuse at each other, fiercely combative.

It was difficult for him to concentrate on the question that dominated his thinking – too many extraneous sights and senses forced their way over him. He walked little more than half a mile, then turned and came back slowly. When he had reached the entrance on the ground floor that led to his apartment he saw the Mini his son drove parked outside, and he went on round to the back of the building where the garages were. He unlocked the door of his own garage, and then the door of the car, on the passenger side, and slid onto the seat.

His hand wavered a moment before he opened the glove compartment. Underneath the duster, where it always was, rested the Mauser pistol. Sokarev took it in his hand, weighing it, feeling the black, hard shape of the butt pressing down onto his palm. The magazine was fastened into position. Live bullets – the power to kill, or to protect. They're dragging you down old man, he said to himself. Pulling you into their own pit, where crude, insensitive violence settles all. What learning, what thought, what intellectual capacity is demanded to ease the stiff and metallic lever of the safety catch and transform a simple piece of engineering into a killing instrument? So vulgar, so alien. To the men who were to accompany him to London the gun would be as familiar as their shoe-laces, their toothpaste, the belts that held their trousers on their hips.

He would take it with him. Whether they liked it or not, those two young men would have to accept it – a part of his destiny he would keep in his own hands. He put the pistol back in the compartment, and covered it again with the duster.

As he paused at the door of his flat, searching in his pocket for the key, he could hear his wife talking, her voice anxious, excited, and the quieter tones of his son. But he felt calmer now, steadied. When he walked inside there was the smile of greeting on his face.

At Victoria Station the Arab pushed his way through the crowds of surging, homeward-bound commuters until he reached the telephone kiosks. He waited his turn, and when the box in front of him was vacant nodded his gratitude to the man who held the door open for him, and went inside. It smelled in the dank cubicle. Perhaps a man had vomited there. Looking up at the board above the phone, Famy read the instructions, found a two-pence coin and dialled the number he had memorized. The call was answered, and there was the vibrant noise of the beeps instructing him to feed his money into the appropriate slot. The coin slid through the mechanism, emerging in a small tray below. For a moment he panicked, fumbled for it, and then pushed the coin again into the machine. A pause, then the answering voice. He spoke the number of the extension they had given him, and heard the click that denoted the reconnection. Another voice announced the number he had just asked for, confirming it for him.

Famy said, 'Mushroom, one has arrived.'

From the other end, curt and hurried, 'Same rendezvous, as if you had been here last night. You know it?'

Famy said, 'Yes, I have it memorized, I . . .'

The line was dead, the voice replaced by the purring constancy of the dialling tone. Three hours to kill. Time to be lost, evaporated. Famy walked out into the late evening sunshine and onto the London pavements. In front of him was a tourists' stall. Union Jacks, dolls in guardsmen's uniforms, postcards of Buckingham Palace, cardboard replicas of 'Gentlemen's Lavatory' and 'Piccadilly'.

His voice seemed diffident as he asked the elderly man sitting on the stool beside his counter, 'Excuse me, excuse me. I wonder, do you have the *A-Z Book of London*? A map called the *A-Z*?'

The man looked at him, boring into his face – not for any reason, just a mannerism. He handed the book to Famy.

'A *to* Z,' he said patronizingly, repeating it. There was a look of contempt on his face. 'Thirty pence, it'll cost you.'

Famy moved away with the book. Across the fast-flowing road he could see a sign. 'Sandwiches and Snacks', it proclaimed. He felt hungry and tired. He waited till a group of pedestrians had gathered by the traffic lights, and joined them as they scurried across the wide space. Safety in numbers. He looked at the huge white-fronted, porticoed houses of Lower Belgrave Street. It was what he might have imagined of London; grand, majestic, privileged. In the café an Italian waiter brought a coffee to his table, and he also ordered some bread and salad. He flicked at the book, taking in the labyrinthine network of lines and words that made up the Greater London area. When his food came he reached inside his coat for the slim diary he carried, and among a jumble of figures in the section for accounts at the end of it selected the top line. It read '77.1.6'. He shouldn't have written those numbers in his diary. The order had been to memorize them. Dani and Bouchi, they wouldn't have written them on paper. But, Famy had been nervous of forgetting. He was aware that for the first time he had broken an instruction of the mission. The sensation of guilt, though faint, caught him as he started to work the code system that he had been given.

He noted the numbers, printed heavily in black at the top extremes of each page, and went carefully through the book till he came to page 77. There was a '1' printed smaller below it, marking a series of squares. He counted through his alphabet, learned years ago at school, searching for the letter that equalled the number 6. On his fingers he came to the letter F. He peered closely at page 77, directing his sight at the square marked laterally by the figure 1 and vertically by the letter F. In the square there was a shaded-in area, a quarter of an inch across, marked 'Waterloo'. They had said the rendezvous would be at a station. If for any reason, his briefing had gone on, it is not suitable for a rendezvous to take place you should go straight to the accommodation. But that was not desirable. He checked with the figures for the accommodation code. '173.65.162'. This time he turned to the back index of the map, sought out page 173 and began to work his way down the extreme left hand column of street names. The sixty-fifth in the descending order read, 'Englefield Road, N.1. 4C 46.' The accommodation address was 162 Englefield Road, on the fringes of Islington and Dalston in North London.

A transcript of Famy's call to the embassy was hurried up to Jones's office.

'There's no chance of a trace,' said the man who brought it. 'Lasted about fourteen seconds, the whole thing, and that includes fumbling with the money, and getting transferred. There's a fair bit of background noise where the call orginates, probably a public place, but that's where most of the phone boxes are. It's not inside a building, anyway.'

'Definitely, we can't pick up a call like that?' Jones queried.

'Not a cat in hell. No way at all. Need an awful lot more than that.'

'And the voice?' persisted Jones.

'Need more time with that. Foreign, and we can go a bit further than that. Not USA, not North European, not African, not Asian. I'd put in a bid for Mediterranean, not Latin but East.'

'Thank you,' said Jones, and the man made his way out of the office.

There were those in the department, trained to work at phonetics and speech, who would be able to pin-point the origin of the caller, or at least the region in which he had spent time long enough for it to affect the vowels and consonant construction of the syllables. It would take them no great time, but Jones was certain that whatever they came up with would merely be the professional confirmation of what in his own mind he already knew.

So he had arrived, their little friend. Missed his first appointment, but was now in and ready to make up the lost time for the rendezvous. Right codeword, right part of the world, and ready to meet up with this sodding little Provo.

Jones reached across for his white telephone, the one which carried the department's main number and an extension. The phone beside it was red, and carried a separate number, left clear for incoming calls. He dialled nine for an outside line, and then his home number.

'I'll be late, dear. No, it's just come up. Usual old story, isn't it? I say I'll be late, but it's conceivable I won't be back at all tonight. Boys all right? Good. I'm sorry . . . I always say that. Mean it though. Love you. 'Bye darling.'

There were two files now. One for the embassy calls, one for McCoy. He took them both with him as he went down to the basement. In cubicles sat the men who listened to the calls that the Director General had authorized as suitable for monitoring. He pulled up a chair beside the man who listened to the number he was concerned with. The man greeted him silently, plugged in a separate pair of earphones, and passed them to him. He offered Jones a cigarette, which was declined. Then they waited, concentration building up, the metal of the earpieces digging into Jones's flesh, as he waited for the next call.

He reflected that there was no complacency among his small team. They were too old for that, too well-versed. Each of them appreciated that they were starting late, catching up in a few hours on the homework it had taken the enemy weeks, perhaps months to prepare. There was never enough time in this business for indulgence. Always running from behind, handicapped, catching up against the passing of the calendar.

The major from Intelligence Corps was able to tell Duggan little of McCoy that was not already apparent. He enjoyed his retirement, and the gratuity the army had given him. He devoted his attention, once directed towards interrogation, wholly to his rose garden. He had been there in semi-darkness when Duggan had called the cottage in Wiltshire, and the former officer's mind was more attuned to the problems of green and black aphis-fly and its risk to his blooms than to the young Irishman he had met so many months earlier.

'He was a hard little bugger,' he remembered. 'Very cool, difficult to shake. Cut above the usual cement-between-the-ears boyos. We had more than one session. Didn't budge him at all. Things had got pretty easy for them by then; clamps were well down on what we could do by the stage we got our hands on him. He didn't tell us anything.'

Duggan read him over the first section of the report from Northern Ireland intelligence.

'I didn't see any great political leanings. So few of them have,' said the major. 'He reacts to orders, like most of them. But he's tougher, harder. Has a lot of hate. Patient. One of those that would lie up on the hedgerows for days at a time ready to set off a bomb under an armoured truck. Plans well – we know that from some of his operations. They're a hard breed down there in South Armagh, harder than anywhere else in the bloody place.'

He paused, seeking for anything else that could be of use.

'One thing. If you're looking for him in London. He had a sister, a bit older, perhaps a couple of years. Worked in a hospital, somewhere in London . . .'

Duggan prompted him.

'. . . Well, the girl went a bit haywire. McCoy thought she'd been in the wrong just by coming over. We were told that from other sources. He didn't think she should be working across in the mainland. Seemed quite a normal girl, apparently,

88

then got mixed up with a load of hippies. Packed her nursing in and went to live with them. He didn't approve of that. They're a very Puritan crowd, the hard-core Provos. I tried to talk about it to him, tried to shake him up a bit, get him angry. Didn't work. Water off a duck's back.'

'That could be very helpful,' said Duggan.

A courier came by car with the report, decoded, from the meeting at RAF Akrotiri. Fairclough had to come down to the lobby of the building to sign personally for the plain buff envelope that carried only his name on the outside. He waited until he was back in his office before looking at the contents, and then read the typed sheets with attention for detail. It was very thorough, but then SIS in Nicosia were well known for their exactness.

He buzzed through to Jones's extension, received no answer, and tried the outer office. Helen had not gone home.

'He's down below. Eavesdropping. Said he won't be up for some time. He asked me to stay behind. Said there might be some typing to do, some reports to make up.'

Annoyance surged through him. His own girl had disappeared hours ago. Jones's girl was always there, never went home, watching them the whole time when they worked late, amusing herself at their expense.

'Get a message to him,' Fairclough said. 'As soon as he's taken the business down below, we need to see him – Mr Duggan and myself. Say whatever time he's through we'll be waiting.'

When he'd rung off he too phoned his home to

warn of a late departure from the office. Duggan had already done the same.

'Here it goes, sir,' said the man hunched intently in the cubicle, stretching his bulk closer over the machinery. Jones could hear the amplified beeps through his earphones. He winced at the noise.

The man reacted to it, without turning round. 'Have to have 'em up full blast. They can whisper and you've lost the lot while you're fiddling the volume.' He had switched on the tape recorder, the two wheels revolving steadily and without impatience. A third man was behind them, holding to his mouth the receiver of an open telephone to the GPO exchange nearest the embassy.

'It's McCoy,' muttered Jones as the Irish voice came through. The man behind was speaking into the phone, urgently. Jones heard the switch made to the extension inside the embassy, heard the code-word given, and the single sentence in reply before the connection was broken. It had been shorter than the earlier call, by two to three seconds.

'Not a bloody hope,' said the man who was standing at the back. 'It gives them next to nothing to work on.'

'Didn't say much anyway,' Jones spat the words out. 'Two hours waiting for that. Used the code-word, though – that's all.'

His notepad carried a few hastily scrawled words. 'Mushroom – same as yesterday, but confirmed.'

Helen was standing by the outer door of the basement when he emerged. She said, 'Mr Duggan and Mr Fairclough want to see you. They said they'd wait till you were through with whatever . . .'

'Get them to my office, and quick.' And he was past her, hurrying along the corridor, not waiting for the lift, attacking the broad central staircase, three steps at a time.

From among the crowd by the mobile tea trolley Famy watched McCoy. The Irishman stood in front of the high wooden board that gave out the destinations and the times of the trains from Waterloo Station. He was wearing the right clothes – shirt correct, draped coat correct, sign correct. Nervous, that was as it should be. Not furtive, but anxious. Passengers swayed round the fair head of the Irishman as he swept the concourse, searching for recognition, and his contact. While he waited Famy reflected that this was a completely new departure for him. He had had no contact with foreign groups in the camp: older, more influential men in the movement had, but not Famy. If it had happened as planned, Bouchi would have been the one to go forward. But Bouchi was in a morgue.

Famy drank his tea, his hands scalded through the fragile side of the plastic cup. His eyes were never far from the Irishman, but intermittently they strayed to take in the rest of the concourse, watching for any other man who might linger overlong. He took many minutes to be satisfied, then began to make his way forward.

He moved deftly, picking his way through the running commuters, avoiding confrontation. McCoy saw him some fifteen feet away, and stiffened. This time it was the Irishman whose breathing came a little faster. His contact was just a few seconds away – a slightly-built figure, with dark chocolate skin, short, well-groomed hair and brightly dressed. A stranger, something separate. McCoy watched him roll his hips and sway past the mass, saw the head turn once for reassurance and look behind, and then he was close, and pausing, and then speaking.

'The mushrooms are—' Famy broke off. 'I think you are here to meet me?' There was a questioning in his voice. The word they had told him to say, how stupid and idiotic it sounded, spoken by a grown man in the chaos of a railway station.

McCoy just said, 'Come on. No need to hang about. Let's move.' Then, as an afterthought, 'You speak English, understand English?'

Famy nodded. Like all these British, they never believed anyone knew anything but themselves. McCoy was on the move, the Arab half a step behind him. The Irishman pushed a path for himself toward the steps that led down to the bus station in the street below. Almost out into the open again, he shortened his stride and said over his shoulder, 'Where are the others?'

'It is just me,' said Famy.

There was a tint of suspicion in the way McCoy tilted his head towards the other man. 'That's not what they told me,' he rapped out staccato. 'They said there'd be three of you. They told me I'd meet three men.'

'It is just me,' repeated Famy.

'What's happened to change it?' McCoy hissed the question, hurrying again now, confused.

'Read your papers of today. Read of the events in northern France. When you have done that it is simple.' McCoy shook his head, his lack of comprehension overwhelming. They were standing at

92

the bus stop, the street ill-lit from the lights above. Famy went on, 'There was a shooting, at a roadblock. Yesterday in the early hours. My friends did not survive, only myself.'

McCoy turned round fast, his body close to Famy. Shorter than the Arab, he looked up into his face. 'Dead?' the one word, very quietly.

'They did not survive,' said Famy.

'Is it called off, then, is it over? Finished, the plan?' McCoy was speaking fast, but trying to keep his voice suppressed.

'It is not over. There is no possibility of abandoning the plan. We have been launched. It is not infrequent there should be setbacks. But it is not a thing to talk of here. Later, we can talk.'

McCoy shrugged. He wanted to say more, but it was difficult against the unfamiliar logic spelled out in the curiously pitched voice of the other man. McCoy noticed he ran his words together – and very precise, very clear. Like some text book, not natural.

They waited in silence for the approach of the big double-decker bus. What sort of game is this? thought the Irishman. The team shot to pieces, and this little bugger carrying on as if nothing had happened. Daft, bloody mad. He saw the face of the other man – masked, unemotional – staring down the road. Out of their bloody minds, this bugger and the ones who set it all up. What can one man, what can two achieve compared with four? Four was the minimum number, all agreed and locked up, that had been. Should have been more, but for the problems of shifting a bigger group. And now it's halved, and this idiot says it goes on. God Almighty, put some sense into these thick buggers' heads. He mouthed the oaths, silently rolling his tongue round them, savouring and enjoying the words that somehow diluted the anger he felt. When the bus came he motioned with his head that they should take it, and went up the stairs to the top deck. A couple sat half-way, and the two men took the front seats, Famy pushing his grip underneath his knees.

'We can talk up here,' said McCoy.

'There is no problem, my friend,' said Famy, his voice gentle and lilting as he pronounced the words. There was no rush as he spoke, only a calmness. 'We two are sufficient. There is a plan? I was told there was a plan that could be executed. That is correct?' McCoy nodded, numbness setting in along with the knowledge that he was no longer in control, that the tall stranger had taken command. 'If there is a plan, we can execute it,' said Famy. He broke off as the bus conductor arrived at their seats. McCoy paid, and pocketed the thin white paper strips he received in return. Famy went on. 'He is only one man, the one we seek. He will be guarded, but not thoroughly. If we are determined there is no difficulty that can arise.'

There was no more conversation as the bus jolted its way from stop to stop, leaving the heart of London far behind and climbing the hill beyond King's Cross to Islington's Angel. The upper deck filled, taking on the teenagers disgorged from the cinemas. Occasionally McCoy looked sideways at the Arab, and realized that the man who sat beside him showed no interest in the journey, that his eyes never shifted from their relaxed unseeing gaze straight ahead. The bright fronts of restaurants, advertisement hoardings, pin-table arcades, cinema hallways – all passed him by. A group of drunk, noisy West Indians, loud and aggressive, gained no reaction. He's like a train, thought McCoy, on course, all signals green, and couldn't give a damn about anything else. The Irishman tried to put himself into the same situation. New city, contact man he's never met before, close to his target, half the back-up dead behind him, and the bugger doesn't even turn his head. Not a drop of sweat on his head, no perspiration round his balls making his trousers too tight so he has to wriggle for comfort. Just relaxed, as if he's on a coach outing.

The time he had shot the paratrooper was very clear to McCoy. He could recall his nausea as the soldier, in his airborne smock and red beret, had come into sight. He waited so long for him, but when the soldier came he'd hardly been able to focus his eyes down the smooth, crisp barrel of the Armalite. Sweat ran in rivulets under his vest, fashioning freezing paths of movement across his skin. Then the soldier had called to the sergeant patrolling in front of him, a remark that McCoy had tried to overhear, and in the effort recognized his concentration slipping away. He'd fired then, watched the soldier heave and clutch at himself, seen the disbelief that comes before the pain and death. He sprinted then, fast with the adrenalin pumping through his veins, and for hours afterwards, even in the womb-like safety of the barn where he lay up after missions before returning to the farm, he had panted with the excitement, close to exhilaration, the moment when he had fired. A near-orgasmic movement of release as the butt of the rifle thudded into his shoulder, his finger coiled on the trigger; he could relive it hour after hour.

But this bugger sitting next to him was something different. It's animal when you don't care, thought McCoy, unnatural when you don't feel the tension. Sub-human. The Irishman had read of these people when they went into Israel. Suicide squads, *kamikaze*, there to kill and be killed. Take the greatest possible number with you. He had seen the pictures on the television of them training with the explosive packs strapped round their waists. Madness, or motivation – McCoy didn't know which. And the man beside him with the vacant, contented eyes – would he be one of them? Had to be, didn't he? Could be certain of that. One of the hard, mean bastards.

'We get off here. Next stop,' said McCoy. The two men gripped the backs of the seats as they made their way down the centre of the bus to the staircase. They waited by the top step till the bus had come to a halt. On the pavement they began to walk, Famy fractionally behind McCoy. After a hundred yards McCoy turned left, then realized the Arab was not beside him. He turned and saw him pressed against the wall of the pub on the corner. Bloody play-acting, said McCoy to himself, and walked on. He'd gone another fifty yards before the running feet caught him up. The explanation was not slow in coming.

'Makes certain we are not being followed. To wait a moment at a corner when one goes on. The tail will hear the feet, and have to keep going. That way you spot him. Nobody is following,' said Famy.

The street was made up of four-storey Victorian terraced houses. Up to fifty years ago these were middle-class homes, complete with maid and cook to work in the basement kitchens and to sleep in the attic bedrooms; expensive and sought-after. But those families had long since abandoned the houses as ghostly, costly white elephants, and fled to the cheaper, more territorially secure suburbs. The houses had disintegrated into flatlets owned by landlords who lived far from the premises. McCoy stopped outside a house at the far end of the street.

'Just a word of explanation,' he said. 'We thought about this a fair bit where we were to hole up. We've tried to find quite a new territory this time. None of the haunts our people use, the regular dormitories. It's what we call a "commune" here. Young people, who just couldn't give a fuck for it all and drop out, absolve themselves of the rat race, they say. This place is up for sale, one property owner selling to another, and it's sitting empty. The kids have moved in, taken over, till there's an eviction order, till they get chucked out. But it's safe, safe for us. People come and go at all hours of the day and night. Nobody asks any questions. Just don't get involved with them – don't ask questions, don't give answers. Just keep to yourself, and no-one will bother you. I've got them to clear a room for us, when I thought there were four. Just don't let them bother you, and remember, nobody gives a damn who you are here.'

They walked up the paving steps to the front door. McCoy pushed the handle and the door swung open. They were met with a flood of hard-rock, shrieking music.

Inside the diplomatic bag sent out of the embassy that night was a cryptic note, in code and in a high-security sealed envelope. It would be flown the next morning to a North African capital. Upon receipt the envelope would be transferred again to Beirut. A telephone call would then be made to the newspaper offices of *Al Nahar*. The call would be person-to-person from the commercial secretary of the embassy in the Lebanese capital to a particular writer. The message that the man code-named 'Saleh Mohammed' was now in London would then be just a drive from the camouflaged tent of the leader of the PFLP-General Command. By Sunday evening he would be aware that his plan was still in motion.

Under the harsh fluorescent light the files in front of the three men who sat round the desk had begun to thicken. Every half-hour or so Helen would bring in the mugs of coffee on which the department seemed to exist. The men's jackets were off, their ties were loosened at the collars and their hair dishevelled. Twice the secretary had been called in to type out assessments, handed her without word by Jones. They were all tired now, weary from the strain that had begun more than twelve hours earlier, but aware that no sleep could be taken until the next day's plan was prepared.

Jones knew the danger of exhaustion, had seen it sap men, make them vulnerable. That's how it had been in the war, the last half dozen raids before the end of a tour, but he'd been little more than a boy then. More than thirty years later, and close to the decreed age of retirement, the similar work load was still expected of him. But there was no way around it. No point in mobilizing the forces at their disposal – police, detectives, army – not until there was a plan, something for the masses to do. And that was the problem that he knew confronted him: to find the shape of the threat. Then, and only then, could the big battalions be drawn in. He'd begun to wonder more frequently what retirement would be like, how he'd feel the day after they'd given him the silver pen, or the cut-glass decanter set, or the shining gardening kit: no train to get on in the morning, no conferences to prepare for, no problems . . . he didn't know whether he would welcome it or not. But irrelevant that night.

Past midnight Jones dialled the home number of the Director General. It was rare for him to be called at home, let alone at that hour. To the head of the department, one of the triumvirate who sat on the Joint Intelligence Committee, Jones spoke with deference. He sketched through the outline of the papers that confronted them. The taped conversations, the identification and background of McCoy, the arrival and rendezvous with the unknown man, the Israeli warning. The 'DG' liked his briefs kept short, and listened without interruption as he sat pyjama-clad on the side of his bed, his wife of thirty-one years asleep beside him.

'Suggestions?' the DG asked at the other end of the line.

'Perhaps you could come in tomorrow morning, sir,' Jones replied. 'Have a conference with us. Then I think we should meet Special Branch with a view to hunting the Irishman. The Israeli security attaché will have to be brought in – get the lines buzzing a bit on the newcomer. We'll have to do a card check on airports and ferries, though that will probably narrow down simply to the Channel ports. This

Israeli professor comes on Monday, in the afternoon. There's not a lot of time.'

'Right. Thank you, Jones.' The winds on the Sussex Downs wrapped round his house, the central heating was long off, cut on the arrival of spring. The DG shivered. 'I'll be in a bit after eight. Give me a few minutes, then the three of you come in at eight-thirty. Get some sleep in the meantime.' He rang off.

Jones repeated the instructions. Duggan and Fairclough shuffled their papers together.

'Not worth making much of a move at this time of night,' said Duggan. 'I'll doss down in the office.' Fairclough agreed. As they were leaving Helen came in, alerted by the scraping of the chairs on the lino fringe of the carpet.

'What time in the morning?' She said it casually, matter-of-fact.

'Eight-thirty, my love. We're seeing "DG". You might as well make it then. Far to go tonight? Or Jimmy's, is it? He's the lucky man?'

There was no trace of a blush, just a light laugh. 'Jimmy said he'd sit up, make me some cocoa.'

Lucky bugger, thought Jones. 'Tell lover-boy not to burn the candle too hard. Might be needing him before too long. All fit and fighting fresh. Tell Jimmy that.'

And she was gone, leaving him with the task of setting up the canvas and metal bed – that fitted so snugly when collapsed into the bottom drawer of his filing cabinet, and which took such an age to make sleep-worthy.

Chapter Six

The music went on throughout the night. It blasted
its way through the walls, through the floor boards
and under the door, finally merging in the room
around the two men. Famy tossed and rolled in his
sleeping bag, heaving it about on the narrow canvas
sun-bed. They were high in the building, with the
walls angled by the roof, but still the noise sought
him out, wresting him from sleep. A few feet away
McCoy lay still, impervious to the noise, his breathing regular and heavy. For the first hour, after he had
undressed down to his underpants and crawled into
his envelope-like bag, the Arab had sought refuge,
burying his head under the cushion McCoy had
given him. But there was a stale smell of perspiration
about the faded material. His nostrils had turned and
curled and he had hurled the cushion across the
room and then tried to find comfort by drawing
himself down into the bag so that his ears were
covered. The bag at least was clean. New, with the
price tag still on it.

There were no curtains covering the window and
the moon threw sufficient light into the room for
Famy to make out its bareness. Rough, uncovered

boards, indented with nails, peeling floral wallpaper. A length of flex hanging twisted from the low ceiling; a bulb but no shade. In a corner a bulging plastic bag, and around it a scattering of orange peel, newspapers and cigarette butts. Apart from the sun-beds, and their clothes and their bags, there was nothing else. His shoulders felt the cold of the great unheated house.

When he'd arrived, they'd offered him food, talked of beans and stewed meat and bread. He'd declined, and watched the Irishman help himself from a scarcely-washed plate. Later he'd relented sufficiently to take a cup of milk poured from a half-empty bottle. That was all he had allowed himself.

He had waited out in the hall when they had first come to the house while McCoy had entered a downstairs room, and over the music made himself heard. Famy had not been able to distinguish the words. A group, a foraging party, had come to look at him, to survey the visitor. Without meaning to he had smiled at them as they stood by the door. They did not come closer, just watched and evaluated. Long, dank hair, falling straight to their shoulders, boys distinguished from girls by their beards and moustaches, but both in the uniform of tight jeans, sweatshirts and jerseys. Some had worn sandals, others had been barefoot. There were beads and badges embroidered on the clothes. Famy had been able to look over their shoulders into the rest of the room and in the candlelight had made out others, either sitting on the floor or draped on chairs, all intent on him. McCoy had not led him in, but up the stairs to the room.

There was no life like this in Nablus. Some might live unwashed and in clothes that were little more than rags, but not from choice. No-one sought such degradation, or made it a purposeful way of life. In the camp up the hill on the Jerusalem Road, where existence was married to the open drains, where a roof was corrugated iron, where walls were fashioned from wooden or cardboard packing-cases, there was no satisfaction at the awfulness. There was simply no option. Those who lived there had come in 1948, bred their children there, built their shanties, and when the Israeli advance had rushed further forward nineteen years later the movement had been too fast for them to walk on again and seek a new refuge in new filth on the far side of the dividing Jordan river. The tanks had outstripped them.

But the Irishman had said it was safe to stay here. That was sufficient, while the operation went ahead.

There was movement below the floor. Doors opened and closed; he heard shouts on the landings. And then the undulating and controlled heaving of a bed, starting softly, rising minutes later to a frenzy. He had listened, almost ashamed, his mind conjuring the faces and the forms of the olive-skinned girls he had known in Beirut, whose arms he had touched, their gentle skin sensitive to his fingers. He strained to listen, drawn by the steady, driving persistence of the sound. The half-sleep left him. Imagination delving into fantasy; coiled bodies, searching and passion and closeness, enacted in a near room. It was almost nauseating for him to imagine anything so precious, in that stench, in that dirt. In the camp there had been girls – not many, and they had slept in their own tents. They joined in the laughter and the gaiety, shared the training sessions, but at night they left the men to sleep alone on their close-packed trestle beds. In his student days there had been girls too, beautiful, supreme but with mothers awaiting them as the city darkened. He had never slept with a girl, had never known the reality of his imagination, and now close to him two of these creatures, with their smears and the hair, coupled. And then the sound died, and the house was at rest.

It was nearly dawn, when the thin grey light had begun to penetrate the room, that he was alerted by the turning of the door handle. If he had been able to drift back to sleep he would not have noticed the action, as it was done quietly and with care.

He lay very still, tense, eyes like slits, watching the entrance to the room. He saw his coat and trousers, suspended from a metal hanger, move towards him as the door opened. The door was heavy, and the hinges made the sparse, scraping sound. Famy controlled his breathing, reducing it to the same pitch as McCoy's, and watched a darkened shape glide without sound into the room and across the boards. For a moment there was a silhouette against the window and he could make out long hair, and the shape of a coat thrown shawl-like over shoulders, then the figure merged into the blackness of the far side of the room and went beyond his power of vision. A small shaft of light – a hand torch? – at the edge of his sight field, and he was aware of hands pulling open and probing inside his grip-bag. Then the light was doused, and the sound of the feet on the floor boards became muted, as if uncertain where next they should travel. The figure went across the room, back toward the door, hesitating there, at his clothes, those that were not beside him. There was a chink as his belt clasp was shifted, and a smooth rifling of a hand inside his trousers. And then there was the sound of the catch being fastened again, the door closed. Yet there came no movement of footsteps away from the door immediately. He stayed motionless in his sleeping bag. Waiting to see if I am aroused, he told himself. Like a rat that comes for the cheese and lingers by its hole to see if the dogs are out and have the scent. Fifteen seconds passed, perhaps more. Then the noise on the landing, the shuffling of bare feet, finally lost, emptied into the hugeness of the house.

Famy found he was sweating, cold moisture on the folds of his stomach, dampness in the hair at the back of his neck. He would have given anything for the company of Dani and Bouchi, for the presence of his friends from the camp, someone in whom he could confide, someone other than the stranger in the other sleeping bag across the boards.

The fool had said it was a safe place, a place where he could relax, where there would be no requirement to remain vigilant twenty-four hours in the day. Half a night, and both his possessions and clothes had been precisely and systematically searched. Should he have intervened? Thrust himself at the intruder? But how would he have done it? The bag was a strait-jacket, so how to create the element of surprise? It could not have been accomplished, he told himself. He lay in his bag, waiting for McCoy to wake and the morning to come.

It was past seven on his watch when the Irishman began to struggle his way out of the sleep. Famy leaned over to him and shook his shoulder, firmly, communicating his impatience. McCoy awoke, eyes focused instantly.

'What is it? What's the bloody matter?' he said.

'There has been someone in here, someone has been in the room.' Famy said it with urgency, seeking to impress with his information.

'So what? People come and go in these places. Looking for somewhere to doss down, kip for a bit.'

'Not like that. Someone has been to search – the bags and clothes. To examine.'

McCoy stared hard across at him. 'Been in here, giving us a look-over?'

'I was awake,' said Famy. 'I could not sleep, and someone came in, went through the pockets. I didn't move, pretended sleep. Nothing was found. It was about two hours ago, just before the light began to come.'

McCoy forced his lids further open, bruising them with the motion of his arm, and sat up. His white skin seemed curiously weak and without sinew till the body swivelled, and Famy saw the reddened, puckered mess of a bullet wound, on McCoy's left side, just below the rib cage.

'Probably just some bugger on the scrounge looking for a few pence . . .'

Famy cut across him, excited, talking fast, 'Nothing was taken. I couldn't see all that was searched, but no sound of money being taken. My trouser pockets, they were looked at, the money remains. It's the wrong place for us here, not the place I was expecting, not *familiar*.'

'Well, it's here you're bloody well staying.' McCoy

was close to shouting. 'You'll stay where I bloody well say, and that's here. It's an out-of-the-way, quiet, no-questions place. If some sod comes wandering about in the middle of the night frightening you I can't help it. Shouldn't believe in bloody fairies.'

'And if you're wrong?' Famy asked.

'If I'm wrong? What the hell does that mean? What I say is we're better off here than with the usual crowd, the ones who might want to know about us – our bloody lot.' He quietened suddenly, recognized the anxiety as genuine, and became anxious to allay and calm. 'I'll ask around downstairs, put a bit of heat on, but gently. There's all sorts of buggers just drifting round these places, looking for a bed, or for something to pinch. Nothing extraordinary about the night. Remember it's London you're at now, and it's Saturday, and the man you want is here on Monday, whatever it is you call him . . .'

'Al Kima.'

'Whatever that means.'

'It is the man who grows mushrooms. The Mushroom Man. My friends would like me to meet him. They would believe that I would avenge them.'

Crisis over, calmed the little bugger down, chance of more sleep. McCoy turned away from Famy to face the wall.

'There's nothing much to do today. Lie up. Tomorrow we start working. For now it's sleep we want, there's nothing today but a walk round the university. Tomorrow it gets interesting.'

The Irishman could not see the gleam in the other's eyes, the brightness that comes from an erotic and compulsive anticipation; the dream of the shudder of gunfire, blood smears on the concrete, the international headlines, and the adulation in the tents far away in Fatahland.

When Famy looked again across the floor of the room he saw McCoy was asleep, with his left arm high round his head to shut out the light, so that the bullet wound below was exposed. The thought of it bruised the Arab. He who had come so far, and who now assumed leadership, was virgin and unconsummated, had never known the reality of conflict. He could not know how it would affect him, the moment when it came. Famy lay on his back staring at the ceiling, while deep in the sleeping bag his legs trembled.

Jones was padding down a ground-floor corridor at the back of Leconfield House on his way to the canteen kitchens. They'd be empty, but he could heat a kettle there and make himself a cup of tea with the tea bags he kept in his desk drawer. He was without either shoes or socks, having washed his socks last thing before getting into bed. They were still damp, and he would leave putting them on till the last minute, before the walk up the stairs to the early morning meeting. After the tea he would shave, make himself presentable. The way it was supposed to be in the department.

As he stood facing the window, running the water from the taps into the opened top of the kettle, he saw the Director General's Humber turn into the narrow entry to the underground car park, wire portcullis raised as the vehicle was expertly manoeuvred by the young man in the front. In the back there was nothing much to see, an opened newspaper masking the figure, well down in his seat.

*   *   *

The alarm bell, furious, demanding attention, woke Helen.

She reached forward, pressing herself up with one hand, the other straining across Jimmy toward the bedside table and the offending clock, till she found the button and the silence. He hadn't moved all night, the bastard. Sprawled on his back with his eyes tight and hermetically sealed, mouth open, his pyjamas buttoned protectively up to his neck. Bloody good weekend entertainment you make, Jimmy. A great porpoise up a beach, with no prospect of another high tide. She made one more concerted effort to work some life into the marooned carcase next to her, slipping her hands beneath the material and working with her nails at his chest, slowly and with consideration sketching out small patterns of the skin. Jimmy slept on.

'You're bloody hopeless,' she told him, mouth close to his ear. 'Understand, *hopeless*, a great dump of garbage. Come on, wake up! Stir yourself!'

No response. She moved her hands lower, indenting a line where the beginnings of his paunch slunk down to his hips. Then there was movement. Convulsive, total, as his arms came up and around her, gripping the shoulder blades, pulling her down onto him. His eyes opened for a brief flicker, then closed again, and his arms went slack.

'Better, Jimmy, fractionally better. One out of ten for trying, zero for everything else.'

He hadn't seen a razor the day before, nor the day before that, and his chin was close-set with a tight brush of hair. It bit into her skin, a myriad of needles.

109

'Not so fast, lover-boy, or we'll have the bloody department wanting a blow-by-blow account if I turn up with half my face scraped off by your beard.'

He spoke for the first time, but as if the effort were all but beyond him, the ultimate struggle. 'It's Saturday, you're not going in today, and what bloody time did you get here last night? I'm sitting here half the bloody evening waiting for you.'

'I'm going in today, and I'm going in now. Jones's special request. There's a big flap, all hands to action-stations.' She slid out of his grasp and swung her legs over the side of the bed. She wore no clothes. Wishful thinking, you silly bitch, she told herself. Leave him past midnight and you're always the loser.

Jimmy had begun to take an interest. Not in me, she thought, wave him the boobs and the backside, but it'll take second place to the department. He was half up, almost sitting.

'What's going on, what's the flap?'

'Don't worry, lover-boy, you're included in the cast. Some hit-and-runners reached inside base with a nice plum. Yiddisher target all to themselves, and second, third and fourth floor are running round like it's Declaration of War Day. Big enough for the DG to be arriving before breakfast, then a full scale bit of summitry at zero-eight-thirty hours on the precise stroke.'

He was still trying to focus on her: rounded, pink, but not clear lines yet. Striving for concentration. 'What way is it for me?'

Helen moved off the bed toward the chair draped with her clothes, and began to pull them on. 'Don't know yet. Jones mentioned you just as I was pulling out in the wee small hours. Said he might be needing you. All fit and fighting fresh. Be bloody lucky, won't he? That was all he said, and I was just on my way. Wasn't social chat, I was on my way then.'

'He didn't say anything else?'

'Nothing at all.'

'Bloody fine message for crack-of-dawn Saturday. What am I supposed to do? Sit here all through the weekend hanging on the edge of the phone waiting for him to ring?'

'That's what you do every weekend. God, these tights smell. Not as though anyone will notice. They all slept in. Jones, dreary old Duggan, Fairclough, all doing the boy scouts' bit, kipping on the premises. They'll all be high, smelling to the ceiling. I'll be in good company.' She eased her skirt into position, and grimaced as she looked at herself in the mirror.

'Look like a bloody wreck,' she said.

Jimmy called across from the bed, 'But he said nothing more?'

'Patience, lover-boy, patience. They'll be in touch. It's just that one hell of a panic started up yesterday. Huddles, chats, meetings, files for me to type, despatch riders bombing over from the FO . . . God, I'm late. Never get a taxi at this bloody time, and I said I'd be in. Have to take the car. Now be a good lad, go quietly back to sleep and shed some of that load, so you sound all sweet and sober when the gaffer comes on for you.'

'One more time,' he said. 'Give us a kiss and tell me again what it's all about. Come on.' He said it quietly, the thickness of his voice evaporating.

She leaned over. Let him kiss her on the throat.

111

He was considerate enough not to spoil her make-up. 'I don't know much. Really. But there's an Israeli coming over to stay here, comes some time next weekend, and they've hooked on to a couple of boys. One's IRA, the other they're not sure of, but Phonetics say he's probably Middle East. The code-word they're using is something involving "Mushroom", and the man they're having the flap about is a nuclear scientist. Seems a nice easy equation. Quite a pretty little code-name, better than all those Greek goddesses we're forever calling our fiascos after. But don't tell Jones what I told you. Let it come to virgin, suitably surprised ears. I'll see you tonight – I'll try not to be late again, and we'll cook something.'

Helen stepped up quickly, gave the prone figure a wave and was on her way out of the flat. Early enough not to meet the neighbours on the stairs, stupid bloody looks they gave her. Two years she'd been coming now. First time after a department party, and Jimmy too drunk to notice she'd driven him home, and waking in the morning and taking his time to remember who she was. And then a habit had set in, and she'd come more often, and taken to cleaning up, and washing his smalls, and cooking him meals. The department directed both their lives, and the few chances of contact with people who did not share an existence governed by the Official Secrets Act ensured a curtailed horizon of friends. They began to accept each other, enough to make love in a perfunctory and clumsy style that satisfied the immediate needs of Jimmy as much as Helen. There was no talk of marriage.

The curtains were still drawn together. Jimmy switched off the bedside light, darkening the room.

Be a bugger of a day, he thought, waiting for the telephone to ring the summons. Be by it all day in case Jones called, just as Helen had said he would, just as he always did when there was something rumbling at the department. Wouldn't go out, not even to stock the larder, not even down to the off-licence. Whisky was thin, drained after last night. He could see the bottle over on the table, by the divan in the living part of the room. Barely an inch left, and it had been two-thirds full at the time she should have come back last night.

There was not much else on the table; just the ashtray, a big, cut-glass effort, and piled high with cigarette ends, stubbed and strangled to extinction, and the water jug. He could remember that he'd started by mixing it with water, but the last two inches they'd been neat. Constant refills, the way it generally worked out when he sat up late at night on his own. Need another bottle if any possibility of another late night. But couldn't leave the phone, not if Jones was going to call. There was a nerve-breaking ache in his head now, splitting it from side to side, and a deep throbbing somewhere far inside and behind his temples.

Jimmy lay back, trying to shut out the pain. This was the way it worked out. A big scene down at the department, high level stuff, top men nattering to each other, twisting their knickers, and at the end of the day finding a place for Jimmy somewhere in the set-up. Hadn't been anything for four months, not since the MP, little grovel-merchant. Represented sixty thousand miners and their families and cohorts up in the West Riding. Smug little sod, with too much to say till they worked out the links,

113

the Hungarians, how he afforded the London flat, the rendezvous points, what he had to offer from the Select Committee on Defence Expenditure. Found it only after Jimmy had slipped the kitchen window at Division Bells' time in the House, picked the lock of the drawer in his working table, and pocketed the over-filled, concisely documented diary. Must have missed it, the little bugger, but he'd never reported it. Just looked crestfallen, as if he might weep when they read the charge out. Asked for his solicitor – lot of good that would do him.

But life had been hard since then. The department's retainers didn't go that far. For Jimmy existence on the fringe of the department had started a long time ago. Recruitment was haphazard, following few fixed patterns and depending mainly on personal recommendation.

Jimmy owed his connections with the Security Services to his actions on a glorious moonlit night on 24 August 1944. He was aged nineteen, with the exalted wartime rank of Flight Sergeant (Rear Gunner) in a Lancaster bomber squadron. He flew in 'Charley Apple' off one of those eternal concrete runways that littered the flat Lincolnshire country-side. The whole eight-man crew, officer included, had bitched about flying that night.

'Should have their bloody heads examined, those desk bastards,' the pilot had said.

'Sitting bloody duck for whatever they send up,' had been the contribution of the navigator.

Jimmy had been neither old nor experienced enough to add to the condemnation publicly, but he had recognized that the cursing was counterfeit for fear. They were more than a hundred and fifty miles short of the target when the night-fighter was guided on to them. Jimmy had had a fleeting glimpse of it before the firing started, enough time to shout a warning and bring his own machine-guns to bear. Then the cannon began to rake the airframe of the Lancaster. Fire was quick to follow, and then the order to abandon the aircraft. It took Jimmy what seemed endless stretching minutes to realize that the heavy canopy through which he should have made his individual escape would not move. There was one other way out; he crawled more than sixty feet down the length of the belly of the plane to where the roaring wind drove an entry through the forward escape hatch. Six men had already jumped into the night that stretched more than three miles beneath. As Jimmy had been about to lever himself into the hole he saw the movement beyond the flapping door of the cockpit. Then the pilot, edging his way toward him. There was a look of surprise on the officer's face, and he had shouted something like, 'I thought they'd all gone,' and his attention was turned from the effort of movement and the pain from the fire that had caught at the upper fabric of his flying tunic. But Jimmy had not heard him. The words were lost in the noise of the wind and the tearing metal as the superstructure of the aircraft struggled to hold itself together in the face of its unnatural and contorted descent.

They had jumped virtually together. Jimmy first, then the officer. It was the first time for the rear gunner: only the tower and the simulator before. He had felt the moment of stark panic before he had pulled the metal hoop fastened to the harness across his chest, and then had followed the decisive and successive sensation of the jolt of the parachute opening, the surge upwards as it billowed out, the silent descent, and then the terror as the earth catapulted up to meet him. The officer had landed less than a hundred yards away, the fire on his body extinguished by the air-rush of his speed of fall.

They had barely disentangled themselves from the cords and webbing of their parachutes when the German soldier reached them, shouting instructions and calling to his colleagues across the fields. Not a front-line man, but middle-aged, a reservist. Jimmy had gestured into the middle distance behind the soldier, and as the man in his inexperience had turned, so Jimmy's heavy flying boot went into his crotch. The German jack-knifed, and simultaneously the hard outside edge of Jimmy's right hand came down on the bare and exposed inch of the man's neck, between the helmet and the thickened collar of the great-coat. The German had died instantly and without a whimper, giving Jimmy and the officer time to fade into the sanctuary and shadow of the trees. When light came the next morning Jimmy had seen the pilot's face, seen the raw, mashed damage, the legacy of the clinging cockpit oil. The sight had not unduly upset him. He had been sympathetic, interested, nothing more.

The pilot's name was Philip Willoughby-Jones. He was two years older than the rear gunner, and was never to forget the speed and ruthlessness involved in the death of the German. He would never put out of his mind the fresh pleasure that played in Jimmy's eyes, reflected by the moonlight, before they reached the trees, nor the adulation of success that encompassed his young downy mouth. Via the French Resistance they had been smuggled to the Spanish border and after their return home had lost touch – there had been different postings, different stations. Following the war, when Jones became a full-time deskman with the department, he had let it be known there existed a man who could kill without scruple.

His assessment of Jimmy had not been disproved.

The nearest police station to Englefield Road is some six streets away and to the north, beyond Dalston Junction and close to the Balls Pond Road. It is a forbidding, grey-bricked building, dingy and in a general state of disrepair. Inside attempts had been made to brighten the cavernous passages and inter-view rooms with quantities of paint; they had been largely unsuccessful.

Police Constable Henry Davies, alsatian dog handler, nine years in the force, was going off duty. That in itself did not entail much work, just signing the time sheet, confirming that his over-night reports were completed and ready for the Day Duty Inspector. It had been a quiet night: no pub fights, no premises broken into. Time for home now – to his ground-floor flat to sleep through the daylight hours, with Zero out in the kennel beside the coal box.

As Davies passed the main desk at the end of the front hall with the dog on its lead, head pressed close to his left knee, the sergeant, old and cheerful in spite of the surroundings, spoke to him.

'Off home then, Henry? Not been much for you tonight.'

'Not a damn thing, Sarge.'

'Seeing Doris this weekend?' He'd need that for his dossier, knew every damn thing about everyone, the old boy.

Davies paused near the door. 'No way, she's staying in through today and tomorrow. Won't be coming out till Monday.'

'Need a good bath and all, then,' said the sergeant. 'I don't know how she does it. Nice clean girl, living with all that muck.'

The constable smiled. 'She doesn't seem to mind. Gets a bit deep about it all, says it's what police work is all about. Laughs at me for lugging this piece of dog-flesh about.'

'Well, I couldn't do it. Might manage if it was nine to five, Monday to Friday. But not living in among them twenty-four hours, weekends and all.'

The sarcasm was gentle and kindly meant. 'No-one's going to ask you to blend into the hippie scene, now are they? Not your style, Sarge. But seriously, she says all the coming and going is at the weekend. When she was at the place behind the Angel they got the pusher at the weekend. You have to be there the whole time – part of the furniture.'

An old lady moved across the hall towards the desk, diverting the sergeant's attention. Lost her bloody cat, most likely, thought Davies. He gave the dog's lead a slight pull, and the alsatian was up off its haunches. They went together to his van.

He had told Doris, but only half-heartedly, that he wasn't that keen on her living in the commune, and she had dismissed it – told him it was a damned sight more interesting than driving round with a dog for company. But he'd see her on Monday when she came out of the half-world that she'd infiltrated, when she came out to file her twice-weekly report.

Chapter Seven

It was Lord Denning who wrote in his report in the wake of the Profumo scandal: 'The Security Service in this country is not established by Statute, nor is it recognized by Common Law. Even the Official Secrets Acts do not acknowledge its existence.' Since its conception back in the late sixteenth century the department has insisted that its moves and practices are cloaked in total secrecy. For years it was successful, and the Security Service remained shrouded in mystery, with its operators able to congratulate themselves that they had found a near-divine formula for the working of the department. But all good things come to an end, and that very secrecy, once so jealously protected, had now brought the Security Service into hard times. Politicians looking for economic savings in the 1960s and early 1970s found a familiar scapegoat to carry the burden of financial cut-backs; few of them understood what went on in Leconfield House, and those that wanted to discover the strange activities of the personnel there were actively dissuaded from pursuing their inquiries.

The numbers of men employed in the department

shrivelled as fewer funds were channelled towards them. Worse followed when their political masters decided that the autonomy of the service should be curtailed, and appointed a career Civil Servant to take charge. Only recently, after a series of publicly-castigated mishaps, had the Prime Minister reverted to tradition and put a senior man from the service itself into the Director General's office. His identity was unknown to the mass of the population, and was covered by a 'D' Notice, requesting that the media keep it confidential.

The present DG spent much of his working day wrestling with the budget the Security Service was allowed by Parliament, striving to keep his force efficient, while at the same time remaining solvent. It was a soul-destroying job, and one which he detested. Nor was he paid much for his pains – slightly less than the Fleet Street average for a middle-ranking columnist. But inside the department the new man had revitalized morale simply because his subordinates knew that the man who now controlled them understood their work, was sympathetic to their problems, and was always available. The Irish problem had also played its part in lifting the tempo in Curzon Street. Instead of their dealing almost to the exclusion of everything else with the activities of the Iron Curtain embassies and the huge Soviet trade mission on Highgate Hill, an extra dimension had been brought into the work. On top of that came the more recent wave of Arab terrorism throughout Europe. The DG could note with satisfaction that the building no longer operated on a five-day week, and that many of the heads of key sections were at their desks through the weekend, even in high summer.

The Director General was a short, heavily-built man.
Spread across his desk, occasionally breaking off to
pencil a few words on a pad, he scanned the files
that had been left for him to digest, his eyes only a
few inches from the paper. There was monumental
concentration, head quite still, seeking for flaws in
the arguments, high spots in the information. He
believed totally in paperwork, required it to be short
and explicit, but demanded all relevant facts to be set
out in the files. He had hooked his coat over the end
of his chair and undone the top button of his shirt,
while his tweed tie hung down loose at the neck.
He smoked incessantly, non-tipped and one of the
strong brands, drawing deeply till there was hardly
enough of the rolled paper left for him to hold
without him burning his fingers.

Promptly at eight-thirty came the knock at
his door, and Jones, followed by Fairclough and
Duggan, came into the bright first-floor office. The
DG gestured to them to pull up chairs and continued
to read the last pages of the file on Ciaran McCoy.
The section heads made a half-moon as they sat
down on the far side of the desk, and waited for him
to finish. The office was bare, but not to the point of
being Spartan: there was a picture of the Queen –
the Annigoni print; a water colour of a bowl of fruit;
a table littered with yesterday's newspapers; wall-to-
wall carpets (as his position decreed); and heavy
plain curtains drawn back to let in the sunlight. Not
much to gaze at, but they all felt the after-effects
from the night just past, and none was in the mood
for day-dreaming or staring at irrelevancies.

When he had finished the DG closed the McCoy

file, piling it neatly with the others. He threw an eye quickly over the notes he had made, and then looked at the three men facing him. He could see their tiredness. A short meeting was required.

'There's not much time, gentlemen,' he started. Voice calm, easy, fluent from his Welsh background. 'Our guest here on Monday night, his public appearance on Tuesday, and the flight out undecided between Wednesday and Thursday. We can probably ensure that he goes on Wednesday. On what we have at our disposal the threat seems real enough. There is one factor we should consider before recommendations are made to the Home Office. If this were simply an IRA affair saturation protection would probably see us through. They tend to like to make it home all in one piece, so if they see the odds placed heavily against them they like to try again when conditions are more auspicious. But there's the added factor of the Middle East involvement. Different people, different philosophy, more prepared to go with the target. If the other half of the team is Arab – Palestinian – then we must accept he is prepared to die along with our scientist friend. It makes the operation of protection infinitely more complicated. The suicide killer always has things stacked in his favour. It means for us that we have to widen the number of people involved, and mount a much wider screen than I would otherwise advocate. That means police, uniformed and CID. Thoughts, gentlemen?'

Duggan spoke. 'This McCoy is a hard operator. Given them a long chase across the water, but he's on strange ground here. It's reasonable to suggest he'll need a safe house, somewhere he can hole up with the other man. He has two alternatives. He can go in with the usual crowd. Provo supporters, that lot. On the other hand he can go elsewhere, somewhere right outside the norm. The only line we have on that could be some connection with his sister. She's no longer in London, back in the Republic, but she went through a spell in a commune, one of those in North London, but drifting. McCoy was reported as disapproving, but it could have given him the contact.'

'Half the raids the Special Branch mount are aimed at communes,' said the DG. 'It's a good suggestion, but it'll take time to check out, and that's one for the police.'

'Presuming that the Palestinian has joined up with McCoy – and we have to believe that from the rendezvous call,' said Fairclough, '—then we can just about guarantee that he's dependent on McCoy for his accommodation, and probably for the guns too. We've had the French report in overnight, and no firearms were found in the car, the one that was shot up and burned out. If the third lad made it away from the car there's little chance he could have carried the necessary firearms, explosives or whatever for three men. And it makes sense that the Arabs would provide the attack team, the Provisionals, what local knowledge they needed.'

'It's strange they should have chosen McCoy, then. No history, no past form of operations in London or anywhere else outside his little patch. But with his associations no problem with firearms if he wanted them – plenty of access, could all be fixed. No problem there.' The DG was thinking aloud, picking his words carefully and slowly. 'The firearms would be McCoy's part. But what we have to consider is this. If the original team is decimated, and the one man wants to go on with it, how far does McCoy involve himself?'

'He's a killer,' said Duggan decisively, without hesitation or doubt. 'It's clear from the file. He'll think about it, he'll try and make sure he walks out of it, but he's a killer. He won't step back, not unless the odds are right against him.'

'And our unknown friend will need him?'

'He's essential,' said Duggan. 'The Arab, whoever he is, needs him – and badly. But the two make a formidable threat. Quite a handful.'

'To become more general' – with a slight wave of his hand the DG terminated the conversation – 'to delve into the theory of the attack: what brings these two together? No common ideology . . .'

'Necessity only,' said Duggan. As the protégé of the head of the Security Services, and one whose career was well mapped, and his future charted, he had the confidence to speak his mind. 'The Palestinians must have the accommodation and transport, and if it's provided locally then the trails can be that much better covered. It's infinitely more satisfactory from their point of view, particularly if they can also travel clean of firearms. Same for the Provisionals: they'll have become involved through the advantages that will come to them. They've tried hard enough to get their hands on Iron Curtain weapon systems . . . Europe's difficult as a supply source; nothing coming direct – they don't want to know over there. The American market is inadequate, and difficult on resupply. But the Middle East offers them a major opportunity. If they pull this one in successful harmony then it'll be a guarantee that Kalashnikovs, rocket launcher RPG 7s, perhaps even a SAM 7 missile will be turning up on the border for the boys in South Armagh and Tyrone. I'd put it down as a straight swap – immediate help by the Provos, and they get top-grade hardware in the close future. And talk to any army man, not HQ but the guys in the field, and ask them how they'd feel about having that sort of gear on tap for the opposition.'

'And the man Sokarev? . . .'

'Important to the Palestinians, big coup if they drop him. Irrelevant to the Irish. If we lose him – heaven forbid! – the chances are the Provos wouldn't even claim him, nor their part in it.'

'And this bomb that the Israelis keep so much under the table, and that our Mr Sokarev is credited with, what state is that in?'

'The Americans call it the "screwdriver" state. That's a good description. Probably not assembled, but way off the design bench. Just needs putting together.'

There had been enough talking, the DG decided. He straightened in his chair. 'I think we'd better get the following done this morning. Details on McCoy to all police stations in London, particular reference to communes. Run a check on all immigration forms coming in via ferries from Boulogne yesterday, that's for Ports Unit of Special Branch. Liaise with the Israelis, the security attaché – not here, though. Fix a meeting with him at Home Office, and don't let him think that he's running the show. Jones, I'd like you to co-ordinate. Final point. I'd like a man on the ground beside this professor night and day, not just Special Branch – they can look after themselves – but one of our own. So we know what's going on.'

Jones spoke for the first time, mock hesitant, a smile on his face. 'There's Jimmy.'

'Is he on the bottle or off it at the moment?'

'About half-way. He'll fit the job.'

'There are plenty of others,' said the DG.

'He's the best of them.' It was Jones's opinion. None of the other men in the room was prepared to make an issue from it.

For differing reasons both Fairclough and Duggan were disapproving of the choice, but neither spoke. Jones's loyalty to the men who worked for him was familiar to his colleagues. It was recognized there was a personal bond between the section head and Jimmy; the detail of it had never been explained to them. But to criticize the judgement that Jones had made of his man would be futile, and both stayed silent.

The DG nodded. He knew Jimmy, had known him for a long time, liked his results, stayed ignorant of his methods. He said, 'I'm going to see the Minister this morning. I'll be back at lunch-time. If you want me, try about a quarter to one. That's it, gentlemen. Remember, there's very little time.'

From the outer office Helen called the home number of the Commander in charge of Special Branch, and put him through to Jones. Copies of McCoy's file together with the fingerprint and photograph folder that had now arrived from Northern Ireland were sent by motorcycle to Scotland Yard. The conversation also served to activate the search of the immigration forms, thirty-nine thousand of them, representing the number of persons who had crossed to Britain on ferries from Boulogne the previous day.

Helen also called the Israeli embassy, introduced herself as Home Office, left a number – the direct one to Jones's desk – and asked that the security attaché should call back as soon as he had been located with a view to arranging an urgent meeting in mid-afternoon. Next she traced the Assistant Commissioner (Crime) to a golf club in North Hertfordshire. He arranged to see Jones in his office at Scotland Yard immediately after lunch. That would set in motion the sifting of scores of reports and observations made by undercover drug squad detectives who worked in the communes. The conversation with Jones was impressive enough for him to scratch from the four-ball game he had arranged, make his apologies to his partners, and drive home for a morning's work on the telephone before going to London.

Lastly she raised Jimmy, still waiting beside the receiver, but dressed now. His trousers were creased at the back of his knees, his jacket had great lines carved across the flap at the back, and the shirt was not quite clean. But he was dressed. Would he come in at four-thirty? 'Course he bloody well would. And after that? She didn't know. Going at it like a lot of maniacs, she'd said, and rung off.

The Cabinet Minister who rejoiced in the title of 'Secretary of State for Home Affairs' liked to keep in touch with his constituents. On Saturday mornings he held a 'surgery', where the electors who had returned him to Westminster for the past eighteen years could come to him with their problems. His opponents claimed it was simply window-dressing, and that as he allowed each of his 'patients' a bare four minutes there was little that could effectively be talked about in that time. Clogged-up drains and the lateness of school buses was about all that could be managed. Anything as detailed as council house rents or the redundancies at the local car-body factory could not, to the relief of the Minister, be dealt with in the limited time of his schedule.

He had dealt with fifteen constituents in the straight hour that he set himself, and was preparing for the drive across country to the hall where he would eat a sandwich lunch with the faithful and make a short speech, when the Director General of the Security Services was put through on the telephone in his agent's office on the first floor of the constituency headquarters. On matters of state security the Director General had direct access to the Prime Minister, but there were occasions when that was not suitable. Going too high up the ladder too fast, and then leaving no-one senior to fall back if the initial contacts with Government went sour. The DG liked to leave his options open, but it was rare for him to seek an interview outside normal working routine with his Minister – rare enough for the Minister to be puzzled, and to be left confused after he had arranged that they should meet at the hall and talk while the tea and food were being consumed.

When the Director General arrived in mid-morning he was shown into a room behind the stage of the hall, and he waited there among the piled chairs and old scenery props for the Minister to come in.

'I'm sorry to trouble you,' he began.

'I'm sure you wouldn't have done so if you hadn't thought it important.' The Minister was wary of the other man. Security was fraught with whirlpools in the political ocean; when everything was going well you never heard from them; they only surfaced when the gales were blowing.

'I think we're running into some bother, something you ought to hear about.'

The Minister acquiesced. The Director General could see he was nervous, uncertain of what was to follow and fearful of its implications, and his voice was subdued as he explained the situation.

The Minister felt trapped. 'What do you want me to do?' he asked.

'It's not so much a case of doing anything, sir. It's a question of your knowing what's going on, what the situation is.'

'How important is this Israeli?' The question was barked, staccato.

'One of their backroom men, not a well known personality. Named David Sokarev. They regard him as critical to their nuclear programme. He doesn't work on the power station side, but on the civilian programmes. He's with the other crowd, the ones they don't talk about. Sensitive man, sensitive work.'

'Is it an important meeting?'

'Not that we know of. We haven't seen a guest list yet – this has only been developing since yesterday evening. We'll have that sort of thing by tonight. But there's nothing to suggest it's world-shattering . . .'

'Which it would be if the bastards get to him.' He lingered, concentrating his mind on the problem. Always security providing the problems, never any

130

good news, always anguish and heart-searching. And now, with not one of his Civil Servants within fifty miles, with the Prime Minister touring Lanarkshire, a snap decision to be made. I know what this blighter wants, he thought, can read him a mile off. Wants me to tell him he's doing a grand job, let him run off and take charge on his own, and when the fiasco comes, when the scandal breaks, then he can tell the committee sitting under the learned judge 'in camera' that the Minister was aware of the situation right from the start. No way you get me that easily.

'The Prime Minister should be told of this. He takes a great interest in Israeli affairs. He'd want to know. I'll do that. My first reaction is that the Israelis should call off the visit. If it's not an important meeting, not an important personality, then what's the point in risking him?'

'You won't find that so easy, sir,' said the DG. 'Foreign Office have tried that one, down the more tortuous channels rather than the ambassadorial ones. Got a straight shut-out on the suggestion. But I agree it would be the easiest solution to our problem. I'd be grateful if someone could let me know how the suggestion is taken.'

The Minister shook the other man's hand, and walked back into the hall. The plates were empty by this stage, and the tea was getting cold. His words were awaited. He prided himself on talking off the cuff, without a note, but by now his mind was clouded by the conversation that had just terminated. It would be a bad speech.

As the sun rose that Saturday morning so it moved beyond the compass of the attic-floor window to the

131

room that housed Famy and McCoy. While its bright-ness and warmth streamed through the glass the Arab had dressed, pulling on his clothes secretively and with a shyness that came from never having been separated from his people before. As he dragged his trousers on he had turned his back on the Irishman, who still lay in his sleeping bag picking at the dirt that had accumulated beneath his finger-nails. McCoy called across to him not to worry about shaving. 'Don't want to look pretty in here. Doesn't fit with the rest of the surroundings.' And then a quiet laugh. After he had dressed Famy paced about the room, taking in its length in a few strides, going continuously to the window to peer down on to the street below, then walking again. He waited for some movement from the other man, and was loath to go beyond the door on his own. The street fascinated him, indistinct voices reached up the height of the brickwork as he strained to hear what was being said. The dogs that ran free cocking their legs at the lamp-posts, the black men and women and children, the house along to the right where the old façade had been painted a bright scarlet, the wooden window fittings and the door in vivid yellow – all were strange and beyond his experience.

Beneath him there were more sounds – the music had started up again. It was not so vibrant as when they had arrived, he told himself. That was reserved for the night-time.

Never far from his mind was the image of the darkened, cloaked figure he had seen in the room. He felt a sense of frustration that the Irishman had not taken what he had said more seriously, and felt affronted by the casualness with which his

132

revelations had been greeted. And when the sun was gone, and McCoy still showed no sign of moving, Famy had just squatted down on the sleeping bag and waited for him to get up.

'You can go downstairs if you want to,' McCoy said. Famy shook his head, irritable at his own reluctance.

'They won't eat you, you know. They're just ordinary kids.'

'I'll wait.'

'Please yourself,' McCoy said. He lit a cigarette, smoked it with consideration while Famy silently watched, flicked the ash successively onto the floor, and then when it was spent ground the tip out on the boards. Then he climbed out of the bag.

Standing in his underpants and vest, he stared directly at Famy.

'Have you done this sort of thing before?' he said, not much more than a whisper, but demanding an answer. Famy wavered, avoiding the other man with his eyes, reluctant, hurt.

'No. No, I have not before. It was planned that I should have moved into Israel, that I should fight there, a mission over the fence into the North. Then they had the information on Sokarev, and his visit, and all was changed for me. I was taken from the original plan.'

'Have you been in action before? I mean, have you fired a gun – in anger?'

'Only in training. I have never fought.'

Famy struggled to control what he thought were the inadequacies of his answers.

'It'll be difficult to get near the bastard, you know that?'

'With preparation, there is always a way.'

'You don't mount a thing like this on wishful fucking thinking.' McCoy showed his impatience. 'You have to know what you're about. You can't just breeze in . . .'

'It is unnecessary to talk to me as a child.' Famy cut McCoy in mid-sentence. His speech was clear, soft, almost sing-song. The Irishman retreated.

'Don't get me wrong. I wasn't suggesting . . .'

'Well, don't speak to me as if I were a fool. If you want no part in the rest, say so now. We can separate – your role forgotten.'

'There is no question of that.' McCoy stopped. The voices and music carried up to them. Neither spoke for four, five, six seconds. Then McCoy said, 'I say there's no question of that, I'm under orders. From the Army Council. They've made a decision, and they'll stick to it. They won't go back on it. Our Chief of Staff has given his word.' He smiled, weak at the side of his mouth, feeling the cold on his skin.

The relief flooded through Famy. He reached out and patted McCoy's shoulder, girl-like, but a gesture meant as affection and gratitude.

'What do we do today?' There was excitement in his voice.

'I thought this afternoon we'd take a look at the university. Can't do that on a Sunday, all the students are back in their digs, in their lodging houses. There won't be many of them about, but a few. Would have been better yesterday if you'd showed up on time. Don't worry, I'm not blaming you. You were a bloody genius to make it here at all. I've got a car, and tomorrow we go down into the country. Where the guns are. I've got some grenades.

We don't use those much, but I was told to bring them.'

'We know about them,' said Famy.

'We'll try and hit at the meeting. It's a public place. Should offer the best hope.'

'In Lebanon they thought there might be two opportunities. The meeting and at the airport – not as he is coming in, but when he leaves.'

McCoy said, 'The airport will be sealed, it's difficult there. The best chance has to be at the meeting. How close do you need to get to him?'

'As near as is necessary.'

'There has to be a way out.'

'We have not come here to escape. We have come to kill Sokarev.'

McCoy fumbled with his socks, turning them inside out, trying to decide which one belonged to which foot. He felt the chill of the moment. Could see again the pictures. Those arching bodies spilling from the windows of the flats at Beit Shean, crumbling on the paving below and welcomed there with knives and axes and tins of petrol, and then the smoke and the flames; the sack-like shape pulled from the wreckage of Tel Aviv's Savoy Hotel. Palestinians who had gone 'as near as was necessary'.

'There has to be a way that leaves us a chance of escape,' said McCoy.

'Perhaps,' said Famy, and the Irishman left it there. He was a madman, this Arab, a suicide merchant. Well, good bloody luck to him. But what to do about it? Couldn't back out, couldn't fade away from it. Orders too implicit. Just at the time, he'd hold him back. Make his presence felt then, and when the shooting came do it with a bit of skill, with an aimed shot, not close in and blasting over open sights.

But they were not a team, and both men longed for the companionship of their own.

When he had dressed McCoy led the way downstairs. They saw no-one till they came to the front hallway, when McCoy opened the door into the main room that faced out on the street. The conversation in the room, carried on in a series of separate huddles, went on uninterrupted, but eyes and heads and bodies turned to look at them. Like the bloody zoo, thought McCoy. He stood in front of the open door, staring back, waiting for someone to speak. They had little resolution against his gaze, and one by one the sitting, standing, crouching youths returned to their own groups. All except one girl. Famy noticed her before McCoy, then the Irishman saw her. Not pretty, rather plain, McCoy thought. A long, loose black dress, and a heavy woollen jersey pulled over her shoulders, shapeless, protection against the cold but nothing else. Ugly witch clothes accentuating the dullness of her skin – devoid of make-up, empty of anything feminine.

Doris Lang had noticed that the two new arrivals were out of place from the moment they had come through the door of the house the previous night. She was trained to observe and make deductions from what she saw. These two did not fit the pattern that governed the other young people in the commune. She had seen the Irishman's complexion – too bright, too countrified, too healthy for life amongst the drop-outs – had noticed that his stature and bearing were divorced from those of the hand-to-mouth hippies. There was too much command in his face for him to belong to those who could not cope with the pressure of the life outside. This one, she had decided, was strictly a transit traveller, on his way through, and using the commune for a particular purpose.

She could also sense the nervousness and unease in the movements of the willowy, dark-skinned man who stood a pace behind. He too did not belong there. His hands must have been sweating, because twice he rubbed them against his trouser-legs. He had cold, purposeful eyes, that roamed without settling across the room, always coming back to her. It surprised her that she had found nothing in their possessions last night to give her any indication of their business in the house.

She felt the two men's eyes boring into her, and turned away, unwilling to appear too curious. There was marijuana smoke drifting, cool and gentle, from the far side of the room. Smoking today had started early.

Chapter Eight

The car of the Israeli Ambassador came to the back door of the Foreign Office.

It was a Mercedes, low on its wheels because of the armour plating that was standard for senior members of the country's diplomatic corps. Unlike the principal transport of other embassies it carried no suggestion in the number plate as to the identity of the passenger. There was a large radio aerial attached to the rear of the bodywork at the side of the boot, and this maintained communications with the embassy building set back from the private Kensington Palace Road. Most ambassadors accredited to the Court of St James travelled with just a chauffeur for company, but in this car there were two other young men, both of whom had been issued with licences from the Home Office to carry Uzi sub-machine-guns. These lay on the floor, one in the front beside the driver, one in the back beside the Ambassador and covered from careless gaze by coats. As it had made its way through the traffic the Mercedes was shadowed by a powerful three-and-a-half-litre Rover, unmarked, and in which sat two men from the Protection Division of Special Branch.

When the car pulled up the bodyguard in the front of the car stayed in his seat, his hand a few inches from the hidden Uzi. The man who had ridden in the back with the Ambassador unlocked the door, climbed out, scanned the pavement where it ran down from Birdcage Walk towards the Horseguards Parade, and nodded. The Ambassador got out quickly, and had been shepherded through the narrow door in a matter of seconds. Both he and his bodyguard ignored the special Branch man who had also stepped onto the pavement. The London detective assigned to the Israeli embassy was used to that, familiar with being treated as an unnecessary bystander, there to make up the numbers, but not to be consulted.

Through the working part of the week a liveried official would have been there to escort the Ambassador to the second-floor office where the Under Secretary who specialized in Middle East Affairs now waited. But at the weekend there was simply a man in a dark suit. The wide passages were darkened, electricity switched off to save money, leaving the portraits of the great British Foreign Secretaries that lined the walls mysterious and shadowy.

'Thank you for coming, your Excellency,' said the Under Secretary, as the door closed behind the Ambassador. The Israeli said nothing.

'The Minister would like to have been able to see you personally. It is regrettable, but he is out in the country, and cannot return to London in the time we felt was available.' Liar, thought the Ambassador. More likely up to his thighs in a trout stream somewhere in his beloved Yorkshire.

'On the basis of the information with which your

139

own Security Service was able to provide us, and because of additional information that our own departments have obtained, the Minister has asked me to request of your Excellency that further consideration should be given to the visit to Britain of Professor Sokarev.'

The Ambassador said, 'You say "further information". To what end?'

Spell it out in words of one syllable, thought the Under Secretary. God protect us, they're a gauche crowd.

'With a view, Excellency, to deciding whether or not the visit should continue as planned, in the face of what your service and ours regard as a serious threat.'

'You are asking me to recommend to Jerusalem that the visit be cancelled?'

'I am asking you nothing. I am merely suggesting, on the direction of my Minister, that you might wish to reconsider the value of the visit.'

'There is only one set of circumstances which would lead me to tell my Government that in my personal opinion Professor Sokarev should cancel his lecture on Tuesday night and bypass Britain.'

The Under Secretary inclined his head, and the Ambassador went on.

'If I were to believe that the police forces and other agencies of Britain were incapable of providing the necessary protection for Professor Sokarev, then I would suggest to my Foreign Ministry that the visit should be cancelled.'

Cunning fox, the Under Secretary said to himself.

'There is no question of that. We will provide protection . . .'

'Then there is nothing further to discuss.' The Ambassador's voice was cold. 'When you report back to the Minister about our conversation I would be grateful if you could relay a sentiment of my Government. We are not prepared to be taken simply as a nuisance-child, a bothersome problem that will go away if the door is barred to it. Professor Sokarev has been offered the hospitality of a learned and illustrious body in your capital. We intend to make sure that he honours the engagement. The rest, my dear fellow, is in your hands.'

The Under Secretary bridled. 'You must understand that I was passing on a request from my Minister.'

The Ambassador smiled, without friendship, puckered his eyes fractionally, and said, 'And I will pass on to my Minister that the British Government will be providing – what was the word you used? – yes, "adequate protection". Perhaps you should know, since it seems you have not been informed, that while we have been discussing the suitability of the visit the security attaché at my embassy has been talking with the relevant people on your side on the very question of Professor Sokarev's safety. At times like this, Under Secretary, it is liaison that is needed.'

He turned on his heel and made his own way out of the room.

In the early afternoon McCoy took Famy from the house and to the car parked fifty yards up the road on the far side.

'I didn't bring it down to the station last night,' he said. 'It's nicked – stolen – and that's too public a place to leave it lying around. It's all right in a street

141

like this, half the bloody motors here have separated from their log books.'

It was a two-door Ford Escort, painted green and unscratched, 'M' registration. 'I got it over in Wembley, that's on the far side of London, out in the suburbs, night before last. Goes OK, though it's a bit small.'

Famy looked at the car, disinterested, and waited for the passenger door to be opened for him. Soon they were heading past Islington Green and stopping at the lights, indicator clicking, ready to turn right down the Pentonville Road and then into the main university complex. And as they drove McCoy realized the extent to which he was involved. It had begun simply, and without complications; providing back-up, assistance. The shooting in France had changed that, and ensured that if he carried on with the enterprise it would be as an equal partner.

There's no bloody help from this bastard, he thought to himself. Talks in spasms, then goes silent, just gazes into bloody eternity, like no-one else exists. Doesn't give a damn whether we come out of it or not. A different war, the hedgerow actions that he had perfected among the fields of South Armagh. Political assassination . . . something that his Active Service Unit had never contemplated. A soldier or a policeman, or a local Proddy councillor, that was different. That was attrition.

This was a totally new concept to him; a killing on such a grand scale that the shock waves would fill the world headlines for a week. It was one thing to drop a Para, to blow a Woolworths, to take out a policeman, but this . . . And he was being drawn into it, he recognized that, and thought even now that the point of retreat was already lost. He was experienced, had known the tension of guerrilla combat in the hills round Crossmaglen, had fired the cumbersome RPG 7 rocket launcher at the tin-fenced, screened and barricaded police station on the edge of his town, had given orders, had had men follow him. And yet this other man who had known none of this was directing him, controlling him – and had out-stretched him in commitment.

Perhaps it was the hate. He'd heard of it, read about it, the simple hatred the Palestinian hard-men felt for the Israelis, and he knew he couldn't match it. Even in the cage at Long Kesh when he had paced beside the interior perimeter wire and watched the camouflaged uniformed soldiers in their watch-towers, traversing their machine-guns, and jeering down at the men below, even then he could not hate to the exclusion of all else. When these people blasted their hostages, threw their grenades without hesitation, without remorse, into cinemas, they put themselves beyond the reach of McCoy's under-standing. His men could never do that. There had to be a purpose to killing. Every victim ought to *know* why he would die at McCoy's hand. But just for the sake of it, just for the gesture . . . that was not enough.

At the bottom of the Euston Road, in the last lap to the university, he asked, 'Why this man? Why Sokarev?'

There was no urgency in the reply. Famy said, 'Three times the Arabs fought the Israelis and were shamed. At their Yom Kippur we fought them again and surprised them with our technique and with our bravery, but we did not win. The next time we fight

143

we will do better, and the time after that we will have greater success. One time in the future we will have them close to defeat. Then they will have no option, then they will threaten their ultimate weapon. They will tell the world of their bomb, how they will use it to survive. Sokarev is an architect of that bomb. To us he represents a symbol of what would be their last throw in desperation. We feel if we kill Sokarev we have demonstrated that we fear nothing from them. If we can eliminate a man so much at the centre of their whole basis of national survival then we have achieved a great victory.'

'There'll be others, others who know as much as this one man,' said McCoy.

'That is unimportant. It is not Sokarev's knowledge that we will deny them. It is the symbol that we attack. It meant nothing in manpower for Israel to lose her athletes at Munich, nothing to lose their attaché in Washington, the man here in London we took with the letter-bomb. It is the symbol that matters. That we can prove to them that we are at war, that we can strike where and when we please.'

McCoy was still silently repeating to himself, 'Bloody maniacs' when he drove past the Students' Union building, and pulled up outside the massive mausoleum structure that marked the administrative and academic centre of London University.

'Just relax. Take it easy. If anyone asks, you've left some notes behind, coming back to get them. But don't look furtive, look as though you belong,' McCoy said as they walked up the great cement steps and into the building.

Famy said quietly, 'Do you know which entrance he will use?'

'No, there are a stack of them. This is the main one, the natural one, but there are alternatives.'

There was almost a tranquillity about the Arab's voice, as if it belonged to someone who has had a great rest, and woken refreshed. His breathing was relaxed, unhurried, as he peered round him in the echoing, high-roofed hallway.

'But the room, we know which room he will use?'

'It's marked on the invitation.' McCoy pulled his wallet from an inner pocket. From it he took an embossed square of card, and smiled as he showed it to Famy. 'It's the real thing,' he said. The Arab recognized the name of David Sokarev in ornate, copperplate writing in the centre of the card, followed by a string of initials. He saw also the words 'Lecture Room D, ground floor, Fourth entrance to the Right after entering the Main Hallway.'

'Where did you get it?' Famy asked.

'Acquired it. Long story. I'll tell you some time.'

'What time does he arrive? And when does he speak?'

'He'll come about fifteen minutes before the speech. There's a reception, sherry and sandwiches – he'll probably arrive at the end of that. He's due to talk at eight.'

But Famy was not listening, just scanning the corridor, taking in the pillars, and the various shadowy entrances that led off the hallway to offices and other lecture rooms. He was assessing cover, the room he would need, the speed at which a man could travel across the floor space, the angle required to see him if he were to be surrounded by guards and the welcoming committee. Without seeing the room, he had already decided there would be no possibility of gaining direct admission to the lecture, particularly with the bulky firearms that would be needed for the killing.

'It has to be from outside,' he said, vaguely and to himself.

Famy turned and walked back down the hallway and out into the light. He went left across the car park to the edge of the building, then moved down its side, his attention locked on the windows that were fitted just above the level of his head. Massive, functional and intimidating in its grey strength, the building towered above him in a narrowing column to the topmost point from where half London could be viewed. The fortress to which Sokarev would be brought. But there had been a way, hadn't there, into every citadel? Brick and stone and cement in themselves do not provide protection, Famy thought. There will be a gap, if only one caused by the error of man.

The construction of the lower floors was in the form of a giant and flattened cross, the main doors at the north end, the lecture room off to the west extremity of a protruding arm. Famy hurried across from the front toward the wall where the lecture room would have its windows set, and in his step there was a lightness and excitement. They had taught him the art of what they called 'using dead ground', moving in terrain which was denied to the vision of the enemy. Those who stood at the main door would have no sight of the windows he wanted; the butting corner would deny them. And where would they accumulate the security men that

146

would come with Sokarev? They would be with him inside, and they would be at the doors . . . He came round the corner, McCoy following blindly but uncomprehending, and again there were windows and beneath them cars, all closely parked and near to the wall. He noted that and was satisfied.

He glanced around him, for the first time a trace of anxiety showing, then scrambled on to the bonnet of a dark saloon. It gave him the elevation to see inside the lecture room, across the rows of pew-like benches, and to the lectern which on Tuesday night would hold the typed notes of David Sokarev. He jumped down from the car.

'Would you go inside,' he said to McCoy, 'and if there are curtains draw them across this window, the middle one of the three?' McCoy stood his ground, confused. 'Just do it,' the Arab said, his voice rising. 'Just this window and draw them tightly. So I can see where they meet.'

He waited a full two minutes after McCoy had gone, then the curtains swished their way across the broad window. He noted that when they closed they were completely together, letting no light escape from the room. He bent down hurriedly, picked up a small stone from the gravel, scratched the wall at the place where the curtains had met. Almost immediately the drapes opened again. While he waited for McCoy he repeated the scratch in the wall over his original mark. This time he drew a six-pointed star a little more than four inches across from tip to tip. He was still smiling about it when McCoy joined them.

'We must get some gloves,' Famy said. 'Thick ones that will withstand broken glass, cover the hand and the wrist.'

147

In the mind of Abdel-El-Famy the assassination plan was complete. Beautiful and totally simple.

The drugs scene in London as in any major capital is a brutal and violent one. A below-surface cancer invisible till the skin of society is scraped. Young detectives like Doris Lang, who attempted to infiltrate the market and supply the evidence required by the courts to convict the 'pushers', went through extensive and thorough training before they abandoned their conventioned trim clothes for those of the teenagers and drop-outs among whom they would now move.

She had been on a three-week course to learn the medical side of the menace, to be taught the arts of survival in an alien society, and had spent two concentrated days in a gymnasium with an instructor who taught self-defence. She was a capable young woman, used to looking after herself, and the Detective Inspector to whom she reported had few fears about her personal safety. What he was looking for from her was, first of all, patience, and, when that was rewarded, detail.

She had seen McCoy and Famy leave the house, and then spent twenty-five minutes reading and gossiping casually and inconsequentially with her new friends before she excused herself and left. On the stair landing on the floor immediately below the room occupied by the two newcomers she had stood stock-still for a full minute, listened to the sounds of the building, convincing herself that in the upper reaches of the house she would be alone.

She had been disappointed with her earlier search in the small hours. She had used the time on the

148

clock that her training suggested, just after 4 a.m., when the psychiatrists say the human physique is at its most vulnerable and yearning for deep sleep. But she had recognized that this search could only be a cursory one, though she had weighed the chances of her discovery as being slight. In daylight she could be slower, more observant.

None of the locks to the rooms was fitted with a key, and she was able to turn the handle and walk in. In her left hand was a small memory-pad and a pencil stub. She worked through the men's possessions for twelve minutes. Much of the time was spent rearranging the clothing in the Arab's grip-bag and McCoy's old suitcase so that they would not detect her hand among the socks, and the underclothes and the shirts. She found no papers belonging to either man, no passports, letters, driving licences; no hint of their identity.

There was nothing remarkable in the clothing she looked at that lay in the case. It was the contents of the grip-bag that fascinated her. The clothes in themselves were unexceptional, except that every maker's tag and washing and cleaning instruction had been removed. Not pulled away, but conscientiously unstitched.

She wrote that down on the pad, beneath the times of arrival and departure, and the descriptions she had taken of the two men. She felt the frustration that came from the failure to explain their presence in the commune. Perhaps, she thought, their trip today would provide her with something, perhaps when they returned there would be papers which she could find if she came again in the cold, desolate hours before dawn.

At Scotland Yard Jones saw the Assistant Commissioner (Crime) in his office close to the operations room on the fifth floor of the building. As a result of the meeting two considerable and widescale programmes would be put into operation. First, a dragnet to try to locate and then arrest the man McCoy and his unknown partner. Second, the gathering together of the security necessary to protect the Israeli professor when he visited London. It was the first plan that took the majority of their time. Jones sketched through the information the department had collected in the previous twenty-four hours, in some instances withholding sources but allowing the policeman a detailed picture of the circumstances that surrounded the threat to Sokarev. He emphasized the faint but possible connection between the Irishman and the North London communes.

'You have a difficulty there straight away,' said the Assistant Commissioner. 'We have several under surveillance – from the outside. I can call that sort of information in at any time. If your men are in one of those we can identify them from the logs very quickly. But there are others where we have people living on the inside. I've been on the phone this morning and I'm advised that there are seventeen where that applies. They tend to come out on Monday mornings. There would be a fair deal of opposition if you were to ask me to break all those covers and get the officers out this afternoon or tomorrow. You appreciate a great number of detailed inquiries are going on through these channels. I think to justify such an action I'd need rather more positive information than you've been able to provide me with.'

The Security Service is a force without powers. It can only request. Jones looked pained, acting up a bit. Face set with disappointment.

'I'm sorry, Mr Jones. Tell me it's essential, tell me an address, give me something clear, and we can act. I think that's reasonable.'

'Is there no other way of getting them out other than destroying their position – your people's?'

'What's your suggestion?' The Assistant Commissioner threw it back at him. Like so many others who rarely came into touch with the Security Services, he distrusted them, remaining unconvinced of their effectiveness.

'I don't have one,' said Jones. 'Not ready at hand.' He felt tired, anger growing at the man across the desk, who was so unable to comprehend the scale of the problem – more concerned with marijuana and cocaine than political assassination.

'I'll think about it, ask around,' said the Assistant Commissioner. That was the concession. Trifling, thought Jones. And half another day gone, and nothing new to show for it.

The security attaché of the Israeli embassy was late at the Home Office. Jones's ill humour was not helped by the lack of any apology. But he recognized there were times to bite on it, not to make the scene he would have liked. And the Israeli brought information – time-tables of Sokarev's movements, hotel and room number, invitation list to the speech.

'And he will have two men with him from our own Protection Division of the Foreign Ministry. I can give you their names. Joseph Mackowicz and Gad Elkin. You know it is our policy, Mr Jones. Since Munich we have become more aware of the dangers. They are expressly charged with the safety of the Professor.'

That was the best news of the day, thought Jones. If the applecart goes then those two bastards will be picking up the load along with me. Nice to be in numbers.

He told the attaché what was known of McCoy. The Israeli said, 'With respect, I would suggest from my observations of your own problems and my knowledge of ours that one we have to fear is not the Irishman. If the other man is a Palestinian that is the creature we have to be on guard against.'

Too right, Jones said to himself. And no name, no description, no fingerprints, no file, no bloody history at all.

'We should meet again tomorrow. Same time, and here?'

The Israeli agreed, and Jones hurried to his car, and drove fast back to Curzon Street. It was his complete lack of knowledge on what should be his next move that fanned his impatience. His job only rarely required such a frenzied reaction as was now demanded. It was a sensation he had not experienced before, and he found himself looking at his watch as if the very minutes that slipped away were precious and should not be lost. It was a new form of warfare in which he had become involved, where his enemy was insignificant in stature and strength, had none of the force and intellect that his own side possessed, and yet was an enemy which dominated, and took the initiative. For the first time in close on three decades in the department he felt a sense of fear and helplessness.

Just before the light faded in the flat the boy suggested it was time for him to be on his way. David Sokarev was not surprised. It was a long, exhausting drive between Beersheba and the IAF fighter-base on the road beyond Afula. He knew his son would be on duty in his flying suit, waiting in the squadron ready-room at five-thirty on the Sunday morning on three-minute warning. He would need the sleep, and the drive would take three hours, even in the tuned-up Mini.

As the boy stood up from the chair on the balcony that looked over the town Sokarev said quietly to him, 'There is a matter I want to talk to you about. Can you come to my room? It will not take long.'

And when they were together inside the room Sokarev spoke to his son, shyly, without confidence.

'Don't interrupt me – not till I have finished. And I have not told your mother this. There is a threat against me when I go to London. There were two men from the Foreign Ministry who came to see me two days ago. They are to guard me, and they told me. It is not an important visit. I had been looking forward to it. Just one speech, and the chance to meet old friends and talk. Talk with different people. But it is something that could be cancelled, and the world would not topple. I do not know how to react to the situation. If there was a risk I would have presumed the Ministry, the Government, would have cancelled the visit themselves. But they have not done that. They have just sent men to tell me that I will be guarded. That is all there is. But what should I do?'

He looked at the boy, pleading, seeking for assurance. But his son answered him predictably enough in the language of a serviceman who executed orders, believed in the inviolate authority of his commander.

'If they did not think it was safe they would not allow you to go. You are too precious to us all, Father, for them to risk you if there was a real danger. If they have not suggested that you cancel, then you should have no fear.'

Sokarev kissed his son on both cheeks, easier in his mind now, dismissing the thought of a telephone call to the Director of Dimona, and together they came out of the office. But the gun, he would take that anyway.

Jimmy had shaved, put on a clean shirt, a suit and the old squadron tie. Finally he cleaned his shoes, and then made his way to Leconfield House. He'd sat in the outer office beyond Jones's door for more than half an hour, exchanging small talk with Helen as she typed, while he waited for his appointment to be kept.

Jimmy was past fifty, and grey-haired. There was not much flesh on his face – the years of living and fending for himself alone had seen to that. There were dark, blotched patches, fierce and red, on his cheeks, not as bad as before he went to the clinic but still evident. A blood vessel had fractured in his left eye, leaving an oasis of crimson in the extreme corner closest to the bridge of his nose. He was tall, and not overweight – partly because he exercised in

154

a private gymnasium, partly because his life style denied him regular food and meals. Helen could see he was ill at ease, almost nervous, as he constantly shifted his position in the chair. Come on, he thought, don't keep me bloody hanging about all day. It was the time he loathed. The time that elasped before he was briefed, before he was back inside the team again and part of the new operation, when his mind was racing with unsubstantiated ideas. Leaves you like a vegetable, in limbo.

Jones came in, nodded to Jimmy, but spoke first to Helen.

'Any messages, anything new in?'

'Nothing,' she said. 'The DG would like to see you before six. He rang through. Nothing beyond that.'

Jones masked his disappointment. He walked through to his office, opened the door and asked Jimmy to follow. Inside he offered him a chair, and then went to his own behind his desk. Jimmy could see the pile of slim cardboard folders on the desk top.

Jones was expert at setting out the skeleton of a problem. He took Jimmy through the information that was already available. He wasted few words, and there were no interruptions.

'That's the background. Not everything we have – you can pick that out of the paperwork when we've finished. In ideal times we'd concentrate the major effort on lifting the bastards before they hit, but as you'll see from situation reports that we've been doing we're cold on that score.' Just as Jimmy would have wanted it, thought Jones. When the rest of us are getting tired and looking to steer clear of the big ones, Jimmy'll be cheering from the top tower. Proper job for him, one to tax him, one to test him.

We're different people. Jones accepted that – the one played-out and trying to avoid the fracas, the other leaping about like a schoolboy. Not quite a smile from Jones. 'We have to be prepared for an actual attack, and I want you, Jimmy, to be right beside our Israeli brother. Adhesive-close, not out of your sight except when he's safely locked in the bloody loo. He'll have his own men with him, a cattle herd from Special Branch, all falling over each other and arguing protocol, but I want you a little bit tighter on him than any of the others. Normally we wouldn't still be in on a thing like this, it would be straight police, but the ramifications are too big if it goes wrong. So you have no doubts about your position, Jimmy, I'll spell it out. If you see anything that bothers you, you act. If you see a gun close to him, you shoot. Don't concern yourself with the bloody paperwork, or the rule book.'

Jones looked thoughtful. Needed to be stronger than that, needed to elaborate, leave him in no doubt, owed it to the man at the sharp end. 'And if you hit some poor devil out for a walk in the park with his dog, we'll cover for you.'

'You always say that,' Jimmy said.

Would he cover? . . . Would he, hell. But it was a form of words. Means not a bloody thing, Jimmy thought – what they feel they have to say. And if the balloon filled up, what price immunity then? In the courts like every other bugger, and double-fast.

'What I need, Jimmy,' Jones went on, ignoring him, best way with Jimmy. 'What I need is the very clear knowledge that I will be informed of every movement Sokarev makes. I don't want it via the

Israeli embassy, I don't want it via Scotland Yard, I want it from you.'

'If everyone is twisting their knickers at this rate, why isn't the visit called off?'

'God alone knows. If anybody else does they haven't thought fit to tell me. The Israelis have known for some days of the risk, they haven't opted for cancellation.'

Jimmy left it there. He could see the other man was close to the end of his patience, not ready for a gentle chat on the theoretical.

Jones said: 'I'll circulate your name to the Israelis and to the Special Branch, and have it backed by the Home Office. You'll need some time to work through the papers. Tomorrow I'll want you with me when I see the Israelis. They'll want to run the whole bloody thing. The DG is mildly anxious it doesn't happen that way. You'll need some weapon practice – fix that for the morning. You'd better get back to your place now and pick up some clothes. Fairclough, Duggan and I are sleeping in. You'd better join us. You can have Helen's room.'

As Jimmy walked through the outer office he stopped beside Helen's table.

'Unlucky again tonight, sweetheart. We're all kipping on the job.'

Chapter Nine

After they left the university building McCoy drove across the artery of Tottenham Court Road, and in the maze of side streets behind the Middlesex Hospital found a small Indian restaurant. They spent a long time over the meal. They talked over the abstract background of their lives – the Irishman mostly, with Famy listening, while they picked and pulled at the chapatis, toyed with the rice and the sauces and meats, and fractured the popadums into tiny lasting pieces. And then they took coffee, and after that more beer, as the evening went by.

McCoy talked of Crossmaglen and Cullyhanna. He spoke of the sharply-rising hills, with the farms that barely supported life, of the large families, of the economic hardship. He told of the fierce independence of the people who lived there, how they had transferred their old enmity of such everyday figures as the customs men and the tax collector to the soldiers of the British army. He related the story of Mick McVerry, killed in the attack on Keady police station, how they had placed nine gunmen round the building, and a rocket launcher, and how McVerry had been shot down as he planted the bomb against the building that when it went off had left a complete wing demolished. He'd been in the 'Kesh' then himself, he said, otherwise he would have been there. Famy had raised his eyes inquiringly when McCoy mentioned the Kesh, and the Irishman launched into his stories of the prison where he had been held – how they, the prisoners, ran the premises. How they held their courts, and punished those they deemed guilty. How they organized their escape committees, dug their tunnels, worked their switches with visitors. How they held their weapons and explosives classes. How they jeered the Governor as he made his rounds. How they rioted and how they went on hunger strike. How they dominated Catholic opinion in the province outside the wire.

Famy had listened, uncomprehending and disbelieving. He tried to suggest that this was something the Israelis would never have tolerated behind the high yellow walls of the maximum security prison at Ramle, where they held the *fedayeen*. There were so many things McCoy said that amazed Famy. No penalties against the families and property of those arrested on terrorist charges. Detailed fire control orders for individual soldiers. A piece of paper that gave each soldier the circumstances in which he could shoot. A hundred paratroopers locked up in Crossmaglen police station whose food and ammunition came only by helicopter because it was too dangerous to drive lorries there – too many culvert bombs on the roads, too many control wires in the ditches. But what astonished him most of all was that McCoy was there sitting across the table. 'Why, when they had caught you, when you had done these things, why did they release you?'

And McCoy had just smiled, and laughed, and known it was not possible to explain the gestures of the Secretary of State for Northern Ireland to a man whose knowledge of guerrilla warfare was based on that fought against an enemy as hard and intransigent as the Israelis.

McCoy wanted to talk and Famy was relegated to passive audience. On to the politics of the Irish Republican Army, Provisional wing. Then he spoke of six counties, and twenty-six counties, and thirty-two counties, and of Ulster, which he said was theoretically nine counties. And regionalism and Federalism and Fianna Fail . . . The Arab was lost. As his mind drifted from the slowly slurring speech of McCoy he reflected that about his own cause there was nothing complicated, nothing that could not be taught to a child, nothing that could not be understood by the simplest in the camps.

Because we know what we want, he thought, we are prepared to strive with sacrifice for our victory. Not in a pathetic cowboy world of minimal heroics, shooting down one soldier and claiming that as a victory, killing one middle-aged policeman and believing that changed political strategy; that is no way to fight. Perhaps because they do not know what it is they struggle for, they cannot steel themselves to acts that will shock on the grand scale. But this Irish boy will learn. He will understand what it is to kill when the diplomats of every major capital in the world will react. He will find out what it is to earn the hatred of one half of the world, the gratitude and adulation of the other.

But Famy enjoyed it, felt the security of the restaurant around him, realized that no eyes were transfixed on him, that he belonged to the scene, and was amused at the conspiratorial whisper with which McCoy kept up his patter of exploits. It was not till McCoy was paying the obsequious waiter that Famy thought again of the darkened figure that had searched his room last night, and of the girl who had stared at them as they left the large house back in the mid-afternoon.

When they were in the car, Famy spoke of that.

'We will sleep in different places tonight. You go to the far wall, and I will be close to the door. If someone comes again they will have to move deep into the room, and I will be behind them.'

She had seen them come in through the open door of the living room. They had paused for a few moments as if undecided whether or not to join the main group, and she had heard their voices, indistinct against the record-player. Then she had heard them walk away toward the stairs, and the sound of their feet as they went up. Through the early part of the night, every half-hour or so, she had turned away from her book to look at her watch, waiting till the time was right. Gradually the room emptied, as singly or in pairs people drifted toward their mattresses and sleeping bags in the rooms above. When nearly everyone had gone, and there was no longer the music and the conversation to keep her company, she felt the cold. If she went to bed early the lack of any heating in the house did not show itself, but by the small hours the warmth of the day had vanished, dissipated in the high rooms and the

161

old walls. Few in the building spoke to her, but that was the life style they chose. If she had wanted to talk she would have found people willing to listen. As she did not she was left to herself.

She wriggled inside the hard wool of her jersey, screwing her muscles closer to her body, fighting to maintain the personal warmth that seemed to be steadily eluding her. There was a child crying on one of the upper floors; it generally did, most of the night. Its mother had little to give it but a vague animal affection. In the days she had been in the commune Doris Lang had grown to hate that woman for her incompetence and her carelessness in the way she treated a two-year-old. She yearned to intervene, and every time dismissed the possibility as being out of context with her cover. Probably hungry, poor little bastard, trying to grow on toast and warmed tins of beans and spaghetti.

At a few minutes before four, the last of those who had sat up in the room with her stretched, and staggered, as if sleep-walking, towards the stairs. She was used to lack of sleep, and was able within moments to drag together the concentration she had allowed to fade and leave her. It was papers she wanted, indications about identity, about purpose – the reason these two unlikely figures, out of shape with the other jigsaw pieces of the commune, had come to spend their time there. Her watch showed just past four o'clock when she slipped out of the room, and went slowly, with great care, testing each footstep, toward the attic.

She wore rubber-soled tennis shoes. They had a dirty exterior, had long been without any whitener, but were totally efficient for moving without noise.

With one hand she hitched up her long skirt to prevent it from brushing against the steps. Outside the door of the attic she paused again, listening to the night, to the sounds of traffic, of the heavy breathing of deep sleep, of the distant chorus of an ambulance on emergency call. From behind the door there was silence. Complete quiet. She eased her hand on to the rounded handle of the door, pushed it open an inch, waited and listened again, then went in.

Famy had not heard her on the stairs nor on the landing. But the movement of the door handle mechanism alerted him, the most minute of sounds, as the bar was withdrawn inside the old, unoiled lock. From his half-sleep his eyes focused instantaneously on the white handkerchief he had tied to the handle on the inside of the door. He could see that, however blurred and grey it was in the near-dark. He saw it move, fractionally at first, then swing out, opening into the room. Then his sight of it was obscured as a silhouetted figure came past it. He felt sweat rise high up on his legs, and the sticky cloying moisture search over his skin, finding havens in his armpits, in his groin, behind his knees. He fought to control the regularity of his breathing.

They are in no hurry, thought Famy. Waiting their time, waiting for the light to become natural, easier. Then there was movement again, and with it the soft scuffing of material on the floor. That told Famy that his intruder was a girl, and as he strained into the nothingness of the room he pictured the one he had stared at downstairs with the pale white face, and the hair that had not been brushed, and the

163

cumbersome dress that would reach down to the boards. His own part of the room was the darkest, but the street light made vague shapes at the end where McCoy slept. He could see clearly the girl's outline as she approached his sleeping bag, saw her bend down and open his case, heard her hands among his clothes.

That she had found nothing that she sought he could understand by the way, unhurried, unexcited, she put down the top of the case. Then there was indecision, confusion. She looks for me, the little whore, thought Famy. Remembers where I was last night, is searching with her eyes, but she'll need the torch over here. He closed his eyelids tight, unwilling to risk the involuntary blink if the light should suddenly come on. The footsteps came closer to him, warily, seeking out the ground, testing the pliability of the boards. They were very near when they stopped, and on his face he felt the thin beam of the torch.

He had put the bag close to his head, and he could feel her breath on his face as she bent low over him, painstakingly sliding back the fastener. She shifted a foot, leaving it just three or four inches from the sleeping bag, then her hands were inside the bag following the line of the torch. It was as she straightened to move away that Famy thrust his hands from under the cover of the bag and grabbed at the leg that was closest to him.

For a moment his fingers were lost in the folds of the skirt, until, just short of panicking, he felt the hardness of her ankle. His whole weight followed, dragging her off balance, pulling her down. The torch fell to the floor boards, clattering and then shining its beam away from them. The surprise was complete. By the time she had realized what had happened she was on the boards, face down, her right arm twisted high behind her back, gripped by Famy, whose knee was indented into the pit of her back. The shock had been too great for her to scream.

'McCoy! McCoy! Come here.' He hissed the command out, and the other man stirred on the far side of the room.

'What is it?' the voice came low across the floor.

'I have the little bitch, I have her here.'

There was a flurry of movement and McCoy crawled through the darkness till he bumped into the mass that was the girl and Famy. His hand reached out for the torch, which he shone into the pale, fear-stricken face. She tried to swing her head away from the light, but he grasped at her hair, and as she cried out he pulled her back into the beam.

'Get your fucking hands off me,' she spat the words at him, and with his free hand he hit her hard across the mouth, and the metal of the battery container caught her lip, bulging and reddening it until the skin broke, and the trickle, highlighted by the softness of her skin, made its way down to the side of her throat. She started to struggle then, without feeling the pain in her head as McCoy clung to her hair, and oblivious of the numbing ache in her arm where Famy had twisted it behind her. With her other hand she reached into the void behind the light, and her fingernails found the flesh of McCoy's face. She heard him cry out in a mixture of pain and astonishment as she raked her nails across his cheeks. The hand let go of her hair, and before she could affect the grip across her back McCoy's foot had lashed into her head. She tried to turn away, but again the foot came, guided now by the light. Accurate and vicious, striking through the long hair that offered no protection to her ear.

Then McCoy was on his knees beside her, hands in her hair again, and this time there was no resistance. She moved her head toward him, following his will, and saw the long weals across his face, saw his eyes, alive with rage.

Famy tightened the grip on her arm, so that she convulsed, then lay inert, the struggle over.

Famy said, 'She searched your things, then mine.'

'Roll the bitch over.' McCoy was panting, and they pushed her so that she lay on her back. The Arab had his weight across her legs, high on her thighs, and he had pinioned her arms to the floor above her head. She closed her eyes and felt McCoy begin to search her. He started at her neck and worked quickly and expertly across her body, running over her breasts, down her waist, rough and uncaring till they fastened on the notebook in the pocket at her hips. Fingers forced their way inside the fold of the material and pulled the pad out. She opened her eyes fractionally and saw him peering at her close, tight hand-writing, flicking the pages over, torch close to the paper.

'What does it say?' said Famy, impatience growing as the other man concentrated.

'She's a bloody tout,' said McCoy.

'What's that?' said Famy, his voice rising.

'An informer. A spy. There are names here, people living in the house, times and dates of arrival. We're here too, when we came in, when we went out

166

yesterday. She's a clever little cow. You've no tags, no maker's marks in your clothes, right?'

'We took them out before we came.'

'Well, it's written down here.'

McCoy waited, the big eyes delving into the young face beneath him. She could sense the chill in his voice, horrible and without pity.

He said, 'Who are you? Tell me why you came.' The glazed, fear-filled face peered vacantly back toward him and beyond.

'Who are you, you cow?' He hit her again, this time with the edge of his hand, finding the tip of her chin bone, jerking her head back, banging it on the boards. Still she said nothing, and he struck her with his fist clenched hard into the softness below her rib cage. She gasped for air, fighting to force it down into her lungs, tried to draw up her knees from under the Arab to protect her defenceless body.

'You'll get it again.'

She started to try to speak, but there were no sounds at first, just the effort. Her chest heaved and writhed before the words came. There was a final act of defiance.

'Get off me, you pigs. I'm a police officer. Get your pigshit hands off me.'

The thought in Famy's mind was immediate. Just two days earlier on the road to Boulogne the police had been waiting for them. Now here, in the supposed 'safe house', the police were again close to him.

'How did they know?' he shouted. 'How did they know we would be here?'

McCoy saw her reaction to what Famy had said, the flick of her head forward to stare at the shadowy

167

face above her. It was that movement that sealed his resolution. His hands came down, settled on her throat, and tightened. She tried to speak of drugs and hippies, but the air was already denied her. Then there was nothing, only the sinking, and pressure of the hands and the blackness when she tried to see.

When McCoy had finished he realized that Famy was no longer beside him. It had been easy. In the world in which he moved and fought the penalty for touts was clear-cut. There was coughing in the far corner.

'Pull yourself together, you stupid bugger,' he said. 'Get your things in your bag. We're moving out.'

The house was quiet, at rest, as they went down the stairs, through the door and on to the street.

While McCoy drove, fast and with studied concentration heading south toward the river, Famy sat rock-still beside him. The Arab's mind was moving at a pace. It was the first time that he had encountered violent death, and the speed with which life had been crushed from the girl amazed him – its simplicity, its suddenness. And the doubts he had felt about McCoy had vanished in those few seconds. When the time came the Irishman too was prepared to kill. Famy knew, and it was a feeling he had not entertained before, that they were now a team. In the darkness of the attic bedroom the links between the two men had been irrevocably joined, and with that his last lingering uncertainties about the success of his mission had gone.

'Where are we going now?' Famy asked.

McCoy did not take his eyes from the road ahead.

'Down into the hills south of London. Into Surrey, where the guns are.'

'And where do we sleep?'

'We sleep rough tonight and tomorrow. We have to ditch this car, get another. Come back to London on Tuesday, probably late. This car will do us for a few hours more, but when the balloon goes up we'll have to have another.'

'How long do you think before they find her?'

'Some time, not immediately. And when they do they'll have the bloody commune on their hands. And they won't make much headway with them.'

'It was necessary to kill her.' Famy said it quietly, but as a statement.

' 'Course it bloody was.'

'She knew who we were?' The question again.

'Shouldn't think so.' McCoy sensed the other man's surprise at his answer. He went on. 'Probably there on the drugs scene. Could have been bomb squad and out Provo-hunting. You've got two alternatives. Bluff it out, or the other. And when you start knocking shit out of the girl that narrows it down to the other.'

'How far do we have to go?'

'About another hour and a half. Get some sleep.' It was an instruction. McCoy wanted to drive without chatter in his ear.

Famy closed his eyes. The Irishman, he thought, he would be able to sleep. But with himself there was no possibility of it. As the car jolted its way along the road the image that endlessly repeated itself was of the girl and her eyes that bulged and pleaded, and of the hard calloused fingers on her neck.

But the killing of Doris Lang had not gone entirely unnoticed.

The woman who had nursed her child to sleep a floor below had been unable to sleep herself. She had lain with her eyes wide open, staring at the ceiling. The sounds she had heard baffled her at first. There had been bumps on the boards above, a half-stifled scream recognizable as such though short and cut off. There had been hurried footsteps across the floor, then the noise of struggle, then shouts, too muffled to understand. There had been scuffling, indeterminate and difficult to follow, and then quietness before the footsteps came hurriedly past her door. The main door had slammed and there had been noise on the pavement, and the sound of a car starting up and driving away.

She had clung to the child that slept, not prepared to go and see for herself whatever had been left in the room. It was light before she summoned up the courage, and by then the men had been gone nearly two hours. When she did go, her child left behind on the mattress still curled foetus-like in sleep, her screams, hysterical and piercing, woke the building.

Henry Davies was drinking tea in the police station canteen. It was thick, strong-brewed, laced with sugar, and hot. He could only sip at it, but always regarded his early morning cup as the essential way to end night duty. He had signed off now, but usually spent fifteen minutes in the canteen, waiting for the day shift handlers to come on, to exchange a few words of gossip and police talk with them.

He had heard on his radio of the flap on the far

side of the area covered by the station, but a dog had not been required, and he had methodically continued his patrol, checking factory, shop and warehouse doors.

He was sitting on his own when the sergeant came in.

'Lad, the DI's been on the radio. Wants you down Englefield Road. Number one-six-two. Wants you down there as fast as you can.' It was the standard joke in the station that he called everyone under the age of forty 'lad'.

'What for?' Davies asked.

'I don't know,' the sergeant lied, but did it well, and Davies couldn't read it. 'He asked specifically for you. Slip on down there, lad.'

They'd radioed ahead when he drove out of the station yard, and the Detective Inspector was waiting on the steps of the house for him. There were three police cars parked haphazardly at the side of the street, and a small knot of half-dressed onlookers. Davies got out of the car. A constable who stood on the pavement and who knew him looked away.

Then the Inspector walked toward him, unshaven, roused from his Sunday morning bed.

'I've bad news, Henry. I'm very sorry . . . It's Doris. Some bastard's killed her.'

He stopped, letting the words sink in. He saw the mask of overt self-control slide across the police constable's features.

'When did it happen?' Davies said.

'Early this morning. We had a call about forty minutes ago. I've identified her. Do you want to go and see her, Henry?'

'There'll be all the cameras there, prints. All the bloody paraphernalia. I don't want to see her like that. Not with them all working round her.'

'Is there somewhere you can go?'

'I'd like to go to her Mum's. Has she been told?'

'Not yet.'

'I'd like to go there, then. Thank you, sir.'

'I'll get someone to drive you round. Fred can come down and pick up your motor, and take your dog home and give it a meal. You can collect him tomorrow.'

'Do you know who did it?'

'I think so. But they're long gone. Two of them. They're telling us a bit inside. More than they usually do.'

The inhabitants of the commune were herded into the main living room on the ground floor while the coffin with Doris Lang's body in it was carried down the stairs to the unmarked hearse. The Detective Inspector watched it go, then walked back into the room. He had spotted the spokesman for the group, older than most, a fragile and defiant figure. He called him out and went with him to the room behind, used as sleeping quarters. Blankets were strewn on the floor in the position they had been left in when the screaming had started.

'You've been helpful, quite helpful, before I was called out. I want it to go on that way.'

The other man looked up at him, without responding.

'The woman who found the body, she tells me two men left after she heard noises upstairs. Some time after half-past four. Who are those two men?'

The man said nothing, but instead spread out his fingers and pushed them through his hair.

'Now, don't mess me about, sunshine. It's a murder inquiry. We get impatient quickly.'

'We knew one of them.'

'Which one?'

'One was an Irishman.'

'I said, and I said it clearly, don't mess me about. I haven't got all bloody day to be playing games.' Their two faces, the one bearded and with traces of acne, the other stubbled and tired, were less than a foot apart. The man from the commune looked away, then said:

'There was a girl who used to live here. Eilish McCoy. One of the men was her brother. He's called Ciaran. I know because she once showed me a picture of him, in a sort of uniform. Taken back in Ireland. He just turned up here about a week ago, asked for a room, said he had some people coming. Said they needed . . .'

The Inspector said, 'Somewhere quiet, somewhere to lie up?'

'Something like that.'

'And the other one, the second one?'

'We never heard his name.'

'Was he Irish?'

'No.'

'Look, boy, last time, don't screw me about.'

'I'd say he was an Arab.'

'And no name, didn't McCoy call him anything?'

'They didn't mix with us. They were either out or in the room. The second one only came the night before last. There was no name.'

173

'You say McCoy said he had "some people coming"?'

'He told me there were three others, only the one showed up.'

A detective came into the room. In his hand, held gingerly between thumb and first finger, was a four-by-two-inch notebook.

'It was over in a corner. Left behind. It's Doris Lang's writing, no doubt on that. I've seen it in the station. Her week's log of the comings and goings. Seems she searched these buggers' room on Friday night, again yesterday afternoon. There's a bit about what she found, and a description of the two men. Proper detailed one.'

The Inspector went out of earshot into the corridor and said to the detective, 'Get on to division, tell them to call Special Branch, and shove over all the stuff on McCoy. And tell the people upstairs to get a move on, we'll have half bloody Scotland Yard here by lunch-time.'

When he reached his office back at the police station an hour later the desk sergeant was there to greet him.

'There's been a man called Jones on the phone for you. One of the spooks from the Security Service. Said something about a notepad. Wants to come up and see you as soon as you've ten minutes to spare him. Number's on your table.'

'Coming up in the bloody world, aren't we?' said the Detective Inspector as he went into his office.

Chapter Ten

Like an incoming ocean tide that thrusts its way into rock gullies and crevices so the name of Ciaran McCoy swept through the many departments of Scotland Yard. Photographic section, fingerprint section, Special Branch and its Irish section, Murder squad, Criminal Records, Liaison Regional Crime. The name was telephoned to the Commander in charge of Special Branch, and to the Assistant Commissioner (Crime). Meetings were hurriedly convened, and at the centre of them were the suitably doctored files passed on from Leconfield House the previous night. The photograph of McCoy was rapidly reproduced, and despatched to all police stations in the Metropolitan area. The photofit team began work on a compilation of the unknown Arab's features, using principally Doris Lang's written description, written by a trained hand, and also including the sketchier accounts of his appearance as given by the occupants of the commune. Teleprinter messages from the Royal Ulster Constabulary headquarters at Knock Road on the east side of Belfast carried more information on the Irishman. The decision was made to release the picture of

McCoy at lunch-time for the Independent Television current affairs programme that would be on the air at that time, and for a BBC newsflash.

That was when Norah saw the picture.

Her father always insisted that the television should be on during the formal eating of the Sunday roast, because he liked the farmers' programmes. After the music had faded away and the end-title shot of a threshing machine had disappeared behind a hill the screen went to black before the appearance of the 'Newsflash' symbol. The three people round the table, Norah, her mother and her father, all stopped eating and turned their attention to the set, food still on their forks. The item lasted a minute or so, the first forty seconds taken up by pictures of the comings and going in Englefield Road. A police-woman had been found in a commune. Dead, strangled.

'Bastards,' Norah's father muttered to himself. 'Bloody bastards.'

Police were anxious to trace a young Irishman. Name – Ciaran McCoy. The picture came up then, and stayed on the screen for twenty seconds. Half this time had elapsed before Norah recognized the boy she had lain beside at the swimming pool, the boy she had kissed, and who had left her so abruptly last Thursday night. She could see it was a police photograph, a man just taken into custody, aggressive and caged. But it was still the same man, the lines of a mouth whether set in anger or friend-ship change little, only superficially.

'Little swine,' her father said. 'We should string them up. Only thing they understand.'

Norah had said nothing. She put her head down

and close to the food lest her parents should see the tears that welled up in her eyes. She had bolted her food, made an excuse and run through the front door. She walked endlessly that afternoon, conscious of an overwhelming feeling of shame, of having been dirtied in some way.

When Jones came back from the police station he brought with him photostats and transcripts of the notepad. Duggan and Fairclough were waiting in his office.

Duggan said, 'He's blown it, hasn't he, our little boyo? Lost his safe house, lost his base. His picture will be plastered everywhere by tonight, all over the television, and front pages of the papers tomorrow. And now he's running, concerned with his own survival. Not what you'd call an auspicious start for what he's after.'

'Meaning what?' said Jones.

'That it may well be over for him. His concentration now is how to stay free. Does a man in his position go walking through a police cordon, cordon forewarned, cordon with a description? Does he, hell! He stays out. Packs it in.'

'That's one viewpoint.' Jones acknowledged the argument, but looked sceptical.

'The other view takes a different course,' Fairclough joined in. 'If we look at the Palestinian, or Arab, or whatever he is, we can come out with a different answer. He's been through a crisis before, in France on Thursday, and he's still on the move. Look at it from his point of view. If he doesn't go on what does he go back to? They won't welcome him with open arms back in his camp. He'd be a miserable failure. Fiasco. It's when the suicide mentality breaks through. The harder the going gets the more he will be prepared to risk his own life in order to succeed.'

'And the conclusion from that?' asked Jones.

'The conclusion from that is that the Arab is now extremely dangerous. Tiger in the long grass with half his guts shot out. He's a killer still, more so, only thing we can be certain of is that. But he's at a disadvantage, and that's positive, and consolation for us.'

'The picture of one of them, detailed description of the other. Available to every man round Sokarev. That stacks the odds a bit against our two friends.' Jones was able to smile, rare over the last two days. 'But if the Arab wants to go on what about McCoy?'

Again it was Fairclough, hunched forward in his seat, using his hands to emphasize the points he made. 'One of them has killed this morning, but they're both in it together. The critical factor is whether they fall apart, how much of a bond they've made. From what I've read of McCoy I think he'll stay in, right up to the end, providing he thinks there's a chance of living through it.'

Jones wondered how he could be so sure, and envied the younger man the certainty of his opinions. But it was not a time for sarcasm, or for academic discussion. So many of them had breezed through the department over the years, knowing all the answers, having an explanation for every half-truth situation. The ones that stayed on were the ones who recognized that there were no simple answers in the business. The problem was – and

178

Jones could see that much – that this wasn't the operation the section heads were familiar with, inexperienced at tangling on the short-term affairs. They were pretty good when they had the space to spread themselves, to get through on the inside, to win time to build up the overall picture. But this was a sprint, and didn't really depend on men like himself. Hadn't much to contribute. When there wasn't any time the whole thing came down to Jimmy's level. Who shoots best – us or them? That's why he'd brought Jimmy in on the effort. He liked the man in a distant way, was vaguely fond of him, but to be dependent on him, to recognize he had more to offer now than Jones himself, that left a taste in the mouth.

Jimmy took considerable care over his firearms.

For close protection work he favoured the PPK (Polizei Pistolen Kriminal) Walther. And this was the gun he drew from the armoury, set behind reinforced walls in the basement of Leconfield House just beyond the area used by the monitoring team. The PPK was a small weapon, manufactured with great skill by the workers of the Karl Walther factory at Ulm on the Danube in West Germany. Its length was little more than six inches, its weight slightly over a pound. It was not new, manufactured in 1938, and had come into the department's collection after the war, but the armourer had maintained it with studied attention, knowing that this, among all the others, was the weapon that Jimmy asked for on his occasional visits to the underground room. On most occasions the gun had been returned unused, but a few times the armourer had noticed the magazine no longer contained its seven shells, and that the barrel needed cleaning.

The two men had talked about Jimmy's choice at the time that the newspapers were full of how the PPK being used by a Royal detective had jammed during a kidnap attempt, and how it had been withdrawn from use by the bodyguards. Neither the armourer nor the marksmen had been impressed by the reasons made public for the switch-over to the British-made Smith and Wesson, the traditional police weapon. Jimmy's loyalty was unmoved.

With the gun signed for, and two dozen rounds along with it, Jimmy drove north to the police firing range in an old building the far side of Euston Station. There were policemen there, members of a pistol shooting club, complete in denim overalls and earpads, firing at targets twenty-five metres across the floor from the painted white line that ran across one end of the range.

Jimmy showed his identification card to the instructor, and the policemen were called back to the shadows away from the shooting line. They watched as Jimmy loaded the magazine, then stood apparently relaxed facing them and away from the human-shaped target, gun pointing to the floor, loosely held against his trousers. The instructor let fall a box of matches. By the time it had bounced twice and come to rest Jimmy had twisted, body crouched, knees bent, two hands together outstretched and both on the butt of the pistol, and his first shot had hit the target. Three more followed.

'About a six inch group,' the instructor said, and Jimmy acknowledged expressionless. Where else did they expect the bloody things to be? He went to the side wall, by the door, waited a moment for his legs to loosen, then flung himself forward on the floor, rolling all the time before there was an instant of steadiness and he fired twice.

'Eight inches or so apart, both in the chest area,' said the instructor.

Jimmy fired all twenty-four rounds. Some in near-darkness, some with a bright light shining at his face, some on the move, some stationary. All hit the target, each a puckered hole in the torso area.

'Bit of a bloody show-off, isn't he?' said one of the watching policemen, but his whisper was overheard by the instructor, who walked across the room to him.

'Look, boy.' His voice was booming, the result of deafness accrued from eighteen years in the under-ground range. 'There's a fractional possibility he might miss. And there's a fractional possibility you might hit. That's the difference between you and him.'

Jimmy was well pleased with the morning session, and it was over quickly enough for him to fit in a drink before he was due back at the department.

The two of them were asleep in the car.

McCoy lay on his side across the front seats, head just beneath the steering wheel. Famy was curled up in the back, his coat off and covering his shoulders. The car was parked deep in a grassy clearing, far from the road and visible through the high summer foliage only to someone who approached to within a few yards of it. There were many such places in the line of Surrey hills between Guildford and Dorking that block the route to London. Later they would become a haven for Sunday walkers and picnickers, but in the early morning the two men had the clearing to themselves.

'We must sleep now, any time we bloody-well can get it,' McCoy had said.

They missed the breaking of the dawn, then the darkness gave way to the half-light, and then the sun began to cast its shortening shadows across the grass. They didn't see the rabbits that came to eat and preen themselves, or the fox that hastened them back to their burrows. It was the noise of children that aroused them. Two boys, little more than ten years old, faces pressed against the steamed-up windows of the car, peering in at them, and running giggling away as McCoy started up from his sleep. He swore inaudibly, and tried to collect his thoughts as he gazed around him. There is always that moment immediately after waking before the bad news of the previous night is remembered. McCoy couldn't immediately place why he was in the car. It came to him soon enough, and with the realization came the memory of the events of five hours earlier.

He shook Famy. 'Come on, lover-boy. Time to be on our way.'

'What's happening? Where are we?' Famy too had woken confused.

'Out in the countryside, taking in the sunshine. Remember?'

Famy inclined his head slowly, deliberately, understanding.

Neither saw the two boys who lay in the thick grass bracken watching the men as they rubbed their eyes and stretched and pawed at the grass, throwing out the stiffness that had accompanied their awkward, limb-twisted sleep. McCoy beckoned with his hand, an abrupt gesture, and the two began to walk the length of the clearing to the path that meandered away among the pine trees and the birches and the undergrowth.

'It's a fair walk, and I don't want to hang about,' said McCoy over his shoulder as he led the way. Neither wore the shoes for the country paths, and both slipped and stumbled where the rain had made the surface muddy.

They walked in silence for more than twenty minutes. Then Famy noticed that McCoy was slowing down his stride, searching for a sign. When he found it he stood still, pleased with himself, beside an old, rusted-up pram chassis.

'That's the first marker,' he said. 'It's easy enough from here to find the place. We go fifty paces now down the path. Measure them out, and we'll be just about there.'

Famy let the distance between them grow as McCoy, his step accentuated by the care he was taking, marked out the distance.

'At home,' said McCoy when he had counted up to fifty out loud, 'we have to hide our guns. We keep them out in the countryside, but somewhere you can get them night or day, so you need markers, so you can find them on a path in the dark. Has to be straightforward and obvious to the man on the pick-up, but giving nothing away to the Brits. Now look, and what's the most prominent tree close to us? Has to be the one with the ivy up it, easy to see, would show up by torch. That's the main marker. Now we have to look for something else that's off the path but equally clear . . . stands out just as much. You walk round the tree, trying to line it up with something that stands out. Right? If you draw a line between this tree, and the big one, over there, the one the lightning hit, you go on and into the bank. There are rabbits' holes all the way down and along the bank. Well, what we're looking for is the hole in the straight line beyond the two trees.'

He walked forward past the ivy-coated branches, past the dead tree. 'The Brits are too bloody impatient to work it out like this. But once there was a chap on the television, and his men called him "Sniffer". He found more of our guns than any other soldier in the province. And what did the buggers do with him? Sent him first to the Tower of London on guard duty, then packed him off to Cyprus for nine months.'

McCoy was still laughing as his hands sunk into the rabbit hole. Famy watched fascinated as they emerged again clutching the whitened plastic of a farm bag.

'I had to dig the hole out a bit,' McCoy said. 'But who's going to notice fresh earth at a rabbit burrow?'

He pulled the bag out onto the bank, scanned the path in both directions, listened for a moment and then, satisfied that they were alone, started to unwind the sticking tape that sealed the top. From the bag he took three rifles, small, narrow, seemingly ineffective by their very abbreviation. Each was only marginally more than two feet in length, with the steel skeleton of the shoulder-rest bent back alongside the barrel. He placed them on the plastic, handling them with delicacy and concern, and with them two bulky cloth bags.

'What are they?' asked Famy.

'It's a version of the M1 carbine. World War Two,

American. These are the paratroopers' ones, with the folding stock. They wouldn't give me Armalites, the bastards, said three was too many. These are old, but that doesn't mean there's anything wrong with them. They were test-fired ten days ago, across the water, then stripped down and cleaned . . .'

Famy interrupted, anxiety in his voice. 'There were no Kalashnikovs?'

'We never get a sight of the bloody things. They've tried to bring them in, but we haven't had any reach us. Our stuff is American. One of the reasons our big men got involved in this was to try and guarantee a supply of Kalashnikovs.'

'To you it will sound ridiculous, but I've never trained with any other sort of rifle,' said Famy.

'There's nothing wrong with these. They've packed enough coffins. Three hundred range, more than we need. Fifteen-round magazine – if we need more than three we're screwed anyway. Small, light – just about six pounds. The Yanks ran off more than three and a half million of them in the war. They're untraceable.'

'Why only three? There were going to be three of us, and then you.'

McCoy was taking loaded magazines from one of the cloth bags. He looked up and into Famy's face. 'You were going to do the shooting. The deal was that I looked after the accommodation and the motor. You looked after the rest.'

'And now?'

McCoy laid the magazines out side by side, twelve of them. 'Well, it can't be done by one alone,' he said, still gazing directly at Famy, 'so we'll need two of them, and have one spare.'

185

There was a huge smile across Famy's face as the strain of the last few hours fled from him. God, the bastard's been suffering, thought McCoy. He's had enough bloody hints and not believed them. McCoy opened the second bag.

'We may not have done you well on the rifles, but on the grenades we've the best. We get a lot of our stuff via the dealers in Holland. These are Dutch, called the "V 40 Mini", less than half the size of a normal grenade. Tiny, but the sales talk is sensational. Four hundred chunks flying out, hundred per cent casualties guaranteed at ten feet. It's what we want, something for close work, not a bloody great bomb that'll demolish half the audience but one that can land nice and near your man, and take him out.'

There were twelve of them. He held one in his hand, nestled in the palm where it fitted snugly, less than an inch and a half in diameter, and deadly. McCoy packed the grenades and the magazines back into their separate bags and dropped them into the bigger plastic one. The rifles followed, and he again taped the top, and then they both walked up the path towards the car. McCoy's mind was now tuned to the next batch of problems. Transport. Where to ditch his present motor, where to get another? And where to sleep, where to lie up for the next two days? Famy could see he was thinking, and did nothing that might break the other's train of thought. He felt complete confidence in the Irishman who carried under his arm the vital weapons that would be used against David Sokarev.

The Prime Minister cut short his Scottish weekend and flew to Northolt, the capital's military airfield.

His surprise move aroused little press speculation among the journalists covering his foray into the north. It was generally believed, and not denied in official circles, that the country's economic plight had led to the abbreviated schedule. It was less well known outside his immediate entourage that the workings of the Security and Intelligence Services that were ultimately answerable to him fascinated and exhilarated the Head of Government. In his first-floor office, overlooking the immaculate flower-decked gardens of his Downing Street residence, he met the Director General of the Security Service.

The Prime Minister was prepared to listen to the exposition of the problem, and hear the results and actions that would follow from the series of meetings that had gone on through the morning between the police and officials from the department. He had shown concern that at this stage of the operation no leakage of information to the press should happen, he required maximum detail on the two potential assassins, but already knew of the remarks passed between the Israeli Ambassador and the Foreign Office. When the Director General had finished the Prime Minister turned away to the window, searching for the words he wanted, weighing them before speaking, face serious and intent, pencil twirling in his fingers.

'There is a chance, then, that a massive screen round the man will deter any attack. When I was in Germany for the football some years ago they adopted that policy. Total saturation. Nothing happened, and whether they were successful or not we have no way of knowing. But I think from what you say you don't believe that to be a likely eventuality, the deterrent. We will now move, Director General, into the realm of what is called "Late-at-night-thought", not to be attributed to this building. I would like to think that should the Arab, if that is what he is, be taken prisoner, arrested, that he would violently resist such action, and that in his escape attempt he should be shot dead. We've had one package of hostages on a VC10 sitting it out in the Jordan Desert, we've had another VC10 wrecked at Schipol, we've had another held at gunpoint in Tunis. I don't want a fourth. I don't want to have to hand this man over at the point of a rifle with a plane-load of lives at stake, and that is what will happen if this man is taken and put through the courts. The Irishman in that context is unimportant.'

The Prime Minister wished the Director General luck, smiled bleakly at him as they shook hands, and showed him to the door.

In their small bedroom the Sokarevs were both involved in the packing of his suitcase for the visit to Europe and the United States. While his wife took the clothes, folded them and laid them on the bed, Sokarev placed them with care into his old suitcase. He chided her against giving him too many shirts, and spoke of the services of hotel laundries, but she said she was not concerned with that, and had her way. The shoes, the shirts, the underclothes and the socks, pyjamas and dressing gown, a thick jersey, all went into the case before his two suits. The suits were the only two he possessed, one for best, for making his speech, one for wearing during the day. And for travelling she selected his jacket and a pair of slacks and hung them out on the edge of the wardrobe. When they had finished the case was bulging and both of them had to press hard down on it for the locks to fasten. The case meant something special to him, and he had cared well for it since it had brought his many fewer belongings to Israel on the long journey from Frankfurt thirty-nine years ago. It was rarely used and treated with consideration, and had taken on special importance for David Sokarev, because his father had bought it for him, and carried it to the station, and handed it up into the train before waving goodbye. His father had disappeared from view as the train had pulled out from the platform, lost in the pall of engine smoke, and had then returned home to wind up the family affairs. He had been full of promises and assurances that he would follow his wife and son to Israel when that was completed. David Sokarev never saw him again.

The key that locked the case had long since been lost, and Sokarev used a wide leather belt to hold down the top in case the clasps should fail during the journey.

She fussed around him that evening in the bedroom. It was a rare event for him to be away from home for anything more than a single night, but she could see that the anxieties and worries that had oppressed him two and three nights before were now something of the past. They laughed with each other, and smiled a lot and sometimes he put his arm round her shoulders, and he talked of the friends that he would be going to see in London, men that he had met on previous visits or who had come to Israel, and with whom he corresponded. When the packing was finished he went to his study to work on the draft of his speech while his wife moved to the kitchen to cook his dinner; it would be something light with cheese, as he liked it.

He wrote the speech in spidery longhand, frequently crossing out what he had already set down and placing the corrections in smaller writing over the top. He would talk on the need of his country for atomic power to ensure self-sufficiency in the fields of agriculture and industry and reduce the necessity of oil. It would not be a fine speech, he knew that. He shared the problem of many brilliant men in that he found it arduous and awkward to cannibalize his detailed laboratory work into the language of a lecture theatre. He had sketched what he would say – unsatisfactory, but the best he could manage. There would be no mention of the energy of the atom when directed for military purposes, and in the well-mannered and professional group to which he would be speaking there would be no questions on that count. It was understood. Accepted.

He had worked for more than an hour, and was still regretting that Anna would not be accompanying him and that he would be dependent on a typist from the embassy in London, when the telephone rang.

'Mackowicz here,' said the distant voice, after Sokarev had given the number. Thoughts of neutrons and atomic piles and reactors fled from him, as his mind cleared. In their place was nothing. Clouded, vacant and hesitant.

'What do you want?' his voice showing the resentment he felt at the other man's intrusion into the private oasis of his study.

'I was just ringing to make sure that all would be well for you tomorrow.'

'There are no problems,' said Sokarev.

'You need have no fears of the visit to London. The British authorities are taking many steps to ensure that no incident will take place.'

'I have no fears.' Sokarev spoke sharply.

There was a pause at the other end of the line. What more do you want to say? thought Sokarev. Why burden me at my home? For the next ten days you will be there to hold my hand, dictate my movements, govern my actions.

'I will be picking you up myself tomorrow . . .'

'But I have a taxi ordered. It is all arranged. There is no need.' He was close to anger.

'It has been decided that I shall take you to Ben Gurion. Elkin will be with me. You can cancel the taxi.'

'Who has decided it?'

'It has been decided in the Ministry, by the superiors in our department.'

Sokarev sank back in his chair, the telephone still to his ear. There was no fighting them; they had taken charge. The depression surged again through him. He was weak, pliable again in the hands of the young men who would accompany him, a toy passed from hand to hand.

The younger of the two boys that had played in the clearing in the early morning saw and recognized the picture of McCoy when it was shown again at tea-time on television. His father telephoned the village policeman. There were a series of calls that followed the sighting, and from County headquarters at Guildford some twelve miles away a tracker dog was sent. Special Branch officers drove down from London, and in the fading light the dog found the rabbit hole where McCoy had secreted the rifles and grenades. It had taken the labrador a long time to discover the hiding place, but eventually he stood by the entrance whining and impatient. The policemen had moved with caution lest they should disturb the footprints in the fresh soil. They would return again on Monday morning for a more detailed examination, but in the meantime the ten yards' square in front of the hole was covered with plastic sheeting, and a constable was left to spend a lonely night to prevent interference with the evidence.

From Scotland Yard the report of the identification and subsequent discovery were passed on to Jones, along with the conclusions that had been drawn from the find in the woods. So Fairclough had been right, and Duggan wrong in his assessment. The bastards weren't running, they were on course still, and visiting a cache. Collecting something. And only one thing they'd need such a hiding place for. They'd have their guns now, thought Jones. He looked at the picture of McCoy on his desk, face puffed out where he'd tried to distort his face as the shutter had gone on the army camera – old trick, to try to make the official record useless. Hard, mean face, thought Jones. The Photofit picture of the Arab was with him now, fresh from the printing press, and alongside it an artist's impression in semi-profile.

Jimmy came into the office, following his knock by a couple of seconds. Jones could see the well-scrubbed chin and cheeks, bright and shining, knew it was the sign of too many at lunch-time and a head under the tap. Cold water, to regain control. Jones pushed the pictures across his desk towards Jimmy and said, 'Those are our little boys. Get those bloody faces stuck in your mind.'

Chapter Eleven

From behind the steering wheel Elkin watched Mackowicz emerge from the doorway of the flats carrying the professor's case, and a few steps behind him came Sokarev and his wife. He saw the scientist kiss his wife hard on both cheeks and cling to her for several seconds before breaking away and almost run to the car door Mackowicz had opened for him. She stood and waved long after the car had gone away up the road, but through his mirror Elkin could see that the passenger in the back never turned his head. The face behind was taut, stretched with emotion, that much Elkin could see before he settled into the long, winding road to Ben Gurion Airport.

There was little talk during the journey: Mackowicz tried several times to get conversation going, but was rebuffed by Sokarev. By the time they were through Kiryat Gat, nearly half-way there, he had given up and sat quietly beside Elkin, leaving the passenger to whatever thoughts with which he cared to occupy himself.

The two security men were not unused to this. It was frequent that men who required bodyguard protection should resent the presence of those sent to ensure their safety. If the man didn't want to talk then that was his concern, thought Mackowicz; he and Elkin had enough to concern themselves with.

They had been out of Israel on this duty before, but always in a bigger team, once with the then Prime Minister Golda Meir, when the detail had been nine men, once with Abba Eban in his days as Foreign Minister, when there had been four others. This was a different situation – just the two of them, which made their success or failure more dependent on the effectiveness of forces completely outside their control. In particular, when they had travelled with the Prime Minister they had been in sufficient numbers to organize a complete security screen around their charge. They had not been obliged to rely on the departments of the countries they visited. But when they were simply a pair they would be forced to accept the guidance and knowledge of the British police. It was not the way they liked to operate.

Their selection for the task of watching over the small, stout man who slumped across the back seat of the car was no accident. Both were expert shots with hand guns, and both were thorough and painstaking. When the threat had become known they had been the two obvious choices. The Head of the Protection Division of the Foreign Ministry had had no doubts that among the men under his control Mackowicz and Elkin were the most efficient and professional. They travelled light, just two canvas bags in the boot alongside the professor's larger bag. They contained a few changes of clothes, while the suits they wore in the car would see them through the public functions. In one bag were the files, marked 'secret', that contained all the available Israeli intelligence information on the threat, and a complete dossier on Sokarev from his blood group to details of his family and his financial arrangements. In the other bag, wrapped in shirts, were the personal two-way radios that would be modified to the wavelengths of the Israeli embassy by the resident communications and wireless expert, and the issued firearms.

They had left at seven and turned into the driveway of the airport seventy-five minutes later, which left them a little over an hour before take-off. Sokarev could sense that the two men in the front of the car understood his hostility to them. He was dominated by feelings of isolation and loneliness, and an inability to communicate with the two men with him. They were so much younger, so assured. There was nothing to talk to them about, no mutual point of sympathy. Killers, he decided: so how different were they to the men who awaited him – if the fears were true? Cloaked in legality, given the seal of approval, how much were they separated from the terrorists? Both groups killed from a sense of duty, both acted without hesitation, ferret-fast. He recognized that he was afraid of the men he had been given as travel companions. Only the gun could give him confidence, his own gun, the unused Mauser, and that was a step into their world, one with which he could never sympathize, barely understand. It rested in his coat pocket, beside his spectacle case, awkward, forcing out the material of the jacket, the single magazine in his inside breast pocket placed within the fold of his wallet.

The baggage check took half an hour. Thirty

minutes of shuffling the cases forward inch by inch as he stood behind a crocodile of blue-rinsed lady tourists who even at that early stage of the morning were strident in their retelling of alimony suits, lost husbands and necessary hysterectomies. He was surprised he was not taken through a side door and spared the routine, but neither Mackowicz nor Elkin made any move to suggest that that were possible. When they came to the young man in the orange jerkin who was searching the cases it was only Sokarev's that was opened. When it had been checked, closed again, and scribbled on with chalk his bodyguards produced their identity cards, exchanged a quiet word with the airport security man, and were allowed on their way to the ticket desk. Sokarev felt the indignity, near-humiliation of it. Elkin saw the chin jutting out and the thin-lipped anger of his mouth, and said – not with pomposity but a degree of kindness – 'It's routine, Professor Sokarev. It's nothing pesonal about you. All passengers are searched. All, that is, except us. We carry papers and equipment. Perhaps it would not be suitable for those to be seen by others standing in a line. So we go through. If it is of comfort to you we are all searched when we leave Heathrow.'

Sokarev fumbled for a reply, unnerved by the accuracy with which the other had interpreted his thoughts.

From the ticket desk the three of them walked toward the staircase that led to the departure lounge. Sokarev noticed now that Mackowicz was to his right, Elkin to the left. Not out of my own country, and already they have taken up their positions, he thought, leading me like a prisoner under escort. They dwarfed him, eyes already watchful and rotating through an arc. Elkin's jacket was buttoned, and Sokarev could see the bulging shape of a strap-fastened holster. They went through passport control, the official barely looking up as he flicked through the passports, stamped them and handed them back.

Elkin said, 'You have to go through the body search now, Professor. We again are excused that. We will collect you on the far side.'

In front was a long row of curtain-fronted cubicles where from time to time a young man or woman, also in an orange jerkin, would appear. Like a whore waiting for trade, thought Sokarev. And the next customer would step inside and the curtain would be drawn back. Once a man, swarthy in complexion, was led back out of the cubicle, his face betraying self-consciousness as he walked in his stockinged feet, the security man behind him holding his shoes outstretched, as they went to the counter that contained the X-ray equipment.

It was the embarrassment on the face of the victim that jolted Sokarev's mind to the weight in his pocket. It was a situation he had not considered. He had not thought out how he would carry the Mauser on board the aircraft; he had vaguely presumed that his escorts would be with him, and would see it as a *fait accompli*, looked pained for a moment, perhaps have shrugged, and allowed him to carry on. The curtain was opened again, the man gestured him to come forward.

He stood with his legs apart and arms outstretched shoulder high. There was fear now. Fear of discovery. The fear that comes to a small boy caught stealing, found playing truant away from school.

The hands started at his collars, feeling under the material, tested the area under his armpits, loitered for a moment on the shape of his wallet in the breast pocket. Sokarev thought he was going to be sick. He watched as the wallet was taken out and opened. The magazine lay there, pristine, unbelonging among his papers. The security man stiffened, set his face, muscles tensed on the top of his wrists.

'Do you have a pistol to go with this ammunition?' said the security man evenly.

Sokarev nodded. 'In the pocket,' he said, still keeping his hands out. The hands found the Mauser there, withdrew it sharply. There was a moment when the security man's eyes were off him as he checked the breech of the pistol, assuring himself it was not loaded.

'I am Professor David Sokarev. I am a nuclear scientist. My work is at Dimona. My flight is to Europe . . .' Waves of wretchedness overcame him, and his voice tailed away. His eyes were now fixed on the floor, not caring to see the keen gaze of the man who stood close to him in the cubicle. When he had collected himself sufficiently he went on, his speech barely audible. 'There are two men from the Foreign Ministry travelling with me. They are to guard me. They are waiting on the far side. I had not told them that I was taking the weapon.'

Ten minutes after they had taken Sokarev to the offices of the security department of the airport Mackowicz was shown in. His face was controlled, betraying no emotion, and he spoke in a huddle with the senior officer there. He never looked once at the Mauser that lay on the desk, the single rectangular magazine beside it. Whatever business was conducted Sokarev took no part in it. Then Mackowicz walked to the door, opened it and waited for the scientist to go through. When they were alone in the concourse Mackowicz said, 'It was unwise of you to try to take the gun through. There is an important thing that we must now establish. Neither my colleague nor myself would consider ourselves fit to make judgements on your work, at which you are an expert. We expect that you would treat us with similar generosity. We do not expect you to make judgements on security matters. If you have no confidence in Elkin and myself you are at liberty, as you have been since we got to Dimona, to telephone to Jerusalem and explain your objections to our superiors.'

The voice scythed through Sokarev's defences. He shook his head, staggered now by his own stupidity.

'I am sorry,' he said. 'It has been a great strain, since you came to see me.'

'We are responsible for your security. We have the right to demand your full co-operation. There will be no repetitions of this situation. Not when you are in our care.'

Sokarev's head was down on his chest as he shambled after his captor towards the lounge seat where Elkin sat. The three men sat in total silence till the flight was called, the guards reading newspapers, the professor staring emptily through the windows and out on to the tarmac. He felt he wanted to discard the whole journey, go home to his wife and to his laboratory and shut out for ever the nightmare world of guns, searches and terrorists. When the flight was called Mackowicz was up first, athletically rising on to the balls of his feet, then he bent down and took the professor's arm and helped him out of the low leather seat.

Elkin said, 'I think we should remember, Professor, that we are going to be together for some time now. Whatever has happened is in the past. It should not linger on.' And he smiled. Sokarev attempted again an apology, but Elkin shook his head.

'It is in the past. Forgotten.'

They walked together down the steps, and past the young soldier who wore an automatic rifle slung across his shoulders, and out into the blazing heat of an August morning in Israel. The sun beat into Sokarev's eyes, causing him to pull the lids together to keep out the very brightness that sprang up at him from the tarmac. Away to the front, acting as a giant reflector, was the 747 Boeing jet, its white underbelly and roof gleaming in the harsh light. There is no going back now, thought the scientist. There is no escape. Whatever happens now it is out of my control.

Sokarev mounted the steps to the plane. Mackowicz and Elkin were a pace behind him.

Along the corridor from the control room, and high in the Scotland Yard tower block, they had taken over the main lecture theatre for the Monday briefing of all those detectives and senior uniformed officers involved in the hunt for McCoy and his colleague and in the protection of David Sokarev.

Jimmy sat at the back, far behind the rows of neatly-clipped necks, looking down on the proceedings. If anyone had turned to watch him they would have detected a faintly bored, disinterested face – that of a man who has been through it all before.

Not that Jimmy ever felt totally at ease in the company of policemen. And they didn't react well to the presence alongside them of what was virtually a freelance operator, unconditioned to their code of discipline and their rule books.

The details read out concerning the timings and locations of the visit failed to hold his attention. A big man in uniform did the talking. Like evidence in a dangerous driving case, thought Jimmy. Solid, monotonous, dull. Never make it on the stage, you won't, brother. Drawing on the blackboard isn't much better. All those lovely coloured chalks. How they adore it, like dressing up for the pantomime. Green lines and red circles and blue crosses.

What a way to go to war. Has McCoy got a big map, does he stick his finger in it like bloody Rommel? Can't fight these bastards with maps and diagrams, old soldier. Looks good, sounds good, doesn't work that way. There's only one place you'll get Master McCoy and his little friend, and that's beside Sokarev. That's the only place those bastards will show. Wasting your time with all the motorcades and all the escort riders. Doesn't happen there. Happens when he's on the pavement or at the speech. Stands to reason, if you're planning a show like this for a dozen weeks, you're not going to risk everything on the off-chance you might manage a pot shot during a cavalcade. And when the old drone had finished, time then to get up to the university, and have a look, and come back via the hotel, and still have some minutes to spare before the plane arrived. Should have done the reconnaissance yesterday, Jimmy-lad, not been in that boozer half the afternoon. Should have given the place the look-over, not a thing that ought to be done in a hurry. Should have been thought out, Jimmy.

He knew it, didn't have to argue the toss about it, and comforted himself only with the thought that he would be close to Sokarev. Human wall, and no pension rights. But perhaps it was a safe old number, for all that. Whoever heard of the bodyguard catching it? JFK, RFK, right down to Faisal; all had the detail round them, who lived to file the reports on what went wrong, and still had time to go to the funeral.

Forty men in the room, all of them brass, and how many taking orders . . . another three hundred, four hundred? And they're just two. What real chance have they got?

That was where Jimmy's thoughts came to a stop. Below him, pinned to the side of the blackboard, were the pictures, McCoy's and the man whose name they still searched for. Nasty, rough bastards, Jimmy said to himself, very hard, very serious people. And what do we have against them? This crowd, dragged in from murder inquiries, bank robberies and demonstrations on Sunday afternoons in Trafalgar Square. His eye rolled around the room. Many of the officers were taking notes, all listened intently, following the speaker as he took them slowly through the maps and diagrams. If these two bastards decide to come in close, thought Jimmy, then this lot'll find themselves in a different league. They'll wish they'd never got out of bed.

The big jet had swung out over the sea, deep and distant beneath them. Sokarev saw the beach at Herzliya, could make out the people on the sand who looked up at the wallowing giant as it surged toward its cruising altitude. Four and a half hours would take them to London, thirty-one-thousand feet and a cruising speed of six hundred miles an hour, hurtling across the Mediterranean, then the Italian coast and the huge expanse of France before the descent and the shoreline of Britain.

Elkin sat beside the window, his charge beside him, and then Mackowicz in the aisle seat. Sokarev dozed till Mackowicz's voice overrode the hazy thoughts he was entertaining, and he opened his eyes. The man talking to his guard was like a replica, thought the scientist. Same assurance, strength, poise and ease of movement. And wearing the same heavy jacket, even in the sweat-making atmosphere of the cabin, to hide his gun from the sensibilities of the passengers.

Mackowicz turned to Sokarev. 'We used to work together, this layabout, Elkin and I. Then he took the easy life. He just flies with the airline. Logs more hours than the pilots.'

Sokarev said, 'I did not know that you people were on board . . .'

'Two, sometimes four. Always two. We have no option. The orders are very clear. Our planes are not to fly to Arab countries. If there is a hijack attempt all you can do is shoot, and hope.'

'And the pressurization, what if that is broken?'

'The pilot will dive. He will try and throw the terrorist off balance. He will also attempt to get below ten thousand feet. If he is unsuccessful and there is a fracture then there is a disaster – nothing he can do. So he falls for two reasons: to get below the pressurization problem but also to confuse the man or woman, give us time to act. It has all been practised.'

'And the passengers, what of them?' asked Sokarev, impatience in his voice.

'If they are Israelis they will understand. If they are not . . . then they use another airline.'

'But the guns you have. The moment you fire you will puncture the fuselage.'

'The bullets are restricted velocity. You need have no fears, Professor, it has all been worked out.'

So they were at war. Even in the womb-like casing of the airliner they were in a state of conflict. Not great armies, just tiny fragments of platoons. But just as lethal, just as capable of inflicting misery as the big battalions. Sokarev reflected that the front line was now under two hours away. It might be in a car on a three-lane motorway into the capital, it might be the pavement outside a hotel, it might be a lecture hall packed with distinguished academics. It was a new war as unfamiliar to him as it was commonplace to the men who now rested, their eyes closed, mouths sagging in relaxation, on either side of his seat.

Jones was a long time staring down at the twin pictures that lay on his cluttered desk. They'd found their way to the top of the pile of files and maps of central London, and the plan of the university complex and the surrounding streets. He supposed he was expected to loathe the pair, have a great and consuming hatred of them, but it never worked that way. Before they'd pushed him into 'Middle East' he'd laboured for a dozen years on the Soviet Bloc (Czechoslovakia) desk – where the then DG said the real work was done. Not hard to remember the attaché, trade of some description, that they'd picked up after months of trailing and surveillance. Was reckoned to have been a big man – 'incalculable damage to the national interest' was what the judge had said – but he hadn't seemed that formidable in the interview room of the police station they'd taken him to after the lift. Rather ordinary, more anxious that someone should give him a cigarette than anything else. Hadn't said anything, of course, just smiled at their questions in an apologetic way, embarrassed that they had to play such games. The Section had used a major manpower quota to track him, classified it as a 'priority' operation, and Jones was one of those closely involved. Afterwards it was just anticlimax, unimportant, devoid of stimulus.

He wondered how much different he'd find McCoy and his friend, whether they'd be any more fearsome face to face than the quiet little man from Prague. McCoy was easier to evaluate; his photograph had been taken in custody and his eyes and mouth showed all the aggressiveness of a trapped man. But the other picture, that was the one that held Jones's interest. Quite a pleasant mouth the Photofit and the artist had given him, and eyes that were large and not set with fear. Hard to see him as something special, something to be exterminated, because the threat he carried was so contagious. Didn't look like the rabid fox he was categorized as. Just a boy, really, and nothing in his features to betray his potential.

Helen came in, no knock, walked across the room and peered past his shoulder at the pictures.

'Those the clever pair, causing all the fuss?'

'Those are the ones.'

'And you've set the big, bad Jimmy loose after them?'

'Slipped his collar, right.'

'And how good are they, compared with our Jimmy-boy?'

'They'll do all right. They'll give him a good run, he won't have to worry about that. He'll get his full out of them.'

'And then they'll send him home in one piece?'

'Probably,' Jones said. Before she went back to the outer office he saw the whiteness of her cheeks. Should have taken it more gently. But it was the one point that nagged at him, worrying at his composure as to whether Jimmy would beat these two at the close quarters where he was certain they would meet. It was difficult to believe in the danger if he stared at the face with the close mesh of curled hair the police artist and the eyewitnesses had given to it. To find the real man he had to go to the file, and that was still sparse and without flesh to hang on the skeleton information they had so far accumulated.

He took a drawing pin from his desk drawer and used it to hang the Arab's picture on the wall beside his filing cabinet. Where he could see it at any time he wanted, where he could study it, learn from it, understand it.

The effect on McCoy was less violent than on Famy. The Arab looked with ill-concealed horror at the pictures blazoned across the front pages of the papers. They were standing outside a small newsagent's shop in South West London beside a bus stop where they hoped to board the transport they needed to return to the inner suburbs. The pictures had been blown-up hugely, and in the squat popular papers covered half the front page. There were banner headlines, screaming at them across the pavement: 'The Killers', 'The Most Wanted Men in Britain', 'Have You Seen These Men?'

'Don't bloody gawp at them,' hissed McCoy in Famy's ear.

'It was that notebook. The one that we left behind, that is where they have taken it from,' said Famy.

'Bullshit. They'll have talked in the commune. Got my name there. That's a Northern Ireland picture of me, taken when I was nicked. They've got an artist to do yours from all the descriptions. It's not particularly good, yours.'

'It is sufficient for them to discard many men. They have given a height, and a weight, the general detail. Not adequate for a positive identification, but enough to come close. And they have the clothes, the trousers and shirt that we still wear . . .'

'Get back, can't you? There's no place better for anyone to spot you than if you're pressed tight up against the damn thing.'

'They have no name on me,' Famy said, as he moved away from the shopfront and the two men resumed their position at the back of the queue.

Famy felt the uncertainty again that had dogged him throughout his first hours in London. It should not have been happening in this way. They should have been safe and secure in the house, not needing to venture out, dependent on the Irish-man for their supplies. There was to have been no question of them hanging about in crowded streets; orders had been specific on that point. Every time a man or woman or child turned to him he imagined the dawning of recognition, and he shuffled his feet, attempting, badly, to maintain a casual, relaxed front. How do people make the recognition? he wondered. How can they translate something so distant from their lives as a wanted picture in a newspaper into the flesh-and-blood beside them on the street? It's a difficult and long step to take, Famy told himself. It would take great certainty, requiring a person to peer again and again to convince himself he were right, and that there was more than similarity with a picture he had merely glanced at.

To McCoy it was a less awesome experience. He was accustomed to having his picture in the front pocket of the bottle-green RUC uniforms and the camouflage tunics of British soldiers. He was familiar with life on the run, avoiding capture under the very eyes of men who had studied his features. But he realized a fundamental danger in their present position. The newspapers put two men together, identified them as a partnership, and that was how they were travelling, in tandem, linked to each other. But isolated, moving as loners, how much safer they would be. It was turning over in his mind when the single-decker green bus pulled in at the stop, and the queue moved forward. They must separate, but where to? It was easy enough for him, but what to do with the Arab? Couldn't have him wandering the streets solo, insecure and liable to panic. So what to do with him? There was no immediate answer, only a vague plan, slowly taking shape.

McCoy bought the tickets from the bus driver, and they made their way to the back seats where they would be behind the other passengers, where their faces would suffer least exposure. Famy had the grip-bag, containing a selection of both their clothes, and the rifles, magazines and grenades. It was heavy, and the handle straps strained against the metal hoops that held them to the framework of the bag. His own case had been left in the boot of the Escort, packed with some of his own clothes, some of Famy's. The car itself was off the road in the woods that surrounded the Surrey town of Esher. It would be difficult to find, and he had prised off the number plates, throwing them far into the undergrowth. The ground had been hard, the tyre marks slight, and anyway they had brushed the ground with hazel saplings, leaving a light scuff covering the trail of the wheels.

As the bus made its way toward Hampton Court the two men sat in silence, McCoy working on his next move, Famy suffering from the tension of having seen the photograph and the drawings. By the time they had become locked in the traffic flow McCoy spoke, low and direct, talking from the side of his mouth and close to Famy's ear.

'We have to separate today. The danger lies in us being together.'

There was startled surprise on the other's face, the flash in the eyes that suggests the feeling of being betrayed. McCoy saw it.

'There's nothing for you to worry about. But we have to be apart for today at least. There are eight more hours till darkness, when we should meet again.'

Famy turned his head, the tightly clamped lips giving warning of his suspicion. 'Where would I go? What do I do?' he said.

'I don't know yet. We can talk about it. But we have to get apart. The two of us together is too much of a risk.'

'We could have stayed with the car in the woods . . .'

McCoy cut into him, anxious lest he should lose control and sacrifice the initiative to the Arab.

'It would have been possible. But we could not take another car there, and we have to change motors. We have to get a car in the town. In the country they can block you too easily; it would be reported faster.'

Famy did not reply.

'Look, you silly bugger,' McCoy was talking quickly, urgently – 'I've told you I'm in this with you. You don't have to worry. I'm not bolting on you. It's a judgement I've made, and a necessary one. Am I going to ditch on you now? Think about it. After the girl, after taking you to the guns, am I going to bunk out?'

Famy nodded. He was exhausted from four nights without adequate sleep; there was no spirit in him for argument.

'Where do we get off?' the Arab asked.

'Further on there's a town – about another fifteen minutes. There's tubes and trains there, cinemas. Whatever you want.'

'And you, where will you go?'

Famy saw the hesitation, and had the ability to sense a lie.

'I'll just lose myself for a few hours,' McCoy said,

'till the night has gone. Till we can meet up and get a car.'

Again the Arab had no reply. A sense of loneliness and isolation welled up inside him. How far could he trust the Irishman? He was unsure now, certain there was a further reason for the split, certain that he was not being confided in. What could he do? On a bus, where ears would flap and quicken if he raised his voice? He was powerless.

Five stops later McCoy rose out of his seat and went down the length of the aisle. Famy took his cue and followed. Then they were out on the pavement, amid people who hurried past them, intent on their own business. The two men stood for a moment before McCoy saw a tea bar down the road and across the street, and began to walk toward it.

'Just round the corner and up the main street, that's where the cinemas are. There's one there that shows three films, separate theatres, all divided up. That'll lose you for some time, and it's dark in there, you'll be OK. We'll meet back in the tea bar. Eight o'clock. Now don't just walk around, get somewhere like the cinema and bloody-well stay there.'

Famy looked at him as they went in through the door of the café, quizzing McCoy with his eyes, searching for the truth of the other man's decision. He found no answer.

When McCoy left the grip-bag and its contents stayed with Famy. 'Safer with you,' he'd said, 'tucked under your legs in the cinema. Out of harm's way, better than me lugging them around.'

He ducked out into the sunlight, and vanished beyond the doorway, hurrying along the pavements, side-stepping to avoid the crowds of lunch-time shoppers. Free of the bugger, he thought to himself. Free at last without the nursemaid millstone round my neck and pulling down. The relief at being on his own again flowed through him, a river that has broken a dam and finds again the dry stone bed, its expression rampant and without check. He was half-running when he reached the supermarket.

McCoy went inside, through the electrically-controlled glass sliding doors. The cash registers, a bank of them where the girls punched the keys and took the money, were at the far end. He took a basket, put a single bar of chocolate in it, something that would stave off the hurting pain of hunger, and walked down past the stacked counters and shelves to the queue that had formed for the privilege of paying. He watched the girl as she deftly handled the bags and packages and tins, eyes never on the customer she served, always on what she took from the wire baskets and put down on the flat surface beside her, while her hands played the numbers on the machine. Her face was set, expressionless, dedicated to the task of extracting the right money, giving the right change.

When he put the basket down the slim hand was there in an instant, pulling clear the chocolate, while the girl mouthed the amount that showed on her machine, as a tiny row of trading stamps reached out from the mechanism.

'Hello, Norah,' he said, very quietly, conscious of the people behind him bustling and impatient at being delayed. She looked up at him. There was startled recognition, then fear, like a rabbit's because she was sitting down and he loomed above her. Taut,

213

strained, wide eyes pierced into him. The will to say something but no voice.

'I have to see you.' He angled the words to give the stress of dependence, and waited for her to react.

'What are you doing here?' Bewilderment, but conspiracy also, hushed so that the words would carry no further than the two of them.

'I have to see you,' he repeated the words, only with greater insistence. 'Outside, make an excuse. I have to be with you this afternoon. I'll be outside and waiting.' He put down two ten-pence coins, the amount shown on the cash machine, took the chocolate and walked back out on to the street.

On the far side of the street he waited. Twenty minutes, perhaps, then she was there looking for a gap in the traffic. Blouse and jeans instead of the overall she wore for her work. Just before she saw the opportunity to cross she looked across to where he stood. His smile was not returned, and then she was concentrating on the cars and the lorries.

He took her hand. Soft, small, fitting inside his fist. He kissed her without pressure on the side of the cheek, and felt her drag herself back from him.

'You didn't tell me inside there. What are you doing here?'

'I've come to see you.' Inadequate, need more than that.

'You've seen the picture. You're in the papers, on the telly.'

'I know.'

'Well, what have you come here for?'

'I wanted to see you, girl. I wanted to be with you. I wanted . . .' He did not finish. What could he tell her, that he had to get away from it? That he wasn't just a machine, a killing apparatus. That there was a need for a break, to get away from the awfulness of the running, from the concealment and the chase and the ultimate confrontation. There was a girl on the farm near Cullyhanna, and a place in the gorse and bracken on Mullyash Mountain where she would go with him and let him talk to her and love her and relax with her, till the sleep came and the understanding. Then he could go back to his war. But how to tell the little shop girl from South West London that a man who fights must one time fall asleep in arms that hold no danger? That the time comes when the company of men is repulsive and rejected? Another day beside that bloody man and he'd come to loathe him, not through any fault of the Arab's. McCoy knew there was no fault in him. But it did not lessen the need to escape, and to exist again in the world which he had denied himself.

'I needed to talk to you, somewhere where we could be alone,' he said.

They walked together through the town and into the vast open expanse of the royal park. There were roads that cut across the landscape, leaving great segments of virgin ground covered by sprouting grass, and the delicate-shaped fronds of the bracken, where the sun shone down. And there were woods where the birches and oaks filtered the light and cast a haze of shadow. It was as he had wanted. He had found what he sought.

They went deep into the bracken, along a path used only by the big red deer that scampered and leapt as they approached, making good their escape.

He put his coat down on the broken stems and they sat together. There was no horizon beyond the immediate wall of green that surrounded them, hiding them from all eyes. McCoy sank onto his back, reaching up with his arms and pulling the girl down onto his chest. Her head rested underneath his chin, and against his mouth he could feel the strands of her hair, and there was a scent to them, freshly washed and clean. They lay there a long time, and his thoughts were of the hill farms, and the other girl who was dark and more heavily built and who comprehended the need for release that overwhelmed him, and of the buzzards that would circle and swoop above them across the hills of Armagh County.

It was Norah who broke the spell.

'It is you they are hunting? It was your picture on the TV that we saw?' Frightened, small voice, and his dreaming reply failed to take her fear away.

'It was me. I'm the one they're looking for. They're a long way behind me, and they won't find me.'

'But you killed a girl, strangled her, that's what it said.'

'What do you want me to say? What do you want me to pretend?' He rolled over onto his stomach, and leant on one bent elbow above her, his free hand in her hair, stroking, caressing it into shapes. 'It has nothing to do with your life. It is something separate. I won't tell you I didn't, and you wouldn't believe me if I did. There's nothing I can say, nothing you should know.'

His hand came down from her hair, and a fingernail flicked carelessly at the plastic buttons of her blouse, held by frail cotton to the material. He saw the tears coming, the tightening of the muscles close to her eyes and the reflection from the moisture that ran beside her nose, and found a track that skirted the fullness of her cheek and then was lost on the grass. He came down to her mouth and kissed her, and there was no room for her to back away. She felt her body pressed hard against the unevenness of the ground. And his hands began to go free, and search out the places they quested for. When they had unfastened the clasp behind her back and removed the soft protective covering on her breasts, she put her arms round his neck, and, sobbing, dragged his head close down beside her. She could not account for her actions, could not justify the tenderness with which she ran her hands over the harsh bristles below the hair at the back of his neck, could not reason why she flexed her legs slowly apart in the hope that his hand would find its way. When she opened her eyes his face was very close, and he kissed the lids, closing them, and there was just the darkness and the sensation and the knowledge that the hands were moving again, demanding ownership, seeking new territory. The button slipped loose at the waist of her jeans and she wriggled as his hands eased them below her knees, and still there was the darkness and the desperate requirement for him to move on. He lingered at the scarce-formed line that led down to the gentleness of the soft hair, and she moaned his name without sound into the roughened cheek joined to her own. When he came into her there was pain, and a power she had not known before, and she writhed and tried to escape. But there was only the thrashing, pinioning weight that held her, till at last he sagged, spent and exhausted.

Norah lay on the ground unmoving, the sun playing on her skin, the wind blowing its patterns, while the man beside her slept, his face with the quietness of a child's, the smoothness of his skin broken only by the tramlines worked by the nails of Doris Lang.

From the bank where he had changed a ten-pound travellers' cheque, Famy looked for the red cubicle he now identified as a telephone box. It took him fifteen minutes and brought him back to the railway station he had walked past when seeking the bank. The bag was heavy, and it was with relief that he dropped it down onto the floor of the box. He closed the door behind him, and felt in his pocket for a two-pence piece. He had no difficulty remembering the number, nor the extension to ask for when the switchboard operator answered. As he had expected, the figures of the extension were given remotely and above the crackle of the connection.

'It's "Mushroom" here,' Famy said.

There was a scuffling on the line, the sound he recognized as a receiver being placed against the material of a shirt or jacket, and indistinct words spoken into a void. Clearing the room, thought Famy.

'What is it you wish to say?' the telephone was active again.

'I wanted to know whether there were further orders, whether there were new instructions.' Was that all he had telephoned to discover, when there was no chance of further orders? His tone echoed the hollowness of his request.

'Nothing has come through.'

Famy paused, waiting, wondering what to say. He could not speak of his desolation, his fears, of the horror of seeing his picture in the newspapers.

'Nothing at all? There is no word from home?' Perhaps the man at the embassy sensed something of his feelings, recognized the helplessness of the other.

'There is nothing, but that was not to be expected. It is the style of the leadership to allow a free hand in such matters. Your arrival has been communicated.' There was a sharp click on the line, and the sound for a moment was blanked out. In less than a second it returned, and Famy was able to hear the breathing, regular and unemotional, of the man he spoke to.

'There are difficulties?'

'It is so confused now. We have lost our place, because of the girl . . .'

The voice cut in, interrupting. 'There was a clicking noise on the line. We must not speak any more. Ring off, and move away. Do not stay near the telephone. Very briefly, is there anything else?'

Famy was confused. He had heard the noise, but had not interpreted it.

'The Irishman. I do not know at what stage I can trust him, whether I am better on my own. We have the guns now, but . . .'

'Is there nothing of importance that you have to say? If not, ring off.'

'. . . it is the Irishman. He said we must separate for today . . .'

'Ring off. And get away from the telephone box. Right away from it.'

The voice was at shouting pitch, and the line went dead, returning to its continual, miasmic purr. The urgency had at last communicated.

Famy picked up the bag and ran from the station hallway.

Chapter Twelve

With the talkative, restless Jimmy out of the office and on his way to the airport for the reception committee, Jones's room had reverted to its normal hushed calm. He was poring over the files, alternately concentrating on the growing information on McCoy and the maps and plans that covered the Professor Sokarev visit when his internal phone rang.

'Monitoring section here, Mr Jones. Your embassy number is on. Chatting away. We've routed through to intercept . . .'

He did not wait to hear any more. He ran through the open connecting door, past the desk where Helen was typing, and out into the corridor. Fifteen paces to the staircase, not bothering to wait for the lift, and down the six flights in a headlong race to get to the basement before the call terminated. He was panting when he arrived. Inside the cubicle the big man was hunched, checking the dials for sound level as the tapes beside him spun slowly round. The spare earphones were already plugged in, and Jones jammed them lopsidedly over his head.

'They've just heard the intercept switch go. The embassy's trying to wind it up,' he was told.

He was in time to hear the reference to 'guns', then the shouts of the other voice. One more half-hearted sentence and the line was cut.

A white telephone on the table inside the cubicle rang and Jones instinctively reached and picked it up.

'Intercept here. The call was made from Richmond, a public telephone. Checking the location now.'

Jones dialled the special number that had been assigned to the Scotland Yard operations room that was concerned exclusively with the hunt for McCoy and the unknown Arab. He spoke briefly, passing on the relevant material. No more, and rang off. Time to get out of their hair, leave them a chance to get moving. Best break we've had, thought Jones. Something real to bite on for a change. They played him back the tape, which he heard through four more times.

When he walked into Fairclough's office Jones said, 'The nerves are fraying a bit in the team. The Arab on to the embassy, doubting McCoy. Says he's been left on his ownsome, and doesn't like it. Sounded depressed, miserable, not having a happy time, wanting instructions from home. But he says they've retrieved the guns, which confirms that stuff from the hills we had in last night. But he sounded unhappy, really miserable.'

'Did he say whether or not they were still going to have a go at it?'

'Nothing about that. Said McCoy had told him they must separate for today.'

'Well, that's clear enough then. And not bad

thinking. They're more vulnerable like that, together. They'll resume harness tonight. I suggest they're still operational.'

Jones made a slow way to his own office. He knew what he had to do when he reached its quietness and sanctuary – had to understand them, had to find a way into their thought processes, had to make the men who were just pictures and closely-typed words into human beings. That was the way, the only way, you could anticipate their next decision and action. But they were so remote, and he so out of touch with their world, that he evaluated his chances as minimal. That was why he was not hurrying.

In the town on the outskirts of London police radios had begun to chatter instructions, locations, descriptions, facial features, clothes. Men were hauled from traffic duties, serving summonses, investigating larceny and vandalism.

The Chief Superintendent who controlled the local police station concentrated deploying his men in three directions. First, he blocked all major roads leading out of the area; that was his major and initial priority. Second, a van-load of police took over the hallway of the station that served British Rail Southern Region and London Transport District Line Underground. Third, he concentrated cars not involved in the roadblocks in the centre of the town, cruising and observing the hundreds who swarmed on the pavements and around the shops. Revolvers were issued to car crews leaving the station, the required and formal paperwork left till the end of the day. When he was satisfied that the town was sealed as well as possible in the time, he came on the radio net himself to issue a clear and uncompromising instruction.

'The man we are searching for is dangerous, is probably armed, and should not be approached by any police officer who is unarmed. If you see him call in; we'll have the reinforcements you need.'

That was the message that first excited the radio ham who sat in his terraced house whiling away the time till his night shift began at the Hawker Siddeley factory down the road in Kingston. He ignored the stringent code set down by the Wireless Telegraphy Act that forbade any member of the public to listen to police messages and make use of them, and left his set tuned in to the area police frequency. He had turned the set up when he had noticed the rapid upsurge in traffic, and was in time to hear in full the words of the Chief Superintendent. He had a list of the numbers of the news desks of the Fleet Street papers, and being a conscientious man, had taken a note of their edition times. The *Daily Express* were traditionally the best payers for news tips, and there was no need to explain from where the information originated.

As the net was closing around the town, Famy was paying his money underneath the glass grille at the cash desk of the cinema. James Bond was in town – double feature.

'You've nothing to fear. Just do as we say, don't hesitate, whatever it is, and everything will be fine. The British have a big force out. Our own people from the embassy will be close by. But do as Elkin and I say with no questions.'

Those were the last words Mackowicz said to

Sokarev on the flight itself. Then the plane finished its long taxi, and the doors to the stiflingly hot cabin were at last opened. Other passengers were already in the aisle waiting to leave when the chief steward and the man that Sokarev knew as El Al security transposed themselves across the corridor, leaving the route to the steps clear for Mackowicz to lead, followed by Sokarev and Elkin. The scientist saw the resentment etched in the faces of those delayed, and wondered why people always looked so hurt and embittered when they have just success-fully negotiated an air flight. What have they to face, he thought, that justifies their puckered and peevish stares, and all because they must wait another seventy-five seconds before following down the steps?

It was a comfortable, gentle heat, not aggressive like that in Israel, that greeted them on the tarmac. And there were the Special Branch men. Six of them forming up, three on each side of Sokarev and walking with him, faces turned outward, toward the black Mercedes of the embassy that waited close to the steps. The security attaché spoke briefly to Mackowicz, shook his hand and then came alongside the professor.

'There are people to welcome you, sir. They are in the lounge at the terminal building.'

Sokarev started to speak of his baggage.

'Just give me the tag, sir. On your ticket. It will all be taken care of while you are in the terminal.'

As the car started up Sokarev could see two heavily-laden unmarked vehicles take up position in convoy behind. He sat in the back seat squashed between the attaché and Mackowicz. Elkin was in the front with the driver, and between them another man who was middle-aged and had a faded, autumn look in his features, a man to whom nothing had the freshness of surprise. From the window Sokarev looked into the expressionless faces of uniformed policemen who waved and gestured the car across the traffic lights. There were dog handlers in the background, and men who stood in civilian clothes but with their right hands resting on the top buttons of their coats. More policemen were at the entrance to the VIP suite, tall men in their serge-blue uniforms, who discussed his progress from the car to the doorway via handheld radios, and who failed to meet the almost apologetic smile that he gave as he walked by them.

They sat him down in an easy, low-slung settee in the suite, choosing one far from the door, and a lady in black with a white apron brought him tea with a china cup and saucer and offered him with her other hand a plate of biscuits. She at least returned his smile, muttered the word 'love' to him and was gone through a doorway, not to be seen again. The man who sat in the front of the Mercedes was moving across the room toward him. Sokarev could see that his suit was old and uncared for, there was a nick of blood on his collar, his tie was sufficiently loosened to reveal the top button of his shirt, and his shoes had been cleaned but in haste and without thoroughness.

'The name's "Jimmy", sir. Security. I'm to be with you right through your stay here. I hope we'll get along. Which are your men?'

Sokarev gestured first towards Mackowicz who hovered close to his shoulder then pointed to Elkin who stood across the room by the door.

'There is Mr Mackowicz and Mr Elkin. I am glad to meet you . . . Jimmy,' he laughed quietly waiting for the other to offer a surname. None was forthcoming. 'I had been told that I would be offered help on the visit. I am grateful to you.'

'There's more than just me, sir. About another two hundred. The ones you'll see, at any rate. But I'm the one you'll be aware of. I'll be beside you the whole way.'

'You'll have competition, then,' Sokarev quipped, warming at his first impression of the man. 'Mr Mackowicz and Mr Elkin have told me they booked those places for themselves.'

'Well, it should be crowded then. Which is about right.'

Thank God, thought Sokarev, they are not all like those men that have come with me. This one at least I can talk to. He has a sense of humour, not like those who pad round in my wake, with their orders and ultimatums and their soured faces. He could see the man who called himself Jimmy talking out of earshot with Mackowicz, folders passing between them. All the men in the room were in huddles, talking, chattering like sparrows, exchanging sheets of white paper, drawing them from folders of green and blue and red and brown. And I am the supernumerary, thought Sokarev. Nobody talks to me, nobody has even the time to say a 'hello', or a 'welcome'. Everybody talks about me, about my movements, my sleep, my meals, but I am not consulted. Even the one that joked with me has nothing substantial to say. All that is kept for Mackowicz. If I wanted to attract attention I would have to shout, throw an epileptic fit, take my trousers off. Otherwise they would all go on as if I did not exist. Perhaps for some I am an exercise in strategy, a game to be played with, and when the time has come for me to leave I must be packaged up, shipped home, and then forgotten. For others I am a source of anxiety. Not that they would mourn David Sokarev if his body lay in the gutter; what they would mourn would be their careers, their futures, and above all their reputations.

He was far away and enjoying the self-pity when the security attaché spoke to him.

'We have your bag now, Professor. We are ready to leave.' His tea was half-finished in the cup. It mattered to no-one. The circus was ready to entrain. It was not intended David Sokarev should delay it.

A reporter with the airport news agency, Brenards, with a clearance pass that gave her access to the area of the VIP lounge, saw the convoy leave. She was there to interview a prominent industrialist returning with major export orders from the United States. Courteously but firmly a uniformed policeman told her she was not permitted to go within twenty-five yards of the lounge doorway. She had already watched the cordon stiffen up, seen the drivers start their motors, taken in the scale of the police operation when the little man was brought out of the VIP suite. He was barely visible between the larger bodies of the Special Branch men who hemmed him in. As soon as the last of the guards had clambered aboard the cars were on the move. She would not have known by what airline the passenger who warranted so much attention had flown with if she had not recognized the features of the El Al station manager. When the cars had gone she had moved up beside him and asked him the identity of his passenger. He had shaken his head, given no explanation, and turned on his heel to walk back to his own transport. There are few things that irritate reporters, even trainees, as much as the studied brush-off.

Her telephoned call to her news editor reported 'massive security, an unknown and anonymous Israeli VIP, police tracker dogs on the tarmac, an escort of armed Special Branch men, the waiving of customs formalities, and a high speed convoy into London'. The news editor liked it too, gave it a further gloss of his own, and put it on the wires, along which it would be carried to the newsrooms of all Fleet Street papers.

Immured between the shoulders of the security attaché and Mackowicz, Professor Sokarev saw little of the countryside bordering the M4 motorway between the airport and central London. If he strained his head there were occasional glimpses of fields and football pitches before the cars sped on to a stilted flyover, and only the roofs and upper office windows of the taller buildings were visible. He could sense the tension that now gripped Mackowicz, the way he peered into the cars that they passed, or, when they slowed, clogged in traffic as the motorway narrowed from three lanes of traffic to two, the way he heaved himself across the window pressing his whole upper torso against the glass. Sokarev had stared in the other direction for the moment or so before the convoy had started off, while the bodyguard had loaded the heavy black-painted pistol before returning it to his shoulder holster. It was an unpleasant, angular weapon, outside the scientist's experience, and he was unable to give it a name.

In thirty-five minutes they were at the door of the hotel that had been chosen for him. More detectives were waiting here, easily recognizable. His own car had jerked to a halt, and Mackowicz had said in his ear, 'Don't stop, don't hesitate, straight inside.' Then an arm had taken his and half-bundled him through the moving swing doors.

Across the hall a man stood with one foot in the lift, holding the button to keep the door open. Sokarev was kept moving, across the lavish carpet, then bustled into the lift. As the doors closed he found himself pressured by the shapes of his own men, the attaché, the one who called himself Jimmy, and the elegant, dark-suited fellow he presumed to be from the hotel. They went to the fourth and top floor. At the extreme right-hand end he saw two men rise from their chairs, one of them turning to unlock and open the door of a corner room. The pace was maintained till the door slammed shut behind him.

'Welcome to our hotel, Professor Sokarev,' intoned the man in the dark suit. He spoke with the necessary formality that concealed the management's displeasure at playing host and having responsibility for such a guest. There had been no breath of this when the reservation had been made, no mention of policemen, or of detectives who wanted to sleep in corridors, watch the front desk, and slump in lounge chairs. That had all started early in the morning, too late to insist on a cancellation.

'There is a connecting door to the other room and your two colleagues.'

One room only for the two of them, thought Sokarev. The attaché read his thoughts.

'At night one will be sleeping, the other awake. They will take it in shifts. In addition there are the men outside.'

Soon the group dispersed, the manager through the main door, Mackowicz, Elkin, Jimmy and the attaché into the adjoining room. Sokarev was alone, able to unstrap his case, and begin to put in the drawers the clothes that his wife had folded with such care. He could reflect that whatever fears he himself entertained for his own safety they were matched by the anxiety of the Security Services of Israel and of Britain. The realization chilled him.

Next door Jimmy was on the telephone, through to Jones, and the other men waited in silence for him to finish speaking and then relay to them the latest information. Jimmy gave nothing away to those who looked for a sign. He listened poker-faced, said he'd be in later that evening, and rang off.

'There's been a flap since Friday morning, but it's really buzzing now. Bit over an hour ago one of them called the contact man. We've traced the call to the south-west. They're saturating a town called Richmond. Nice, comfortable, posh place. And it's crawling with coppers now. They think there's a good chance they have the bastards bottled up. But then they always say that. And then make the excuses twenty-four hours later.'

'How many of them are there?' Elkin asked.

'Just two,' said Jimmy. 'One from Northern Ireland. Cut above the usual grade. Good record, good operator. The other we think is from your part of the world. No name, but we've a face, not a bad

231

one we think, to fit to him. He's a bit homesick, made a phone call he shouldn't have. That's how we're pressuring them right now. Special Branch will be round in about twenty minutes, an inspector; he'll have the files and the pictures for you.'

Jimmy sensed he was the odd man out in the room, that they wanted to talk in their own tongue, discuss their problems among themselves. It was the time for him to assert himself, make the position clear. There must be no doubts, no misunderstandings.

'My orders, gentlemen,' he said, 'are very clear. I have to be beside your man every moment he's out of that room. Not five yards, or four yards, or three yards away from him. Right beside him. My orders are very explicit on that. He's not to leave this building without me knowing it. This isn't a scene you'll run yourselves. We are in charge, and you will listen to us. And a final point. If I see something out on the street and open fire and hit the wrong bloody target there'll be a hell of a row, but it'll blow over. If one of you does it, you'll be in court before you know what's hit you; it'll stink for months. So go a bit careful.'

Jimmy went out into the corridor – to have a smoke, chat up the Branch men, and to allow the men he'd left behind in the room to vent their feelings. With amusement he heard the raised voice that he recognized as Mackowicz's rich in aggrieved anger, and Elkin's quieter but in a harmony of protest, and then the calmer tones of the attaché soothing the hurt pride, salving the wounds.

That poor little sod in the other room, Jimmy thought. Lonely, frightened and going through this hoop just to make one bloody speech. He could just as well have put it in the post, all neatly typed out, and everyone would be just as wise. But that's not the way it works. He's going to stand out there like a tethered goat, put out as bait, with us up in the trees and him praying we get the bastards before they get him.

Jimmy went back into the room. Mackowicz was still hard-eyed, uptight; Elkin was a bit better, not much, but they both knew where they stood. The attaché had done a good job. Their clothes were already scattered around the room. The radios and the Uzis were on one of the bedspreads. They were settling in.

'No appointments tonight, right?' Jimmy said to the attaché.

'Correct. He was to have dined at the university. We've put that off, said he had a heavy cold. He'll eat in the room tonight. He'll be tired from the journey. Tomorrow he can stay in till we go out in the evening.'

'And Wednesday to the States?'

'He goes to New York on Thursday. His arrangements there are from that day. We saw no reason to change them.'

'I hope he likes his room then,' snapped Jimmy. 'Because if he's going to be here for an extra day that's where he's going to have to stay.'

The wind had raised its pitch, gathering power and determination as it swept across the great open spaces of the park. It sought out the body of McCoy where he lay, shirt unbuttoned to the waist, forced its currents across his chest so that in his sleep he shivered, and wriggled to hunch his frame and protect himself. And then he woke. He saw the girl beside him with her clothes still in the casual disarray that he had left them, legs outflung, arms behind her head, staring vacant and uncaring into the deep distances of the sky.

He looked at his watch. Past seven. Less than an hour to the rendezvous, and the light beginning to drift away. The afternoon had been lost, and soon would come the cover of darkness that he needed for movement.

'Come on, girl. Time to be on our way.' He said it without noise, but there was none of the tenderness in his voice that she sought and expected. She lay motionless, unwilling to look at him.

'Come on, girl. I said it was time to move.' There was a cutting edge in his voice, sharp and unfamiliar. She reacted, fumbling with her jeans, pulling them over the slight hips. She turned away from him to contort her arms round her back to refasten the clasp he had unhooked. He brushed the grass and dried earth from their clothes and together they started to walk toward the heavy wrought-iron gates, through which the cars flowed in and out of the park. They walked in silence, Norah with her head down, avoiding him.

They were still a hundred yards from the gates when McCoy saw the policemen operating the roadblock. He counted six of them. One was far in the distance on the road toward the town waving his arm languidly in the air, slowing and warning the oncoming traffic. Another had a clip-board and was taking down registration numbers. Another talked to the drivers, peering inside to scrutinize the passengers. A fourth and fifth searched under bonnets and in the boots of the cars, and a sixth sat in a police car facing away from the block, his engine ticking over. McCoy understood the scene. Last man there for a break out, revved and ready to give chase. It was professional, he accepted that.

Too many for anything routine. Too heavy a force for local crime. Then he thought of Famy. Unwilling to be left on his own, nervous of what might happen to him if he were abandoned to his own devices for just a few hours, suspicious of where McCoy had gone. And now the roadblock; not a casual one, but thorough and painstaking. He had to be sure where the bloody Arab was, had to know what had happened.

Stretching on either side of the gates were the eight-foot-high walls of matured brick that ringed the park.

'I can't go through the check,' he said. 'I have to get across the wall, somewhere away from the main roads, but near to the town.' The girl hesitated, uncertain. The policemen would hear her if she shouted. One scream and they would be running, sprinting towards her. And what then? That was where the equation defeated her. What would she say? Tell them the man they sought had lain with her, that she had opened her legs to him, pulled him down onto her?

She was not long in deciding. She took McCoy's hand and led him across the grass, cut short by the sheep, past the great oak trees, and then where the wall dipped down following the contours of a gully she stopped.

She had chosen well, he could see that.

McCoy reached up to the top of the wall and levered himself a foot or so off the ground. It was perfect. The wrong end of a cemetery where the trees grew close together, where the leaf-mould and grass-cuttings had been piled against the bricks. He slipped over, landing easily on the piled vegetation. He put his right arm back over the wall, grabbed Norah's wrist and heaved her over the barrier. They crouched behind one of the big yews, the necessary precaution till he was certain they had not been observed.

'I want somewhere that I can lie up, somewhere safe,' he whispered to her.

'Just out of the cemetery there's a building site they've cleared. There's nothing there now. Just scrub and that. What are you going to do then?'

'Get me there, I'll tell you then.'

They walked along the narrow tarmac path between the disordered rows of stones, past the jam jars that held single wilting tulip-stems, skirted the fresh rectangular shapes of earth, and came to the gate.

'Where to from here?' McCoy said.

'Across the road, and about a hundred yards down, that's where the site is.'

'But there's a bloody great fence round it. I can't climb that on the main road.'

'Down at the side, the second turning, no-one'll see you there.' She was involved now, part of his team. The moment of crisis had gone. She would do as he told her, he had no doubt of that. Usually did, the little bitches. He sensed he now had in his possession something quite priceless. He had a courier. Someone who could run for him, who could be his eyes and ears. God knows why they want to dip their fingers in, he thought, but they do. Don't think it out, too stupid to do the addition and multiplication.

There was traffic on the road, but no policemen. He had his arm round her shoulder as they waited for an opening and then crossed. They fitted a conventional image, boy and girl, out for a walk, fond of each other, and very distant from the picture any motorist who saw them might have had of a hunted killer of the Provisional IRA. They walked down the side road, not fast, taking their time. McCoy spoke to her closely, and anyone who saw them would have imagined it was endearments he was whispering against her hair.

'Listen carefully,' he said. 'Do exactly as I say. Near the station there's a tea bar, on the far side of the road, toward the river. You'll find a man in there, a darkie. Taller than me, no moustache or anything, short hair. He'll have a grip-bag with him. Just say the word "Mushroom" to him, and tell him to follow you. Take him through to here, not on the big roads, down the side streets and get him here. And tell him to go carefully.'

'Is he the other one they're looking for?' Norah said it with excitement pitched in her voice.

'I've told you. You don't need to know. Just go and do it, girl. The way I've told you. If he's not there, wait for him. At least an hour. But get him here.'

He scanned each end of the road. Empty, deserted. Then he was on the buckling, bending wire, monkey-like, before he tumbled down on the far side and was gone. She heard his running feet crashing in the undergrowth, and after that nothing.

From his seat in the cinema Famy heard the sirens in the street outside. He remembered the urgency of the instructions over the telephone to set distance between himself and the station, and he huddled in the darkened seat as the raucous noise blotted out the soundtrack of the film whenever the police cars passed outside the cinema. He bit at his fingernails as he watched the Technicolor heroics that filled the screen. The images meant nothing, failed even to divert his attention from the problem that now preyed upon him. It was the immediate problem of survival. The bag was there against his legs, reassuring in its bulk, and he quietly slid open the zip and felt with his hands for the cotton surface under which were the awkward, angled shapes of the grenades. He lifted one out, small, the size of a shrunken apple, and put it in the pocket of his coat. The rifles were too large, too cumbersome, but one grenade would be sufficient to stave off immediate pursuit. It could be concealed, not like the guns, and it gave him the confidence that he would need to walk out into the unknown of the middle-light of the evening.

Sometimes his thoughts wandered back to his friends, the men he had hardly known, but whose companionship in the short-term he had valued, to Dani and Bouchi. Their laughter on the plane out of Beirut, the banter about Nablus and the olive groves as they had driven across France, and the fear that had bound them on the route to Boulogne. He recaptured again, so that it overwhelmed him and blotted out the meaningless antics of the celluloid pictures, the blood of his friends that had spattered and soaked the seats of the car. He could still hear Dani's words. Their exhortation before the colour in his soft brown cheeks had faded to the greyness that preceded death. The words knifed through his subconscious, controlling him, providing the momentum he needed to go on.

He left the cinema before the completion of the second film. He'd already seen well into the second reel, and the story had still not attracted him. But his motives were clear. He wanted to be away before the big rush to the doors, and the exit he chose was at the side. It was simple reasoning that if a hunt for him were in progress that the entrance hall of a cinema would be an obvious place for them to look. With the bag in his hand and the grenade in his pocket, he slid back the iron bar that kept the fire door shut. He went unnoticed and without impediment.

It took him many minutes to make his way to the rendezvous. He walked with a shuffling, almost sideways gait along the front of the shop windows, ready to spin his head toward the loaded shelves of merchandise on the occasions that the squad cars cruised past. There were men on foot too, and to avoid them he twice entered shops, mingling in front of the counters till he had seen through the plateglass windows that the danger had passed. With each step he took there was greater confidence. They're stumbling about, he told himself, uncertain what and whom they seek, thrashing in the dark.

In the café he took a seat at the back, again sideways on to the door, so he could observe the comings and goings and at the same time swing his head away should he wish to obscure his face.

He saw the girl come in, noticed the nervous, switching eyes that took in the customers sitting at the tables and on the stools at the counter. The look of grateful recognition she gave him stiffened Famy and his hand moved instinctively to the pocket that held the grenade, his fingers seeking out the circular pin that was the safety device of the V40. He stared at her, hand clasped round the metalwork as she came close, eyes riveted to her pale, pretty face.

She bent down toward him as she reached the table. She was trembling, and when her lips moved, at first there was no sound.

'Mushroom.' She blurted it. 'He said you were to follow me. I'll take you to him.'

And Famy understood. Why had he been so anxious to split up that afternoon? Needed a girl. Not a woman who would reason things out, but a girl who would follow blindly where he led. Dangerous, he thought, but probably better than someone older. As she turned back toward the door he saw the hard-etched creases in her blouse. Not bad, McCoy, he thought. A roll in the grass and you have the loyalty of the whore.

She took him through the back streets of the old town, climbing the hill over which sprawled the fashionable residential homes of the previous century. Past almshouses and churches, past homes that had been neatly outlined in white gloss, past blocks of flats where those for sale were advertised as 'luxury' on the estate agents' boards. Sometimes the streets were narrow, in other places they widened out, but none of them was busy with cars. There were children playing their games with balls, men walking in company to the pubs, women hurrying home with their baskets of late shopping, and no policemen. Famy held the girl's hand, and she let it rest there, inanimate and without feeling. But it was better that way, more secure. They went mostly in silence, Famy occasionally speaking, but meeting only non-committal response.

In front of them was a wall and daubed on it the words 'Park Hill was Home to Me' – a relic of the time there had been a great house set in its own grounds on the site, and when there had been protests before the demolition men came. Now there was only a tangle of bushes, cut-down trees and neglected shrubs.

'That's where he is,' she said. Her voice was detached – as if she realized, thought Famy, that her usefulness was expended, and was resigned to it.

'It's time I was getting home, my Mam'll be spare. Going out of her mind.'

'Where do you live?' asked Famy.

'Chisholm Road. Just round the corner. At twenty-five.'

'I hope we see you again. You have been very kind to me . . .'

She was away running into the night. He was different to the other one. More gentle, wouldn't have hurt her like that Irishman. But probably wouldn't have done anything, sat there all afternoon pulling grass up. It still ached where McCoy had been, and there was a bruised, raw feeling at the top of her thighs. And he hadn't used anything, the bastard.

241

Chapter Thirteen

Even as security-conscious a building as Scotland Yard is susceptible to leakage of classified information. In the drably-painted ground-floor press room the crime correspondent of the *Express* heard the first whispers of the mounting of a major security operation to protect an unnamed Israeli VIP.

The anonymity of the man being guarded was broken by the paper's science correspondent, who had received an invitation seventeen days earlier to attend a lecture by Professor David Sokarev of the Dimona Nuclear Research Establishment. His casual call to the Israeli embassy's press spokesman, and the flat refusal to his request for information on the professor's itinerary, served to confirm that Sokarev was the man being subjected to intensive security. The Brenards' report of armed Special Branch men at the airport to guard an El Al passenger added further colour to the story. But it was the chief sub-editor's intuition that turned the story into the front-page splash. At his desk where he collected the various typewritten sheets and the agency copy, he began to shuffle together what had up to then figured as quite separate material. He had in his hand the stories now catchlined 'Sokarev' along with those on which he had scrawled 'Manhunt'. And it made good sense. Heavy protection of an Israeli nuclear scientist married with a vast police dragnet for a known Provisional IRA killer, travelling in the company of an unidentified Arab.

By the time the third edition was on its way by van to various rail terminals the headline 'Arab Death Threat to Israeli H-Bomb Scientist' blasted its way across the top of the front page.

The Prime Minister's anger when he read the story before retiring to his Downing Street flat for the night was stonily rejected by the Director General.

'No leaks from this department,' was his riposte. It was his policy to strike an independent posture for the Security Services, and one thing with which he was traditionally quick to show intolerance was ill-informed criticism of its work.

'From what you've told me, sir' – the deference was purely formal – 'I think you'll find it straight-forward reporting of a series of facts visible to any trained eye.'

That went some way to calming the Head of Government. 'But it doesn't help the position,' the Prime Minister said.

'There's not very much that does help the situation in times like this.'

'What I mean,' said the Prime Minister, 'is that if anything happens to this man Sokarev after this, we are all going to look almighty stupid.'

'That's a fair point, sir,' the Director General replied.

Not a great deal to say after that. Only the obvious, that they had problems, that they were coming from behind, that there was huge ground to be made up. The silences grew longer, till the conversation reached its natural end. He wished the Prime Minister a good night's sleep.

So they'd the wind up in Whitehall. It always amused him. Meant the telephone would be going every five minutes in the morning. Politicians crawling in on the act, and nothing they could do about it. For that matter, he thought, not much any of us can do. He checked with Jones, still in his office too, but with no new developments to report from Richmond. It would be a long day tomorrow, long and trying.

Before they had set out into the darkened park there had been fierce words between Famy and McCoy. Ostensibly it was over the question of whether or not they should leave the seeming security of the undergrowth at Park Hill, but in effect it concerned the leadership of the two-man team. Famy had wanted to stay put, and was impressed by the semi-concealed basement of an old, long-gone building that McCoy had been hiding in while waiting for the Arab's arrival. The Irishman was for getting on the move immediately.

'We have to sleep somewhere tonight. We have to have some rest, and this is as good a place as any,' Famy had said.

'With the police about we have to quit, get out and fast,' had come the answer from McCoy, who was accustomed to command, was used to men reacting to his orders without hesitation and arguments. He had assessed his colleague sufficiently, felt the time of deference had died its death.

'We are completely hidden here. We would not be found.'

'All we are doing is staying inside whatever cordon they've round us. Giving them time to get organized, bring in reinforcements. It helps them, louses us. And in the morning, at first light, there'll be dogs, helicopters, the whole bloody works. They know we're here. Christ knows how, but they know it, and we have to shift our arses, and on foot, and in the dark.' McCoy was suppressing his wish to shout, turning his voice to a subdued snarl.

'But they will concentrate their efforts while they believe in their information. When they have been unsuccessful they will relax. Tomorrow it will be easier to move; we should stay till tomorrow.' The top of his cheeks were flushed red. Famy stabbed with his finger at McCoy's chest to reinforce his point.

'They don't work that way, little boy. They're bloody policemen, not soldiers. They do it by the book, solid and thorough, they don't get bored and go home to put their feet up . . .'

'You have endangered us,' Famy interrupted, unwilling to let McCoy dominate. He threw his ace card, unsure where it would take him, what dividend it would bring. 'You have risked us. And what for? So you could lie with that girl for the afternoon . . .'

'Shut your fucking mouth,' McCoy spat the words at him. Famy could not see him, just hear his breathing, feel the closeness of his body. 'Shut your face and don't open it again. And just think back a bit, over what you've done today, try and remember where they picked you up.'

The memory of the agitated diplomat on the far end of the telephone seared through Famy's mind. The sense of shame was too great for him to tell the Irishman what had happened. He was defeated.

'Where do we go?' he said. McCoy made no capital from the submission, applied no salt, and spoke with the heat gone from his voice. Silently Famy thanked him for the concession. The pivot that controlled who dominated the team had shifted – it was inevitable given the circumstances, and irreversible.

'We're going on foot into the park. There's a place near here where we can get over the wall. It's a couple of miles across. If we keep off the roads we'll be all right, and out the other side. Another couple of miles, and if we're lucky we'll get ourselves a motor.'

Famy followed as McCoy led, blindly. The truth of his situation was clear to him; without the Irishman he was doomed. He could yearn till it bled for the companionship of Dani and Bouchi, for the warmth of comradeship at the camp in Fatahland, but on his own in another continent, in a strange country, he needed the Irishman.

They blundered across the rough ground, tripping on fallen branches, stumbling in water ditches, always seeking the total black void away from the lights of cars. Once they saw the revolving blue light on the roof of a police car and flung themselves flat on the ground, and waited long after it had gone before resuming their progress. They climbed the chain-link fence that demarcated the boundary between the park and a golf club, handing over the weighted bag, one to the other, made their way across the greens and fairways till they came to another fence which shielded a neat, tended row of back gardens. They went with care over that fence, having sought out a garden into which no lights shone, and then were out in a short and rounded cul-de-sac, well illuminated by the tall sodium lights.

McCoy said, 'I'll go ahead. Twenty yards or so, and on the other side. You take the bag. That way we're not so bloody easy to notice. And go slow. Look as though you belong.'

They walked another hour and a half till they were in the wide and deserted Wandsworth High Street.

'Somewhere off here,' said McCoy. 'Out of the main stream we'll collect a motor. The new ones'll have locking devices on the wheels. We want an old one, something with a "D" or "E" or "F" after the numbers.' They were together now, the immediate threat of the police cordon far behind them.

'It was easy, as it turned out,' Famy smiled, shy, wanting to end what tension still existed between them.

'There's no way they can stand shoulder to shoulder round a town that size. All they can do is block the main routes and hope to luck. If you keep your cool you'll win.'

McCoy didn't regret the hard words of their clash. Be something wrong if we weren't at each other's throats on a caper like this. Not enough sleep, not enough food, eyes running the pavements over your bloody shoulder half the day. Less than a full day to go, and then, Holy Mother . . . the mad scramble to get clear of the sodding place. No clear escape route, not like it had been planned. Should have been sitting quietly in that attic hearing the fuzz and the politicos spouting on the radio, spieling their inanities to the goddam reporters. Should have been all ready and waiting, safe in the nest at the top of the house, stacked up there while the temperature stayed cool. And now . . . Where to go now? Where to shift to, where to lie up? . . .

One at a time, my Provie boy. Let it work itself when you get there. Get the priorities sealed up first. But this bloody carry-on is not the way you do it. You don't stand up in Crossmaglen market square and blast a para and then wonder where you'll scarper. Doesn't work that way. You plan it all out, think about it, have your watchers and your spotters and the woman who'll take the gun in her pram and the man who'll leave his back door open and the car that'll be waiting. You don't leave it to chance. Donal hadn't a route planned when he fired – seventeen and couldn't read. He'd died in the alleyway behind his house, and everyone in the section shot him, big, bloody guardsmen, and they'd laughed. Sean hadn't thought it out when he drove the bomb to Newtown Hamilton and they stopped him at the check-point. Wasn't usually one there, not on that crossroads, and he's fifteen years in the Crumlin Gaol to think on it. The bloody eejit way of getting stuffed, he'd told his men, to be out on the business without the preparation. You don't survive if you're in a hurry.

They'd expect something better of you, Ciaran McCoy, he thought. Piss themselves laughing in the boozer. Off on the big one, off on the spectacular, and no plan out. The beer would swill round their guts but there'd be no tears if the bastards shoot you, no protests if they nick you alive and lock you up the rest of your natural. Drink themselves stupid and talk and talk, and all to say that Ciaran McCoy had done a job across the water, and hadn't thought the way out. They'd hiccup and belch their way home, down the streets off the square and think: 'Stupid little bugger, and him the one that was always telling the rest.'

But there'd be no more trouble from the Arab. He saw that, the way Famy followed him, like a dog, half a step behind, frightened of disapproval. There'll be no more shouting. He'll do as he's bloody told.

Off the main roads the streets were deserted. Television had played the national anthem and was now quietened, the bed-time cocoa had been taken upstairs, the doors locked and bolted, cats shoved into the night. No-one curious of the sounds came to an upstairs window as McCoy prised open the bonnet of an ageing Ford Cortina. From his pocket he drew a packet of cigarettes and took one out. He slid his thumbnail down the join where the two ends of the paper met and brushed out the shredded tobacco, then squeezed off the filter, letting it fall into the gutter. With one hand he felt across the iron frame on the top of the engine till his fingers, guided by knowledge and experience, rested on the vital terminals. Into the gap between them he inserted the sliver of paper. Without asking he moved to Famy, took the grip from him, unzipped it and pulled out a shirt. He placed it against the triangular glass partition at the front of the driver's window, paused and then smashed his hand against the cotton. The blow was sufficiently muffled. There was no alert from those who slept in the houses around. The glass tilted on its axis. There was room for him to insert his hand down alongside the interior handle and carefully release it. When he had opened the driver's door he leaned across and freed the block on the passenger side, then motioned for Famy to take his seat. When the Arab was there, door closed and the bag on his knees, McCoy returned his attention to the engine. Again his hands moved across the greased bulk searching for the rubber, nipple-like button that he needed. When he found it he glanced again toward Famy, gave him the half-smile that meant success, and pressed. As the mechanism shook into life he eased the bonnet down and slipped into the driving seat. There was a last look up at the undisturbed drapes across the windows and he had edged the car out into the road and driven off.

He headed east, away from the policemen who shivered, bored and listless, at their roadblocks.

'Piece of bloody cake,' he muttered to himself.

'What now?' Famy asked, cautious and uncertain of the Irishman's mood.

'Get some distance behind us. About half an hour's worth, and across the river. Find somewhere off the tracks, and get some sleep. We'll need a garage when it's light where we'll get some keys to this bloody heap. Out on the other side of town where there are woods and we'll lose ourselves there for the day. We don't come back into town till the evening.'

Famy nodded. He was conscious he was being told what he needed to know, nothing more. No frills on it, no embroidery, and above all no discussion.

McCoy sensed the mood.

'Don't fret yourself, lover-boy. This is your day, not mine. I'll get you there. I'll prop you up just when the curtain rises. You think about that and leave the transportation to McCoy. Don't concern yourself with how we get there. You'll be on hand, just when you need to be, to see your man. There's a

250

lot to get through before that, but it'll come soon enough. The time won't stand back for you, it goes on its way, till it's you and your man. And don't go ballsing it on me.'

McCoy laughed, selfish and introverted. Private thoughts, not to be shared, and as they drifted along the broad empty vistas of a deserted night-laden city he sang, quietly ignoring his audience. They were songs of his movement that passed over his lips, soft, delicate, finely woven words of death, martyrdom, adulation for the fallen hero. They're all like that, he thought bitterly. Need to be stiff, cold, and shrouded before the music-men get round to you. Get their fiddles and accordions out then, when the grass is sitting on you. Not before. Don't find you the price of a pair of shoes till then. But let some bastard soldier gouge your guts out, and they'll be round the clubs, strumming and crooning your name. That's the way of the music-men. Never a song about the living, only the dead. Only the little bastard stupid enough to get in the way.

He'd walked at Donal's funeral, tramped his way far behind the family, deep in a mass of bodies and far from the army cameras and snatch squads, hidden and anonymous, and made a lone exit from the graveside while orations and epitaphs were in full flow. But they had an effect on him, those great and endless trails of silent men and women who formed the processions behind the cheap box, draped with the flag and surmounted by the black beret. He could recognize the emotional dragnet that caught him up and welded him further into the cause. When they buried one of his men there was immediate retaliation – a soldier died. It followed as inevitably as night after day. Clear, easy to understand. But the death of the Israeli – was that worth getting blasted for, put in the box, was it worth the journey, bumping on the shoulders across the long, ill-cut grass of the churchyard? Never heard of the sod, hardly knew what he looked like, one piss-poor photograph. Fat, insignificant little bugger, living on the other side of the world. Just an order, McCoy. Leave it at that, and leave the thinking to your superiors. Do as you're told, obey your orders. Somebody else's war, this one, but can't be fought unless McCoy stands in the line. Famy would die, no hesitation, but Ciaran McCoy, what would he do? How hard would he press home his attack? His mind was too tired to react to the intricacies of the problem. Shelve it. Pray Jesus that it doesn't come to that. And if it does . . . ? Think about it then.

Famy was asleep when McCoy brought the car to a halt. They were back north of the river, and the rough ground behind the flats would suit him for the two to three hours before the growing dawn and the light of the day would drive him once again to seek obscurity and a more settled hiding place to while away the hours before David Sokarev was to make his speech.

It was hours now since the planes had come. Without warning, the sound of their vast thrusting engines left far behind as they swooped over the hills, flying the contours of the ground, hurtling towards the plotted co-ordinates of a map reference. Young men, expert and trained in the sunshine of far-away Arizona till they could handle the multi-million dollar complexities of the Phantom cockpit, straining with their eyes for the criss-cross of wheel tracks on the sand five hundred feet beneath them, then searching for discreet, camouflaged outlines of the tents before they let loose the awkward torpedo-shaped cannisters containing the petroleum jelly that had been given by a nameless scientist the title of 'napalm'. The pilots carried their planes away toward the next target that had been designated, and so did not see where the cannisters landed. The navigator would twist his body – difficult in the all-encompassing, padded-out 'G' suit – but he too would recognize only the column of thick black smoke and have no knowledge whether the mission had been successful or not.

The leader of the General Command was in his tent. The stubbled, worn face resting on his clenched hands. There was a candle held upright in a Pepsi Cola bottle, on the same table where he leaned his elbows. The light faded and rose, at the whim of the cool night that eddied through the flap on the tent, finding the flame and bending and brushing it. It was a time that he loathed and detested, a time when he was helpless and unable to hit back. Four men dead, burned beyond recognition, life cut short as they had screamed. And the technology of his enemy, his speed and his knowledge, took him far away from the puny retaliation possible to the men on the ground. Nothing, only the oaths and obscenities shouted into the dirt as they had lain in the fragile cover between the rocks and waited for the echoing noise to pass. And the men who had died, buried already, not deep down – the parched ground prevented that – but hurried into shallow pits at dusk.

His subordinates, recognizing the signs that he wished to be alone had left him when he had retired to the tent. Others would care for the morale of the young men who had filed past the bodies, would take care that the sight fanned their hatred of the enemy across the border. There was a solitary piece of paper on his table brought by the journalist from Beirut, who had visited and left before the arrival of the jets. He had read it over and over again, keeping the information even from his closest colleagues, savouring among the disaster and horror of the day the news that it carried. The one they called Saleh Mohammed was there, on target and meeting his rendezvous contact. The best boy that he had, the one he had willed to survive.

It would devastate them, he knew that. A plan of such detail and skill that he had hugged and kissed the shy bespectacled recruit who had worked on its conception, not a youth who could go himself across the border, the right claw foot controlled that, but one with brains and with foresight and who had talked not just of the operation but of its consequences, its wounding potential to the state of Israel. It would hurt them, twist behind the nation's rib cage . . .

The old man who acted as his bodyguard came noiselessly into the tent.

'Some food for you, Ahmed. It is time to eat. One cannot sit and starve and grieve.' He was the only one in the camp who would call the leader by his given name. It went back a long time, eight years. They had held the house together at Karameh when the Israelis had swarmed in brigade strength into the refugee village beside the river Jordan ten months after the Six Day War. It should have been so easy for them, but for the first time the Palestinians had stood and fought. The cynics said it was because they had been left no escape route. There was truth in that, but for once the *fedayeen* had not thrown down their guns and surrendered. There had been mourning in Israel when the casualty figures were announced, more than twenty dead, more than seventy wounded. There had been dancing in Amman as the captured Centurion armour was driven in triumph through the ancient, winding hill-streets, and among the Palestinians there had been much to remember and heady praise and the start of resistance. The hours in the wrecked building, hammered by the tanks and hitting back with the rocket launchers and the Kalashnikovs, had forged the bond between the two men, one a leader and the other a follower. The relationship had not changed. It was acceptable, and the old man knew when he was required.

He put the plate in front of the leader. A mess of beans and rice and sauce with lamb's meat cut in small squares.

'They have had their day, the Israelis. We will have ours. There is no sudden way to victory,' said the old man.

'What they have accomplished against us is a mere nothing to the blow that awaits them.' The old man was rarely taken into the leader's inner confidence. He said nothing and arranged a spoon and fork alongside the plate in front of the sitting man. 'Within the next hours, perhaps as long as two days,' the leader went on, 'we shall hit them so that they yelp like dogs.'

'Across the border? With a burden of sadness. He knew the risks, had cleared too many bundles of the possessions left behind by the suicide squads.

'Across many borders. Far from here. Bouchi, Dani and the third one, you remember? They went to Europe. Bouchi and Dani are dead, the other alone has gone through. He is on course, on target. Today or tomorrow he will move, and then the world will know of him.' He spoke the words hurriedly, interspersing them with pauses as he scooped up the food from the plate, cramming it without finesse into his mouth. He did not look at the man that stood behind him. When the plate was cleared he sat back in his chair and addressed himself to the empty screen of canvas to his front.

'His target is David Sokarev. Of the utmost importance to them, but a man of whom you will never have heard. He is from the world of science, of the very fundamentals of science. He concerns himself with the structure of the atom, and with the breaking of the atom, and with the release of its energies. They are jealous of their anonymity, these men, they do not seek to be answerable to their fellow species. They hide themselves away like slugs underneath wet rocks. It is rare for them to emerge into the open light, but Sokarev has come out. To London. That is where we will meet him, and will kill him.'

The old man watched as the leader turned toward him. He saw the excitement in the eyes, deep and brown and shadowed in their sockets. Not since they had waited for news of the raid into Kiryat Shmona when the orders had been to eliminate as many of the enemy as were within range of the guns, men or women or children, had the old man seen a similar look – the fanatic awaiting his fulfilment.

'Eight bombs they have, perhaps nine by now,' the leader went on staring into the other's face, the voice quavering on the verge of self-control. 'Not big – the size of Hiroshima and Nagasaki. In a city they would kill ninety thousand, up to one hundred thousand. Suck the air from their lungs, burn the bodies of our people, blind them, maim them, infect them so that those that live from their breeding would produce grotesque mutations. They would not make what their American allies call the "clean bomb". They will not waste effort and expense on such refinements. It will be a weapon of filth and of poison, and it is their ultimate defence. They hide behind it in the knowledge that the very mystery of its existence gives them strength. The man that we will shoot is the man who has created this bomb, loved it, succoured it, spent his working life refining the effectiveness of its yield.'

'And when he is dead, what will have changed?' said the old man.

'It will take the elimination of Sokarev to awake the world to the Israeli power. When he is dead and the news has been carried from continent to continent the world will wonder why the Palestinian people have chosen to exact retribution on one who seemed so mild, so harmless. And we will tell them why he was chosen, we will tell them of Dimona, of the plutonium schemes, of the reactors there. And with their knowledge so too will come their fears. Fears of a mushroom cloud settling the "Middle East problem", as they call it, fears of an annihilation more ghastly than the world has experienced since

257

its cleverer men developed this horror. All the world will be talking about the bomb of the Israelis, not just the peasant peoples but in the embassies and the chancelleries and the senates and the palaces. There will be demands for inspections and controls – the Americans will want that if only to silence their critics. If their bomb is muzzled their ultimate defence is taken from them, and then they are weak, then they can be beaten. All their men are replaceable. Dayan was replaceable, and Sharon of the Canal, and Rabin, and Eban, and Peres, all have others who wait to take their places. Sokarev, too. Other scientists can move behind his desk, but nothing can replace the bomb. It is final, the complete answer to their defensive strategy when future war goes against them. If it happens as we believe it will, if the governments of the world demand to know of this weapon, exercise control over it, then ultimately Israel will lose and go down stripped of her last and most powerful weapon of defence. That is why we will kill Sokarev.'

The old man ran his fingernails across the bristle of his chin, pondered, his brows lined with deep confusion.

The leader smiled like a man who has outlined to his friends his plans for the conquest of a woman they all consider beyond reach. The older man had not heard him talk in that way before.

'It is strange,' he said quietly, 'how the death of a man can move the world more than the life he has so long striven to perfect.'

He let himself out of the tent, taking the plate with him, and was gone, moving his way with familiarity across the sand, bypassing the ropes that held the tents. The night was very clear, a slight moon and the endless abyss of stars.

The leader snuffed out the candle with his thumb and forefinger, and stripped off his denim coat and trousers. He felt his way across to the narrow canvas bed and edged his body under the single blanket that he allowed himself. He had no difficulty in finding sleep. The images of the four burned carcases had long since passed, and he dreamed of the small, sad-faced man whose picture he had seen. And the face dissolved into terror, and there was a gun blotting out the picture, and he could hear the man's scream and then the staccato roar of the automatic rifle.

Beyond his canvas walls the camp was quiet. Only the shuffling movement of the sentries and, at the village a mile away, a dog calling for its bitch.

It was past three on the Tuesday morning when Jimmy returned to his flat. He had been conscientious enough, nothing to drink, and he had made his calls. He had been to Leconfield House and reported back to Jones, he'd returned to the hotel and seen that Sokarev was in his bed. For half an hour he had padded round the hotel checking the fire doors to convince himself they were closed to outside entry, satisfying himself that the Branch men were in position. He had spoken briefly to the Israeli who was sitting up; the one called Elkin. The other slept noisily in the bed close to where they had talked in whispers. The connecting door to the scientist's room was open, and the Uzi lay on the bed beside them. They talked inanities, Jimmy cheerfully, and Elkin with caution, as if unsure of himself with the strange man. Jimmy had said he'd be back by early morning

259

and repeated that under no circumstances were there to be visitors allowed to see Sokarev or that the man under threat should be permitted to leave his room.

There was a Branch man in the corridor outside the room, another beside the lift-shaft, two more in the ground-floor lobby of the hotel. Too many for them, thought Jimmy, hopeless for the opposition. It relaxed him enough for him to wander out of the front door easy in his mind that no harm could come to his charge during the night.

From the hotel he drove south and west for twenty minutes till he reached Richmond. The roadblocks were in position still, searching the cars travelling in the other direction. He found the police station easily enough, in a side street close to the bridge where the scent of the low water river drifted up to him. It was a chill, damp night, and he hurried from the car across the parking area at the back of the station to the rear door. There was a bustle of activity there, an ants' nest into which a spade had pitched.

In more normal times there would have been three, perhaps four officers on duty, whiling away the darkness and waiting for their reliefs to come in. Instead the lights were on, blazing throughout the building; corridors were noisy with hurrying men – some in uniform and some in plain clothes; teleprinters chattered messages to and from Scotland Yard; telephones rang. At the front-hall desk Jimmy showed his identification card, and watched as the bored features of the sergeant who looked at it awoke with interest. He was ushered up two flights of stairs and shown the open door of an office where a group of men sat round a table. The air was heavy with tobacco, the flat surfaces littered with maps and plastic coffee beakers.

The senior officers didn't waste Jimmy's time. He was grateful for that. They explained what they had done, in what they were currently involved, what they planned for the morning. It was thorough and painstaking, and left nothing out. They showed him where they had already searched, where their road-blocks were in force, where their patrols, foot and mobile, were operating, the locations of the houses they planned to raid at first light. But he could read the answer he was looking for in their drawn, humourless faces. There was none of the anticipation that catches hold of a huntsman's eyes when he thinks he is closing on his goal. It was routine, good routine, and that he conceded, but there was in-sufficient material for them to go on, and they knew it, and understood that for them to catch the men whose descriptions were plastered across the district they would need extraordinary luck. Policemen don't expect luck, don't count on it, Jimmy knew that. He sensed that for all the effort being put into the search there were few in the room in which he sat who expected that the night would be crowned by success.

As he drove back to the flat he could reflect that it had not been a totally wasted journey. Jimmy liked to know where he stood and the monotone description of the police action in the town had provided him with the information he sought. They were loose again, the two little bastards. Free and with their guns and with a plan and inching their way closer to the target. They had two full days in which to launch their attack. When they're that close, Jimmy boy, then they have to be in with a chance. No doubt about that. You're enjoying it, you little bugger, he said to himself, it's the way you would have wanted it. You'd have crapped yourself if they'd been picked up, and you'd had to hand the PPK in, unsoiled and unused. Nobody likes a fox that won't run, that goes to earth too fast, and you, you're looking for a good long ride and a good kill at the end.

He let himself into the flat, took off his shoes by the door and tiptoed into the bedroom. Helen was there, scarcely covered by the sheets, arms and legs heaved apart in the abandon of sleep. Not a stitch on her, poor girl. Destined for disappointment again. He undressed, letting his clothes mingle on the carpet with hers, and eased his way on to the bed, careful not to wake her. Something in his presence must have aroused the girl. She hooked an arm across his waist, feeling out the crevice underneath his armpit, but she did not waken, and Jimmy lay still till sleep came to him too.

He never found it difficult, not even on the nights before he might shoot or be shot at, or when another man's life might rest on his wits and alertness. There was no tension. Killing was not important to Jimmy, which was why the sleep came to him fast, which was why Jones championed him, and why the Director General tolerated his presence on the payroll.

Chapter Fourteen

It was the cold that woke Famy. He had been in a half-sleep, tossing under his coat in the back seat of the car searching for warmth, wriggling to escape the chill that had settled on his body and gnawed its way beneath the light cotton of his clothes. For a few moments he could not place where he was as he stared up at the roof of the car, then swung his head up to peer through the window. There was a noise, but far away, the sound of children shrieking to each other, the revving of starting cars. Beyond the glass he saw the tired untidy shapes of the tower flats, grey and streaked from years of exposure to the weather, soaring up in composite and identical rows to high beyond his view. There was a woman there shouting into the void instructions to a man going to his work. Between the flats and his own position were the lines of prefabricated garages, and then nearer still seven feet of chain-wire fence, buckled and bent where children had scaled it. To the far side of the rough, broken ground where the car was parked was another fence and beyond that a railway line. There were other cars alongside, but different from the Cortina, without bonnets, without tyres, wheels even, doors gaping open, deserted as useless and too complicated to dispose of.

Famy stretched to see over the back of the seat, anticipating the huddled shape of McCoy prone across the width of the car. It hit him a cruel, winding, sledge-hammer blow. The emptiness that he saw. He rose on the back seat, jerking his sleep-stiff limbs forward searching for confirmation as the messages raced through his brain. Two seats, gear handle, steering wheel, dashboard, nothing else. The sweat started to run. He peered again through the windows, turned round in all directions, before sagging down upright on the seat. With a quick movement he felt for the grip-bag and ran his fingers over the outside till they rested on the hard shape of the rifles. The guns were there, but where was the bastard Irishman?

The argument and the hard words of the previous evening came back to him, and the long silences as they had walked and then driven through London. You cannot trust any but your own, he should have known that. Putting trust in a stranger, one whose involvement was no more than partial, it had been madness. Famy felt a great exhaustion sweeping across him. On his own how could he go forward? Was it possible to continue by himself? He started to cry. He had no strength to fight the tears, interrupt their path to the stiffness of his collar. He had not wept for many years, not since his youngest sister had died at the age of a few days in the front room of the bungalow in Nablus. But he had been only a boy then, and since adulthood he'd prided himself on his ability to keep his emotions tight and controlled. But that the Irishman had left him asleep and defenceless, betrayed him, made an escape without having the courage to face him directly . . . that was a total wound, painful and throbbing.

He opened the door of the car and eased himself out. His watch showed past eight and the sun was coming high from behind the flats, casting great shadows and playing patterns on the weeds that grew unchecked on the open ground. He walked warily away from the vehicle taking in his surroundings till he came to the opened gateway which led to the made-up road and further away to the lines of sand-brick, terraced houses that lay behind the long tin fence. There were more people there, none concerning themselves with the tall young figure who watched them. As his eyes played on the short horizon of chimney tops and television aerials it took him little effort to realize that he had no knowledge of his whereabouts. They had driven a long way since crossing the bridge, he had known that as he jolted in the seat with the motion of the car. Then he remembered the *A to Z* street guide he had bought, that had stayed in the grip, and he looked for a street name that would help him to identify his location. It would be at the far end of the line of houses, where the junction was. But there were too many people out on the pavements readying themselves for work and school and shopping. Later they would be gone, and that would be the time to walk the whole length of the street to find its name.

By the time he turned on his heel and drifted slowly back toward the car his mind was made up. There was no possibility that he could follow the path of abject defeat taken by the Irishman. When the men of the General Command went across the enemy's border there was no retreat if they were cut off and surrounded short of their target. They stood and fought and died where they were trapped. Few returned to receive the adulation of their comrades after a successful mission, none returned to admit failure. Failure and surrender were the cancer growths in a movement such as his; despair would be close behind, and hopelessness, and then the victory for the enemy. If we lose our courage, he thought, we can lay down our rifles, fold away the denim fatigues and go back to ploughing the fields of Lebanon and Jordan; we will never see the hills of Nablus and the groves of Haifa.

There was a poem he had read in Beirut, written after the degradation of the Six Day War. One verse alone remained in his mind, clear and without complication.

> People may be divided into two classes, those
>   who grin
> Vacant and lopsidedly,
> Who've given in,
> And the rest of us who grin
> To prove he isn't there,
> The worm within.

It would be a sentence of death to go on. A conscious and measured decision. But it had been so for his brothers at Beisan, or on the sea front of Tel Aviv, or at Nahariya. They had stayed to die, had accepted its inevitability. He felt a great calmness after his mind was concentrated. The tears ceased to roll on his face, and deep in his belly the tightness had gone.

There would be no insinuating, creeping rottenness, no worm.

Mackowicz did not inform David Sokarev that a visitor had arrived at the hotel expecting to take breakfast with the scientist. He was left in his room playing with the toast and the little packets of butter and the plastic marmalade jars, unaware of the heated dispute being fought out in the lobby. When the tall, white-haired, upright figure of Sir Humphrey Talbot, Fellow of the Royal Society, glasses half-moon and far down the bridge of his nose, had come to the reception desk and asked for the Israeli's room number a Special Branch man had folded the newspaper he had been reading and walked to Sir Humphrey's shoulder, indicating to the girl behind the desk the information should not be given.

'Can I help you, sir?' His voice was pitched low, inaudible to the other guests who milled about the counter handing in keys, seeking directions, writing travellers' cheques.

'I don't think so.' He turned back toward the girl. 'Young lady, I was asking you the room number where Professor Sokarev is staying.'

'He's not taking visitors, sir,' said the detective.

'And who might you be?' snapped the other man, already in poor humour at the frustration of the delay, coupled with the early hour he had risen in order to travel from his home in Cambridge to keep the appointment.

'Detective Sergeant Harvey, Special Branch, Scotland Yard. I'm afraid the Professor is not able to see anyone this morning. It's a very clear instruction we've had, sir. I hope you haven't been inconvenienced.'

'Of course I've been inconvenienced. I've come up from the country to see the man. I have a letter from him inviting me.' Sir Humphrey reached into his faded leather briefcase, riffled through the papers, and with a look of triumph on his face produced a single-page letter. 'There, read that. Very simple, I would have thought. Clearly typed and with his signature at the bottom, on headed paper from Dimona.'

The detective read it through, motioned for the visitor to wait, and picked up a house phone. He spoke quickly and out of Sir Humphrey's earshot, put the receiver down and came back to Sir Humphrey's side.

'One of the Professor's colleagues will be down to see you directly, sir. To explain the position.'

'But he's travelling on his own. It says so in the letter . . .'

'I think you will find that things have changed somewhat, sir, in the last few hours. Have you seen a newspaper this morning?'

'Of course I haven't. Not read one anyway – just glanced. Been travelling, haven't I?'

'If you had, perhaps it would be clearer to you, sir.'

The lift door opened and Mackowicz emerged. His jacket had been hurriedly put on, tangling with his shirt collar. At least he's hiding his shoulder holster, bloody cowboy, thought the detective. Might have shaved by this time in the morning. Mackowicz read the letter, and handed it back.

'I regret that your journey has been unnecessary.

268

Professor Sokarev is receiving no visitors before his speech this evening. I'm sorry.'

Sir Humphrey's voice rose in anger. 'But this is absolutely ridiculous, damned ridiculous. I've travelled half-way across southern England to get here at the Professor's invitation, and you, without even the courtesy of introducing yourself, tell me I shouldn't have come. What sort of nonsense is this?'

'My name is Mackowicz, I am with the Professor's party. I can only repeat my apologies that you were not forewarned by our embassy that it would be impossible for Professor Sokarev to keep his appointment with you.'

'I demand to speak to him on the telephone. He's an old friend.'

'That, too, I am afraid, will not be possible. He is taking no calls. I am sorry, sir.'

Sir Humphrey was not used to being spoken to in such a way. He was accustomed to deference, a smoothing of his way. He was uncertain how to react toward the young man with his open shirt, casual leather jacket and a day's growth on his chin, who met his gaze so unswervingly.

'Well, when in heaven's name will I be able to see him?'

'Are you going to the Professor's speech this evening?'

'Of course I'm going. I'm chairing the damned thing.'

'There will be an opportunity then,' said Mackowicz. 'I see from the Professor's letter that he was expecting you to drive him to his speech this evening. That, too, I am afraid, has been changed.

But at the university you will have an opportunity to meet with him and talk.'

'And perhaps you would be so kind as to inform me the reason for this lunatic carry-on?'

The detective sergeant handed him a morning paper. 'You seem not to have taken in the news, sir. Perhaps that will help you to understand our problems . . .'

'Of course I've seen the headlines, but you're not for a moment considering that I pose a threat to . . . ?'

Mackowicz cut him off. 'Because of the situation it has been decided that the Professor will receive no visitors. There are no exceptions.' He went back to the lift and disappeared. Flushed with embarrassment, Sir Humphrey walked to the door and the Special Branch officer settled again in his chair, moulding into the background, inconspicuous and unnoticed.

Four floors above, Sokarev had finished with his breakfast, and paced dejectedly about the room. Elkin was now asleep and Mackowicz made poor company. More than an hour to go before the typist came from the embassy to take the dictation of his speech, but that at least would distract him from the company of the young men and their sub-machine-guns and radios and who shuffled about with their fixed, humourless stares. The speech would take the morning to prepare, and after that perhaps he could sleep. There would be many distinguished men of learning to hear him in the evening, and he wished to be at his best and most incisive. An afternoon rest would help.

*   *   *

Jimmy slept late, deep in a meaningless dream that involved images of the countryside, hedgerows, overgrown fields and the animals who made their homes there. He fought to retain it against the increasing competition of the daylight that surged through the window, curtains not drawn. Silly bitch, he thought, when he woke up, always leaves them open, probably undresses there as well, right in front of the glass, handing out orgasms to half Holborn.

He hadn't noticed it when he'd come back to the flat. Stayed up too long. Too much talking with Jones before going to the hotel and to Richmond. Bloody man didn't seem to want him to go. Wants to be loved, Jimmy could see that, lonely boss-man with all the chaos piling up on his desk and having to rely on someone else to steer him through it. Jones under strain, talking more than he usually did, fidgeting with his pipe and pulling at the skin at the graft points below his mouth, reddening and irritating the lines. And he'd wished him luck when Jimmy went on his way. Never done that before. It had been a bit ridiculous, a sort of paternal send-off, and Jimmy not three years younger and as much in his twilight as the other man.

The girl was still sleeping. One of them always was – it seemed the most consistent fact about their life together. They laughed about it to each other, and cursed privately. She looked good, always did when she was asleep, and too vulnerable to be woken. She'd be late already for the dingy room where she spent her days sandwiched between Jones's office and the corridor. He wouldn't wake her yet – Jones could wait. It wouldn't do any harm, slave labour he had from the girl. Jimmy told her that often enough, and she ignored him. Jones could get impatient for one morning, wouldn't take her so much for granted.

He reached across her prone form, careful not to disturb her and deny to the girl the deep relaxation of sleep that showed in the way her mouth had drifted open, awkward but at peace, too many teeth showing. Not at your best, sweetheart. There were lines beside her lips, alongside her eyes, under her chin, that in a few hours would be camouflaged by the cosmetics. Jimmy wasn't concerned with that; the rivulets of age that were forming on her features caused him no dismay.

From the bedside table he lifted the telephone receiver and dialled the number of the hotel where Sokarev was staying. When it was connected to the top-floor rooms where the Israelis were encamped Jimmy recognized Elkin's voice, softer and more conciliatory than the other bastard's. He sounded cheerful, said they'd had an uneventful night, that their charge had woken, taken his breakfast and was now working on his speech for the evening.

'And no visitors, under any circumstances, right?' Jimmy said.

'That is the instruction. A guy came and wanted to see him, a scientist. Mack dealt with it. He was a bit bothered, but left.'

Jimmy shuddered at the prospect. He could imagine the tact that Mackowicz would have employed to make his point.

He said, 'I'll be down quite soon. A few things to sort out, but it'll be before lunch, and for God's sake no room service or anything sent up from the kitchens direct to the room. If he wants something

272

he'll either have to do without or you get it yourselves.'

'There's enough of your police outside the door to
serve a banquet, cook it, and wash the dishes afterwards.'

'Don't worry about them. They're there to make
up the numbers, make the circus look good. Do it
yourself. I'll be there round about twelve.'

Jimmy crawled out of his bed and made for
the bathroom out through the door and across the
corridor. There wasn't much else of the flat, just a
kitchen. Bachelor Towers, and he wanted it that way.
He needed someone like Helen to visit, once or twice
a week, and clean the place up while she was waiting
for him. But not to live there, they'd be on top of
each other, arguing, pulling hair out, claustrophobic.
It was not a bad arrangement. Gave each sufficient
companionship, and the minimum of commitment.
Those in the department who knew them both and
who knew of the limitations of the arrangement
put the bond down to a mutual passed-over loneliness. Jimmy would have denied that, perhaps
violently. Helen would have smiled and changed
the conversation. It was generally agreed among
their friends that neither allowed the relationship to
impair their individual effectiveness at the department.

After he'd shaved and scrubbed with his tooth-
brush to eradicate the taste of last night's cigarettes,
he dressed. He did it slowly and with thought, as if
getting himself prepared for an important engagement, an interview for a new job, an evening out
with a girlfriend. But it was the clothes themselves
that let him down. His trousers were heavily creased,

not just at the seams down his legs but all over, a legacy of the night-time hours that they had lain crumpled on the carpet after he had kicked them off. The shirt that he chose was clean, not worn yesterday, but it had been on his back for many other days before that and the collar showed the frayed outline where the cotton had rubbed worn against the unshaven bristles on his neck. A button was missing, but would be hidden by his tie. The socks too were clean, unholed, perfect, and he could smile quietly and secretly to himself as he pulled them on. Three pairs he'd bought, one of his few concessions to the semi-domestication Helen had tried to enforce on him. Beside the bed were his shoes, brown and lace-ups. The toes were scuffed and needed the attention of polish and a duster. He pulled the handkerchief from his trouser pocket, checked to see that Helen was still asleep, and then rubbed the white cloth square hard across the leatherwork. She'd seen him do that once and screamed a protest. His habits hadn't changed; only now he employed discretion.

From the drawer of the table on which the telephone stood he took the pistol he had drawn from Leconfield House, and the shoulder holster apparatus that was his own. The holster, of strengthened black plastic, fitted across his upper back and chest like a carthorse harness. It had been made to fit, and until he placed the gun itself in the pouch provided he was hardly aware of the straps that looped round his arms and across his back. But the gun gave the holster a weight and presence. His jacket hung across the chair he had draped it over, and when that was worn the PPK and its props were decisively hidden. Same tie as yesterday – RAF Escapers Club. Nothing dramatic for the motif, just a pelican bird, and not many who would pass Jimmy on the street would know its meaning.

He shook her shoulder, gently and with a kindness that few who knew him casually would have guessed he possessed.

'Wake up, girl, time to be on our way.'

'What time is it?' She said it sleepily, resisting the intrusion, eyes squinting into the sudden light.

'Bit after nine.'

'You pig!' she shouted, scrambling from the warm security of the bedclothes.

'It's a beautiful sight to start the day with.' Jimmy was laughing as she struggled to cover her thighs and breasts with the scraps of lace and nylon that she scooped from the chair near her side of the bed.

'You're a pig, Jimmy. A mean, miserable pig. All bloody dressed yourself, and not calling me. Jones'll be off his rocker when I drift in at this time.' She wriggled her long legs into the trousers she had used the day before. Jimmy didn't like her keeping spare clothes at the flat, so what she arrived in the previous night she went out with the next morning.

'Won't do him any harm. Let him sweat a bit,' Jimmy said.

She said nothing else, fiercely concentrating on her dressing and then the attack on her face in front of the mirror. Hunched over it, eyes intent on the reflection as she worked the pencils and brushes around her eyes. The lipstick she put on with a bravado that ensured disaster. There was a low oath, in a pitch she seldom used, as she tidied the indulgence with a flick of the Kleenex tissue that had remained overnight on the dressing table.

'Are you coming down to the speech tonight?' Jimmy asked as they stood on the pavement beside her Maxi car.

'Only if I'm needed. I don't want to be there just to rubberneck. I don't know whether Jones is going.'

'I'd like you to come, might want the car there. If I've one from the department I'm saddled with the damned thing. If you come, slot in behind the convoy and when we've dumped the little bugger back in his bed we can shove off somewhere. I can call you later on.'

'There can't be much chance of Jones going. He may want to be at the Yard, or by his phone, but it's not like him just to be there if there's no purpose to it. There's enough of the thickies, you included, lined up for the evening without him shoving in and getting in the way.'

'Whether he comes or not I'd like you to be there with the car.'

She unlocked the driving door and sat far back into the seat. As she fastened the safety belt across her chest she said quietly and with a suspicion of mockery, 'Want me to see the hero boy in action? Roy of the Rovers defies Amazing Odds. Triumph of Virtue. Good wins through. That it?'

When it came to needling Jimmy she was the great expert.

'Bugger off to your boring office,' he shouted. 'I'll call you, and I want you there. If you want a bloody meal on the house, that is.'

The car was away and lost in the traffic, leaving

Jimmy searching the street for a black cab. They were not easy to find in the final throes of the capital's rush-hour, and he paced impatiently for a full fifteen minutes before he could hail one and then sprint a weaving path between the oncoming cars to the other side of the road where the driver waited for him.

When they were on the move Jimmy sagged deep into the seat, half-aware of the scurrying masses going about their business beyond the Perspex. This was the ideal guerrilla country, the perfect territory on which to wage the sharp and cruel form of warfare that the enemy had perfected. Thousands of faces were swept past his vision from the window, their preoccupation with their own affairs total, their knowledge of the threat minuscule. The perfect, unnoticing hiding ground, where anonymity remains a virtue. In this huge, ant-like society what hope could there ever be of selecting out just two who were different from the rest by the virtue of the fact that they had declared hostilities? Where to find them – where to start to look?

There can only be one killing ground. The one right beside David Sokarev. Not ten yards from him, or even five, but right up against his shoulder. Jimmy felt no sense of fear at the prospect of physical injury. What screwed up his guts was the possibility of failure. It always dogged him, that horror. That he would end up the ultimate loser. He could picture the little man with the blood and the surprise in his face, and the look of betrayal that would dominate his eyes. That would be the awfulness for Jimmy. The unmentionable and unspeakable disaster, if he lost Sokarev.

By the time he reached the hotel where he would spend the rest of the day before leaving for the Senate House, the very image of failure and the chance of it that had crossed his mind had rendered him irritable and tensed.

From where he crouched inside the small car Famy saw McCoy appear round the corner from the street and walk warily towards their hiding place. Twice he looked behind, to satisfy himself he was not under surveillance. He jogged the last ten yards to the car.

Under his arm was a brown paper bag, and he reached inside his pocket on the left of his trousers when he reached the window through which Famy stared at him. McCoy took in the numbed astonishment in the other's face, and the sad, emotion-drained look in his mouth.

'I've got the keys. No problem, an old fool in a garage up the road, spilled him a yarn and had them straight away. Got the whole bunch and said I'd return them later. Piece of cake. I've got the gloves we need for the window, too, motorcycle sort with protection half-way up the arm. Made of leather and bloody expensive. Hope your mob are good on expenses.'

He laughed, then let the humour dissolve as Famy's face failed to react.

'What's the matter?' McCoy said. 'You look like someone's just parachuted you into bloody Jerusalem.'

'I thought you'd gone,' Famy whispered, frightened of the words, but with no option but to speak them.

' 'Course I'd bloody gone,' said McCoy. 'I told you last night we'd need the keys. You said we'd need gloves. What's special about that?'

'I thought you'd gone for all time. That you were not coming back.'

McCoy spat back at him, 'How many times do I have to fucking-well tell you? We're in this to-gether. I've told you that. For once in your suspicious miserable life try believing what you're told.'

He stomped round the car, angry, kicking at a tin and clattering it away across the stones and debris of the site. Famy climbed out of the car.

'I'm sorry,' he said. 'It was shameful to doubt you. I am abject to you.' He paused, letting the seconds of confrontation flitter away. 'How do we spend the rest of the day?'

McCoy nodded. He had the imagination to feel the Arab's sentiments on waking in the empty car.

'I should have woken you. Forget it now. We stay for the rest of the day. It's as good as anywhere. We'll go direct from here to the Senate. No sense in just moving about unnecessarily. What we need now is some sleep. I don't want to be yawning and look-ing for my bed tonight.'

The few tourists who had gathered on the pavement across the road were unaware of the identity of the man who stepped from the black Humber car and hurried into the extended and tranquil-lit hallway of 10 Downing Street. No better informed was the police constable on the door, nor the morning-suited usher who glanced from the proffered card to the book listing the day's appointments of the Prime Minister, and matched the printed name on the card he had been given with the typed list that rested on the lobby table.

The Director General was taken by lift to the flat on the top floor that the country's senior politician had turned into a miniature home when pressure of work prevented him from using his more substantial town house. It was well known that the Prime Minister's wife disliked having her living rooms trampled on by Civil Servants and Members of Parliament and visiting delegations, and so when her husband had early business to conduct he 'slept over the shop' as he delighted to tell those who called on him at the start of his day.

He was at breakfast, but immaculate and ready to present a public face, the absence of a jacket to cover his waistcoat his only concession to informality. As he pushed the marmalade onto his squares of toast he motioned to the Head of the Security Services to take a chair opposite and pushed in his direction the china coffee jug.

'I've seen the Home Secretary this morning,' the Prime Minister said. 'He's told me what the police are doing concerning the Professor and his problems. I wanted to know your feelings about the affair as we go into these crucial hours. No minutes to be kept or anything like that, just your opinions and what your own department's state of readiness is. That sort of thing.'

The memoir business into which political leaders entered with such enthusiasm on retirement was sufficient to keep the Director General on his guard. He regarded the Prime Minister's request for information as legitimate, but saw no need to expand at too great length.

He chose a cautious path, describing what the other man would already know. He started with the police operation at the hotel, listed the precautions that would be taken to transport Sokarev across the city. Official-style decoy car driving from the hotel at high speed, while the target left via the kitchens in a closed police van, switching to a more formal type of transport in the concealed yard of Tottenham Court Road police station before arriving at a normally locked side entrance at the university main building. He spoke of the scale of the escort that would be used during the transit period, and also of the numbers of men on guard at the building and of the search procedures that had been adopted inside and outside the hall where Sokarev was to speak. He mentioned the gelignite-sniffer labradors, and the metal detectors that plain-clothes troops had employed before the room was sealed the previous night. He talked of the police liaison with his own department that had been set up. He went into the degree to which invitation holders to the lecture had been vetted, and lingered for a moment on the problems of body searches without giving offence to the members of some of the most learned institutions of the country. He touched on the convoy and the protection screen that would be used to return the professor to his hotel. And then he stopped and waited for the Prime Minister's questions. They were not slow in following.

'Well, that covers the police side of things. Everything in fact that the Secretary of State told me. What are you doing?'

The Director General was in no hurry. His long

pauses could be infuriating and he knew it, but did nothing to alter the pace at which he delivered his answers.

'I have the men who head the various departments involved in constant meetings, and they have a liaison line to Scotland Yard. We have endeavoured to provide the Metropolitan force with all information, relevant information, that is at our disposal.'

'Do you have a man on the ground with Sokarev?'

'I have a man right beside him. He is my direct liaison with the police protection force and with the Israeli Foreign Ministry protection team that is accompanying Sokarev.'

'What sort of man?'

'Experienced,' said the Director General.

'Experienced in what? Running an office, liaison, Arab affairs?'

'He's a marksman.' The Prime Minister stopped, swinging his head from the window to stare directly at the DG. A piece of toast remained uneaten, half an inch from his mouth.

'There are enough police there for that, surely? I would have thought that you would have put a senior man with liaison capabilities rather than a gunman.'

The Director General was patient, leading a small boy through an alegbraic problem that he might one day answer, but not in this school year.

'I have placed a "gunman", as you describe him, alongside Sokarev because the greatest risk to the life of our guest is close-range shooting. The man I have there is far in advance of anything the Metropolitan Police can provide. He will not be taking a subordinate role in this day's movements . . .'

'It would seem,' said the Prime Minister, 'from the way you have dispensed your priorities that you regard an act of violence as a major possibility.'

For the first time since he had sat down the DG poured himself a cup of now lukewarm coffee. Before he began to drink it he said, 'Considering the known opposition I regard it as inevitable.'

Chapter Fifteen

As David Sokarev walked through the door of the lecture room in the Senate building of London University he came unnoticed. He was late, and the attention of the three hundred men who made their living from the study of nuclear physics had long since been diverted from the huddle of plain-clothes policemen with their bulging suits who blocked the only entrance.

He was close to half-way down the side of the room and heading toward the table adorned only with a stand microphone and a glass water jug sitting on a tray between four glasses when those he had passed reacted to the short figure in the grey suit who shuffled past them, hemmed in like a convict by the taller and more heavily-set body-guards who jockeyed for space at his side. There were few who had come to listen who had not read their morning papers, listened to radio news broadcasts or watched a television news bulletin. All day the headlines had blared the information that a major terrorist plot existed with the sole purpose of assassinating the scientist now making his way the length of the room. Those who first recognized him, from the pictures they had seen in the last few hours, or who had met him in the past, rose from their seats and began to clap. Within seconds the entire room had taken their cue from those who had initiated the applause. The noise spilled into a cheer, self-conscious at first, the men used to working in silence and unaccustomed to venting their thoughts in such public manner. Those that were close enough saw the sad eyes of Sokarev, saw his tongue run with anxiety over his lips seeking to moisten their desert dryness. Perhaps the acclamation confused him, but as he turned to look behind to gauge the size of the room his feet became entangled and he pitched forward a few inches before one of the many hands of the men who surrounded him arrested his stumble.

By the time he reached the top table everyone in the room, excepting the security men, was standing pulping their palms together in a concerted gesture of solidarity. The smile that dawned on his face was one of helpless gratitude. He tried not to look as they beamed and shouted their support for him, instead contenting himself with cleaning his spectacles, and when that was exhausted sorting his notes for the address.

It all meant little to Jimmy. He had permitted Mackowicz and Elkin to flank the scientist and had positioned himself a pace or so behind. That had been the inner yoke of the shell around the Israeli. Beyond had been the Special Branch men, six of them, two car loads who could get no closer than five to six feet from the man they had been ordered to protect. Now the shell fragmented as the guards moved to their appointed places. The only door had been locked behind him, a plain-clothes and unmistakable police guard on either side and equipped with walkie-talkie personal sets to co-ordinate any turning of the key. There could be no sudden surprise entry from that quarter.

The two Israelis were at the raised table, Elkin standing to the side the door was found, Mackowicz opposite and close to the windows now draped in brown velveteen curtains. Jimmy saw that Mackowicz had brought his macintosh; warm summer evening, clear sky, indisputable weather forecast of sunshine for at least the next three days. The coat, held across his thighs, meant the Uzi was concealed there. Wonder if he's put the catch off, thought Jimmy, put one up the spout. Down the long walls that stretched the length of the room were four of the Branch men, two on each side. The remaining two were at the far end, facing Sokarev and the committee that had assembled to host the meeting. Nine armed and trained men in the room. Has to be enough, Jimmy said to himself, has to guarantee it. But the knowledge that Mackowicz had the sub-machine-gun grasped in his right hand aggravated him. Without permitting anyone in the packed ranks of seats to observe his action he drew the PPK from his holster and held it low behind him against the wall, and positioned himself so that he faced the windows, and could see Sokarev to his left and the men by the door to his right.

When silence at last settled on the hall the chair-man rose to speak. He had already glanced with as great a force of anger and contempt as he could command at Mackowicz. He found no reaction, but his experience of the morning in the hotel lobby still stung.

'Ladies and Gentlemen,' he threw his voice to the back of the hall, correctly gauging that some of the elderly might have difficulty in hearing in spite of the amplification system. 'It gives me the very greatest of pleasure to welcome to our gathering this evening that most distinguished of colleagues from the State of Israel, Professor David Sokarev.' He paused, and the clapping began immediately and with great fervour, till Christ-like he raised his hands to quell it. 'I think we are all aware that the Professor has done us a great honour in coming to visit us. If we believe only a half of what we read in our daily journals then there is no doubt in my mind that Professor Sokarev has displayed great courage in coming to our shores to honour this engagement. I think we can accept that in the highest offices of our land the dangers that Professor Sokarev is running are believed to be genuine – witness the number of gentlemen with us this evening who I regret whole-heartedly are going to find this evening's lecture extremely tedious.' There was a ripple of laughter as the greyed and balding heads of the audience strayed around the walls searching out the men with their close-cut, two-button suits and suede shoes. But the laughter did not last, and it was at best brittle and nervous. The presence of the interlopers was a factor beyond the experience of the men who had come to listen to the professor.

'Because of the difficulties that have surrounded Professor Sokarev since his arrival here I myself have not yet had the opportunity of speaking to him, but when I extended the invitation that he should come and talk to us I suggested he might care to discuss in our company the distinguished work connected with

287

lasers that has been associated with his name. Now whether that is what he has eventually decided on, I do not know . . .' It was clear the chairman had more to say, and Jimmy was prepared to shut out the rest.

The gun, he had now decided, was unnecessary. It could rest as easily in the holster, enough of the melodrama. He turned to the wall, as a child does when it wishes to urinate out of sight of adults. With the PPK again weighted against his chest he faced back into the room, wondering how many had seen his movement. The speech of introduction droned on. Jimmy felt himself beginning to relax. Two moments of priority danger, he told himself, and one already successfully negotiated. Arrival and Departure – those were the hitting times for the opposition. Not in here, not with the screened and searched and checked-out audience. The departure would be the time for maximum vigilance, not Jimmy's phrase but Jones's. And Helen was out there waiting. Soft and comfortable. She'd follow them back to the hotel, and when they'd dropped Sokarev off, all tucked up in his pit, they'd go back to the flat together, and stay awake together.

The policemen who were beyond the locked door, outside in the corridor, shared Jimmy's feelings. They had formed a close knot together, sufficiently at ease to light up their cigarettes and talk about the ordinariness that dominated their lives. Mortgage rates were swapped, the cost of holidays, gossip about superiors and desk men. And in the creeping darkness beside the towering shape of Britain's largest university complex the officers posted there also felt an easing of the tension that had gripped and alerted them at the time the professor had driven to the building. There would be ample warning of his exit. Then the pocket radios would chatter and there would be the noise of the car engines revving. Time enough to supervise their closely chosen watching points. One group had gathered at the main entrance, dwarfing and formidable. Another had drawn together by the the side door through which Sokarev had entered the building. From neither position was it possible to view the windows of the lecture hall; that part of the building butted out too far for them to see beyond its corners.

The constable who had been assigned the duty of watching the windows of the lecture hall now lay at McCoy's feet. He had not been armed, and even if he had carried a gun he would not have had the opportunity to use it. Nor had he spoken into his radio, attached to his tunic lapel, before the crashing blow came down on the soft rear area of his head, below the line of his reinforced helmet and where skull base and vertebrae come together. It had been mercilessly simple, Famy advancing with his tourist map, stuttering ineffective English, distracting the constable's attention as they peered together at the street divisions while McCoy moved cougar-quick with the metal tube of plumber's piping. The thieves' charter of keys McCoy had gained at the garage in the morning was next employed. A parked car opened, hand-brake released, and the vehicle pushed in silence to the place of the scratched star underneath the window.

Famy saw the Irishman never looked at the sprawling figure beneath him. Again the glossy coldness that meant there would be no hesitation at the

289

moment of contact, and all who trespassed in their way obliterated without concern. It was as he would be when the time of firing came. Famy was aware of the flooding excitement bursting through him. Now at last they would savour victory, triumphant over endless obstacles. It was the ultimate moment of his mission.

McCoy said, quietly and slowly, so that he did not have to repeat it, 'There's been one round of clapping. That's the entry. The next one means he's on his feet. We go, straight then.'

Famy extended the shoulder rest of the M1, locked it in its extended position, checked the magazine was in place, cocked the gun – quickly and fearfully lest the noise of the mechanism would arouse curiosity – and eased off the safety catch.

Beside him McCoy had pulled the heavy black glove on to his right hand, the metal tube grasped in the grotesque finger-shapes. But no gun; Famy saw he had picked up no weapon.

'You should have the other M1 with you,' he hissed, amplifying his worry.

'No need. Your pigeon now, remember? I'm going to give you the clear shot, then it's all yours.'

'It will be a famous success for our people . . .'

'Keep that fucking nonsense till you've hit the bastard.'

They heard the swell of applause build behind the blackness of the curtain, prolonged fierce clapping and shouts. Famy went up the back of the car and on to the roof that buckled and heaved under his weight. He needed to steady himself with his free hand, nerves gripping at his legs. McCoy came the other way, climbing over the bonnet and stretching up past the windscreen till both stood together, uncertain of balance on the shifting platform. They were exactly above the mark Famy had drawn against the wall, and level with the join of the curtain. The Irishman pushed his face close to Famy's.

'Remember it then. When I've done the window and got the curtain back he'll be forty-five degrees to you. And don't bugger about. If they all start blasting chuck the grenades. Right?'

He waited for Famy to bring the rifle up to his shoulder in the aim position, waited till it was snug against the shoulder and the right cheek, and then smashed the tubing into the expanse of glass. Famy winced away from the noise as McCoy's fist, protected by the glove, beat at the obstinate and remaining slivers still fastened in the mortarwork of the frame. The hand grabbed for the curtain and pulled it back; instinctively Famy lunged forward, still in the fire posture, raking the brightness of the room for his target.

Where was he? Where was the whore? Which was the one he sought? Which of the uncomprehending, blank faces that had turned and now stayed motionless and transfixed peering at the source of the commotion? The answer was not long coming. The man who stood at the table while all round him sat, the man who had begun to cower, who knew the blow was near and sought to avoid it, who could not urge his muscles to follow the racing orders of his brain. That one, that one was Sokarev.

Famy steadied to fire, aiming for the chest where the white shirt and the dark tie disappeared into the greyness of his suit. So big, so easy, through the shape of the gunsight.

'Speed it up, for Christ's sake,' screamed McCoy, and as the finger closed round the trigger, squeezing as he'd been told, Famy twisted his gaze to the agony of impatience on the Irishman's face.

When he looked back he saw the man at the far end of the table thrusting a way toward Sokarev, and the man closer to him was wrestling with a coat swinging the billowed shape of it up toward his shoulder.

Famy fired.

As the curtain exploded with the noise of the breaking glass, Jimmy's hand moved to the holster under the breast pocket of his jacket. His fingers found the harshness of the handle, fastening on the ridging there to aid his grip. Then there was the protruding gun barrel, barely thirty feet from him. The pistol was coming fast, out in front, arm extended, level with the eyes as he heard the shout from far in the night, and then the first shot. Fractionally later Jimmy pulled the hair trigger, without finesse and conscious of the need not for accuracy but for a volume of shots. Some were to hit the curtain, some to disappear he knew not where.

Jimmy had fired six times, shouting all the time in the direction of Sokarev.

'Get him down. Get the bloody man on the floor. Get him under the table.'

Elkin reached the scientist first, taking off in a leap when still five feet from him to pinion Sokarev to the floor among the tangle of chair and table supports and feet. Jimmy saw the chairman sag in his chair and then fall forward, casually and without effort onto the open surface of the table.

Again and again the rifle at the window fired and with each succeeding shot Jimmy was surer in his knowledge.

'He's missed, the little mother fucker, and he knows it!' It was almost a shout, exhilaration at the contact, half-smile playing on his mouth. But the eyes were cold – focused, taking in the scene around him.

The two Branch men along the same wall as Jimmy had begun to fire, not standing but crouched in the taught posture, classic but slower. He's not going to take it, too much for him, it'll finish him, the little rat, thought Jimmy. He saw Sokarev far under the table, Elkin covering him, saw Mackowicz bring the Uzi to his shoulder, rid himself of that useless coat, and he began to make for the door. He had reached it, elbowing aside the policemen, shouting for the door to be opened above the nerve-shattering noise of the long burst fired by Mackowicz, when from the corner of his eye he saw the puny, dark grey and rounded shape loop its way from the window toward the top table.

Mackowicz far back in the room shouted the one terrifying choked word, 'Grenade!'

It bounced, seemingly consumed with inertia, onto the floor between the table and the front row of the audience's seats, made a gentle parabola before bouncing again and then rolling unevenly, toward the shelter of the table where Elkin protected Sokarev. Mackowicz jumped for it. There was a moment when he was airborne and Jimmy could see the grenade wobbling, nearly stationary, then it disappeared beneath the big body. Stillness, fractional but complete. Then Mackowicz was lifted high toward the ceiling, Jimmy did not see him fall – he was through the door, now unlocked and running toward the main entrance.

The detonation of the grenade was still battering in Jimmy's ears as he went down the corridor through the confusion of the milling policemen. Because the shots and explosion had come from inside the lecture room every man, in or out of uniform, saw it as his duty to crowd as close as physically possible to the source of the gunfire. Behind Jimmy as he shouldered his way through the advancing charge came a cry for 'Stretchers.' He knew where to go. He dug his heels into the soft gravel immediately outside the doorway, ran out into the night and to his left and then swerved again to get himself along the side of the building and to the marksman's position. In the shadows far in front he saw two men jump from the roof of a parked car and start to run for the low boundary wall that separated the university precincts from Malet Street and the free-flowing traffic. Still sprinting, Jimmy fired – stupid really – carried away with the cowboy game, only one shot, and the magazine was expended. There was a shot in return, wide and high and to the right, barely close enough for him to distinguish the 'crack' that signalled its incoming. As his finger moved uselessly on the trigger, bringing home the message of his wastefulness, he slowed, couldn't get close now, not with an empty bloody shooter. Across the road he heard the frantic, piercing sound of dispute, and the noise, belatedly, of a car revving. Jimmy was panting now, out of condition, not enough time in the gym, striving to fill his lungs with air.

'Helen. Helen. Where in God's name are you?'

It seemed deep eternity before the car pulled up sharply alongside him.

'Get out. Get out of the bloody thing.' His voice came in short staccato bursts. She hesitated, disorientated by the distant noise of gunfire and now the heaving wild-eyed form of Jimmy.

'Get out, you stupid bitch. Get out of the bloody car.'

She began to unfasten the clasp of her safety belt worn across her body. Always in position, however far she went, reflex. Jimmy wrenched open the door, took hold of the collar of her coat and pulled her from the wheel. One action, out of the seat and clear of the door. The background cacophony; of police whistles blowing, of a radio screeching with static, of orders bellowed. Jimmy had taken her place and the car was already spinning in a one-hundred-and-eighty-degree half-circle as he headed for the one gap in the wall and toward where he had seen the running men and heard the starting car.

Seventy yards in front the Cortina struck out into the main stream. It was a laboured movement, that of a winged animal, one certain in the knowledge that it must escape but with its limbs damaged and impaired. Jimmy heaved with relief. He was in contact, the vacuum space between the cars would lessen. He cut right from the centre of the road to avoid a racing police car, light revolving, siren at volume, travelling in the other direction. Flashed his headlights, but it was past him, his gesture unseen by driver or navigator. No system of communication from Helen's car, no radio telephone. He pulled out again, avoided the bus that lumbered in front and cursed that the girl had

purchased a slow-acceleration family car. But the gap
would close.

The Cortina went through the traffic lights on
red and was in Goodge Street, long, Georgian and
geometric, heading south. Jimmy followed, was
faintly aware of a car skidding to an emergency stop
to avoid collision, and settled himself easily into
the seat. Not good yet, Jimmy, had you with your
Y-fronts on your knees, not often it goes that way,
but it'll get better, and the little bastards up front'll
wonder what hit them. The PPK rested on his lap.
Another magazine was in his jacket, right pocket. He
would wait for an opportunity to reload.

They had run from the window close together, Famy
with his head bent round, covering the area behind
them, the small rifle ready to fire, ready to head off
pursuit, McCoy leading with his right arm pressed
hard against the upper shoulder. When Famy had
turned once to fire away into the distance McCoy
had savagely pulled him forward, destroying his
aim.

'It's distance we have to have. Hang on here and
we're screwed.' The words sobbed out, but with little
tone as they emerged from the clamped and pain-
creased mouth.

When they reached the Cortina McCoy had thrust
his left hand across his body into the opposite
trouser pocket and pulled clear the laden keyring.
It took him several seconds to select the one he
wanted, small and bright and fresh-cut. He tossed it
to Famy.

'You drive,' he said, and flung open the passenger
door, left unlocked when they had parked the bare

forty minutes earlier. Should have left the keys in the ignition.

Famy had the rifle to his shoulder. It was small, a child's toy, too insignificant to be a killing weapon. The people who had paused on the far pavement did not believe in it and now stood and watched – not with great fear, nor petrified beyond movement, but curious. Famy was jolted from the image by McCoy's words.

'Come on, you stupid bloody eejit. You'll have to drive.'

Still Famy held the rifle up, peering over its sights, watchful of pursuit.

'Shift yourself, you bastard.'

Famy lowered the rifle, and held it at his side, as a man who walks with a stick, and is resting. 'I cannot,' he said.

McCoy seemed not to have heard him. 'Don't piss about. Get behind the bloody wheel.'

'I cannot drive.' Famy said it slowly. Humiliation, abject and total.

'Course you can bloody drive,' McCoy's voice rose in exasperation and temper.

'I don't know how. I have never driven.'

McCoy waved his right arm in Famy's face. 'Can't you see, there's a bloody great bullet in there? Stop farting about and move the car off.'

'It is impossible. I have never driven. I cannot.'

The monotonous recitation slid home to McCoy. The obscenity he yelled at the Arab was vicious and wounding. McCoy ran round the car and draped himself into the driving seat. He laid his right arm along the wheel for support and from the street light Famy could see his face whitened. With his left hand

McCoy inserted the key into the ignition, and then put the car into gear. By pushing his whole body forward he was able to turn the wheel toward the direction of the road before he could bring his left hand into play again with the gear stick.

Famy wondered whether the Irishman would faint. He wound down the passenger window and looked back across the road, rifle aimed again. In his jacket pocket were three grenades – he could run his fingers over them. Grip-bag in the rear, where it had been left, more ammunition, more grenades, needed the reassurance, and then the car was moving. He cringed as they went through the lights, bracing himself for an impact that did not happen. And another car came through the lights, clearly visible to him, unmistakable.

'Another car followed us,' near-panic, near-hysteria.

'What am I supposed to do about it?'

'I cannot see it now, not as an individual car, there are just lights.'

'Forget it,' said McCoy. 'If it gets close blast it. If not forget it.'

McCoy could tell that his concentration was slipping, felt the weakness drifting uncontrollably over him. The wound itself fascinated him. Little to see, but he glanced obsessively at it. Just the neatly driven hole that lay in the centre of the blood patch where the cloth had darkened and stained on the upper forearm. The pain ebbed, rising only when he tried to use the hand, and then sliding into numbness when he rested his fingers on the wheel.

'Did you get the bastard?' McCoy said.

They were on the move now. If he did not have to

go fast, and drive under pressure, then he could manage. If there was pursuit . . . There was a vagueness, an absence of care, caused by the loss of blood, but that was the option that he did not care to consider.

'I don't know.' Famy's reply was little more than a whisper.

' 'Course you bloody know. Either you saw him go down or you didn't. You know when you've hit a man, the way he goes.' McCoy said it with patronizing knowledge. Seen at first hand – the way a man was raised in the air, thrown up rag-doll and the way he then slumped out of control, unable to protect his head. There was a lapse of the co-ordination that maintained the living.

'It was difficult to know.' Famy paused. He studied the road in front, the thinning traffic of late evening in central London, then glanced behind. Only a myriad of jumbled lights, some stationary, some on the move, none so close as to threaten danger. Famy wanted to explain, wanted the other man to understand. 'I was about to fire at Sokarev when you shouted. There was distraction. As I fired there was a man across the room who began to shoot. One of the men pulled Sokarev under the table, I was firing all the time he did that, but he was on the ground and then was gone from my sight. The man who sat beside Sokarev, he was hit . . .'

'Big deal, they'll be singing and dancing in Beirut if you've drilled a Brit geriatric.'

McCoy was almost amused at the other man's discomfiture. And it was a failure, that much had penetrated to him, through the cloud and the haze. Without his wound he would have felt savage hatred at being associated with the fiasco, but the injury dissipated his anger, rendered it obsolete.

'. . . There was shooting from the wall facing us. Three or four men. And the bodyguard near the table, another one, not the one that went to Sokarev, he had the small machine-gun. He had started to fire when I threw the grenade. The grenade would have taken Sokarev, but the man fell on it. Then I could see nothing. He just exploded, and then there was smoke. The men who were shooting had an aim by then, one could not stay at the window.'

'One of those bastards took me.' There was finality in McCoy's words. To Famy it seemed the pain of the inquest was over, and the car was still moving. McCoy could cope with the disability. Famy watched the cars behind and those alongside but could find nothing to sustain his earlier anxiety. He put the M1 on the floor, under his legs, easy to reach but invisible to any driver who might glance at them casually from an adjacent car.

McCoy said, the trace of a smile playing at the side of his mouth, 'I thought this was the one where you stood up and had yourself counted, where you took Sokarev, or they took you. Bugged out early, didn't we?'

'It was impossible to continue shooting with all the firing from the wall.'

'Hand gun stuff, not accurate at that range. Lucky shot that hit me.'

'You started to run, and you were pulling at me.'

'But it's not my war, remember? You could have stayed. You were the bloody marksman. I'm just the chauffeur. So, why did you do the scamper?'

'I couldn't see any more . . . only the smoke . . . I

couldn't aim.' But Famy knew they were just words. There was no recollection of making a decision to run. He was already moving long before the awareness of it. There had never been a moment when he had the choice, choice of life and death.

They had swung to the west now, and the traffic was lighter as they navigated a bypass route which avoided the heart of the city. McCoy was able to keep the speedometer flickering a path between twenty and thirty miles an hour.

'They won't react well, your masters. Won't have wanted you hanging about able to fight another day and Mr Bloody Sokarev coming out clean.' McCoy was turning the screw. Knew it, and enjoyed the process. Retribution for his pain.

Famy stayed silent.

'My crowd wouldn't take kindly to it – not with all the investment. If it's cocked then it would have been better it had never started. Victory for them, bad news in your parish.'

McCoy was talking as if to himself, softly and winning no response.

'The Provies have their own way if it doesn't work out. If it's yellow, if the bugger sprinted to save his neck, then it's court martial. Not as formal as all that, nothing pompous. Half a dozen guys, in a barn or in a garage. Sentence comes a bit formal, though. Hood and a pistol-shot behind the ear. Leave a note on them too, so the next lot know why.'

Famy had his eyes closed, lids tightly drawn together, but was unable to shut out the message as McCoy expanded.

'If it's just because they didn't think, mucked the scene, then it's easier. Call it knee-capping. Bullet through each, from the back. They walk again, but they never run, and they stand out from the crowd because they're on sticks for weeks. The Proddies, the other mob, they're worse . . . use a Black and Decker. It's a drill, used for putting holes in the wall. Takes longer than a bullet – obvious isn't it? But they're real bastards, those Proddies.'

Famy said, 'There was one who went into Israel, and came back alone. All the rest were taken or killed, only this one survived and they found his Kalashnikov had not been fired. And they took him with ten of his friends to the open ground. He had a start of fifty metres, and then his friends began to fire. They all had to shoot, and the guns were checked afterwards, and they were watched to see they did not shoot wide. He did not go many metres, and it only happened once. There was no need for a repetition.'

'You'd better think of something good to say,' said McCoy. The game had gone far enough. There were other preoccupations for McCoy. Where to go, what to do about the wound? All men who go to the lonely war, the guerrilla's war, have a common fear, multiplied in their fantasies till it controls and dominates them. It is the horror of sepsis, of gangrene, of the putrefaction of their flesh. McCoy needed a den, where he could go and curl his legs and watch the entrance, and be safe, and needed it for many days, with hot water and clean towels . . . What to do with the bloody Arab? No place for him in the den, the lair for one only. Perhaps kill him – easiest solution, attractive. Something to think on, half an hour more for the driving, and a decision by then.

The problem engrossed him as he drove, and

Famy too was quiet, but with what thoughts McCoy neither knew nor cared.

For a full three minutes after the firing of the last shot Elkin covered Sokarev's body. When the scientist tried to move and shift his suppressed left arm from under his body the security man firmly pressed him down again flat onto the polished boards of the floor. There was a great calmness about Elkin's face, and the eyes were very clear, traversing the room for any further threat, and outstretched in front of him as an antenna his arm and the service revolver he preferred to the Uzi.

The Branch man who had taken a position nearest the table had bent down and asked the one inevitable question. Was Sokarev hurt? Elkin had shaken his head.

'Keep him there, then,' the detective said. 'First we'll clear the casualties, then empty the room. After that we'll work out how to shift him.'

Sokarev was aware that his legs were trembling, uncontrollably, the flesh of his upper thighs lapping together, and he was powerless to stop it. He could remember little of what had happened, just the noise of the window, and then the sight of the shortened barrel of the rifle poking and weaving in the curtain gap, locking on to him. He could recall the moment that Elkin had hit his legs and pulled him down, and then the horrific, unending exchange of gunfire. He had seen Mackowicz dive and lie still and then lift off into the air, and his ears felt pierced by the sound of the grenade.

The stretchers came fast. That on which the chairman lay was covered, end to end, by a grey hospital blanket and left at the far end of the room. What remained of Mackowicz was beside it. The policeman who had helped the ambulance team to lift the Israeli's disembowelled corpse onto the stretcher had vomited as soon as the pink and softened organs were covered over. The ambulances had come from University College Hospital less than half a mile away. It was to there that seven casualties were hurried; four suffering from gunshot wounds, one from grenade shrapnel injuries and two from coronary heart attacks.

The detectives had already started to examine the fire position outside the window when one of their number, walking beside the car used as the platform, stumbled on the body of the constable. When they lifted the young man onto the stretcher it was with care, a degree of gentleness, conscious they were handling their own.

In strange, shuffling silence the guests were ushered from the room and across the wide corridor to a similar lecture hall. Their patience was requested and it was explained to them that though they would not be detained for long it was impossible that they could be allowed to wander from the building while the large-scale search of the immediate area of the university was still under way. After the door had been closed on them few had anything to say. The conflict between Israel and her neighbours was not a thing that many understood. For a few moments they had been exposed to the unfamiliar; but the experience would do little to aid their comprehension.

When everyone had gone Sokarev was helped to his feet. They stood him back to the wall and hemmed in by policemen, Elkin right beside him, the gun still in his hand but resting against his trouser pocket. Later they brought him a glass of water. He found he could scarcely hold it, and Elkin took the glass and put it against the professor's lips and tilted it to such an angle that some spilled from his mouth and dribbled onto the front of his suit.

Jones had stayed in his office alone that night. Helen, vague about her movements, had been gone three hours. From a long way down the empty corridors he heard the laboured footsteps of the messenger from communications. Too old to hurry, and why should he in his ignorance of the message he carried to Room 3/146? He was a little out of breath when he knocked on the outer door, and surprised that the Section head had bounced across two offices to be there to snatch the paper from his hand. There were no thanks from Jones who now concentrated on what the other man could see were three bare lines of type.

They didn't explain much. An attack on Sokarev – unsuccessful rifle fire and an explosion – casualties, large local-scale hunt started for two men – no immediate result. In his office again Jones sagged back into his chair, read the message three, four times, looking unsuccessfully for any word or interpretation that he might earlier have missed. And nothing from Jimmy. Where was he when all this was going on? Why hadn't he intervened? Why hadn't he called? Half the reason for the man being there was that he'd be on the phone, so the department wasn't relying on the police for information. Should have called in by now. He swivelled half round in his chair and looked at the picture, in deep shadow now because of the angle at which the lights were hung. Pretty little boy, nice smile, big eyes, neat head, looked as harmless as a butterfly, but he'd concealed the wasp sting. Bloody-near pulled it off, him and that Irishman. Jones felt a great sadness that pulled him down, his head deep in his arms on the table. What was the point of it all, when all the king's horses and all the king's men could be pushed off centre-stage by that little rat? Shouldn't have been an equal contest, shouldn't have been allowed to throw the sucker punch, and he had, and nearly won.

The Soviets sniffing round the Defence establishments, or the Czechs, or East Germans . . . they were so straightforward. Bit of a game when you became involved with them. Reckoned on the odds, didn't they? And if they didn't think they could win they didn't come in. But this little sod, he hadn't worked out his chances of survival – couldn't have done, or he'd have stayed at home – and yet he was in there kicking. Jones didn't know what his feelings were toward the young Arab. Probably there was a tinge of admiration, that of the older man for youth which does something no longer possible for the other through age. But it was balanced quickly by the anger and frustration that the Arab had put them through the hoops, and laughed at them and lived.

Had to be brave, too, Jones acknowledged that. The old labels weren't any good. Courage if he was from your lot, fanaticism if he was on the other side. He'd learned the futility of the tags when he was still young, when he saw an ME 110 night fighter with its two-man crew peel away in its tail of flame, known they wouldn't survive, and known too that they'd pressed their attack long after the chance of success had vanished. They were brave men, and they were the enemy, and they'd earned respect, and been prepared to die. The Arab had been prepared to die too, as a sacrifice for his army, whatever bunch of twisted idiots they turned out to be. And all such a waste, and everyone scared out of their wits by the implications of it all – everyone except his Jimmy.

The telephone broke in, shrill and insistent, bursting over the quietened room. Helen on the line, chill and matter of fact. Jimmy in her car . . . hot pursuit . . . a get-away vehicle disappearing from the scene . . . God only knows where he's gone . . . shots in the street . . . she was coming back to the office. Just the staccato statements, without emotion or involvement, and then she'd rung off. Jones put the receiver down. Funny the way she'd used Jimmy's name, usually a laugh when she mentioned him, but not this time. Jones, long sensitive to intonation and emphasis, noted it, and wondered what the hell she was doing there anyway. Then he put it from his mind. Unimportant, silly girl – should have stayed at home. His thoughts were surging with Jimmy. Just what he would have wanted, he thought, the big challenge and the chance to prove himself where all else had failed. And he'd have to kill them, wouldn't he? Have to kill the Arab. Only way now.

Under pressure Jones would normally have resorted to the palliative of work, buried himself in the paperwork of the operation, twisted his mind away from the generalities with the specifics of detail. But he had no function now; it was all out of his hands. There was nothing he could usefully do. That's how far down those bastards have brought us, he thought, right down to the base area, where the Jimmys are waiting.

He screwed up the teletype message, crumpled the paper in his fist and tossed it unsuccessfully in the direction of his waste-bin.

None of the photographers and television crews who had been covering the arrivals and who were scheduled to film the departures had any worthwhile pictures of the event. Now they crowded against the side door from which they believed the Israeli scientist would emerge. A fierce argument broke out when a police inspector called them to silence and informed the gathering that under no circumstances would flash bulbs or arc lights be permitted. Thirty voices were raised in protest, but when they died the inspector's message was even more explicit.

'Gentlemen,' he said. 'I am not prepared to have the person of Mr Sokarev either impeded or in any way illuminated on this step. If you think about it there's no way I can say anything else. If you don't play ball you're down the station, charged and in court tomorrow, and I wouldn't vouch your cameras will survive.'

The Prime Minister, called from the dinner table, suffered three agonizing minutes of uncertainty. The first message relayed to him by the Commissioner, telephoning from Scotland Yard, merely stated that there was heavy shooting and an explosion inside the room where Professor Sokarev was speaking. More details would follow.

He had waited for them alone in his personal

office, unwilling to face his guests again before he knew the worst. When the telephone rang again he expected catastrophe, but was told that whereas there were casualties the professor was not among them. There was no more reliable and confirmed information.

He had barely resumed his meal when his Parliamentary Private Secretary brought in a folded slip of paper. The Israeli Ambassador was demanding a meeting, and that night.

'Put the bloody man off till the morning,' he said, and motioned for the butler to replenish his glass. 'Right to the top,' he urged.

Chapter Sixteen

It satisfied Jimmy that the car he tailed should be unaware of his presence. Like a marriage, tied together, but neither showing any indication of the bond that linked them. It was as it should be, professional but not easy, not one for the kids in the department – they'd have been up close, blowing the contact, but Jimmy kept back from the other car, leaving it room to manoeuvre, far from the bumper and the rear red lights that shone at him, that gripped his attention. No question of an attempt to ram or force it off the road. Idiocy if he tried it. Would leave him with two men to handle, both armed and with all the dangers of losing them both in a foot chase. It was better this way. Eventually the bastards would stop and that would be time enough for him to make his presence known. They went slowly, and so were not hard to follow, yet he was surprised that there was not more speed and more effort to put greater distance between themselves and the university. Jimmy sought to interpret his opponents, fancied he could understand them, all part of his training, but this lack of urgency confused him.

There was a roadblock outside Richmond. Uniformed police, torches, arms waving, but all in the lane that ran toward the city and with no interest shown in the cars that travelled the other way, from the direction of London. Typical, thought Jimmy, no bloody liaison. The wireless nets must be jammed with traffic on what's been happening, and nobody's told these poor sods that the birds have upped and flown, and that the only purpose of the law being there is because they might come back to the nest to roost. It was a wide and open road, well laid down by a fully endowed local authority with a grass space with bushes and small trees separating the two routes. Slow as it was the car he followed went through, carried by the flow, too fast for him to shout and attract the attention of the policemen on the other carriageway. No chance of stopping, couldn't risk severing the thread that bound him to the Cortina.

The PPK was loaded now, empty magazine discarded on the floor by the foot-brake. It had not been difficult to rearm the pistol, and he now weighed in his mind when would be the moment to open fire. Perhaps when they stopped the car, when they were out on the pavement and unaware, when he was in the darkness of the saloon and they were in the open, free for him and naked, illuminated by the street lights. A possibility, a good one. Attractive because then there was the chance that they would be close together, and the burst of shots might cover the two of them. When the traffic closed and he was but two or three car-lengths away from the Cortina he could see the two heads. That of the driver bent low, in supplication over the wheel, the other more upright and turning every two minutes or so to look behind him. How did they rate themselves? Jimmy wondered. He knew where he'd have put it. Fifty-fifty, at best. Escaped but hadn't taken the professor. Perhaps not as good as fifty-fifty. Chap needed a score to measure his performance against, important that, competitive world. Not as good as evens, Jimmy reckoned. Perhaps only the professor counted. Buggered it up, hadn't they? And for all the security they'd won their surprise – must have wanted the surprise factor above all else, and they'd achieved that. Good groundwork, but the rest screwed. Not like McCoy, that, Jimmy thought, not if you read his file. Couldn't have been him on the gun, must have been the other bastard. Taken too long, hadn't he, not the way you'd have done it, Jimmy, you wouldn't have left the rifle hanging through the window half the night. Silly bastards. Should have been on champagne now, and instead they're running, and don't even know what's right up their backsides and waiting to belt them.

Jimmy could see they had slowed in front of him. Nearly there, he told himself, but they must be unsure of the right turning. Lost their way, but they wouldn't be in the side streets unless that's where they're heading for.

The pistol was in his right hand, flat against the wheel. His window was down. Not long now, my little darling. He muttered casually and without emotion, but would not have denied the excitement.

To kill the Arab or not. It had bounced round McCoy those last miles into the town. Famy was expendable, and from the way he turned and fidgeted in his seat

312

was aware of it. Knew what his own people would do to him if he crawled home, the surviving straggler, in the first true flush of failure. Better off face down on the refuse of the building site, with the weeds and undergrowth and rats for company. Had had his chance of immortality, if that mattered to him, and had messed it. The alternative, to rot in a cell as a lifer in the Scrubs, and no-one coming in a hijack jet, the freedom bird, to lift him out and take him home. Good-for-nothing, wasted material. A bloody great beacon of a fiasco to his colleagues and commander – McCoy liked that, rolled off his tongue well. He'd be paraded, sunken and sheepish, through the British courts, after the spooks had finished with him, after the chatter, after the 'debrief'. Be a killing for the Ministry of Information back in Jerusalem, worth a public holiday to them – 'Day of Arab Balls-up'. And the bugger knew it all, could see that from the way he sat, misery from ear to ear, the little chokes, the set firmness of the mouth. And his chances of making out on his own, getting clear, McCoy assessed them as minimal to nil. If he needed his hand held for the attack, how much more would he depend on the nanny protection for escape?

McCoy was close to resolve when Famy broke the long silence that had permitted the flow and insinuation of the Irishman's thoughts.

'You are going to the girl's home, right? To the place where you hid when she came for me? That is the place that I will leave you.' Perhaps he looked for reaction, expected surprise, but there was none from McCoy, just eyes on the road, hands on the wheel, and the bead of lit sweat high on the forehead.

'There was an idea when we were planning the mission at home, that the attack should be mounted at Heathrow, at the airport as he flew to the United States. It will be harder without my friends, but it is the only possibility. I will go on foot, across country, to the airport. They told us that it was not difficult to gain entry to the perimeter, and I will see the El Al land. He will not board till the end, and I will have time, with the rifle, to get as close as I need.'

'Impossible.' McCoy never moved his head, just the word of dismissal.

'It is not impossible, only difficult. I have the resolution now, not earlier but it has come to me. It was different earlier. I have now the will that I should have possessed when Sokarev was on the gun. But it was the first time that I had ever fired on a man. It is not easy, not the first time. It is not simple to stand and expose oneself to gunfire. I have learned much in the last hour, more than they taught me in the camp. More in the hour than in three months.'

'They'll gun you down before you set foot within two hundred yards of the plane, and you don't even know which one it will be.' Perhaps McCoy was less certain of himself, the quietness of the Arab disconcerting him. There was a strange confidence he hadn't witnessed before, something novel, delicate, and which he did not wish to fracture.

'The plane will be the one that is most heavily guarded. I have ideas, and there are many grenades. The Israelis say, and they are right, that if one intends to kill there is no favour to be found in starting far back, relying on aim and the steadiness of the hand. The Israelis say you have to be close, body to body, that you have to be prepared to die yourself.

314

They are correct. They are experts in the art of killing, and we are not. We can only learn from them.'

'We part company then. It's not part of my game.'

'Your side is more than complete. You carried me to the target, you placed the rifle in my hand. You have fulfilled your order. As long as I live I shall remember you with friendship.'

No risk of that being long, thought McCoy. Right hornets' bed we've put our stick into. But if the boy wants to go gloriously that is his concern. Not the style of Crossmaglen. Happened once in Ballymurphy, up in Belfast, when they were all twisted after Internment, and half a dozen guys went for a trot down the road and firing Thompsons from the hip at the biggest pile of sandbags and bunkers you ever saw. Had their bloody heads blown off, one after the other. Did anyone thank them for it the next week, or the next month, or the next anniversary? Did they, shit. Just called them 'eejit bastards'.

'I'm going to the house,' McCoy said. 'She'll put me up somewhere. I have to wash the arm. Doesn't hurt so much now, but it needs cleaning. Last time they had me over the border, into Dundalk General and on the table with the knife in less than half an hour. You can't bugger with gunshot, have to clean it.'

'Where will you put the car?' asked Famy.

'At the end of the street by the house. It's a dead-end, no-one'll see it there, come looking for us. We'll do the goodbye bit then.'

He'd hesitated at several of the road junctions in the last half-mile, searching for the landmarks of the streets known from the single occasion that he had

315

walked the girl to her front door. And then there was the spread of ivy on the end brick wall, and the tree with the white-washed number on it, that was cancered by disease and that would have to be cut. She had said it was a shame, for the tree. He turned into the girl's road.

After McCoy had stopped the car he reached awkwardly toward the back floor space of the car, feeling for one of the M1s in the grip-bag and for another magazine. From the cloth sack he took two of the grenades, slipping them into his pocket where they banged together, making a dull, hidden noise, without the ring of softer, less lethal metal. The gun he crooked under his shoulder Then with his left hand he opened the door of the car. Famy waited for him, then pulled the bag over his seat. His rifle was loose, trailing one-handed as he walked round the front of the car. Simultaneous with McCoy he was aware of the light of another vehicle that turned into the street, and reacted as fast as the Irishman in shielding his firearm alongside the silhouette of the leg.

'Stay still till he's parked and switched off,' McCoy snapped at Famy, concerned at the intrusion, wanting to be on his way, unwilling to face interruption. They were both illuminated by the powerful undipped beams that blazed at them from twenty yards down the road. There was a sense of foolishness, of conspiracy that was unnerving.

'As soon as he's gone, disappear.' McCoy tried to take control, knew it was for the last time, but pride dictated that at this moment, even as he relieved himself of his commitments and responsibilities, he should still lead. 'It's been strange. Not much to say now . . . but I'm sorry, for your sake . . . and I mean it . . . I'm sorry it loused up . . . What's the matter with the bastard, why doesn't he kill those bloody lights? . . .'

McCoy felt the searing surprise of pain as the first bullet struck his shoulder. It spun him half-round in the fraction of time that it tore a path deep into the softness of the flesh, smashing into the boned strips of his upper ribs, before disintegrating, the aerosol of smoothed and roughened particles. Famy reacted well. Crouched beside the car door he fired six aimed shots at the car, hunting for the lights, seeking to destroy them, and when that was complete blasting into the darkness above his memory of the bulbs. He paused, studied the silence that had spread at desolate speed across the street, and grasped for a grenade. Pin out, lever free, left arm extended, and then he hurled it, as the instructor had taught them, overarm and toward the car. The moment before the blast he saw a shadow, down low near the pavement, scurrying for the protection of the nearest front garden.

Drunkenly McCoy regained his feet and lurched through the wicket-gate to the front door of the girl's home. With his rifle held one-handed and high he hammered at the wooden panelling. There was one more shot, but wide and far into the night, insufficient to deter him.

'It's a pistol. Out of range, give him a few more. Have the bastard keep his head down. And listen: when we get inside just do as I say, don't bloody argue.' Famy saw he was ashen, his face screwed tight around the mouth and chin, the reaction sharper and more acute than the previous bullet had achieved.

The door opened. Silhouetted by a light from the back of the hallway was the girl. There was an older woman behind her. Further back a man, top collar button undone, staring without understanding.

McCoy pushed the girl savagely to one side, sending her spinning onto the carpet. Satisfied that Famy had followed him in he kicked back with his heel and heard the door slam behind him, the Yale lock engaged, the portcullis down on the outside world of the street.

'Whoever the bugger is that's out there' – McCoy was speaking only to the Arab, ignoring the others as if they did not exist, had not yet been reached in his agenda of priorities – 'he's seen us both go in. Double yourself out the back, through the kitchen door, over whatever fence there is, and run, run till your legs won't carry you. I'll hold here with this crowd. It'll take the fuzz light years to work out what to do, and all the time they'll be thinking it's the two of us that are sitting inside. It'll give you hours of start on the bastards. But don't hang about now. Move yourself . . .' The pain came in a great spasm, seeming to catch hold of the wound and pluck ruthlessly at it before letting the sinews fall back into their torn but ordered place. 'For Christ's sake don't mess me, be on your bloody way.'

Famy said nothing, just ran on past them. Past McCoy and the girl, past her parents. The light from the kitchen ceiling threw the small garden into shape and he saw the fence, five feet high and sixty feet away. He trampled through some plants that clung to his ankles then swung himself onto the wattle-embroidered barrier and was over. There was a path, and beyond his eyes nothing but darkness.

When McCoy spoke again it was with great deliberation, his defence bunker against the flowing agony.

'I have a rifle, fully loaded, twenty-six rounds in the magazine. I have hand grenades. There will be no hesitation in killing you if you do not do exactly as I say. And any bloody heroics and the women get it first. The old one right at the start. If the police come, God help you.' The girl, upright now, and joined in fear to her mother, began to weep – quick, sudden, little choking sounds, delicate convulsions at her throat, head hanging. 'You, father,' – McCoy gestured with the rifle barrel to the man – 'You're to go round the house. I want all the outside doors and windows locked, and I want every curtain in the house drawn, and I want the keys brought to me.'

He looked at them for the first time, turning his head from face to face, lingering on each till they averted their heads, unable and unwilling to meet and sustain the gaze of the deep, hate-consumed eyes. 'I've explained it then? And it's understood? Don't mess me about. Don't play games with me. I've said what it means if you fool with me.'

As he took the mother and daughter upstairs he could hear the noise of the locks being turned, the bolts driven home, and the curtains sliding on their plastic runners. He was so very tired, so near to sleep. He yearned for it, for an escape from the pain, and the awful hallucination of fighting in another man's army, another man's war.

On all fours Jimmy edged his way along the pavement toward the end house of the terrace. Helen's car was alight, flames careering through the interior.

In a few moments it would explode, when the heat reached the petrol tank. Shouldn't have happened to her, not her pride and joy, only bloody girl he knew who washed her motor, poor cow. He went without haste, feeling the growing heat playing at a distance on the seat of his trousers, watching all the time at the house, expecting the gun, the black barrel. Next round due, bell should be clanging, and he was short of seconds, no-one to hold the stool – but no-one that he would have wanted there. What you joined for, Jimmy-boy, the licence to play the grown-up games. He saw the curtains in an upstairs room abruptly jolt across the window frame, noted it as an essential step in the protection and precaution process against siege and eventual attack. Nothing else he could register on, and then he smiled to himself, nothing but the tacky and small pool of blood, reflecting, by the front gate. One of the bastards with problems. The Irishman, it would be his cupful. That was the one he'd aimed for and who had spun against the bodywork of the old Cortina too fast for him to be on the evading kick. The move of a man who's been hit, and the blood, the amount of it, that meant an effective and hurting wound. 'Incapacitating' was what old Jonesey would have called it. Cuts the odds, getting on to an even chance now, Jimmy. One by one the lights were doused in the house. Good thinking again – obvious, really – but meant the homework had been done, necessary if they want to see out. Only have to move the curtain a fraction of an inch and they can see the whole street, while they stay hidden, invisible. Four houses down and on the same side of the street a front door opened and Jimmy could see a man peering at the burning car. Others would follow when curiosity over-whelmed the baser instincts of self-preservation and the barricading of doors in response to the gunfire.

The man backed away when he saw Jimmy's gun, seemed to see it before he fastened on to the crouched figure beside his hedge-enclosed front garden, and hurried toward his door, seeking to shut out the threat. But Jimmy was faster, had his foot there, his worn leather taking the force of the swinging woodwork.

'I want the telephone,' Jimmy said. 'And while I'm talking write me the names of the people in the end house, this side, everyone who might be in the house at the moment. And don't go back on the street, not unless you want to make the front page of the papers, picture and all.'

For the man it was instant nightmare, too consum-ing for him to question Jimmy's identity, and there was the gun. Meekly he led the stranger to the back room and pointed to the telephone. It was an auto-matic response that led him to subdue the volume of the television programme he had been watching. Fingers spun the dial. Jones's direct outside line number.

'Jimmy here, Mr Jones. They're holed up in Richmond. Chisholm Road, just by the park. One's in difficulty, not fatal, but he'll have a hard time. They've rifles and grenades, same stuff as earlier. Police aren't here yet, but they'll be coming when the local worthies report gunfire up and down their discreet little track. First impression is that they know what they're at, taking all the basic pre-cautions . . .'

Through the house Jimmy heard the penetrating

wail of a police siren. He put the telephone down without explanation and ran back through the house and front door, careering into the centre of the road to wave down the patrol car. He saw the officers inside flinch away, then remembered he still held the PPK. He showed them his plastic-coated identity card – the answer to all problems – with the black and white mugshot from the days before his face filled out with age.

'Don't go any further,' he snapped. 'First thing, one of you get round the back, the other clear the street. Boyos from the London effort tonight are in the end house, one on the right side. They're littered with hardware, so go careful.' As an afterthought he asked the obvious. 'Have they issued you with fire-arms?'

The policemen were both young, not out of their twenties. They shook their heads, apprehension running deep.

'Well, don't just sit there. If you haven't got them it's tough. Showbiz. One of you'll still have to shift round the back, the other call up the bloody cavalry.'

Within a quarter of an hour the house was sealed to the outside world. Police marksmen with FN rifles had taken up positions outside across the street facing the house. Others lay in the garden at right-angles to its front door. Four were against the back fence and with them were the local force's two attack-trained alsatian dogs. A portable searchlight, short and tubular, erected on a tripod, and powered by a noisy insistent generator, projected its high-intensity beam against the face of the house. The building itself was eerily still, as if contaminated by plague, quarantined, no movement and no noise around it, great shadows thrown on the brickwork by the roses that the family had so carefully nurtured. At the bottom of the street were the fire engines, motors ticking over, blue hazard lights circling perpetually, and further back the ambulances with their rear doors opened and the red-blanketed stretchers laid ready at the roadside. This was where the other residents of the street had gathered. Adults still dressed, children in their night clothes and wrapped in anoraks and overcoats against the chill of the evening. There was little talk among them, just the overwhelming sensation of shock that such a thing should happen in their street, in their private preserve.

The order had already been issued that no instruction concerning reaction operations should be broadcast over police short-wave radio, and no information issued to the press unless from authorized police public relations at Scotland Yard.

'We have to cocoon them,' the station superintendent said. 'Cut them right off till the VIPs arrive and announce the Great Plan. In the meantime no sense letting them just twiddle a few knobs on a radio set and have an earful of what we're up to.'

'Who's coming down?' asked Jimmy.

'Half bloody London. They're leaving the PM and the Queen in charge, far as I can make out. The rest are hot-footing it over here. Assistant Commissioner, Home Secretary, Defence people, a man called Jones from your crowd, scores of them.'

'Let's hope they bring some changes of socks,' said Jimmy. 'They can take a long time, these things.'

'It can take a long time or it can take five minutes.

That's a political decision.' The superintendent walked away.

In the back of the official car that sped south-west out of London toward Richmond Jones felt an overwhelming sense of relief. Had the pair of them boxed up: that had been the gist of the message from the Scotland Yard Operations Room. Would just be a matter of sitting it out, waiting for them to get tired of their predicament once they'd been convinced of the hopelessness of their situation. Might lose a hostage or two – unlikely though, and anyway they were expendable, weren't they? Probably get everyone out alive; it was reasonable to assume so on past performance. That would tie it up neatly, avoid the martyrdom that Jimmy would want to award the Arab. No more killing, no more slaughter, and a finish to this lunatic hysteria that had been gripping everyone in the department the last five days. And the department had done well; that would have been noticed.

The Prime Minister sat at the end of the table, the cigar nestling in the fingers of his right hand. It was unlit and little more than a theatrical prop, but he liked to have it there, particularly when decisions had to be made. There were four other men at the table. On the Prime Minister's right the Commissioner of Police for the capital and the Permanent Under Secretary for the Ministry of Defence. On his left the Director General of the Security Services, and further away a middle-ranking Civil Servant from the Home Office.

The Prime Minister had opened the meeting –

begun as his dinner guests were still finding their way on to the pavement outside Number Ten – by asking the Commissioner to report on the latest situation at the house.

A detailed, clipped account. Without waste, no adjectives for effect, rhetoric removed. The policeman concluded, 'It's basiccally a classic siege situation, of which we have some experience of our own but on which there is much international information to fall back. They have three hostages, they are proven killers, one of them is confirmed injured. As yet we have no demands, but it's early for that. They'll follow, and when they do they'll be wanting a plane out. These men are liable to be in a highly unstable condition after their failure earlier in the evening. In my submission, time as much as anything else will calm them down. Otherwise you have a potential bloodbath.'

The Prime Minister shifted his weight, faced the Director General.

'I've not much to add to that. Except that we believe that our man has wounded . . .'

'Your marksman,' the Prime Minister interrupted, 'the one that you put such faith in.'

'. . . our man has wounded the Irishman, McCoy. Our assessment is that McCoy would probably be the more skilfil of the pair, in the tactical sense, that is, but that his resolve may not equal the Arab's. We would believe that if it came to a shoot-out in the house then the greater threat to the lives of the hostages and of the storm party would come from the Arab.'

So ridiculous, thought the Prime Minister. Intelligent men, all of us, people to see, work to be done, beds and families to be getting to, and all sitting round a table in the seat of Government discussing the form, the betting card on who kills best – the Celt or the Oriental. Nonsensical.

'Mr Dawson, we move into your realm. What are the considerations we have to weigh in contemplating the storming of the house?' The Prime Minister was looking past the Director General to the young, lean and shadow-pallored man who had to that moment taken no part in the discussion, only scribbled comprehensive shorthand notes on a small lined pad.

'With respect, sir' – Dawson spoke at a speed that matched his writing, not looking up from his papers, but in a low voice so that the others had to strain forward to hear him – 'the business we face is not that different to the proceedings of the Lord Chief Justice's Court. We can only deal with previous case histories, with other judgements. It is unlikely that there will be special circumstances that will give us an option that has not faced other authorities here or on the Continent or in the United States when challenged with the same problem. I submit that we have to look at the solutions that have been attempted or discarded in the past. First, the best documented: the Olympics attack. In Munich the Germans were confronted with an end-of-terrace building, but they were dealing with a larger group of hostages, and many more men in the attack squad. The Police President of the City considered the use of incapacitating gases and eliminated them as too slow. They also considered gaining access to the house next door and placing explosive charges against the common wall and blasting an entry that

326

way. This was rejected, too: potentially dangerous to the hostages and also unsatisfactory if their exact location in the building could not be pin-pointed. So they relied in the end on luring the Black September team into the open and assulting them with selected marksmen. Result: a fiasco. In the United States, in the Washington Court House siege, the authorities took their time, stalled. After many hours they managed to provide a key to the hostages, secreted in the supplies they were permitted to send in, but they had some high-quality people imprisoned who were able to make decisive use of the help given to them. I think that is unlikely to apply in this case. The Israelis themselves – and they believe they have a certain unmatched expertise in these matters – stake all on heavy frontal assault backed by diversionary fire, heavy fire. They risk everything on speed and finely worked-out timing. You will be aware, sir, that the terrorists die, but they take a high proportion of the hostages with them. Probably unacceptable in our circumstances.'

There was no shuffling of papers, scraping of feet, stifled coughs. Dawson was the expert, with a mastery of a vague and untested subject. It was easy to see that on his ability and conclusions rested the lives of many.

'The Dutch faced a different type of situation in the prison siege at Scheveningen in the autumn of 1974. They determined to enter one heavily locked door, the only point of access to the prison chapel. But they had certain knowledge through eye-witnesses and electronic aids of the precise positions of hostages and captors. They waited till they were satisfied the terrorist faction had been lulled into

327

false confidence, then used a laser beam to burn out the lock, accompanied by massive diversionary noise. That operation was completely successful. I should stress that British experience is in the field of the waiting game. It is the tactic most generally advocated. As a strategy it is probably applicable more to the domestic problems of criminals or IRA-type terrorists, less useful in dealing with international groups – Palestinians or Red Army of Japan. If you freeze the latter type out you are then faced with the legal processes and the probability of reprisals with the aim of freeing your prisoners.'

'How soon could we mount an effective attack on the house?' The Prime Minister wanted it over, completed. The other men could see that. Easy to recognize, the fear of a drawn-out bartering for life. Endless negotiations as they had witnessed in Germany and France and Greece and Italy, and then government capitulation to the power of the automatic rifle, the primed explosives.

Dawson said, 'It's well documented that the most favoured time for assault is just before dawn. Give or take a few minutes, but it's round four o'clock. Doctors will tell you that medically this is the time of least resistance – it's when the elderly die, the blood gets colder then. And we start with the advantage that these men will be tired. They have been under pressure for many hours now, since the weekend. They need to rest. If one is hurt then that puts greater stress on the other, but he too must relax at some stage. So tomorrow morning – it could be done then, as soon as that. But the earlier you attack the greater the risk. Whatever their capabilities these two men will still be attempting maximum performance.

You would be leaving no time to wear them down, blind-alley them.'

The idea of the laser appealed to the Prime Minister. He talked frequently in his public speeches of the need for technological advance in the country; his opponents said he was obsessed with gadgetry, more interested in the machines of industry than the men and women who manipulated them. He was close now to the decision for which the four men waited.

'Two questions, Mr Dawson. Could we produce the laser by the time tomorrow morning that you have specified? And what sort of diversions would you think necessary?'

It was William Dawson's value to those that he advised that he seldom answered unless certain of his information. The availability of the cutting beam caused him to hesitate before committing himself.

'Probably we could get a laser from industry, certainly from Imperial College. It does not have to be a particularly refined or sophisticated model. Whether the necessary authorization and personnel could be obtained in the next five hours . . . ? As for the diversions, I would suggest considerable noise for five-minute periods, every twenty minutes or so. Engines revving, fire brigade sirens, shouting radio chatter. Build it up, then let it fade, but keep it up in the pattern through the night till the small hours. They'll be accustomed to it, familiar, by the time we want to use the laser, its noise covered, it would take about fifteen seconds to open the front door, not more.'

'You have the authorization, Mr Dawson. Get the damned thing.' The Prime Minister was bubbling now, effervescent, decision-taking, the broth of politics. Facing the Civil Servant who sat beyond the police commissioner, he said, 'Mr Harrison, I want the Special Air Service to assault the house in the small hours of tomorrow morning. I would be unconcerned if the Arab should not survive the entry.'

The commissioner reacted quickly. 'With respect, this is a Metropolitan Police district. Several serious crimes have been committed in that overall responsibility area, and we are quite capable through our Special Patrol Group of mounting the necessary assault. It's a slur . . .'

'Commissioner,' said the Prime Minister coldly, folding his spectacles, the discussion completed. 'I am interested in results, not sensibilities. If you ask Mr Dawson I am sure that he will explain in great detail that one of the few successful legacies handed down by the Munich police after Furstenfeldbruck was the certain knowledge that in future all similar operations should be placed squarely in the hands of the military.'

The messages went out, coded and fast. Thirty-five minutes after the Prime Minister's advisers had taken their leave, and still short of midnight, the SAS anti-hijack force had been lifted by Wessex helicopter from their base camp in Herefordshire. They represented some of the most highly trained and resourceful troops in the British armed forces. There was little equipment stowed on the floor of the helicopter, just an awesome variety of firearms.

The spasms in his shoulder came and went with increasing frequency as McCoy moved about the house, so that he needed to steel himself for the onset of pain that caused him to stop and lean against the nearest wall. There was much movement, much that he had to do, aggravating the wound, but his persistence was uppermost. Structure had to be built, the rest would come after that. He took the parents upstairs, one at a time, and laid them face down on the beds, one in the main sleeping room and the other in the spare bedroom. It required great effort for him to rip up the top sheet of the front room double bed into the narrow strips that he sought. Using his undamaged hand and his teeth he tore at the lengths that he needed to tie them. Neither of the elderly people was in a state of mind to resist him, too horrified by the suddenness of the incursion. But if they had then one well-placed blow would have won them their freedom. As it was they obeyed meekly and followed exactly the orders that he gave. When they were prone on the beds he bound their hands behind their backs, threatening to each that he would be watching the lifetime partner, and that if he heard the sound of attempted escape then he would kill.

When he had finished he felt his strength drain until he was totally weak. Mingling now with the pain was a rising nausea. He flopped back against the wall behind the headboard, on the sparse single bed in the girl's room, his feet on the yellow coverlet, smearing it with street dirt. He angled his body so that his weight was borne on the left side, and in that hand he held the rifle, pistol-like, the shoulder support still folded. Like a grotesque interloper he dominated the tiny room, blond hair dishevelled and lost in a myriad of Medusa patterns, his face, with its colour from the fields of South Armagh now vanished, showing only the anger of the eyes and the ferrule lines of exertion. The stains on his jacket were not rich and red but stark, damp and soiled. He had laid the rifle across his lap and pulled from his pocket the grenades, which he placed beside his hip. The good hand, the one he now relied on, resumed hold on the trigger guard of the M1.

Till she followed him into the room the girl had not seen the wounds, but when he shifted on the bed, awkwardly and seeking the comfort that the pain denied him, the blood run was visible, and she saw too the twin holes in the cloth. She sat on the end of the bed.

'Why have you come back here? What do you want of us?'

'Time, my little girl. Time for a friend.'

'For the Arab?'

'Time for the Arab. Time for him to stretch his legs, get on his wings.'

'He has gone?'

'You saw him, he's moved on. Further to go than I have. This is where I finish; his post is a long way yet. It's as if he hadn't left the starting line. He's the whole course to run. I'm his handicapper. Big Ciaran ensures he starts in front, out ahead of the bastards. That's the way it is, my little cash-machine girl.'

No need to talk to her, nothing could be said that mattered, just an empty face and fingers that punched a till. Meaningless. Time to think of yourself, Ciaran-boy. Famy off on course, but the fences are higher and the ditches are deeper and they've extended the track, the bastards. We held all the cards, he thought. Now we've none of them, and the silly bugger's gone on, and to his death, and he's taking you with him. His eyes were open, but he did not see the girl, just stared to the darkness of the ceiling. He wondered how he'd go, how death would close in on him. Had thought it might be in a ditch, or in the mess of a farmyard as the cordon tightened, or on the high wire of the Kesh, or being pulled by the legs from a sniper pit by a para. But never thought of it like this, not in a room eight by ten with rabbits and daffodils on the wall, and the smell of scent and a folded nightdress under his arse.

But even as the the barometer of pain circled to hideous levels, so the preciousness of life remained hard to pass up. His eyes closed, clamped shut, his upper teeth hard down on the bottom lip, and he waved with the rifle barrel for her to come closer. He put the gun down beside the grenades and began to drag with his left hand at the jacket. She slid along the bed to him, and as he levered himself away from the wall she looped the jacket over his shoulders and down his arms. Once he cried out. When the jacket was off and he was free of it she dropped the garment on the fluffed, sky-blue rug. He rolled on his side, doubled up and panting for relief.

'Get some water, and something to clean it.' She barely heard the words. She was gone briefly, and came back into the room with a saucepan, the steam rising from it, and a wad of bright cotton wool. When she switched on the light he opened his eyes again, and then, with his help, she took off his shirt. With care she lifted his vest over his head. The blood had caked far down his chest – dark, dried rivulets leading to his navel. With the swabs she worked her path closer to the neat, circular wounds in the flesh.

Not much time on the arm, priority to the shoulder. She felt the skin tighten, striving for escape as she neared the place of the second bullet's entry. Instinctively she pulled him forward so she could clean the expected exit wound in his back, and saw only the skin, unbroken and stretched across the tightened back muscles.

'It's still in there,' half a statement, half a question.

He nodded, and for the first time she saw him smile.

'It has to come out. It'll kill you.'

'All in good time,' said McCoy. 'The lad has a long way to travel. I want him far on his journey before the heavies find it's just wee Ciaran McCoy that's holding the baby.'

'What will they do, the police?'

'They'll huff and puff a few more hours, then they'll call for surrender, and we'll do nothing, then they'll have a bash at us ... Switch the light off!' His voice was suddenly urgent, incisive. When the room was in darkness again she could listen. Close by, down the road, there was a roar of a heavy engine as if the driver was pumping his foot up and down on the accelerator. Across from the window muffled shouts. She eased the curtain back, giving herself visibility of the road immediately in front of the house.

'There's nothing moving there,' she said.

There was some brightness from a street light, augmented by the searchlight beam, and though his face was half in shadow she could make out the line of his features. 'Why is it necessary to do what you have done to my parents?'

He anticipated her. 'They stay tied, and they stay separate.'

'They couldn't do anything, they couldn't hurt you.'

'I said they stay like that . . .'

'You said the police would break in. How soon?'

'Not for a day or so. They'll want time to work out a plan. Take them half a week.' He reached forward with his left hand and took hold of her arm, then pulled her so that she stretched across the width of the bed, and his head sank into her lap where her thighs came together. He remembered the afternoon in the park. Not thirty hours before, yet half a lifetime. In the darkness his breathing slowed and he lay still. Had to rest, had to go back to Cullyhanna, had to climb the hills again.

'Why didn't you use anything yesterday?' she said.

'I don't know,' said McCoy. 'I don't know.'

Chapter Seventeen

Once the doctor had gone they left David Sokarev alone in his room.

The tablet he had taken, washed down with tap water from the tooth mug, had taken effect quickly, bringing on the drowsiness that conquered the terror of the earlier part of the evening. After the noise-filled, siren-blasting convoy had carried him to the hotel they had hurried him to his room, aided his undressing and readied him in his bed for the arrival of the Jewish doctor. Elkin had hovered close and maternal as the doctor bent over his patient, but Sokarev could see that his bodyguard's calm acceptance of the situation was waning, to be replaced by a morose silence. The lion had lost its mate. The two men had hunted together, worked, planned, eaten and rested together, bound in their opposites by comradeship. That was all destroyed now, by a pathetic and harmless-seeming grenade.

The assurance and confidence around the scientist when they had left for the university was another casualty of the attack replaced with a diffidence that alternated with the fraying tempers. The Englishman should have been there, the one Sokarev remembered above all others, the one with only a given name and with the old suit. He was the one who had promised he would be beside Sokarev, who had made a joke of it all, who had laid his professionalism out for all to see in the very relaxation he had demonstrated since they had met. But he was absent, the one who was needed now. The man among all others in whom Sokarev had believed, in whom he had placed his trust. There had been a promise.

Sokarev felt a great helplessness, isolated and remote when he spoke from his bed, the neatly folded hotel blankets high up against his striped pyjamas and across his chest.

'Where is the Englishman, the one who called himself Jimmy?' It was an interruption and cut across the low-pitched conversations that were being pursued out of his earshot across the width of the room.

'He left in chase,' said Elkin. 'After Mackowicz was killed he ran for the door. He had been shooting, there is no word of him since then.'

'He said he would be with us. Continuously.'

'Well, he's not here. No sign of him. Running the streets, no doubt, trying to pull back something from the chaos. But something dramatic it has to be, after what has happened. The security was like a sieve. Disorganized, unprepared. A shambles they made for us.'

He came close to the bed, words barely under control, spitting his anger. 'You can understand, Professor, that from now it will be we who supervise all movements. There will be no more outsiders making decisions, no more delegation. The Englishman that you want beside you made a grand speech about "responsibilty" to Mackowicz. Where is Mackowicz now? Where is the man who gave those orders?'

The Special Branch Inspector, already feeling the ice wall that divided him from the Israelis, made no comment. Irretrievable situation. No verbal points worth scoring, and short of currency anyway.

With the arrival of the Ambassador the men had withdrawn through the communicating door. The Ambassador, not attempting to disguise his fury, the security attaché, Elkin, two more men from the embassy that Sokarev had not seen before but who carried hand radio sets. They closed the door after them, and the English policeman, unwanted and ignored, made his way into the corridor outside. Last to go had been the doctor. Just a specimen to them, thought Sokarev. Like a box of bullion, to be displayed when necessary, shifted when convenient. Not to be consulted, not to be taken into confidence. In the last minutes before the pill took its action he heard the raised voices seeping through from the next room. Shouting, and Elkin's voice loud and demanding to be listened to, the security attaché attempting to act as intermediary and being driven into irrelevance by the deep, clear-cut words of the Ambassador.

The point at issue was simple enough: the movements of Sokarev. Elkin insisted on an immediate return to Tel Aviv. The Ambassador with his superior diplomatic rank but without the specific responsibility for Sokarev's safety, required clearance from Jerusalem before the visit to New York could be cancelled.

338

'It is impossible to justify the continuance of his journey,' shouted Elkin.

It is a way of life in the Israeli community that title and position count for little when the question of security is at stake. He could browbeat a senior diplomat in a way unthought of throughout Europe.

'If they can attack here they can attack in the United States. One of our men has died already that this one speech could be made. How many more do we lose protecting him if we go to America? And for what . . . ?'

'He goes for precisely the reason that he came here in the first instance. The threat was known, but we do not bow to threats . . .'

'He was a scientist, not a target dummy.'

'. . . The decision was made at Cabinet level that he should come. We will not be cowed by these people.'

'Before, that was a reasonable risk. Not now. They did well tonight, those bastards. That they missed was our luck. No credit to us. Luck, and Mackowicz.'

'The decision must come from Jerusalem.' The Ambassador spoke with finality.

'The decision is easy, Excellency. Very simple, no doubt you can answer it for me. Which way is the Professor more important? A household name, famous, and dead; a martyr to the cause of the survival of our country. That is one option. Or more important in his office, in his anonymity, with his papers and his tables and his work. It is sad you cannot consult with Mackowicz, he would pick between the options.'

There was a purple, veined flush high on the Ambassador's cheeks. He turned to the door. 'As I have said, the decision must come from the Foreign

Ministry. I will relay your comments, and they will have consideration.'

'And what of Sokarev? What of his ability to go on? Will that have consideration?'

But the Ambassador and the security attaché were gone. Elkin looked at the two new men who were to share the room with him, then twisted away lest they should see the tears that now lapped at his eyelids. Like a brother to him, Mackowicz. An elder brother, protective, dominating. And now without his stomach, intestines splayed to the winds. He crumpled himself full length on his bed. That Sokarev was alive and breathing heavily a few feet away was an inadequate consolation.

The Ambassador, an experienced diplomat, was well versed in the art of self-preservation. His request to Jerusalem for guidance contained no suggestion of his own, and added with prominence the concern of Sokarev's remaining bodyguard. The coded reply he awaited, a jumble of numbers, arrived in the embassy communications room within two hours. After it had been deciphered it was brought to him.

XXCLL478219

FOREIGNMINISTRY JERUSALEM

001 8208 PERSONAL FOREIGN MINISTER TO AMBASSADORUK ITEM HIS EYES ONLY ITEM AFTER URGENT CONSIDERATIONS SOKAREV'S MOVEMENTS EYE INFORMING SIMULTANEOUSLY AMBASSADORUSA TO ANNOUNCE CANCELLATION OF ABOVE'S TRAVEL AND SPEAKING ARRANGEMENTS IN NY AND OTHERS ITEM SOKAREV SHOULD REUTRN ISRAEL FIRST AVAILABLE NON-STOP ELAL FLIGHT ITEM WE

DEMAND FULLEST SECURITY DURING REMAINING
HOURS SOKAREV'S PRESENCE UK PARTICULAR
LONDON HEATHROW DEPARTURE ITEM YOU WILL
ISSUE STRONGEST PROTEST TO UK GOVERNMENT AT
LEVEL NOT BELOW FOREIGN MINISTER PREFERABLY
PRIME MINISTER AT LAX UK SECURITY STRESSING
FULL INFORMATION AND WARNING PROVIDED BY
OUR SECURITY SERVICE PRIOR SOKAREV ARRIVAL
ITEM WE REQUIRE PUBLIC EXPRESSION REGRET ITEM
COMMUNICATION COMPLETE
XXDYY478219

Alone in the flat in Beersheba the scientist's wife
heard over the Israeli Broadcasting Corporation's
final radio news bulletin of the attack on her
husband. The information came without warning,
as the news media transmitted the story faster
than those Government authorities responsible for
her husband's welfare could react.

In desperation she tried to telephone first her son;
on operational standby and not available to take
messages. Next her daughters; both out of their
student hostels and not expected back till later. The
Director at Dimona, an old friend; away at a conference in Tiberias. The seemingly endless lingering
of the disappointments as she waited four times for a
familiar voice to come on the line, and on each
occasion had her hopes dashed, took a heavy toll.
She sat in David Sokarev's chair, beside the fire that
would not be lit till the winter came and the cold
over the desert and waited for the early morning
light still five hours away. That she knew her man
was safe was of some small help. What caused her to
sob soundlessly into the half-darkness of the centre

341

of the room was the knowledge of the deep fear and terror he would have suffered. So inoffensive, so mild, without enemies, without a voice that was ever raised in anger. Buried away in a cramped office, insulated against the hatred and hostility that lay rampant beyond the wire fences of Dimona. But would his work, and the implications of his study, provide him with an insight into this obscenity? She wondered. The preparation of the bomb itself, awful, grotesque, multi-destructive, would that have prepared him to confront the viciousness of the last hours? It was not his way to see the bomb as a finished and completed article of war. Just figures and notes on paper. Drawings that were meaningless to others. Long hours and days and months of work. Calculations and equations.

He would not have understood. He had been too long absent from the world of men who now fought round him to take and protect his life. He would be alone, defenceless. That was why she wept for him.

The Special Air Service squad were brought to Chisholm Road in two Black Maria police vans from an improvised helicopter landing pad on the football pitches beside the main road that ran out of Richmond to the south. They wore full-length black dungarees, were not encumbered with webbing and equipment and none boasted badges of rank on their upper arms or shoulders. They jumped casually and with ease from the open doors at the back of the vans, and then the heavy canvas bags were handed down.

Jimmy stood in the shadows and watched them. Not youngsters, but most of them still half his age, hair cut close, clean shaven, disinterested faces visible only when the lights rotating on the roofs of the fire engines illuminated the path across which they walked. The killing squad. Different to Jimmy, not self-taught as he had been. Trained and practised, funded by Government that their expertise should be developed. Selected with care and toughened and primed. Taught not to act independently, but in the pack, deadly and irreversible when the leash was slipped. If they felt excitement they did not show it, just trooped after the one who was their leader across the road to where the Home Office man waited. Some squatted low over sheets of paper held flat on the pavement, others stood in a circle peering into the area lit by torches.

William Dawson was a thorough man. He took them through the diagram of the outside of the house, all windows and doors marked in red, first the ground floor, then the upper storey. The squad said nothing, two taking notes, the others watching and silent. Then came the plans of the interior of the end-of-terrace home. Drawn to scale. Red marking the doorways again, and blue crosses on those that the neighbours had reported to be fitted with locks and bolts. Fingers ran along the routes of the hallway, the stairs and the landing. Occasionally those at the back would crane their necks up the street to relate the floodlit frontage with the paperwork. Jimmy stood half a dozen paces back from the huddle; Jones was far behind him at the steps of the police control vehicle.

Dawson was talking, fast and coherent, sketching the plan he had described to the Prime Minister. Diversions, and time factors, and entry points, and opposition capability, and of the laser. There were precedents, and case histories and suggestions. The attention that the squad gave the Civil Servant was the accolade that he had done his work, was as expert in the planning as they would be in the execution.

When the group broke up it was to appointed tasks. Four to unload the firepower they had brought with them, to lay the weapons out and to load them. Four more to begin a scrounging expedition among the fire brigades, for ropes and axes and the fifteen-foot ladders that would carry them to the first-floor windows. The officer and his sergeant detached themselves, and in the company of a ranking police officer made their way past the front doors of the houses, traversing the front gardens, working closer to the house that they would storm. When they had seen the front they moved, silent and catlike, through another house and across its back garden till they came without warning on the police who watched the rear of Number 25. From the outside there was little to tell them of the situation beyond the brick walls. All curtains drawn, windows darkened.

'They had the light on a bit ago. In the front, upstairs, the small room where the girl sleeps. It was off within a minute. The men across the road from the front think the curtain there moved once, but it's bloody difficult to be sure. It was when we first started the noise business that the Home Office chap wanted. The second time we did it nothing happened, not that we saw. There's been three more times we've used the noise since then, and nothing. No movement that we've seen.'

The Chief Inspector was depressed. That this was not police work he acknowledged, was grateful he was not asking among his men for volunteers for an attack party, but the very competence and hardness of the new arrivals had shaken and concerned him.

'What chance have you got of getting those people out alive?' That was the nub of the problem as he saw it, and he raised the question as they slipped back toward the concentration of vehicles and men.

'Can't say,' replied the officer quietly, as if their voices would carry. 'Depends where the family are, whether they're together. What state the wounded fellow is in. How much speed we can muster. If we're fast enough there's a good chance. The theory is that it's difficult for a man to turn his gun on his hostages as we're coming through the door. He has no protection. He goes with them. There's not many relish that – that's what the handbook says, at any rate. But it's all theory. There's nothing cut and dried.'

Before they reached the fire engine closest to the house, and where men in uniform had gathered, and where there would be ears to listen to their conversation, the officer said, 'Don't misunderstand me, but isn't there some question about priorities? The hostages aren't at the top of the list as I see it. If they were we'd be talking, negotiating. Spinning it out. I have the priority as the two blokes. If we get the family out that's a bonus. Hitting those two buggers in there is what we're here for.'

Jimmy's eyes had seldom left the house. Its very ordinariness fascinated him. Uninteresting, unremarkable, undistinguished. Forty-nine others like

345

it in the road. An inhabited box. Lived in by people who were stereotype-produced as the bricks and mortar they surrounded themselves with. And their visitors, they also were from the depths of mediocrity, without identity – totally irrelevant without the guns and the grenades. The only things of significance about them were their rifles and the explosives. But that to Jimmy was muscle, that was the core of terrorism. It was this power that lifted the nonentity onto the pedestal he sought. Jimmy had heard that in a lecture in the department, had listened – which was rare – and agreed. Behind him was the Home Secretary, arms either akimbo or flattened against his backside as he looked solemnly at the tarmac and heard out the Assistant Commissioner. Only one reason he's here, thought Jimmy, the hardware. Doesn't matter how screwed up are the little bastards with their hands on it, the hardware brings the big men out. To all of them standing round the house with their guns and their dogs and their truncheons McCoy and the Arab were just pictures, two-dimensional, black and white. Not to Jimmy. Jimmy had seen them, seen the character of their faces, the shape of their mouths, the slouch of their movements. And Jimmy had tried to kill them that evening, counted himself unlucky that he hadn't. It tied them together, Jimmy and McCoy and the Arab, in a perverse but brutal liaison. And they had seen him, twenty yards away, and there had been the rifle fire and the thrown grenade. So they knew each other, understood the stake money. When he looked away from the house Jimmy could see the SAS men making their preparations. But these were outsiders, not a part of it till little more

346

than an hour earlier when their helicopter had lifted off from the far west.

Jimmy walked across the road to where the army officer stood, concentrating on his notebook. He tapped the other man's shoulder and pushed forward his identity card. The officer glanced at it, and acknowledged him by diverting his gaze to Jimmy's eyes. He's impatient, the bastard.

'Jimmy's the name. From the Security Services.'

'George Martin, Captain.'

'I've been on this one. Full time. Since the flap started. I'd like to go along with you.'

There was a faint smile at the extremes of Martin's mouth. Not quite as tall as Jimmy, looking up at him. Unsettling, unhelpful, difficult to communicate. Jimmy went on, 'I'd like to go into the house with you. I know what they both look like, could be of use to you.'

The smile broadened. 'Sorry, father, no passengers this time round. If you want to come and identify them after there'll be no problem.'

'Don't give me the father crap . . .'

'And don't get in my way. We've work, and no time . . .'

'Listen,' said Jimmy, face close to the soldier's. 'I'm in the protection team. Right beside Sokarev, the Isracli, this evening, appointed to guard him.'

'You're a touch off course then. Nobody told us he'd joined the party in there. I'd have thought your best place was at the hotel holding your baby's hand. Must be looking for a bit of a lullaby after the hoop you put him through tonight.'

Your cool's going, Jimmy. Double fast, like it always does with these uptight swine. 'If it hadn't been for me he'd be in the morgue now. And when you get in there you'll find one of the bastards half-dead with my bullet in him . . .'

'Come to the wrong chap, then. It's the Birthday Honours you're looking for. I don't hand medals out. Right now I'm busy, got my hands full, and no-one goes in alongside my team. Understood?'

'You stupid bastard,' said Jimmy.

The captain smiled again, almost a laugh, and walked away.

It took Jimmy some minutes to find Jones. He was in a group among men of equal status, discussing the problems that confronted them. How to introduce before the scheduled dawn attack the fish-eyed visual surveillance lens that would arrive in a few hours from London, the merits of the various audio-electronic devices that were available, the question of news releases. Jones was rarely in such company, unfamiliar with the bright excitement his companions felt at whiling their evening away waiting for whatever disaster or success the morning might bring. He felt his years shackled to the desk had cheated him of something he vaguely saw as precious. Too much time on paperwork, while the knowledge of the techniques that dominated the world of his new companions was denied him. That he was accepted among them pleased him, but he recognized it was not because of his contribution but through his rank and title. And then Jimmy was at his side, pulling at his coat, just as he was in mid-sentence, and drawing him away. Jones saw the warning signs, noticed the blink in Jimmy's left upper eyelid, knew it from years back. And Jimmy launched off: 'Bloody army, bloody pigs. I've been with this one right the way through, did you well tonight, bloody well, and now I want to go in there and finish the bloody thing, and that little prig, the bloody army man, treats me like I'm out for some bloody Cook's Tour. All patronizing and "Come in when we've finished" and that crap.'

'What do you want to go in for, Jimmy?' said Jones.

'To finish the bloody thing, finish what started this evening.'

'Be in at the killing, right? That's what you want?'

'Right first time. I bloody started and . . .'

'It's not a quota job, Jimmy-boy. You don't need notches on your pension book. What's the matter, short this year on your numbers? You're not a policeman. You haven't got to get twenty traffic bookings a month to hold down a reputation.'

'You mean you're not going to tell them to count me in?' There was doubt in his voice. Jones had always backed him in the past. Why different now?

'Of course I'm not. What do you expect me to say? I've got a man on my books who's a bit short of stiffs this month. Comes out in a rash if he doesn't nab a couple each thirty days. Snap out of it, Jimmy. You've had your scene tonight, done well. You should be off home, and in your pit by now and sleeping so you're not a zombie tomorrow when God knows what happens.'

'Straight bloody heave, then?'

'If you see it that way, Jimmy, that's your problem. But do us all a favour and shove back to town so you're not knackered in the morning.'

'I thought there'd be some bloody clout from you,'

Jimmy was shouting, his words carrying across the still of the night, loud enough for those who could not avoid hearing to shuffle their feet and cough.

Jimmy swung on his heel and walked through the rope cordon, side-stepped the newspaper and television photographers, past the sightseers who would wait till there was any action of any sort at whatever advanced hour. He walked down the hill toward the town. There would be a taxi rank there and then there would be the hotel close to the flat where the night porter would fix him up with a half bottle. As he went he wondered about the life and times inside Number 25. He thought of McCoy with the hole in him, and of the Arab. Pictured the faces as he'd seen them in the glare of his headlights the moment before he'd fired. Wondered how they'd cope when the military came in. Wanted to be there, missing his bloody treat, and God he'd deserved the party. The tin that he kicked in his frustration careered clumsily and raucously down the road in front of him.

She knew that if she moved McCoy would wake. It was awkward, half-propped on one arm, and lying across the narrow width of the bed, with the weight of his shoulder and his head flattened against her stomach. His sleep was light, punctuated by convulsions when he twisted his body over from right to left, felt the pain, and swung back onto the undamaged arm. The wound through the upper chest was near to her head and it oozed strange and unknown fluids that showed in the half-light as opaque dribblings. Sometimes she turned her eyes away from the hole and its debris, but then her imagination took over and besieged her more fearfully than the reality. Nightmarishly she could see the stunted column of lead striking the softness of the skin, could feel the splitting and carving of the tissues and wonder at the sensation of the fragments making their uninterrupted passage in the void beneath the flesh. And he had said it would all happen again. Had told her that they would come. Policemen with rifles, more bullets, bursting through the door, kicking their way across the tiny floor-space, brushing aside the white-wood and wicker chair on which she had laid his stained jacket and shirt and undervest. And what would he do when they came? His rifle was half under his legs, still held close to the trigger guard by the left hand. So small, and beside its shallow length the grenades, miniaturized. They didn't have the scale and size for her to believe in them as killing weapons. Too sparse, too insignificant. But when they came, when the police came, he would try to fire, try to pull the absurd circular pin on the grenade. And they would shoot. They would be quicker, organized, without pity. Then there would be the profusion of holes, beating formations in his chest, slicing through the rib cage that showed clear as he lay in his sleep. When they came it would be to kill, not to capture. Norah knew that.

Even had she not been so tired she could not have analysed her feelings for Ciaran McCoy. 'Love' was the magazine word, written in stories with windswept hills and boys who were dark and tidy, and girls with wasp waists and unbuttoned blouses and long hair. Infatuation she understood, read of it in the agony columns, real enough, able to match it with her own emotions; the boy last year who worked under Father at the factory. Temporary and heartrending, nice to cry over. But McCoy, this was something unique for her and surpassing her understanding. She could not envisage herself in love with a man capable of such horror as the strangulation of the policewoman whose picture the television had shown, not in love with the man of the hateful, animal-wild eyes imprinted in her mind from the newspaper picture. Yet she had lain with him in the grass of the park, and taken him in her arms, and pressed his head against her breasts, and said his name, and felt the warmth and the pain of him deep between her legs. And he was to die. Snuffed out. Shot dead by the guns of men in uniform.

Norah reached down to the floor, to the square of carpet that covered the centre of the room inside the vinyl surround, and felt under her bed for her shoes, careful not to disturb his sleep. All her shoes were under the bed; the room was too small to provide the adequate cupboard space she required. Two pairs were there, her evening going-out ones, and the flats for work in the supermarket. Further under were the back numbers of the magazines that came on Thursday mornings, and that caused her to linger in bed and be late for breakfast and run for the bus. She straightened, gently and slowly, taking time till she could ease out the pillow that had nestled in the small of her back. Together they were sufficient. First the magazines, then the shoes, then the pillow. With one hand she steadied his sleeping head while she wormed as far back toward the wall as her body had room to move, and then there was the space for her to build the counterfeit lap. The height was the same, and when she eased his head onto the softness of the pillow his eyes stayed tight shut, and there was only the forced and erratic breathing.

She was not betraying him, she told herself, only offering him salvation. This way he would survive. Go out of her life, that was inevitable, but survive. On her window-sill were the keys to the outside doors he had brought upstairs with him. It was easy for her to select the one that opened the front door.

Past three she saw on her watch when she stepped out on to the landing of the house and went barefoot, and on her toes, without sound towards the staircase. At the head of the stairs she stopped to listen to the light noises of the house. McCoy's breathing, audible, painful. Fainter movements from the rooms where her parents lay.

Pray God he doesn't wake, she said to herself, and eased onto the first step.

Famy had gone over the wall and into the park. Once inside he ran till his legs would carry him no further. Fast, hard and direct toward the southwest, sprinting so that many times he had plunged without warning into bushes, stumbled in the grassed-over drains. His hands were cut, and there were tears round the knees of his trousers. The rifle made it difficult, clutched as a talisman, with only one hand free to protect him when he pitched forward. But McCoy had made the sacrifice. McCoy had stayed behind to win him the distance he now sought to put between himself and the pursuit. No idea how many hours' start he would have, whether the hunt had in fact already begun, whether it would come at dawn or not for a full day. But the Irishman had sacrificed himself, probably given his life to gain him the ground he now swept over. It clinched his motivation, and when his legs sagged under him he rested only for the muscles to tighten, the control to be regained, before starting once more.

When the brickwork of the park wall swung away from the direction he sought, exhausting its usefulness, he looked for escape in the streets and roads outside. It took great effort for him to force his way up onto the summit of its height, and he toppled rather than jumped onto the ground on the far side. Soon he was out of the cover of the trees and under street lights, passed by late traffic, and running by houses where lights still shone and from which came the flicker, blue-grey on the wallpapers, of television sets. When he came to the river he walked along the bank, anxious lest he should miss the bridge marked on his pocket-book map. But when he had found it he quickened his step. There would be no more such barriers for him now, the map showed that, just a network of streets and roads and gardens stretching across his path, separating him from the great open space of flattened concrete that was the airport and from which David Sokarev would fly.

He knew his way, was unerring in tracking his route. Every ninety-five seconds a jet-powered passenger airliner roared above him on its descent to the tarmac, red and green belly lights flashing the message to the Arab far beneath that he was on his course.

Chapter Eighteen

It was the policeman crouched in the shadows of the doorway directly opposite Number 25 who first heard the faint sound of the bolt being withdrawn behind the door across the road. He stiffened into an aim position, his FN rifle at his shoulder, barrel pointed across at the floodlit porch, and talking all the time into the radio clipped to his tunic. Within seconds of his first message he could hear the scraping of activity around him, others alerted, more marksmen preparing themselves. The superintendent's voice was relayed to him over the miniature loudspeaker set into the same instrument. Disembodied and unreal came the instruction, 'If the men come out, shoot. Only if their hands are up and they are obviously not armed do you hold your fire. If they have hostages with them, shoot. Under no circumstances are they to reach the darkness, either of them.'

All right for him to say that, the policeman thought, all right if you're down in the control vehicle. The door edged open, two inches at first, time for the constable to ease off the safety clip on the right side of the rifle, an inch or so above the magazine. He was sweating, could feel the moisture on his hands. He'd only ever fired in practice, and the last time eight months before. Then the door swung fully back on its hinges, but the light from the beam down the road came at such an acute angle that the hallway was only a black rectangle of darkness. He strained without success to see into it. They'll come in a rush, he told himself, all together, the parents and the girl in front, the men behind. And his orders were to shoot. God help us all, he thought, lips bitten tightly, hands shaking, causing the sight on the end of the barrel to waver in gentle helpless meanders. In normal times he drove a squad car; a marksman's role was something he had never taken on before. Only his eyesight, that was superb, qualified him for the shooting position he occupied twenty short paces from the doorway.

His finger tightened around the trigger, and then he saw the girl come from the shadow and hesitate on the step. There was a surge of relief through him. At least the bastards were not right behind her. It would give him a chance to miss her, perhaps hit them. Very quietly, little more than an aside, he broadcast her progress along the four yards of paved path to the front wicket-gate. Here again she stopped, and the fifteen rifles that had covered her as she walked forward traversed their aim back to the dark recess of the doorway.

A hundred yards away and watching now through binoculars the superintendent called into his microphone, 'Tell her to get into the middle of the road, and keep the bloody door covered.'

The constable stretched up, straightening his legs against the stiffness that had long crippled his knee joints. The girl wouldn't have seen him yet, wouldn't have seen any of them, would be bewildered by the silence and the emptiness of the street.

'Keep walking,' he said, more staccato than he would have wanted. Nerves, he put it down to. 'Come out into the street, hands high. Out in the middle.'

Still the girl seemed unaware of his presence, simply obeyed the commands. She came to the centre of the road, and the constable could see her glazed eyes, could see the bloodstains, too, on the white of her blouse, the scattered hair strands, and the uncertain steps. Like a sleepwalker, he thought, like someone learning to walk again in a hospital. 'Walk down the road, and slowly. There's a rope across it about a hundred yards down. They'll meet you there. And don't run.' The girl veered to her right, and began to walk, and the policeman's concentration returned to the open doorway, rifle grip marginally relaxed, waiting.

When she reached the rope a host of hands greeted her. Under her shoulders lest she should faint, hands of comfort around her back. She felt weakness till two detectives frisked her, and she was alive again, backing away from the fingers that ran down her body, circling her waist, on the inside and outside of her legs. 'Just formality,' said the voice behind her, but close and reassuring, and then there was one arm around her, strong, protective. She made no effort to stem the flow of tears that wracked her as they led her to the control van. They helped her up the steps, and the superintendent muttered to his men, 'Keep it very gentle. When she starts to talk I want it coming easily. Rush it now and we'll screw it for all time.' He was old enough in the business of interrogation to know that hasty, capsulated and impatient questioning could cause the girl to freeze, make the progress endlessly slow and confusing.

They gave her a chair, and the superintendent said, 'It's Norah, isn't it?'

She nodded, blank agreement.

'Tell us what's happening, Norah, in your own words.'

She smeared her arm across her upper face, diverting the tears, snuffled, and started to talk. Her voice was very low and the policeman and the SAS captain who had crowded into the van had to stretch forward to hear.

'He said you'd attack, and when you came in you'd be shooting. You'll kill, I know you'll kill him. You'll murder him in there.' The faces of her listeners were impassive, showing no reaction. 'I couldn't see him die, not like that. He's hurt, there's a terrible wound, blood . . . and he got me to clean it. He's sleeping now, he was when I left him . . . I made a pile for his head so that he wouldn't know I'd gone. He needs help, needs a hospital. I thought if I let you in you'd take him alive, you wouldn't shoot him.'

Behind her a detective whispered, half to himself but not subdued, 'Little cow. Little bitch.' She seemed not to hear.

'The door's open. He's up the stairs, in the small room at the front. It's my room. He's on the bed there. Asleep. He doesn't know I've come. He'd kill me . . .' The tears came again and her head sank forward on the smallness of her chest.

The army captain leaned close, one question to

358

ask, 'What sort of guns does he have? Where are they?'

'There's a rifle, a little one. It's in his hand, and there are some grenade things. They're beside the rifle, that's all he has.'

'Norah, listen, because this is very important if we are to help this man' – the superintendent spoke softly, paternal, a voice to be trusted – 'you have to tell us where in the house is the other man. The one on your bed is the Irishman, where is the other one, the Arab?'

She looked into the face that was very near to her, tired and haggard eyes, stubble beginning to show, white collar fringed with grime. So he knew what he was up to, the man McCoy. She wanted to scream with laughter. It was as he'd said it would be. Buying time for his friend, and how much purchased? How many hours? Four, five perhaps? And they didn't know. Tricked by a man with one good arm and half his chest shot out. All these coppers, and McCoy had done them. But there was no hysteria, too exhausted for that. Only a slow smile that rimmed the bottom of the young fresh cheeks almost of sympathy.

'He's been gone a long time,' she said. 'He went right at the start. Just ran through the house. There's only Ciaran . . .'

'Bloody hell,' said the superintendent, kindness evaporating from his mouth.

'We'll go and get the bastard.' The captain said it over his shoulder, already half out of the van.

The superintendent sat back in his chair. 'And you haven't come to tell us this to save your father and mother, haven't mentioned them. Nor to help the troops who were going to break in, less than an hour from now, and risk their bloody lives. Not on your list, right? Only thing that matters is that Ciaran gets his bloody treatment. Straight in on the National Health. Makes you want to puke.'

She was satisfied with herself now. They saw the defiance come to her, chin jutting out.

'So where's the Arab?' Different tone, harsher, games completed.

'He didn't say. Just ran through the house. Went through the back. Hours ago.' The last spat out with relish.

'Where to, for Christ's sake?'

'I said, he didn't say. Ciaran said the whole thing was to win him time.'

'And how long have you known him, this McCoy?'

'Two weeks.'

'And you knew what he'd done?'

'I knew.' And she smiled again. Pretty smile, the superintendent thought, pretty face. Just as they all are when they meet their McCoys. Screwed her, and screwed her life. Par for the course. He climbed out of the van to begin formulating his plans for the manhunt that would not get operational till first light, still more than ninety minutes away.

The split board that Norah's father had so long meant to repair betrayed to Ciaran McCoy the approach up the stairs of the SAS sergeant. The creaking whine when the soldier eased his weight onto the divided wood broke through the thin sleep, causing him to sit up sharply, a reflex before the agony jolted him down. He was aware of the rifle immediately, nestling in his hand and pressed to his thigh, but when he motioned his shoulders seeking

the shape and familiarity of the girl he realized
she had gone. He took his hand from the butt of
the rifle and felt the pillow and the shoes and the
magazines. Confirmation if he had needed it. There
was a whisper from the stairs, a hiss for quiet, then
the drumming of feet, the moment of assault. For
a fraction of time he had capability to make the
decision that would determine whether he raised his
gun and armed the grenades, or whether he submitted . . . but his mind was incapable of clear
thought, and his instinctive reactions too dulled.
When the sergeant came through the door, finger
poised on the trigger of the Sterling sub-machine-
gun, McCoy lay where he had slept, gun barrel
prone on the bedspread and offering no threat. That
he lived through those three seconds as the SAS man
acclimatized himself to the light of the room was
dependent on the soldier's training and expertise,
and his knowledge of when it was necessary to
shoot, when not. He assimilated the atmosphere
of the room, saw the crumpled figure, the barrel
that pointed nowhere, the hand removed from the
immediate proximity of the grenades. And then there
were others crowding into the bedroom, three, four
and five more, standing high over McCoy. The light
was switched on. One pulled the gun from his hand,
removed the bullet from the breach, scooped up
the grenades. They ran their hands over McCoy's
trousers, checking him for more weapons and lifted
him without violence from the bedclothes before
ripping back the pale blue sheets. When they laid
him down again it was on the hard-coiled springs of
the bed.

Ciaran watched them as they worked quickly

and with thoroughness round the room, no words spoken, acknowledgement that each knew what was expected of him. End of the road, Ciaran boy, but not the end his imagination had ever entertained when he played his war games. He'd thought they'd shoot. Flattering himself. Couldn't take the great Ciaran alive, without a whimper, without the mighty bang-out. Too big just to finish up this way. Deceived himself. Unimportant, though, and he didn't care. Get so tired, such exhaustion, that you don't give a damn what happens. Glad in a way that it's over. Whichever way, with the living or the dead, un-important, just the relief that it's completed. And the Arab had had his start, had his opportunity. And he must go through it all again, the poor bastard. And on his own. And you're out of it, Ciaran boy, clear and finished and safe.

The captain bent over him.

'Get the doctor up here.' He said it without emo-tion, matter of fact. 'Pity the bloody thing wasn't six inches across. Would have saved us all a load of trouble.'

Through the door McCoy could hear the voices of Norah's parents, frightened, gabbled and seeking the reassurance of the soldiers. There were feet on the staircase, a diffusion of voices, orders being given, and then the arrival of the doctor.

'Make a habit of this caper?' The doctor had his hand on McCoy's pulse, but his eyes, puckered with the distress of an old man, wandered from the wounds to the already healed scar in McCoy's side.

'I don't mind shifting him,' said the super-intendent. 'But I don't want him under anaesthetic yet. He's some talking to do before we get that far. We'll chat to him in the ambulance and when they're cleaning him up.'

The father and mother were still on the landing when they carried McCoy, bound to the stretcher, past them. They looked at him as if staring at a rodent, vermin. Hate-consumed, but schooled by fear. The progress down the narrow stairs was difficult and slow, and before they were half-way, and manoeuvring on the bend McCoy heard Norah's mother, plaintive and appealing.

'Where's our girl? What's happened to our Norah? What did he do to her?'

You'll find out soon enough, thought the Irishman. It amused him, and without the pain he would have laughed. You'll find out and wish you'd never asked, and if they tell you you'll wish they hadn't. Always the same. Always the girls in tow, attracted like dogs to a bitch's fanny, flies in a jam pot. And always they cock it up. You're not the first, Ciaran. Just like the big boyo in Belfast. Took his bird along when they holed up in the big posh house, in the posh road and she still went in her slippers and curlers to fetch the morning milk from the corner shop. Rest of the road had it delivered. Gave it away a mile off, once the copper on car patrol spotted her. Got him nicked.

He was still wondering why the girl had betrayed him when the stretcher party carried him out onto the street.

There were television arc lights there. They'd allowed the cameramen up from the corral at the bottom of the hill. Give 'em a show, McCoy. Give 'em a picture. Don't let the bastards see you down. The spotlights were aimed at his face and blanched the skin on his bared chest, accentuating the whiteness that surrounded the bullet hole with its sparse patch of covering lint.

He shouted, 'Up the Provos,' and the policeman holding the stretcher handles behind his head jolted them hard, sending the rivers of pain flowing fast and deep. Bastards. And all up to the bloody Arab to wipe the victory smile off their faces. The bloody Arab and his Mushroom Man.

Before they lifted him into the ambulance McCoy had lost consciousness.

The cures he'd been on, the expensive, the unpleasant and the not-so-cosseted varieties, had never lasted for Jimmy. The craving and desire for excess of alcohol, a dose sufficient to immunize him against pressure and anxiety, remained, lingering and nagging in his life. They'd tried most of the accepted methods to wean him away. The health farm in Hampshire had cost the most, and lasted the least time when he was back in the outside world. The withdrawal programme practised at the clinic behind Brixton Station had been the most ferocious, the most scarring and the longest-running. But each broke down at the stage when Jimmy went back to his breadwinning and the sepia world of his activities demanded some softening. He was now a low-capability drinker, a short-capacity man. When rational he could recognize the problem, when angry and disappointed he turned away from the consequences.

The flat had been empty when he returned. Helen was not there, gone to her own place. Could hardly blame her, didn't know what time he might have shown up, or in what state of tiredness. Bed hadn't been made from the previous sleeping. Washing up not done, never was, tea leaves settled in an eddy round the plughole of the sink. Clothes not picked up. If she'd come back she would have done the tidying ritual. But at least he wouldn't have to tell her about the car. Insurance? . . . Didn't know, be some difficult talking. She'd hate him for it. Couldn't blame her. Pride and joy . . . and up in smoke.

He unscrewed the top of the bottle, cheap brand. Filthy expensive by the time he'd paid the porter his chip, lose it all on expenses. They looked at them hard in the department, but he could lose that, hadn't eaten all day, funnel it through there. Straight, no water. Tap water would be warm, and he hadn't filled the ice-cube box in the fridge. About an inch to start with, four gulps, needed forcing down, coiled up his guts, blazed a trail through them. Sagged in the chair, the easy one, springs still kept in check by the upholstery, feet just reaching the table, laces at eye-level, loosened his collar. Coughed a couple of times then corkscrewed his body forward to reach the bottle and the first refill. So tired, seemed to have been moving for ever. No thoughts, just wanting to shut it all out. Jones pulling his bloody rank, the SAS captain, and those bastards in the house. Should have been your day, Jimmy, and yet you're sent home early, and told to work a bloody shift pattern.

At first the telephone was an accompaniment to his thoughts. It took time for it to communicate urgency, and even more for it to instil the submission required for him to give up the comfort he had established for himself and hobble across the room to the table beside his bed. He deliberated whether to answer, but discipline won through. He picked up the receiver and gave out the number, had it right too, which surprised him.

'It's Jones here, Jimmy. It's all over down at this end.'

'Congratulations.' Jimmy had difficulties, the word was slow coming.

'It's not like that, Jimmy. We have McCoy, but the Arab's gone. He's loose.'

'Not so bright then. Which clever bastard let him slip?'

'He went when you were there, Jimmy, so cut the quips, before the cordon . . .'

'I was on my bloody own, wasn't I? Can't be round the whole house. He didn't come through the front.' All the same, bloody buckpassers brigade.

'Don't come the maudlin, Jimmy. No-one's criticizing you. It's a statement of fact. He's loose with a minimum of five hours' start. I want you at the West Middlesex, and now. Not hanging about, but down there now. They're patching McCoy up, and we're keeping the surgeons off him till we've had a preliminary. After that he goes under, has his surgery, and they dig your bullet out of him.'

'Leave the bloody thing there.'

'Don't screw me about, Jimmy. We have to know what the Arab is at. McCoy has to tell us.'

'You've got others who can go and do it.' Why wouldn't the bloody man get off the line and leave him to the bottle and the chair? Why Jimmy, why not one of the young ones who fancied their hand at interrogation? Budding Skardons all of them,

366

looking for another Klaus Fuchs to break, looking for a reputation.

'Jimmy, stop waffling, stop boozing, and get off your arse. The Yard's down there. I'm on my way. I've sent a car for you, be at your door in about ten minutes. Put your head under the tap and be there. I want you to talk to McCoy, that's all.'

Even with the drink Jimmy knew why he had been called. Just like Jones, the way his mind worked. Who'd be on the same wavelength as this Irish bastard, who'd be able to frighten him, or win him, or batter it out of him? Not a copper, not one of the bright lads transferred from Intelligence Corps, not old Jonesey himself. Another thug, that's what he wanted, and put them together. Two rats, both hungry, in the same hole. Two cockroaches disputing the one patch.

Jimmy sat up, breaking his cat-nap as the car drove through the wide gateway and into the hospital forecourt. Sleep when you can, basic rule, fit it in with the opportunity, always the same when the other lot dictate the timetable, hold the initiative. Time now to regret the whisky, hadn't been much left in the bottle, motion of the car didn't help. Head spinning, uncontrollable circles. The half-light was beginning to simper through and the nineteenth-century blocks were heavily outlined against the coming dawn. Blue and white signs pointed in every direction. CASUALTY. MATERNITY, X-RAY, OUT-PATIENTS. Ward names, recalling local dignitaries and benefactors. He saw the police van and the group of uniformed men outside casualty, and the car pulled up there. Jones was waiting for him.

He saw Jimmy's appearance and winced, distaste on his face.

'We don't have long. The surgeons are impatient. Want to get their hands on him. Police haven't had anything out of him. Laughs at them. He's weak, but should survive. Reckons he's the cat's whiskers – probably the morphine.' Jones led the way through the corridors beyond 'Casualty', past the red-eyed junior doctors and nurses who whiled the night away waiting for the road accidents and the self-damaged drunks. By the staircase there were plain-clothes men, cigarettes cupped in their hands, the whole place deathly quiet and accentuating their echoing steps. They went up the stairs onto the first floor and towards the ward entrance to their right.

Jones said, 'Fifteen minutes' maximum. You and me. I'll take the notes. Just get the bastard talking.' He showed his I/D card to the two policemen outside the door short of the main communal ward area, and went into the private room. It was barely big enough for a bed, a table and an upright chair. They'd worked a small chest in there as well, and the two men had to ease their way round the obstacles to get to the bedside. There was a nurse sitting at McCoy's feet, short and West Indian, her feet dangling above the floor, waiting the requisite time before removing the thermometer that stuck out like a battleship's gun from the Irishman's mouth. The two men said nothing, allowed her to examine the thin glass tube, write down the results of her study on her clip board, and go when she was ready. She moved past them, avoiding their eyes, and went out into the corridor. The detective who had been sitting in the room followed her. Jimmy took the nurse's place on the bed, Jones the vacated chair.

Picking at his nose, Jimmy said, 'My name's Jimmy. I'm here till we've finished with you. After that you'll get the surgeon. But not until we've chatted. Doesn't matter to us whether it's ten minutes, ten hours, ten days . . .'

'That's not what the doctor . . .' McCoy spoke with a faintness, whispering.

'Fuck the doctor, McCoy. The medics come back through that door when we say so.'

'They said—

'Well, they got it wrong. Don't you follow in their tracks. We've all the time in the world. You haven't. You're short of an exit wound, right?'

McCoy turned his head toward Jimmy, managed to lift himself fractionally so that he could see into the eyes, grey-blue and pitiless, rimmed with red. There was a man like that in Armagh City, came to do the executions, seemed to matter less to him than culling a pig on market Thursdays.

'I know about that bullet. I fired it. Not a good shot, should have killed you. Was ahead of you all yesterday. Fired first at the meeting when your gun was still waving about, followed you out, trailed you all the way. Then you gave me a good clear shot while you stood on the pavement, couple of bloody gooks. Pathetic stuff, McCoy, and you supposed to be an expert. Short of men on your side of the water, are they?'

Good stuff, Jimmy-boy, thought Jones. Nothing to write down yet on the pad, but setting him up well. Kicking the boy's vanity, needling him and hard.

McCoy could remember, though his concentration surged and ebbed, the time the army had lifted him years before. There had been a roughness, but a certain set of rules about it all. Pinioned him not gently, but they'd never given him the fear that they'd kill him. This man was different. Not a soldier, not a policeman . . . different. An enemy.

'Wasn't me on the gun.'

"Course it wasn't you on the gun. That was the sharp end, wasn't it? Didn't expect you'd be there, didn't expect you'd be standing by the window when we all started blasting. Left the man's bit to the kiddie, did you?'

'Famy wanted to shoot, that's what he came for.'

Jones's pencil started to move, first words on the virgin paper. A name at last to put to the face. Not really important, but tidier. Made it all neater when you had a caption for the picture. And all those hours they'd put in just to get the name, and now they had it it was irrelevent – not worth a damn alongside the usefulness of having the face. Jimmy would have registered it, too: it would have given him the kick he needed to get on top. Be no stopping him now.

'He's worse than you, and that's fucking useless.' Jimmy's voice was quiet, casual. As if the conversation were about the visiting centre-forward between strangers on the terraces. McCoy could follow the technique, was aware of it, but too tired, too hurt, too drugged to combat his adversary.

'He's not finished, the boy.'

'Only because he's running. Running with the mess in his pants, and the bog paper in his hand.'

'He'll bloody show you, you Britisher pig.' Out in the corridor where nurses and doctors waited, gathered beside the police guard, they heard the Irishman struggling to shout. They looked at their watches, noting how much longer the questioning could continue.

'He'll show us how fast he can run.'

'He's not finished. What do you think I stayed behind for? Why hole up, if not to give him time? I wasn't there just so he could scarper. He's set to blast you, you and the Yiddisher.'

Jimmy laughed, exaggerated, loud, ridicule. 'He'll never see him.'

'He'll see him and he'll get him.'

'What do you think we're going to do, you pig-thick ape? Parade him up Whitehall? Stick him in a coconut shy? You had your chance, and you buggered it.'

'You can't keep him close all the time. He'll have to put his feet on the ground . . .'

'There's only one place.'

'Right,' hissed McCoy. Jimmy could see him quivering, chest shaking, breath panted in the emotion of the dispute.

'The airport. Up the steps the little man goes and your hero makes his last stand,' Jimmy gabbled the words out, maintaining the momentum. McCoy was with him.

'Right, right first bloody time.'

Jimmy said nothing. Sudden, total silence. The noise stillborn, the voices aborted. McCoy's eyes closed tight shut. The enormity of what he'd said, slow in dawning then overwhelming. Betrayed him. Ciaran McCoy, volunteer and officer in the

Irish Republican Army, had betrayed him.

'Holy Mother of Jesus, forgive me.' His lips barely moved with the formation of the words that Jimmy did not hear.

Jimmy stretched off the bed and walked towards the door, Jones a pace behind. He said, distant, matter of fact. 'The surgeon only gave us fifteen minutes. We reckoned that would be enough. And we were right, Ciaran, we've four and a half to spare. So it's over to his tender hands now. Hope the bloody knife's blunt.'

McCoy did not see him go. In his life he had never known such abject misery.

The diversion along the park wall and then the search for the bridge crossing of the Thames had cost Famy a considerable detour, switching his journey from six miles to nearly nine. The pale shiver of light was spreading as he came to the cohorts of warehouses and offices that marked the outer perimeter of Heathrow. He felt new confidence now that he was alone and on his back the new clothes, blue jeans and a pale-green shirt. It had been a clear night and the housewife who worked a long day's shift had seen the opportunity to leave her husband's washing out on the garden line. A bonus for Famy as he had gone on his way. New clothes that would render obsolete the description given to the police in Richmond.

Famy recognized the danger of moving too far a distance inside the airport before he had solidified the cover that he regarded as essential to protect himself later in the day. The detail he had studied and accepted as he had run. Now all he needed, he told himself, was time. Time to move to the position that he must have. Time to be ready for when the El Al landed. Must be there for the first one. They'd take him out, send him home, rid themselves of Sokarev. And so easy to know, once he was there. Can always tell when a big man is flying, or one they think highly of. The security, that's what gives it away, what makes it so obvious. But had to get there, and then stay and wait and watch; watch for signs that meant Sokarev was coming. Had to get there, to where the first El Al flight would take on its passengers, and then be patient and observe, and look for the security men; the hard-faced men who would tell him the quarry was close.

In Fatahland they would be waking now. In the tents set among the scrub and the rocks his colleagues in arms had passed a night spent dreaming of an opportunity such as he had been given, awaiting it as their own one-time destiny. The new day would be coming over the camp. The same sun rising across the mountain to the east of Nablus where the road ran on down to the Jordan valley, where his father would be out of his bed, and his mother already in the kitchen outhouse behind the bungalow, and his brothers dressing for school. And in Haifa and Netanya and Ashkelon and Beersheba the Jews would be waking too. All would say his name when the next evening came. Some with adulation, some with resignation, some with detestation. The blow he prepared to strike would be mighty, to many millions it would shatter the foetid complacency, and to those who lived on the far side of the wire and the minefields and who longed to cross over he would bring hope and aspiration.

There was a pounding of excitement, close to purest happiness.

Inside the perimeter he skirted the road that ran adjacent to the runways and across the acres of dividing clipped grass, keeping back from the vague traffic flow, seeking the shadows. He appeared to any who might notice him as one more from the ranks of the thousands of immigrant workers, the lifeblood of the airport, on his way to another day at work, washing dishes, sweeping concourses, cleaning lavatories. His bag seemed not to weigh so heavily, the roar of the big engines lightening the load. He was very near to the estuary of his mission.

Back in Lebanon they had told him about the tunnel that was the sole route from the outside conurbation to the heart of the airport complex. They had showed him a photograph of its entry, pointing out the footpath that ran separate to the vehicle road. If there was security that path could be guarded – too simple, too easy, and risks should not be taken, not when the scent was so strong. He saw the bus queue, a short hundred yards up the hill from the entry tunnel, a straggled line of brown faces, of turbans and saris, many carrying the bags that contained their working overalls, bags that were so similar to the one that rested by his feet when he joined them. Infiltrate where you will not be noticed, that is what they had told him; there is a time for combat uniform and a time for camouflage. And the bus when it came would take him to the central terminals. He must look there for the canteens and rest rooms where the workers gathered for their breaks. He must look for a man whose job, whose appearance, and whose identity papers would give Famy the passport to the tarmac where the Jumbo would refuel, reload its seats.

One man, one man from so many who would be there, one man alone would be necessary.

Chapter Nineteen

The bus was hideously slow through the tunnel. Worrying its way down the underground passage, sandwiched between the cars and lorries and coaches, it had no speed, no hurry, no urgency. Flashes of illumination thrown into the interior from the big yellow lights fastened to the angle where the sides met the roof, causing Famy to turn outward toward the windows, obscuring his features from his fellow passengers. There was little talk on the bus. The eyes of the inmates were remote and insular, men and women compartmentalizing themselves from their seated neighbours, minds dulled by the time of day and the anticipation of the boredom and frustration of their service tasks through the next nine hours. They were soft, thought Famy, unthinking fodder, with neither the power nor desire to question the humiliation of the role that had been awarded to them. Poverty of initiative, absence of hope. Facing another day of averted eyes, stumbling submission, far from their own country. Plucked from a great distance and brought here to serve. Pathetic people, without the arm of Famy and his strength, incapable of insurrection, shackled. And they would have little comprehension of the Arab, fail to understand his mission and what he tried to achieve for them. They would be unable to accept that the M1 and its hitting capability represented a blow for them, as much for them as the men and woman and children in the Chatila and Sabra camps. Did not all colonialists support the Israeli State? They paid lip service to the enemies of Israel, but only superficially, only for their gasoline. There was no sincerity. The white man identified with the Jew. When the day was over and they sat again on the bus that would reverse its route and they went back to their homes, how would these people have reacted to the operation that Abdel-El-Famy planned for the last hours of their work shift? Too stupid, most of them. Few would acknowledge that his act was for them, for all the majorities that lacked wealth and opportunity. They were trapped, these people, as trapped and imprisoned as the Palestinians. Without homelands, without fields, without flocks, without expression. It is a day-dream, Famy; tomorrow will be the time of dreams, tomorrow . . . but today there is not time. The bus increased its speed, surged into the brightness at the end of the encasing tunnel, and pulled up the hill in the selected lane that would direct it to the central airport building.

They swung across the traffic lanes, paused at the traffic lights, and then turned right toward the bus shelter where the night shift workers waited. Inside the bus many were already standing up, lifting their bags with them, and the sudden jolt of the brakes as the bus finally came to a standstill made several lose their balance. Then they were hurrying down the aisle, afraid of being late, and in their rush they swept Famy forward with them.

He watched the way the men went as they left the bus halt. The procession had divided, men taking one course, women another, a splitting of the human confluence. There were other buses behind him, more in front that had already disgorged and were pulling away, and the stream took him toward the opened double doors of the red brick building surmounted by the blue-tinged windows of the octagonal control tower. There were signs beside the entrance. 'Canteen' and 'Admittance to staff Only'. No security checks, none that were visible anyway, but it was early for that. Nothing sensitive here, no threat presented. But it suited him well to be out of the rising sunlight, anonymous among the mass of people who belonged to the System. They would not be looking for him here. It was a place where he could rest, where his legs that ached and protested could relax, where he could doze and regain the sharpness of thought he must have by mid-afternoon.

The woman who served him at the long counter was surprised at the way his cup and saucer rattled as he carried them away from the cash machine. She put it down to nerves. Like half these Asians, she thought, scared out of their wits, and what do they have to do? Only clean out the loos and push a broom round. It amused her, gave a cherished feeling of superiority. But she was wrong. There was no fear in Famy now. That his hand shook was from the strain of carrying the bag for so many hours, fingers entwined around the plastic strap. But no fear, not now he was without the Irishman. And

378

confidence is of critical value to the assassin. The killer has to believe in his prowess as much as his cause, must believe in his ability as much as the God-given right to exact retribution. Those who saw the unfamiliar face sitting at the clothless table by the window would have latched on to the great contentment on his features, the gentleness that comes from peace of mind and the patience to consume time. He was now a more dangerous and potentially lethal figure than at any time since he had landed in England. He had come to terms with his mission, and with its implications. He was ready to kill.

He put three spoonfuls of sugar into the coffee, stirred it slowly and looked about him.

Along the Great West Road leading toward London from Windsor huge queues of traffic formed up behind the military convoy.

Land-Rovers front and rear, fifteen three-ton trucks, each carrying twenty soldiers. Alpha, Bravo and Headquarters Company. Grenadier Guards, long lines of battle honours stretching back into three hundred years of history. Thin red-line tunics of the ceremonial discarded for mottled camouflage denims, the uniform of urban guerrilla warfare of the streets of Northern Ireland. Four hundred men in all. FN rifles. General purpose machine-guns. Hand-held Carl Gustav rocket launchers. All there to protect one man from the hands of an equally solitary threat. Many times the resident Battalion at Windsor Barracks had practised on exercise their recent responsibilities of Heathrow security, but there was a tightness and silence about the men who sat on the slatted seats in the backs of the lorries. Never before had they been told the risk was real, confirmed.

Interspersed among the trucks were the armoured cars of two Hussar squadrons, Saladins with khaki cloth tied across the muzzle of the big gun, and the Saracen personnel carriers.

Police reinforcements were being mobilized from Divisional forces in the Metropolitan area. More would come from the rural Thames Valley strength. By nine in the morning the perimeter of the airport would be sealed, the concourses would be under guard, the tarmac patrolled. Later the plans for the security of the El Al flight to Tel Aviv would be thrashed out in the squat police station on the far side of the tunnel where the various security forces would set up their control and communication posts.

The Prime Minister had rubber-stamped the guidance from Home Office and Defence. Saturation. Forces of such strength that the Arab would turn his back on his target, dismayed. Box the bastard out, deny him any chink of light, any opportunity to attack.

Through the window Famy saw the deployment. Little strung-out columns of troops. Rifles carried warily and diagonally across their bodies, letting the bustling civilians fan out and find a path to the side. Some were draped in the belts of machine-gun ammunition, worn in cross-over sashes. One man in each patrol hunched forward to compensate for the weight of the radio set perched high on his back. Among the conventional throb of the traffic he heard the piercing and complaining squeal of the big Rolls-Royce engines of the armoured cars, and saw the pedestrians out on the pavement pause and stare at them. All had read their morning papers, heard the radio news bulletins. They would wait for the five-minute call, for the show to begin. And all would stay for the curtain call. It amused Famy. One against so many. No-one to share the footlights with him. After a while he became tired of watching the criss-cross motions of his enemy, and finished his coffee. He walked back to the counter, ordered a fresh cup, and with it a sandwich filled with dried and crumbling cheese and slices of over-ripe tomato.

There were many hours to be consumed before it would be time for him to move, but the sights beyond the window fanned his confidence, spread it as a bushfire. His best hopes were confirmed. The troops and the guns had not come just to hunt down Abdel-El-Famy. There was another more cogent and potent reason. The Mushroom Man would be travelling, on course for their rendezvous. The fly into the web, the lion toward the pit. And all the soldiers and police would be as extras, as onlookers.

From the next table he took a discarded newspaper and read a version of the previous night's events. His English was adequate, sufficient for him to understand what had been written. He was 'fleeing', he was 'probably on drugs', he was a 'fanatic'. The public were warned to keep away from him, not to 'have a go', told to phone the police if he were sighted. Guns had been widely distributed to the police. He would be shot on sight, the journalist had written. On the front page there was a smudged and meaningless picture of the house where he had left McCoy, a policeman there had a rifle in his hand, and the story was topped with the news of the capture of his friend. Described as 'late news'. He read that McCoy, though injured, would live, and he was thankful. But they do not understand, he thought. There is no word of Palestine, no word of the bomb, no word of the camps and the suffering. It raged through him so that he wanted to scream at those who shared the canteen with him. Do they care so little for Palestine that they take no trouble to understand why? Why do they think we are prepared to die? Stupid, goat-shit bastards, do we enjoy death? Can there be no sanity in what we do? Can we never be right, justified, driven beyond the boundaries? And then his temper calmed. On the centre pages of the tabloid was a photograph, blown large, of David Sokarev. It was more recent than the old snapshot they had shown him in Lebanon. He could dwell on the face in a way that had not been possible in the split seconds that he had peered into the artificial light of the hall. Remember it closely, study its detail. There will be little time when he is between the car and the steps, and he will be hurrying, and there will be men round him. Recognition must be instinctive, not as it was in the hall, when his eyes had to search. Faster this time.

He would know him. Whether he was crouched low, whether he wore a hat, whether he had his coat collar turned up, however fast he went, he would know him.

The alcohol Jimmy had drunk in the small hours needed greater time to disperse through the bloodstream than Jimmy had permitted. Short of sleep and still wound at wire tension he came to the hotel. The adrenalin that for a short period had fought and overcome the whisky for control of his veins as he confronted McCoy was now bested. Johnny Walker supreme. His head ached with the pressure, trying to break out and expand from the confines of his skull. Splitting pain, and self-administered. Wanted to rest, wanted just to fold up and sleep it off. But no rest was permitted. Told where he had to be, and that was with Sokarev. Back on course again, Jimmy, taking orders, doing as the gaffer said.

The Branch man in the foyer recognized him from the previous day, nodded a greeting and described his passage into the lift over a small radio transmitter. New, that, souping things up a bit, and so they should. On the fourth floor he was met again, quizzically and with suspicion, by a man he had not seen before and who blocked his way down the corridor to the Israelis' rooms. Jimmy fumbled for his wallet and searched among the folds for his card. Should have been able to spot it straight away. Knew where he put the bloody thing, but couldn't find it. Always put it in the same place, but where? And then it was there, clearly to be seen where he should have looked in the first place. Jimmy mouthed an apology, embarrassed. The detective was clean-shirted, shaved, dressed for work. And you, you look a bloody wreck, Jimmy. A shambles. The policeman examined his card, searched back again into Jimmy's face, handed the card back and stepped sideways to allow him through. There were more men outside the doors of the two rooms. They would have seen the initial checking, but went through the routine again. Bloody coppers. Jimmy knocked on the first door, opened in response by Elkin.

The greeting was mutually cool. Had to be after

last night. No source of congratulations. Jimmy noted that the curtains of the room were drawn, bedside light on, no possibility of anyone outside the building being able to see inside the room – basic precaution, as it should be. Everyone learning what it's all about. There was a new man slouched on the far bed, the Uzi not more than six inches from his right hand. Elkin went straight into the attack, had been accumulating it.

'It will be different from yesterday. We have taken charge of the arrangements. Any plan will go through us, be approved by us.'

'You'll do as you're bloody well told.' Hadn't expected the assault that fast.

'After last night we make the decisions.'

'You'll make the decisions when you're on that fucking aircraft . . .'

'We left it to you, and it was a fiasco.'

'You'll be told what's going to happen, and if you don't like it you can get out on the pavement and walk to the airport.' When Jimmy shouted the sledgehammer reverberated behind his eyes. He closed them. All so bloody daft, childish. When he forced the lids hard together he could squeeze out the pain. 'Calm yourself down for God's sake.' He spoke like a man who wants to end the full drama of a domestic row, wants to pack it in and forget it by the morning. 'Did you sleep last night?'

Elkin shook his head. Bags big and bulged, sack full, spreading to his cheeks, high red flush beneath them, eyes above soft and watery. Been crying, Jimmy saw.

'We have the Irishman. Only leaves the one other. Fancies himself at the airport when your man goes out this afternoon. Be out of his depth. Less chance than a chicken in Biafra. He's no hope. They'll be working out a route later in the morning, nothing for you till that gets in the pipeline. You should put your head down till then.'

Elkin walked back to his bed, sat on it heavily. Jimmy recognized he would struggle to stay awake and lose. Poor sod, doesn't rate us – and why should he? Fearful what we'll cock-up while he's kipping. And everyone so bloody tired, never known an operation when they weren't all walking round like zombies . . . what Jones had said, wasn't it? Stupid old bugger. Jimmy took off his coat and slung it on the floor, lifted the pistol from the shoulder-holster and pressed it into the waist of his trousers before dumping himself into a brocaded armchair. He had thought that sleep would come easily to him, pleaded for it, aware of how much faster the incapacity of exhaustion came to him as he veered between middle and old age. But the liberation was not at hand, and was made harder by the still figure of Elkin on his bed. Jimmy willed himself to follow, but without success. And his head throbbed, with the blood scarlet flashes across his vision.

Beyond the partition door David Sokarev too was asleep. Jimmy had heard no movement, no creaking of restless bed springs, and turned the door handle giving himself a few inches of vision. Like a little angel. No nightmares, the pills had seen to that. Dead to the world, blanked out, insensitive to it all. Pray the drug keeps him there. Met a man once in a pub – where you meet them all, Jimmy – in his cups, deep. Said he'd been a prison screw. Once done the death cell stint. Hadn't volunteered, the sick list had seen him on the rota, usual guys not available. Not the actual night, but the one before. And the man had slept, and they'd all marvelled, and known the news the governor had brought the previous evening. Even slept through the shift change, and the new screws had tiptoed in. They'd let his breakfast get cold, fearful for him when the protection of sleep was gone. He'd been a crude bugger, the one who'd told him the story, but different when he spoke of this. And the more that Sokarev slept the better. Cushion him from the carry-on. Only bloody defence he had. A weak face he had, unprotected, with its old man's stubble.

And by the late afternoon Sokarev would be gone, and his hands would be washed and he'd be back with his girl, and no phone calls, and he'd retrieve the bottle. God, he wished his head would call a cease-fire. He'd be in lousy shape in the afternoon. Lousy.

Famy had studied many of the men who came into the canteen through the early and middle morning. Some he dismissed immediately as being of no use to him, others he toyed with for longer, examining their features and their build, before rejecting them too as unsuitable for his purpose.

It was gone eleven when he saw the man he wanted. Indian, correct height, at a little below six feet. Youngish, early twenties, and not yet filled out with the obesity of his race. A turban, good because it distracted from the facial images, white and cleanly furled. A faint moustache, hardly visible, but there was time for Famy to use his battery razor and match that. White overalls, emblazoned across the left chest with the British Airways sign and, more important, specked with oil spots and smeared with grease. Maintenance. A man who worked on the engines, tended the beasts when they were tethered, had access to them when they lay crippled. And where did the work go on? At the piers, on the tarmac, on the big concreted open spaces where the aircraft sojourned. Access dominated his thinking. The need to find an identity that ensured access. A job that provided access to the hidden and secret areas denied to ordinary civilians, the ticket behind the wire fences and the control points.

Famy left his table, and holding his bag moved across the floor of the canteen toward the table where the Sikh sat, solitary, unaware of the man who approached him.

As his car drove away from the cul-de-sac of Downing Street the Israeli Ambassador's concern was defused. He had taken his security attaché with him to the meeting with the British Prime Minister, but in the event had left him outside the heavy oakwood doors to the personnel office. Alone for an hour with the British Head of Government, he had discussed the previous night's attack. They had moved on from the past to the plans that had been drawn up for the departure of David Sokarev in the late afternoon.

'The Prime Minister put it to me,' said the Ambassador to his companion, 'that his Government could in no way be accused of dragging their heels on this matter. He said it was his personal order that preparations were made for an assault on the house where it was thought the terrorists had taken refuge.

He said that the safety of the hostages was put at secondary priority compared with the need to avoid negotiating with these people. I cannot counter that. It was to be done as we would have hoped. And they have been fast with the interrogation of the one man they hold. They tell me that the Arab will attempt a final attack at the airport. It is admitted that there was laxity at the university, but I have assurances that it will not be repeated. It would have been difficult for me to relay the instructions of the Foreign Ministry.'

The security attaché was unconcerned with the private diplomatic innuendo that had passssed between the two men out of his hearing.

'What are their plans for the airport?' More important, to what had his civilian master, short of a military background, agreed?

'They have moved troops to Heathrow. Guardsmen and light cavalry. They are bringing in more police. There will be around a thousand men from their security forces, many armed, they tell me. The Prime Minister informs me that the Arab is in possession of an M1 carbine with a maximum effective range of three hundred metres. Therefore they will put an army and police cordon in position of a circle with a radius of four hundred metres around the jet-liner. There will be no admittance inside that area other than to vetted personnel, our own people, and the security men. The plane will already be loaded when Sokarev boards . . .'

'How is he transferred to the airport?'

'It is the assessment of the British that a motor convoy is the best method. There are many points of entry into Heathrow, and they maintain that it would be impossible for the Arab to be correctly positioned, and knowing which one they will use. I see no reason for disputing that. It is their hope that the demonstration of force will be so great as to deter the man until Professor Sokarev is safely in the air. After that they will concentrate on his capture.'

'So again they have not consulted us.' The attaché spoke evenly, not looking at the Ambassador, watching the oncoming traffic.

'They have consulted me.'

'You are not an expert in these matters.'

'That is offensive.'

'You would not know whether there were flaws in the plan or not.'

'Where are the flaws that your experience warns you of?'

'How can I tell? How can I estimate? I had hoped to see the plans. Discuss them. Negotiate them. Be given alternatives, told of the contingency fall-backs. There is no chance of that now.'

The Ambassador was silent, thoughtful of the way he had committed himself so few minutes earlier. Career, future, promotion to permanent position in the Ministry in Jerusalem, all might rest on the agreement he had made with the Prime Minister. The attaché said nothing else. The point had been made, there was no value in returning to it. They would do their best, the British. Probably haphazard, but their best. Only they were not experts. Europeans did not understand the Palestinian fighters, were naïve in the new science of counter-terrorism. But so proud of their integrity, so determined to make their own decisions. And their own mistakes. So there had been no talk of decoys, or of helicopters, or of military aircraft. Do they comprehend the resourcefulness of the assassin who is prepared to die that he should reach his target? He doubted it.

Mohan Singh was happy at the other man's company. It was rare for him to have conversation during the early lunch-break when his shift pattern decreed he went off sooner for his food than many of his work colleagues. The stranger listened to his problems, to the description of his life and his education, the circumstances that had brought him to England, and his difficulties in finding a job as rewarding financially as the one he now held. He spoke of his family – his wife and the three small children – how they lived in two rooms at the back of an uncle's house in Hounslow, how he was obliged to send money back to Amritsar to maintain his elderly parents. He was not aware as he chattered on that the man with him spoke little, just nodded and smiled and encouraged.

There was not long, Famy knew that. Sitting at the table already for fifteen minutes, there for another fifteen before the approach. How many more before he returned to his work? High wall clock turning, not much time. And all the while the plans racing, wasp-fast, through his mind. They had more coffee. Famy going up to the counter and collecting the two cups. His hands no longer shook, relaxed and supple now, fingers eased, pliant . . . He set the coffee cups down and inclined his head to hear again what the Indian wanted to pour out to him. He had no feeling about the clear knowledge that he would kill this man. He was as nothing. An arcade machine, activated by a coin. Not an enemy, not a friend, just a carriage to take him to his destination, to his destiny. McCoy would have done it better, but McCoy had made the sacrifice for him, and he must fulfil his trust.

The man was tedious to Famy. Grumbling but frightened to be considered in that light, without the courage to fight for what he wanted. As a carpet that complains but cannot shift itself from the trampling boots. He would die quickly, compliant with his fate. The Indian had finished his coffee, coughed and cleared the sinuses of his nose, loud and guttural.

'I must return, or I will be late for the afternoon's work. It has been nice . . .'

Famy interrupted. 'I have to wash my hands. You will show me the lavatory?' A stranger, helpless, needing a friend.

The Indian responded. 'I will show you. It is difficult to find if one is new here.'

They walked together down the corridor further into the building and away from the canteen. Twenty yards, perhaps thirty, and round two corners till they came to the door with the male, trousered symbol set high on it.

The Indian smiled, 'It is here. Not easy to find.'

His inclination then would have been to leave and walk away, but Famy spoke quickly and at the same time pushed open the door, moving inside.

'I would like to see you again. Where could we meet?' Mohan Singh followed him. Famy was no longer listening, was taking in the layout, the cubicles at the far end of the long side walls past the stand-up urinals. There was a man there, nearly completed, heaving his hips to shake off the last drops. He would be gone in a moment. It was not a place that men delayed beyond their business.

At the washbasin, the water running loud, inter-fering, he pretended not to hear.

'Wait a minute. Till I have finished,' he said over his shoulder. In the mirror he saw the man move toward the door, heard it slam in his wake.

Famy swept the water from his hands onto the front of his jeans and spun to face the Indian. No words now, and how many seconds before another man came in? The Indian had started to talk again when Famy's forearm, swung from far back, hit him on the protuberance of his throat, at the Adam's apple. A gurgling, choking moment of protest. Surprise in the eyes before the misting of insensi-bility. Famy caught him as he collapsed and pulled him, limp now and unprotesting, to the furthest of the lavatory cubicles. Then through the door into the constricted space in front of the pan. Not dead yet, not a body. But had to be killed, had to be silenced. He worked the shape in front of him so that the head faced inward and he had room to close the door behind him and fasten the catch. 'Engaged' it would say to any who came. And he would hear the door into the main corridor if it were opened and an intruder entered. That would hold him up. He had waited all morning for his man and now was impatient.

He closed his eyes, settled himself as if in a moment of prayer, seeking the strength that now was essential, knuckles whitened, nails in his palms. He raised up the Indian's head, took the turban from it, placed it carefully on the door hook, particular not to disarrange it, aware that he would not know how to rebind it. Then he pulled the zip fastener of the overalls down to the level of the upper waist and clawed the arms of the garment from round the shoulders till it rested in a concertinaed mess on the Indian's hips. The overalls as much as the turban were too vital to be defiled if they were to serve his purpose. And now he was ready. A fearful clarity, in slow, stopped motion. He lifted the head again and with all the force in his shoulders slammed it down on the hard polished white china of the rim of the bowl. Once, twice, three times till the bone of the skull no longer resisted the impact. Crude, irreversible damage was what he sought. He could not hold the man in the upright position any more. It slumped onto its knees, blood finding independent paths into the water held at the bottom of the pan, suffusing pinks and reds together.

There was no movement. The man had become matter. Insignificant, finished. Famy heaved him once again upward so that he could observe the hurt he had inflicted, and more practically to see that the ribbons of blood had not passed onto the overalls. These he stripped off, twisting the body, lifting it, pushing it so that he could slip the garment down its length and over the shoes. It had been a hot day, and the Indian wore only a singlet – deep-stained now – and pants underneath, not clean and with their own faint smell that competed with the urine stains on the floor.

He left the body still kneeling but with the head deep in the pan. An obscenity, but necessary to remove totally the horror of the face and the damage that he had brought to it. In the breast pocket of Mohan Singh's overalls he found the small, plastic-coated polaroid card, read the name of the man he had executed in the cause of Palestine, and looked at the photograph, unrecognizable from the smashed features of the man he had killed. Three minutes later, now wearing the overalls, he climbed up over the dividing wooden wall and into the next cubicle. He hurried across to the washbasins, scrubbed his hands in liquid soap to rid himself of the few blood-spots that rested there, then checked in the mirror that the turban was straight and still fastened. His bag was where he had left it, under the basins.

Out in the corridor Famy glanced at his watch. If the Jumbo were on time it would be landing in three hours and forty minutes. There would be another sixty minutes of refuelling. He had far to go, each step more hazardous than the last. And he had killed for the first time, the first time in his short life. There had been men who had slumped in his gunsight in the lecture hall, but they were different – abstract, unconnected. This was with his own hands, using his own strength, his own will. It had been the irreversible step, and he had taken it.

Chapter Twenty

It had been four years since the British had first awoken, and then tardily, to the threat confronting their premier airport. The familiar continental backdrop of patrolling troops and armed para-military police on the runways and in the terminals had been thought just another European eccentricity, until the Guards and their armour had deserted Windsor and rolled into Heathrow for the first time. Many had seen that as an erosion of something peculiarly British, a departure from a way of life long established, a further weakening of the nation's aloofness from the violent habits of its neighbours. But times changed, and the troops came more often, the frequency of their alerts reducing the bizarre appearance of their initial arrival. And the British Airports Authority, the managing body for the 2,700 acres of billiard-flat grass and concrete that played host on a summer's day to close on a thousand aircraft, had called its charge a 'national defence priority', and written in an annual review of the 'formidable tasks posed by the new warfare' of terrorist attack. Familiarity, though, dulled the fascination of the armed men, the excitement died its death. Twenty million passengers came and went each year, and few could boast to their friends of having seen a rifle, a semi-hidden pistol handle at the hip of a policeman, let alone a light tank.

So on this Wednesday there was again a refreshing novelty about it all, and enough sunshine to bring out the crowds. Those who were flying arrived earlier than they otherwise would have done. Those landing lingered in the anticipation of an event. Around the army, the work of the airport continued uninterrupted; but ears were cocked listening for sirens and gunfire, and above all the ceaseless drone of uninformed and ceaseless rumour.

The turban felt strange and unfamiliar on Famy's head. Not that it was heavy or ill-fitting, but as a constriction, the mark and uniqueness of an identity that he had not fully taken over. The overalls were right, loose and baggy, presenting no pressures on the shape of his body, and masking the rifle now pinioned, barrel down, in the belt at the front of his trousers. It was one of the small pieces of advice that they had given to him: secrete a barrelled weapon in the very front of your body. The hands always search at the sides, examine the flanks. The grenades would have been harder to dispose of on his person had the Indian not carried the small, yellow lunch box in the pocket of his trousers. The V40s wrapped well in the greaseproof paper that the nameless and faceless wife packaged round her man's food.

Famy walked toward the security check-point between the two giant structures that formed Terminal Three. 'Departures to Right', 'Arrivals to Left,' and straight ahead the pendulum bar, unmistakable in its red and white message, with the notice slung beneath, large and decisive, 'Stop'. Beyond was the inner world that he had to join, the realm of the loaders and mechanics and airline personnel, passengers excluded unless they moved in their corralled herds on specific walkways. The BAA security man, blue uniform, white-rimmed cap, operated the movement of the bar from a glass-cased booth at the side. A soldier had crammed in beside him, and there was a Land-Rover behind daubed with the standard NATO camouflage parabolas. More soldiers beside the barrier itself. They were relaxed, confident, safe in the knowledge of their numbers and their firepower. Briefings had passed that down to them. Battalion commander to company commander, company commander to platoon commander, platoon commander to section leader. The word had been spread, circulated. One man was the risk. They had his picture in their minds, the description of his clothes.

An Indian in British Airways livery went no way toward fitting the requirement for vigilance and care that had been stressed on the Guardsmen. They looked in the bag, but cursorily and laughed when he asked in a voice, high-pitched by nerves, but which they took to be the flavour of his homeland, whether he should remove his turban. As they waved him through he shouted to the men in the booth.

'Good luck.'

And their smiles turned to the sneers of the young. A thousand against one. So who needed luck? With those odds half a day more and the rifles would be back in the armoury and they'd be in the pub under the castle wall. They watched him go, and their attention was taken up by the next vehicle. An airport catering van, and there was the need for the tedium of climbing inside and searching.

Pier 7, they had said back at the camp, was the one where the El Al would come to rest. Right at the extremity of the glass and prefabricated buttress down which the passengers would walk to the aircraft. Some days they would board through the tunnel that billowed out from the main construction, sometimes they would walk a few yards across the tarmac. One thing was constant, they had said, always the El Al was removed and remote from the other aircraft. Nearer to him was Pier 6, clogged with its quota of Jumbo 747s . . . British Airways, Pan American, Trans World Airlines, Japan Airlines, Middle East Airlines. He skirted them, measuring a distance that would cause no offence, draw no attention to him. Neither too close to the machinery nor so far out on the tarmac that his basic unfamiliarity with the surroundings would be exposed.

There were more soldiers to his front, and an armoured car dwarfing them. Awaiting an arrival. Sitting and crouched among their packs, close to the one who had unslung the burden of the radio. Watchful, but not yet on alert. They had been right at the camp, and he praised their thoroughness, wondered where they accrued such information. This was where Sokarev would come. There were police standing in separate groups, distant and unwanted by the soldiers, a lesser force, while dogs sat with patience beside their handlers. As he crossed beyond Pier 6 more of the reception group came into his view. Two more armoured cars sheltered under the raised flooring of the further and final pier. Big, ugly, powerful. Huge engines. Mounted machine-guns silhouetted against the sky. Firing power, hitting power, killing power. All there for Abdel-El-Famy. Twice he had seen the wounds on McCoy, seen his man's blood flowing from his body, seen the pain take his face. But they were pistol shots, not fatal, not lethal. Different to the force and velocity of the weapons that were now arrayed in front of him. These were stopping guns. Men did not climb up again, did not drive cars, did not see another day-break, not when they were struck by this power. The M1, difficult to forget, pressed against his groin, was unequalled. Only the Kalashnikov could compete – superior perhaps. The rifle he had been trained on, a soldier's rifle, a rifle of war. Trained? Trained for what? So easy in the dry heat of the camp to talk of war, and to wave the farewells to the men who went without hope of return and whose places at the trestle-tables would be filled by others with the bright eyes and the solutions and the unquestioning confidence. But what war was this? In an alien, hateful world. Reviled. Hunted. A war with only one victory, consummated only with the death of Sokarev. And if toward that victory Famy died it was of no consequence. Erased without trace if the big rifles took him. That Famy was prepared to die for Palestine was not important. An aggregate of irrelevance. Forgotten with the last tremors of his heartbeat, as if he had never been. But in the camp, would they not care there? Only from success can the martyrdom come. Success and only success, no other criteria. As in a dream he walked, argument and counter-argument punching and confusing him, seeking answers his intellect could not provide. Why knowing the forfeit did he strive so willingly to be remembered? Why, when we know we will be dust, worm fodder, do we seek so hard to be recalled in friends' minds and in their voices? Famy did not know, did not have the comprehension. He yearned only to be mourned. But understood the currency. To be remembered with tears, then Sokarev must die. Only then would they weep for him, the boys with the abyss-brown eyes who shared his tent in the camp.

'Where the bloody hell do you think you're going?' – strident, beating in through his fantasies. The voice was rough, aged and foreign to him. 'Get out the bloody way.'

Famy was rigid. Horror at discovery, disaster. His eyes flickered, body still. The fork-lift cargo transport was five feet away from him, directly in his path, painted strident yellow and blue. El Al colours.

'You want to look where you're bloody going, mate.'

'I'm sorry,' Famy stuttered the words.

'Not half you won't be sorry, not if this lot runs over you. What do you think those bloody lines are for, the white ones? 'Cos it's for trucks, right? Trucks' corridor.'

'I was watching the soldiers.'

'Stupid buggers, goofing about because of this Arab and the Yiddisher. If you worked for El Al you'd see enough of them. Troops, police and their own crowd and they're right bastards . . .'

Famy had recovered, was steadier. He was not one of them, this man. An employee, but not of their blood.

'It will be a big show this afternoon, all the troops and things, when the Israeli comes.'

'Not here it won't.'

'But when he boards there will be great security, surely?'

'Not putting him on here. Stands to reason. They're not bloody fools, these people. Load up here, taxi on to 28L, across to the VIP suite, lift him on, and up, up and away, and the squaddies and coppers can go home.'

'I didn't know there was a VIP area there.' Fishing, Famy. Deep, black water, unable to detect what is nibbling at the bait, uncertain of the reward.

'The new one. The one the old girl uses when she's off to Balmoral, where they put Kissinger down, right beside Cargo.'

'I'm sorry that I was in your way.' Famy smiled, and turned and began to walk toward the nearest British Airways plane.

A fleet of company trucks hovered underneath the fuselage belly. There would be a lift there. He would say he was urgently required at Cargo. It would only take a man a few minutes to drive him, and he would be close then. As close as he needed. Within range, within the range even of his M1.

The fleeting relief to which Jimmy had succumbed was broken by the arrival of Jones in the hotel room. He was aware of the voices, dim and thudding through his consciousness before his eyes reluctantly took in the scene, lids prised apart in protest to the sounds. Elkin looked to have benefited from the rest. He stood now on the far side of the room and close to Jones. They were examining a sheaf of typewritten sheets. The security attaché was with them, and before he let his presence back with the living be known Jimmy accepted that the conversation was between Elkin and Jones, attaché on the outside, present but not partaking of the feast. No sign of Sokarev. Poor bugger, thought Jimmy, still holed up in his patch and waiting to be consigned. Wonder they don't give him a waybill, stick a number on his arse and freight him home. His head still hurt, not as acutely as before, but intermittently. Take the bloody pledge, man. Your age, and still don't know better.

Jones acknowledged him. Not with friendship, not with warmth, just recognition. Doesn't really like me, after all these years, tolerates me around. Accepts he needs me today, knows he won't have to go through the charade tomorrow. That'll be the ditching time, usefulness used up. Quick handshake it'll be, then piss off and don't show your face till it's been under the long-term tap and washed the bloody booze out. No obligation, not till the next time, till there's a bit of filth that needs scooping off the carpet, a drain that needs cleaning that stinks too much for him to put his pure white hands down.

'Glad to have you back with us, Jimmy,' Jones said. 'I was summoning the courage to kick you, you've been snoring like a sow in labour.'

'Why didn't you wake me when the confab started?'

'Nothing too complicated there, and you were much too pretty to disturb. Mr Elkin and I have gone over it.'

Pompous bugger. Wasn't like that when he wanted McCoy talked to. Means he thinks it's a piece of cake from now, all sewn up and can't go wrong.

And it had to be. He'd be a gutsy bastard, the Arab, if they saw him again. If he puts his nose into this crab hole, then you'd have to hand it to him.

'What's my part in this show from now?' Jimmy asked, still slumped in the chair.

'You travel with him to the airport. Hold his hand all the way. Take him carefully up the steps, fasten his seat belt, and last thing before they shut up shop you vamoose down the ramp again. Very simple, very straightforward.'

'Where's he going from?'

'South side, the VIP area. The plane will taxi across from Terminal Three and lift him up right under our supervision. For once it's all planned, nothing for your right index to get twitchy about.'

'What news of Famy . . . ?'

Jones was growing irritable. Not pleased at being spoken to with such lack of deference in public, in front of foreigners, strangers.

'No word of him. But the airport's sealed. Troops, police, armour, no need for you to be worried.'

'It's not me that's worried. It's not my job that hangs on knowing where the little runt is.'

Six thousand men work at the Heathrow Cargo terminal, there to despatch and unload more than a thousand tons of freight a day. That an outsider, an alien, should be in their midst would not be noticed.

Famy squatted low on his bag in the sunshine in the front of the big British Airways transit shed. There were others around him, watching the soldiers in the distance, statuesque and guarding a circle of empty tarmac. He spoke to no-one, nor received any words of greeting or inquiry. It was of no concern to

403

him, he did not seek communication and conversation. More troops on the corner of the building before the open ground that stretched to the white wooden fence that shielded the bungalow VIP lounge from his sight. The presence of the turbaned stranger would not arouse comment; freighters were traditionally the veterans of the fleet, converted as their passenger days were exhausted, and it was accepted that maintenance was in frequent demand.

There was a warmth in the air, and in the distance the shapes jumped and bounced and faded, made hazy by the heat. He had to blink to hold his concentration on the big plane in full view across the tarmac. The sheen played and gleamed on the outline of the El Al jet less than six hundred yards from him. He could make out the armoured cars, black in shadow against the light, and occasionally the figures of the soldiers around them would press into focus. Beneath the upright zip of his overalls the rifle worried against his body. It hurt, and would continue to hurt. There were many minutes before the plane would be ready to take Sokarev on board. He felt a curious calm now. No anguish and no stress. The desire to dream and fantasize was conquered. All so very clear. In limbo, sucked into a void, and awaiting the inevitability of the rendezvous. It was beyond interference.

Sokarev was past complaining or feeling any degree of independence as they led him through the kitchens of the hotel and then into the delivery area where food and provisions were unloaded in built-up bays. The escort seemed to the scientist to be too preoccupied with their problems and anxieties to explain or justify the departure plan that had been decided on. The van that waited was painted blue, unmarked and with the windows smoked to prevent those on the outside looking in. There were five men with him to share the two rows of seating behind the driver. The security attaché, still defensive and introverted. Jones, who ignored all around him. Elkin, fidgeting, willing the journey over, the Uzi across his knees and constantly referring to his wrist-watch. Special Branch convoy co-ordinator, talking all the while into his handset, and then fiddling with the dials as his answers came back in differing volume. And there was Jimmy, picking with a match-stick at the dirt under his nails, with his coat open, and his gun exposed, and his head down thoughtful and concerned, and not sharing his mind. Behind was a car, more Branch men, and with them the replacement for Mackowicz, unhappy and pained at being separated from his man.

It is as if they are punishing me, thought Sokarev. As if I am in some way culpable for what has happened. He was still tired, not rested by the capsule that the doctor had given him. They put me out of their way while they worked out their plans, needed me absent, and the easiest way was with the pill, he told himself. But it does not bring real sleep. And he recognized that the men with him were tired, had seen it in their faces, and in their clothes, the way they snapped at each other, their impatience. The equation for him had often been proved in the work at Dimona; tired men operate at reduced effi-ciency, and that frightened him. He felt a shortness of breath and searched for air, loosening his collar and slipping off the suit jacket he had put on for the journey. All the ventilation slats in the van were closed. He would have liked one open, to release the engine fumes and the body smells, but did not feel he had the authority to ask for it. Incapable of soaking up more humiliations he sat in his seat and suffered till he felt a shiver in his limbs and deep under his clothes, and a feeling of cold and sickness. There was nobody to tell.

In the yard of Hammersmith police station, a third of the way to Heathrow and behind closed doors, he was transferred to a car. There were escorts front and back, but nothing for the casual observer of the convoy to recognize.

The security attaché now drove, Jones and Special Branch crowded into the front beside him. Sokarev was sandwiched between Elkin and Jimmy.

As they climbed onto the pillared flyover that they had crossed two days ago Sokarev felt a tug at his sleeve and looked at Jimmy.

'Don't take too much notice of these buggers,' Jimmy said, for all the car to hear, 'they're all as shit-scared as you are. And will be till we've waved you on your way.'

Famy's whole being was riveted to the movement of the big jet. Three hundred and fifty tons of it, making the solemn progress from the end of Pier 7 toward the axis of the runways. Two Saracens came in front, where he could see them, dwarfed by the huge concentric lines of the nose. Small cockpit windows, high above the ground, where the pilot and his crew were sitting. All of them able to see him, but not capable of recognizing the face of their enemy. Remember Dani, remember Bouchi, remember McCoy. Endless, indistinct, faces played through his vision, sometimes blotting out and obscuring the reality of the plane. The faces of his friends, of those who believed in him.

The plane was waved inside the cordon of soldiers. More armoured cars were awaiting it, policemen beginning to scurry, and the wind brought the talk of their radios, faint but recognizable. The soldiers faced out of their arc, stern-eyed now, keyed up, expectant. The nearest was barely twenty feet from Famy. A corporal, two blackened V-stripes on his tunic arm, self-loading rifle, water bottle, emergency field dressing strapped to his webbing belt. Famy saw his hands as they cradled the rifle. Finger on the lip of the trigger guard, thumb for the safety catch, a movement of a second and the gun was armed, deadly. The soldier did not return his stare, gazed through him, used to being looked at. The Guards always were. And his position, the square of concrete on which he stood, had chosen to stand, made him Famy's opponent. As inconsequential as that, where a man placed his feet. That decided whether he would kill or be killed.

'Juno turning into Hatton perimeter entrance, sir.'

Corporal on the Land-Rover radio set to his company commander. The major raised his hand in acknowledgement. Bloody stupid names they always gave these affairs.

'Sunray getting it on the net?' the major asked.

'All getting it, sir, not just the CO, the convoy's hooked into all stations.'

'Put out the Instant Readiness.'

'Roger, sir.'

The major saw beyond his cordon a line of civilian trucks and cars and lorries held back a quarter of a mile from the plane. Have to wait till the show was over. No non-involved persons inside his line, perfect field of fire around three-sixty degrees. Just about perfect, anyway. Only the corner hangar of the British Airways cargo complex jutting in and breaking the geometry of his protective circle. Saw the loaders there, standing and sitting and watching, anything for a chance not to work. Shouldn't have been there, but no harm done. The corporal dominating them. No need to throw his weight about, make a scene, have them shifted. Saw the turban, creased and clean. It stood out in the light, the sun playing on it.

He turned toward the VIP suite past which the convoy would come.

The cars came fast down the straight line of the inner perimeter road, motorcyles in front, and all oncoming traffic blocked far ahead. Sokarev saw the arrowed signs to the right marking the route to the VIP suite.

Jimmy said, 'Just about there now, sir. No farewells out on the tarmac. The car goes right up to the steps and you're to be straight onto them. Don't stop. Don't hesitate. Just go straight on up. Inside don't look out of the windows, just get into the seat. They're not going to hang about, you'll be straight off.'

Sokarev did not reply. Jimmy could see the nerves on his ageing face, wrinkles accentuated, eyes wide open, staring, but at nothing, and the lips clamped fractionally apart, breathing coming in irregular sucked heaves. Poor sod, not taking it well. Ten to bloody nothing his legs will freeze half-way and we'll have to carry him on.

The convoy swept past the low-built lounge with its decoration of hot-house plants. Marigolds and snapdragons and embryo rhododendrons. In front was the Jumbo.

'Goodbye, Elkin,' Jimmy leaned across Sokarev, hand outstretched. It was not taken. The Israeli's attention was outside his window, fingers clamped on his sub-machine-gun.

The cars spattered through the gap in the fencing and raced toward the jet. Jones found himself reflecting at the vulgarity of it all. Big men, hunched and crammed together on the seats. All so difficult to take seriously, just a game for grown-ups. Only Sokarev playing, though. We're all in with the spectators, thought Jones, it's only the old man who goes onto the field. No dignity in the moment, nothing of the third floor at the department, and Jimmy lording it over everybody. Intolerable, really, and he'd have to be spoken to. The plane was huge now in its silver closeness, dwarfing them, a fortress in its own right. And the steps were there, in position, waiting for them.

The stiffening of the soldiers, the way their hands quickly changed the grip on their rifles, fingers to the trigger guard, telegraphed to Famy the imminence of the arrival.

His right hand ferreted down inside the overalls for the safety mechanism of the M1. Already cocked, already a bullet nestled in the breach of the firing chamber. A hundred yards to the steps of the plane.

Take twelve to thirteen seconds. The problems were fading, over everything a devastating simplicity. When the cars came into sight that was when to start running. Fast, but weaving, ducking low, and the shot when the man was at the base of the steps. Bank on chaos. However much they have prepared for you, they will never quite have expected the presence, that was what the men had told him in the camp. There will always be confusion; it is the greatest weapon in your hand, they had said.

Three cars in the convoy, snouting round the corner, braking because of the angle they were negotiating. Famy was on his feet.

Without hesitation, a continuous rippling movement. He pulled the zip fastener down the length of his chest. The Guardsman was barely aware of his action that produced the rifle before the bullet hit him low in the muscle wall of his stomach, throwing him back and clear from the path of Famy's sprint.

In front of him, as if in slow motion, the doors of the car were opening, the men in their suits jumping out. Unaware, they don't realize. The insane exhilaration that he had achieved surprise. Run, weave, duck, maintain the rhythm, give no-one a clear sight. When do the bullets come? How long? The bundle in grey, half out of the car, helped by the darker suits, reluctant to come, slowing them down, impeding them. The first bullet spat into the ground close to his feet. Fools, idiots, crazy men, firing low. Halfway there. Sokarev in sight, his head clear, the body half-shielded by the men around him. The orange groves, upright, regimented, before the spring brings the sun of Palestine to make fertile their leaves and their fruit; merging together the fantasy of the trees and the sharpness of the men as he pounded his way forward.

More bullets now edging closer, the little puffs of nothing in the concrete and the hostile, honed whine of the ricochets off the concrete. And the ranging blast, wide but creeping, of the big machine-gun. Sokarev near the steps, wrestling with the men around him. They taking him toward the plane. Doesn't want to go, the little bastard, wants to crawl and hide and bury himself. The moment to shoot.

In full stride Famy flung himself, arching forward in a swallow dive, with a strange grace, onto the tarmac. His knees and elbows took the impact, ripping at the cloth that covered his body. The gun was at his eye, down the barrel, down the needle sight. Eyes smarting with the pain from the fall, blinking the moisture out. The man in the grey still struggling. He fired, finger released the trigger. Knew with that deadening instinct that he was wide, high as well, knew it even as he felt the jolt in his shoulder, heard the empty clatter of the discarded shell case. A moment, breathtaking, of silence, then again the machine-gun.

No more to see of Sokarev, so still everything in front of him, no man standing. Gone, all of them, at a stroke. Disappeared, vanished. At the steps no target.

Four in a burst they teach the soldiers to fire when they feed the belt into the machine-gun. More than that and the barrel waves too greatly for the accuracy to be maintained. One in the right foot, two in the calf, fourth in his hip. As if a man with a pickaxe was striking him. Not aiming at a rock face, but at muscle, vulnerable tissue, and the delicacy of his flesh. There was nothing in his hands, only the flat oil-smeared

411

concrete for his fingers to grasp at. The rifle was far to the front, pitched clear, beyond reach, beyond his chances of hope and salvation. In the distance, and to his ears the words echoed and had a strange quality, came the ordered shout, voice of command.

'Stop firing.'

Between them Jones and Elkin carried Sokarev up the flight of steps to the plane. The strength he'd summoned earlier to resist them had gone. Elkin at his shoulders, Jones at his thighs. Both men panting, and the narrowness of the steps preventing further aid.

Jimmy rose from his knees where he had taken cover in front of the scientist between the steps and the door of the car, and began to walk toward Famy. Slow paces, all the time in the world now, the end of the stampede. Around him soldiers were lifting themselves from their firing positions, uncertain what to do, and uneasy in the sudden silence. So many of them, and so many rifles and revolvers, and only this one enemy in contention.

He saw the eyes of the prone man still locked on his rifle, tantalizing, out of range, far from the capability of heroics. Jimmy swung his foot, lazily and without care, and kicked it noisily into the middle distance.

'Good try, boy,' Jimmy said, quietly spoken, a private remark. Famy watched him, awkward from the ground, neck stretched back, face unmarked. 'Good try. Just not good enough.'

Jimmy raised his voice so the Arab could hear him.

'McCoy told us you'd be here. Told us this morning. We didn't think you'd get this far. But it wasn't far enough, boy. One shot you got off, just one. Way off target. Looked good, looked dramatic, but set yourself too much. Should have been an aimed shot. Never works, all the running around, not with a pop gun like that, anyway.'

He saw Famy smile, overcoming the pain, mouth moving but no sound.

'That was what they gave you, the M1? Not very generous, not very suitable. Would have liked something with a bit more guts, right, boy?'

Famy nodded, slight movement, agreement. As far round as his eyes could see the men were now advancing on him, soldiers and police, their guns no longer aimed. Pointed at the ground and the sky.

Jimmy put his hand in his pocket, under the cover of the cloth, and when it emerged the PPK was there. He saw Famy begin to squirm away, trying to move, but pinioned by the damage to his legs and his hip. Whimpering, like a dog that expects a beating but is too trained to run from the threat.

'Don't make it difficult, boy. You knew what it was all about when you came on the joy-ride. And you did well, considering.'

Jimmy fired into the centre of the pale brown forehead, below the clear white rim of the turban. Even with a moving target he was usually accurate.

The noise of the shot was drowned by the four fan jet engines of the taxiing 747.

From beside the car, still stationary, still with the engine ticking quietly over and with the front and rear doors open, Jones had watched it all. There had been words that he'd tried to say, some sort of call, helpless and faint, for Jimmy to come back, but the roar of the engines prevented his being heard by any other than those immediately beside him.

He had seen the pistol in Jimmy's hand, small and blurred in the distance but silhouetted as a recognizable shape against the great emptiness of the tarmac. He hadn't looked after that. The plane was turning toward the runway, its power rising into deafening, ear-blasting crescendo as it eased its way clear of the group of men with their dark suits and hardened eyes.

'Bloody good job and all,' muttered the Branch man, whose eyes had never wavered from Jimmy and who now stared over Jones's shoulder.

Jones swung back. Jimmy walking toward him now, the one he knew just by the name of Famy abandoned and unmoving behind the erect and brisk figure that was soon close enough for him to see the almost boyish grin of satisfaction that wreathed the mouth. Cat with the cream, thought Jones, as if he's scored a bloody try at Twickenham.

'Bloody good job, the way it should be every time,' the Branch man said again, and Jones bit on his lip, unable to speak his mind, out of step with the mood.

Well, they'd had their money's worth out of Jimmy-boy this time. Earned his retainer, hadn't he? There'd be a mass of paperwork to be getting on with, the predictable escape mechanism, and Jones went in search of a car heading for Central London. Knifing through his mind the continuous thought . . . it was what they'd wanted, it was what they'd asked for, those bloody politicians with their directives from on high, and they'd been gratified.

*   *   *

414

In the first-class cabin, occupying two seats at the rear, were Sokarev and Elkin. The pilot had swung the plane hard round and lined himself on to the 3,600-metre-long Runway 5, given precedence over all other flights. Clearance from the control tower was immediate, and the aircraft hammered its way into the slight wind down 28L.

Just before the moment of lift-off Sokarev whispered, straining to Elkin's ear, that he felt sick.

'Don't worry,' Elkin said. 'It's all over. It's finished now. We are going home. There is nothing more to fear.'

They were all going home. Mackowicz in the tin box on the freight deck beneath them, Elkin who had been his friend, Sokarev who had been his charge. The security man noted the pallor of the scientist, and the perspiration on his balding head and the way that he struggled to reach upward to direct the cold air nozzles toward his face. When they were airborne it would be easier. He told himself that, and settled back, deep, into the comfort of his seat.

Chapter Twenty-One

At first the pains were slight and concentrated in the centre of his chest, but the nausea and desire to vomit were uppermost. As Elkin slept beside him Sokarev was able to worm a path over the legs of his bodyguard and into the aisle towards the lavatories. He'd had little food and his retching was painful and hard. By the time they were flying over the Mediterranean the pain was spreading in area and intensity, and still Elkin's eyes were closed, insensible to the outer world. When at last a stewardess noticed Sokarev's distress he was doubled up in his seat, his hands across his body. Over the loudspeaker system of the aircraft the chief steward called for a doctor.

Elkin stood out in the aisle now, for once helpless, unable to offer aid to the man he had been ordered to protect. The doctor reached low over the heaving form of Sokarev, whom they had stretched across the two seats, centre arm rest pulled out.

When he stood up the doctor, young and in a T-shirt displaying the name of Hamburg where he had been holidaying before joining the flight, asked if anyone were accompanying the passenger.

'He is subject to severe coronary attack?'

Elkin nodded, unable to speak, stunned at the revelation. Now of all moments . . .

'Has he been under strain?' The doctor's voice carried the hush of concern.

'He is David Sokarev.'

'I don't know the name, I have not been in Israel some weeks.'

'He is the one the Arabs tried to kill. At the airport and before that last night.'

'The reason for the troops? The passenger on the far side of the airfield?'

'Yes.'

'He has been under severe strain?'

'Total strain. They were trying to assassinate him.' Enough of the talk. There must be action that can be taken.

'He needs morphine,' said the doctor.

'And . . .'

'And I do not have morphine. I do not carry it with me.'

Elkin looked away from the doctor, down to the pain on the professor's cheeks. 'Call the Captain,' he said. 'Get him off the deck and here.'

The pilot, mid-forties, shirt sleeves, grey hair, a decision-maker, offered no options. 'We go for Ben Gurion. Lebanon and Cyprus are nearer, but are out. Beirut, obviously, Larnaca is too short for the plane. Athens might save a few minutes, but it's marginal and the facilities at home are superior. We have a little less than an hour till we are down. The necessary people will be waiting.'

The doctor said aloud as he bent once again over Sokarev, 'He is an old man to have gone through all

417

this. Overweight, not equipped to take such turmoil. The bastards always hit when they are not expected.'

Elkin could not reason why he spoke. There was no need, no requirement, but he replied. 'We have known for some days that an attack was planned. The Professor has known too.'

'And you took him, and you exposed him? Knowingly you brought him to Europe? At his age, in his condition?'

'A decision had been taken.'

'There is no wound on him. Remember that. You and your people will have to make your own decision if he dies. You will have to know who killed him.'

There was darkness round the jet as it whispered on its way, ten miles every minute toward the coastline of Israel and the landfall.

On the intercom the Personal Assistant announced that the Prime Minister was calling from Downing Street. With resignation the Director General cleared the papers that obscured his notepad, took in his hand a sharpened pencil, and raised the receiver of the telephone. He heard the Prime Minister being informed that the link was now through, that the other party was waiting. There was quiet in the room, fitting for the moment before the verbal assault that he had anticipated and predicted to himself. It was an understatement that the Prime Minister was furious. Voice raised. The head of the Security Services held the telephone a clear inch from his ear.

'It was turned into a clear fiasco by your man.'

'In what way, sir?' Don't give the blighters an inch,

418

don't get into the apology situation, don't make it easy for the inquiry.

'In what way? Because of what your fellow did on the tarmac. Right out there in the middle, with half the bloody world looking on.'

'You'll have to explain, sir.' Stall the inevitable. Let the heat cool, then counter-attack.

'Don't play the fool with me. Your man has executed – only word for it – this Palestinian, or whatever he was, right out there, in public . . .'

'Your instruction was quite clear, sir. You did not expect the Arab to survive our contact with him.' They'd be taping at Downing Street, nice to get that on the magnetic ribbon.

'Not like that. I didn't expect him killed like that, not . . .'

'He had grenades on him. Live and primed. He was still capable of using them. His hands were moving. He could have used the grenades.'

'You're justifying your man?'

'His target was still armed and dangerous. My operative made a quick and correct decision. More lives could have been lost if he had hesitated. He acted quite correctly.'

'It makes our position fearfully difficult.' Always the same with these politicians. Can't take it on the chin, can't ride a right hand, weakening already. The Director General had the telephone close again, against the lobe of his ear. 'The shooting of this fellow could have very grave repercussions.'

'I think that our man would have felt that faced with the circumstances that confronted him the actual danger to life was of paramount importance when compared with the possible diplomatic repercussions.'

Abruptly and without further comment the Prime Minister rang off. The Director General waited for his line to clear then dialled the extension to Jones's office.

Long into the evening Jones sat in his office, alone at his desk. The coffee in the beaker remained undrunk and sealed with a skin surface. Helen had gone now, eyes reddened and aware of the conversation he had had with Jimmy.

Sod it. Cock Robin kicked the fucking bucket. Bloody waste, a man like that going, getting the chop. Still full of sap, years more of it. Awkward bastard, couldn't deny that, but then Jones had always fancied he alone could handle him. Bloody-minded when he wanted to be, but not just now. Had gone with his own dignity, hadn't made a fuss, just let the blade run through the timber, and keeled over gracefully and without protest. Hadn't argued, just accepted it, made his excuses and disappeared out of the door toward the basement to check his gun in. Jones had seen him from the upper window walk out into the street and stride away toward the underground station. Could have had a car home, but not his style to ask for one, not when he'd just had the push. Typical of the way the bloody department exists. DG couldn't do it himself, had to get a minion to scrub the dirty pants, rinse the unmentionable stains. Told him what to do, told him what the PM wanted, and he'd carried it out. To the letter, careful and in copperplate, he'd done it . . . and that was why Jimmy was walking home. On the scrap heap and the best man they had.

Didn't any of the stupid bastards understand the

new warfare? Gone past, the Queensberry Days. No rules that governed this combat. Have to fight the McCoys and Famys with their own kind . . . Would they have left Sokarev half dead for an ambulance team to cart away? Would they, shit? He thought he'd never see Jimmy again. Wouldn't be the way of the department for him to have further contact with a man he'd fired. Went back a long way, lot of years, lot of late nights and talk and togetherness. Now all screwed up because of a little swine from God knows where in a place called Palestine that doesn't exist.

When he telephoned home his elder son answered. Wife out at the Women's Institute Committee. They'd had their food before she went. Didn't think anything had been left for him. No reason why it should. It was a clear week since he'd last phoned and said he might not be home that night. It had been the best bloody week in his time at the department and it had ended all loused up. And he scratched and worried at the irritation of his scars.

The detective had to screw his legs under the wooden chair to leave room for the nurses who worked round McCoy's bed. They fussed and pecked at their patient and then went in crocodile line out through the door. There was light from the car park outside and shadows thrown against the wall. For what seemed an age, frighteningly long to the policeman, the Irishman lay still, unmoving, unblinking on the crisp white of the bedclothes.

When eventually he spoke it was too dark in the room for the detective to see his face.

'What happened to him?' The words were slow in coming, spoken so faintly that the other man had to lean forward, cursing in his mind the murmur of the distant traffic.

'Did he make it?'

The detective was uncertain what he was allowed to say, and kept silent.

'Did he get the bastard?'

Conscientiously the words were written down.

'Did he get him? For Christ's sake, tell me.'

'He tried and he didn't make it. Shot a soldier, fired on the Israeli. Missed. He's dead now, they shot him on the tarmac.' From the bed there was a deep, heaved sigh, then only the regular, drug-controlled breathing. McCoy said nothing more.

Through the haze of images there was a certain hard-won precision. Of how the news would spread from Cullyhanna to Crossmaglen, what the talk would be in Forkhill and Mulaghbane, what the men would say in the hills round Slieve Gullion and Lislea as they nestled in the bracken and grass and watched and waited with their binoculars and their Armalites. And he felt against the clamminess of his arms the white tiles of the cell walls that would be his. There would be bars and heavy doors, and iron-shod feet, and uniforms, and he would slowly rot away, praying and hoping each night for the mercy of sleep.

Behind the barman and hidden by the inverted spirits bottles the radio played music from the BBC Northern Dance Orchestra. Jolly and conventional and designed to cheer the customers of the pub. There was much noise in the 'Public', and the swill of beer before closing would soon be under way. There was talk of the day's affairs, not of the economy, not of inflation, not of sport, not of the boobs on the inside pages of the tabloids. Attention was gripped to the events of the airport. To be expected . . . the picture of the Agency man with his telephoto lens had made the final editions of the London evenings. Not much detail, but the figure on the ground, and the man above him with the gun were recognizable enough. The art department had helped with the gun. The photograph justified the headlines – 'Execution' and 'High Noon at Heathrow'.

Jimmy sat in the far corner, near the door, solitary, uncommunicative and now on his fifth double whisky. He was slumped low with his head close to the glass and his eyes deep in the amber, watching the stillness of the liquid, following its reflections, amused by the shapeless patterns of the bubbles that rose from the diminishing ice cubes. No bitterness. Just a sense of regret. Passing of time. Ending of an institution.

The barman rang the big ship's bell hanging above the polished counter.

'Last orders, gentlemen. Last orders. One more gulp for the road.'

Compulsive for Jimmy. Never could resist the last one. Had to have it, rain or shine, success or cock-up. He was on his feet, pushing with the throng, thrusting forward his glass with the rest of them. The signature tune of the news headlines rose and faded above the shouting and demanding. First words indistinct, drowned by the big man wanting the big round. Fatuous face, filled out with beer and distended sub-skin veins. Heard the word 'Sokarev'. Heard the words 'Heart Attack'.

'Shut up,' Jimmy yelled. 'Shut your bloody faces.'

A score of faces were turned on him, saw the power of his eyes, of his chin, of his shoulders.

'. . . an hour after Professor Sokarev had been admitted to the intensive care wing of a Tel Aviv hospital it was announced by the Foreign Ministry in Jerusalem that the efforts of doctors to save his life had failed. The Professor, who was aged 53, was one of the country's principal scientists working at the nuclear centre at Dimona in the Negev desert.

'In London, Scotland Yard have still not given any details on the unnamed security man who shot dead an already wounded Arab terrorist on the tarmac at Heathrow after the unsuccessful attempt on Professor Sokarev's life this afternoon. But our political editor reports that Government ministers are demanding disciplinary action against . . .'

His deep, raucous, baying laughter shook the bar. Head well back, face taking on the crimson of exertion, body shaking. And all around the faces of hostility and reaction.

'What's so funny about that?'

'Nothing to bloody-well laugh about.'

'Warped little bastard.'

'What's the matter with him? Half pissed.'

He ignored them with grand contempt. So bloody funny. Hilarious. Laughed till it hurt in his guts, till the pain came to his chest and was laughing as he stumped out into the coldness of the street. Cheated them all, you little bugger. Denied the bloody satisfaction to Famy and McCoy. Fucked the triumph of our side. What price now, Mr bloody Elkin, or Jonesey. How much champagne already downed, and what now? . . . A fair old belch there'd be back at the department. And you, Jimmy-boy. He screwed you, too, and after all that. All the bloody heartache, all the bloody pain. You screwed everyone, Dr Sokarev, sir. The whole lot of us. Both sides. Didn't know you had it in you, you crafty little sod.

The flat would be empty. There was no hurry to approach its loneliness, its vacuum. Slowly Jimmy made his way down the pavement, and the hiccups were intermingled with the laughing, and that soon faded to little more than a giggle.

Failure had been a familiar bedfellow. So many missions launched with high expectation, and rarely the wounding blow that they sought. Barely a fortnight without the young men departing for their objectives, erect in their confidence, and then hard on their heels the devastation of disappointment. Undisturbed beds, unused mess tins, shortened ranks on the morning parade. And when does frequency become inevitability? When does the dimness phase into darkness? When is there no longer hope of success? The leader of the General Command had been brought the transcript of the World Service news from London and had read without comment of the death of Famy, the survival of Sokarev, the flight of the El Al jet from Heathrow. He had walked into the sands seeking solitude and absence from the new recruits. It had been a good plan, he reflected, and he had sent good men, but it had been insufficient. He stood more than an hour as the dusk came down over the desert, so still that an earth-coated mouse ran close to his feet as it meandered a path to the ambush of the adder. And the killing was quick; startled eyes, frozen movement, and the job completed. The land where the

425

soft, and the gentle and the harmless did not survive. He yearned for the snake's speed and resolution, remembered the cold, unfeeling and mechanical strike of the reptile and craved the ability to impart the simplicity of that minute brain into the minds of the men who would leave the camp before midnight and drive in the jeep to the frontier and walk forward toward the minefields and the wire and the enemy.

When the night had advanced and the stars risen he made his way back to the camp and went and sat with the four who were eating together with their friends, perhaps for the last time. He hid his depression behind humour and quiet exhortation, and made no mention of the news from Europe. When the time came for them to leave he walked with them to the jeep and hugged them deep and kissed each on both cheeks, and watched the tail lights till they were too distant and had gone among the shallow hills. Afterwards, in his tent, he lay on the canvas bed and read again the operational plan on which they had been briefed. He was close to sleep when the old man pulled aside the tent flap and illuminated by a storm lamp came across the floor to him.

'They have been monitoring the Israeli broadcasts. Sokarev is dead. He died tonight in Tel Aviv . . .'

'From what?' The confusion of the leader showed. Half-sitting up in the disarray of his blankets he said, 'The reports made no mention of his being injured.'

'The Israelis say he was unhurt in the attack, but he suffered a heart seizure on the plane.'

'So it was not us, not by our hand?' He sank back

onto his roughened pillow, the momentary excitement extinguished.

'But he is dead.'

'But not at our hand.'

'We sought to kill him, and he is dead, and . . .'

'Listen, old man.' Weariness crept tantalizingly and irrevocably through him. It was not the time for discussion. 'Listen. His death is unimportant if it was not at our hand. We had to show we had the power to strike successfully at him. Instead we showed we were not capable. That is no victory.'

'We could say . . .' and the old man, mindful that he had been interrupted before and aware of the leader's failing attention, let his words tail away.

'We could say nothing. To make people of whatever country, wherever in the world, aware of the mushroom clouds that can rise over our men and women and children then we had to be triumphant in our attack. We were not. The mission is over and completed. Sleep well, old man.'

When the light had gone and the tent flap had been folded back into place the leader turned toward the canvas side that was close to his face. And before he slept he thought of the lights of the jeep and the bright furnace eyes of the men he would not see again.

THE END